ISBN 978-0-9756342-0-2 (Paperback)
ISBN 978-0-9756342-1-9 (Hardback)
ISBN 978-0-9756342-2-6 (E-Book)

First Published (2024)

Mortuus Carnem

For the horror and gore hounds out there, you rock!

Prologue

The year is 2056. The world is plagued with an apocalyptic outbreak. Things started going awry in 2034, when scientists worldwide discovered a new parasitic insect species with physical characteristics similar to that of the common mosquito and wasp. Its shape and size were similar to the toxorhynchites (the world's largest mosquitos), while its striped markings on the abdomen were identical to the ones found on the apis melliferra (the common honeybee) and the or European wasps. However, this new parasitic species had an odd behavioural pattern. It, the parasite, dubbed 'Mortuus Carnem' by a now dead man named Carter Elrod (in Latin), which translates to Dead Flesh, reason being since it was attracted to the rotting and dead flesh of humans and animals. It's proboscis, as tough as stainless steel, acted not only as a needle to inject its venom into the skin of the deceased but as a borer to easily tunnel through dirt and even wood, so it could easily drill its way into sealed wooden coffins. It mattered not how broken or decayed the corpse was, the end of their proboscis was diamond sharp. Once it broke the skin of the corpses and spewed their venom into the deceased bodies, the corpses would reanimate with sometimes horrific results. The deceased would rise with no memory of their former self, devoid of any emotion or control over their actions. Pure mindlessness, broken husks doomed to forever wander the earth with an unresting hunger that could never be sated.

However, because a living specimen of the parasite was yet to be captured and studied, the reasons it was able to reanimate the dead remained a mystery that citizens would hopefully be unearthed sooner or later. The buggers were crafty and found ways of escaping human confinement.

But even before the discovery of the mortuus carnem the planet had become victim to the greed and power-hungry corruption of humankind. Warring countries were constant and desperate humans fought tooth and nail over limited resources. Then along came the mortuus carnem which aided in quickening the process of killing the earth and its inhabitants, turning the once abundant planet into a dead one.

Now in 2056, Earth is nothing more than a barren wasteland full of ghost towns with minimal resources and very few survivors. The only buildings properly functioning were the science facilities. This is where most of the wealthy people have taken refuge. They have a reasonable number of resources: supplies such as food, and some medications in order to help them stay alive.

The poor and less powerful people on the other hand are forced to navigate the highly dangerous streets where the dead roam, to find safety in abandoned houses with little to no help with their chances of survival.

The once beautiful planet called Earth was becoming more inhabitable with each passing second. The virus caused by the mortuus carnem was transforming the dead into walking corpses, or more commonly known as the 'Undead's'.

Fortunately, the few science buildings that were inhabited by humans have provided a genius solution to decrease the numbers of the flesh and brain eating undead ravaging the world.

Scientists and doctors worldwide and facilities such as The Great Facility of Science and Medical Research (located in the United Kingdom) had warily theorised plans and ideas to take back Earth.

To go with this process, hunger drugs (using a wide range of liquids and objects ground together with a pestle, like the venom of copperhead snakes, human dandruff, marijuana, hydroxyzine, and scabs from a recently deceased person) for the sole purpose of reducing the undead's ravaging appetite for brains and flesh for up to five hours.

The zombies under the influence of the drug would be taken into the mess hall of the facility by soldiers who had the responsibility of finding certain zombies to be brought into the facility where they would be left out for scientists, called Bonders. The bonders had the important job of being inside a prison cell-like room with their undead subjects. The bonders would train them to become as human as possible, teaching them about humanity, themselves, and everything else they may have forgotten from the many years of being dead. The bonders had to use physical and emotional contact with them, talking and communicating with them in different ways in hopes the undead's could learn to become more human like, while the race for a vaccine and cure went on. This kind work with the undead was later given the term of Bonding.

The process of getting an undead to regain its humanity and become human again, seemed impossible to some people. Others that held high hopes were left speechless by how revolutionary the concept was.

Some undead's were, of course, failures but there were also some that were successful in regaining lost shards of their humanity. These bonded undead's had to undergo a series of training and tests that ensured they no longer wanted to eat humans and could be integrated back into society.

The undead bonding concept was dubbed by some people living in the facilities as the answer to their prayers. But to the soldiers who were ordered to bring in the undead's from the outside, the whole idea of bonding remained in their minds as a sick fantasy. As part of the UK army they were ordered to bring in certain undead's for the bonding studies.

The effects of bonding aimed to turn around the infection of the mortuus carnem; its entire purpose is to drive the undead back into their state of humanity, not just with personality but in appearance using what is known simply as The Surgery.

The Surgery, is a tricky and otherwise disgusting business of changing the rotting decayed flesh on the living cadavers with new clean flesh, giving them a more human like appearance. However, obtaining the fresh skin is easier said than done. The best and only solution the scientists could agree on was to use the skin of recently deceased people before the mortuus carnem had got to them. Uninfected skin is crucial in the study and surgery of turning the dead back into normal people again for an unknown amount of time, so as soon as word got out that someone had died from causes not related to the mortuus carnem, the scientists ordered the soldiers into action; to take the recently deceased bodies into the hospital ward for the Surgeons, where they would begin removing the uninfected skin to prepare it for when a bonded zombie is ready for the surgery. A complicated but otherwise successful process that was hoping to be the saviour of the dying human race.

Chapter 1

Alexander Fredrickson strode through the barren hospital-like corridors towards the holding cells of the Great Facility of Science and Medical Research. He buttoned up his white lab coat over a long-sleeved black top. Fredrickson was a stern-looking man with no-nonsense brown eyes, sharp features, and a neatly groomed haircut to match, that was showing small traces of grey hair at the roots. Having turned forty-eight in the month of September day eighteen. He was, for his age, considered the most experienced scientist within the facility having studied zombie bonding for six whole years and co-wrote a book about the process of Zombie Bonding titled: <u>The UK Mechanisms for Infected Subject Reintegration and Bonder Training Manual</u>.

He spent day and night, having around ten cups of coffee to keep him awake and alert while he studied in the secluded room, which he happily called his office at the end of the bonding hallway (his office was a small but simple enough looking room with a desk, filing cabinets, wall shelves for books and ordainments).

There was a large overbearing window behind his desk to look at the world that was once ripe with life as well as his other belongings strewn about the room, he had five copies of the Training Manual which he had co-wrote with his good friend Charles Mansfield. There was a door which connected to a small storage room with a mattress, pillow, and duvet where he would sleep for the nights. It was safe to say he knew his way around the bonding process and had the strict, and arrogant ego to match, giving himself quite the reputation around the facility, often bragging about how things had to be done, and pinning himself above everyone else with his charisma that often intimidated those that weren't as confident as him. He often liked to abuse his power over people, seeing that it was a perfect way to get new aspiring bonders in shape. So, even if his intentions were good, his execution sometimes wasn't.

He'd been sitting in his office at the end of the bonding hall when he received a buzz that alerted him to come to the mess hall to receive a new subject. So, Fredrickson left his office and walked down two flights of steps, to retrieve a new zombie subject by a man named Ryan Winsome – someone whom he didn't really share eye-to-eye with – who'd made the call to him with a sing-song tone that Fredrickson had found irritating. When he was down the steps and the floor that he needed to be on, he strode down a blinding white corridor where he bumped into a blonde-haired woman wearing a ponytail, brushing against her shoulder as he made his way to the mess hall, without turning back to apologise to her, he pressed forward even as the woman called out from behind him 'You gotta work on that Fredrickson.' She'd said in a strong Australian accent, but he paid little to no attention to her as he kept his eyes ahead of him as he maintained the goal in his head of getting this new zombie. He'd been advised by a Bonder's Bellhop intern named Carl Boyle that his new subject was female and she was suspected as being in the over seventy AOR category, otherwise known as Age of Reanimation.

As Fredrickson reached the end of the corridor and stepped into a dankly lit room with large dusty tables strewn around where people used to have their food in, but since the arrival of the mortuus carnem, this mess hall had now been used as the place where bonders met their subjects. He observed a scrawny, balding looking guy clearly waiting for him, known by the way his hand shot out in an expected handshake and the excited smile of anticipation on his face. Fredrickson hadn't seen this man before, so suspected that this man was the intern who'd identified that AOR to him was Carl Boyle, man, judging by the enthusiasm on his face, had been told a lot of stories about Fredrickson, great ones at that and it seemed to Fredrickson that this had been a moment that Boyle had waited for upon arriving here, whenever that was, Fredrickson didn't really care. To this young balding man, having a chance to meet Fredrickson seemed like a fever dream, for he'd wanted a chance to meet up with the GFOSAR's top bonder as soon as he had come to the facility and had heard about Fredrickson's reputation. Boyle was the type of man who wanted to meet anyone who had a good reputation about themselves, because a good reputation surely meant that the person was a good person and good at their job, right?

Fredrickson looked at the hand in front of him briefly before brushing the man off (much to Boyle's dismay) and approached the black-haired female zombie he'd been teamed with, ignoring the balding man's very presence as if he wasn't even there to begin with. Fredrickson was in no mood for pleasantries, he just wanted to retrieve his latest subject and go back to his office to assess who he'd be working with for the next few days or weeks or even months at most.

The zombie female was quite tall, standing at the same height as Fredrickson who was already six feet. She wore a black t-shirt with some flaky mud and bloody splotches and some dirt-stained tan-coloured shorts that reached just below her knees, running with minor rips. Like all zombies, there was always a distinctive feature in regards to how they died which the scientists had come to refer to as the Death Mark something that had been named by Fredrickson's friend Mansfield before he moved away. Frederickson immediately observed hers was very evident. Clearly due to her death mark being a large gaping hole through her stomach which had torn through her shirt leaving it a large "O" shape exposed. He took in more details of the woman's state, the gory opening in her stomach he ascertained was more than likely caused by a firearm and without a doubt the obvious cause of her death.

Fredrickson had become acquainted with firearm damage as taught to him by one of his superiors (Taylor Paxton) before she passed away after her body was mysteriously found near the shoreline of the Tower Bridge in 2052. The death mark in the subject's gut, was clearly missing her pancreas, ribs protruded at odd angles and most of her small and large intestines were gone, leaving broken fleshy tubes dangling in the open hole. Dirt from the grave had replaced the blood. The zombie woman's skin a sharp greyish brown colour coated with old faint scabs of decay, had sunken and shrunk to the bone showing her skeletal frame. By her appearance Frederickson calculated that this woman was most likely buried in a coffin-less grave evident from the amount of dirt and muck over her, as he had always hypothesised that if a corpse was inside a coffin when they awoke as the undead, their bodies would be clean – absent of all the dirt and grime.

The zombie woman appeared as if she was in pain or at least was feeling a heavy amount of physical discomfort as could be seen by the way her posture appeared weak and unsteady, making her stumble from side to side as she swayed around uncontrollably as if she had been administered a heavy dose of Bacardi without her consent and the way she was making silent moans as she swaggered around. It was clear she would've collapsed like any drunk person if her arms hadn't been hoisted up by the two young looking men at her sides.

To Frederickson this observation of drunken swaying was the most apparent sign that she'd been administered with quite a heavy dose of the hunger drug before being presented to him, so these two men had at least done the right thing and for safety purposes, and given her the drug before she would be transferred over to Fredrickson. Fredrickson observed her head that drooped down low causing her to stare at the ground. He couldn't see her face underneath that curtain of black hair, and if he was going to assess the age of this woman, he'd have to get a good thorough look at her face.

'Why is she looking down?' Fredrickson wondered aloud as he blinked while fumbling at the base of his chin at this female zombie that was to be assigned to him. He was curious as to the why this certain zombie couldn't seem to hold herself upright without support. She swayed her head like she was wasted on the strongest vodka to come out of the best pub in Moscow. It was evident they'd probably over done the hunger drug dosage and it made him curious as to why. He looked down at her hands, seeing how they were clenching and unclenching in the air as if she wanted to grasp something that only she could see. This hand movement gave Fredrickson an oddly eerie feeling about it that he didn't quite understand. He couldn't help but feel a slight discomfort around this one zombie. The way she slowly swayed back and forth on the spot made his spine chill, it was almost like he'd seen this kind of drunken posture before from a movie, like when a person plays the dumb idiot for the first half, only to reveal later on that they are actually smart, like scarily smart. He couldn't explain why, but he got a sense that this woman zombie was hiding something from him, something he didn't like and couldn't determine. He couldn't help but feel a strange anxiety looming over him when he stared at this frame that shimmied from side to side. Was that why he felt like ghoulish hands were caressing his spine and making him feel that chill? Was this zombie woman just acting and playing the part of being heavily doused with a strong dose of the hunger drug? Fredrickson shook his head. No, it *couldn't* be, because this woman was undead and unbonded, recently plucked from the streets and chosen for him to bond with. That was the only explanation he could come up with. He would find out this woman's identity through the bonding process.

Boyle opened his mouth to give a response to Fredrickson's earlier question, but his voice was quickly overshadowed by another voice, this one sounding snarkier and with a cockney hint in his accent. 'Bitch was a savage one.' This new voice said, breaking Fredrickson away from his thoughts. Fredrickson closed his eyes in annoyance. He didn't need to look up to see who the owner of this snarky voice was. He instantly recognised the voice as belonging to Ryan Winsome. Fredrickson rolled his eyes when he heard the man's cockney voice, thinking back to rule 2.5 (treat the undead subject with dignity and respect). Winsome was a caramel haired man with green eyes and a mousy moustache above his thin rat-like lips. He smirked as he approached the mild and quiet Boyle holding the zombie from behind. 'Well, according to one of those military diggers outside…' he pointed behind him with a cock of his thumb to the door which he had come out from. 'But because we're just so nice to the legendary Alexander Tomas Fredrickson, we gave her a stronger dose of the wonder drug! (1.2. ensure both safety of bonder and subject) It tots knocked her, "dead," if you know what I mean, but ey if ya won' ta see er face. Though I warn ya' she ain't a pretty thing.'

This snarky man with his mousy moustache was Fredrickson's least favourite colleague, the one who'd called him down to the mess hall to retrieve this zombie. Winsome chuckled to himself, he seemed to enjoy pushing

Fredrickson's buttons as it was with all of their other previous encounters. Winsome showed up to annoy Fredrickson and Fredrickson would reward him with a scowl or the occasional insult. But Winsome didn't mind, this was all a game to him – a game which he'd enjoyed greatly.

Winsome snatched the zombie away from Boyle, he fisted the zombie woman's hair with one hand; he tugged a knot of the zombie woman's hair making the zombie woman let out a small grunt of discomfort. Boyle seemed to withdraw a bit at Winsome's violent move on pulling the zombie woman's head up. 'Careful, Ryan,' he murmured in a hushed tone, 'we have to treat the undead with respect, it's what's written in the book Mr Fredrickson wrote. Remember? rule 2.5.'

But Winsome just rolled his eyes at this intern's weak attempt to take the fun away from him. He looked back at Fredrickson, presenting him with one of his usual sly, cocky grins – the type that Fredrickson loathed.

'Better doc?' he gibed allowing the drugged zombie's dead eyes to stare into Fredrickson's chocolate brown ones. The look was one of adulterated starvation. He had an alarming impression that this zombie never got her fill out there amongst the other zombies; that whenever she would shamble over to a newly deceased body that had been occupied with other hungry zombies like her, a fight would issue and she'd be left to shamble off as a defeated loser, mindless and constantly starving. So, it wouldn't be strange for Fredrickson to think that she'd be more than eager to get the first taste of this professional and feared human man before her. If she was so hungry, she wouldn't be picky and anyone that was alive would do.

The zombie's pupils were a light tint of grey, almost white colour with heavy bloodshot sclera's (the eyes of the dead). Her face was a mess of decay and flabby skin, the nose was skeletal and this close, Fredrickson noticed a few small spiders had made her their home by the faint cobwebs that clung inside her nostrils. Her lips had withered away leaving her with a mouthless gape that exposed her rotting and missing teeth – a death grin exposed over the course of time. Fredrickson then took a step towards her and inhaled her scent – it was a step he hated – but it was crucial information to smell a new subject and to jot the info in the paperwork, that way if things went well, he could purify her bonding room to give her a more sweetened, more pleasurable smell. The smell from her was reminiscent of the stench of burnt sizzling dead flesh on a fire pit. He took a step back and grimaced, covering his nose with his hand and gagged even though nothing came out. She smelt fucking disgusting, almost like she'd fallen down a hill and rolled into a pile of discarded cat excrement or had been showered in the chemical thioacetone which clung to her like crows to a hit and run carcass. He gagged again, but kept his nose covered. 'Did you find out the Age of Reanimation of this woman, and when she died?' Fredrickson questioned Winsome and the other scientist whom he now remembered as Carl Boyle. He clearly didn't have time for small talk as he had an important job to do, and anything to get away from Ryan Winsome, whom he had a vivid distaste for. Boyle was silent the entire time as he kept both his hands seized on his side of the zombie woman's arm. He didn't want to say anything else to Fredrickson when Winsome was already talking for him and humiliating him in the proceedings. He gripped her tightly by the arms in a way that gave Fredrickson the impression he was worried someone was about to get hurt or killed. When Fredrickson looked at Boyle up and down, he noticed that Boyle seemed like a responsible and reliable chap, so much that he'd wished it had been just Boyle who had sent out the call to him to fetch this woman and not Winsome, wishing that Boyle had come alone so that he wouldn't have to deal with Winsome and his stupid remarks. But because Winsome was working out his mouth at every second and stealing Fredrickson attention away from Boyle. It was becoming hard to keep his eyes on Boyle.

'Why, are you asking me, Alex, my friend?' Winsome smirked at their side. 'You're the one that's quote-unquote *big* in zombie research and shit like that. How am I supposed to determine the ages of a rotting sack of decomposing flesh?' he shrugged. 'All zombies look the same as any other rotting cadaver out there. All I do is get the meat sacks from the diggers owside and decide who they go to. Ya know, like a bellhop directing you to ya room number, my role is like tha equivalent of that, only instead of luggage its zombies. And you, Alex, have been chosen to be this lucky one's teacher since everyone boasts about you being so amazing and all that crap.' He paused, taking a great deal of satisfaction when the wooden face in front of him changed to one of annoyance. Winsome smirked in satisfaction at this. He continued gloating and teasing Fredrickson whilst gesturing to the man helping him to keep the zombie on her feet. Winsome, much to most of the Bonder's disgust was in charge of the zombies once they entered GFOSAR earning him the title of Bonder's Bellhop. He, however, spent most of his time passing his duties on to others like Boyle and generally just liked pissing everyone off in the process. It left everyone wondering how he had ever gained the position in the first place.

Fredrickson raised his eyebrows at the smartarse, 'What is your goal, Ryan? Why must you insist on pushing me?'

Winsome laughed and flashed Fredrickson a sly wink and said, 'Because it's fun seeing the frustration swell up on your face. And besides Carl here, has only been around for like thirty-two days, so of course, he's nowhere near as amazing as the country's most renowned, Alexander Fredrickson. He's got the job of supplying the good shit to ya Bonder's.' He gave a mocking royal bow. Boyle turned away, flushing pink with embarrassment, 'aaaaaand like me, he often gets assigned to the Bonders Bellhop post of choosing which zombies go to who. Am I right Carl?'

Boyle said nothing. He was looking away from the conversation between the two men as if he wished that Fredrickson would just take his new subject and leave, because he was more humiliated by Winsome rather than irritated. His chance of meeting the legendary Alexander Fredrickson was ruined by Winsome and his cocky mouth.

Fredrickson rolled his eyes and huffed with irritation at his cocky co-worker, his patience for Winsome was always a thin layer of ice, and this encounter was no different from all the other times Winsome pushed him, his eye twitched slightly before he shot an arm forward and seized the zombie's right arm; the arm which the balding, quiet Boyle was holding. Fredrickson violently wenched the zombie over to him forcing Boyle and Winsome to release her or fall on their faces.

'Who stuck a cork up your arse pops?' Winsome shrugged his cockney accent coming out at the word arse; he threw his arms up as if surrendering to the police.

Fredrickson at that moment really wanted to clock Winsome but restrained himself for the better of his reputation. 'Do everyone a favour and get out of my space, Ryan. We're amid an apocalyptic crisis here. I got no time for smartarses such as yourself breathing the same air as me.' Fredrickson growled at Winsome. Before he left the two men, he looked over at the intern with a fresh set of eyes, eyes that almost looked sympathetic, 'I'm sorry that you got pinned with this arsehole.' He said before he wretched the zombie woman closer to his side. Despite Fredrickson's usually keeping himself calm and collected around his colleagues, hoping to maintain his professionalism, he tightened his grip on the walking corpse's arm, turning his back to the two young men and angrily skulked towards his office situated at the end of the holding cells to the left.

Holding onto the zombie's right arm he led the way into his office, roughly tossing the zombie against the entrance doorframe like she had no purpose. Fredrickson strode over to her and grabbed a shackle that was bound to the wall right to the door to his office. He placed the shackle around the woman's neck and closed it applying his safety rule = 1.2. The Bonder accepts full responsibility for their own safety and the safety of the undead subject. So, if she was to wake up and felt hungry, she would have to get out of that restraint if she wanted to get to him. 'Don't you dare think about trying to get me when you wake up, that is if you want to break your spine.' He mumbled to himself as he went over to his desk. She stood silently for a moment then began uttering small soft groans and moans clearly still under the trance of the drug.

Fredrickson fumbled around his shelving and desk of drawers for his bonding paperwork (since the computers at the GFOSAR were either broken with parts missing or had old updates, making them slow and inoperative, so writing practical paperwork was often required), he knew that he should've had more time to properly organise his desk before he had gone downstairs to meet his new subject. He wasn't usually this disorganised and when he saw the state of his desk, he felt somewhat ashamed that he had allowed it to get in this state. He sat down on his office chair, picked up pieces of papers scattered about on his desk while occasionally he glanced at the zombie to see if there was motion… nothing. *They really must have knocked her out, I hope she doesn't die on me again before I begin the bonding process,* he thought to himself.

Glancing at the zombie woman with her dirty black hair draped over her face, he marvelled for an instance how her appearance seemed to be like something that he'd seen one night when he was younger.

He'd caught a tram from London to Greenwich to go to what used to be his home at the time, he got off the tram when he spotted a lady with her hair covering most of her features on the opposite side of the road. At first, he thought that maybe she was just some woman hoping to catch a tram home herself, but when a tram had driven past without stopping, she was gone. Fredrickson wasn't a believer in ghosts, so he'd simply shrugged off the image of that woman as just his eyes creating a mirage for him in the late night. And yet, seeing his new zombie shambling around with that shackle around her neck and her hair draping her face had made Fredrickson remember that strange encounter on this strange night all those years ago.

Fredrickson looked over into the small room where his bed was for a second, wishing that he could just have a small snooze. But he knew that he wouldn't be allowed to, so he sighed and looked back at his new subject, only this time, another strange image appeared to him. He imagined her head snapping and rolling off its post, fall to the floor and roll in front of him, revealing a sharp toothy grin, with those wide eyes behind that curtain of hair that stared into his own, finishing with the grinning smile contorting in soundless speech which if Fredrickson imagined saying something cryptic like, 'It won't be long until death comes looking for you, Alexander.' Fredrickson gulped and turned away with haste. He shut his eyes and counted for five seconds before he took a deep a breath and regathered himself, he took a tissue from the box on his desk and blew his nose and disposing of the damp tissue on the small rubbish bin on the right side of his desk. He took hold of his papers and growled a frustrated 'bugger,' as a few of them slipped through his fingers to scatter on the floor at his feet. 'Dammit,' he muttered angrily putting the papers he still grasped back on his desk. He dropped to his knees sliding the messed-up papers together, so they were nice and neat but not in order. He slammed them on top of the others on his desk, feeling one of his violent fits beginning to bubble. He could handle one page being in the wrong place, but when he had to deal with Winsome and when more than one page was muddled up, that was something Fredrickson couldn't remain calm about and he had to let his fury out somehow. 'Goddammit! Fuck me!' he seethed, balling his fingers into fists from the untidy mess in front of him; The pages are fucking everywhere,' he raged, feeling an intense urge in his blood to pick up his chair and throw it. He instead calmed enough to fall violently back into his office chair, taking a few big breathes in order to simmer the angry demon inside him.

He'd often struggled with his temper and tried breathing exercises to help keep his temper under control – sometimes they worked, sometimes they didn't – but thankfully, this time it did work. Calmer now, he began sorting the papers making sure they were in the right order, then fumbling around he grabbed the pages he needed for his research, sighing, and muttering under his breath, 'Don't need any more fuck-ups.'

Fredrickson then gripped his chest, closed his eyes, and took in a few deep breaths, remembering that he now had a zombie in his office with him and that sudden outbursts from bonders could result in zombies lashing out at them. He had to remain calm, at least until he got a cell for the zombie. He glanced up from his paperwork, he had a feeling something was off. The room was silent, no pained moaning was coming from the zombie; she was silent as a rock… *Had the drugs worn off?* Fredrickson thought with curiosity, he moved his head up to check on the female zombie that he'd left near the right corner of his office entrance and let out a startled yelp. He leapt out of his chair with such alarming speed that he knocked his chair over and he fell on his buttocks.

The zombie had silently shuffled her feet over to his desk which was about two and a half meters away from where he'd left her and the shackle that he'd put around her neck was dangling against the wall where he had left her. How the hell did she do that without his knowledge, like an owl flying soundlessly in the night air to catch a stray field mouse. How did she get out of that shackle around her neck without a key and how did she do it without him hearing it? Had she been stalking him like a jungle predator eyeing its next victim? Was that the reason behind why she was so unnervingly silent upon creeping up to his desk? *How? How? How? Why? Why? Why?* Were the types of things that were going about inside Fredrickson's head. Whatever the reason behind her stunned silence, she was standing at the foot of his desk and staring dead into his eyes, a scary feeling was inside them that made Fredrickson's heart almost stop. He didn't like the way she was staring at him, those eyes made him uncomfortable and the way those pale grey pupils stared deeply into his without so much as a single blink just only added to the discomfort he felt.

Chapter 2

Thick strings of saliva trailed down the zombie's lipless mouth showing those rotting teeth covered in muck, and all sort of nasty things that could've been her previous meals. She clenched her jaws and emitted hungry growls sounding like a distorted and guttural version of a motor engine, more than enough to tell anyone that they ought to back off and get out of there. And when zombies were starving, they would leave nothing on the bones. The remains would look like they had been snacked on by a pack of scavenging hyenas.

Fredrickson knew what was going to happen as he'd experienced the wraith of a hungry zombie many times before. But there was just something wrong and heavily ominous about this one zombie. How did she get out of the shackle around her neck without a key and how did she manage to shuffle to his desk without him noticing? He didn't like the way his thoughts ran rampant like that and he dreaded the idea that maybe, just maybe, his new subject wasn't as braindead as the rest of the undead. He could almost sense it when he stared at those pallid grey eyes – she was smarter than she looked (much smarter) – she knew what she was doing and she'd continue to exceed his expectations further down the line if Fredrickson managed to restrain her and put her into a cell for when the bonding process would begin. But first Fredrickson had to restrain her and get her into that cell.

Considering what had just happened in the process of a few minutes and how his new subject had released herself from her bounds and moved over to his desk with quick and owl-like silence, Fredrickson tried to not let the trepidation overwhelm him. He relaxed his features as best as he could as if he were lecturing his pupils on what they should do when the hunger drug wears off and their undead subject becomes hostile with hunger. But inside his heart was running on a race-track. He was scared, terrified even. But he knew better than to allow himself to be swallowed up in fear, he'd dealt with this kind of thing before. So, he would just administer the same techniques he'd used with his previous subjects. 'You don't scare me. I've done this plenty of times before you, why should you be any different?' He scoffed, trying to sound brave and unperturbed, even if his heart was on that track, telling him otherwise, telling him to call one of the guards such as Robert Boson to come and restrain her for him. But Fredrickson was not a coward and the type of man to not get his hands dirty – if one was to become a bonder in the first place – they would need to get their hands dirty. As if on impulse, Fredrickson spat at his latest subject, watching as the ball of spit hit her on the heavily desecrated left cheek. But the undead woman showed no reaction to being spat at, she just stood there, glaring at him, and growling that broken motor-like sound. He sat back in his chair, his body now frozen, glued to its current position. He took a deep breath. He knew what he needed to do, keeping a calm visage and to not allow himself to show strong emotions such as trepidation or anxiety as strong emotions could be dangerous – drugged zombie or not.

Then after a few gruelling seconds of her standing there, glaring and making that hideous guttural noise, the zombie woman reached out her long rotting hands with those bony fingers, grabbing hold of Fredrickson's coat collar she pulled him towards her with such an incredible strength that Fredrickson's eyes widened with wonder and yet in horror. Just as quickly as she'd outstretched her arms to grab him over the desk, her hands clenched around his throat as if to strangle him, her heavily decayed features morphed into one of adulterated hatred, a hatred that he couldn't understand and one that had caused him a great deal of discomfort. Being so close to her face now and smelling that rancid stench of rotting meat in her breath, he could've sworn he heard this zombie woman hiss out "liar" as if she'd known or seen him before when she was alive and had known what he'd done, or perhaps she was recalling something that happened before her death. But he didn't know if he'd actually heard her say that or if his mind was just playing tricks on him due to the trepidation in this moment of danger. Despite the dread that had engulfed him, he took the logical route and went with the idea that the fear was causing him to hear things that he knew nobody else could her. Fear has a habit of doing that to even the most hardened of people.

The woman then let out a guttural bellow which sounded like a sputtering motorbike and pushed Fredrickson so violently into a wall that Fredrickson had heard a sound of something breaking and books and medical trophies falling off the wall shelf. When Fredrickson staggered to his feet, he looked behind him and saw a hole in the plaster where he'd been thrown and some of his medical research books and two trophies commemorating his bachelor's degree in science and medicine had fallen to the floor. He would have to clean these items up and find some way to block the hole in the wall next time he was in his office. But that hole though… he couldn't help but think of that hole. This caused Fredrickson's face to animate with shock when he came to this sudden realisation, he took note of the immense strength that this female skeleton possessed, it was staggering as much as it was scary. The undead were truly interesting as much as they were terrifying.

The woman then advanced on him, her movements were janky and stiff, almost like she was a puppet. Fredrickson could've picked any moment in this open window to move and call someone to restrain her, but Fredrickson's feet were nailed to the floor. He couldn't move! *Goddammit! Move! Move!* Alexander Fredrickson tried to move his feet, but each effort was fruitless, he was stuck there. Stuck and waiting for the female skeleton to make her way over to him in only a few short puppet-like strides.

She was in front of him now. He was breathless as he gazed into those pale grey eyes, transfixed by them as if they were crystal balls foreshadowing his death. He could see the hunger inside her eyes and how she had yearned consume him here, in this room. But Fredrickson couldn't allow that to happen. If he had another window, he might just be able to fend her off and show her who is supposed to be pulling her strings in the operation.

The female zombie threw her hands into the scruff of his collar again and this time she lifted him up. Her strength was remarkable as he felt his feet levitate from the floor and dangle helplessly in the air. He was weightless, like a ragdoll, his body had felt like it was made of loosened fabric as his body was yanked across the desk scattering the recently tidied papers. Was she playing with him? It sure felt like it.

His eyes were as wide as golf balls and his lips were trembling as he felt those cold, flayed bony fingers grasp his throat (he'd dealt with strong zombies before but *never* skeleton zombies with strength like this!). He watched as the zombie woman opened her lipless gapping mouth impossibly wider ready to bite down on his head, intending to crush his skull with her teeth and slurp out the succulent juiciness of his brains (the drugs had defiantly worn off). Abruptly, Fredrickson felt a rush of adrenaline enter his body. The sensation was like the time he'd been cutting vegetables, and accidently dropped a kitchen knife which impaled his foot. Reliving that painful accident had finally caused his survival instincts to kick in. He balled his fist and punched at her on the side where he'd spat. The zombie woman released one hand from his throat to clasp at her cheek where she'd felt the impact of his fist. Fredrickson wanted to seize this moment to try and pry her other hand away from his neck, but he couldn't grasp the time to do so. The female skeleton had recovered quickly and instantly resumed throwing her hands around his neck, hulling him over the desk, knocking papers and other desk equipment over as she brought the man over to her so she could kill him and eat his brains. Thankfully though, Fredrickson guarded his throat with his own hand, so when she tried to grab him again, she grabbed his hand. She squeezed at his hand, trying to yank it away. Her disgusting fingernails were chiselling themselves into his skin, prompting Fredrickson to bite his bottom lip and let out a hiss in discomfort. But Fredrickson wasn't intending on being lunch just yet, not when he had an important job to do. 'Damn you, I'm trying to help you! Don't fight me!' Fredrickson hissed through his teeth. He knew he shouldn't be fighting with his latest subject like this. But he knew he'd have to get a drug into her gob, and he wasn't going to administer it while he was in the custody of her grip. He had to fend her off somehow and make her stagger enough to give her a pill. He darted his eyes downward to her stilts holding her up and threw a foot into them, he then raised his foot a little higher and kicked at her chest, causing small pebbles of dirt and grime to fall out of her and making her stagger a bit on her legs. He punched and pushed, doing anything he could to shove her away, to keep her teeth from latching onto their intended target. They struggled back and forth for what seemed like hours but were mere minutes, her trying to pull him closer and him shoving with all his might to keep her jaws at bay. He knew even the smallest of a bite from her would be his end. He never liked relying on others, but he knew that this was something that he'd require aid with. So, he called out for help but knew the likelihood of being heard was slim as he liked his solitude and kept an office far away from the rest of his colleagues.

After some intense fighting and struggling, Fredrickson was beginning to feel numb and was tiring. It was a grind to keep back a durable and strong zombie such as this and he wasn't sure if he'd be able to keep this up any longer. Most of his strength had abandoned him, leaving him with the heart-stopping feeling that this was it for him, that he was going to die. But he was stubborn and clinging onto life for as long as he could, even if most of his fight and strength had left him, he was going to keep fighting until he could get her drugged. Not wanting to get in the way of those teeth he continued to push at her throat with all he had whilst reaching into his breast pocket with his freehand praying he'd remembered; *Rule No.1; Always have Hunger drugs with you, how many times had I taught this to new bonders*. He thought to himself. Feeling the pill in his fingers he felt a flood of relief knowing he now had a chance. He grasped the pill in his fingertips and pulled it free from his pocket. He shot his face back to the woman as she snapped at him and clutched at random parts of his chest. Fredrickson held the pill in his fist and the snarling female back with his other. He kept a hand on her neck, doing his best to keep her head at some distance away from him. He made a sharp turn and manoeuvred his body so that he was standing behind her. Then he used his weight to his advantage and shoved the female into his desk. She made a small guttural grunt as her exposed damaged chest hit the wood of the desk. He was filled with a wave of confidence that he had her where he wanted her. Then in a risky move, Fredrickson wretched her hair back, causing her to open her grimy toothy maw for him, Fredrickson then held the pill above her gaping mouth for a moment and then he dropped it inside her mouth. He pulled out the chair and stepped back a bit only to shove her into the desk once more, this time the side of her face was on his desk.

He bent his body over her from behind holding her down to the desk with all his weight. Clasping her forehead and chin he held them tightly down together encasing the pill inside her mouth. Now she just had to swallow it.

'Come on swallow it you bitch!' he hissed, struggling with the zombie as she thrashed around against him, she growled a howling animalistic sound as she struggled against his weight. Luckily, he was a little larger in frame than her, otherwise he knew with the strength he'd felt from her earlier that she could have easily flung him off her. But even with those facts inside him, he was determined to win this fight, as long as she would swallow the pill, that would tell him that he won and she was his. He continued to hold onto her forehead and chin as tight as he could using all the strength he could muster, continuing to lock the pill in her mouth. There was no choice but to wait for her to swallow it and he prayed that his strength would hold out for that to happen. After what seemed like an eternity of him holding her this way and her struggling, his arms aching from his efforts he heard her make a swallowing noise (bitch finally swallowed the motherfucking drug! *Ha! Good riddance*). She moaned weakly, showing her defeat as if she understood she'd lost. Then her struggling came to a sudden stop.

Panting like he'd just tried his luck on the rodeo bull, Fredrickson unclasped the zombie's chin and forehead catching his breath again, she stood slowly from the desk and returned to the previous slumped state with her eyelids flickering tiredly. 'You are one stubborn corpse.' He addressed her shaking his head. He grabbed a wad of tissues from a box on his desk and used them to wipe the sweat from his face.

'Regardless of how stubborn you are, I will see to it that you're bonded with and outside on your final journey to becoming human again.' Fredrickson then grabbed her wrist and took her back over to the wall where he had shackled her earlier. He chained her again and watched her for a few careful moments before he went back to his desk. Making sure she still appeared compliant by casting a few glances at her and making sure she was still chained up and doped. When he was satisfied, a scant smirk appeared on his face and he leaned down, grabbed hold of his paperwork that had spilled to the floor during his struggle with her. He checked it was all still in good order, took out the papers he immediately needed and made his way back around his desk, this time keeping a careful eye on the zombie the whole time putting the pages together in the way he'd left them before the struggle with his new subject. Holding them under his arm, Fredrickson pulled out one of the drawers and took out a teal folder. He opened the folder and slipped the papers inside before closing it and putting it under his arm.

He approached her pausing slightly to check her for any sudden movements, he sneered at her as if expecting her to jump at him. Nothing. Good. Fredrickson unlocked the shackles around her neck with a key that he kept in one of his pockets in his lab coat. Fredrickson seized her wrist, looked her up and down then he started walking away, pulling her along with him. They made their way as swiftly as her drug state allowed back down the corridor to the ward which held the Zombie cells for the zombies going through the bonding process. They crossed the room making their way around people and zombies alike, with people taking glances and muttering things around him and his latest subject. But Fredrickson paid no attention to the gossip of his colleagues as he made his way down the path. He took this time to glance at the zombie again checking cautiously for her state of compliance. Noting no change to her state of drugged mindlessness and absence of violence as he proceeded down a corridor housing the zombie cells stopping abruptly outside a cell door numbered B-35 which stood for Bonding No. 35. Zombie cells usually consisted of just a small room with a bed, an interrogation table and two chairs. The cells weren't much but it's not like zombies need a homey place to live; they're dead so it wouldn't matter, though sometimes arrangements were made to make cells more respectable if the subject was behaving and bonding well, such as getting pictures, a few desk nicknacks or things to keep their minds occupied such as toys, books or tablets to play music on. But usually for the first half, bonding cells were plain and simple. He checked her again before entering a code into the keypad on the wall beside the cell door near a large glass observation window. He muttered the number as he put in the code "1-9-8-0" and the door buzzed open. He shoved the zombie into the cell where she took a few stumbling steps to right herself and then stood swaying in the middle of the room. He closed the cell door shut and peered through the large glass window set in the door for observation. He waited for the familiar buzz to show the cell had locked. He continued to watch his new subject for a while and as she swayed under the effects of the drug. She didn't do anything else that had caused much interest to Fredrickson, so he huffed and walked away.

Zombie bonding will begin tomorrow. I'm intrigued about finding out who this woman was before she met her maker, he thought to himself.

Chapter 3

People who aimed to become Zombie Bonders needed to follow a strict criterion, such as taking in a few lectures by a superior such as Fredrickson, needed to do some theory work and keep notes of the dot points from the book _The UK Mechanisms for Infected Subject Reintegration and Bonder Training Manual By Alexander Fredrickson and Charles Mansfield_ (the latter works over in Washington D.C to repel the undead and train the Americans in the ways of bonding) that bonders had to abide by, these dot points were to include specific rules and protocols that all bonders must obey. There were 13 in total outlined in the SEPTER model Fredrickson had created: Safety, Ethics, Procedures + Protocols, Training Evaluation and Release. Further to Frederickson's SEPTER model was his five mechanisms.

-    Mechanism One: Dismantle to Refrain (D2R).

-    Mechanism Two: 28 Day Neuropathy Rebuild (28Nb).

-    Mechanism Three – Emotion Regulation and Conditioning (ERC)

-    Mechanism Four – Complex Consciousness and Behaviour Training (CCBT)

-    Mechanism Five – Integration Animation Evaluation (IAE)

Bonding sessions usually take place in the months of February, April, June, August, October, and December. Despite Christmas been in December; it was just easier for the Bonders to work during every second month of the year because they would all have a practical month of bonding with their zombies which could sometimes be tedious and time consuming (depending on how the zombie acts) and a month of theory an equally boring task of filling out forms, rereading through notes gathered during bonding sessions, occasionally having board meetings about how they were going and if they're zombie was going to be either a failure or a success by explaining how their zombies were behaving, if they were listening to their bonders and if the zombies were starting to show physical (more lively facial animations) and mental progress (decision making). But mainly bonders opted to use these scarce months for a much-needed break away from their zombies if all they're theory and scribbling in records was completed, in which they would be able rest up and spend the rest of the monthly holiday to their own leisure. The zombie files were a series of lined papers sealed inside a folder which had stored a dossier file, which had a photo of the zombie as well as other pieces of information in regards to their appearance, citizenship, DOB, DOD etc. then these files would temporarily be stored away in record books and filed in the facility library, to be plucked out and consulted by other bonders as a study of the signs of good and bad zombies along with techniques on how to deal with issues when they arose, and when the other bonders were done with the records, they would be transferred back to the bonder who'd written them. The weeks and sometimes months of paperwork depending on specific notes bonders gather on their zombies would also allow bonders to take a much-desired break from the exhausting task of trying to tame and bond with a zombie, while also consulting with other bonders and exchanging tips on how they could bond at a reasonably steady pace with their zombies, because the theory work was of the upmost importance when it came to being a zombie bonder, you had to have a keen eye for detail and a tendency to be practical and think outside of the box when it came to bonding and the facility in which the bonders worked at tended to be very picky about the individuals they chose to become bonders. This could become mentally draining on the bonders, who'd have to continually deal with outburst of aggression from their subjects, along with learning difficulties as they started to become more human like, but even during those outbursts, they had to be with them to try and calm them down and resolve it humanly. But if the paperwork had been completed and checked off at the briefing room by the highly qualified such as Fredrickson himself (he marked and checked his own notes without needing to go to briefing, but he only went there to teach new bonders on how to correctly write their reports). This was payment for the bonders, instead of cash. They'd be granted the time to have a break from all the work, put their legs up and rest assured, knowing that they had half a month to themselves and were free to do anything that they wanted in the facility, as long as it was safe and it didn't revolve following the Winsome route by teasing the zombies as they sat in their cells in silence. Not that anyone would follow in the steps of the Winsome anyway, because he was the village idiot that everyone disliked. So, in order to get that time off to relax, bonders needed to work on their notes and get them marked off by their superiors. If their notes were detailed and up to date, they were qualified for a break. There were twenty-six bonders at the GFOSAR in total.

The survivors that sought refuge in the facility would often wonder why the Bonders worked over Christmas day and the other important holidays, it was a common wonder why the Bonder's didn't take time off their work to spend Christmas with their remaining family members or have a day off for their birthday. But if one were to see things from a Bonder's perspective, they would be able to work out that the bonders saw their work as the only option and means to help humanity survive and the survival of the human race was far superior to these holidays, so birthday's, Christmas and wedding anniversaries were unimportant, when the lives of billions were on the line, the human race would do anything in their power to ensure a means of survival. But if bonders wanted to let their fellow colleagues know that they were another year older, they would say that it was their birthday and nothing else, just a simple, "It's my birthday today" was all that was necessary.

They were living in a dying world, where seeing a former dead relative walking around had now become the new normal. Christmas and Easter weren't as important as the bonding of zombies, AKA the solution into the Mortuus Carnem epidemic. The only thing that was celebrated was when a zombie showed human-like intelligence and a capability to return to their humanity and live a life that was once ripped from them. So, when it came to Christmas, the closet thing they got to a gift from Santa was their zombie showing the electrical cords of humanity. And if the zombie was doing well according to their bonder's notes, they would be given an early Christmas present in the form of a frozen brain.

Chapter 4

The day was October 1st, and the time was 7:32 in the morning. Fredrickson opened the drawer in his desk, took out that teal coloured folder, opened it, took pages out and began prepping his paperwork for his first session of zombie bonding with his female zombie. As Fredrickson stood and put his chair under the desk, he pondered. He knew that in order for this zombie to work and for him to finally live up to his reputation of "best Bonder in the GFOSAR," he had to change, his methods had to change. He needed to be in more control over his emotions and violent outbursts.

Before leaving his office, Fredrickson made the decision to pick up his old jar of antidepressants from the wall shelf which had his zombie bonding training books. He unscrewed the lid and fished out a pill. Without water, he plopped the pill into his mouth and washed it down with his spit before leaving his office to begin his work with his new zombie.

Whilst Fredrickson steeled himself for today's session of bonding with his yet to be named zombie, he passed by one of his colleagues: a young brown-haired spectacled woman with matching kind eyes and soft, clean, tender round features by the name of Marilyn Kolen. Fredrickson looked at her for a moment as she strode past him, clutching a clipboard to her chest, her head lowered. She didn't say anything to him as she went by. Fredrickson had the idea that perhaps she hadn't recognised him. Fredrickson liked Kolen. He thought she was a bright young lady with a big future ahead of her. Even though Kolen was timid and sensitive, Fredrickson liked her nonetheless and thought she was one of his best pupils.

Kolen was the youngest bonder to date. At the mere age of twenty-eight, she was lucky to even obtain a position as a zombie bonder when she first met Fredrickson who saw a deal of potential in her, saw that she was loyal, could see that she wanted to do something to help the cause, could see the grief struck inside those kind brown eyes. He saw someone whose dreams had crashed down upon her and that she was here to try to rebuild herself and to start again instead of giving up and letting her failures swallow her up.

Inside those grief-stricken eyes laid an enthusiasm to make the world a better place, and that was something that Fredrickson liked to see when people came into the facility to become bonders. He wanted enthusiasm, even if it was hidden behind grief. He wanted someone who would be loyal and wouldn't contradict him. He wanted someone who'd listen to him and take careful heed of the things he'd say. He saw those things in Kolen, that was why he liked her, because there weren't a lot of bonders around that had shown as much loyalty and attentiveness as Kolen. In a place like The Great Facility of Science and Medical Research, simply known as GFOSAR, there was a stigma that with age comes wisdom. This was partly because being so young and inexperienced could result in disastrous occurrences. Luckily for Kolen she'd won over her employers regarding the argument of her age. With a lack of people wanting to take on the dangerous task of bonding, along with her enthusiasm, loyalty, and explanation that she was desperate to make a difference she'd joined the fight to help mend the wounds of the broken planet.

She had no zombie bonding experience but made up for it with her eagerness to learn this basis of what she'd be getting herself into in Fredrickson's classes which she'd taken notes of, listening closely to Fredrickson's brilliant SEPTER model that spilled out her mentors mouth and jotting down the key factors that she'd follow when the time came for her to get her own subject. Kolen was a very organised young woman who took a great deal in keeping up with everything Fredrickson had put her through (another thing that he liked about her). So, she wouldn't be late for lectures and other important meetings, Kolen would put on an alarm to wake her at seven o'clock. But not only was Kolen on head when it came to being organised and had notebooks full of the procedures and protocols Fredrickson created and taught, she'd completed her first aid courses in her youth and had some experience with mental therapy during her college and university years back at her home and believed she would be a valuable asset to the team as the facility was in need of someone with heavy enthusiasm, and as Kolen had put it during her first interview back in late May of 2051, "I like to use gentle precision with those I work with as it would be unwise to rush things. I believe that patience is key in this line of work. Precision and patience is what wins the race. And not to brag but I'm also a fast learner if you would like to see my university degree." Kolen was born in Middelburg in The Netherlands and arrived in England only five years prior during early March of 2051. She had learnt English two years prior to integrating to the UK.

Marilyn Kolen was a widow at the tender age of twenty-eight. She still wore the silver wedding ring on her right hand which had **26-12-49** engraved on its inside, which she sometimes stares at and fumbles with sadly. Whenever she found herself in a lost state of mind and the memory of the heart throbbing last time, she saw her husband Jacob in her mind. He'd become infected by the mortuus carnem shortly after Kolen had made the decision to tell him she was finally ready to start a family, something Jacob had wanted for years. Kolen was always an innocent, sensitive woman who liked to keep to herself and couldn't face confrontation, her late husband had been good for her in that regard. Whenever confrontation found Marilyn, Jacob would be there to stand up for her. So, when on that fateful day when word reached her that her late husband, Jacob Kolen had passed away from a stroke only to be reanimated by the mortuus carnem parasite as a lumbering hungry zombie, Kolen being the timid type, couldn't bring herself to gun down the man she'd married and loved. She remembered getting a call from Jacob's twin brother Nico who had fretted that Jacob was "awake" and was acting strangely,

"He's become violent and very aggressive and has tried to attack and eat me! I had no other option, there weren't any weapons around, so I had to knock him out by waiting for him to come into a room and slamming the door in his face. Then I dragged him outside and tied him to the big tree with some rope and tarp. I'm sorry Marilyn, I would do it myself… but Jacob loved you deeply and would talk about you a lot, so if someone is going to put him out of his misery, I think it should be you."

At first Kolen had thought that this was some kind of cruel, insensitive joke that Nico was pulling on her, as Nico had a thing for scaring Kolen. Nico was a good actor. But Kolen had discovered that this had been no prank and that Nico was actually telling the truth for once. Kolen had come home to find signs of a struggle with overturned furniture and broken glass and pottery littering the floor. Some of the pieces of glass had blood on them and Kolen couldn't discern the blood belonged to Nico or Jacob. But regardless of whose blood it belonged to, Kolen was now scared and frightened. When she'd gone outside to the backyard as that was the place Nico said Jacob was, Kolen was horrified to find her dead husband whom she'd watched get lowered into the ground two months before, tied up to a tree, tarp around his body and rope holding him and the tarp to the tree. Kolen had just stood, tears brimming down her cheeks as she stared helplessly at her dead husband sharply darting his head back and forth, snarling and thrashing against his restraints madly. The zombified Jacob saw Kolen and he snapped his teeth at her a few times and even managed to free one arm from the rope and tarp, and with that arm, he tried reaching out to her, all while he continued snarling and gurgling as saliva sprayed out of his mouth. After about ten heartbreaking minutes of crying and staring at the revelation that her husband had become some walking dead man hellbent on eating anyone he could get his hands on, Kolen decided she couldn't stand another second with her now zombified husband. She ran back into the house, packed up all the money and valuable items that she could find, then fled the house, went straight to an underground rig which a lot of people had been going to.

This rig asked for cash and Kolen paid everything she owned. Satisfied with the money, Kolen was able to get into a boat with a large group of people looking to get out of the country. On this boat with others like her, Kolen set out of Middelburg to London after hearing frequent chatter on the boat about a place dubbed the GFOSAR where experiments with the undead were being conducted in hopes to save the human race by teaching those infected and reanimated into becoming human again, and hoping to remember their former selves before they danced with death.

At this time the mortuus carnem was well established throughout the globe with many taking matters into their own hands to prevent their loved ones from rising. She, however, had been unable to bring herself to grant him eternal peace by the chosen form of putting a bullet through his skull, choosing instead to flee from her homeland crossing into the UK by boat and taking on citizenship in England.

She wished for some different way to assist those like her beloved that had become infected, which led her to begin her immense three plus years of theoretical training with GFOSAR to become a zombie bonder since it was vital to have at least 2 years of Frederickson's theory and training, plus an induction and onboarding process that introduced them to the bonders quarters and cells, available equipment used, the hunger drug stations, the physical condition of zombies and a list of notes that she'd have to record when the time came for her to receive her first zombie. Seems like a handful, but it was important that new bonders knew everything that was crucial to bonding with zombies. During those 2 years of training under Fredrickson's lectures and with about seven other pupils in her class. And about three weeks on the tenth of September 2054, Kolen had been present inside a cell with another bonder named Olio Garcia who had agreed to let Kolen be in the same room as she bonded with her zombie named Queen, Kolen had stood in the background with a pen and notebook in hand, getting an insight into what she'd have to do when it'd be her turn to sit in front of a zombie.

So, today was a very special day for Marilyn Kolen, as this was her first time working alone, she'd yet to receive a zombie to bond with until today, in this exact moment, on this day Oct 1st 2056.

It was just after seven in the morning when the young Dutch woman had arrived at the Mess Hall. There, standing in the middle of the room in a circle of tables and chairs stood Carl Boyle. This time he was alone and didn't have Winsome chewing in his ear with sly remarks about the bonders. Kolen approached Boyle with a smile, she tilted her glasses above her nose when she looked down at her new subject. She was presented with an old decomposing legless zombie, intestines smeared with dirt and worms hung below an exposed ribcage. At first Kolen thought she might lose her breakfast upon sight of seeing the legless zombie and all those wriggling worms slithering around that ribcage. But after turning away and coughing into her fist, she quickly recovered as she read in the training manual prior and remembered reading about the various physical zombie appearances, so thankfully it didn't take long for Kolen to bypass the intestines wriggling out of the zombie's severed body.

The zombie was brought over to her in a rusted wheelbarrow and had clearly been stuffed half dead with a recent dosage of the hunger drug.

Kolen looked over at the bald, red-faced man who was holding the wheelbarrow by the handles. Kolen noted the arms of her new subject which were lolling out the sides of the wheelbarrow.

'I thought about it carefully, since it's your first-time bonding Mrs Marilyn Kolen, I figured you should start with something simple so decided to give you a crawler to bond with. I've read that Crawler types are fairly easy as they don't have legs and can't really move to attack you.' Boyle said as he bit his lip, turning his eyes away slightly, an attempt at trying to hide his overpowering red face. He had an overwhelming feeling of love for the chocolate-haired spectacled woman in front of him. She was beautiful just as she was kind-hearted. The moment Boyle had seen her politely step out of his way (when most people would just bump into him) when Winsome was giving him a tour of the place, he knew that he'd developed some kind of childish crush on her. Because it was hard to find beautiful and kind women these days. Carl Boyle held up the rusted green wheelbarrow by the handlebars and looked away from her slightly. 'I-Is that alright with you la-lass' he stammered, not noticing his Irish accent had slipped out in the last of his words.

'Ja, it is completely fine. Thank you' she giggled from watching Boyle turn into his own interpretation of a human beetroot. 'You are awfully kind, Carl. You didn't have to present me with a crawler because this is my first-time bonding with a zombie, but you did it anyway because that's just the kind of man you are. I hope you get a raise if raises are a thing here at the GFOSAR.

Boyle's eyes flashed and for a moment, Kolen had seen the blush spread around his cheeks so quickly that she couldn't help but put a hand to her mouth to stifle another giggle. Boyle looked away, biting his lip a little harder. Finally, after she decided that she'd better get back to work instead of teasing the Irish Bonder's Bellhop.

Underneath the white rimmed glasses which she wore, she scanned the state of the crawler lying in the wheelbarrow, looking up and down at the slumped body lying motionless, regarding two faint lumps coming from the chest and the excess of decay in the body.

Without looking at Boyle, she stated her thesis. 'I believe this zombie is a female by the faint breasts and is over the forty-year AOR by the few scabs and the dead grey skin? Although it isn't good to make assumptions about the undead regarding age and death. My assumption is that this crawler zombie could've had a brutal death, either by being torn apart by the legs or maybe, caught under a lawnmower? The last one is unlikely, but I could be wrong. I'll let her tell me when she gains more intelligence with the bonding process.' Kolen looked back at Boyle who was silent with brightly coloured cheeks and biting his lip so hard that his upper lip was white. She had to stifle another giggle. She smiled at him warmly. 'Again, thank you for choosing an easier subject for me to work with, Mr Boyle. From what Mr Fredrickson told me during my two years of training and from what I learnt observing Garcia, zombie bonding has many different twists and turns, the zombies can turn the tables on you when you least expect them to like he said, 'they have more potential than others think they do'. She gave Boyle one more smile, and then walked over to take the handles of the wheelbarrow from his grasp, saying goodbye to him, and waiting for him to stammer out his farewell to her, Kolen parted away from him. Kolen left the mess hall and went to the elevator, furthest down the left side of the facility. She knew she wouldn't be able to get the wheelbarrow up the stairs, and even if she did, it would be wasting time getting each wheel over a step. So, Kolen took the smart option and took the elevator up to the bonding cells on L3. Keeping the wheelbarrow ahead of her, she navigated her way past people, moving the wheelbarrow left and right to avoid people walking past until she reached a cell labelled B-12. She reached out to the keypad next to the door and typed in the code 1-9-9-2, the lock buzzed, opening the cell doors. Kolen noticed the step in that was preventing the wheelbarrow from entering. 'It's never simple,' she mumbled to herself as she thought of ways she could get the wheelbarrow over it. She pressed down on the wheelbarrows handlebars so the front wheel hung idly in the air, then using her weight she pushed the wheelbarrow forward making an awful grating noise. It roared through the halls as it dragged forward without the assistance of the wheel. Some cries emanated from the cell doors along the corridor, the zombies within the cells clearly didn't appreciate the sound. *Sorry... sorry...* Kolen thought guiltily to herself as she looked back at her subject, expecting her to wake up. Nothing, not even a stir. Good. With the front wheel now over the step she set the wheel back down to the ground. She pushed the wheelbarrow into the cell, the wheel now taking the weight and was finally ready to begin her first experimentation.

Kolen lifted up bars of the wheelbarrow so the crawler zombie slid easily out of the wheelbarrow and onto the floor. She blinked at the zombie, watching it lay there for an instant and then turned and wheeled the wheelbarrow back down the step leaving it outside the cell in expectation of someone else collecting it.

She then sealed herself and the zombie inside cell B-12. Turning, she took the time to examine the crawler on the floor, still apparently doped on the drug.

Kolen picked up her subject from the floor, being mindful to keep the head and teeth away from her own, and carried her over to the gurney attached to the wall and laid her down gently on it. 'Well,' Kolen began nervously, clapping her hands together and rubbing them. Considering you're my very first zombie to bond with, I guess I should give you a name.' Her heart was pounding with nervous excitement as she grabbed the chair that was tucked under the interrogation table. She dragged it behind her over to where a steel gurney was set against the far wall and placed it down just in front of it. *Bonding today will start on the bed, well, the introductions at least,* she thought to herself. To prevent the crawler from launching out at her if it returned from its dazed state, she took the leather belt straps that were underneath the gurney to restrain the female crawler to the bed itself. Looking her subject up and down and finding not much of a body to attach to the bed, she settled on the decision to reach over and put one of the belts around the neck of the crawler and clipped it to the other side of the gurney. She did this to the other strap, looping it around the crawler's chest and tightening the straps so that she was certain that her crawler wouldn't get away. 'There,' Kolen said, lightly patting the crawler on the ribcage. I hope it isn't too uncomfortable for you.' The zombie didn't react to her at all, allowing Kolen to do what she felt was necessary to her subject while she was stuck in her drugged-up state.

Kolen blinked and feeling a tinge of sympathy for the now restrained zombie, she reached out with the insane urge to untighten the straps around the zombie's chest area as she was worried that she might be hurting her subject. *I don't want to hurt her and make a bad first impression on my first zombie. Maybe if I just loosen the strap around her neck.* But then remembering the rule about safety in her training thankfully she threw the idea away, instead leaving the zombie restrained. Kolen put on a positive face, even if seeing the straps tightly clasped to her crawler's neck and chest did bring her some discomfort, she knew it was best for her safety to keep the crawler tightly strapped, even if she did at first think that her crawler looked harmless and that bonding with her was going to be a simple and straight-forward.

Then she remembered Olio's words after she'd finished watching Olio work with her zombie. 'The undead are cunning and will try to trick you, watch for these signs, Marilyn. You have to treat them with respect, Rule about respect, and do no harm, yes, but you should also give them boundaries, keep them restrained until you start earning some trust from them, then slowly begin to loosen those restraints.' *Olio was right, I should keep her restrained until I start developing a mutual trust with her*, Kolen thought to herself. She then returned to her work and thought where to start?

Kolen looked at the ceiling idly as she tried to think of a suitable name for her crawler. She put a finger to her lip and tapped it thoughtfully. Then, finally a name which she'd thought would fit came to her and she looked at her drugged zombie with cautious enthusiasm. 'How about, Ace, like the number one card?' Then as if realising the important impact an Ace playing card had in her life, Kolen sniffled and wiped a small tear from underneath her glasses, her fingers instinctively went to the silver ring on her finger, remembering her late husband Jacob, who was always a fan of card games; poker, solitaire, spider, SNAP!! Anything as long as he got to use cards. And his favourite cards were the Ace of Clubs and the Ace of Hearts. So, the name of her first zombie seemed fitting, even if she felt the weight of depression on her at the memories of her beloved Jacob. She shook the memories loose and instead focussed her mind on what was in front of her.

The female crawler zombie stirred. The crawler's eyelids slighted until she opened them fully to stare over at her bonder. The crawler zombie laid back silently, her withered lips trembling, and her black tongue lolled out from her mouth as if she was already trying to say something in response to her name christening. 'A-A-c-ceee' the crawler zombie now known as Ace moaned in a voice that was a mixture of a frog croak, and a cat hiss yet distinctly human and yet it was spoken in English and not in incoherent moans and groans, also known as *ZOMBLISH.*

Kolen ceased her own mutterings and stared in utter shock at Ace. She felt her eyes sting from the tears as they splashed onto her glasses. She hurriedly wiped them away removing her glasses to clear the splodges of droplets on the lenses before quickly placing them back on her face to peer again at Ace. Kolen's mouth dropped in awe. The chocolate eyes underneath her glasses widened with surprise from hearing the zombie respond to her. As Kolen stared, her mouth remained unresponsive; she was felt speechless, and didn't notice paperwork slipping from her hands to the floor. All she could do was stare at Ace with wide eyes of surprise; taking in a breath Kolen finally spoke. 'Can you understand me Ace?' Kolen questioned with a glimmer of hope that her zombie would respond to her. An answer that would confirm that indeed Ace could understand. Kolen made sure to keep an eye on her crawler, as she approached the gurney she was strapped to.

Much to Kolen's disappointment, Ace didn't reply this time, so Kolen found herself moving in closer still. But Kolen got a wee bit too close (bad idea rookie), she hadn't paid attention to the faint hungry snarls that were coming from Ace's mouth. Kolen reached a hand down with the urge to unstrap the leather collar around the crawler's neck due to the un-expectant human connection which had flowed from their interaction. As she reached for the collar it was then that the new bonder learned a valuable lesson: Ace tried to snap at her, her teeth trying to find Kolen's flesh. Kolen stumbled back away from Ace, the collar and straps thankfully doing their job of holding Ace in place, preventing her from reaching her intended victim and doing any damage to Kolen. Kolen stood back. A surge of adrenaline passed through her, followed quickly by regret as she watched with sad eyes as Ace continued to struggle and thrash violently against the straps, and collar around her neck, making loud yells and shouting things that made no sense, and protesting to be unstrapped because she was starving and needed some living meat.

Kolen sighed wanly; she straightened her glasses, her mouth closed into a frown, backing up further from the gurney she sat back in the chair watching Ace continue her struggle, her fingers playing nervously at her straight chocolate brown hair.

'I guess it was wrong of me to hope for this bonding to work just like that. This'll take some time, but we'll get there soon, Ace, I promise you that. I promise that you will feel the joy of being alive again' Kolen frowned. She just continued to sit there on the chair starring at the half lipless mouth on the crawler's scabby face. Her head and mouth were making odd jerking movements as if she was trying to reach out and bite down on a slab of invisible meat hanging just in front of her hunger induced eyes. Saliva was crawling down Ace's cheek, falling to the ground in small droplets of foul-smelling spit. Kolen observed her zombie's desperate effort to getting the straps off her neck and let out yet another sigh. She felt foolish for the incident and made a silent vow to herself not to do that again.

Seeing the scattered papers on the ground, she leaned over and picked them up, sorting through them one-by-one neatly in her lap whilst watching Ace still desperately thrashing and struggling against the bonds that held her.

Kolen held the papers in her hands and made the effort to force a smile of hope onto her face. 'Alright Ace. Let's refresh and start this over again, shall we?'

Chapter 5

Fredrickson sat on his chair in cell B-35, staring with irritated eyes and huffing in annoyance at the zombie opposite him. She slumped in her chair, drooping her head low, so low that her temple was touching the table as she swayed drunkenly, dragging her temple across. Fredrickson could see there was a small wet streak of drool escaping from her mouth.

He crossed his arms and leaned back against his chair and wondered how she could be sitting there considering the amount of hunger drugs she'd consumed today. He'd given her two drugs just to be on the safe side and to not have any more surprises from her. But even if he did give her two dosages, he knew and expected her to be able to sit up straight, as it was usually when zombies had three pills that they wouldn't be able to sit up straight. So, Fredrickson wondered why his zombie was doing this if she'd only had two.

It would humiliate and frustrate him more if she fell off the chair and passed out, he thought. He sighed, leaned back over the desk, and jotted her behaviour in his paperwork, as it was important to note the behaviour so he could see if there'd be any changes in future sessions. Fredrickson did this idly, noting that she hadn't displayed any emotion or movement ever since he'd thrown her into her cell after their last session's fiasco. It was also the same time when he considered applying his own rule – he'd have to give her a name, a name that is simple and recognisable. Because Z20 was not a good and recognisable name, each of the subjects he worked with had their own unique name.

He glanced at her as he tried to think of a suitable name for her, but he couldn't think of anything. The way she continued the same groggy swaying movement and the parting of those black weeds around her head as she dragged her temple across the table made him consider giving her an inappropriate name, such as "Waif." But he shook his head and said, 'you can't stay drunk like this forever.'

He thought back to their first meeting when the drugs had worn off, and she'd made an attempt to attack him. 'You do realise that I'm only trying to help you, feel the same way as if you were alive again… so you need to help me by bonding with me in a civil manner, and I'll help you to feel the sun again,' he added before muttering under his breath. ("Useless waif") 'Because the last thing I need is one more stubborn zombie. I've had a gut full of working with stubborn zombies. I want at least one fucking zombie that will bond with a grade that I mark as a success. Is that too much to ask for?' Fredrickson said, he thought about his medication and the attitude he possessed during those subjects that had ended up as failures (failures that he had caused). He'd get so worked up and angry that he'd forget his own rule, Rule 2:4 about maintaining a calm exterior and emotional regulation in front of a zombie, and he'd unintentionally sabotaged his own bonding process by lashing out at his zombies for not doing what he wanted them to do. So, if he wanted Z20 to be a success, he knew that this time he had to be better; he had to be the one to change. He had to be more restrictive with his emotions if he was going to come out with his first success story. He leaned back in his chair and fiddled with his pencil, twirling it around his fingers.

Frederickson took a deep breath, then decided to start again. If he had to change for the better, he might as well make a start now. He ruffled through his papers before setting them neatly down in front of him, sighing at the impossible task of bonding with a zombie so drugged up she probably couldn't understand what he was saying. Despite her drugged state and his irritation at her minimal movement, he forced himself to smile, not an overly jovial one, just a small grin that showed him that he was at least feeling a bit hopeful for what he could get out of his female subject. He expected great things from his new zombie, and despite his reputation as the GFOSAR's senior bonder, Fredrickson wasn't perfect; he lacked patience and was often quick to hit his angry button, resulting in a hostile outburst, which had often resulted in most of the zombies he'd worked with being failures; startled by his sudden outbursts.

But thankfully during the recent weeks before meeting this female subject, Fredrickson had been taking antidepressants for his anger problems. He also tried frequent breathing exercises in order to keep his mental state in check. He should've taken a Valium before starting the day. If he was going to make this zombie a success, he needed to be calm and change his bonding method.

He took a deep breath and still maintained that slight grin, even if he, himself, wasn't feeling the urge to smile.

'Let's just begin the bonding with an introduction,' he said as he put a fist over his mouth and lightly coughed into it. He cupped his fingers together, placed them down on the table, opened his mouth, and introduced himself, 'my name's Alexander Tomas Fredrickson. I'm aware that you don't remember your name, considering you've been dead and rotting in your coffin-less grave for over seventy years, so that can be forgiven. I know this because I have bonded with over nineteen zombies throughout my job as a zombie bonder, and you, madam, are my twentieth. But, looking back on those nineteen subjects, it was actually me that had made things harder for myself, and I'd been the one who had turned them into failures. But I hope to be different this time. But if I'm to change, I'll need your help. So, let's hope that you're different and that we can regain a sense of trust for each other.' Frederickson thought about the gaping hole in her stomach, 'we'll fix that stomach as well as the rest of your body when your personality develops. That'll happen when you start to meet the eligibility standards for surgery 2:11 he added. 'But for now, this is only to fill you in on what's going to be happening here.' He considered not bothering to tell her the rest, but because it was something he had to tell each zombie, he couldn't refuse (and because he was earnest about his job). The learning process on zombies was varied over the course of the bonding procedure; some were fast learners and only took half a week, while some were slow and would take months for a single zombie to learn one thing. But it was always the same procedure with zombies; the first bonding day was simply an introduction for the bonder and zombie to get to know each other. The second day and the days following day one resulted in the bonder deciding to use their skills and time to bond with their zombies. The last bonding days, which could be any day, all really depended on the working relationship the bonder and zombie had for one another; the last day could either lead to the zombie being disposed of or being sent into the wild to try and live a life that was taken from them.

'You have been brought into this facility known as the GFOSAR to be experimented and tested on. My job is to bond with you as a zombie bonder so you will remember your life before. Sounds good? Of course, it does. So, if you help me, I will help you, and vice versa. Do we have a deal?' Fredrickson finished and watched as the zombie tilted her head so her face could be seen through the hanging veil of her hair. She moaned, her head suddenly dropped to the table, and a loud thud echoed throughout the room. Fredrickson raised his eyebrows and scoffed while muttering to himself. 'Of course, we do; it's not like you can object to me now; you're here with me, and that's that. I'll be back tomorrow.' He sighed, tucking his paperwork under one arm. He stood, grabbed the top of his chair and, scrapping it against the floor, moved it to the corner where he'd retrieved it from. He headed towards the cell's only door, then hesitating, he turned back to the zombie. She seemed to notice he was still there as she slowly raised her head from the table, looking at him with her dead eyes, and a string of drool dripping from the corners of her mouth; Fredrickson looked away from her, thinking. 'I can't keep calling you zombie or Z20 now, can I? You need a name,' he pursed his lips together and looked idly at the ceiling light as he tried to think of a suitable name. He tried to think of scientists from history that had names that could fit. Then he thought of an American philosopher and neuroscientist, and a grin instinctively made its way onto his face as he believed that he'd found a suitable name and one that he would associate with greatness.

'I guess you'll be known as Sam.' Named after the late 2038 philosopher Samantha Tiliaski.

Chapter 6

The second of October marked the day when another bonder who'd worked alongside Kolen recently received a zombie to bond with; the bonder was a wise but quiet fifty-seven-year-old Norwegian man with Prussian blue eyes and greying black hair named Henrik Losnedahl. He began his training as a zombie bonder two years ago. Because of the detailed teachings by his experienced instructor and reading through the training manual, he was faithful that he would be apt to work just as well as Fredrickson and the other experienced bonders that he had the pleasure of learning from. Henrik Losnedahl had been wide awake when he'd gotten a knock on his office door informing him that it was his time, that he'd been called into the mess hall to retrieve his first zombie, who was over the six-year AOR. He opened the door to greet the young male Bonder's Bellhop with pale blonde hair outside his door with a friendly handshake and matching smile, but he didn't say anything in the way of response to the Bonder's Bellhop standing before him. But the pale blonde man didn't seem to be offended by the fact that Losnedahl hadn't said anything to him. Instead, the man just smiled heartily at Losnedahl and, put a playful hand on his back and spoke with a comforting tone, 'You're going to knock it out of the park, Henrik, I believe in you, friend.' After the two men exchanged their goodbyes, Losnedahl went back into his office to grab some books and then put them into the cell that he would be using for his bonding sessions. He set down the books and left the cell. He began descending down the steps to the mess hall where his new subject would be waiting for him.

Losnedahl entered the mess hall where a well armoured solider with a scraggy brown beard that reached well below his chin, standing in the centre of the mess hall, wearing a black bulletproof vest and an old-fashioned

WW2 helmet that looked like it'd once been a relic of a history museum had been waiting for him to collect his first zombie.

Losnedahl and this solider glanced at each other in silence. The soldier let out an irritated grunting noise and shoved a body in front of Losnedahl. The zombie was in handcuffs and was lightly swaying, a little unsteady on the feet. Losnedahl noted that the zombie looked to be a young boy with grey skin and jet-black hair.

Without exchanging a farewell glance at each other, Losnedahl took the young zombie boy's cuffed hands from the soldier and escorted him out of the mess hall, down the hall, up the steps to the bonding cells, and put his new subject into cell B-01. It was the closest cell to his office with his office situated on the far-left side of the hallway, just in front of the stairway that led up to the laboratory section of the GFOSAR and the cell just at the end of the hall.

Losnedahl skipped greeting the zombie boy. Instead, he got straight to the examination of the subject he had to work with. Losnedahl gazed into the boy's eyes, which were a pale grey (bloodshot scleras usually don't appear until a zombie is much older). The zombie boy only had a few minor scabs on his arms, legs, stomach, and face, but significant amount of horrendous-looking scabs around his fingernails; translucent-yellow discs, slimed, thin and untethered from the cuticles. But other than those details, Losnedahl thought the boy's body looked quite alright and wouldn't need a lot of delicate surgery to fix his body.

Losnedahl continued his examination, looked his zombie up and down, from the black hairs on his head to the toenails caked in soot on his feet, Losnedahl was able to calculate that the boy was around sixteen years old. But as to how he'd died was up for debate. This was something that Losnedahl couldn't work out. Still, he was hopeful nonetheless that he'd find out later, hopefully when his zombie was able to remember. Losnedahl bonded differently with the boy, bonding at a slow pace with BSL; even if teaching his subject, the basis of BSL, would be a slow and taxing process, Losnedahl didn't grow impatient, and he saw that he could be successful in his methods of bonding if he just took things slow and was careful not to rush things (slow and steady). Losnedahl named him Linus after he wrote the name down on a piece of paper, naming him after one of his favourite Swedish singers, Linus Lindholm of Jontez, whom he'd often listen to during his early teenage years. Losnedahl and Linus communicated with sign language with the use of BSL tutorial booklets, which he had ready on the desk, and the occasional hand gesture instead of talking because Losnedahl had no tongue with which to speak; this he had been living with for most of his life, he wasn't born without one, oh no… what happened to Henrik Losnedahl and how he came to lose his tool for taste and speaking was a story that still haunts him and isn't one for faint hearts.

Henrik Losnedahl was born in Florø in Norway in 1999; he had the misfortune of having an inhumanly cruel alcoholic as a father who, during one night of heavy drinking, cut the baby's tongue as punishment when his mother killed herself shortly after Losnedahl was born. His sadistic bastard of a father named Joakim had been drinking continuously for some time after his football team had lost their final against Belgium. His violent outburst unfortunately aimed at the new baby boy who'd been born in the opposite room. His father had an undying love for sports (more than his own wife and newborn son), took the games seriously, and got very vocal and hostile when his teams didn't win. Joakim had serious problems with his anger, which he couldn't control or simply didn't want to control for the better of those around him. He was often violent and would be a ticking time bomb if things didn't go right for him, making it a wonder how Losnedahl's mother had even married him in the first place. Losnedahl had been given the name "Henrik" by his mother, who he'd been told by a late old friend that the name was said to be as angelic as his father was violent. Losnedahl had never had the chance to get to know his mother, as within forty minutes of his birth she was dead, and a steaming Remington shotgun was on the floor next to her.

Due to his father's violent drunken outbursts from the other room and the pain of childbirth, and the pain that would soon befall the pair of them together when Joakim decided to take out his anger on them, she'd caressed and cradled him lovingly, lulling him to sleep, and then grabbed the Remington which she'd bought solely for this purpose and placed it in her mouth.

She'd laid her head tenderly on his, hoping the blast would kill him too because she didn't want him to grow with Joakim's drunken abuse. Her tears fell onto the Remington's barrel as she made her final goodbyes to the cruel, disgusting world in which she and Losnedahl would be expiring from. 'Fuck you, Joakim, I hope you rot in prison,' she spat right before, 'I'm sorry.' She'd wept as she closed her eyes, letting her last tears roll from her cheek. She pulled the trigger, sending two loud shells through her head, splitting it apart.

Baby Losnedahl screamed from the exploding noise as his eyes opened to his mother's blood sprayed all over the walls. Young Henrik, not even an hour old, got the blame by his father for his mother's suicide. Joakim had entered the room in a fury after hearing the loud explosion and seeing his wife's headless body slumped on the couch with a newborn crying baby resting in her stagnant arms.

Joakim went into the kitchen to grab a kitchen knife. Back in the room he seized hold of baby Henrik's tongue and sliced it off clean (gagging and choking, Auntie Annette knocking and investigating), and miraculously, after such trauma for an infant boy… he survived.

Joakim Losnedahl had died shortly after Henrik's thirtieth birthday, and Losendahl relished the thought that someone as cruel as his father was where he belonged (in hell).

Now, at fifty-seven years old, Henrik Losnedahl had dedicated his life to doing some good for the world by becoming a zombie bonder, and despite the unnatural amounts of domestic torture he'd suffered at the hands of his father Losendahl strived to be a good person, to become a man whom his mother and aunt would be proud of, which was one of his reasons for becoming a bonder. He wanted to make a difference, to have a positive influence.

Losnedahl shook off all thoughts about his missing tongue, the cruelty of his father and his long-dead mother. In his training Losendahl communicated with the boy zombie in the only way he could, through sign language, writing down words before showing Linus the object, such as writing the word "Pen" on a sheet of paper and then placing the pen underneath the word. Then he'd use BSL to sign the word for him until Linus was finally able to sign the word back to him. After a few days Losnedahl gave out a thin smile of hope, knowing that while he'd been rendered permanently mute from his father's sick abuse, he was still able to contribute to humanity's survival and the zombie bonding process. He wasn't just a liability, a man without a tongue, he was a zombie bonder who used British Sign Language to get the job done.

Chapter 7

Another bonder the same age as Fredrickson sat in the chair, pen and paper in hand, looking groggily at her subject. Cansu Aksoy, was a tan-skinned woman with dark eyes and short, straight hair. She'd originated from Izmir in Turkey. Cansu had been bonding slowly with a male zombie over the 70-year AOR, which had one arm. She chose to communicate with her subjects in two languages; Turkish and English. Why she'd chosen this method was anyone's guess, but it was suspected Cansu wanted bragging rights because she spoke both languages fluently and sometimes shifted from Turkish to English whenever she felt like it. Or perhaps because she wanted her sessions to be a bit more interesting, seeing as Cansu was a woman who seemed easily bored of the mundane and needed entertainment in her life. She'd been living in England for eighteen years, so she was more than fit to call herself a British citizen even if English was her second language and she'd often prefer to speak her native tongue.

So, for a way to make things more interesting for her, this approach of bonding in two languages seemed a more natural approach for her; even if others around her thought it was complicated and was making things harder for herself, they didn't bother to protest her to stick with just English, as Cansu didn't value her time in distractions and it didn't help that Cansu Aksoy wasn't exactly the best person to talk to anyway, as she almost consistently had a wooden expression on her face and always spoke in a dry, simulated tone as if she was a robot. Either way, Cansu wasn't perfect, and neither was anyone else living in 2056.

Cansu was forced into leaving the country of her birth back in 2038 when the numbers of the undead had spiralled out of control; completely taking over the country of Turkey. Much like the Nazi genocide in WW2, the country and 93% of its population had died and now belonged to the undead. Turkey was among the first countries infected by the mortuus carnem parasite. Bodies started rising from the ground in droves as soon as the first sightings of the mosquito-like parasite were reported on social media, and the numbers quickly became too much for the Turkish military. Since then, the plaguing numbers of the mortuus carnem raising the dead had spread throughout the entire country, giving Cansu little to no other choice but to move to the United Kingdom, one of the few countries still habitable by the living as the Brits had made strict protocols and they were right onto declaring a global panic as soon as word got out of more than 1,500 zombies were roaming around and causing chaos.

Cansu missed her hometown of Izmir greatly and often had dreams about returning back to it just so she could grasp the taste of familiarity because she wasn't a fan of living in England. But she was always hushed up and reminded that Izmir was a playground for the undead and, therefore, wasn't safe. Still, Cansu didn't much care what other people. She kept to herself a lot of the time, and wasn't great at interacting with people.

Cansu Aksoy was the last person to turn to if you need bonding tips and advice. Back before the mortuus carnem outbreak, Cansu had lived the life of a troublemaking rebel who often found herself in the backseat of a police car for being a public nuisance, spray painting cars, annoying pedestrians by getting in their faces and sometimes dining and dashing with her friends around 2033.

Cansu was the tomboy type who was often seen wearing either green or red denim. As a teen, she owned a red skateboard with a flaming blue skull and had a knack for causing trouble, pulling pranks on the public, and just acting like an annoying fly to everyone who crossed her. But one day doing a 3am challenge by herself, Cansu's days of rebelling against the law were quickly cut short with an accident which had led her to lose three of her fingers (pinkie, ring and middle), when she got her hand stuck on a broken conveyer belt in an abandoned car factory which still had around 30% of electricity which had escorted her hand to a large grinder and which had grinded up her three fingers like potatoes, making it almost a miracle that she didn't lose her entire hand. Recovering in the hospital, the trauma and loss of her three fingers had caused her to completely transform her personality due to PTSD. From once a rebel into a bored, sarcastic shell of her former self who didn't have any light in her anymore. She'd lost her friends because they weren't fond of her sudden and sullen change in personality, but she didn't seem to notice they were gone, almost seeing them as simple worker ants in a continuing growing colony. Due to the PTSD and whenever she looked down and saw only her index and thumb, had caused her to become the opposite of her former self, closed up and reclusive, rarely opening up to anyone. Sometimes, when her fingers were mentioned, Cansu would say in a blank voice, "Cut off, accident." And then she'd move away from them, leaving the questioner shrouded in even more darkness about her past and the reason behind her missing three digits. But it was known to not try to push Cansu because she was just so wooden and closed up.

Cansu had started working with her one-armed subject a day after Fredrickson got his new zombie and had no trouble in naming her zombie Ziya, after one of her old best friend's three-legged Anatolian Shepard who would sometimes sit on a grassy patch watching them skate down in the skate park… part of her old life.

Ziya was an elderly male zombie who looked around his seventies, according to Losnedahl's calculations, and like Cansu's old friend's dog Ziya, who'd been missing a leg, her zombie Ziya was missing an arm.

Cansu couldn't help staring at the zombie with tired, sleepless, slow-blinking black eyes. She felt no emotion about seeing the zombie missing an arm, she just found that her heart was empty, and she couldn't feel any sadness or empathy whatsoever ever since she lost three of her fingers.

Cansu was lethargic, like she hadn't slept properly in a year, and was considered an insomniac. She observed the details and death marks around her zombie. But despite her constantly having a tired expression and being very slow with things, she was professional none-the-less,

Cansu pulled out her small notebook with a blue swimming dolphin photograph on the cover from her breast pocket and dotted down with her pen the state of decay her zombie was in and his supposed death marks. Ziya not only had one arm, but he missed a shit load of the wrinkled skin on his top half, making him look like he was gruesomely turned inside out over the time of decay, so all that remained of him was his exposed, rotting muscle. Ziya was recorded as being one of the oldest zombies that'd been brought into the GFOSAR to be bonded with, aside from Fredrickson's zombie Sam. Ziya could've died during the late seventies or even early eighties, judging by the long 1970s pants he was wearing. And by looking at the strings of rotten flesh hanging from the missing arm, his death could've been something like he had it pulled off by something with inhuman strength, or worse, she speculated… this poor older man could've got it caught in a large blender which would have shredded it, or had it wholly flattened by a steamroller, crushing it like a watermelon, spraying blood everywhere and making this old guy die an unbelievably painful death.

If that's the case, I sincerely apologise, she thought to herself from just staring into his rotting exterior with a blank, tired expression as if she craved a hot cup of cappuccino. Even if she didn't show her emotions through her face and body language, deep down was where her emotions shone, and she was feeling pity and sadness for this man, even if her body didn't emote to it in the same way her mind did. Because the idea that he was missing an arm had made her think of her own missing fingers. Despite not emoting in the same way as her peers, she felt a bit of a connection to her elderly one-armed zombie named Ziya, and maybe he could help her to become more open about herself. Maybe…

Chapter 8

Two days (4/10/56 had passed since the introduction of the bonders with their newest zombies. The process was going through a tedious and slow pace for rookie Kolen. Ace, her crawler was making a scene that anyone passing by her cell would be able to see and perhaps laugh at, much to Kolen's dismay. Ace was flaying her arms around like she was in some sort of disco rave and was yelling and saying rubbish that made not even a lick of sense, like, "Tima has ga flu bog!" which had both embarrassed and confused Kolen majorly, but she still tried her hardest to get Ace to settle down and listen.

Losnedahl, on the other hand, with his zombie Linus, was having a complex session. Because he had no tongue, he couldn't precisely formulate words, and he'd mistakenly forgotten his card with the BSL alphabet on it. So, Losnedahl had to quickly leave Linus alone in the cell while he hastily went into his office to fetch his BSL alphabet chart out from the second drawer of a sand-coloured filing cabinet, which he keeps near the door to his office. Once he had his chart, Losnedahl raced out of his office, flashed his card on the key panel and went back inside the cell. He sat down with his young zombie and letting out a relieved breath that he'd gotten back in less than five minutes, giving him the opportunity to refresh with his chart now in hand.

Cansu's sessions with Ziya were always slow. She lacked a certain kind of enthusiasm.

Fredrickson, however, began his seventh working day with Sam. He flashed his card and entered the cell only to be left stunned as if he'd just received an electric shock, when Sam, in lightning speed, stood up from her seat, knocking the chair over and waved at him with a bubbly enthusiasm that Fredrickson never thought he'd see from an undead, let alone, one that he was bonding with.

Her heavily bloodshot grey eyes were wide and broad; those withered, almost non-existent lips appeared to stretch out slightly, managing what had looked to be a crooked, toothy smile caked in grime and filth in his direction. He'd never seen a zombie smile, not ever… and he honestly wasn't sure what to make of it. His thoughts had become scrambled, and his emotions and feelings had been mushed together and served on a plate, looking like a formless blob of yellow, red, blue, white, and grey. Fredrickson couldn't blink, couldn't take his eyes away from the sight before him. It was as if she was elated to see him again, giving him the impression that if she could talk, she'd say something in a beaming, cheerful voice along the lines of, "Hi! Mr Fredrickson, how was your morning? Did you sleep well? Are we going to talk about my past life today?"

He felt that his heart had just skipped two beats as he struggled to process what he witnessed. Standing behind the steel desk was the zombie, the same one who'd wanted to devour his brains upon their first meeting and now that same zombie was standing in front of him smiling, actually smiling at him, while moving her raised hand in a swift friendly waving gesture. He'd never seen an undead smile in a way that seemed to show a raw sense of joy.

Fredrickson gulped. 'He-Hello Sam.' he muttered as he cautiously approached the desk. He pulled out a chair and sat, placing his paperwork on the desk while keeping a visual eye on Sam's unclean crooked smile. That smile unsettled him, making him think of a mentally unstable serial killer in a thriller/crime movie based on actual events. 'You can sit down.' he told her, jerking his head slightly in the direction of the chair opposite him, his eyes never leaving that ominous crooked smile. Sam's scary, broken smile instantly snapped back into her idle frown after Fredrickson told her to sit, her waving hand lowered to her side; she sat and grabbed the sides of her chair and pulled it inwards to face him across the desk. They were now sitting eye-to-eye; the smile was gone, allowing Fredrickson to collect himself and start the day's session.

'So, Sam, do you remember what you've learnt with me so far?' Fredrickson asked, rummaging through his papers to find a blank piece. He was longing to see what kind of progress Sam had made, hoping she'd remembered how to read and write. He'd taught her both bases on day five and wanted to see how much she'd understood. Sam put her fingers on the A4 paper and slid it towards her. She reached her hand out and took the blue pen from his hand with a human gentleness that sent shivers up his spine. Fredrickson watched her with awe and fascination. Her eyes were fixated on the paper, and he dropped his gaze upon it, waiting. The black-haired zombie gripped the plastic lid of the enclosure with her teeth, pulled it off swiftly, and spat it like a bullet randomly to the ground, it ricocheted, bouncing to the wall and back to the floor again, where it rolled to a stop at Fredrickson's feet underneath the desk. He glanced at it for a second, ducked his head under and then up, knowing that it was best to waste no time, he steadied his usual attention on Sam and what she was writing down on the piece of paper he had given to her.

When she'd finished, she dropped the pen on the desk and locked her fingers together, resting them and permitting Fredrickson to read her note. Although it looked messy and like a toddler had written it, it was still readable and understandable. It read; hAllo MIZZtA fRadrACKsON. Iz LERN ABoT tAlky an ritiN WIT penz. Iz CAT spek tHo buT iz Fel Sarter AlWeady tanks to Yo missta fracdracksoon, PleZ teCH me mAOr. Fredrickson stared at the words written down with jaw-dropping amazement, so amazed that he had to re-tell himself that it was a zombie who wrote this for him even though there were significant spelling errors and had unnecessary caps during some words. Sam, as she had said in her note, was indeed getting more innovative, and by most polished bonders like Fredrickson, it'd seem foolish to stop the process and dispose of her now, not when she could be the cure to the pandemic.

Fredrickson was harder and, on a rare occasion, more abusive towards his zombies with his training than any other bonder. His temper resulted in the permanent death of many of the zombies he'd dealt with. To him, they'd turned out to be failures and that he would require for those failures to be promptly disposed of. Those failures were sent away with the hovering bodyguards that frequently clung around the facility between their duties. And much like disposing of them, the soldiers were also the ones that went out into the dangerous world beyond GFOSAR; tracking down zombies for the bonding procedure. It was a hazardous business as they had to beat them into submission before returning them to GFOSAR. They would then hand them over to Carl Boyle, who was now in charge of administering the drugs into the zombies' mouths and keeping them compliant as Boyle took his job more seriously than Winsome ever did, and his position as Drug Administrator seemed to be the facilities way of promoting him. Winsome liked to hang around, watch the process throw around some orders and make unnecessary jokes about how the drugs would knock 'em bitches dead, which Boyle had learnt to ignore.

But when the time comes, and a Bonder requested disposal, their orders of disposing of failures (usually the ones that remained zoned out through every session and would learn nothing) was simple. Fredrickson had witnessed it once, and it had reminded him of a scene from a war movie where prisoners were lined up and executed by firing squad. Rumours sometimes spread throughout the facility about these "failures" and that maybe it was from his lack of patience and not the zombies' ability to learn. One thing was for sure, and that was Fredrickson was resilient and determined to have a zombie that he could name a success. But even so, despite Fredrickson having a constant feeling in his gut that all zombies he worked with were going to just end up on the failure's checklist, there was something about his latest subject that he knew wasn't like the rest; that smile and wave had been a prime example of this, and the way she'd instantly reverted back to her old ways as soon as he had opened his mouth made him uncomfortable.

Sam was *different*. Different in so many ways that he never thought possible.

That part was prominent enough. Her behaviour, which seemed to be sporadic, had begun to send shivers down his spine, leaving him feeling cold; it'd even come to the point that looking at her was terrifying. Frederickson knew this zombie was dead, but something about her felt off. *I'm a man of science; why am I letting this brain-dead woman affect me in such a way?* He dared to inch a little closer and bent his knees to meet her face. *Those eyes*, he thought to himself. Grey, dead, cold, but there's a flicker behind that veil, a live, fat worm of hateful fire.

A trickle of impending doom ran down his spine like the first cold drizzle from a morning shower. *Is she hiding from me? Is she pretending to be affected by the drugs? Whatever she's doing, I don't like it, and I will find it out, one way or another, I will find out whatever the hell she's planning.* He thought as he peered up into those empty eyes, feeling a strong sense of unease, which resulted in him retreating back into his original stance, his hand clenched at his chest. *She has progressed this much in only seven days! Something isn't right about this; something isn't right with her…*

Fredrickson looked down at her message again, and the more he read through it, the more unsettled he became. She had thanked him and had done so politely, then requested from him more teachings. All this was in the short twenty-nine-word sentence that was meant to see if she could even form one word and if she'd learnt anything from the last few days with him. Out of all the rotting corpses he'd worked with in his six years, he'd noted that none had ever thanked him. She'd already toppled all the zombies Fredrickson had worked with, and that was a good thing in his book. Sam is a fast learner he thought to himself.

Fredrickson stayed planted in his seat. His body couldn't help but tremble; as much as he wanted to stop, he couldn't. His eyes darted across the words written down on the paper in blue ink, staring at the sentence, making an unknown fear swell up inside his lungs like helium blown into a balloon. He didn't know if he was supposed to be scared or elated. He felt a mix of both.

'Alright, Sam.' he started with a gulp, 'I'll come back tomorrow to tutor you some more.' His voice was stricken with joyous fright; he'd never been so afraid and yet so radiant over a single zombie before in his life! There was something unnatural about the rapidly quickening pace of Sam's developing intelligence that was unsettling, yet at the same time excited him. One side of his consciousness told him to stop and have her taken away and disposed of but the others begged to differ, wanting to continue their work. He felt that the good half was telling him to continue working with her.

He longed to see how far she'd progress with the proper guidance. He'd achieved so much when it came to bonding with her. Her progress was something every bonder, either new or old, should be buoyant with; she was slowly reaching towards the clouds and her goal of becoming human again.

He felt that abandoning her at this astonishing stage of evolution and fast learning would be a fucking stupid idea. He knew in his heart that his childhood idol, Albert Einstein, would chastise him for even thinking of it. That thought alone gave Fredrickson the courage to continue on with his work with Sam. Even though the bristles on the back of his neck rose at the thought, his inner instincts told him not to continue.

'Tomorrow, I'll bring you some physical books to read. I don't know why we still have these fossils in this day and age,' he added in speculation. 'And some more paper so you can write down what the words say in the books. If you have trouble with what they mean, just tap the desk, and I'll tell you because you aren't capable of speech yet... sadly.' Fredrickson added. He shuddered, feeling a sudden cold breath on the back of his neck, but still, he tried to keep up the pace of work. But he felt he couldn't continue with the rest of this session; his mind was all over the place, he considered that maybe some time alone in his office or having Valium to soothe his nerves. Perhaps tomorrow will bring a brighter and better session for him. He fetched up his paperwork, wearily eyeing Sam. He worried that she might turn on him when he least expected it, as she'd done during their first meeting in his office. It was then he remembered that he'd been lax with administering her hunger drug. It suddenly came to him like Winsome had backhanded him on the head (*Yo Alex, mi old compadre, ya know Sam has gone two days without the good stuff? It won't be long until she sees the Fredrickson main course on her menu*) jogging his memory that Sam hadn't had her usual daily dose of hunger drugs for two straight days! A very risky move on Fredrickson's part that could've cost him his life if Sam continued to go full bonding days without drugs. Zombies usually take up to two hunger pills a day, for the first two hours and then at the end of the session, but, due to Fredrickson getting distracted by her progress and other important matters, which wasn't like him, he'd seemed to have forgotten all about the drugs, until now! His pocket still contained her four pills inside, meaning that he'd risked his life and forgotten to give them to her. He baulked at the thought she hadn't had any drugs since day five! With that fact aside, he wondered about why she hadn't attacked him again. Had she no intentions of acting up on him? She showed no signs of being hungry, and that was scary... if she wasn't showing signs of hunger now... when? She also appeared to be playing the part of a drugged-up zombie to fool him, a fact that scared him considerably... This exploration of intelligence without being drugged every day wasn't normal... and it was a scary thought that she possibly knew more than he thought she did... who knows... she might've even remembered her name but refused to tell him, leading him down a rabbit hole of questions into how much knowledge of her past life she actually did know, but wasn't hinting into anything, wanting to continue to drive Fredrickson into trying to find the answers to those questions.

The red capsules, known only as the hunger drug, were for the undead only, not for human consumption. Once taken by the zombie, whether it be an animal or a human, the drug worked to sedate the raving hunger of the zombie. Sometimes, it did more than banish the appetite. Causing a *knock'em dead* response (which Winsome had dubbed it), this usually happened if the dosage of the drug was high — causing the zombified body to have no choice and feeling or no mobility or hunger whatsoever. The zombie under the influence of the drug would just stand still, sagging around, without purpose or response to anything nor any surge of hunger for the living. That was why bonders needed the pills with them at all costs, and it was vital to drug them twice a day; this kept the bonders and all currently residing in the facility safe.

Fredrickson flashed his ID card in front of the scanner to the door; hearing it buzz open, he flew out of the cell labelled B-35. He didn't notice he dropped some of his hidden papers inside the cell. His heart pounded full of adrenaline; seeming to do backflips inside his ribcage, he appeared to lose his usual professionalism for keeping an eye on his paperwork. At his moment of retreat, Fredrickson felt only Fear with a capital F. It surged everywhere inside of him, and this was when his mind concluded what he really thought of Sam. He may be known for being hard on the zombies and having a lack of patience for their slow learning, yet he knew that this had nothing to do with that but more about how she made him feel.

Fredrickson was a man who gave off the impression of fearlessness and instilled a confidence in rookies like Kolen. Administering an impression that he could handle any obstacle that came at him and that he ruled his line of work with an iron fist, but this time, it was different. He was different. This was the first time a zombie had made him well and truly uncomfortable, the first time one had made him a genuine sense of fear around them, afraid to continue with the bonding process and just give up zombie bonding altogether. He was fearful and wary of Sam, and he couldn't understand why. He hated this feeling, the feeling of being scared and wanted to toughen and straighten his nerves but thinking of that rotting twisted grin and those written words made fear engulf him. Yet, if he were to bottle up that fear for a minute and look at things with a logical perspective, with her progress and rapid learning, it had scared him almost as much as it delighted him! *Could I finally have a successful zombie! In all my six years working here, could I finally have a success story?* He thought he was on the cusp of doing something great and that she was somehow the key to genuinely bonding with zombies, not only creating the mindless shells they'd already had some success producing. While he wasn't as keen on working with Sam as before, he knew he had to continue. He knew that he had to see her development over the course of his sessions with her; yes, she may do something that might freak him out inside, but he was willing to take that risk. Anything in the name of science and the future of humanity.

Frederickson quickly gathered his things and flew out of the cell without so much glancing back at Sam through the cell's window, not wanting to shift his gaze to her for a mere second as her face scared him; that twisted, rotten grin gave him shivers. While standing outside B-35, he'd found the solace and time to calm his nerves and settle his beating heart, allowing it to relax; still, he took some time to catch his breath, which sounded similar to the panting of a dehydrated dog that was well in need of a drink after having a good run.

Finally feeling calm, he straightened the collar of his lab coat, exhaled a deep breath, and started making his way back to his office. As he passed by Sam's window again, he was unaware of her, silently pressing her hands onto the glass; bloodshot zombie eyes scowled, watching him with an intense flare until he turned the corner to no longer be seen by her. Fredrickson barged into his office with enough force to make the door slam into the wall and create a deafening crash. Fredrickson stormed over to his desk and tossed his clipboard with his remaining papers on his desk. He still wasn't in a suitable space of mind. He threw his arm across a filing cabinet, resulting in books and papers flying across the room to lay scattered across the floor. He stomped over to the far wall to glance at his erratic reflection in the oval-shaped mirror hanging there. His hair was unkempt and messy, and he had panic ensued, perspiration dripping down his face and protruding from his body. He knew this was the result of the fear Sam had ensued. His fear had turned to anger as his temper came loose, he was unimpressed by the way he'd reacted today, and he hated showing vulnerability… especially to a zombie. 'C'mon Alex, you *FUCKING WEAK SACK O'SHIT*, get a fucking grip on yourself!' he roared at his reflection, punching the wall missing the mirror by mere millimetres. 'She's just a fucking zombie! Get a grip, stop being such a motherfucking pussy, and face her like a man! You've dealt with scarier zombies. She hasn't lashed out at you yet! So, stop this farce and be the bonder you know you could be!' Fredrickson continued to cuss at himself; his aggravation grew as he focused on the emotions of humiliation and embarrassment he felt. Unable to hold his feelings further, his last remaining surge of anger was taken out on the mirrored wall, kicking it hard until the pain in his foot threatened broken toes and his knuckles bled.

Finally calmer, he convinced himself that he must stop beating himself up and sit down and relax. He stood for a while, breathing hard and turned to thoughts of ways he could've ended the session better. Finally calmer, he ventured over to his desk, and pulled out his chair, where he crumpled down into it like an athlete, exhausted and caked in heavy sweat. Opening a drawer, he took out a navy-blue tissue, using it to wipe the pulsating sweat from the stress and his outbursts from his face and his body. He disposed of the handkerchief in the bin as it came to a dripping mess of sweat and snot, and he couldn't be bothered cleaning it, so he preferred to use another fresh one. He leaned back into his chair, slid his sweating palms down his dripping face, and wiped his moist hands over his knees. The familiar, blunt heartbeat thrum pulsed in his temples as if a bottle had been shattered over it, giving him one heck of a screaming migraine that pulsated through his head at an uneven rate that he rested his head in his hands using his fingers to massage his eyelids as they throbbed too like he'd been stung by a bee. He felt exhausted, like a man who'd worked a total of ten hours of work with no break, yet the day had just begun.

It was at this moment when Fredrickson decided he required something that would cause his mind to linger away from the topic of Sam and her disturbing grin and the toddler-scribbled letter because there was something about those scribblings and that crooked grin that had caused his flesh to bubble with goose pimples.

He sat in his office alone, cheeks resting on fists, trying to distract himself. He thought about going to the ground floor and buying some distilled water from one of the vending machines, but he quickly thought against the idea as he didn't feel like making the trip all the way down to the ground floor and trying to work out those stupid vending machines. So, he just sat on his chair alone, listening to the faint murmuring of people outside his office and the faint shuffle and squeaks of feet on the linoleum floor. He wheeled his chair around and looked out at the grey clouds and the landscape, which once used to be lively and full of significant business buildings, skyscrapers, construction sites and cars, trucks and buses that moved through the streets like ants on a coordinated path. Fredrickson sighed and closed his eyes; memories of when he was twenty-eight then came back to him, giving him that much-needed distraction from his freaky subject and the terrible landscape in which he and so many others currently lived.

The year was 2038 before the UK had been introduced to the ungodly effects of the mortuus carnem parasite, was already due for death, due to political corruption, increased taxes, rent bills, diseases, mindless criminal activities, and natural disasters, with some people on social media calling out that *Mother Nature is pissed*, which wasn't all that far from the truth, considering that in just three months apart from each other, Tripoli in Libya was hit by an earthquake in early February of 2037. In May of the same year, Derna was hit by a tsunami. Still, it wasn't only Libya that got the wrath of Mother Nature, Switzerland in November 2035; it was targeted by a devastating fire that had left most of Bern a blackened scape of burned trees, ash, and animal skeletons. Money and greed ruled the world and assisted in turning the once lively country upside down. With the increase of bills and people being ugly to each other, there was always something that people weren't happy about, these often led to these sporadic cases of crime and random accounts of murder such as stabbings and shootings.

Fredrickson had grown up in a terrible time – but it was the life that he'd known – as awful as it was, he didn't mind. As long as he could go about his business undeterred, that was the main thing he cared about. *You don't bother me, I don't bother you*, was his motto.

Fredrickson's lips shifted slightly upwards at the thought of when he was younger. While this was the exact distraction Fredrickson wanted, the memories changed direction for the opposite effect that Fredrickson had wished. They had caused him nothing but sadness and grief as he continued down the path to the thoughts of his late wife, Deborah.

Deborah Fredrickson was a humble and quiet woman, born into poverty to the Mikalsson family, who couldn't afford to pay the increase weekly £550 of rent for their apartment, which was already littered with cracks in the walls and ceiling and the furniture was either cheap or broken, such as one armchair which had a spring poking out of its left side. They'd been forced to move out to the streets to beg for money, blankets, and food. And yet, despite the deplorable conditions that she and her family had to live in, she still managed to become the most kind-hearted woman Fredrickson had ever met. Before meeting Fredrickson, her life was one of desperation and a struggle for survival, often pickpocketing and stealing money to provide food, shelter, and some warmth, which she had hated, but she knew that it had to be done if she was going to have some chance at survival in the world around her and her family. As for Alexander Fredrickson, he wasn't always strict, with a big red button for frustration and anger. He used to be a pretty reasonable, respectable man who was a little egotistical and liked to brag about his money and ocean-side house. He was living on a wealthy sum of money in a decent home with a sea-side view. In those days, £4,500 per week living in an expensive five-million-pound house with everything a 2038th person could possibly want, especially living in such a harsh and populated country. It was customary for him to leave the bank with seven grand in his wallet, which he sometimes fawned over and admired, though rarely, Fredrickson would spare a ten for a nearby charity such as a cancer foundation.

On one particular morning of coming back from the bank with a six-grand cheque folded in the pocket of his suit pants, Fredrickson happened across a haggard woman with fiery red hair, busking alone for tips near the local ROKIT clothing store. The rags that she wore were ripped and had working patches, making her look like she was a time traveller from the medieval period, yet little did he know that she'd later become his wife.

The lone young woman with the fiery red hair named Deborah Mikalsson had been covered head-to-toe in dried mud, yet when she looked up at him, pushing her red locks out of her face, Fredrickson almost had the sense that she was a one-hundred-pound note that someone had accidentally dropped into the mud. Underneath the grime, Fredrickson saw beauty that he'd never seen in a woman before; her blue ocean eyes blinked desperately back at him, and her skin appeared soft and smooth even under the dirt. Fredrickson had knelt down so he could see the expression of lonesomeness and sorrow plastered on her pale, thin face.

Fredrickson couldn't help but feel sympathy for her. She'd looked up at him with those beautiful features caked in grime. She held out a tin can up to him, a bold word with TIPS written in black marker across it. She spoke to him softly, mousy, 'Please, mister... could you spare twenty pounds? So, I'm able to get something warm to wear for the night?' The scene reminded him of *Oliver Twist* from the classic Charles Dickens story. Young Fredrickson had looked into the tin can she was grasping and saw that it was bare. He'd felt a warmth rush through him and had dared to reach out, moving the strings of hair that draped her face to take in and then admire the beautiful complexion of Deborah's face. That gesture had been what had made him decide with impulse, to run his fingers across Deborah's wrist until he found her hand and clenched it. She'd opened her mouth to protest, stilling as Fredrickson had shushed her with a finger to her lips. He remembered smiling while looking into her eyes, letting her can drop to the ground. He pulled her gently to her feet, leading her away, talking to her about a better life as he led her to his large luxurious home at the oceans-side.

He'd welcomed her inside, and almost instantly, she was greeted by the smell of warm tea. She saw a room with nice furniture, plants, a sheepskin white rug and a comfortable-looking lounge with a crocheted white and green rug laid over it. Seeing that this was all new to her, Fredrickson took a small step forward and held out a hand to her, smiling comfortingly, telling her that things were okay and that he was going to get her some food and cleaned up. Deborah took his word for it, timidly wrapped her small, skinny fingers around his, and allowed herself to be escorted into the house, accepting his invitation. He showed her around the house, and then he set her down near an old-fashioned wood heater, which he thought provided him with solace and tranquillity when he watched the flames dance around. He gave her a nice warm bowl of chicken stir fry, ran her a warm shower, and prepared some fresh new clothing for her in the laundry basket. He'd even given her her own room with a beautiful, warm place to sleep, saving her from the bitter chill of the night. He'd not known then that she would stay and he would fall so deeply in love.

Fredrickson had then dedicated his life to her; he gave her money, food, and all the clothes she could desire. It'd only been a matter of a few weeks of living together that it was clear they were meant to be. He'd asked her on a whim, and she'd accepted. Fredrickson was more than happy with the arrangement, and they'd married on the eleventh of August in 2040. She'd been the most stunning bride he'd ever seen. Under his care, she'd gained weight, turning her from a skin and bone homeless mess into a curvaceous beauty. But this was during the terrible year of 2038 ... and shortly after, a few days after their wedding

and experiencing their first nights of marital bliss, Deborah
had confirmed with her newly wedded husband that she
wasn't yet willing to conceive a child, which had
disappointed Fredrickson, but he'd agreed and wasn't going
to push her into doing what he wanted. Later, he found out
that Deborah suffered from infertility and that she couldn't
have children even if she wanted to. The life she'd had on
the streets had been hard on her body, and to be brought
into a new, completely different one had put a lot of stress
on her. Stress, which she couldn't deal with.

Deborah passed away in the bath on the twenty-
sixth of September at 1:54am after overdosing on the
sleeping pills that she'd been prescribed for her recurring
nightmares. Fredrickson found the empty pill bottle lying
on the floor, along with Deborah's diary and a pencil next
to it. When Fredrickson read through the final entry in the
diary, he was distraught to know that she was going
through a lot of mental stress that no amount of money,
food and expensive clothes could fix, and it had cut through
his heart like a scalpel, making a surgical incision and he
sat by the tub with her lifeless corpse, holding her diary to
his chest and sobbing, knowing that he hadn't done
anything to help her, to properly help her... She was given
a traditional Christian funeral that Fredrickson barely
remembered attending. Witnessing his wife's coffin being
slowly lowered down into her grave, he'd cried
incoherently into a tissue provided for him by Deborah's
Swedish father, Benjamin Mikalsson, a man he barely
knew but shared in his grief. Fredrickson returned home
after the funeral came to an end, and there, he wept harder,
missing his companion, lover, and wife.

Fredrickson awoke himself out of this memory of
grief into the present day of 2056. He slapped himself
awake after the memories threatened to become too

confronting, sniffing quietly and wiping away tiny teardrops with his thumbs and fingers.

'Get a grip over yourself, man; now isn't the time to take a stroll down memory lane; you're working right now.' He ordered himself quietly. Shaking his head, trying to get away from the awful memories of his wife's funeral. 'Oh, my dear Deborah, I would give anything to hold you again. But time hasn't been fair on me, my sweet; my heart is not whole without you; it's empty, and only you could fill it up. He'd wished they'd met sooner. Where he could've saved her from her distress. He cursed himself; I would've gotten you well if only you'd told me what was wrong. I could've gotten you the therapy that you needed. He sighed in anguish at the thought that haunted him still. *Oh, please be at peace with God, my dear... please keep that coffin of yours hard to hold against the mortuus carnem, he thought. Because I wouldn't be able to bring myself to put you down even if you become one of those walking corpses... I miss you every day, Deborah and I still love you with all my heart; just please be safe inside that coffin... don't turn into one of those freaks.* Fredrickson prayed, knowing that it was pointless. It didn't matter how many prayers to God he made; they would't be answered, and because life in a zombie-ridden world was not kind to prayers... anything could happen without people knowing. Things didn't just blow over if you made a prayer to God. What God? God wasn't there to grant prayers. Instead, the people of the apocalyptic mortuus carnem-ridden world relied on their chances of survival and fate, and sometimes fate wasn't kind. Fate was cruel and barbaric, another way of saying that their lives were going to end with death and tragedy.

Chapter 9

There was a sound of paper being rustled that echoed throughout the cell. Fredrickson looked down and noticed that his hands started to tremble, and so was the piece of paper he was holding. *What the hell? What's wrong with me?* He thought to himself, being so overwhelmed with a spark of terror that was almost paralysing. His thoughts were a mixed bag of different thoughts and harrowing memories that he wasn't thinking very clearly when he'd ended the session so suddenly, based on his own accord and feelings, which he agreed with himself, were not pleasant. Fredrickson knew that he'd come to regret this decision later on as it was unlike him to leave a session early due to fear. But it was too late to turn back; he'd already collected his things and left the cell. He knew that it'd been in the best interests of himself and Sam that he finished up earlier than the rest of the bonders. It was absolutely crucial to stay calm during the sessions, even if you had the shittiest of days. Especially at those times when someone pissed you off, or someone close cashed in one's chips, making you depressed and feeling like nothing could get any worse. As a bonder, it was crucial you bypass those emotions, put them aside for when the session was over and instead put on the act of dexterity as a replacement for your other emotions. To get something out of the drugged, dumbass reanimated corpses controlling one's emotions was paramount as sudden flashes of sadness, anger, and even happiness could confuse and startle them. Startling a zombie is the strict rule ALL bonders must avoid; startled zombies came with catastrophic outcomes, which came with only one solution, resulting in the zombies being taken away and permanently disposed of.

Fredrickson felt, unlike the previous day, that he now had the patience to steady himself. He held his chest, breathing deeply until he could feel his heart slowing down its panic-enthused beats. When he'd finally gotten himself in order, he thought about his pay check, knowing that he wasn't going to get paid much for this abysmal session. He took out his credit card and stared at the expiry date, 27/12/2050; his card had expired six years ago and was useless. Even so, he kept it as a memento of how much the world around him had turned upside down and with the fall of the government and order as soon as the mortuus carnem and the undead reared their hideous faces to the world. Yet he was a professional, a bonder, nothing more, and bonders didn't care for the reward money they earned, so he scoffed at the idea of getting a pay check and put his useless expired credit card back into his pants pocket. Money wasn't essential and needed more use. It was really only used to purchase food and drink from the operating vending machines (there were chefs too who were trained in recipes from other countries such as Korean, Indian, Swedish, German and so on, but they rarely cooked food unless a particular order was made for someone and cooking those specific orders sometimes took up too much time, though if a bonder had finished their duties for the day, they could always come down to the kitchen and make an order) around the facility, which usually was things small like protein and muesli bars, potato chips, bottled water, cordial and fizzy drinks, sometimes if bonders felt like something organic, they could get small bags of sliced apple, banana and orange from refrigerated vending machines, as well as small punnets of berries such as strawberries, raspberries and blueberries which were grown down in the kitchen's private greenhouse. But usually, the thing that would keep them going would either be a cup of coffee or tea and a few small muesli or protein bars, which bonders could snack on throughout the day.

However, on a positive note, and something Fredrickson had missed out on when it came to the discussions the bonders had after each session. Results were showing that some of the zombies were actually showing signs of humanity. It didn't matter if it wasn't their own (the main thing was they were showing it!) and displaying intelligence to their ALIVE tutors that matched the intellect of a small child, either by demonstrating an understanding of particular commands, showing emotions, or the ability to use objects such as cutlery to cut and eat their food if in a more civilised manner. Not all, however, were this successful. There were still those that weren't teachable; no matter what the bonders did, they could not help but grant their zombies the gift of thinking. Such zombies were sent away to be permanently disposed of.

Zombies tagged for disposal were taken away by trained individuals called Bodyguards who patrolled the facility's floors, watching and maintaining the safety of the bonders and everyone else in the building that hung around the GFOSAR's many corridors. They would forcefully take the zombie from their cells, chain them hand and foot, and place a metal muzzle, which was strapped over their mouths, a preventing measure from biting anyone and spreading the infection. These zombies were then taken to a broken elevator shaft, notorious throughout the facility for its use of zombie disposal, earning it the nickname "Elevator to Hell," which measured a whopping total of 357 meters from top to bottom. Situated on the sixth and top floor of the GFOSAR facility, the soldiers would place the screaming (sometimes drugged) zombie just in front of the Elevator to Hell, aim their rifles at their head and fire, shooting the zombies dead in the head. The Doomed zombie would fall into the Elevator to Hell, or the soldiers would unceremoniously kick them over the edge, making the now dead, ill-behaved zombies fall, landing on a growing mountain of rotting, stinking undead bodies. This was yet one method the soldiers used to dispose of the untrainable. But that wasn't the only method of getting rid of a bad zombie. If the zombie was far too violent and just wouldn't die with the emergency drug, would be harshly dragged out of the cells with a snare pole tightly wrapped around their necks, enough to dig into the skin. The soldiers would then drench them head to toe with whatever flammable liquid they could find, flick a lit match into the zombie caked with the flammable substance (they did this outside) and watch them blow up in a fantastic display of bellowing flames. It was always an incredible feat to the survivors inside who couldn't help but feel them an enormous ocean wave of satisfaction to be hearing the pained screams and howls of a zombie that is being burned because they knew that the zombie, whether it be he or she would be burnt to a charred pile of ash. If the fire didn't char them like expected, one loud blow to the head with a shotgun certainly would!

Cansu Aksoy had found herself with such a zombie. Ziya was ill-behaved, refusing to work with the middle-aged Turkish woman despite her best efforts. She even tried going as far as emoting human expressions in hopes of trying to make Ziya understand, but nothing seemed to work. If he wasn't going to behave, she saw no reason to keep going, and once her mind was made up on something, she stayed with it and saw little reason to continue her work due to her lack of patience and tendency to give up with the slightest sign of a stubborn zombie. Without Cansu's control, Ziya was causing mayhem in the cells. Making a continuous ruckus, slashing his only arm around madly, slamming it into things much like a pissed-off silverback gorilla. His loud moaning was accompanied by the sound of him throwing and knocking things over. His moaning and growling were heard by Winsome, who just happened to cross by Ziya's cell with one Robert Boson, one of the elite bodyguards that roamed certain rooms and patrolled hallways, keeping a close watch of the bonders from behind the glass.

'Well now, Cansu must be having some fun with that one-armed old geezer,' purred Winsome. 'From where I'm standing, she sounds like she's doing more than bonding and is getting a little kinky with the old one-armed fucker. Am I right, Bob?' he winked slyly, nudging the big black man's side playfully. 'You think the two are fucking?'

Boson glared at the small, moustached man next to him and rolled his eyes irritably, clearly finding no amusement in the joke that was "supposed" to be funny. Well, at least according to Winsome, it was hilarious.

Do you seriously think you're being funny? Honestly, grow up. Men like you make me sick.' Boson growled. Boson knew Winsome's reputation as the village idiot of GFOSAR, having been pre-warned about his antics. At first, he took them on advisement. Still, he treated him usually, yet eventually, Winsome became the most despised and irritating man Boson had ever met.

But Winsome just continued to playfully prod and he nudged Boson in the side - a little harder this time. 'Hey, come on, Bob, where's your sense of humour and adventure?' Winsome kept elbowing Boson in the side until the big black man decided that he'd had enough and seized Winsome's wrist, which seemed pencil-thin to Boson and twisted it around, causing Winsome to hiss through his teeth in pain. 'Okay, okay, uncle, uncle!' cried Winsome weakly, prompting Boson to sneer at him with his piercing brown eyes. 'Get lost, Ryan.' He snarled at the small, moustached man before he opened his fingers, releasing Winsome's wrist. Winsome looked at him as if this had been the first time that Boson had laid a hand on him. He cradled his aching wrist, and then he scampered away like a fox being chased away by a cat.

Robert Jeremiah Boson was a six-foot-six hulking black man who, like Fredrickson, had a short fuse. He'd been hired as a guard for GFOSAR, and with his mass and guns alone, he fit the profile well. He was intimidating to those who were thinking of crossing the line and breaking the rules of the GFOSAR (Winsome being the exception… much to everyone's dismay, as he appeared not to find Boson the least bit intimidating). Boson wasn't always full of fury; before the mortuus carnem, he was a well-respected, highly profitable football player for the Chicago Bears in America. He'd had a wife who was of Aboriginal descent whom he'd met when she was eighteen, having moved to America from Australia. They, in turn, had produced a daughter: Mimi, whom he loved with all his heart, and he'd fit into the life of a family man with joy. His life in Chicago was everything a decent man with a beautiful, loving wife and a cute kid could want. That was until Boson had returned home full of pride and enthusiasm after winning the 2034 Cup, a satisfying win over the Dallas Cowboys by just one point. His wife and daughter hadn't been able to attend the game, so when he arrived home, he sought them out to relay his news. As he stepped foot into his and Nanina's bedroom, he found his worst fears had leapt out of his head and into the real world. He dropped the golden winner's cup upon seeing the ghastly sight staring at him in the face! Someone had broken into his home while he was en route home and murdered his precious Nanina by a fatal stabbing. At the same time, he'd only been no less than a few minutes away from pulling up in the driveway, "Na-Nani-na." he croaked out his wife's name as he stared wide and teary-eyed at the battered corpse lying on their bed, her stomach riddled with bloody stab holes that spilled out around her and… "Oh no… No…' Boson fell to his knees upon seeing the stagnant body of his six-year-old daughter, Mimi's petite body curled up next to his wife with a pillow over her face. Someone had smothered her with it! What kind of sick fuck asphyxiates a six-year-old girl! Was the first thing that had gone through his head when he saw his daughter's lifeless eyes, which stared up at the ceiling.

Then, while Boson was in his current state of shock, he could hear rustling footsteps coming from within the house. Boson stood up and left his wife's and daughter's bodies to investigate. He went into the living room, and that was when he caught the perpetrator, currently in the daring act of trying to steal their safe, which held the sum of $64,997 inside. Boson snapped; his eyes twitching, his biceps bulging, and his teeth clenched, and right then, a new persona in him was born; he wasn't waiting any longer to let it out if it was to be unleashed, it would be here, the beast would be let out of its cage upon this intruder who had done the unthinkable thing of murdering his wife and child and was now trying to make off with his safe! How fucking dare he! It was bad enough that this man had his wife and daughter's blood on his hands, and now he was going to be a petty thief and try to take his money? This was something that Boson could not let slide.

Full of nothing but pure, seething anger, grief, and blood-red hatred from seeing this hooded man with a knife trying to take his prized safe, who had already stolen the most valuable things in his life. Robert Jeremiah Boson wasn't going to allow this murdering thief a second to take another breath. Hell, he wasn't going to leave the Boson house. Robert Boson made deftly sure of that. Boson propelled his body at him, going for the tackle, knocking the knife out of his hand, and holding him down with all his weight. Because Boson was a hefty man of six feet six inches and muscle, escape wasn't an option for the murderer … his life was done. Boson had no sympathy for the man and wasn't reasoning about the consequences of his actions. *"YOU CUNTING BASTARD! YOU MOTHERFUCKER! I'LL KILL YOU! I'LL KILL YOU!!*

I'LL KILL YOU!!!" He roared as he began punching at the perpetrator with the full force of his mighty, hungry fists, pounding his heavy fists as the man cried. It didn't take long for the man's face to become black and blue, and it didn't take much longer for a cracking sound to come from the man's face and echo through Boson's ears like a sadistic tune which he savoured as the perpetrator's bones caved in from his heavy blows resulting in a gruesome demise and a shattered skull which had blood spilling out of it at an uncontrolled rate.

Boson ended a man's life that day, but he didn't feel guilt; he knew that he'd sent the man to where he belonged, hell and allowed Nanina and Mimi's souls to pass on into heaven.

He couldn't remember how long he'd sat between his beautiful wife and child, pulling them as close to him as he could. Then, finally waking enough from his grief to call the police. His head just kept playing over and over; his wife had been stabbed, his daughter asphyxiated, and they were gone forever. Two months later, in December, Boson had retired from Football forever, buried his wife and child and left the scum of America. Leaving the memory of his family behind. Moving to London in the UK, he'd taken a job as a bodyguard, which is where he found himself still. Robert Boson made a living in making sure that everything was in check and rules were obeyed. It made him feel some control in his life so he could take his mind off the harrowing experience that had happened to his wife and daughter back in America. Scientists and survivors were now his responsibility to keep in check while ensuring that the Bonders were safe as they went about their work with their zombies. While Boson would've preferred to continue living his days as a footballer for the Chicago Bears, he knew that because he'd taken that man's life and with the death of his wife and child – he knew that he could never return to that life again, being a bodyguard and patrolling the GFOSAR and looking after the bonders as they worked was better than nothing. Even if he would occasionally have to deal with an irritating fly named Winsome and the frequent zombie that needed to be disposed of. Things are never the same when tragedy and the mortuus carnem are involved.

Chapter 10

'Allah kahrestsin! Stop, Ziya!' screamed Cansu; for once, she was showing actual emotion as she tried putting a restraining muzzle over her elderly zombie's neck. However, Ziya had none of it, and he wasn't going to allow himself to be restrained like a dog so easily. He was done listening to her deadpanned tone and seeing that consistent wooden expression. Working alongside Cansu had been torture, and he wanted out and away from her, even if it meant being disposed of; he just wanted to get away from that robot in human flesh. Cansu Aksoy wasn't the bonder for him; he made damn sure she knew it.

He disobeyed her every order, purposely misbehaving whenever he could so that he could prove something to her, that she wasn't the right person fit for the job and that she'd be better suited to something else that wasn't bonding or anything to do with talking to people. With his one remaining arm, Ziya grabbed the desk from one of its sides and yanked it to the left side of the cell. It hit the wall with a loud crash, which sounded like an explosion, sure to grasp some concern for the neighbouring zombies and bonders. Despite being an old zombie and only having one arm, he sure was strong, throwing the steel desk to the side with little effort.

'Ziya! Ya sonofabitch!! I've just about had a gutful of this! I'm trying to help you gain your humanity again! Don't you want that? If you do, stop this shit, and just let me do my job and help you!' Cansu hissed as she backed up from the angry Ziya as he swiped at her with his one arm. Growling and snarling as if in demand of a chunk of her.

He seemed to be asking for her to do her job right and show him some emotion in her voice. But Cansu managed to release her cat-like reflexes, ducking his arm's swing, and finding an opportunity to jump behind him. She pushed him down hard to the ground with her body weight, pinning him with the use of her right elbow to the back of his neck, her left hand holding his face to the floor, demanding that he kiss it. Next, Cansu did something that wasn't known to her and screamed out for some assistance. 'Yardim! Ziya is a failure. I need him disposed of ASAP!' she shrieked, punching a big black button labelled in bold white letters EMERGENCY near the cell door and waited for someone to come while she did her best to keep a tight hold on Ziya, his head held so low to the ground that he was basically lapping at the floor.

Cansu was kneeling on his back, pinning him with her weight. All the while, he continued to thrash and struggle about under his normally poker-faced bonder's weight.

And as luck would have it for Cansu, it was Boson who'd been patrolling nearby and was the one who'd heard the clamorous amount of noise coming from cell B-29, knowing that quite a severe scuffle was going along inside it. He barged into the cell like a startled rampaging elephant and, seeing the situation the Turkish woman was in, jumped into the fray, more than willing to aid her in the struggle.

Cansu rolled off the elderly one-armed zombie, and she made a haste move to get back to her feet and to allow Boson to do what she'd called him here for. She took a scant moment to regain her breath, hands on her knees and wheezing. Cansu stood up straight; she took a small step backward where she watched in stoned-faced satisfaction as the beast of a bodyguard grabbed Ziya by the one arm and hoisted him upwards with such violence that it was a wonder that Ziya's other arm didn't tear off. Boson lurched the elderly zombie up to his chest, and before Ziya could whip around and turn his sights onto the bodyguard that had him, Boson had one of his large, black hands in a fist and caved it down upon the snarling Ziya with a brick-hard THUMP on the head. The impact was hard enough to make a muffled cracking sound as he'd just cracked his skull with one hard punch to the back of the head. Yet Ziya slumped still out cold with one punch, his arm still held by Boson while the rest of his body was lowered to the floor.

Cansu's mouth quivered. She could hear the echo of her teeth clattering. She put a hand to her bottom jaw to stifle her trembling mouth and those chattering teeth. As soon as she knew everything was under control and Ziya had been knocked unconscious or dead (again), - as that was quite the blow to the head - she took one of the red pills from her lab coat breast pocket and handed it to the big black man. Boson took it without a second thought. Holding Ziya's head up high, he squeezed the zombie's jawline, forcing him to open his mouth. Then, she jammed the hunger drug home before slamming his jaw down with brute force till he heard him swallow the drug.

'Keep or dispose of?' Boson asked Cansu Aksoy.

'Dispose of. Ziya is of no use to me anymore, Mr Robert.' She replied with her usual deadpan voice. Her personality returned to her (hooray… the robot has been rebooted), and no other emotions, such as the adrenalizing fear and heart-pounding frustration, remained. She erased them from her mind without a trace of them ever being there in the first place. She had no time for such trivial thoughts and emotions.

'With pleasure, ma'am.' Boson replied, nodding his head without hesitation, Boson grabbed the muzzle from where it lay on the floor. He unceremoniously placed it over Ziya's head, tightly buckling it in place. Harshly pulling Ziya up by the white tufts of hair on his head. He held his arm back behind his back, forcing him to straighten his stance and find his feet in his now drugged state.

They began walking from the cell, Boson escorting him past the other cells containing the bonders and their zombies. Ziya tried to look up for one last glance at his kin, his fellow zombies, as he knew he was to be disposed of. His former bonder had some time ago explained what would become of him if he didn't comply. And he knew she'd finally requested (most likely, he'd be set on fire because that is what happens to nasty zombies here), and he was going to his final death. As fate would have it, that's precisely where Boson was taking him: outside to be doused in a carton of kerosene.

On their way to the stairs that'd eventually lead to L1, they passed by other zombies. They were currently on L3, the (Zombie Bonding Level), the place that Ziya had found as home, if only for a very short time.

Linus, the boy zombie in cell B-01, was too doped on the hunger drug to care about his surroundings and the fuss that Ziya had been causing. A blind elderly zombie named Wendy in cell B-30 curiously looked around in the direction where the noise had once come from as if she was trying to pinpoint its exact location. Perceptive Spot in cell B-09 curiously tilted his head, asking his bonder what the ruckus was. Ace, the crawler in cell B-12, had been screaming long after Ziya was drugged, and now they passed in opposite directions in the hall. Ace, now when silent as the drug took effect fell off the chair and passed out.

And then there was Sam who was by herself in cell B-35 after Fredrickson just up and left her after their strange interaction and occurrence she didn't quite understand at the time. However, she was unlike the other zombies, who had different reactions following Ziya's ranting earlier. She was quietly sitting at the desk, displaying a very eerie human-like behaviour. She was carefully reading through some pages that lay before her on the desk. Frederickson's life and personal feelings were written in explicit detail, things truthfully, he'd want to keep to himself. Yet Sam took her time going over the pages, again and again, ignoring the sounds of Ziya's distress, not caring what that meant for her fellow zombie.

Chapter 11

On the eighth of October. There'd been a rumour floating around the building that one of the bonders, Olio Garcia, had gotten up to this stage and had a success story whose name she'd yet to mention or confirm if the rumour was, as a matter of fact, true. But this was only a rumour, but who knows – sometimes rumours turn out to be true. The bonding was now going at a reasonable pace, with hopes of returning the forgotten humanity to this handful of undead individuals. Once, these undead individuals had some humanity in them and were able to do things such as using cutlery, speaking, using manners, and behaving respectably. In other words, turning them into civilized citizens which was something that would strengthen the hope of saving the dying world they now lived in. If subjects continued to show signs of success to their bonders, they'd be escorted into the medical ward of the facility, and then the newly bonded zombies could have their reconstructive surgeries, which would give them a more human appearance.

From then on, they'd be released upon Zone 5, into the desolate streets to begin the mission their bonders had trained and prepared them for. The plan was a bold one with these zombies trained to help the remaining living; to find those that were in hiding and assist them in regaining their confidence and help the plight of rebuilding a better new world and to train the zombies in Zone 5 to be more human, to consume human foods and to prove that they are capable of living as a human again, building them into subjects of a better world. One where both the living and the undead could coexist together in blissful harmony. The living could start over again in repopulating the Earth and restore her to her original lively state of water and greenery, and maybe some industrial spots, pubs, and other social gatherings, all with the much-needed second hand of their undead partners.

It would be a peaceful world of order and prosperity, where zombies and the living could work together side by side – and maybe down the line, a cure could be in the works – or at least something that would have the opposing effect on the undead. Instead of the mortuus carnem turning them into mindless, brain eaters. Perhaps a cure could be injected into the bodies, turning them docile and instantly making them civil. But that was a massive MAYBE and an even bigger IF.

Inside the GFOSAR, the bonders woke up to the blaring sound of their alarm clocks inside their Harry Potter-esque closet room, alerting them that it was time to get up and get to work. They rose with groans and yawns as they had to leave behind the comfort of their warm cocoon-like resting positions, and warm blankets. They only had single beds in their small closet-like rooms, so any funny business was out of the question as the rooms were small and could only hold one person inside. But that was okay because the bonders didn't think much about sharing their beds with the others in the facility. However, most of the survivors that sought shelter away from the dangers of the outside and the consistent fear of a lurking undead putting them on their dinner menu had to sleep on the floor, where they would have to huddle up to each other just to keep themselves warm because the GFOSAR had limited space, beds would be assigned to the ones that worked in the facility. The beds would be for those who were trying to save the remaining members of the human race, according to a broad sign hanging up from the ceiling near the entrance of the building. So, if survivors wanted to find a good place to be safe and not be in the way of the bonders, scientists, surgeons, bodyguards, etc, they had to be happy in the basement, as that was mainly empty and unusable.

Therefore, it was the perfect place for survivors to stay and spend their time, safely with other people like them.

There were only a few liveable houses with beds of comfort in the dying zombie-riddled world of 2056. Most of the houses outside resembled a war zone. They looked like a nuclear bomb had hit them. No longer were they homey interiors; they were just a pile of burnt rubble. But despite the houses being uninhabitable, there was a redeeming factor about them. Some still contained a quantity of food, water, and medical resources. If a person was lucky enough, on the rare occasion, it would be sufficient that he or she could even use some of it to trade at one of the shops that hadn't gone to shit yet. And that was always good to know about if you were on the streets, fending for yourselves and loved ones.

On this October morning, Cansu Aksoy jolted awake as soon as she'd heard the familiar buzz in her office, letting her know that someone had prepared a new subject for her. She flew the covers off her, got dressed and left her closet room. Despite losing Ziya yesterday, Cansu was ready to receive another subject. However, her experience with the elderly one-armed zombie was making her think about her priorities, that maybe bonding wasn't for her, and that she should possibly resign. But that would just be ignorant. She couldn't go home as her country was infested with the undead, and she couldn't go outside where it was a massive risk for those who weren't adapted for survival or knew their way around firearms, and Cansu didn't want to throw herself into the line of danger yet. So, she considered that it would be best for her to keep her position as a bonder, even if she didn't enjoy it – *it was better to be in a room with one drugged-up zombie than outside with dozens of rabid ones,* she told herself.

Cansu made her way down the steps to the mess hall where everyone collected their new subjects (it was a wonder that the room didn't have a name change at this point, perhaps to ZOMBIE COLLECTION AREA or NEW SUJECTS, but suppose name changes weren't necessary). Here, when she walked through the room without a door, she met with a spectacled, red-haired, freckled woman named Martha Velcisco, who'd given Cansu a large yawn, but not because she didn't like Cansu; her large yawn was for a different reason altogether. Underneath those large black-framed spectacles, which looked far too big for her small, slender face, were drooping blue eyes that had bags underneath them from lack of sleep, but that was one thing that Martha struggled with; she just couldn't get to sleep no matter how much she tried.

Martha was an insomniac; she hadn't slept in over three weeks and was often seen holding a cup of steaming coffee in one hand. This was no different for Cansu, as when she came in to see Martha, she'd seen that cup of coffee in her hand, which she took occasional sips from. Martha had chosen another zombie for her as she was holding the handle of a rusted grey wheelbarrow in her other hand. Cansu stepped up and looked at the body slumped in the bucket. On observation, Cansu could immediately tell that it was a crawler and in a similar state to Ace, but this one was a male, like Ziya. Martha explained to Cansu in the best way that she could (without sounding lethargic) that her new subject had died and lost his legs a few days ago, making him one of the more recent undead. Cansu nodded and ordered for the latest zombie to be taken up to the cells so the work could begin. And without another word to Martha, she strode away purposely to wait for the zombie to be delivered. Unlike the others, she wasn't one to do things for herself and expected every command to be followed.

Meanwhile, Cansu got her latest crawler at the same time that Kolen started her eighth working day with her crawler, Ace. She was astounded by what her crawler had accomplished in just those eight days. She'd mastered the capacity of speech! Yes, there were gaps in the phrases she would say, and the grammar and ability to speak a complete sentence needed to be more there.

So, "Hello, how are you?" Would be, "Ello, how you?"

Despite the grammar flaws in Ace's speech, Kolen found it fortunate that they were making splendid progress. Progress to make up Kolen's mind about rewarding Ace with something special; it was always good to reward a zombie once in a while if they were well-behaved. She'd chosen something all zombies couldn't get enough of… the one thing they always fight for, like lions, when it came to hunting the living for food.

Kolen re-entered cell B-12 after she had left temporarily, claiming to Ace she'd forgotten something important. She felt a little anxious in hoping that Ace would like her present. Drawing in a deep breath, she pulled a plain cardboard box from behind her back. It wasn't wrapped up in any fancy birthday or Christmas paper, and that was okay; zombies like Ace didn't care for brightly coloured wrapping. She had, however, taken the time to write on it with a black marker. *To ACE From M. Kolen* was scrawled over its front in her neat handwriting. Ace stared at the box with a sleepy, drugged-out expression and then at her bonder in a questioning manner. Kolen was smiling at her; her eyes from under the glasses were calm and yet apprehensive. She recollected the instance that happened on their first bonding day, which caused her to feel a bit on edge about how Ace would react to her gift.

She did struggle quite a bit to keep up the act of a calm persona on her smooth, youthful mug, but who could blame her? She was about to give Ace her first reward. So, it was forgiven that Kolen was feeling both nervous and exhilarated, and the smile she gave her zombie had displayed her precise emotions with apparent accuracy as she gently placed the box on the table between them. She then sat down opposite Ace and gently pushed the box over to her with her hand, still smiling bravely as she presented the present to her. Ace studied the box, examining it and peering around all sides. Kolen could tell that she was curious about the contents inside the box, yet her face didn't appear to show her curiosity, zombies very rarely showed expression of their emotions unless it was anger. Instead, Ace presented with a tired and zoned-out expression, most likely due to the small amount of The Hunger Drug still required for them to work together.

'You've been just amazing with the bonding, Ace! There's just no other way I could put it. You... You rock, girl! So, to show how impressed and happy I am with the way you've been learning. I thought I'd give you this present as a token of our friendship and the progress you've gone through to get this far.' beamed Kolen. She smiled and tilted her sliding glasses upward on her nose. Ace looked at the box again and sniffed at it, her eyes suddenly lighting up, yet apprehensively looked at Kolen, appearing confused. Kolen did the honours for her and opened the box lid, gesturing for Ace to look inside and accept her gift.

Ace reached forward in her wheelchair, the green plaid blanket over her missing legs creasing from her stretching forward. She reached her arms out and grabbed the sides of the box, pulling it closer towards her and peering inside. Thinking that she'd be disappointed, Kolen nervously bit her lip. Turning her head away, she fiddled with her brown hair, considering the possibility that Ace didn't understand the meaning of her gift and why she'd given it to her. But hey, like Fredrickson said, "zombie bonding has many different twists and turns", so anything could happen while working with them.

She looked up as Ace's joyful sound was heard. Much to Kolen's delight, she looked over to see the crawler's dead eyes now wide and awake with ecstasy as her eyes stared into the box. Kolen was just as surprised as she was, beaming with excitement at seeing her zombie's joy firsthand. A zombie displaying such a genuine emotion as happiness had never been documented before. She continued to watch Ace reach into the box, pulling out a huge glass jar full of a light pink fluid and something sloshing around inside of it. Containing a freshly dissected human brain. For Kolen, seeing a human brain sloshing around in a jar was a disgusting sight. Still, to Ace, it appeared it was the ultimate gift that she could ever receive.

Kolen had sourced the brain from the contamination room in the facility's lab earlier. There were few of these, and they were only meant to be given to zombies as a one-time treat to show that their bonders were pleased with them bonding well and behaving themselves as ordered. Then, after this one-time brain treat, they'd be given more human-based foods such as vegetables and animal meat like lamb, beef, chicken, fish, and pork. 'FOOOOOODDD!!!' Ace whooped with joy and satisfaction from seeing the human organ in-cased inside the glass jar. Timid, little Kolen, couldn't help but cry tears of proud elation. She chuckled in delight at her now radiant zombie, who was closely hugging the jar containing the brains to her chest like it was her most favoured possession.

'Here,' Kolen held her hand out cautiously. 'I'll help you open it'. Ace looked at the jar and then at Kolen's hand.

Kolen, obeying the crucial rule of not startling Ace, took her time for Ace to comply. It shocked Kolen, making her jaw drop, and her eyes widen when Ace actually held the jar out to her instead of snatching it and keeping it to her chest like Kolen expected her to do.

Kolen carefully and attentively took the jar away from Ace's clinging rotting fingers. Holding the jar to her chest in a grip, twisting and turning at the lid she found had been tightly screwed on. Beginning to worry, she observed Ace, concerned that Ace's patience may not hold. It finally gave way after Kolen swore she could feel her palms bubble with blisters, and she sighed in relief. She took the lid off, smelling and contorting her face, grimacing at the disgusting odour of dead and soon-to-be rotting brains that assaulted her nostrils and tried not to gag. Putting the lid and the jar on the desk, she pushed the jar back over to Ace. Yet when the jar was within her reach, Ace's pale grey dead hand rammed itself inside the glass jar with such force and ferocity that Kolen suddenly felt a little unsettled.

Ace grabbed at the brain like a starving child who hadn't eaten in days. At first, it refused to come free, with Ace moaning in frustration. Not willing to give up, Ace tugged at the brain until she managed to pull it out with one hard pull. Next, Ace displayed the most common behaviour of the undead, stuffing the freshly dissected brain down without hesitation. High-pitched moans that sounded like musical delight ruptured from Ace, the likes of which Kolen had never heard before from a zombie. Kolen looked away, clutching her lilac shirt, as a sick feeling enveloped her stomach; the sight of her zombie eating a brain reminded her of a wild, starving animal. When the sounds ceased, she looked up to find Ace smiling with a look of ecstasy on her face. Blood coated Ace's decaying fingers, exposing smiling teeth, dripping onto the desk and the floor. Kolen composed herself, pushing her glasses up her nose to their needed position. Nervously, she patted down her blouse as Ace started to lick at the residue on her fingers.

'I hope you enjoyed your treat Ace since you've been such a good girl.' Kolen gulped when the sound of licking and slurping stopped, only to be replaced by the sound of Ace's hungry breathing.

Kolen turned around, observing the expression on Ace's face; her wide eyes full of insanity, a bloody dripping smile of teeth completing the gruesome picture. Surprisingly, Kolen held her own. Gaining the courage to put a hand into one of her lab coat pockets; she took out a clean white cotton handkerchief. Knowing it was a risk yet being unable to stop herself with slow motions, she went about lightly dabbing the clean handkerchief around Ace's chin. Much to her surprise, Ace didn't move or try attacking her. She didn't even flinch, even when the cotton hanky touched her chin. Ace seemed to steady her hunger as zombies were known to never feel full; they were known to always be hungry. Kolen couldn't help but grin at the gentle, almost child-like gaze Ace was giving her. It gave her a sense of relief that Kolen liked as she fumbled with the silver ring on her finger. Ace sat patiently; the kind gesture never once flickered away or faltered, allowing Kolen to lean over and lightly dab even her bloodied teeth with the now blood-soaked handkerchief.

Kolen couldn't believe her luck; she felt like hugging Ace but made sure to keep her excitement to a minimum. She was feeling amazing; her heart was beating, and her fingers were shaking with joy at her zombie and their interaction over the gift. So, this is what it's like to be a successful zombie bonder? Kolen thought as her face and body swam with confidence.

When Ace's face was dry and absent of blood, Kolen removed the blood-soaked handkerchief and placed it back into her coat. Kolen couldn't wait for the next stage of the bonding process. If Ace continued behaving brilliantly, she'd have bragging rights. 'If you continue on this road of becoming smarter and human-like with my help. Not to brag,' she added. 'We will need to do something about your decaying flesh; isn't that exciting? With surgery, you can look alive again!' Kolen explained, a wistful smile on her lips. She felt excited thinking about the future of the good zombies that behaved; by the looks of things, Ace was just about ready to undergo the procedure, and she couldn't feel prouder.

Chapter 12

In cell B-09, the only Australian bonder in the building, Lisa Ark, felt a sense of wonder with her subject and the development her subject was going through. For one, she'd noticed that her zombie seemed to be more on the docile side of things; even without the administration of the hunger drugs, her subject never seemed violent or aggressive. Even as she bonded with him, she couldn't help but feel awe whenever she'd come into B-09 and to see her subject sitting up straight, his hands in his lap, as if he was patiently yearning for her arrival. Either way, he provided his bonder with a consistent feeling of astonishment and a sense of "safety" whenever she was with him.

Even though he was one of the undead with a similar goal as all the other undead husks outside, Ark couldn't help but feel like she was in a safe place whenever she entered the cell seeing him sitting quietly and patiently for her. Because it had reminded her of the times when she'd saved people from a dangerous neurological disease. Seeing her zombie sitting there patiently, waiting for her, and curiously tilting his head in her direction when she entered made her think of the many times when she'd dealt with child cases and whenever she'd turn off the anaesthesia and feel the sense of achievement when a child's eyes would flicker open and ask her if they were okay, providing Ark with the wonder in knowing that she'd saved the life of one of the innocents. That was why Lisa Ark felt a sense of safety whenever she was with her zombie, because whenever she looked at his towering slender form, she saw one of those children on her operating table, just waiting for her to turn off the anaesthesia so that he'd wake up and ask her if he was okay, to which she would reply with a smile and stifled tears, telling him that he's alright and that he was free to go back home to the people that loved him.

Her tall male zombie, whom she'd named Spot, shared some similarities to Kolen's crawler (who seemed to have been pulled apart) when it came to identifying the cause of death. It was reasonably easy to identify the reason behind Spot's demise, as the evidence was staring Ark straight in the face (literally). Spot had the top half of his head missing, and his appearance resembled the similar look if a child had taken a paper cut-out of a man and snipped half of his head off with some scissors, leading Ark to think of plausible possibilities of how such a thing could've occurred. Eventually, she came up with two possibilities, one: he either could've killed himself with a blow to the head with a shotgun. But the jury was out on that plausibility because the exposed sides around his mouth were straight and appeared to be cleanly cut, not rough and jagged, which usually was the case from the aftermath of a shotgun blast, so this ruled out the idea of a shotgun blast. Secondly, she thought it could've been that he'd had something sharp and fast-moving slice half his head off in some freak accident. This would have made his demise an instant and painless death, though a very shocking one for anyone who'd happened to witness it; this theory seemed more palpable. Ark looked him over like a broken leaf that'd been slowly eaten away by a ravenous caterpillar. She hoped for his sake; it'd been the second conclusion, and he'd not suffered as by the white buttoned blouse and black overalls which he wore. Ark had the idea that he'd probably been a decent guy in life and that he would've been well-loved.

As Ark sat on the chair in the cell, looking Spot up and down as he continued to sit silently and patiently with his hands in his lap, she couldn't help but think back to the day when she'd received him from Boyle. Ark determined that he was well over six-five in height. So, when she'd seen the state of the zombie that would become hers, she'd almost fainted from the feature that defined him and made him a staple in her mind. Seeing that he was without the top half of his head and the way his tongue drunkenly lolled from side to side. It reminded her of an octopus feeling for its prey with one of its tentacles. She wondered how the zombie could walk around without half his head, let alone how he'd be able to eat and hunt for food. Seeing her stress, Boyle immediately offered to get her another zombie, one that comprised of a full head. Being a pretty gullible man who never liked seeing the discomfort in women.

Ark had been quick to overcome the sight of Spot and remembered responding to Boyle's proposal of getting a subject exchange. 'It's okay, Carl,' she said 'I can still work with him; I was just a bit shocked when I saw him. I've never seen a zombie before with the same death mark as him. When you described him through the intercom, saying he was half headless, I thought you to be a little bonkers or that shithead Ryan had put you up to it.' There had been more discussion regarding the appearance and AOR, but overall, their conversation was relatively short. Ark took control of the zombie; and given Boyle a grateful smile as she approached her tall, imposing, half-headless male zombie and tenderly took his large, skinny hand from the balding man. Then Ark left the mess hall, escorted her subject, lead him up the stairs and through the maze of corridors, avoiding any collisions with people and to the bonding cells.

She'd come to the cell labelled B-09, fingered the combination into the lock, hearing the buzz as the door opened, then assisted her new subject over the step inside. There, she led him over to the table, pulled out his chair, gently grabbed his arms and lowered him down; she had put his hands in his lap; her bonding method was to show respect and tenderness to her subjects. Then, when he was seated, she went around the table and sat on the chair opposite from him.

Ark's first impressions of her new zombie were grand. Taking her usual stance to bond, telling him in a soft and friendly tone. 'From now on, you're to be treated as if you were someone who had a place in this world. My name's Lisa Ark, and I'm your bonder. Not only will I be your bonder and responsible for you, but I'll also act as your best friend until it's time for you to leave this facility. But that will only happen if you cooperate well with me; if so, you'll be rewarded, and I'll make a compromise with one of the surgeons to do something about your missing top head half. But that'll happen if we grow a steady friendship and you bond well with me. Alright, now that introductions and the basics are done, let's begin.'

From here on, she'd welcomed him into the procedure like a long-distance friend and named him Spot upon noticing an odd-looking circle-shaped mark on the veins on his right arm; just a simple brown spot, a birthmark? Or perhaps it was a wound he'd sustained from his living days that hadn't completely gone through the healing process due to his death shortly after receiving it? It didn't matter how he got it; it was a minor thing that didn't contribute anything to his bonding. Ark simply shrugged it off, ignoring it entirely after she'd given him his zombie name; it now had no consequence to the process.

Ark glanced up at a digital clock mounted above the door behind her, and she thought that she'd try a little experiment with him. It was when the time came for the hunger drugs to wear off. But Ark wasn't going to administer him with another; she wanted to see what he would do. And she wasn't disappointed; she did get a response, but it wasn't what was typical for most subjects when the drugs had worn off. This was the moment when Ark noticed the difference between Spot and her previous zombies. 'This is new,' she remarked, taken back by the surprising feat (she may have a winner here), that Spot didn't seem violent or showing signs of hunger like most of the zombies, which left her gobsmacked. She pursed her lips, broadened her eyes, and nodded slowly at this revelation. 'My, my, aren't you a patient one,' she said, complimenting him on his placid demeanour.

When the drugs wore off, she half expected him to start tensing up uncomfortably, swinging back and forth against his restraints or at least violently swishing that tongue of his around to show her that he was craving. But no, she got none of that. He just continued to sit silently and patiently in his chair, not moving so much as an inch. Seeking no urge to leap up and try to hurt her, not presenting as violent and aggressive like the others she'd tried working with before. It was as if Spot faintly had some shreds of his former humanity left. The drugs, it appeared, were helping it surface above his undead mind. Yet it seemed highly impossible for that to be a thing because he lacked a brain. Aside from the missing top half of his head, another fact was that he was categorised in the five years AOR. So, it was probable that he still had some parts of his humanity deep down inside.

However, you never knew when it came to the undead, as Ark had written in one of her previous notes with one of her last subjects named Drongo, who'd been disposed of about two months ago due to a violent outburst similar to Ziya. *Once they regained some semblance of smarts, enough to understand communication at least, the sonofabitches were found to be full of fucking surprises. Some could even surpass some of the living regarding intelligence, which was always a good sign.*

Ark had discovered more than a few little surprises while bonding with the tall Spot, that he was heading that way and could be one of the rare cases of zombie bonding done right and that he might actually be a success story and would be a step forward into bringing humanity in the right direction. But one can hope. One can hope.

Chapter 13

Back in B-35. Sam was bonding with Fredrickson much faster than any zombie that came before her and far quicker than any zombie Fredrickson had worked with. He wiped the perspiration from his forehead as he stared into those dead eyes. He almost couldn't believe his luck and felt he ought to thank Winsome and Boyle for giving him such an excellent subject who was bonding well with him. It was outstanding how much she'd defied his expectations. While Spot and Ace were getting good grades and were exceeding their bonder's expectations based on the records, he'd read about them. They couldn't par with the progress that Sam was going through, and Fredrickson still couldn't believe his luck and that maybe, for once, he was finally going to have a success story and rights to brag (if you keep this up, I will be maintaining my reputation as the best bonder in the GFOSAR). Fredrickson looked down at his notes and saw that he'd written the word, excellent under the <u>HOW IS THEIR BEHAVIOUR?</u> Paragraph. Although when he considered how he'd gotten her to this stage, he jotted down that he'd prescribed her at least three pills a day for every hour, dulling her hunger while also being mindful of taking at least one Valium in the morning before going into the cell to start the day, making the bonding process easier for both his and her parts – he wasn't in the risk of being attacked – she wasn't in the risk of him having a furious outburst at her if she didn't do what he wanted. So, if he abides by his medication schedule and takes his Valium, he should be calm for his sessions.

By getting rid of the raging hunger and taking his medication in the morning before work, Fredrickson ensured that Sam listened to his every instruction and order. So, a Valium, some water, and some well-needed rest the night before were sure to fix that. Now he was working with Sam, he thought about incorporating some of the techniques/mechanisms that he'd used when working with his past zombies but decided to think outside the box for Sam, seeing where it would take her if he mixed things up a bit, maybe that was why his previous zombies were failures because he always followed his own training and never opted for something different to try with his zombies. How lucky for Sam that she would be the first subject to change Fredrickson's usual daily process.

Fredrickson had upheld his part of the deal. He'd said that he'd provide her with some books to read, and he'd done just that. He'd entered the cell carrying a plain white tote bag with six books inside, all written by authors spanning over different periods and all ones that he'd read. Bringing six books instead of one allows Sam the gift of choice. He took the books out individually, setting them down on the table in front of Sam and letting the zombie woman take a brief moment to study the different covers before her. 'As you can see here, Sam, I held my end of the bargain and have brought you six books instead of one. Now, you choose which ones to read. Of course, you won't be able to read all of the ones you choose in one day; I'm not expecting you to even finish one in a day, heavens, no; you can read them in your own time, at your own pace when I'm not around. So, instead of sitting around and waiting for me to return in the next session, you can open the book you've chosen and start reading through it at your own pace. Also, here.' Fredrickson reached into one of his coat's many pockets, procured a small plastic strip with some blue and black checkerboard paper, and put it in front of her. 'You'll need this if you want to stop reading and remember where you left off. You can use that to mark your page. Handy things they are, bookmarks. I use them all the time whenever I'm reading a book.

Now then, let's see what we've got here.' He pointed to the first book on the table, looking at her earnestly. 'This one is The Cat in The Hat by Dr Seuss, a silly picture book for beginners. It's a very childish one, but it's good for those learning the basics of the English language and good for children. Personally, I'm not a fan of Dr Suess and the silly rhymes. But this isn't about what I think but about you and teaching you these things again.' Frederickson then pointed to the second. 'This is Fantastic Mr Fox by Roald Dahl, a book directed at children yet with some adult themes; however, Roald Dahl was a childhood favourite of mine.' Fredrickson pushed this book forward a little across the desk before continuing. 'Next, is William Shakespeare's Macbeth, an absolute classic. Although you may not understand it, Sam, and I wouldn't blame you if you don't; most people don't.' Fredrickson stated matter-of-factly. 'It was written as a play around the year 1609, and Shakespeare isn't really touched these days as he was back then. But it's worth a try.' He added, hopefully pushing the book slightly forward before indicating the next book by tapping its cover. 'The Stand by Stephen King is a long story but, nevertheless, a true masterpiece. Personally, it is one of my favourite books and one I often recommend.' He added, pushing it further forward so it nearly hit the tips of Sam's fingers resting on the desk. Then he continued on quickly, 'I also have Jurassic Park by Michael Crichton. If you like dinosaurs then this one is the one for you. And finally, I got Harry Potter and the Philosopher's Stone by J.K Rowling,' he stated, pushing both books forward before adding, 'A story about magic, witches, and wizards. Popular with all ages, though, not me, I always preferred Tolken's Lord of the Rings and Hobbit over the Harry Potter series.'

Fredrickson sat back on his chair, crossing his arms, waiting for a response from Sam. 'Choose one of these books to read, Sam, but only one. And I suggest you write down any words you don't understand. It will give me an opening to the things you do and don't understand while also letting me into the kind of person you were when you were alive.' Fredrickson instructed before taking a black ballpoint pen from his breast pocket and a small black notebook with an orange tiger printed on it. He placed them on the desk in the middle of the second and third books and pushed them gently towards her. Sam silently studied him for a moment, reading the expression in his brown eyes; she tilted her head as if she couldn't understand what he was asking of her. But this expression was only for a mild second as she then glanced at the six books in front of her; observing the colours on the covers and the thickness of each. She picked up some of them, opening them to random pages, studying the font size and then putting them back down where she looked through them again, trying to choose which one to read. Then, almost absentmindedly, she rubbed at the decayed flesh of her exposed stomach, stroking the destroyed shrivelled organs and touching the spine that was barely visible to human eyes.

'Sam?' Fredrickson asked, curious about what was happening in his subject's head. He tried placing a soothing hand on Sam's cheek as if to calm her. He saw that one of her hands had become a ball and was trembling; she looked stressed, and he wanted to reassure her and perhaps pick a book out for her so that she wouldn't have to feel so stressed about making a decision. But she'd already made her decision and didn't want Fredrickson's help picking a book that was of little interest to her. She smacked his hand away as soon as it was about to make contact, and she grabbed two of the books and slammed them on the table creating a loud metallic echo in the room. Then she pulled them across the desk swiftly towards her as if worried he'd take them away just as fast as he'd offered them to her. An expression of frustration was clearly shown as she glared into her bonder's eyes; she snatched up the notebook and pen and glared at him with eyes that were distrusting of him.

Sam had chosen from the six books were Shakespeare's gothic war tale, Macbeth, and The Stand, two highly praised novels. Both were filled to the brim with death and destruction, ironically much like the events that happened in 2020, when the world was plunged into a global pandemic that Fredrickson had only been a young boy during.

Fredrickson glanced at Sam and the two books she'd pulled over to her and now hugged tightly, and her face was still that canvas of fury. An expression of bewilderment came to him. He noted down her choices in his little notebook, which he kept inside his breast pocket. 'May I remind you that you were only meant to choose one, not two,' he said and reached a hand out across the desk with intent to remove one of the books from her grasp. Sam, however, didn't appreciate being told what to do. She reacted like a spoilt brat who demanded the latest technology and two pairs of highly expensive shoes that their parents couldn't afford. And, much to Frederickson's dismay, snapped at him. An angry snarl escaped her, and she bared her blackened, foul-smelling teeth. Dead grey eyes glared into his brown ones with intense exasperation, sending him a clear message. *Fuck off, Fredrickson! I'm not some kind of obedient dog of yours; I'm my own being! I do what I want. I've chosen these books to read, so I will fucking read them!* Fredrickson withdrew his hand, instinctively hugging it to his chest. The message was received. She softly growled at him one last time and hugged the books, and then, without being told, she scooped the notebook with the tiger, took out one of the pages and slammed it in front of her. She quickly scrawled on one of the papers and then shoved it at him. <u>My to learn wit you, sed</u>. She scowled at him, her bloodshot eyes narrowing in accusation.

Fredrickson gulped and wiped the dripping sweat from his crinkled forehead using the sleeve of his lab coat. If he hadn't moved his hand away, he indeed would've been bitten and would be kissing his job and life goodbye because once bitten, it was the end. When someone sustains a bite, it is all over; no amount of medical treatment could remove the infection, and it usually took up to an hour and thirty minutes for the pollution inside a zombie bite to kick in, painfully killing the individual from the inside and later transforming the person into a mindless husk devoid of emotion and any sense of logical thinking and understanding. It was always something that bonders had to be mindful of to keep their distance from zombie's unless they were high on the hunger drug. 'Jesus, Sam, I'm sorry… I'll let you read your damn books in peace.' he cringed. He folded his arms in a defensive stance as he continued to watch her.

'Fine, read them at your own pace then, but I will say that I still have to be present in this room during the regular eight-hour bonding sessions; I have to observe you as you read and write because it will help me decide whether you're ready for the surgery. But by all means, continue to read them throughout the night and whenever I'm not here with you. Though I expect to see some words that you're having trouble with tomorrow. Understand?' Fredrickson paused and thought for a moment, Sam nodded absently, allowing him to continue. 'Good. Oh, and Sam, I need you to listen to me when I say this, as it is imperative that you know this, you must understand what will happen to you in the future if you continue to display this feisty attitude.' Fredrickson gulped again, fearing that she'd snap at him again for the distraction he was posing; after all, she'd already opened a book and begun reading. To his surprise, however, she didn't turn hostile in the slightest or try to bite at him. Instead, Sam rolled her eyes (*holy shit! She knows how to do that?*) with resentment. As if he wasn't already stunned enough for one day, he watched as she picked up the pen and slid it onto the page, she'd just finished reading; then, she closed the book and slid it aside.

Fredrickson quickly observed that it was Macbeth she'd chosen before looking up to find her glaring at him. The same glare that had never left her face from his first mistake today. It was then that Fredrickson really looked into those bloodshot orbs, and a sinister realisation came billowing through him like he had ten ghosts breathing down his neck. The pale grey tint of her iris and pupils looked like a mountain; streaming from it, her bloodshot sclera seemed like roaring acute flames.

Hell-like, with all its demons residing inside those dead sockets, fiery pitchforks clutched in their hands.

Was this some kind of premonition? Fredrickson winced as he gripped the sides of his chair, cringing back. *No, it's bollocks, nothing but Scott's gittering mank*; his breath faltered as he shook his head until the image of hell became nothing more than just a stupid fragment of his imagination.

He calmed himself before he continued.

'Sam.' he began with a cough, clearing out his throat. 'If we bond well together and you display exceptional amounts of human intelligence in the experience, you'll be escorted from your cell to the hospital ward on L2. Here, you'll undergo treatment by one of our finest surgeons'. Sam now dropped the flaming intensity in her eyes, exchanging it for an expression of attentiveness; she was now curious about what Frederickson had to say. She picked up the book from the desk and placed the pen on the page she was currently reading, using it as a bookmark. 'You'll undergo full-body surgery. This is to assist in making you look alive and human again. We hope that we can be successful in making you look like you formally did before you had your life snatched away. Before you began to wither and rot away in that grave for over 70 years.' Fredrickson paused to make sure Sam understood him, yet at her unchanged expression, he continued. 'Of course, we don't know how you looked when you died because none of us knew you when you were alive. However, we'll try our best to transfigure you from undead to living,' he added, looking down solemnly at his hands before solemnly looking back at Sam. 'I can't imagine what it must be like being dead and inside an open grave. Rotting away… having your flesh eaten by bugs and bacteria.' He looked at her with sorrow and pity in his eyes, 'I could tell your grave was an open one because of that exposed chest of yours and the dirt-caked inside it. Clogging up the flow of the blood. From what I saw during our first meeting, your wounds weren't dressed either, so whoever killed you must've wanted to get rid of you quick without paying for a funeral or dressing the wounds.' Fredrickson pulled his chair out before rising and checking the wristwatch. 'My finishing time was forty minutes ago, I'm afraid I went overtime. I've spent a longer time with you than I should have.' Fredrickson felt sick in his stomach; the thought of how Sam cashed out was disturbing for him. This feeling had him leaving in haste without looking back at Sam as he exited her cell. Not able to express another word or even a goodbye. Not even the usual lecture on what would be happening about the next day, of which he usually went into vivid detail. One detail that refused to be shaken away from his mind was that there was something… unnaturally… disturbing about Sam… while she was a fantastic subject, there was just something not quite right with her, something that he couldn't quite grasp. He didn't want to hang around to find out what it was, further opting him to leave without so much as a glance back at her.

Having been left inside the silent, empty cell by herself, Sam was annoyed. The six books were laid out in front of her. Yet she would have preferred some company. Books couldn't talk and start a conversation with you. Still, Sam didn't have them; she just had plain paperbacks, and she was less than pleased about being left alone without a farewell from her bonder. Fire surged inside of her. Her eyelids were twitching, and teeth were borne, spitting out flakes of spit. Sam clenched, digging the dirt-smeared nails into the skin that peeled like the outer skin of an orange. If she were alive, she would have drawn blood, yet no blood spilled, only a little dirt trickled down her wrists. A deep grumble emerged from Sam's throat as she growled at the automatic door leading from the cell. She didn't like how Fredrickson didn't look at her as he'd left; it was rude, and she hated it. She also loathed him for not at least saying goodbye. She looked forward to having insight into what was to happen the following day; it kept her feeling sane and gave her something to look forward to in this hellhole of a cell. The only other time he didn't speak to her was when he was overwhelmed with fright, causing him to leave the room in a panic. She hadn't meant to do that then but had also felt a surge of power at the fright she'd caused him.

The hellish landscape was back in her eyes; shaking with rage, Sam let out a horrific, unhealthy noise that was full of fury but sounded choked. Feelings and emotions buried deep down into the lowest part of her subconscious ripped free. In her fit of anger, Sam tore herself free from the chains that bound her in place with little effort. The display of strength would've been incredible to behold. Her zombified temper had returned back to her. Not finished with her display of anger, she picked up the desk by one leg. She threw it against the side of the cell, sending the books, blank papers, and her bookmarked copy of Macbeth flying across the room, crashing to the ground. It was now

Sam who was seething and trashing the space around her. Fredrickson had unknowingly sparked something hateful in Sam, something that Fredrickson would come to regret and fear. Sam made another ugly, constricted cry, charging to the cell window, banging the glass with her fists, and slamming her head into the glass in an attempt to crack the glass. But to no avail; the glass was sturdy and bullet-proof, so brute force couldn't penetrate it. She continued to try, however, for a solid two minutes, releasing all the hateful and fuming emotions that she'd rediscovered, taking her anger out on the window of B-35. *Why did you fill me with all these fucking emotions! Fredrickson, you cunt! Why do you punish me by abandoning me! Forcing me to wallow in these feelings! You living fuckers, think you're so fucking superior. Just because you teach us dead beats to be human again, it was you humans that started this whole fucking mess! You're absolutely fucked!* Sam's thought screamed. Sam wanted to scream out her bonder's name, condemning him to suffer for not saying goodbye to her and that he'll soon come to regret his rude exit as she comes back to bite him in the arse about it. But she was unable to scream out words, unlike Ace. She had yet to master speech. Her brain was beginning to switch back on; Fredrickson's sudden departure had woken something up inside Sam, something he thought would be forever lost. Fredrickson had unknowingly given Sam the key to unlock some of the boxes that had been buried deep inside for so many years; one such box opened to reveal a blurred, blackened image of a masculine figure towering above her and what looked like a Boss shotgun directed at her. It was as if someone had connected the wires in her dead brain, flicking on the light switch, illuminating all the memories from the deepest, darkest drawers of her mind. Unfortunately, these were memories that anyone would want to forget.

When Sam finally ceased to express her frustration with Fredrickson leaving her without so much a final glance, she relaxed her tensed body, keeping her fists on the window, taking a few heavy breaths. Sam closed her eyes and welcomed another blurred image into her mind, but she couldn't work out who the blackened silhouette in this image was. Judging by its small size, it was a child, no older than ten. Whoever this figure was, it had provided her with some comfort. Sam stood silent for a few seconds, fists resting placidly on the bullet-proof glass window. She allowed herself to calm down and regain her composure. The child-like silhouette was gone, and Sam was left with all these broken thoughts and blurred-out images that she couldn't reach out for; as much as she had tried, they remained out of reach, growing more distant within each arm she had stretched out. Something was happening to her… she was feeling. The roots of humanity were starting to return, and she didn't know if she liked it or hated it. Sam unclenched her fists, allowing them to flop back down to her sides as she turned to get a clear view of the mess she'd made.

The cell was a disaster; the desk was flipped upside down to the right side of the cell. The six books spread across the floor, some open, some closed; papers were littered all over the floor; most appeared torn and crinkled from the sharp impact hitting the wall.

Sam sighed wanly as she walked over to the flipped desk, grabbing its nearest legs and standing the desk back to its upright position. She stood on the opposite side of the desk, a grating noise rang through the room as she pulled it towards her, returning it back to its original position. Sam then looked towards books, which were now crinkled, with pages bent, yet all seemed to miraculously hold their shape and were still readable as none of the pages were torn, and the dust inside those pages could easily be wiped with one swift hand gesture. She retrieved them from the ground one by one, placing them back onto the desk. Lastly, cleaning up the littered papers and smoothing them into some semblance of neatness, she placed them on the desk. Considering their condition, the pile was as neat as they would allow and sat next to the books that were now in random order. She looked around her surroundings, taking it in a while, trying to tidy the memories forming in her mind, much like she'd just done with the room. Her remembrance of things and the order in which they'd come were still being determined. But that wouldn't be a problem for her because despite occasionally appearing rude and ill-tempered, Fredrickson was indeed good at his job. Regardless of the bumps he made here and there, his teachings were clear, which was important.

Much like her memories, Sam only one hundred per cent remembered the order in which Fredrickson had given her the books. However, she did remember the one she was reading and the other that she'd chosen to read next. Taking them from the pile and set them down in front of her. Then, taking blank papers, she put them aside from the book she was to read first, readying herself to start on Fredrickson's instructions. She was about to grab the pen to sit next to the papers, yet it wasn't on the desk. Sam rose from her chair and retrieved the pen where it lay near the cell door without complaint and making any sounds of irritation. She knelt down to pick it up, quickly examining it to check if it was damaged. It was okay.

She walked back to her seat, the pen resting between her thumb and index finger and sat at her desk. Her anger now forgotten she reopened Macbeth, and starting at the first page due to forgetting the page she'd read previously, she began to read.

Now that she was alone, she lost herself in the pages of the gripping tale of Macbeth by William Shakespeare. (The bittersweet joy of violence and the spilling of the blood of the innocent, and the glorious crimson nectar that was tasted on the tongue; come, my friends, enjoy this moment, savour, and embrace the killer instinct, fight your enemies, and make them tremble under the mention of your name). If Sam had lips, they would be raised in a grin.

Chapter 14

While Sam was in the process of reading through the first few pages of Macbeth, taking the words printed down with a keen and detailed eye. At the same time, a few cells down the hall in B-01, Losnedahl stared at the stony grey face of Linus and Linus stared back at him, both eyes meeting and unblinking as if they were participating in some kind of non-blinking staring contest, with strings of drool leaking from the corner of the boy zombie's mouth which hung there. Linus won as Losnedahl blinked as soon as the drool from the boy's mouth detached and splashed the table; Losnedahl sighed, disheartened, mouthing out the words that played inside his head. *'Please stop staring at me like you have forgotten everything we've done together, please Linus, help me out here. I've written it down so many times already that I can't talk to you like the other bonders here. Please don't do this to me; work with me here. I want to help you; let me help you.'* Losnedahl looked away from the boy to stare at the clock on the wall above the cell door. Typically, he wasn't the type to let things distract him from his work. But even the most focused of people can find their process hindered by something that had happened in their childhood, a past trauma that can come back to haunt them, and in Henrik Losnedahl's case, it was no different. He moved a hand to his mouth and grimaced; his missing tongue was a constant reminder.

Suddenly, Losnedahl shivered like he'd just been transported into a butcher freezer and saw all the hanging meat hooks above him; his shoulders tensed, and he gritted his teeth behind his lips, remembering the daunting things

Anette Svensen had told him concerning his missing tongue and how it came to be. He covered his mouth with a hand and clenched his eyes as one such twisted image emerged from the darkness. It was the image that Anette would spell out for him, about his father's drunken, angry protests and mother's sobbing as she'd taken a shotgun, put it into her mouth and cried as she pulled the trigger, killing herself a few hours after her young son was born. "She hoped that the blast would take you with her, but it didn't, and you survived." Anette had told him that story all those years ago, but she always encouraged him to repress them, not to allow himself to be haunted by them.

But Losnedahl couldn't help but allow them to barge into his brain like an unwanted childhood nightmare. This was one such moment where it returned to plague him. *'Shut up! SHUT UP!! Let me do my job! I work as a zombie bonder! I'm working to give the human race that needed push forward; I'm not going to let you fill me with the shattered memories of what you did to me, you awful, poor excuse of a father. So why don't you just get fucked out of my head!!'* Losnedahl bellowed inside his head, clenching his eyes, tensing his fists, and concentrating hard until he successfully shut out his father's evil protests. Losnedahl cleared his throat and made a husky rasping noise; he grabbed and straightened his paperwork on the desk, carefully fingering through the pages, checking if they were in order; he did this while wiping the perspiration from his head and wiping his hand on his coat. Linus stared at him stupidly, blinking slowly and drooling, lolling from the corner of his lip. His mouth was trembling as if he was trying to speak but couldn't find the exact words because he didn't know any, and because Losnedahl couldn't talk, things were more problematic for him than they needed to be.

Losnedahl calmed eventually with a deep, controlled breath. He clicked his pen several times as he grasped one page from his paperwork. He flipped the page to the blank side and scribbled, his other way of talking without the formation of words. Please don't try to speak Linus. I only gave you a hunger drug nine minutes ago. It usually takes up to fifteen to twenty minutes, sometimes a few hours, for the drug to subside; it depends on how strong the dosage is. The only thing I want you to focus on at the moment is your English with writing and your understanding of sign language. Now, as I can recall from our latest sessions together, I had taught you how to say "hello," "thank you," "goodbye," and a few sentences like "How are you", "It's a nice day today", and so on. It's been over a week now since we first met, and you have been... well, 50/50 is the best way to put it; most of the time, you have been given a strong dose of the drug, but maybe that's just me getting too carried away and paranoid with the hunger drug, only giving you substantial dosages just to make sure you don't try anything. But as I'm sure most of the bonders have mentioned to their zombies, when you become brighter, you'll have surgery to make you look more alive again, and it'll be a step closer to you becoming human again.

After Losnedahl wrote this down on the flipped-over sheet of work paper, he reached into one of his lab coat pockets. He pulled out a laminated card of what appeared to be the sign language alphabet from A to Z and, with pictures of the hand gestures above the letter that they had meant.

He placed the picture on top of the written message; he hoped that Linus would be able to use it to his advantage and hopefully would be able to memorise the alphabet off by heart and do his bonder proud, leaving him more with the language of sign and allowing the lessons of sign to become more accessible for later lessons. Because there were only so many repeats of the same sign that Losnedahl could manage, he hoped that Linus could learn some things on his own when the drugs wore off, and he had time to himself and his own devices.

Linus cocked his head to look at the card and written message; he pulled them over towards him, glancing down and observing the both of them together. Losnedahl sighed with disappointment, seeing that he hadn't made much progress today; glancing down at his watch, seeing that it was six-thirty and made another disappointed sigh as he looked through the papers on his clipboard; it hadn't much progress to show meaning that this session had come off as pointless. *'Another long and tedious day without much to ponder on, bummer,' he thought as he packed up his things, 'I did almost nine hours, an hour, and thirty minutes longer than I should've... I better be getting overtime for this; a nice plate of valfer or lefse or a nice pavlova would do very nicely as payment. Something nice and creamy.'* Losnedahl got up from his seat, feeling his legs were getting cramps, and if he rushed things, he might topple, but he took his time in shaking away the cramping feeling in his aging legs. While he did care about Linus and his position, he did enjoy his breaks because he wouldn't have to worry about signing up with anyone and could rest up his aching legs in his office. He pushed the chair underneath the desk and scooped up the paperwork that he had needed for his assessment, which he doubted required a lot of scribbling.

Losnedahl looked at his subject and smiled sadly. *'My time with you is finished; I've been working overtime; please study those words on my message and the language graph carefully, and please try to learn the alphabet on that card. See you tomorrow, Linus. I'm hopeful that you might be able to work well when left alone. I guess I'll wait and see tomorrow.'* Losnedahl gave a friendly wave before he'd left Linus's cell B-01. But before going for his quarters where he'd rest up for the night (Bonder's sleep in the building, having private bedrooms in their offices), he quickly glanced through the window and saw Linus was staring down at the written message tilting his head as if trying to comprehend what was written down. This fuelled Losnedahl with a glimmer of hope, but he didn't smile at it; he could feel that somewhere deep down inside that rotting exterior was a young boy who wanted to feel alive again. Losnedahl still had a rotten feeling in his gut as he held his head down, looked at his feet, and walked, holding his paperwork tightly under his arm. *The real reason I became a bonder was to hopefully reconnect with my mother; the mortuus carnem parasite would've most likely infected her by now. While it seems cruel and inhumane to wish for a loved one to become infected. I want a chance to meet my mother, even if she is undead and without a head; just an opportunity to meet and at least see her would be more than satisfactory for me. After I finish with Linus, I will make orders to the military to find you again, Mum. Although I never got a chance to meet you, as you died shortly after conceiving me, I remember Aunt Anette saying to me when she would look after me that you were the most amazing, most loving person she had known. I'm fifty-seven now, Mum, so that means I haven't killed myself yet; oh, Mother, I swear to God I will find a way to reconnect with you again, like mother like son. I wouldn't care if you looked horrible with maggots eating away at you. You are still my mother. I will always love you, even in death, even as a rotting corpse. I would give anything to finally meet you.* Losnedahl had prayed to himself, signing himself off and finishing his bonding session for the day before finally heading back into his office, where he sat down on his chair and closed his eyes and buried his face in the pages of his work, exhausted.

Chapter 15

A few weeks had passed since the introductions; it was now twenty-seven October, only four days until Halloween. Bonders were spending most of their time with their zombies rather than spending time with their peers, not even saying as much as a "hello" or prattling on about the progress of their zombies and their level of intelligence. And because their work was more critical, Halloween decorations were nowhere to be found; seasonal holidays were non-existent in the GFOSAR; and even Christmas was treated as just another working day. Christmas was meant to be celebrated with family, and those who lost family members most likely didn't want to spend their family Christmas putting a bullet between their undead family members. So, Christmas, Halloween, Easter, Thanksgiving, St Patrick's Day and birthdays were just forgotten about, which was depressing for those who were desperate for a break and wanted to spend time with the remaining family members and friends (alive ones, at least) instead of their zombies.

But despite it being almost Halloween, it had felt like Saint Nick had come to give them an early Christmas to the bonders who were in charge of these three zombies. These specific three zombies were building up relationships with their bonders and expanding their knowledge of things at a phenomenal speed, so having a fast-learning zombie was the peak of a zombie bonder's career. It was often compared to having Santa come down the chimney and surprise you with some presents for being on the "Nice list." Instead of a Christmas Nice List, the GFOSAR had a "Lucky List." And those who had a success story to tell would also have bragging rights about being on the Lucky List. Two such examples of the Lucky List candidates were:

Ace: although her understanding of her surroundings and the things in the cell wasn't developed yet, and she often tended to forget things that happened yesterday and needed to be reminded, she'd occasionally make mistakes and forget things like her name, her bonder's name and why she was here in the first place. But that didn't worry Kolen; things such as memory would come later because with those obstacles out of the way, the important thing was that she'd already begun to 'speak' and not just with moans and groans like you'd expect from a typical zombie in a movie or TV show, no Ace was speaking actual English words! Words that she must've picked up from Kolen or perhaps Boyle or Winsome while Ace had been waiting to be transferred over to Kolen. Although her English punctuation was bad, and she often misplaced and forgot keywords in her sentences, making most people think she was mentally slow, that was okay because she was a zombie and zombies were known to be slow in brain power. And despite being a little slow, none of that seemed to matter to her bonder because Ace was a crawler zombie who could speak English just as well as a student in prep and having a talker was something that should be appreciated because zombies just aren't known for speaking in a language that wasn't moans and groans. Still, for Ace, she was an exception, and Marilyn Kolen should be proud to be bonding with a talking zombie who'd shown her signs of trust; she was the link that showed other emerging bonders that the undead could still be capable of speech.

Spot: was one of the pleasing, well-behaved, more docile, and most surprising zombies on record; while he didn't look like he could possibly learn anything because the top half of his head and brain were absent. And in her notes, Ark had written about a little expedition to the outside to grab something that would be of use to Spot. She returned with that something for Spot, and witnessed firsthand how her half-headless zombie had changed right in front of her; he developed a personality right at that moment!

Notes of Lisa Ark – 26 October 2056, 5:58am. Going outside.

Instead of going straight to Spot's cell, I woke up early on a cold October morning. The sun was just starting to come up. That early. I wore a casual white buttoned shirt, navy blue jeans, and a grey cardigan. Though call me crazy, but these weren't for going out partying with, oh goodness no. These causal-looking clothes were caked with the blood of the undead, they had rips and tears in them, and often had meaty, rotten chunks of flesh inside the pockets, which gave off the most unpleasant stenches of zombie, so yeah, not the best attire for a party, but it was also good that I was wearing this repugnant getup because despite how disgusting I would smell and with all the looks I would get as I walked through the hall with all the dead flesh and blood over you, it was a good way go outside of the GFOSAR without an army escort and without the undead eyeing you as their next meal. Why? You might ask, would this simple getup work without an escort? To anyone reading this point on, I'll tell you. Wearing these foul-smelling, blood-soaked clothes was a way to trick the roaming undead outside, allowing you to slip right through them undetected. Although you would have to act like a zombie to really fool them – you can walk past them usually – you would still have to smell like them. Though if anyone were to take this rather dangerous route, I would strongly recommend putting on the act of being a zombie. It just makes it a little harder for the undead to spot you as not one of them.

This is precisely what Ark did; after she'd written this first batch of notes onto some lined A4 paper, she left the safety of her office to go down the hall and down the steps, ignoring the disgusted glances she got as she passed by her fellow co-workers. She wasn't afraid of doing things like this because Ark was a courageous and independent woman who had a very strong stomach and could handle most of the things women her age wouldn't be able to comprehend.

She did work as a neurosurgeon back in Australia and saw her fair share of brains and spinal cords during her time; even though she'd almost fainted upon seeing Spot's gnarly condition, that was only because she'd never seen a walking corpse with half his head. But getting over that, she was fine and could take him back to B-09 to bond with him. She'd seen headless zombies but never a half-headless one, so meeting Spot for the first time struck her as a shock more than anything. She knew that despite what Spot lacked in half a head, she could tell that he had potential and that she'd work to exploit it. So, she figured that she'd go on this little trip to the outside to grab something vital for him, an item from the outside that she was sure would help him.

Ark's notes about her trip to the outside in the gnarly attire in search of this particular item for Spot continued on the next page and had taken up a few more pages in the A4 journal.

When I was outside, and past the guards, I started the act of shuffling and moaning. Playing the act of a zombie. I wadded through hordes of starving undead that skulked and sniffled about. I didn't carry a map or phone with a GPS or a gun, as that would be risky if I were to fire it and send the undead on my bacon; the only items I carried were a shovel and torch. If I'm being honest, I did feel like I was on a bit of a suicide mission, and I was really nervous because one wrong move and I would be someone's breakfast. But however anxious I was. I was determined to find what I was looking for without using such devices. But even without the apparent safety of a firearm with me, I did make sure to carry some kind of switchblade in a holster on my ankle for when I would need to produce a quick getaway; I kept it covered with a sock on my foot, although I probably didn't need to conceal it, I suppose I covered it out of habit. I was determined to see this through despite the feeling of my heart thundering in my ribs. I pressed on towards my goal, finding the tombstone that held Spot's top head half inside it and finding his brain, hoping it was intact (my plan would work better if it was intact and undamaged).

After about an hour (I didn't have a watch, so I couldn't tell) of seemingly fruitless wandering around, I finally came to a cemetery that was closest to the facility. Armed with only a shovel and torch, I clenched them tightly in my cold and shaking hands. I would use the shovel or switchblade in the foot holster in case I was found out.

When I entered the bleak, dreary-looking graveyard that was littered with shards of broken wood, cobblestone, and marble, I cringed. There were disturbed open graves everywhere! It was a sense straight from a horror movie. I sucked it up, took a deep breath through my mouth and did my best to ignore them as I stepped into the place where people were supposed to find eternal sleep; my mind was focused on one thing, finding what remained of 'his' spoilt grave. I was trying to find 'his' (hopefully) intact brain. Notwithstanding the broken and chipped headstone, I made sure to flash my light across the faces of the headstones, making sure to check every one of them, trying to find the actual name of her zombie as well as the exact place he was buried in or if I couldn't find 'his' real name, I was sure to look for a spoilt grave which had the top of 'his' head inside. I was hoping that this was the right place. Not knowing how much time had passed since I went prodding through headstones with the handle of the shovel, studying the rows upon rows of open graves.

Finally, I came to a specific open grave which seemed a little larger (as if it was made for someone very tall) than most of the graves I had seen in the third row, which, when I had shone the torch into, I managed to see something that resembled a top half of a head. I was hopeful that this one was Spot's, so I tapped the marble headstone with the shovel, sweeping away the mud that clung to it and taking a few paranoid glances behind me whenever the metal scrape of the shovel contacted with the marble. I didn't want to create a lot of noise that would bring any unwanted visitors to my location.

After I had wiped away as much as I could. I put the shovel down and knelt down to look at the headstone, hoping to see a name, but I was disappointed to see that the name and dates of the headstone were faded and unreadable; they looked like they had been purposely damaged by someone who either was looking to desecrate it or someone who purposely wanted to keep his identity a secret. This seemed peculiar to me at the time. But even so, I looked at what was left of the engravement on the marble face. I wish I had bought a phone to take a photo of it. But I was foolish to not even consider the things I would find and the possibility of taking photos, so the best I could do was write down what I had seen on that tombstone. This was what was on the tombstone, at least what I could make out. **"m ch ved son and a fr en to all. May his soul rest with his ord and sav or in hea en"** *This message only seemed to make me more curious as to the identity of my zombie, and at that moment, I wanted to know what had happened to the grave and why it was so badly damaged. But I told myself that "Spot was back in B-09, waiting for me to start the day with him," and this was what stopped* *me from pondering more about the reason for the grave damage. I took my eyes away from the curious engravement and peered down into the open, empty grave. I was disappointed that I couldn't read the name of the grave. When I looked down at the size of the grave and the large empty coffin and the top half of a head, I was certain that I had found what I was looking for, that this was his grave. I had muttered something to myself when I came to this theory that I had found Spot's grave and remembered muttering something else about how I was going to go about with my plan.*

For starters, I went to the front of the grave; I got down on my knees, squinted and looked sideways through the hole in the coffin, and what I saw inside had looked like teeth, which seemed to coincidentally look similar to the teeth that belonged on the top half of one's head. Now, this was when I was certain I had found what I was looking for. I smiled with satisfaction. So, without saying or whispering a word. I picked up the shovel and began chiselling the sides around the grave, destroying the coffin further and disrespecting what should've been his final resting place. After a few minutes of grinding my way into the remnants of a coffin, I tossed the shovel aside and hopped down into the spoilt tomb. I was quite surprised that the grave didn't smell as bad as I had thought it would; it mainly smelt of damp soil after rain, and it was actually quite refreshing. If someone were to read this, they would think of me as a grave robber. But believe me, I had a good intention for what I was doing, and that was to get Spot's brain, and hopefully, it will help him think more clearly. So, I wasn't digging graves because I felt like it; I was doing it for a reason. From here, I placed the torch on the side of the grave, retaking the shovel, using it to dig and scrape away all the unneeded scraps until reaching the top half of the head. Picking up the torch again, I held it low, lighting up the object inside the coffin; it was exactly what I had thought it was; it was indeed the top part of someone's head, and to put it more clearly, the missing half of someone's head. Spot's head. This was what really made me glow with radiance; "I have done it!" I had mumbled to myself. I had found Spot's grave!

I put the shovel up the side of the opened coffin; I was sure I was smiling like an idiot the entire time. I carefully started digging at the dirt around the head, being mindful not to damage the head as I dug it out from its tomb. When I got the head loose enough, I tossed the equipment aside again, and then I put my hands into the grave, not caring if the soil was getting in my nails. I grabbed the sides of the half-head and pulled at it towards me, once again, probably smiling like an idiot throughout the whole thing. But yet, despite my excitement, I was also trying to be gentle, not to cause any more damage to the head.

I was beaming when I eventually got the head out of the disturbed grave. I stared down at the grimy but smooth features still present on the face, and I could almost imagine what the face would have looked like when it was full of life. I saw a pretty, attractive kid with kind eyes, a perky nose, and thin lips that would be full of compliments. Part of me wanted to kiss that nose. But I didn't because that would just be wrong.

Anyway, I knew that I would have to get back up to B-09 and do some work with her zombie and at least have something to write down. I was haste in my efforts to get out of the grave and collect my equipment. I held the shovel and torch in the same hand while the other hand carefully caressed the top half of Spot's head; at least, I was hopeful that it was his head.

So, with Spot's top head half in my grasp and phase one of my mission complete. I made my way back to the GFOSAR; once again, I had to shamble and act like I was one of the undead to avoid being detected. As long as I would still smell like a zombie, I was sure that I was safe.

To those who read this far. You can call me crazy all you want – but yeah – I did this, and I don't have any regrets about making that trip to the cemetery caked in zombie gore. Because this little trip would turn out to be one of the best things I've ever done, and if any of you read Spot's progression notes, you'll find out why.

Upon returning back to the GFOSAR, Ark made her way over to the central laboratory on L4. She passed by some of the other scientists who were working on the same level; all were exchanging perplexed and repulsed glances at each other upon seeing the sight of Ark's light gold blonde hair wearing the putrid smiling blood-soaked overalls, meaning she'd dared to go beyond the doors of the facility (only the military or those with a death wish were allowed to go outside with the rabid undead). She was clutching half of a very dirtied zombie's head and strutting over to an unoccupied desk. There she placed the head that was missing its bottom jaw down onto the desk, smirking wickedly, ready to conduct another little experiment.

Scientists that'd been tasked with manufacturing hunger drugs and creating artificial prosthetic limbs that sometimes were used in the surgery of good zombies, and if the good zombies were missing an arm or a leg, the artificial limbs would be *Frankensteined* to them, returning their once absent limps back to them, even if it was said a white arm on a black body or an Indian leg on an Asian body, it didn't matter on the colour of the artificial limb, as long as it agreed with the body it was going to, it was the critical thing.

The scientists that'd been working on said limbs had stopped what they were doing to see what Ark was doing up here instead of being down another level with her zombie, Ark knew precisely what she was doing with the rest of her zombie's head; she had all the experience she needed in working with things that needed surgery or transplants.

Ark took off the disgusting, blood-soaked attire and exchanged it for a more traditional surgeon's uniform … something she was more than familiar with. Ark sat down at the desk with the head and recalled her surgical skills and training from her time at the hospital in Adelaide. Ark fingered through a small tray of surgical utensils, took a scalpel, and placed it beside the head. She slapped some plastic gloves over her hands, cracking her knuckles and licking her lips with satisfaction as she retook the scalpel and turned the head around so that the back of the head was facing her; she didn't want to cut a line through that handsome but messy face. Ark started the first stage of her experiment. Without drawing a line to show where she was going to make an incision, she held the scalpel in one hand, the other hand was clenched over the black hair on the head, she pierced it. She carefully made her way down to the bottom.

'Sorry, mate,' she murmured to herself, putting down next to the head the scalpel, which now had a dark red substance on it. Ark licked her lips once more; she moved her fingers in between the cut she had made, and she started pulling them away from each other, spreading the halves apart and removing the skin and handsome features away from the dead scarlet-tinted muscle around the head; she peeled off pieces of the dead muscle until she was left with a skull. 'Sorry, boy.' she uttered, again picking up a bone saw from the equipment tray and putting it to the side of the dirty gore-covered skull, 'sorry about scalping your head and removing the muscle, but I only need that brain of yours.' *You'll thank me later... I hope,* she thought.

Chapter 16

Fredrickson came into B-35 the next morning, which now had an old 2025 calendar of horses on the wall (Fredrickson had asked for it yesterday and had one of the bodyguards install it for him). He was looking at Sam and showing her a new face. And a face that was rarely seen amongst his co-workers. He was beaming, a smile that was ear to ear. 'Guess what, Sam?' he spoke with a tone that was full of uncontained excitement. He pulled out the chair and sat down. He wasn't carrying any of the paperwork that he was usually seen with whenever he entered the cell of his black-haired zombie. But a beaming smile wasn't all that was rare for him. Fredrickson grabbed her gaunt hands over the desk and stroked them lovingly and tenderly with his thumbs. He looked into those pale grey eyes, those non-existent lips, sunken eyes, and her skeletal face, which was drowning in flakes of skin peeling off; he knew that Sam was different; it was clear to him now as he saw her looking straight into his eyes and was patiently allowing Fredrickson to fawn over her bony hands as she wasn't doing anything to remove them. He mentally noted that she was placid with him and showed no signs of malice within her. This excited him and this was one of the reasons why he was completely sure that she was his first success story, and with her being his first success story, he wanted to express his gratitude for bonding well with him by rewarding her. He was staring into Sam's face and felt slightly disappointed to see that she wasn't matching the same kind of beaming interest as he was. But he could bypass that as she was still learning complicated things such as Mechanism 3 – Emotional Regulation and Cognition (ERC) (she might need to see Spot and take some lessons from him). Her dead eyes were full of emptiness as she met with Frederickson's proud sunny ones, dreading the thought that he was going to talk about his birthday and the stupid presents he received or relishing the news of some prick whom he had hated that had died, stupid things that she had no care or interest in. But Fredrickson thankfully saved her from his tedious life story and instead gave her the news that would aid in her future if she was going to be released.

Fredrickson turned her hands over and was lovingly rubbing her flayed palms. He could feel the bones, but that didn't deter him from rubbing them. 'Because you've been fuck all nothing short of exemplary with the bonding process, I'm going to reward you with the special treatment!' His hands were shaking from his sheer wonder at the thought that one of his zombies would finally get the surgery. He released her decayed, emaciated hands and sat them on his lap, clenching them with profound eagerness to get her into the medical ward.

Sam's deadpanned face continued to stare into his chirpy brown eyes; her eyes were blank and unblinking, and her mouth was shut, and drool was seeping out from her teeth. Fredrickson opened his mouth to hint to her about the surgery that was going to take place but thought that it was better to leave her guessing, so he shut his mouth and looked away from those blank, dead grey eyes, instead focusing his attention on her mouth and hands, taking his time in admiring the old decay that was soon going to be replaced with brand new skin that would give her the human-like appearance that was to be expected of the well-behaved zombies. Fredrickson bit his lip excitedly, unable to contain the urge to provide her with the news that she would be heading to L2 to the medical ward to undertake the surgery. 'Ah, to hell with it,' he mumbled to himself as he stared back into Sam's eyes, bubbling with joy. He wanted to hold those bony hands again, but he could still feel his own hands trembling in his lap. 'Do you remember when I said a few days ago that you'd receive special treatment if you bonded well with me and showed me an excellent example of intelligence? Well, judging by what I've written in your record, I can definitely say that you've done just that, and today is the day. So, I'm very proud to say you're becoming more like a human and less of a zombie now, which makes me very glad to be your bonder. So, if you'll take my hand and accompany me, I'll take you to where you'll have new skin grafted onto you. And you will be one more step closer to being released, where you'll commence the final stages until you're officially classed as "human" again!' Fredrickson toned down his beaming smile into a leering grin, offering his hand to her.

Fredrickson watched his black-haired zombie take a moment to study her quarters, looking at that 2025 horse calendar, gazing from the left to the right before cocking her head to the side, her dead grey eyes furrowed with confusion. He wondered what kind of messages were going through her head. She seemed wary, which confused him. He saw her recoil a bit, moving her hands away from him. So, Fredrickson smiled lightly and reassured her that everything would be okay and that she'd look in the mirror once the surgery was over and see a human woman staring back at her. At least, that was what he'd hoped would be the result. He didn't know; he'd never experienced one of his subjects going through the medical ward as a rotting corpse and leaving the ward looking like they belonged on a magazine cover.

Now that she was curious about what the surgical procedure was going to do to her appearance, she tenderly placed her hand in Fredrickson's; she relieved herself from her seat, pushing it back under the desk and traversing around it, hand still in his,

'As soon as we leave this cell, you'll be saying goodbye to that rotting, decaying mess of a body and welcome to a fresh new batch of skin, and if it goes as planned, you should be able to walk off this premise with the body of a human' Fredrickson's eyes twinkled, unable to contain the thought of how lucky he was to get a zombie up to this point. He had butterflies in his stomach, the feeling was just too great; he thought about how long it had taken him to get Sam this far, the decisions he had made were worth every pound. *Out of all the shitty walking corpses I've worked with over the years, by far, Sam has been the icing on the cake, and I feel like a proud father taking his child to work for the first time after all the knowledge she had been learning throughout the schooling years!* He had thought happily to himself.

Fredrickson led Sam past the other bonding cells, keeping a tight lock around her flaked fingers, making sure not to lose her amongst a sea of oncoming bonders and zombies. To save her the trip of walking the stairs, he led her over to an elevator that was still operational, took her inside and pressed the button labelled L2; they would be going down one level into the hospital area. When the doors parted, Fredrickson escorted Sam into a room that was totally foreign to her. Once inside the room, Sam looked around, examining the area that surrounded her; there were desks and tables with wheels that had all kinds of surgical equipment strewn over them, the walls were covered in coloured and some black and white pictures of what looked to be of the former staff members of the hospital ward, which made Sam think that the GFOSAR used to be a simple hospital before it underwent development into becoming a sanctuary for those wanting to keep their hearts still beating and a place where the zombies undergo treatment into becoming more like the average everyday Joe that walks the street. While Sam had her eyes fixed on the photographs hanging on the wall, Fredrickson took the chance to reach into his coat's breast pocket and pulled out a different-looking version of the hunger drug, a purple and red one, meaning it was a much stronger dose than the standard hunger drugs she had somewhat gotten used to taking. It was suggested to turn zombies into motionless vegetables and was only really meant for zombies that were going to go through the surgery. It usually lasts as long as the duration of the surgeries, and depending on how rotten the zombie was, the surgeries could take up to seven to ten hours to do; if that was the case, two purple and red pills were needed because the zombie needed to be in a vegetated state while the surgeons do work on their broken bodies, working to their best to repair dead and rotting flesh and hopefully the surgery would be able to turn Sam into an attractive looking living woman. Fredrickson twirled the pill significantly between his fingers, waiting for Sam's curious eyes to fall upon him. 'Now I'm gonna have to give you a much stronger dosage of the hunger drug; it'll knock you out for a few hours, but it's important that you don't wake up halfway through surgery, seeing someone fumbling around underneath your ribcage' he reassured Sam with a smile, beckoning her to open her mouth so he'd be able to drop the purple and red pill down her throat and wait for it to take effect.

Only a few seconds after swallowing the pill, it had immediately started to take effect; Sam could feel what remained of her dead insides shutting down, her vision became blurred and fuzzy, and her sense of smell and hunger had disappeared as soon as the pill touched the back of her throat. Her limbs had become heavy and were supporting the rest of her like they usually had done; she swayed around drunkenly, tried her hardest to keep herself standing and keep her eyes open, but to no avail, as the purple and red pill did precisely what it was supposed to do; Sam's eyes fluttered, her head drooped and she drooled out the mouth, then her legs eventually gave out, the twig-like stumps unable to support the body and she ended up collapsing. Fredrickson smiled thoughtfully, seeing his now unconscious (even zombies can be knocked out into unconsciousness) zombie lying sprawled over the plastered white floor; he approached her body and knelt down to it; he buried his arms underneath her back and lifted her up in his arms. Sam's rotten body swayed around in his arms like a ragdoll as she was being carried.

We'll get you looking right; after today, you'll be a fresh-looking human,' Fredrickson cooed, even though he knew that she wouldn't be able to hear him or anything for the next few hours, depending on how long the surgery took. He smiled heartily at her decayed sleeping face, holding her carefully as he took her over to an unoccupied gurney where Vincent Grossman, one of the surgeons at the GFOSAR, waited patiently for his next subject to give skin and a living appearance.

Upon seeing him, Fredrickson's warm smile vanished, and his original work-orientated persona returned back to him as fast as the smile disappeared from his stern canvas. He carefully placed Sam's cold, unconscious body onto the surgical gurney, stepping away from the thin-faced surgeon, finding a wheeled chair for him to sit on and giving Grossman the order to do surgery on Sam while he would sit back and watch.

'So, this is the zombie that's been getting such a profound record? This is Sam, the fast learner? The wonder zombie?' Grossman had asked Fredrickson, wanting to confirm that it was indeed her and not another zombie that he'd brought up for someone else; he studied the layers of decay over Sam's body and the tattered attire that she wore before he pulled over a wheeled end table that had a rolled up scroll made of cloth tied up with lace, he untied the knot that kept the scroll rolled up, and grabbing one end of the scroll, he unravelled it across the table, showing it was a belt of a vast assortment of sharp surgical equipment.

'Yeah, this is Sam.' he replied with a wooden expression, not wanting anyone to know that the professional take-shit-from-no-one Alexander Fredrickson was actually capable of showing care and respect for his zombies. 'Try what you can with her; see what you can do in hopes of making that rotting flesh look new and fresh. I have the highest amount of faith that you'll make Sam look alive again. So don't you let me down, Vincent,' he said threateningly, making the middle-aged man a few inches shorter than him gulp. But before Grossman picked up the correct tool for the beginning of the surgery, he plucked out a notebook with a holographic wolf on it and a pencil from his breast pocket; there, he wrote Fredrickson's name and the name of his zombie. He stared over at Fredrickson, who crossed his arms, looking ever so impatiently at Grossman.

'Be-before I do anything to Sam, I-I just need some clarification that you gave her the purple and red dosage of the hunger drug instead of the red normal ones because I don't want her waking in the middle of me cutting through her rotten skin or fawning around with one of her broken bones,' he declared, wanting to disclose the information that he'd memorized from the worksheet that he'd have to fill in post surgery and Fredrickson took his human-looking zombie away with him.

Fredrickson raised a brow accusingly at Grossman, who immediately felt a tinge of regret for asking him the important question that he'd have to ask every other bonder.

'Do you think I'm an idiot, Vincent? Do you think I would be stupid enough to not drug her out before surgery? *If you want proof that I gave it to her, carve her throat out and see the pill for yourself.'*

N-No Alexander, I implore you, I don't think ill of you in any way, it's just I need to ask that to every bonder; it's part of my job; we surgeons have to make sure the zombies have been given the stronger dosage before they can have any sort of incision. I mean, from all I know, you could've administered the red and orange one.'

'I do know how important this is; besides, look at her.' Fredrickson hissed, pointing to the zombie lying soundlessly on the gurney with her arms dangling over the sides, her eyes shut, and she appeared to look like she was at peace. Perhaps she was chasing memories or was having an equivalent of what humans like to refer to as "dreams." Whatever was going on inside that skull of hers, Fredrickson could tell that it wouldn't be a problem for Grossman. 'I see her, Alexander, but I-

'Then you'd be wise not to insult my intelligence, Vincent, by saying that I don't know how things work around here. *You know I have a problem with my temper, so you best keep that pie of yours shut if you don't want to be on the receiving end of just what I can do when I'm angry.* Of course, I know that zombies have to be administered the purple one before surgery.'

'I'm not saying you don't; I just need a yes or no,' he eagerly held the clipboard and pencil towards him.

Fredrickson grumbled in his seat, looking away from Grossman; he hated taking orders from people with less authority than him. Fredrickson snatched the pencil and clipboard from the young surgeon and ticked YES before handing them back to Grossman, who put the pencil into his breast pocket and the clipboard on the table; Fredrickson huffed, crossing his arms and waited. Grossman turned his attention back to Sam, who still lay motionless on the gurney, eyes shut and not breathing; that was fine; zombies didn't need to breathe because they were already dead. Grossman pulled some plastic gloves over his hands, pulled a surgical mask over his mouth and a cap over his head, then he peered down at the sleeping zombie, shovelling the black fringe that blanketed Sam's features, getting a straightforward few of the sleeping zombie's decay and assessing how much work he'd need to do to give her a human-like appearance. 'Alrighty then Miss Sam.' He flickered her a small smile, taking up a scalpel from the surgical belt.

'Why don't we start with the head and face.' Grossman said to himself, making a small incision along Sam's sleeping face. All the while, Fredrickson watched with interest, even if his face didn't show it.

The surgery was a long and taxing process, taking almost up to six hours because Grossman had to fully reconfigure an image of how Sam had looked before she had died. He had to estimate what she would've looked like without a photo. Fredrickson had dozed off while Grossman went from table to table, scouting high and low for the tools he needed and for pieces of skin that he'd use to fix her broken, decayed body. Using a scalpel to cut away the unneeded rotting flesh only to replace it with a fresh coating of undamaged skin, he sowed and stitched the fleshy pieces together in a way that looked like some kind of morbid human puzzle, making sure that they fitted before he would glue them down to her body by sowing them into her lacking shrivelled muscles, and to make sure the Frankenstein-like stitching remained invisible to the living that was unfortunate enough to be living outside the safety of the GFOSAR. He'd use this tan coloured resin substance and gently finger it over the stitches and making them blend in with the colour of the skin to a scarily realistic effect, completely vanishing the stitches from the peering eyes. After the tediously dragging surgery,

Grossman wanted to go the step further into satisfying Fredrickson by going out of his way to dispose of Sam's old tattered attire and replacing them with new ones, a nice black shirt without a large gaping hole and some tan shorts that reached just below her knees.

After the entire operation was complete, Grossman stepped back, wiping tuffs of his wet fringe that were peeking out from his surgeon's cap, away from his forehead, which was dripping with perspiration. At the same time, Fredrickson soundlessly slept slumped back in the chair, arm crossed and head drooped; Grossman took his time to tenderly study the work he had done on the unconscious zombie on the operating table. Feeling more than satisfied with himself and his work to make her look like a living, breathing person, he went over to Fredrickson, snapped his fingers a few times in his ears and woke him up with a start. But before Fredrickson could question him on why he'd woken him. 'I've done it, Mr Fredrickson; I think this might be my finest work to date,' he crowed, peeling the face mask down. He gently tugged Fredrickson on the sleeve of his lab coat, who was tiredly rubbing his eyes with the heels of his palms. 'You better hope that it lives up to my expectation, Vincent, or I'll have your job if it isn't.' Fredrickson threatened, getting off the chair and following Grossman over to the gurney, which now held a stunning-looking woman on it, a woman with raven black hair, sharp but beautiful pale skin, sharp yet soothing eyes, a smooth looking nose and lips that spelled KISSER. She wore a clean copy of her clothes before the surgery and not those rags she came into the facility with. If her attractive face wasn't enough, her arms and legs were now completely devoid of harsh, hideous-looking scabs and heavy signs of decay, and her body looked as clean and fresh as the next living person. Grossman had done exactly what Fredrickson expected him to do; hell, his expectations were exceeded, as Grossman could read it in Fredrickson's stunned expression. Vincent Grossman had successfully turned Sam into a human in appearance; she just happened to be slightly over the pale side, but that didn't matter; as long as she looked like a human, that was fine. When the drug did wear off, Sam rose up from her resting position to be greeted by the sight of Fredrickson beaming and shaking her surgeon's hand. 'Ah, Sam, you're finally awake.' Fredrickson's eyes were wide, and his jaw hung low at his now attractive and, in some ways, sexy-looking female zombie. He turned to Grossman only for a minor second, bringing his eyes back to Sam and her dazzling beauty. 'Show her the mirror', he ordered the surgeon with a stern smile, who, without hesitation and beaming with the idea that he received praise from Fredrickson and with his work on Sam, grabbed hold of the nearest mirror and handed it over to Fredrickson who took it from him and held it in front of her, letting her in on who the person standing in her reflection was.

'I do believe I've captured your style and hypothesized on what you looked like prior to your death. We, of course, don't know what you looked like because we didn't know you before you started to wither away from being underneath that grave for so long, but I believe and hope I've done you justice.' Grossman chirped. Sam took the mirror from Fredrickson and studied the woman staring back at her from inside the mirror. Her eyes were wide, and her mouth hung open; she appeared to be taken back and regretting ever doubting Grossman's capacities, seeing her reflection with clean pale skin with no patches of decay whatsoever; it was like Sam wasn't even a zombie anymore and had just been gifted the opportunity by God to being reincarnated once more as a human, but God played no part in this resurrection, it had been done by a highly trained surgeon who'd spent almost half a day into making her look human again. Vincent Grossman had outdone himself with Sam, achieving his and Fredrickson's goal of completely transforming her, and you know you've done well when you receive praise from the ordinarily strict and professional Alexander Fredrickson.

The two men watched with beaming faces as Sam's lips and cheeks raised. She let out a small moan of pleasure, seeing that her new appearance was even better than she had thought possible, sinking in all those lusting sharp and somewhat seductive details Grossman had blessed her with, giving her the appearance of Britain's next top model. After she was done scoping and checking herself out, still smiling, she handed the mirror back to Grossman, who took it gingerly from her hand and placed it back on the table he had taken it from. After that, she leapt off the gurney and joined Fredrickson at his side, who was once again exchanging an ecstatic with Grossman, who had gone red and looked like he was about to shed a few tears of pure lusting joy, knowing that he was getting praised by Fredrickson of all people.

'You ready to go back to your cell?' Fredrickson asked politely to the black-haired woman, holding out his hand and taking Sam's, making them look like even more than just a boyfriend and girlfriend couple. 'Once again, thank you, Vincent; I'll see that you get a raise for this,' Fredrickson said, nodding back to Grossman, who was now as red as a beetroot.

Fredrickson and Sam left the surgical ward together, hand in hand, but Fredrickson detached his hand from hers and instead brought it down to her buttocks, where he rubbed gently, not really expecting Sam to react since she was well...dead. This kind of naughty behaviour usually meant that the man was horny and wanted to get a little closer to his love by dropping his arm down inside the woman's shirt, sticking his hand down into her bra and touching the breasts, jiggling them up and down. It was usually an obvious sign to the man wanting to get a grasp of more than just his love's breasts and wants a night on the bed. With her, so he could play naughty games with her, but knowing Fredrickson enough, you could determine that he was a sensible man and all the joy of fucking a woman had seeped away out of him after the death of his beloved wife.

As they walked up the stairs (not wanting to take the elevator up this time), he was again leading her past the other bonding cells, moving away from the oncoming traffic of bonders and zombies, slowly returning to cell B-35. But before getting there, they had passed cell B-12 (the cell of Ace the Crawler).

Ace had been bonding well with her rookie bonder Kolen for the time being, learning more of the English language in general, making Kolen feel like she was the luckiest rookie on the planet. But all the positive attitude about learning the English language went out the window as soon as Ace and Sam locked eyes on each other, and getting a glimpse of what the surgery can do to a zombie, seeing Sam looking alive and human again, time seemed to stop for the crawler. The way Sam had walked by her cell accompanied by her bonder in slow motion, it didn't feel her with joy. Sam noticed the expression of loathing that Ace was giving her and smirked; it was a smirk that Ace hated, didn't like and trust in the slightest, a smirk that fuelled Ace with the instinct to kill.

Time caught up with Ace as soon as Sam looked away from her, walking along with Fredrickson and out of sight, but Ace continued to glare in the direction they'd gone, which had understandably unnerved Kolen into what had made her crawler zombie wear a face of sheer... hatred. What was Ace seeing that was making her glare in such a ripe way? 'Ace, what's wrong? You look like someone who saw her rival across the road,' Kolen wondered, yet a little frightened by the intense glow seen in Ace's dead eyes. She waved her hand in front of Ace's rotting face to try to distract her away from whatever it was she was so transfixed on, even looking behind her just to see what Ace was staring at with hot-blooded hatred and loathing. But it was like Ace hadn't heard her or acknowledged she was even there to begin. She continued staring at the right corner of her cell, her thoughts returning to the nightmare smirk Sam had given her.

'I no like her...' she snarled quietly, not taking her eyes away from the window Sam and her bonder passed by (like how Kolen had put it, she did just see her rival, or did she suspect that something bad was going to happen). Kolen's concerned face contorted into one of fear, worried that Ace's strange sudden behaviour was a sign that she was developing something dark and sinister, something that Kolen didn't want to know. She looked behind her again, seeing only a few scientists and doctors passing by, no bonded zombies anywhere in sight. 'Not. One. Bit...' Ace growled again.

Chapter 17

One such example of a zombie with a highly damaged brain currently in the facility and often subjected to being ridiculed for not being able to learn without a proper "healthy" brain, was Kashima; a lanky five-eight Asian zombie that'd been shot in the head at least seven times by what appeared to be a small .38 sized bullet holes in his head, making the brain inside his skull a little on the irreparable side. But if Spot was anything to go by, any zombie could have a chance at becoming human again – no matter how damaged the brain was.

His bonder was a middle-aged Japanese man named Daisuke Kushiro who was straightforward and often times sleep-deprived and depressed as he was rarely seen with a smile on his rugged, sleepless face, which always had bags under the eyes. He was often referred to as the male Cansu Aksoy by his long face and sluggish features that looked like ice cream that had melted in the tropical sun. Another trait that he'd shared with the Turkish woman was that he'd shared a dark past that had haunted him right up until he'd taken one of the smuggler's boats to the UK. He had fled his hometown of Kochi to get away from the guilt that stayed on his skin like a tattoo that he was ashamed of getting etched into his flesh. Fleeing Japan soon after coming to terms with what he'd done to the zombified remains of his wife Haru and his son Nagisa – how he'd hacked them up and doused their already crisp remains with a flammable liquid. This became a valid reason behind Kushiro's endless, sleepless nights of tossing and turning and frequently waking up with cold sweats or his heart pounding in his chest. The start of his horrendous, never-ending nightmares had started at night when he was at home after his shift at the Kochi clinic for the injured. Soon after getting out of the shower and into something that wasn't his clinic smock, he'd received a telephone call (that one call that changed everything) from the school where Nagisa attended and where Haru also worked as a cooking and homeroom teacher. They'd been doing class normally when the accident broke out, resulting in Haru and Nagisa's and two others' tragic demise. It wasn't until two months later when they became unfortunate victims and be resurrected by the disgusting mortuus carnem, with no memory of their previous lives and only two things on their minds: kill and eat anyone they see, increase the spread of the infection. The countless amounts of therapy and suicidal attempts by hanging himself in his office could not free Kushiro from the shards of memory that haunted him. The memory of being informed by one of the school's officials who'd declared that his wife and only child had burned alive during what was thought to be harmless and simple cooking class. Both Haru and Nagisa had died, trying to put themselves out as well as trying to keep the ever-expanding fire at bay until the fire brigade arrived, which happened to be a few minutes too late as when they did arrive to evidently put the fire out, it had been confirmed by one of the firefighters who sought to make sure everyone was out, that there were four fatalities, mother, and son Haru and Nagisa Kushiro, twelve-year-old boy, Kenji Miyamasu and a nine-year-old girl, Yui Ueda. The class had gone normally leading up to this sudden accident, with everyone helping each other out and Haru doing her best to help her son and any other student who was having trouble with preparing some sashimi. It wasn't until Nagisa's bloodhound-like nose picked up something in the air that didn't smell like raw fish; it smelt more like gas. A terrible gas leak below the cooking class, and because of the gas seeping through the floorboards of the classroom and the gas travelling in the air to the hotplates (the hotplate Nagisa was working on), a fire quickly erupted in front of them, spreading fast like a raging, growing demon. The class erupted into a state of terror as Nagisa wailed in pain when he saw that the sleeve of his uniform was now at the mercy of the burning demon clutching his arm. He tried to shake it off and put himself out in with the help of his mother but to no luck. The fire had spread frightfully, burning away at the young boy's arm and making it even worse for both; it had jumped onto Haru's arm like a fiery grasshopper, then jumped onto Yui and Kenji. Haru screamed not only in pain for her and her son but for the rest of her class to flee the building as the fire continued crawling up her arm while she, her son, Kenji, and Yui rocked and rolled on the floor, trying desperately to put themselves out. Both mother and son, Yui, and Kenji, hollered in agony as their flesh sizzled and bubbled as the raging flames consumed their bodies until, eventually, the pain had become too great, and their lives were severed, their strings cut. Kushiro was working his daily shift as a nurse on the other side of Kochi, so he was nowhere near the school and didn't hear what happened until his boss called him over, saying he had an urgent call to take and that it was about his wife and son.

Even if Kushiro wasn't there to bear witness to his wife and son grizzly burning after he'd heard about the deaths when he received that call, boy did his mind and imagination run wild-and not in the best way, delving deep into detail about how they must've felt to see their own flesh bubble and burn right in front of their eyes, and knowing they were powerless to put themselves out, oh did his tender heart snap. The stress of losing the two people he loved most in the world had caused such a deep split in Kushiro that it prompted him to quit his job and contemplate suicide, which he could never find himself going through with as much as he'd imagine their screams haunting his ears. Daisuke Kushiro would visit their graves every day until he decided to take up the bottle and drink his life away, hoping it would spare him the torture of vividly revisiting the haunting imaginative cries and screams they'd made when they died. All this had happened two months before the mortuus carnem found its way to Japan, so it was only a matter of time before it found its way to the deceased Haru and Nagisa Kushiro.

Daisuke Kushiro had been sitting down in his armchair in front of a blank screen TV, holding onto a half-empty bottle of Asahi (Daisuke Kushiro was never a big drinker before the deaths of his family) and about four empty bottles lying next to the armchair, he sobbed his sorrows while drinking his life away… thinking that life was meaningless without a family to raise and support; he just wanted to escape from the cruel world he was living in by getting himself drunk, going for a ride in his car and hopefully drive off the guardrail and into his watery resting place. But God had made a deal with death to give him a second chance at life, delaying his death when his biggest fears (and motivation for the future) had become a reality. While about to drink the last few mouthfuls of his current Asahi bottle, he was interrupted by the exploding pounds and bangs on his door, which eventually led to the door being torn from its hinges and sent tumbling to the ground with a crash, there in the doorway of his and Haru's bedroom room house stood the steaming, charred, foul smelling burnt corpses of his wife and son. The rumours were true! Before he'd quit his job, he had heard rumours of the dead bursting from their graves and attacking anyone on sight. And it just so happened to have happened to the two most important people in his life. The mortuus carnem had infected them and had turned them against him!

Overwhelmed with guilt, self-loathing, fear and anger that he couldn't save them from their fate, Kushiro had no other choice but to kill his own undead wife and son with a katana that had been passed down from his grandfather's great, great grandfather, and to make sure they were dead for good, and that the mortuus carnem wouldn't get them again, he doused their already charred bodies with kerosene. He set them on fire for the second time while screaming and crying, proclaiming how sorry he was that he couldn't save them and how he'd felt like he'd failed them as a father and a husband.

A few minutes later, sweating and wiping away the tears from his face, he was able to return back to his senses and get over the fact that he'd carved up their zombified remains with the family heirloom and burnt their remains along with his house by pouring kerosine which he had inside a canister in the backyard shed over them and setting them on fire, Kushiro couldn't face living in Kochi for another minute. He had decided to move to the first country that came to mind, and the place that he had heard had been in control of the undead. He'd caught one of the last flights to the UK to take a job as a bonder after hearing about it from someone on the street (that you needed to have completed a science or medical degree during some stage in life) and remembering that he in fact done a medical course during his college days and his current job as a nurse, Daisuke Kushiro vowed for a rewrite of his current chapter. He wanted to do more than just sit on his armchair drinking his sorrows away like in the movies. He would get up and do something about the spread of the infection; he hoped that he would be able to aid the human race in fighting back against the zombies infected by the mortuus carnem; the one thing he couldn't do when Haru and Nagisa had perished in that school blaze.

Chapter 18

He was sitting straight on the metal chair, eerily still and silent, immobile like a statue; the only sound coming from him was an occasionally audible splat of saliva as it oozed from his bottom jaw, down his chin and landed rhythmically onto the stainless-steel table below him. He wasn't sure how long he'd waited for his bonder like this; quiet and firmly planted in place, his hands cupped on the steel desk in complete utter silence that if Ark could be here in the room right now, it would feel her with an unnatural tinge in her spine as if a ghastly cold hand had caressed it from above the flesh. But aside from the dripping saliva, he made no such noise as a hungry moan or a gurgle.

Well, how could he? It wasn't like Spot could make much noise to begin with, as he didn't have a fully functional mouth. Hell, he couldn't even eat much like most zombies. The only way he'd be able to consume food would have to be through a straw that was placed into his throat where he would have to drink them out, or the liquidised food would be fed into his throat with a cone flask, so to Spot, the most mundane task of eating was a real struggle, and when it came to the other zombies, eating was the closest thing to human breathing. The fewer zombies ate, the more violent they became. So, during the bonding sessions, this was something that Ark needed to think of; strategies and ways to feed him because while he may not have been able to eat her like other zombies like him, he could still use his brute undead force to snap her neck as if it were a simple fig twig. But even through his obvious physical problems, Ark was determined to have him outside and help others, and she had opted to feed him drugs with either a straw or lifting up his tongue and dropping it down his throat where it could dissolve.

The poor zombie only had half a head. You'd be forgiven for thinking that he'd never be able to learn anything if his brain had been absent from his head. Still, there have been previous cases and records in the archives of some of the bonders in the GFOSAR who had worked with zombies that had no brain matter in the slightest. They were still able to learn the simple things like working out what shaped block goes in which hole and using a fork and spoon to eat food instead of using their hands or just pelting in for the kill. But those zombies were quickly disposed of as using cutlery and eating in a more civilised manner seemed to be the only thing those brainless husks could learn. Spot's silence was eventually reaching a point where he was becoming impatient, and he needed his bonder with him – he started becoming agitated by fidgeting with his fingers – moving them around with erratic and random motions as a clear signal to show that he was becoming agitated, either from loneliness or hunger. Hunger seemed the most plausible answer, as zombies couldn't get lonely. Right?

It was only a few minutes later, after Spot's erratic finger movements, when Ark returned from her work in the central laboratory on L4; she was beaming like a child who had just been told that she'd be getting a puppy or kitten for her birthday. Her heart was pounding with nothing short of anticipation of what Spot would do when he saw what she had done for him and how it would show him how committed she was to him, to helping him on the path to becoming human again. She thumbed in the code for the lock and let herself inside. She strode jovially over to her side of the desk, pulled out her chair with her foot and sat down. There, resting comfortably in her hands, was a large round glass jar that looked big enough to house a decapitated head safely inside. But of course, the jar wasn't empty, oh no, it most definitely wasn't.

Ark had come from the lab clasping said glass jar that was almost to spilling point with some peculiar moss green liquid sloshing around inside, and floating purposely inside was a bunch of bizarre stray wires and cords which were connected to a fleshy looking sponge-like object, the way the sponge-like object moved and pulsated inside the green liquid and with the wires poking out of it suggested that they were keeping Spot's own brain alive inside it. The way Ark had played around with the cables beforehand determined the kind of wires she would put into the fleshy mass inside the brain. And when she'd seen the thing pulse like an electrical twitch she knew she'd chosen the right cords and had inserted them into the brain. More pulses and twitches later, and Ark knew she'd done what she'd set out to do. She'd given a once-dead brain life and the ability to think, which gave Ark a better advantage of bonding with him.

'G'day Spot! Guess what I got for you!' Ark's voice sang, getting Spot's attention, making him turn in the direction of her voice, which might've sounded as sweet as a bird singing if he had proper ears to hear with. The half-headless zombie was unable to see from the missing top half of his head. Still, at least he could listen and grasp a brief summary of things, and if things turn out well for Ark, the brain in the jar would provide more than a bonus for helping Spot learn the ways of becoming human again. Ark tenderly placed the jar containing Spot's brain on the desk in front of his cupped hands; the smile was still plastered on her face, not thinking to check the time on her wristwatch to see if she still had time to work with him or if she'd wasted half of her session outside looking for graves in the local cemetery. 'I've just come back after taking a quick visit to your grave (*at least I'm certain it was yours; I hope for the sake of my experiment that it was yours*), and I dug up something that I think you'll be needing.' She crowed, gently tapping the side of the glass jar significantly. 'So, I went and did a little something to the thing that makes the human and zombie tick, and hopefully, I've reanimated it with science, so it should help us bond more easily. So, my dear Spot, this is my present to you! Fingers crossed it'll help,' she clarified, pulling up her seat and sitting opposite him, taking a moment to drink in on his height, which was around six-foot-six, so when he was alive and with a complete head, he probably would've stood at least seven feet, a giant man that could've been playing for the local basketball team and dwarfing some of his peers; unless they were all tall like him.

Who knows, unless Spot could write down his real name and past life before dying, all those speculations about his life as a basketball player remained the most plausible explanation of what kind of person he was in life, seeing as that was Ark's goal, to uncover the secrets about his life in the same way as every other bonder tried to look for.

'In a way, I wanted to give you something as a token of my appreciation for you bonding with me well, despite not having a complete head like most zombies, and I thought that by returning something familiar that was stolen from you, I thought that it would help you think clearer and have a better understanding of the things I teach you.' Ark's once gleeful smile beginning to fade away as if the reality of things had swept through her like a ghostly chill; it was as if all the happiness had been sucked right out of her when she took a moment to think of a more logical and realistic approach into how Spot would react if he had found out what she'd done into retrieving his brain, poking it with cords and wires, putting it in a moss liquid filled jar called *LUNG* and giving it to him expecting him to be exulting with joy would be insulting to his corpse, since she'd basically desecrated his already spoiled grave.

Ark looked down at her watch, seeing the time, and almost shrieked and knocked the jar off the table, sending it crashing to the floor.

She'd been absent for about four hours! Four hours was too long, and it was vital that bonders spend as much as seven to eight hours a day with their zombies as possible, or they'd be faced with disciplinary measures concerning their craft of work. Being given the sack and tossed to the streets to fend for themselves.

'Oh fuck, because of all the time I spent in the cemetery looking for your brain and the work I did to get the brain here, my bonding session is going to run out in a few hours, and I haven't even started! Shit!' She roared, standing up so suddenly she knocked the chair over. 'I don't plan on getting fired now and tossed into the dead streets! No, no, no. I have to get you ready for the outside!' Ark cried, anxiety creeping up into her voice, backing up from the desk and staring down at the time on her watch in disbelief that she'd been gone for so long and that her employers were going to be hearing about this and were most likely discussing on whether or not to fire her and leave her stranded on the zombie-infested streets. At the same time, Spot would either be given another bonder or, worse, disposed of. Ark couldn't allow that to happen; she didn't want all her progress to cease just because she'd spent most of her hours outside of his cell.

There was another crash, and Ark looked up in horror, seeing that Spot was now standing, tall and imposing, like Goliath, staring down at the small boy with his slingshot. 'Shit!' she cursed at herself. She wanted to try taking a few therapeutic breaths to try and calm herself down, but her mind was too fevered, and she couldn't control the waves of thoughts that she was going to be fired and sent packing into the dangerous outside with no one to help her. 'Goddammit, I've probably startled Spot!' She hissed to herself. 'I know that startling zombies is one of the worst things a bonder could possibly do. Shit, Shit, Shit! Now I've really fucked it up! Spot is going to attack and kill me, and I'll be resurrected as a hungry zombie like him! Motherfuck! Lisa, you dumbarse!' Ark condemned herself with gritted teeth. She knew that she had to remain calm, but how could she? She had startled him, and there was nothing that she could do that would be able to prevent what he would do to her. Readying her fist, taking aim, opting to punch or at least smack herself in the face for getting too invested in her surgical experiment and not taking a moment to think about the consequences of her job as a zombie bonder if she'd been found to not have been spending the seven hours with her zombie. Since Spot couldn't see her, he wouldn't be able to knock her teeth in, and as long as that fact was out there, Ark could injure herself as much as she felt suited, and he wouldn't even know. Though, who was to say that Spot couldn't hear her and the obscenities she was throwing at herself.

Bonders usually get fired or demoted from their position if the reason behind their absence from their zombie was something outlandish and stupid, like making love in the locker room or deciding that they didn't want to work that day and kept calling in sick just to do your own thing. Sick days weren't an option in the GFOSAR. Zombie bonding was a rigorous job, and it needed to be taken seriously at all times, so any funny business was not to be taken lightly; the bonder had to be with their zombie for as much as possible. Ark knew this and wore it with her like a wristwatch.

However, while Ark stood there fumbling through the pages of her unkempt paperwork, she had a white-knuckled fist ready for when she' punch herself in the face, wanting to break the nose or at least make it bleed as he felt that she deserved it. 'I'm such an asshole!' she spat, shutting her eyes, and contorting her face as if she was ready to feel someone's brick-like fist slam against her cheekbones, causing her to stumble back and maybe fall on the buttocks upon impact. Her fist came roaring to the middle of her sharp mug. She vividly imagined already feeling the sharp, stinging pleasure of a broken nose and feeling the cool, moist substance of the blood trickling down her bloody shattered nose and seeping out of the mouth in some kind of twisted human blood fountain, where you put the favourable liquid into where the brain is usually housed. The said liquid would pour from the eyes, nose, and mouth, creating a rather spectacular yet unholy sight that must be seen to be believed.

But lucky for her, she didn't have to feel the agonised sensation and hear the gruesome crack of her nose being shattered by her own hand; the only thing her nose felt was the chilling air that her balled hand had thrown at her, meaning that someone had obviously stopped her from committing such an offence upon herself (but who and why she thought, surely no in their right mind would let themselves into the cell just to stop me from punishing myself). Ark didn't want to open her eyes just yet, probably thinking it was just a visage and that she had indeed punched herself and she was now lying sprawled out on the floor like some crooked starfish in a deep, unconscious sleep. But she could still feel her feet planted on the floor, so she was obviously still standing and very conscious in her mind. So, she tried again, throwing her angry, bared knuckles upon herself again, but she just couldn't get her fist to make contact; she couldn't even get her own fingers to touch her nose. A firm grip was compressed on her arm, and from what she could feel, it seemed that this strong clasp on her was pulling her arm away, banning her from self-harming, all because she realised that her shift was almost over and that she hadn't been with her zombie like she was supposed to.

When Ark eventually opened her eyes to get a glimpse of whoever had stopped her, she was taken back, and her heart may have skipped a few beats upon seeing that her saviour was her own zombie. The towering Spot was standing a few inches from Ark; one of his hands was tightly clasped around Ark's wrist, his tall structure and the way his tongue dribbled and lolled out in her direction as if pointing had made her feel a little uneasy, knowing she was now at the mercy of Spot and if he really wanted to, he could very effortlessly kill her and snap her neck like it was a mere twig because despite looking feeble and brittle, zombies had enhanced strength which was believed to have been the result of the mortuus carnem bringing them back from the dead; not only would the corpse rise as a zombie but they would be granted with enhanced strength and would easily be able to snap bones like tree branches. And because Ark was a simple woman of only 5'8 and an average weight, she knew that she would stand no chance against Spot if he decided that her life had reached its peak and it was now time she was replaced. It was no surprise that tall zombies could've easily fitted the basketball roles in their former lives. Still, it was in this very heart-stopping moment of confrontation between zombie and bonder that Spot appeared to have gotten taller. His threatening size and drooling pointing tongue had caused Ark to shrink, feeling smaller and smaller the closer the tongue got to her. Because he seemed to have no intentions of letting her wrist go, she knew that this was going to be the end of her time as a zombie bonder as well as her final day as a human; he was going to attack her because she'd committed the biggest penalty for a bonder, she had startled her zombie and was going to pay the price for it. Knowing that it would be fruitless to try to fight back for another chance and another day as a human, she closed her eyes once more and gritted her teeth, veins popping in her neck as she prepared for the killing blow.

But it didn't happen.

Confused and unable time to process what had happened next; Spot's tongue reached her and licked her on the nose, making Ark's eyes widen, and her mouth hang loosely as if the tendons holding her jaw together had broken, causing her bottom jaw to hang down at an impossibly low rate. The tall zombie then hunched down, lowered his size a bit and opened his arms wide around Ark. He was still holding onto her wrist, and his other hand was now stroking the fabric of Ark's lab coat; he then started pulling her forwards; that was when he had loosened his grip on her wrist and eventually letting it go entirely, leaving only a mild reddened hand print over her wrist. She took this advantage to bring her arms together in a feeble attempt to shield her chest as Spot closed her exits, pulling her close to his chest and… hugging her. And to boost Ark's current status of confusion, Spot leaned what was left of his head onto hers and was making soft gurgling noises that sounded a little like a cat purring.

It was a given; if Spot could talk, he would say something to his bonder, something that would sound like: *'Don't hurt yourself, Lisa; I don't care what you were doing out there rather than being with me, I know it was for a good reason. If it weren't for you and your mass dedication towards me, I wouldn't have gotten this far in intelligence. I may only have half a head, but that doesn't stop me from thanking you for everything you have done for me. You go out of your way for me, getting my own brain for me to help me. I don't want you to be sad, Lisa. If I were alive, I would do more than hug you now.'* Ark lost her words, her mouth a perfect O shape, unable to think of something to say and unable to twitch as much as a muscle. All she could do was stare in shock at her zombie, as his arms were enclosed around her waist and his jaw resting upon her silky blonde hair, making soft purrs, and combing the fabric on her long white coat with his gault fingers. It took a few quick seconds for Ark to understand precisely what was going on, and this was his way of saying "thank you" for retrieving his brain and returning it back to him wired up and allowing him the joy of being able to hear things more clearly again and able to conjure rational thoughts for himself and for those he would come to care for.

Ark's eyes became wet, and with each blink so much that a tear rolled down her cheek. The muscles in her mouth rose, and Ark was able to produce a vague but very genuine smile; she had dealt with well-behaved zombies before, but none had come close to showing her the same amount of affection she was getting from this particular half-headless zombie, and judging by the way Spot had embraced her and how he was tenderly raking her back with his chipped, musky fingernails, he seemed to show more than just his gratitude for having something that was once stolen returned back to him, the gentle nature of how he caressed her and the somewhat nice gurgling noises that came from his throat as he rested his half head on hers, meant that he was showing was commonly regarded as expert level bonding and the hardest thing for a new zombie to learn, usually taking a few years to get right and on point.

Ark pried her arms out of the cage-like arms and pulled them away from her back, allowing herself the opportune moment to free herself from the undead's embrace. 'Sorry,' she mumbled, wiping the joyous tears away with her thumb. She stepped away from Spot and took about two minutes to study her tall zombie with half a head while he continued to stand still on the spot, completely silent. Her smile widened, and her eyes were twinkling as if her superior had informed her that Spot was ready for a head transplant. She glanced down at the red tattoo on her wrist and thought it would make a good reference for her paperwork, how her zombie had stopped her from knocking herself out, and how her zombie had hugged her and showed her a light but obvious sign of emotion.

It would be a good thing on her record and might end up in her getting promoted and having a higher zombie bonding status.

'You are a very good boy, Spot! I hope you can understand that.' She beamed, but her eyes didn't show the same twinkle as before; they showed one of guilt and loss. 'I just wish I could give you the special treatment to make you look alive again, but sadly, it would be impossible because we lack the parts in the hospital ward… I'm really sorry… the most I can do for you is present you that jar with your brain inside it, hoping it'll help our future sessions.' She blinked and forced the sparkle to return to her eyes again, forcing herself to think about the amazing lessons she would be having with Spot in the future.

'I'll keep returning to you, Spot, and we'll continue to bond as usual. Thank you so much, Spot, for your help! I'll see you tomorrow.' Ark sniffled, wiping the rest of the happy tears that stained her reddening face. She flashed her card over the keypad lock, and it buzzed open; before leaving cell B-09, Ark took another minute to glance back at Spot with a beaming grin, trying to envision in her mind what Spot had looked like when he was alive and if he was a handsome young man who played basketball for his country.

'See you tomorrow, Spot, my amazing boy,' she repeated, considering the urge to blow him a kiss, but hesitated, knowing that he wouldn't be able to see it and understand it at this point, but he would come to eventually. He was a fast learner like Fredrickson's acclaimed subject, and it would take no time for Spot to learn the basics of blowing a kiss and other bits and pieces like that. She pressed the red button on the number pad to shut the cell door behind her while pondering the sad fact that he couldn't show it on his face; she knew that Spot was happy and was making gurgles of pure bliss at the idea of seeing his bonder tomorrow.

Chapter 19

It was 5:24pm on October the twenty-ninth. It had been a long day of sitting back, arms crossed and waiting for the surgery to be complete. Fredrickson left cell B-35 upon gathering his paperwork and finishing another session with Sam, who was now completely unrecognisable. Those who didn't know what lay underneath the fresh garment of skin would be easily fooled into thinking she was just another gorgeous, beautiful woman in her rocking late t wenties or early thirties. One would possibly believe that she was a model at some point in her life as her facial features were sharp, smooth, seductive and clean; acne and skin blotches were utterly absent; she was tall and lean with a perfect hourglass figure; Vincent Grossman had really outdone himself and as long as the bonder was happy with the result of the surgery, so was the surgeon conducting it.

Upon closing the button to seal Sam inside the cell, Fredrickson opened his folder for a quick glance at the mugshot Carl Boyle had taken of her before she had been transferred over to Fredrickson. A smile cracked on his sunny face when he regarded how much Grossman had altered her appearance. How he had transformed a foul-smelling skeleton with rotten ribbons of skin stuck to her as if they'd been glued onto an attractive black-haired woman who could've once lived as a model before she had died. Feeling pleased with himself and how his twentieth working day with Sam had gone.

Fredrickson closed the folder and put it under his arm. He held his head up high and still had that smile on his face. He was in good spirits as he confidently strutted up the long silver hallways, lightly whistling a tune to himself, the before and after image of Sam never leaving his head as he ventured forth into his office to rest up for the night and plan ahead on what he was going to teach Sam tomorrow, as well as informing her of where she'd be heading and that she'd be his very first success story, with her being released to the outside to conduct the very final stages of becoming human again, and once that was clear, Sam would be qualified as a human again! The very idea that she was heading in that direction was making Fredrickson so excited that when he got back to his office, he would do his rendition of a tap dance. Something that he'd never done in front of his colleagues, and usually, whenever he broke out in some kind of dance, it was sometimes to show off how happy and excited he was about something that would happen. She'd come a long way and had learned so much in such a short time, which Fredrickson was profoundly impressed with. 'For the first time in all my six years of bonding, I finally have a successful zombie! *Now I can show the new bonders what a successful zombie looks like.*' He gloated to himself as the memory of their first meeting replayed in his head; how Boyle had the twinkle in his eye upon officially meeting him and how Winsome had made those snarky comments just to try to get Fredrickson riled up. As much as he vented his distaste for Winsome then, he couldn't help but thank him and Boyle for choosing Sam for him, his first official success story, his first privileged rights of bragging to the other less fortunate bonders! One of his personal goals as a bonder was to have the right to brag about how he had a success story, and now that that was becoming a reality for him, he clapped his hands in a jolly way.

During his (for once) jolly journey back to his office, whistling that minor tune to himself. He didn't get far from B-35 when he noticed three silhouettes ahead of him, and Fredrickson, for once feeling like he could talk and strike up a jolly conversation with anyone about even the most bland and dumbest of topics, kicked up the speed in his legs and caught up with them, realising the three silhouettes as Marilyn Kolen, Lisa Ark, and Henrik Losnedahl, who like him, were heading back to their own offices to refuel their energy and plan their sessions for tomorrow. 'Hey! Hey Friends!' He called out to them as he trailed up behind Kolen, who at first flinched a bit, thinking it was Boson or worse… the king of irritation himself, Winsome, but quickly became comfortable from seeing it was Fredrickson, her idol and mentor. Though there was something about the way Kolen looked that didn't match the other two, she seemed nervous, a little more jumpy than usual. But Fredrickson didn't interrogate her on it as he was far too excited and wanted to talk his brains out about Sam. 'Well, someone's in a good mood.' said the blonde woman with the Australian accent.

'Oh, hello, Mr Fredrickson, how nice of you to tag along with us.' Kolen mumbled in a small voice, removing her glasses, and brandishing them, rubbing the fog that clung to the lenses with her lab coat's collar before returning them to their resting place on the nasal bridge. Fredrickson didn't seem to recognise the slight tone of her voice. 'My pleasure, Marilyn,' he smiled kindly. 'Tell me, before you three depart from me to enter your own quarters, I want you to tell me how the bonding process is going for you and how your zombies are going. Are they getting brighter? More human? I want to know everything that you can tell me. I want it all.' He beamed, his eyes darting from Kolen to Ark and Losnedahl, waiting for someone to start and answer his much-interested question. He wanted to hear if someone was having just as success as he was. He liked to hear someone else brag about their zombie just as much as he wanted to brag to them about his zombie.

It was Losnedahl who took the honours of reciting his story about Linus in the best way he could. He pursed his lips together, raised an eyebrow, held up his palm like a straight plate and tilted it slightly from side to side, giving the motion that Linus was around the 50/50 category.

'Why's that Henrik? Humour me.' asked Fredrickson, cocking his head to the side with curiosity. Even if he knew what Losnedahl was going to say, he was feeling gracious enough to show consideration and respect for the tongueless man. So, Losnedahl did his absolute best in trying to explain to Fredrickson through sign language that at random times, Linus would display different emotions and feelings towards his lessons and sometimes didn't show any sort of interest in learning (which had reminded Losnedahl of when he was in high school and dealing with rebellious teenagers who only wanted to do the work if they were interested in the subject). There would be other times when he would be keen to learn new things with Losnedahl, so overall, bonding with Linus was a reasonably slow progress because it all depended on Linus being well and in the correct mindset to learn things, so the best way that Losnedahl could describe Linus was that he was on and off. He elevated his pointer finger and flicked it up and down as if he was flicking a light switch.

'Ah, that makes sense; well, hopefully, Linus will be able to learn more. Just gotta be patient, Henrik, you'll get there.' Fredrickson put a hand on the man's shoulder and nodded to him.

A child-like-sounding giggle came from Ark's lips, alerting Fredrickson. He looked at her with the same amount of curiosity that had been present on his face when he asked Losnedahl about how Linus was doing.

'If I start with Spot, you won't shut me up. So, I'll spare you the trouble and details by simply saying that he's bloody brilliant, and he's even started expressing emotion! Yeah, you heard that right, emotion! How brilliant is that?'

she laughed, biting her bottom lip, and going pink in the cheeks; feeling giddy at the very thought of her subject. 'Just thinking about Spot was enough to make her belly flutter with butterflies, and that was a perfect sign that Spot was one of the good ones and from how excited Ark was at the thought of it; it seemed that it wouldn't be long until it was his time to visit Grossman or one of the other surgeons in the medical ward. Fredrickson looked fascinated, and then his sight drifted to Kolen, who was blinking timidly, biting her lip, and holding her clipboard protectively to her chest; her shoulders were tense, and she was avoiding eye contact with him. Her face was even redder than Ark's. After that quick hello, she hadn't said anything when Fredrickson caught up with them.

'Say, Marilyn, you've gone quiet; anything to say about your crawler zombie, Ace, wasn't it?' Fredrickson wondered, putting a gentle, comforting hand on Kolen's shoulder, which made her flinch, so he took his hand away. The spectacled Dutch woman nodded, confirming that it was her name before opening her mouth and telling Fredrickson the things his ears wanted to hear.

Kolen's words came out as a slight mumble, and Fredrickson had to lean in, putting his ear to her so that he could hear what she had to say. 'W-Well…' she began with a vague stammer. 'Ace has started talking and has spoken even on our first day. However, she can't speak full sentences well like we are right now. She can't do that yet, but at least she can speak, so… I… I'm not complaining about that. If she does try to speak in a sentence like most people, her punctuation often misses words like "is" and "am," but other than that, she has been behaving commendably, and I'm really proud of her as my first zombie.' Kolen finished, returning back to biting her lip again as she walked alongside the other bonders. She didn't even glance at Fredrickson in the eyes the entire time.

Instead, she had been looking down at his neck. The closest she had gotten to his eyes was his mouth. This confused Fredrickson, as he had always known Kolen to look him in the eyes whenever she spoke to him. So, why wasn't she doing it now?

The others didn't seem to notice or register this peculiar behaviour in Kolen, which only added more confusion to the soup. 'Holy shit, I don't remember you saying Ace was a talker!' Ark blurted out, slapping Kolen on the back. Kolen made an audible grunt from the impact of the slap.

'I-I did… it was written down on Ace's records in the archives.' said Kolen timidly.

'Ah! That's why I've never heard you mention it; I'll have to quickly detour to the archives,' Ark beamed. 'Must be easy to have a talker, wouldn't it, Marilyn? Even if, like you said, her speech pattern is a little wonky.'

'A little, but she'll get better; I have faith in my Ace,' Kolen smiled gingerly; she tightened her grip around her folder and looked down at the linoleum floor.

Pleased with what he was hearing (and a little puzzled by Kolen's distant behaviour) and knowing that his office wasn't far away, Fredrickson nodded to the two women and Losnedahl, bidding them farewell and politely pushing through them so he could get to his quarters and prepare for his time with the black-haired honey in B-35 tomorrow.

H-Hey!' Kolen called out to him with a stammer, 'what about yu-your zombie, Alexander? H-How is…' Kolen sounded like she was having trouble saying the name of Fredrickson's zombie, almost as if the name scared her.

Why? Fredrickson wondered. Finally, Kolen managed to get the word out. 'How is Sam going?' Kolen had asked Fredrickson, making him halt almost instantaneously as soon as Kolen had finished inquiring him on the information regarding Sam. She, Ark and Losnedahl picked up their paces and gathered around the brown-haired man with the usual stern, cold expression, curious about his female zombie who had grown quite the renowned reputation for being a fast learner and one of the rare success stories.

'Sam, huh?' Fredrickson coughed to clear his throat. 'Ah crap, where do I even start? *Well, she does scare me sometimes with how she looks at me with those cold eyes, almost as if she's planning something.*' He wheezed, gathering up the memories in his head about her, putting his hand over his forehead and groaning quietly like he had just contracted a massive migraine. 'Where most stories start, Alexander, at the beginning', Ark said gleefully, patting Fredrickson on his back to encourage him to continue talking about the outstanding prodigy known as Sam the Zombie.

Fredrickson closed his eyes and thought long and hard about how he would explain his status with his renowned black-haired zombie. He took a deep breath.

'It's kind of a long story, I'll tell you later at the next board meeting; I really should get back to my office to rest up for the night; Henrik looks like he could use some sleep and is on the verge of passing out' Fredrickson looked over at Losnedahl whose face was sagged and his eyes bagged, he had looked like he hadn't gotten any proper sleep in days; probably due to Linus causing a racket at night and considering Henrik's office was just opposite to Linus's cell of B-01, it wasn't hard to feel some sympathy for the fifty-six-year-old man without a tongue. It could be forgiven why his face often appeared sagged and why he always had some baggage ringed around his eyes. 'Never mind Henrik, he can rest up for the night if he wants to. He is the oldest out of the four of us standing here, so all in all, he should be the one telling us what he wants us to do, like if he wants to hear about Sam or go to bed and shut down for the day.' Ark acknowledged Losnedahl, looking over at him with a calm, friendly grin, waiting for an answer even though Losnedahl couldn't talk without making ugly gagging and gurgling noises, sometimes, on rare occasions, coughing up blood if he tried too hard to speak up. Losnedahl didn't like it when people relied on him to decide what to do just because he was in his fifties and was more mature and rational than most in the GFOSAR. And the fact that he had no tongue just made decision-making even more daunting for him. 'Lisa… Henrik can't talk; remember he's mute from the incident that happened when he was a baby.' Kolen defended Losnedahl, opening her mouth and pointing at her own tongue, using it as a window to remind Ark that Losnedahl was missing one and, therefore, was left permanently mute. 'Oh yeah, crap, sorry, Henrik. Just thought since you're the oldest of us that you should decide on what we should do or you want to do, you know, respecting my elders.' Ark rubbed the back of her neck while laughing sheepishly. 'My memory of first meeting you guys has gone through the tumble dryer a bit. Working with the spectacular Spot has been distracting me from the other bonders and their stories; I seemed to have forgotten about Henrik's "missing" tongue' Ark chuckled gingerly, apologising to Losnedahl, who smiled and nodded without words, saying that he forgave her and that it was a common error people make to him. Ark looked down at the violet-skinned watch on her arm.

'Well, I guess I will bid you guys farewell; I'm gonna go get some sleep and think about my sweet angelic zombie while I rest' Ark closed her part of the conversation cocking her head to Losnedahl and Kolen and Fredrickson, turning her back from them and parting away from them for her office to get some shut-eye. Losnedahl tapped a finger onto Kolen and Fredrickson's shoulders, gave them a humble salute and bidding his farewell to them both, turning and following behind in the direction of Lisa Ark to the end of the bonding cells to his office next to B-01, hoping Linus will be a good boy and keep his pie-hole zipped and allow his bonder to grasp hold of some decent sleep.

'I-I guess since everyone else has parted, I-I should leave too, Mr Fredrickson; it was nice talking to you again; the last time we spoke like this was when you were training me to become a zombie bonder and if you don't mind me saying, if it wasn't for your wise and clear teachings about the zombies and how they are unpredictable, I wouldn't be at the stage I am now with Ace. I really owe you my life, Mr Fredrickson, because your teachings have kept me alive; Ace can speak because of what you taught me, which makes me really happy.' Kolen gushed, timidly moving some of the long locks of brown hair away from her glasses and feeling her cheeks heat up; she looked away from him, embarrassed at the thought of Fredrickson seeing her with such a childish high-schooler blush.

Shortly after getting employed at the GFOSAR, she met her mentor, Alexander Fredrickson, whom she had quickly grown a fondness for and admired greatly as if he were a world-class celebrity. He then taught her to become a successful and safe bonder, learn to deal with the zombies by herself and fight her own demons without help like she had needed for most of her life.

'Well, goodbye, then, Alexander. I hope we get to talk again sometime soon… perhaps when Sam is about to be released into the wild as a living person.' She smiled heartily, waving at him, and distancing herself from him to go to her office while he grinned idly, thinking about how much Kolen had matured since day one. Walking along the lean corridor to his office, he couldn't help but replay what Kolen had said about his teachings about keeping her alive. *I may have taught you the basics of zombie bonding and the things to prepare them, but it wasn't me that bonded with Ace and got her talking; that was all you, Marilyn, and you should be very proud of yourself because I am happy that you were able to achieve something that I haven't yet.* Fredrickson thought idly to himself, watching Kolen grow distant from him with each passing second. He smiled a generous smile as he approached the entrance of his office, let himself inside and stared at the door leading into his bedroom where he would be able to have a good sleep tonight without thinking of anything that would be sure to send him into a raving fit of anger. As Fredrickson settled in for the night, the memories of Kolen's teachings played throughout his head as if being played on a cinema projector; he smiled, wondering aimlessly about the kind of things Kolen would be able to do in the future. He thought about how distant she was around him during their recent talk and thought he'd ask her the reason behind it when they next met. Because Kolen was never like this around Fredrickson. There was something with the way she'd struggled to say Sam that confused Fredrickson, and even if it wasn't an overly big deal, his mind pondered on it. Did Kolen know something he didn't? He would have to find this out when he sees Kolen again.

Little did Fredrickson know that while he'd been talking to Kolen and the others, someone else had been listening in on their cheery conversation, someone had been eavesdropping, building up their intelligence by listening carefully to the words spoken and understanding the meaning of the emotions and topics that were used in the conversation.

Chapter 20

The following day, on the 21st of October, a thunderous bang came from outside his office. Fredrickson slid his hands down his face in annoyance as he was rudely awakened from his slumber to loud, overbearing knocks on his door. He knew precisely who was harrowing at his door by the tone of the knocks. It was none other than Maximillian (Max) Engel, another zombie bonder and co-worker who got on his nerves on the same level as Winsome (while Winsome annoyed him on purpose, Max seemed blind to it), banged and pounded his fist upon his office door, demanding him to wake up and get ready for today and in doing-so taking Fredrickson away from his lovely blissful dream, for once he'd actually had a good dream about the outcome of Sam being released into the outside and the positives it would have on the country. So, for that dream to be taken away from him put him in a very sour mood and one that he did not think his medication could soothe.

It's not a good start to anyone's day, being disrespectfully awoken by another one of your idiot co-workers who couldn't understand that dream time was your time.

'Alexander! ALEXANDER!' that whiney voice outside his office drawled out. Fredrickson ran his hands down his face again and groaned irritably. 'Stop jacking off in there and get up! You're about ten minutes overdue from your session! You, of all people, should know how vital it is to spend as much time with your subject and not miss so much as a second with them. Zombie's brains aren't like ours; they can forget things quickly like people with dementia, so why don't you have the decency to get your arse out of bed and bond with your zombie!' Engel's shrew, high, mouse-like voice burned into Fredrickson's ears as the sound of his door being pounded on echoed and bounced from the walls in his office and bedroom. Just when Fredrickson thought he was going to have a good day with Sam after having that wonderful dream about her possible future, idiot number two came knocking and poured oil into the ocean. 'Great; this is just fucking perfect! The thing I needed is that Engel idiot coming in and bearing his fists upon my door and getting me away from what could happen to my zombie when she's released.' Fredrickson hissed, rubbing his eyes, and sitting up on his bed, which was a simple mattress and grey army blanket stowed away in what was originally the uniform room. He pulled his uniform coat down from one of the coat hangers above him and took time to dress himself just to spite Engel further, thinking that it would be some form of payback for waking him up. But as soon as he got dressed for the day and left the room, Fredrickson soon came into regretting his decision of spiting Engel as Engel's barraging on the door had started to become violent, and his voice became more impatient as Fredrickson left his room rubbing the bags under his eyes and clothed in an un-ironed uniform which had creases and was starting to smell. But he wouldn't have time to clean the clothes because Engel was baring at his door.

'ALEXANDER TOMAS FREDRICKSON!!! WAKE THE HELL UP!!' The dense, irritating, mousy voice screeched, sounding like someone had put razor blades in Fredrickson's ears.

'I AM awake! Christ, give a man a fucking second to get his things!' He roared back as he slumped tiredly over to his desk and fingered through his drawers to get his papers for today. He looked up angrily at the plump silhouette that stood in front of his office window, bearing a striking resemblance to a villain in an animated kid's movie by his ball-like shape and a head that looked too small for his body. Fredrickson had slept in his casual clothes and had a faint odour; he only hung up his lab coat whenever he slept, but he washed his clothes whenever the stench became too unbearable to his colleagues' nostrils. Once Fredrickson was sure he had everything that was needed for today's session, he took a brief moment to blot out Engel's impatient rants and poundings on his door and proceeded to stare out of the open window behind him, glancing down sadly at the barren wasteland that was once his beloved home… was once a place where you could find a ten-year-old Alexander Fredrickson frolicking among the swaying cat tails and swinging joyfully on tyre swings (Fredrickson had grown up with a traditional family that didn't like technology). All that remained of the United Kingdom was the ransacked buildings with broken windows, cracked sidewalks and roads, and traffic lights that were either bent or snapped, leaving the fractured remains on the ground to act as a grim reminder of what the world had become, glass littered the lifeless streets which had started to become overgrown with vegetation only for it to shrivel up and die, leaving a mess of brown tangles and vines. And, of course, the undead were the dominant species now, as they were everywhere. Living numbers were dwindling and would only continue if people weren't careful.

Fredrickson sighed. Just looking at the dead country he was currently living in was making him sick in the stomach. Even when he saw a filthy homeless man covered head to toe in rags trying to outrun about five zombies, only to trip and break his leg, he couldn't help but feel sick as the zombies closed in on him and devoured his guts when he was still alive. Because of being eaten by an undead, Fredrickson could imagine it would be one of the worst ways to cash out. Fredrickson couldn't bear the thought of what it must feel like to be eaten by a zombie. To have your insides torn out and left there to slowly and painfully die or for the infection to pass through the body, turning you into one of the expanding numbers of the undead. That would be a fate worse than death. Being one of the undead. Your only goal is to eat and devour anyone you see, even if you knew them once.

'I won't tell you again, Alexander! Get Your Arse into Cell B-35!' exploded Engel, banging even harder than thought possible into the door that Fredrickson, for a moment, believed that the door might snap from its hinges. At that moment, Fredrickson wanted to ram his fist right into Engel's fat little face and give his balls the boot just for good measure.

'Alright, Alright, I'm coming! Jesus Christ, Maximillian, can you be a little fucking patient!' Fredrickson snapped, taking his papers, and holding them close, double-checking that everything was in the correct order. He hated it when people rushed him into things because it offered more chances for him to forget something important, and when he forgot something important, it would mess with his temper. He probably would've gotten his work and into B-35 in an orderly fashion and had another excellent bonding day with Sam if his morning had been so rudely interrupted by the impatient thirty-six-year-old Max Engel, who had just set off the ticking time bomb in his older co-worker, and because of that, Fredrickson had forgotten entirely how elated he had been yesterday and was officially back to being in his usual angry, short-tempered self, all thanks to Engel impatience. Fredrickson looked at his desk once more, grabbed his bottle of Valium pills, unscrewed the lid, took one tablet out and tossed it into his mouth without dousing it down with water. Why must someone come along and disturb his mornings like this?

Engel had been gracious enough to have lived his whole life here in Britain as he was born here. Even if his name was German, his parents came from Munich, Germany. They had moved from Germany to the UK just before they brought Max into the world with already a decent loan and finance for when he got older and would be able to make expensive purchases for the things he'd claim to need. Regardless, Engel always knew how to strike the wrong chords in Fredrickson and always succeeded in getting him overwhelmed with a wave of searing anger that would give the angriest man a run for his money.

'No, I can't be patient! I can't keep Wendy waiting!' he spat at Fredrickson and thought he was being noble by unnecessarily bringing his eyeless zombie into the argument. Suppose Engel kept using these pointless excuses to get Fredrickson up and shattering the good thoughts in his mind. In that case, he would pay for it as Fredrickson was about 91.9% into losing his mind and was near ready to explode at Engel in a way that would make even Winsome step back into the shadows of his own regret. Fredrickson knew that it wasn't Engel's job to wake up Bonder's, who had slept in; it was no one's job; if they missed time, it was their fault and something they took responsibility for. But Fredrickson thought that Engel just chose to do it because it made him feel powerful. He enjoyed pressuring them to do their job like some kind of teacher's pet cranked up to eleven. And Fredrickson could tell that he irritated others more than just him. But at least Engel had good intentions and was eager to hear about a few bonded zombies being released into the wild to undo the damage they had once done, even if the way he executed them wasn't the best. Case in point: yelling and throwing out insults instead of being more soothing and motivational. It only made it more frustrating when Engel used his zombie as an excuse, like his barraging on

Bonder's doors was keeping him away from his time with his zombie and that he would blame it on them.

'Go to her then! For fuck's sake, Max, I don't have time for your bickering like some spoilt brat who couldn't get the Hot Wheels car he had wanted. You're only wasting time standing outside of my window and accusing me of this bullshit! Christ, it isn't even your job to act as my own personal alarm clock! Why don't you do me the kindness for once in your pathetic life and just get fucked!' Fredrickson roared, 'I'll get ready at my own pace, thank you very much!' He propelled his fist into the wooden paling near the door; there was a crack, and he had popped his white knuckles inside. But Fredrickson didn't seem to feel the warm liquid trickling down his knuckles; as long as Engel did him a decent amount of kindness and pissed off his old hag, Fredrickson would assess to the tissue loss of his injured knuckles, dress them in bandages soaked in disinfectant before cooling his steam down enough so he would be able to start the day with his own zombie.

Fredrickson had never liked Engel for this very reason. However, he wasn't as bad as Winsome; no one was worse than Winsome and joked like Winsome, but Engel really did know how to push the big red frustration button on people; he really did know how to drive people insane and turn them into rage-fuelled lunatics, one might say that Max Engel was a professional aggravator who loved driving people insane and to paint himself as the innocent bystander who was just unfortunate to be in their way.

Fredrickson took a brief moment to block out Engel's bickering, enough for Fredrickson to remove his bloodied fist from the wooden palling and take a moment to examine the damage and tissue loss. Fredrickson looked at his fist and travelled over to his desk, took out a bottle of disinfectant, took out a roll of bandages from his drawer, and put them on his bleeding fist.

After he'd finished inserting the disinfectant on his bandaged fist, he had finally finished getting ready for his session with his zombie; he grabbed his things from his desk drawers, and in case she decided to turn the tables and go rouge on him, he took a small 99. Glock out of his third drawer on the right side of the desk to be on the safe side, and not leave himself open to a set of hungry jaws. When he was confident, he had everything, Engel's shouting and persisting had increased in volume, ringing in Fredrickson's ears, telling him that he had stuck around and was being cruel to Fredrickson by overstaying his welcome. So, Fredrickson decided that enough was enough, and someone ought to show him what happens when people push him over the edge and get him riled up to the point where he could hit someone or, worse, send someone to the hospital with fractures and broken bones. Fredrickson took the door handle in a harsh grasp, puffing steam out of his nose just thinking about Engel, and slammed his arm into the door, causing it to barge into Engel, who stood outside the door like an idiot, seemingly planted to the spot and refusing to weed himself. An ugly snapping noise accompanied by Engel's brief but pleasurable sound in pain. It had sounded like his nose had been dislodged; good serves the sonofabitch right. Engel yelped in pain from the force of the door slamming into his nose by the door. Engel cupped his plump little hands over his nose and mouth to stop the blood from dripping from his now fractured nose. Fredrickson clasped onto his maroon buttoned vest and held him close. He drew his fist back, watching the despair crawl on his smug little face, readying his fist to punch this moron's lights out. Still, Fredrickson knew better than to let the anger overtake him; he would need to wait for the Valium to take effect, so he lunged Engel to his face and threatened him in a deep, infuriated tone that was trying hard to keep the anger inside him repressed. He grabbed the scruff of the small, fat man's collar and held up five fingers to him.

'You're about five seconds into taking a trip to the medical ward with a broken face. I had a perfect daily schedule until you fucked it up!' Fredrickson's eyes blazed as he brought his face closer to Engel's meek, frightened stare. 'If you EVER pull a stunt like this again, Max, if you ever wake me up again before I have my medication, I'll have your nametag and see to it that Robert throws you outside to fend for yourself. Do I make myself clear?' Engel didn't dare open his mouth to say anymore. He quickly nodded, wide-eyed and holding his sore nose. 'Good.' Fredrickson snarled as he tossed Engel, who stepped backwards. Without so much as another word, Fredrickson stormed past the other cells, clutching his paperwork under his arm, venturing over to cell B-35 to begin his session with Sam. His face was lava that was spilling towards a town.

Engel stood silently for a moment, watching as if the world had stopped moving as Fredrickson's image blurred and eventually disappeared behind the crowd of people walking past. Engel held his bleeding nose; the pain seemed to have vanished as he stood unflinching in shock, wondering why Fredrickson didn't go the extra mile into breaking his nose. He knew he'd gone too far as soon as he saw the cords in Fredrickson's neck bulge, which meant that Fredrickson really desired to deck someone, but he hadn't, and Engel couldn't quite understand why he hadn't done it to him.

Engel's mind was stuck on the fact that Fredrickson, of all people, hadn't punched him with enough blunt force to shatter the nasal plates in his nose. Because most people would injure him in some way, especially Boson (he was the big man with the big temper and was the one-man Engel steered clear of and knew not to go out of the way to piss off, because Boson made sure you paid for it), so it was a given for Engel to expect someone to deck him as he frustrated them to a degree where he would be hit for it.

Engel then huffed, using an arm to wipe away most of the blood from his nose before he, too, followed protocol, making his way over to cell B-22, where his blind, eyeless zombie Wendy waited patiently in silence. Engel had had Wendy turned over to him a little later than the other bonders, so he wasn't having as much success with her as as the other bonders were with their zombies. But unlike others, Engel was patient when it came to zombies because he knew that zombies weren't the best thinkers and couldn't think logically for themselves. Hence, they needed help with their learning process, similar to how it is in kindergarten. Wendy was a female zombie that Engel had discovered had died during five-year AOR, making the year on her death certificate sometime around 2051. Engel had been christened with the name "Wendy" after his late grandmother on his father's side: Wendelin Warner was her name, and Engel hadn't much liked her when she was alive. She died early in the year 2034. He would always dread the days when his parents informed him that they had to work and took him over to visit her. After all, said parents had substantial loans and finances to make at the local bank in London, but sadly, Engel wasn't allowed to come and act as a volunteer, opting for any excuse to get away from Wendelin. Because Wendelin Warner had been the only member of his family with the most logical sense. She didn't spoil him as much as everyone else in the family did, and she was known to frequently call him out whenever he committed a felony and when he tried weaselling his way out of trouble with his parents or school. In a way, Wendelin was like an eagle watching its prey and always had a keen eye on Engel, making sure that he wasn't up to anything nasty like nicking a kid's lunch money or cheating on tests. And Engel hated it, which was always a reason he wasn't very fond of her and why he'd decided to name his zombie after her, to display his dislike of the undead and his late grandma. And considering her appearance, she was quite an old drink, looking to be around her late sixties by the cracks of wrinkles on her face and curly white hair. She was blind and had blackened voids where the eyes should be.

Wendy was bestowed into Engel's care with a bloody kitchen knife protruding out of one of her eyes, meaning the possibility that she'd been viciously murdered and that the perpetrator had left the murder weapon inside her eye. Blinding her and killing her. Engel saw potential in Wendy and believed she'd be one of the wise zombies, and he'd train it to become a far better version of his late grandma. Unlike his actions towards Fredrickson and other bonders who sleep in, Engel behaved civilly around Wendy, speaking calmly, and using gentle instructions. For example, he touched her hands caringly and softly when he needed to touch her hands. He'd already developed a relationship with her. Engel already saw a positive outcome if she was successful and released into the wild with a walking stick, so he had wanted to hurry up and make that fantasy a reality and get bragging rights to having a successful zombie. This was one of the main reasons why Engel was so impatient towards his older colleague because he'd wanted to hurry up and be with her badly, even though getting Fredrickson up and riled had nothing to do with being with Wendy. He was just in a foul mood. Engel was one of those individual people who wanted everything to be perfect and wanted everything to be on time, even though it meant telling people what to do and ruining their peaceful morning just to get what he wanted and if it meant pushing Fredrickson into the volcano, so be it. Anything to get Fredrickson over to Sam.

Chapter 21

Fredrickson was livid due to his morning meeting with Max Engel. He had stormed down the hall, his feet heavily stamping the ground, creating an audible echo that sounded like he was bringing a stampede behind him. His face was burning hot when he arrived at B-35. This was a bad sign. He'd need to remain calm if he was going through with the bonding today. He needed to take a breather, to at least give the Valium time to settle in. But his mind was too full of irritation and fury that Engel had forced upon him that he just couldn't stop himself or take a moment to breathe before he entered the cell to begin his day with his zombie prodigy. But that wouldn't happen with how flushed his brain was right now. Why did Engel have to do that to him? Why did he push him because he'd slept in for only ten minutes?

Fredrickson violently punched the code into the number lock, with enough brute force to initially break or at least bend the buttons and create some sparks. He wouldn't give a rats arse about the cost of property damage when his mind was in such a state, if he didn't take his frustration out on a breathing punching bag or rewind back to his office and take another Valium, he could throw all the success with Sam out of the window. He needed to take charge of his emotions if he was going to get through the day. Why was it that individuals like Winsome and Engel took sadistic delight in teasing one of the angriest men in Britain, tilting him off the cliff of tranquillity and into the ocean of rage? What fun did they get out of pushing Fredrickson off that cliff? This was a jigsaw that Fredrickson couldn't find the correct piece for. So, like always. It left him stumped.

Inside the cell, Sam noticed this extreme case of emotion in her bonder's bulging neck veins and the hideous, infuriated breathing coming from his sniffer. She threw up her head to glance at the irksome mask her bonder wore as he stormed his way into the cell and forced the door to shut by pelting his fist down on the red button labelled "door" with such velocity that she could've heard the damn thing splinter. But she didn't flinch. She just sat motionless, staring with curious eyes, more interested in the emotion known as anger.

'Fucking Max Engel,' he upbraided through gritted teeth, not realising he spat out his words and now showed a face similar to a dog with rabies as strings of saliva dribbled down his lips. Sam cocked her head to the side as if curiously examining him and the expression he wore, not saying anything in response or suggesting he sit down and take a breather. Hell, she didn't even make a sound; even a whimper of fear for her bonder's outburst wasn't heard, which, if Fredrickson were capable of rational thought at this time, would find most concerning. On the contrary, Sam had shown very little emotion and displayed little to no fear or dislike for this outburst of anger. She just sat eerily on her chair, not moving so much as a flinch, but who was to say that she was feeling something on the inside and was simply hiding it from Fredrickson.

Fredrickson threw his paperwork down on the desk, stomped over to one of the steel walls on the side, and shot his foot at it, taking out his anger. Sam watched him do so, her eyes never leaving his shape. He leaned over, placing his hands on the wall and taking a vital moment to breathe heavily, taking his time to calm himself and get adequately prepared to do his work.

Fredrickson then closed his eyes and, balled up his fists and bit his lip – he could feel the Valium finally taking effect – he was starting to feel himself calming. This was a good thing. It was good that he began to grab the wheel and steer it away before the vehicle crashed into something else. Fredrickson closed his eyes, gripped his chest, and took a much-needed deep breath.

After catching his breath and staring at the wall for two minutes straight, Alexander Fredrickson finally regained enough composure to banish the sweat away from his forehead with the back of his hand and let out a long sigh. He combed his brittle brown hair with his fingers and straightened his white lab coat. Ashamed he'd allowed himself to become overwhelmed with frustration, Fredrickson kept his head low, veering away from the wall and dragging the chair out from underneath the desk, far enough for him to plant his arse upon. He sighed deeply and ran his fingers through his hair and down his red, sweaty face.

'Sorry about that outburst, Sam. I hope I didn't interrupt your train of thought if you were reflecting about our last session together or your new "alive" appearance,' he said miserably, thinking about how the snapping noise that came from Engel's nose. 'It's just Max Engel… some fat smug-headed guy that grinds on me. And this morning, he…' he paused, thinking of how to piece his sentence, 'really got on my nerves, bitching about this old blind goat he had named Wendy. He can marry the eyeless bitch for all I care, just anything to shut him up and make him fuck off! If I'm lucky enough, Wendy might turn the tables on him and will show him who's the dominant one and attack him and rip his tongue out so he won't be able to bitch and harass anyone again, just like Henrik!' Fredrickson snickered wickedly at the thought of Engel not having a tongue and not being able to speak, blubbering like some bratty kid. Still, he instantly stopped laughing when he thought of Losnedahl and how he'd disrespected him by wishing someone would end up with his fate. 'I shouldn't say that; it was immature and disrespectful of Henrik; now he, on the other hand, is a good man, Sam; I don't want you getting Henrik and Max confused when you are released.' Fredrickson was all bark and no bite; he may say brutal things about people and may have said that he wished someone would drop dead so that they'd get off his case. But, of course, he didn't mean to wish death upon one of his colleagues. But even so, Engel had dipped his foot too far and pushed more than just an anger button in Fredrickson's brain. Engel may have pressed the volcano button, triggering Fredrickson into an explosive fit of furious anger similar to when a volcano erupts, spilling molten lava down its mountainsides. Still, at least Engel didn't press the nuke button to transform Fredrickson into a destructive, violent creature from fiction that would take serious effort to calm down. Thankfully, Fredrickson seldom went into nuke because of the scripted antidepressant drugs provided by his psychologist around seven years back when Fredrickson's anger was almost at nuke if it wasn't for Deborah suggesting that he see his shrink and get him on medication for his outbursts.

Fredrickson let out another controlled sigh, turning his attention to his papers on the desk. 'So, I guess we should begin this session as usual with the things you've learned and know now; thanks to the GFOSAR for providing you with me and, with my help, tutoring you on this path to becoming human again.

Fredrickson did the usual thing he always did during the start of his bonding sessions with Sam. He pulled out a blank sheet of A4 paper from his pile of many documents. He took any colour pen from his lab coat pocket, handing both the form and pen to her so he could observe how her handwriting and spelling had developed during these past twenty-one days (had they improved?

Suppose Fredrickson would find out). A written message would be able to grant him an insight into how she'd developed during his time with her when compared to the first time they'd met, on the 8th, when Sam was but an empty shell of a person up until they'd started bonding together on October 9th right up to now on October 30th, marking their official 21st bonding day.

Sam did as she was told by her bonder without protest. Taking the sheet of paper and pen, she began to write something; what it was, Fredrickson didn't know and didn't really care. Fredrickson's morning was ruined by the ever so impatient Max Engel; therefore, he wasn't exactly in the mood to read scrawled broken English written down on paper by a zombie, so he fiddled with the pistol inside his pocket, waiting for her to finish what she was writing. 'Remember to push the pen and your written work back to me when finished. As you know, it's my job to observe your understanding of things,' he deadpanned, resting his chin on his wrist, watching her spiritlessly, expecting the usual, predictable, broken English. Fredrickson waited for a total of seven minutes and forty-four seconds for Sam to finish writing her passage. Fredrickson noted how long it was taking in his notes. Goddamn, woman. You must be writing everything you've learnt, he thought idly to himself, taking a few glances at her and the passage that she'd been writing.

Sam looked up at him, the usual straight face occurring on her blank but beautiful, regular-looking face. With a final flourish, Sam stopped writing. Her pretty mouth pulled up in a corner, a smirk. She flicked the pen; it skittered across the table and almost rolled off, but Fredrickson stopped it with his index finger, looking at her sincerity.

'Done?' he asked, reclaiming his pen and putting it back into his lab coat pocket. Sam nodded. 'Alright, let's see it.' Sam put two fingers on the paper and slid the written piece up towards him, which he plucked from underneath her fingers, twisting it around so he'd be able to read it; her eyes were trained intensely on him, not avoiding his eyes for even a second, not even blinking.

It made Fredrickson a little uneasy how she stared at him. Even so, he shook his head and looked at the piece of paper, and what he saw written down made his eyes widen. Sam had written the passage in perfect readable English! It had appeared to show more than sixty words, all with ideal spelling and punctuation, as if a high-schooler had written it for a creative short story. Remember that a zombie over the 70-year AOR had written this, and it wasn't known for 70-year AOR zombies to produce such tangible elegance in writing. Fredrickson read the passage wide-eyed and mouth moving along to the words written down:

Hello, Mr. Fredrickson; in case you were wondering, no, I ultimately wasn't bothered by your sudden volcanic episode. A few days ago, I had recently gone through a similar anger episode because I was a little upset about when you left me suddenly on day eight, but don't worry, I have calmed down since that episode. Furthermore, thank you for giving me this look and giving me a chance to read like you. Now I can live among other people like you undetected, like I'm not even a zombie or dead at all. I want to thank you for considering me. I may be over 70 years old, but that is fine. I may used to look all rotten and decaying at first glance, but it does not mean I'm stupid. We, zombies, are more capable of things than you living people realise. So, Fredrickson, I take my hat off and give you my every curtsey. So, sincerely thanks again, Mr.

Fredrickson; I applaud your hard work in getting me this far. Enjoy the afterlife.

The last bit was unreadable to Fredrickson because it was too small for his eyes, but other than being unable to read the previous paragraph, he was left utterly speechless and stunned by this. Fredrickson looked up from the paper at Sam with unbelieving eyes, who continued to sit still, a slight smirk of satisfaction creeping on her face along with narrowed, unblinking eyes. After finishing reading the words written down, he put the paper with the passage down, unable to speak in response. Fredrickson's matching brown eyes darted over to Sam's pale grey ones, feeling a potent mix of emotions, all trundled over each other, making it impossible to handle a specific discernible emotion. Fredrickson couldn't push away the gut feeling that told him that he'd created a mistake when he took the role of working with Sam and wanted to request a transfer for another less developed zombie, a zombie that didn't scare him so much. Her lifeless glance was refined, but it was her eyes; there was a picture inside them that he couldn't shake off, that hellish mountain inside those grey orbs had haunted him and continued to do so. Then, as if he had been smacked on the back of the head by some unseen force, he remembered the firearm in his pocket. He took it out, scrutinised it, and then looked at Sam gingerly as if he felt an eerie presence from just gazing upon that smirk on her face.

But when he looked up and saw those eyes, how they didn't blink and remained firmly on his, he cringed, scooting his chair slightly as if he wanted to get away from her and those… those eyes. Those cunning, twisted eyes. Was she playing him for a fool this whole time? No, she couldn't be; she was another zombie that was being bonded with correctly this time, and she was plainly showing him gratitude for it. In her own unprompted words, she had said in her notes that she was grateful for him and the process they'd made. And there was nothing wrong with that. This was what he'd been working for, wasn't it?

So why the gun? Why was he thinking about aiming it and propelling a bullet between Sam's eyes, ending his time with her? He didn't even know why he'd brought the damn thing in the first place. Maybe it was because he thought that she might have to get used to seeing guns outside? Perhaps she might have to use them outside? He didn't know; he was probably just not thinking clearly, Fredrickson closed his eyes and sighed, soon recovering his scences after he'd felt like he was possessed or something had taken control over his mind and thoughts.

Fredrickson took a deep breath and dropped the pistol on the desk. He settled back into his chair, throwing his hands up to his head and sliding them down his face, his eyes once again finding their way back to the passage written down on the A4 sheet of paper for a few seconds. He couldn't help the overwhelming feeling of merit as he cupped his mouth and stared at the passage with wide peepers. The anger and frustration he'd felt earlier seemed to die in a second after re-reading the passage again for the second time with more thirst. He looked up from the passage to Sam, then at the paper, Sam, paper, Sam, paper, as if he was trying to convince himself that this message was, in fact, written by a zombie that used to be a living skeleton. 'Sam…this… this is brilliant… absolutely brilliant,' Fredrickson spoke through his hand; he could not conceive what his eyes were reading, and knowing that a zombie could write a passage so diligently. It provided him with a sense of pleasure that only Deborah in bed could give him. He felt a smile blossom, his eyes bloomed with exhilaration, pushing the A4 written passage to the side. He put his cupped hands on the desk and stared wide-eyed and dreamily at Sam like she was the woman he had come to idolise as the saviour of the human race. Sam's smirk shunted into a small frown while still retaining the sights narrowed on him. 'Sam, I… I need to tell you something extraordinary' he announced gracefully, studying Sam, who looked back at him, putting her chin in her palms, dispensing non-interest for him and what he had to say.

'When a zombie reaches a specific point such as you have, intelligence-wise, and has transpired through the surgery into looking human again in the same route, it won't be long now until you're ready to leave this facility and re-emerge in the city as a "human," or shall we say, a "successful zombie." And as much as we bonders would love for you successful bonded zombies to stay here with us and help us clean up and be our associates, helping us with future zombies expecting to undergo the same bonding method as you have, but unfortunately, that isn't what happens when zombies are ranked successful and ready to be discharged into the barren wasteland.

Like all the bonders here with successful zombies, I must let you go. But before I do, I will give you the key to your chains and sign the deliverance papers so you can officially leave and venture into the world beyond the GFOSAR. Fredrickson reached into his breast pocket and pulled out a single red antibiotic that Sam had grown very accustomed to seeing and eating.

'I'll need to supply you with enough capsules of hunger drugs to aid in sedating your appetite … for the time being, as I'm sure you are thoroughly aware of by this point. They'll help you do what all bonders come to expect of good zombies, and that is to consume human foods, regaining their human tastebuds again! Hopefully, changing that voracious appetite for brains and flesh.' He paused momentarily, seeming to be lost in thought or perhaps had forgotten his train of thought. Sam tipped her head curiously as to why he'd stopped talking and was inadvertently staring into her eyes with dazed amazement like he'd become frozen in time. She brushed the gauze strapped neatly and tightly around her abdomen, still grasping a rugged deformity of the hole from underneath all the layers upon layers of bandage. I guess that was one thing that Grossman couldn't fix to perfection. Whilst it was covered in bandaging, if one were to touch those coverings, they'd feel a disfigurement that felt like there were no organs or stomach inside. So to hide Sam's Death Mark, it had to be concealed in wrappings and covered with clothing.

'I honestly just can't believe that you've reached this far… you possess no discernible idea of just how hard it is to get a single zombie to this state of aptitude in just this condensed amount of time. Fuck! It hasn't even been a damn month! And you've already displayed phenomenal intelligence in just this amount of time!' Fredrickson beamed as a scant tear trickled down his raised cheeks. 'You seem about ready to face the world as a successfully bonded zombie. I don't see anything else I can do that can improve the state you're currently in. So, before I hand you over to Zone 5 and let you go, free to live your life again as a human, I'd like to close off our final session together by asking some questions concerning your previous life as a living person before your death. That's if you can remember it, of course.' He said, struggling to contain his childish wonder of his first successful zombie and oppression of seeing her go. While he may have hated her during the first sessions, thinking that she was just going to join the ranks of Fredrickson's failures, but over the course of the past twenty-one days, Fredrickson had started to see that Sam wasn't like the other failures he'd worked with. She may not have known it at the time. Still, Sam had spunk, and he admired it greatly. Yes, she may have frightened him on some days, but that was because she was determined to become human again, and he could bypass that because Sam showed an eagerness to become human again that those other failures hadn't. He slid another blank sheet of A4 paper, popped off the cap of a blue ballpoint pen, and handed it to her, allowing her to do the rest and write the answers. 'Do you remember your name?' Fredrickson asked.

Sam shrugged causally, symbolising that she didn't know too well, and Fredrickson noted it down, ticking the tick box on his paperwork attached to a clipboard in front of him. 'What kind of person were you?' he asked another question, still holding some connection to the first one. Sam held the pen close as she began to scribble her answer before holding it up for him to register. She'd written that she wasn't too sure what kind of person she was in life, and that was understandable; she'd been dead for so long that the memories of her past life were sealed deep within a box without a key. Fredrickson furrowed his brow. 'Well, alright then, it seemed that because of what you've been learning here as a zombie, most of the memories have been stored up deep inside the brains filing cabinet, which will need some serious digging into to find, but I'll save you that, and I'll stop asking the rest of the questions. However, there is one question I have to get out of the way,' he furrowed his eyebrows close collectively in an intimidating look of interrogation. Sam smirked at him; her eyes narrowed too, ready for the question as she knew that it might be one of the last things, he ever asked a zombie.

'When did you die? How many years ago was it?' Fredrickson interrogated, hoping that she could give him some discernible kind of evidence regarding her past as that was part of his job. Sam gave him a scant expression that, upon vivid inspection, gave the impression of something… ill-intended. Sam pulled the piece of paper towards her once more and scribbled down her answer but didn't give him the report immediately. She held it for a bit, teasing him. Sam looked at him with seduction, which carried a certain kind of creepiness, revealing different intentions from the more switched-on person to the ones Fredrickson had planned for her. She pointed upward, wanting him to read it whilst standing up. He looked puzzled by this sudden, strange request, but even so, he listened and stood up like she'd wanted, pushing his chair out without question. Now, Sam slid the sheet of paper to him, kneeling over the side of her chair to pull up some documents that she'd kept with her since bonding day three and slid them over to him with a sly grin; she'd kept them with her as before she'd been curious about them when Fredrickson had abandoned them, now she decided to give them back after she'd read through them. She was eerily silent while Fredrickson took the sheet and the papers from her and examined the words she'd written when he asked about her date of death. First, it said; 76 years ago, 1980. Fredrickson's mouth sank, amazed by her ability to remember the exact year of her death. Why that, but not her name, then?, he wondered. Fredrickson then flipped the sheet to the back of the pile of paperwork, and Fredrickson's heart sank so deep in his chest that he almost felt like he was going to faint or, worse, have a heart attack. Sam took the paper with her written passage and circled the last three tiny words with the pen, so the next time he looked, he'd have to pay close observation to the written words. It said: *Enjoy the afterlife!* Did this mean that Sam had been secretly planning to...!

'How...did you?' Fredrickson shuddered; his eyes widened further as the fear Fredrickson had once covered up began to bubble up. Still, he snubbed it as best he could and kept reading through the paperwork, putting his hand over his mouth, and taking a step back in horror, coming to the disturbing understanding that she'd been reading through all the bad shit he'd done in his life, the written A4 dairy entries that he must've accidently taken with him and dropped in the cell on the same day (*how the fuck did they end up in my bonding papers in the first place? And how did I not notice that they were missing from my desk drawers?*). And that the scary thing was that Sam knew all about them. She'd learned about the nasty things he'd done in his life, abusing homeless people, and marrying Deborah because she was good-looking. Sam knew it all! He started to quake with anxiety, his heart pounding inside his ribcage; his breathing became hesitant and full of panic. Droplets of sweat crept down his face that matched the exact same mask he'd worn the day Deborah passed away. 'Th-These are my SINS…' he whimpered, glancing up from the papers in his trembling hands. Then he noticed Sam was holding a pistol, the very same gun he'd brought in the last effort to dispose of her if she ever decided to turn on him. 'Sa-Sam.' Fredrickson quivered about to say something else, but a loud shot echoed in his ears, blotting out his voice.

Steam billowed out of the pistol's barrel as a bullet shot out at such an alarming speed, striking Fredrickson in his apple. At first, Fredrickson was frozen, trying to process what had just happened. Then he felt it, warm liquid spilling down his neck, then the sharp feeling inside his neck. He'd been shot! 'Wah? What the FUCK?!' Fredrickson shuddered, thrusting a hand up to his neck, holding it as blood squirted out of the wound. He could feel the ungodly bullet taking up residence inside his throat and wanted to cry from the pain, but he was unable to. Alexander Fredrickson tried with all his willpower to plug up the oozing orifice in his neck with his hand, putting pressure on it, but the more pressure he added to the wound, the more blood he had pushed out making it hurt a hell of a lot more, doing the complete opposite of what he'd originally intended. He even transferred the bullet more into his neck, which just made things graver on his behalf.

The blood was now beginning to gush out with more force and velocity. Fredrickson felt as if he could pass out from blood loss. Fredrickson's eyes streamed with tears. *This is it! The bitch shot me with my own cunting gun! This is the end of the road, old horse. I'm fucking done! Sam has been playing a role in a twisted game that I didn't realise was being played; she wasn't hoping to get her life back! She was...!* his thoughts screamed with horror. His body was starting to feel weak from the amount of blood he'd lost. He could feel his life slipping away. Why didn't I use the damn thing before her? He didn't know how long he could keep up the exertion to secure his throat and stop it from oozing crimson. His vision was groggy, his hands started slipping from his throat, and he was afraid (was this true, legitimate fear.) He looked through his watery, sickened eyes at Sam, who'd leapt up onto the desk like some feral creature depicted only in campfire stories. She was sitting on balanced knees, smirking down at him sitting meekly on the floor, trying to keep as much blood inside his neck even if he knew it was useless and was dancing a precarious dance on thin ice. Sam then rose tall, stretched out her arms to grope at something in the air that only she could see. But to Fredrickson's dismay, she lowered her arms in front of him as if mocking him, teasing him, showing him that those clenching fingers would go around his neck soon. He imagined the cold touch of her fingers clamping down around his throat, wanting to choke him and snuff the life out of him; he wasn't planning on waiting to feel such a sensation; he knew that he had to get away from Sam, or better, find Boson or anybody to restrain Sam and kill her before she could cause him any more pain.

Fredrickson tried retreating, shuffling his legs in one desperate battle to get away from his zombie-turned pursuer. Still holding his neck, blood seeped through his fingers and out of any open area around his hand, caking his hands red with his own ripe blood. Sam threw herself onto him, pinning him to the ground and pushed out more blood from the impact, squirting splodges of blood onto her face. Being a zombie, and a violent one, by this unforeseen exhibition of aggression towards her bonder, she wasn't at all disturbed by the blood running down her cheeks like tears. She rather enjoyed watching it gush out of his neck, finding his meek effort to stop it sadistically amusing. That was until Sam began to snarl; her teeth borne with drool dribbling from her mouth in a twisted psychopath grin, and Fredrickson took the obvious hint that his life was fucked and that he was going to die in a not-so-friendly way.

Fredrickson took his hands away from his throat, knowing what was going to happen next. But even so, Fredrickson tried one last valiant effort to keep her away hoping someone might walk past the window, seeing him and his struggle. Then they could enter B-35 and help him, disposing of Sam while getting him to the medical bay to patch up. But sadly, he'd been prodding the flame too long, and it was time for him to perish. Fredrickson continued to hold onto Sam's head, pushing her back while the blood proceeded to spill from his neck from where she'd shot him. It was fortunate for him the bullet had just missed an important artery in his neck, but however it did hit a blood artery, spilling out gallons of blood that was sure to fill up a small plastic zip lunch bag.

This was her plan! Sam was buying her time as Fredrickson bonded with her, giving her more intelligence, and even with the intelligence and fresh coat of skin, Sam was intending to kill Fredrickson! She had no desire to become the human race's saviour; her intentions were far worse than Fredrickson could've ever perceived.

Fredrickson sought to hold back against the rabid and violent Sam that he was only starting to enjoy the company of. Still, with every struggle and every ounce of blood lost, the weaker and paler he became as blood started to fill his mouth and he started to choke. His strength leaving him. He wanted to push her off and punch the big black emergency button on the opposite side of the door to let everyone wandering about the facility know that Sam had gone bad and was trying to kill him. Still, Sam had him pinned and he couldn't shove her off as much as he wanted to as everything was hell; even breathing and clinging to life was tough; the more blood he lost had just made things twice as difficult. 'You're a bad, BAD girl...' Fredrickson rasped; it hurt to speak as blood spilled out of his lips.

Now, all the vigour he once had forsaken him; and his arms felt heavy as if they were made of stones, but he still kept up the fight in holding Sam back even if he knew his endeavours were hopeless; he wasn't ready to go down without one last fight. No, Alexander Fredrickson wasn't the type to back down so quickly; he kept it up until his arms were screaming. Tired of Fredrickson keeping her back, Sam seized his arms and pushed them down to his sides forcefully without much work. The man was dying; he hadn't the strength left to keep up the struggle against a hungry zombie. Wasting no more time playing with him, Sam shot her teeth down into Fredrickson's neck like another bullet and sunk them deep inside his neck, tearing a large chunk of his flesh off while he was still stubbornly clung to life. But before he could scream and possibly alert someone passing by, Sam descended her teeth back into his neck once more and began shredding her way through his neck, eating his flesh along with drinking the blood like a cold-hearted feral vampire. The only thing Fredrickson could do was watch, unable to do anything as his life was gradually robbed from him.

When Sam had finished consuming Fredrickson's throat, she wiped her mouth and smiled wickedly at the twitched body in front of her. Fredrickson's bleeding neck was now left with large chunks of flesh gone, his spine visible. He was left in a state so unholy that it was a wonder that he still kept clinging to life. But soon enough, his twitching body eventually stopped working. After a few more seconds, his heart stopped, and he was dead, bathed in his own blood and heartlessly murdered by his highly intelligent, bonded zombie, Sam, who stood before his lifeless body, smiling.

Sam wiped her mouth, licking the blood off her hand like a cat grooming itself and stared at the body of Fredrickson, which lay motionless in a growing pool of his own blood. The unsettling, evil smirk that haunted Fredrickson again spread onto her face. She walked over to his body, feeling no shame for stepping in the red pond around him; she walked over to the number lock on the side of the door. The chains were off her. Sam took one final glance back at Fredrickson's corpse on the floor and chuckled, pinning the code 1-9-8-0 into the lock and allowing herself out of cell B-35. She was free!

Chapter 22

Now, things were only beginning to go South. It was a worse kind of luck for the other bonders in the facility. If they were already having bad times with their subjects, things would only get worse for them because now a bonder had been killed, and a particular zombie had escaped using his card. Fredrickson had never got the chance to trigger the emergency button like Cansu Aksoy did before sending Ziya off to be disposed of. He'd lost so much blood from his throat that it was not long before his cheeks started to lose their colour, his eyes rolling to the back of his head, losing consciousness, which ultimately led to his painful and bloody death.

And now his killer was out of the cell, wandering about the bonding corridors like a lion prowling. Sam grinned with malice, harnessing the knowledge that she was out of her cell and that she didn't have the pestering Fredrickson in the way to stop her intentions and the malevolent things that was cooking inside her dead skull. She was Free!

Smiling with an unearthly glee at the thought that she was finally out of that prison that Fredrickson had kept her inside of, Sam strolled down the (for once) deserted hallways of the GFOSAR full of murderous intent. Waves of pleasure danced through Sam's body. She tongued her new, sharp thin lips and relished the copper salt of Fredrickson's leftover blood on them, her hunger not satiated, her appetite for human brains awakened. She was hungry, hungry for brains. Sam didn't chafe in taking a hunger drug that she stole from Fredrickson during their struggle before he cashed out. Though she knew she would need the pills later. But for now, she just stroked her shorts pocket, which hid the drugs away, putting a bloody hand stain on it. But of course, she didn't care. Sam glanced, eyes browsing around at each independent person and zombie. She caught a glimpse of the three-fingered human-robot marching down the hallway towards cell B-28, unknowingly approaching Sam's direction, alien to what Sam had done in cell B-35. Sam simply looked at the Turkish woman with her usual sagging face and eyes, which looked like they were ready to fall out of her sockets, and her smile broadened. Cansu's head was low, buried in paperwork, as she brushed by Sam, colliding with her shoulder without offering her an apology back. But Sam wasn't expecting an apology either way, and it wasn't like a sorry was going to stop her from the thought of snapping the woman's neck and listening to the satisfying crack the spine would make as it was twisted. It only made her plans work out in her favour when the Turkish woman strode past her as if not registering that she was even there in the first place or the stink that fanned off her like the world's smelliest flower. Sam's plans were coming together, and Cansu would be one of the lucky contenders to see this plan go ahead.

Sam laid back and watched the woman go. She knew it was not wise to attack her on sight like most zombies would, as killing her in the middle of this walkway would draw attention to herself. If Sam was going to get out of this building undetected and without bullet-shaped holes in her newly grafted body. She knew she'd need to lay low and play her cards just right. To put this into fruition, Sam took a step forward to stalk Cansu, ghosting her while hiding her figure away if Cansu sought to look behind her if she was suspicious that someone was following deathly in sync behind her to a cell containing a male crawler zombie who'd been christened with the name, Berk (the French word for Yuck). As Sam stalked Cansu, keeping a steady distance between her, she looked through the glass. She could see that this Berk fellow was doped on the drugs, hiding the obvious factor that he was starving.

She could also see his feet were dangling uncomfortably off the chair, she could see Berk's legs were broken, rendering them useless. Her smile broadened once more, her brows lowered as she began to understand what her goal was, what she'd planned for the rest of the human race, and it wasn't stopping the infection of the mortuus carnem parasite; her ideas for humanity's future were, let's say… the opposite: making blood angels in entrails and sitting on a throne of corpses, laughing manically as the reminder of Britain's population is snuffed out.

Sam thoroughly enjoyed the enticing feeling as she bit down on her pathetic bonder's neck and watched the life leave him. She wanted more. She wanted more blood on her hands, more blood in her mouth. More blood!

Sam waited patiently behind Cansu, watched as she was about to pin the code into the number lock to let herself inside the cell so she could bond with her new crawler. But the urge for more blood was taking over Sam, and she decided she couldn't wait any longer, so it was her time to strike! Sam jumped Cansu, suppressing the Turkish woman by clamping a hand over her mouth so she couldn't scream, not to mention that the smell of a rotting hand underneath surgically grafted skin touching your mouth was bound to make anyone gag. And to Cansu this was made a reality, the only sound she could make were muffled fearful cries as Sam led her away into a small storage room like a criminal holding a hostage at gunpoint.

Cansu flailed around in Sam's grasp, endeavouring to fruitlessly punch and slap at Sam, trying to pry her palm away from her muzzle, but with no prevail, Sam just constricted her grip around Cansu's mouth, intending to suffocate her. But the Turkish bitch was stronger than Sam initially anticipated and wouldn't bite the dust so easily like her late bonder, Cansu clung to life. So, Sam resolved to end it quickly. With one decisive twist, Cansu's neck made a snapping sound and her flaying around came to a dead halt. Sam had broken Cansu's neck with ease and dropped her lifeless body to the ground. Sam then bent down to the body and fished out Cansu's key card from her maroon cardigan's breast pocket. In no hurry, Sam took a moment, studied the photo on the key card, and let out a light disbelieving chortle at seeing the woman on the key card was actually smiling. Even if it did appear fake or most likely forced, it was still a sight to behold (seeing Cansu Aksoy with a smile on her plastic mug). Sam scoffed at the photo, holding it in her hand. She left the room where Cansu Aksoy's body lay and ventured over to Berk's cell. She swiped the card down the slot instead of putting a pin she didn't know into the keypad. The door flung open with a loud BZZT. Sam entered. Sam gawked down and studied Berk, chained up to the wall by his neck like he was an animal in a zoo. The grin never once dissolving from her face, Sam knelt down to the restraint crawler on the ground and prodded at his broken shin, telling him to wake up. Berk sprang to life as soon as Sam touched him. He snarled hungrily, slobbering like a dog with rabies: Sam brought a finger to her lips and blew into it, gesturing him to be quiet. Berk shut up.

Sam caressed the chain that kept Berk near the wall; Berk grunted sadly as if telling her that the chain was too tight and that it was strangling him. Sam knew what she had to do; she yanked at the chain with both hands, hauled at it until it gave way and snapped off its hinges, freeing Berk. The two zombies met each other for about a minute. Berk stared drunkenly at Sam feeling no hunger interest for her as he could determine that she was dead like him just by smelling her. Sam steered the crawler to the open door, communicating in grunts and groans, telling the crawler zombie that he was free and, that he could go and eat as many brains as he wanted and that nothing was going to stop him. Within less than a minute of misuse, Berk was out. He was shuffling and heaving his mutilated body, the bones protruding out, his legs scraping the floor as he left cell B-28 in search of a seasoned human to feast upon.

Sam left cell B-28 shortly after watching Berk become distant from her. The piercing sound of screaming followed, supplying Sam with the wicked sense of satisfaction that Berk had found his first victim: a male doctor who got in his way. Berk crawled over to the terrified doctor and sunk his teeth into the doctor's left ankle, making him cry out from the shrill pang in his ankle. The doctor tried to shake Berk off, but he wouldn't budge, so the doctor hobbled over to the side and fisted a large black button that sat underneath large bold letters: outbreak, letting everyone in the GFOSAR know that there was a breach and that a hostile zombie was lose. The flashing red alert button labelled outbreak triggered an ear-splitting racket that chimed into the people's ears inside the GFOSAR. At the same time, it firmly secured the zombie bonding cells, locking them tight like a rabbit in a trap.

The evacuation alarm gave the haunting message that was loud and shrill, similar to the nuclear explosion that shook Chernobyl, providing a clear signal to those even inside that weren't in the cells, whether it be the wealthy shits seeking refuge in the supposed sanctuary of the basement, or the doctors and nurses, or the scientists and bonders that weren't working with a zombie that they had to flee the structure immediately, as once the outbreak alarm was initiated, nowhere in the facility would be safe until the zombies skulking around had been destroyed by the patrolling soldiers. But this sadly wasn't the case in the GFOSAR; the place wasn't as safe and lucky as people first thought; it may have once been when it was established back in 2027, but that was because they weren't dealing with the dangers and intelligent zombie named Sam. Now they were, and God help them.

This just made things even more entertaining for Sam. It would be easier to annihilate people because of people's panic. They wouldn't fight back because they would be too over-cumbered by their fears and the growing dangers spilling around them. With the increasing number of bites, Sam would give the people, it wouldn't be long until those soldiers were outnumbered by the growing number of unbonded zombies and zombie bonders. It would just make things more fun for Sam to walk freely amongst the panic; hearing screams of terror as people were torn apart. It would be like Mozart to her ears.

Sam caught a glimpse of the American security guard, Robert Boson stomping his way down the bonding cells like a charging rhino, coming to the doctor's aid and kicking Berk off the doctor's leg. Sam fingered her chin, engrossed in how this scene played out. She watched Boson pick up the already infected doctor by the back of his collar and toss him out of his way as if he were a ragdoll, knowing that he'd turn into a zombie in a matter of time.

Boson stormed head first like a quarterback, commemorating his glory days as a footballer to pin Berk down with his large foot, holding him down on his chest and observing the crawler's puny efforts to get away from his hulking captor. Berk squirmed like a fish out of water, grunting and growling to be released. Boson indulged no time and took no delight in the crawler's struggles. He advanced his other foot down on Berk's head and, in less than a second, had spattered Berk's skull in pieces, brain mass exploded out like a cherry bomb in a Jack-o-lantern along with the bloodied chips of what had survived of his head. Seeing this had caused Sam's smile to dribble just a little at the distasteful sight of a late football player overpowering a simplistic crawler zombie before stomping on his head and killing him without so much as breaking a sweat.

Despite not knowing his ghoulish backstory before coming here, Sam felt that this man could not be permitted to live anymore and savoured feeling the hunger surging through her body (no one deserved to live). She elected to stop putting off food by taking the drugs like a good zombie would; alternatively, Sam did the reverse and invested in her primal hunger. Sam licked her lips, eyeing Boson with devastating intimidation, knowing that he would soon join the undead's ranks or see his family again in the afterlife (if there was one). Like Boson had done to Berk before caving his head in, Sam snarled before springing up into a sprint towards Boson like an athlete springing to the finishing line, to which Boson had unmistakably caught notice of issuing in him contorting his face to show more fury, from the first moment he saw he was coming out from her appointment with Grossman, he knew that he hadn't liked her. 'You? Fredrickson should have disposed of you!' Steam billowed out his nostrils in the same way steam boils out of a kettle. He recognised her when he came up the stairs, seeing Fredrickson escorting her out of the medical ward; Fredrickson may have been faithful that Sam was going to be a success, as Boson could read it in his face. Boson knew otherwise and wouldn't let some female zombie slip by him - even if she did look drop-dead gorgeous with a human appearance - she was still that black-haired zombie he'd heard Fredrickson talk about. And surgery or no surgery, zombies were zombies to Boson.

Boson clenched his hand, balling it into a mighty fist and one you wouldn't want to be on the other side of. He drew his fist back, ready to send Sam flying, when she got in deathly close proximity of him. Boson thought his brute strength would be enough to fix the stunning female zombie. But unlucky for Boson, he wasn't a bonder; he was plainly an ex-footballer turned bodyguard to the bonders, so he had no knowledge of the potential zombies can make during their time with bonders. So, when Sam got to within a metre's length in front of him, Boson fired his fist like a bullet toward her. Hoping to strike her and pelt her halfway across the hallway. But thanks to Fredrickson's teachings, Sam prophesied that he would use brute force as a weapon against her. If she were a typical unbonded zombie, she would fall straight for his fist and end up on the other side of the hallway. But Sam wasn't an ordinary zombie. She was smart; could think for herself, like a person. Sam counted Boson's fist and ducked, zipped to his slide, and dodged being penetrated by this hulk of a man by slipping underneath his legs like a nimble gymnast. Sam leapt onto Boson's back, her arms locked around his neck, and showed minimal manifestations of letting go. Boson tried to cope against her by endeavouring to thrust her off his back. 'Get fucking off me fucking zombie bitch!' he howled, swaying around swiftly, striving to shake her off so he could terminate her in the same way he finished off Berk by throwing her down and crushing her cranium beneath his boot. But Sam refused to launch; she kept purchase around Boson's neck, using force and speed to ascend, lapping her legs around his gullet, and holding onto his head while Boson started to panic; his efforts to wrangle her off became more urgent. But Sam still didn't launch; even though she was tossed around like on a rodeo machine, she kept a steady anchor on him. Sam bit onto Boson's bald scalp. Boson felt the searing onslaught of pain on his head and hissed, trying not to yell and show weakness as much as he wanted to. Boson was inaugurated to shake more vibrantly, desperate to get her off, even working to uproot her like a weed with his big hands. But the fight inside him was becoming weaker as the strain was ripening to an unbearable position. Every time he sought to fight against

Sam, she just sunk her teeth deeper into his head, prompting him to a screaming fit. He couldn't keep the fight in any longer but still ventured on. Boson wailed in excessive agony as his energy started to fail him.

The pain was becoming too critical for him to handle. Sam descended her teeth into his head further, and feeling them stop, hitting something hard and bony, she had made it to the skull. She was amazed at how Boson was still standing even with his skull in the open, wondering why he hadn't bought it yet, why he was still endeavouring to cling to life even though he knew it was pointless and that he was pretty much dead as soon as Sam took the first bite out of his head. *'fuck you bitch! I hope you fucking die and go to hell. I hope your remains are burnt to a fucking crisp!'* Boson condemned Sam, which only egged her in wanting to cause more agony to him, seeing his attempts of fighting her and screaming at her did nothing for him and that she took a great deal of pleasure in hearing his pain. The fight was already Sam's victory; she was nimbler and had him at her mercy; it wouldn't be long until Sam decided to cut the wires holding Boson together. She smiled wickedly and chiselled her way through his skull, provoking Boson to cry and scream at the top of his lungs. Sam didn't care about the ear-splitting noise coming out of Boson's mouth; as a matter of fact, she rather enjoyed the sound as if it were music and he was the maestro composing his final piece, bathing in it as she was getting her fill, eating away at Robert Boson's brain. At the same time, his feet stumbled back and forth before he finally succumbed to the floor. Boson had perished as soon as Sam had bitten down into his brain and tore out a chunk, squirting arcs of bright red blood out of his scalp and onto Sam's face, painting her whole face and breast area red with crimson.

Boson's dead body crumpled to the ground like Goliath falling to David shortly after Sam had swallowed the first lump of his brain. Sam went down with Boson's corpse, like how a knight is often depicted after slaying the dragon. She was still latching onto his head like a prized artifact. Sam consumed more of his brain, not stopping until she had finished, eating Boson's entire brain before getting off him, satisfied with her meal.

Sam sought no point in wiping the blood off her mouth; the more blood, the better. She walked away from Boson's corpse without looking back, leaving the other zombies to feed on the rest of him when she got them out with a button at the GFOSAR's main terminal. Sam stopped and peered through the cell labelled B-22, seeing what her old bonder had dubbed the blind old goat and the fat little man she'd heard Fredrickson mention at the start of today. Max Engel pounded on the cell's entrance, imploring to be let out since he couldn't use his ID card to get out since Lockdown was initiated. In tears, he was pleading imploringly, knowing that his blind zombie, Wendy, wasn't fully bonded and that she was just like most zombies that were starving. 'Someone get me out of this fricking cell and help me outta here. I'll make it worth your while!' when Engel saw Sam, he was visibly delighted. 'You, woman with the black hair in front of this cell. Get me out! Please! I'm not ready to die!' he appealed, acknowledging Sam in front of him, staring at him soaked with blood and grinning. Engel only took a minute to see the grey pupils and pink sclera. Now he realised why she hadn't tried anything to rescue him and simply smiled at him. The cognisance socked Engel like a clock to the face. The bitch is a zombie! One that has had the surgery to look human and she was drenched in blood. Human blood!

Engel's eyes widened; he stepped back in horror. 'Oh, God... Ye-Your Alexander Fredrickson's bitch, Y-

Your Sam!' he sputtered, withdrawing from the door as Sam shuffled closer to the window peering through it, watching Engel shitting himself. She waved at him cruelly, and Engel tripped and fell over. Sam glanced at Wendy sitting on the chair, anesthetised on the hunger drug, before looking back at Engel, trembling on the floor. Sam beat the window with her palm and frightened Engel so much that Sam couldn't help but smirk at the darkening circle at Engel's crotch as it widened into a wet splodge. 'No! St-Stay back!' he shrieked, covering his eyes, inundated with so much dread that he couldn't stop his body from shaking, and he couldn't control his bladder from how scared he was. *You like to talk big, Maximillian, making everyone grovel at your feet, but in reality, Max Engel, you're just a pathetic fucking coward!* Came the ghostly voice of Fredrickson that galvanised from inside Engel's head, reducing him into a crying mess to the point of pissing himself and cowering behind his eyes like a scared little boy. Sam narrowed her eyes at him through the glass and smirked sinfully. 'What are you doing?' Engel fretted, knowing by that smirk that Sam had meant to do something awful; he just didn't understand what.

The answer to Engel's paranoia that Sam was evil (that smirk was enough evidence to let people know that Sam wasn't the saint Fredrickson had envisioned), and that she'd do something horrible to him was quickly answered when Sam started to bang the window with both hands. Engel knew this was a bad move as he wiped his head around and squeaked when he saw his zombie stirring and twitching out of her drugged state, shooting her head up with a start to cock it in the direction of the banging and by extension, her bratty bonder's hamster-like squeaking on her left despite being blind, she could hear his rushed breathing and sniff at the air, she could smell the urine in his pants that only seemed to get sweeter, riper indicating that his fear was over the scales; and therefore, she was able to determine where he was just by the bittersweet fragrance that whiffed from his khaki trousers. Wendy snarled; she thrust her arms out in front of her, trying to reach out to wherever she heard that panicked breathing and the smell of urine staining khakis, not to mention that she could almost taste his ripe, irresistible brains. She'd just had to get to him, get out of the restraints holding her back and get him; only then, would Max Engel's brains be hers for consumption. 'Wendy? Oh, Christ... Not you!' he screeched, staring over at his zombie, who thrashed about in her chains. Engel found it troublesome to glance at both Wendy and Sam, who had now begun to put some scary might into her banging of the window, intending to break her way in, free Wendy, and get a front-row seat in watching the blind elderly zombie eat her bonder. Sam snarled, now taking running starts and throwing herself into the window, causing it to crack. Wendy shook about against her restraints, eager to get out so she could kill Max Engel, who was cowering away in the far-right corner, crying his pitiful little heart out. 'Please, God, don't let me die... I don't want to die like this,' the fat man prayed behind sobs, dreading the moment when the inevitable happened and when Sam forced her way into the cell.

Sam's hammering on the glass had created a brief cobweb in the glassware! It wouldn't be long now until Engel is made short work of. Only a few more blows with her already bloodied knuckles and the bullet-proof window would give way. And when that does happen, Maximillian Engel can breathe his final breaths as he is evidently torn to ribbons.

Engel panicked. He was kneeling and praying to a God that didn't exist. 'Please, if anybody can hear me, smite these wretched primal beasts away and save me! I'll be in your debt for life if you permit me passage to live,' he pleaded, thrusting his praying palms up into the air. But nothing happened to the zombies that were trying to get him. He prayed three more times since it was given that the third time would be the charm and wipe out his enemies, but wishful thinking got him nowhere. Sam and Wendy were still present, hungry, and craving him.

Taking into evidence that God had forsaken him and abandoned him, Engel's eyes broadened with tears spattered on his reddened cheeks. The next thing that issued was Engel going into a fit of hysteria; he clamped his eyes shut and clutched at his heart. The dreadful sound of shattered glass and the pieces raining down on the floor below had finally come. Engel stared and bawled.

Sam had smashed the window, the blood of her victims dripping from her knuckles. Engel screamed, falling to the fall, and shuffling backwards as Sam desecrated her own body, making herself bleed pebbles of smelling, shrivelled blood by impaling her hand on a shard of glass. Sam vaulted the window, pushed glass out of her way, and vaulted over the pane, making her way into cell B-22. Sam smirked again; fresh red blood dripped from her lips and chin. She glanced at Wendy and blinked briefly before slowly turning back at the cowering Engel, who curled up in the corner, holding his knees, rocking back and forth, showing how scared he was.

Sam didn't worry if he fought back against her; it was typical for people to fight back against their captures and potential killers. She grabbed his legs and held them up high. She spread them out and gawked down at his wet crotch and back at his face with a grin. To make sure he was in anguish before she and Wendy could do their thing, she raised a foot high above his crotch and Engel, seeing her intentions, shrieked. 'No! Please, I beg you! Not That! I need that! Anything but the pecker!' he urged Sam not to go through with her sadistic plan. That didn't delay Sam from what she planned on doing to him; she didn't care if those around her suffered because the more those around her suffered, the more satisfied she felt. She cared very little for the people who'd tried to bring her back from the dead and give her a new life; Sam had other plans on her mind, and they certainly didn't revolve around saving the human race, her intentions were much darker. Besides, she couldn't shake away the joy she'd felt when she took a life. Sam liked being bad, and killing Fredrickson was only a start; Sam wanted more; she didn't want her old life back; she liked this one because she was free to break and bend the status quo to her will, spill blood and eat all the brains she wanted. Sam supposed that this was one thing she was grateful for when it came to the things Fredrickson taught her; reading about death in those novels seemed incredible to her, and executing her own ways to kill people seemed like an even more fabulous idea. The many methods to take a life were endless, and it gave her great pleasure to conduct different ways of killing someone who was stupid enough to get in her way or try to stop her.

Sam smiled at the cowardly man showing rotten teeth and slammed her bare foot down on Engel's crotch with enough dense pressure to squash his penis so he'd never be able to fuck his dream girl. He'd never be able to take a piss like an average man without the unbearable feeling of pissing razor blades. Engel wailed, rolling to the side, holding his crotch even though touching it was unendurable in terms of sheer pain. Sam's evil smirk grew larger, retaking grasp of Engel's legs, locking them under her arms and keeping him still with a foot on his broken penis underneath his wet pants. Sam began to stretch Engel's legs while Engel screeched so hard that he lost his voice. Sam towed harder at his legs, drawing them more toward her that Engel felt as if he was about to pull the father of all pulled muscles and cramps. Sam pulled harder and harder, gritting her teeth, eventually finding satisfaction, feeling a sudden release of pressure. After that, flesh threatened to tear, and joints inaugurated to disconnect, making Engel wail harder than he thought humanly possible. The pain was just too much for him to handle, but his attacker showed no signs of stopping. Sam yanked harder on the legs, with enough force to punch through a cinderblock until more pressure was released, and Sam pulled them entirely off Engel's body while he wailed, convulsing. Blood spilled out of his stumps, drenching the floor and Sam's feet with blood, causing Wendy's voracious zombie appetite to expand.

Sam proceeded over to blind Wendy, uprooted the chains off her, and left her to feast on her cowardly bonder Max Engel, who was left planted on the floor, covered in a puddle of his own blood. Not even looking back, getting a front-row seat to the carnage, Wendy began to gnaw her way through her bonder, silencing his screams by ending his good-for-nothing life! Sam vaulted the window pane she'd come in from and left cell B-22, proceeding her way down the foyers again (she'd more people to kill, so much more blood to spill); with fresh red blood smeared all over her tainted body. Sam killed scientists, doctors, civilians in hiding and bonders alike that got in her way, massacring the GFOSAR, one of the only places in the world that was genuinely safe and alive. And Sam had destroyed it.

Chapter 23

It wasn't long before the sounds of screams began echoing through the halls. The sounds of bangs and flesh being torn had now filled the once-safe halls. Now, all that was left was death and destruction; all that work into making GFOSAR a safe place had collapsed, and the worst part was that this was one of the only safe places in the country. Now that it had fallen, there was nothing left. No safety. Now, people would have to resort to being scavengers like those on the outside if there was still anyone living on the outside. All it took was one single zombie to escape her confines and wreak havoc upon the place that was meant to save the country and a fifth of the world. The worst part of this was that there would be nothing that the survivors of this bloodshed could do… trying to fight an intelligent bonded zombie gone rogue without anything to defend themselves with was a guaranteed death sentence.

Kolen, Ark, Losnedahl and Kushiro were fortunate (better in here than out there) enough to still be held up inside their delegated zombie bonding cells with their zombies. After the alarm was triggered by the now-deceased Cansu Aksoy, it had caused all bonding cells to initiate lockdown procedures, imprisoning anyone who was still inside in a highly fortified cage! As soon as the alarm was triggered blaring an ear-piercing electronic noise, they were trapped inside their cells, locked up like prisoners at a death camp, or unwittingly becoming contenders to a sick game of who dies first and who goes insane first.

Marilyn Kolen suffered a mental breakage from encountering her first lockdown. She'd flinched and became tense as soon as she heard the outbreak alarm. She huddled herself in one of the corners of the cell and started to cry from the sheer panic of being trapped in lockdown like those rabbits from that scary animated movie that always traumatised her as a child. This was like her worst nightmare come true – to be locked inside a room with someone dangerous and could hurt and possibly kill her whenever they felt like it. Ace was her only company and… probably wasn't the best sympathiser in this situation with all the speech problems and broken phrases. But even so, Ace tried her best to console her bonder, similar to how a child would consult their mother by asking what's wrong and telling her it would be okay as long as she was there with her. So, despite Ace not really knowing what she was saying, at least she was trying to console her panicked bonder instead of attempting to eat her, so that was a good thing. However, that didn't stop Kolen from being pessimistic and fearing that her crawler might decide to turn on her if her drugs wore off. And it didn't help that Kolen could hear those horrible screams outside, drilling into her ears no matter how tightly she clenched her ears to blot them out.

Lisa Ark, who'd been known for her strong stomach and the last person to let panic overtake her, knew that it was best not to let herself be overtaken by fear, as tempting as it was in this situation. She understood that it would be best to remain calm. Because whoever had done this would more than likely want her to be scared and for her to be crying in a corner due to fear. But Ark wasn't going to give them what they wanted. She wasn't going to boil over and act submissive. Instead, she remained calm, despite her rapidly beating heart and was communicating in a civil tone with Spot on how they were gonna get out of there. Even though Spot only had his brain wired up inside a jar of moss-coloured liquid and just half his head, those wires and lung liquid acted in the same way as ears, allowing him to hear without the form of actually visible ears. From what Ark discovered during her sessions with him, he was indeed an excellent listener and would drink in his bonder's words, taking them to account and thinking of ways he could help his bonder in the best ways he could. If she wanted something from him, he'd do it without hesitation. Ark wanted to get out, and she and her zombie worked around to see their escape; Ark theorising on what would be the best cause of action, and if a square seemed to fit inside the cube, she would ask and direct Spot over to what she was hypothesising where she would give him a thorough explanation on how he was going to do what she asked of him.

Henrik Losnedahl was isolated in cell B-01. Linus was with him. But Linus was going rampant, uncontrollably thrashing about in his chains (even though Linus had some fragments of intelligence, he wasn't as bright as the others like Sam, Ace, and Spot. And when faced with something he wasn't accustomed to, he reacted like a typical zombie would), screaming wildly as Losnedahl had become overpowered with loneliness and dread, knowing that it would be risky to try to feed him another hunger drug while Linus was in such an agitated state and with Losnedahl being almost sixty, not having the strength he once had, he knew that if he tried, he'd just end up losing the battle anyway. Fortunately, Losnedahl had done one prudent thing and chained up Linus while sedated on the previous hunger drug for the time being. As in his current state, Losnedahl didn't trust the boy zombie, not when he was one of the 50/50 cases and could turn on him at any minute if he wasn't careful. But the drug's effect had diminished, and now Linus was hungry for Losnedahl. So Losnedahl did the only thing he could, and that was to sit in the corner of the cell and wait for the inevitable, waiting for Linus to break free and kill him without wasting a second. He couldn't cry out for help, he couldn't scream, he could just sit there, silent, giving up. Henrik Losnedahl saw no point in breathing on this Earth anymore. He was mute, and no one would even consider saving the life of a fifty-something mute Norwegian man who couldn't even cry out for help. The planet was dead anyway; it showed zero signs of recovery, and life just wasn't worth it anymore. His head flopped down, and tears rolled down his cheeks, accepting his fate, acknowledging that he wasn't going to survive the night and that he was going to be bitten by Linus and turned into one of the undead. That's pretty much how the world went now: … you're born, live a life of survival, if you're bitten, you die, you join the undead. *Life is meaningless… living a life in hiding, fighting for survival; I should have perished in that blast that killed Mum. My curse was surviving.* Losnedahl lamented to himself, waiting for the sting of the bite that would end his life.

Daisuke Kushiro, much like the late Fredrickson had done, thought it best to come prepared in case of emergency, bringing with him a weapon, while it isn't recommended to carry weapons into the cells, the cautious ones such as Kushiro and Fredrickson thought that it was necessary and that bringing a weapon for self-defence, should have made it into the bonder's handbook. 'Having a weapon would ensure more safety,' had been one of Kushiro's words before starting today's working day with Kashima. Like Losnedahl, Kushiro sat on the floor quietly, staring at Kashima, watching his every move, and blinking every two minutes. Strictly adhering to his tanto knife, which had been passed down from his father and his father's father before passing away fourteen years ago in 2042. Kushiro had drugged Kashima an hour ago, so it wasn't long until the drugs would exhaust, and when that did happen, Daisuke Kushiro would be ready for when Kashima's hunger returned and he attacked.

Kashima was already a bust because his death mark consisted of two bullets in his brain. So, bonding with him was very difficult. But Kushiro emphasised keeping him until he'd dispose of Kashima himself with his treasured tanto knife when the time came, as Kushiro didn't want Kashima to die like the other failures. Even if Kashima was well and truly a failure. Kushiro wanted whoever Kashima was in life to know that he'd died an honourable death instead of being disposed of with disgrace. So, when the time came for Kushiro to drive his blade into Kashima for the killing blow, Kushiro would initiate his original (personal secret) plan of checking himself out.

Back in B-12. Kolen continued to sit in her corner, lightly sobbing to herself. She looked up and around her confinement. 'How are we going to get out of here? The cells are in heavy lockdown. And even if we do get out, how will we get the other bonders out?' Kolen queried beneath the veil of tears, questioning no one in particular. Though she thought that was just wasting her breath, shaking her long brown hair out of her face. Ace was bright but not as brilliant as Sam; no zombie in history could compete with Fredrickson's rouge zombie. If one were to determine a moderately accurate representation of both in percentages, Ace's mentality level would be approximately 31% at most, while Sam's was 100%. And yet, despite the staggering difference in intellect percentage and the patent issues, the crawler still struggled with things such as the basics of speech punctuation, sentence structure, and clarity. Ace did, however, know the one truth before anyone else. That Sam was bad news. All it took was one stare into those lifeless grey orbs for Ace to see that Sam was the end of the peace the GFOSAR had worked so hard to provide for the survivors. And all it took for Ace to see the demons and true nature inside her blackened heart was just that one look, that smirk had been given by Sam just after she had left the surgery with Fredrickson and was heading back to her cell, her bonder alien to what his zombie was scheming behind his back. Ace hypothesised that Sam originated all this, and she was the reason for the lockdown. And because Ace was a zombie, like most of the subjects here, she knew the devastating hunger of a fellow zombie and what it could make the undead body do if not fed. It could be that Sam had triggered the alarm, had killed all those people, hence the screaming and repugnant Velcro sound of meat being ripped from the body, attended by the putrid squelching of organs; all those offences to the ear had made Kolen want to gag

'I no know, ba I am no who attak all dose pleeps.' Ace answered Kolen's question, her speech pattern once again in broken, misspoken English, but what the crawler was trying to get at was understandable. Kolen took her white-rimmed glasses off and commenced wiping the small tears from them before settling them clean back on her face, glancing at Ace with importance. If Ace had a theory regarding who did this and their escape, Kolen was all ears. 'Yes, go on, Ace!'

Meanwhile, in B-14, as the screaming got louder, so did Kashima, who became unstable from the drugs wearing off and from the deafening sounds outside the cell. He began to thrash around in the chains bounding him, pulling, biting, and trying to tear away from them. But before Kashima could free himself and take a swing at Kushiro, Kushiro jumped to his feet and leapt over the desk, crashing down into Kashima, bringing the chair down with him as he tumbled to the floor with his zombie. One of the chair legs struck Kushiro in the crotch area as he descended down with Kashima; Kushiro yelped and gritted his teeth, trying not to injure the sharp pain in his balls. Daisuke Kushiro stood his ground, remaining strong, the tanto knife clenched tightly in his right fist, his left hand rubbing his crotch softly to soothe the stinging feeling. He glared at Kashima, patting the ground to get up. Then Kushiro unleashed the fury of his ancestors, letting out a warrior's scream, imagining he was a Ronin like in all those samurai movies he used to watch as a wee young lad back in

Sapporo. He held the knife above his head and charged, his left hand still cradling his aching crotch. His body slammed Kashima down to the floor again and pinned him down with his knees on his chest. But it wasn't enough to restrain the arms that Kashima had broken the chains to free himself from. He held the tanto knife up high to strike it down on Kashima. But Kashima worked around him. Kashima fought back.

He grabbed the wrist that held the knife and held it up for a temporary volume of time; Kashima seized the hand covering the crotch and bit down on Kushiro's hand with his zombie's teeth. Advancing the infection of the mortuus carnem virus through his blood within a single bite. Kushiro hissed in discomfort, knowing it was all over and it was a matter of time before he turned. The fifty-year-old Japanese man invoked the idea of dying with a warrior's honour and dignity instead of rolling over and giving up like most people would if they were bitten.

With his bitten arm, he pressed on Kashima's face as Kashima snapped at him. Kushiro let out another warrior cry, thrusting the tanto knife up and bearing it down with malicious velocity into Kashima's head, piercing him through the skull; blood seeped through the sides of the tanto knife. Kushiro withdrew the knife from Kashima's crown as the hole in Kashima's had started to pool blood. Kushiro brought the knife pelting down on Kashima again, this time right in the eye! Kushiro kept raising the blade and whamming it back down on Kashima until Kushiro's energy was depleted. His former zombie had stopped moving, becoming a lifeless husk in the middle of the room. Even so, Kushiro kept stabbing at the dead zombie over and over, committing more offence to the dead body, painting his face with droplets of blood that flew off the blade.

Kushiro withdrew from the ruined Kashima, having stab wounds all over the zombie's rotting face. Kushiro slammed his back against the wall, still maintaining hold of the tanto knife in his right hand. He rubbed his bitten, infected hand over his forehead, wiping the blood-soaked sweat away. Kushiro fiddled about his lab coat pockets, not looking for anything in particular. But when his knuckles bumped into something, he examined it with his fingers, and his heart stopped upon distinguishing the object in his pocket.

Kushiro drew a desert eagle handgun out of his pocket. At first, he was baffled about why it was in his pocket. Still, then he remembered he'd put it there the day before yesterday morning in case of emergency; for example, if he'd got bitten, he'd use it as a means to kill himself instead of suffering the painful transformation into an undead; that is until the mortuus carnem sniffed out his corpse.

Kushiro burst into tears at the very sight of the gun; he wasn't ready to depart from the world just yet; he didn't want to die. He tried to get out and help any survivors, but he'd been bitten, and it was all over for him. He could either let the virus kill him painfully on the inside or kill himself and be over with it. He instantly dropped the tanto knife and put the eagle into his open mouth, sobbing his last few tears and taking what was now going to be his final breath. ' Aishiteimasu, musuko no Nagisa-san, soshite aisuru tsuma no Haru-san, mata sugu ni aimashō (I love you, Nagisa, my son, and Haru, my beloved wife, I will see you both soon).' he cried in Japanese. He pulled the trigger.

Chapter 24

Kolen's tears ceased. It was as if the screams and flesh ripping from outside had been turned down as if by a remote control. She scampered to her feet, pulled out her chair, and sat opposite Ace. She put her hands on the table and leaned her body dangerously close to the crawler's mutton chops. Her eyes stared at the crawler, begging for an answer about who was behind this nightmare. 'Yes, Ace, go on?'

'Go on what?' Ace asked absently, forgetting everything that was previously on her mind as if someone had rebooted her thoughts. Kolen's eye flinched a twitch without her control, but she wasn't the type to get irritated and criticise someone for forgetting something important. It would be forgiven because Ace was a zombie whose brain function wasn't at its best, but Kolen hoped they would improve over time. So, for now, Kolen just sighed and leaned back. Ace was still developing, and that was fine. This was something Kolen would just have to get used to, that was if the two managed to get out of the cell to hinder whoever was doing all this. Kolen knew they couldn't stay in B-12 forever because what would happen if Kolen ran out of hunger drugs, and what would happen if Kolen herself got hungry or thirsty or needed to take a dump? What would happen to her sanity? Yes, it was thoroughly clear that Kolen knew she had to get out of there, but the main question on her mind was; *How? Perhaps*, Kolen thought, *I could drug Ace for now and hope for the best.* She considered as she stared at Ace, whose head was moving around in a mechanical circular motion like a theme park ride.

'Ace?' Kolen spoke timidly, 'I'm going to give you a pill. If we get out of here, I don't want you to start attacking me when we get out, okay?' Kolen said wistfully, taking a single red pill out of her lab coat's breast pocket (where some bonders keep the drugs).

Ace didn't dispute her bonder's orders, simply opening her rotten chops, prompting Kolen to toss the drug into her mouth. Ace swallowed the pill and immediately started going loopy; her sense of everything around her disappeared; she no longer felt hungry or anything for that matter, which was a good thing on Kolen's part, though it would be challenging to move a crawler around in a rusty wheelchair if someone had, in fact, come to her aid, at least that was what Kolen hoped. 'If anyone is still out there and hasn't been murdered or worse... eaten.' Kolen cupped her hands. 'Please save us... please... help us.' Kolen lamented, looking over at the bulletproof glass window with the broken steel shutter. If she smashed the window with the steel chair a few times, she might be able to make a hole big enough for her and Ace to make their escape. But that most likely wouldn't happen because Kolen was a pacifist and didn't have an ounce of violence in her, not even enough to break a window. She couldn't even do that. Besides, how in the hell would she get the wheelbarrow out? It would take more than a simple hole to get that out. Kolen placed her hand on the window and looked through the hole in the broken shutter, seeing nothing but a wall with traces of red spattered on it, Kolen couldn't help but think of the worst, did the one responsible for breaching the GFOSAR kill someone outside the cell, or severely hurt someone, causing them to limp and leave a trail of blood behind them? Kolen didn't want to know whose blood it belonged to. Instead, she slid to the floor, hugging her knees, and softly commenced sobbing into them, praying that someone alive would knock on the shutter, alerting her and coming to rescue her and Ace. Because Kolen, like most people, wasn't ready to die.

'Alright, Spot, let's get the hell out of here!' Ark, who refused to allow herself to become bottled up in her own terror, beckoned to Spot, who continued to sit quietly at his desk, holding the jar bearing that peculiar liquid that was keeping his wired brain alive and active. Spot heard her by perking his head up, glancing forward in the direction of her voice; he may not have known the context of what she had meant by 'get the hell out of here', but that wasn't much of an issue, as Spot knew that he'd be able to find out as long as he stayed with Ark and did exactly what she asked of him. After all, he wasn't just going to forget the debt that he owed her for getting his brain and wiring it up for him, allowing him to hear things again, something that would've been impossible if it wasn't for the wires protruding out of his brain like electrical cables and the lung liquid that kept his brain healthy and alive.

Ark smacked herself on the forehead like someone does when they come to a late revelation. 'I feel like such a mindless sheila for not thinking of it until now! Spot, Now I know this is risky, and you could turn on me at any given time. But in order to get out of here instead of sitting ducks. I would unchain you if I had the keys (bonders are instructed to keep the keys in their office and are only allowed to unchain the zombies when they either go out to be disposed of, have surgery, or, on the infrequent, rare occasion, are released into the wild to live another life). I'm gonna need your size and undead strength to free yourself from those chains and assist me in breaking this bulletproof window as well as the window shutter. After we get out, we'll find Alexander and the others if they're still alive and if their zombies haven't eaten them. You with me, boy?' Spot tilted his half head to the side before nodding, confirming that he understood, obeying her orders like a loyal, obedient dog. Spot wanted to do anything he could for his bonder, to repay her in any way, no matter what it was; if Ark required it, he'd do it without protest.

He grabbed the chains securing his legs (he didn't need eyes and a whole head to see the chains bounding him; he could feel them around his legs) and ripped them off with his enhanced undead strength. The reason he hadn't done it before was that he'd been under the influence of the drugs, and mainly because he wasn't a hostile zombie like most and it wasn't like he had somewhere else to be. Therefore, he saw little reason to break them. Recent zombies around the 5-to-10-year AOR would be classed as the strongest of the bonded zombies. As they got older, showing their age with decay, they got weaker. However, some were still stronger than most average humans as it was believed that when the mortuus carnem infects it provides some kind of physical adrenaline, allowing it to run and overpower a human with little effort.

Ark picked up the steel chair that she sat on during her bonding sessions with Spot and flung it as hard as she could at the bulletproof window, splintering the glass with a few scant cobwebs but not so much to make it shatter. She gathered the chair again and hurled it a few more times into the window while Spot remained motionless until the scant cobwebs grew into cracks, and those cracks grew into a sizeable hole for her and her zombie to get through. 'Alright, Spot this is your time to shine! I want you to use your strength to break through this shutter!' Ark directed; she tenderly took one of Spot's wrists, escorting him over to the front of the shutter whilst stepping on the broken window glass underneath, making a sound of glass breaking under their feet. It didn't matter, though; Ark was wearing shoes with good foot padding while Spot wasn't, and it didn't matter to him that he was stepping on the glass; the sharp feeling in his feet garnered no reaction from him.

Spot wanted to make Ark happy. He found that he was forever endebted to her after what she did by getting his brain back to him, helping with his learning and helping him develop feelings. Spot did precisely as requested by his bonder (and maybe his best friend). He stretched out his hands to touch the steel stutter before him so he knew what Ark wanted him to destroy. Spot summoned his inhuman strength and struck the shutter with brute force. Ark accumulated the jar carrying Spot's brain inside so both would remember. She stepped back and watched Spot fight and bash his way through the shutter, creating thunderous bangs that echoed through the bonding cells, causing a dent that he caused to grow and expand within each brutish offence.

'Atta boy Spot! Destroy that screen and get us out of here!' Ark cheered, seeing a hole in the shutter begin to appear. Spot jimmied his fingers through the hole in the shutter, proceeding to break it apart with all his mustered strength. The opening got larger, eventually ripping in two separate ways. Spot tore the two halves of the shutter, creating a hole large enough to be deemed an exit from cell B-09.

'Excellent work, Spot!' Ark said, sauntering and handing him his brain jar. 'Now let's get the hell out and save the others... That's if they're still alive and haven't had their guts ripped out and eaten by the zombies that are now skulking about the GFOSAR,' said Ark, crossing her fingers, hoping that she and Spot weren't the only ones left.

Losnedahl continued to sit by the corner of cell B-01, begging he could just die; he didn't have a gun to grant him that wish. He didn't have anything that would be of any use in putting an end to his life, so his only means of escape would be the young zombie in front of him. Fortunately, Linus was essentially out of the chains. However, because his zombie appeared to be around the young age of sixteen, he wasn't as strong as the adult ones, hence why it took him quite a bit to free himself from the restraints restricting him, but even so, Linus was out, and the mute man was right in front of him, his for the taking. Losnedahl just starred. He blinked slowly, waiting for his demise to come in the form of teeth.

Forgive me, mother, whom I have not met. You would most likely want me to stay alive and survive against this apocalyptic war against the living and the undead, but alas, I'm not strong enough and not phyhically built for this kind of scenario. I can't escape the inevitable. While he may not have been around when Sam had killed Fredrickson, Cansu, and Boson or around any of the deaths, it was only a matter of time until the panic became apparent more bodies started to pile up around B-01. As soon as the lockdown was initiated, he was stuck in this cell, which had become a prison. *My fate has been chosen. And I shall die here in this lonely cell waiting for Linus to take apart my insides and eat them while I can only watch, unable to make a sound. No one will be able to hear my gagging screams of pain as I lay dying by being eaten alive. I wouldn't even be able to cry... I'm so sorry, Mother if I was such a burden to you; I never meant to hurt you when you gave birth to me. I don't want to be a zombie for the end of my days... But this is the cruelty of fate; it's a bitch.* Losnedahl made a final prayer to his mother, accepting death. Linus made one last devastating wrench on the bounds, and he was free from one of the chains.

But lady luck was on Losnedahl's side. Death wasn't ready to collect him just yet. He was going to live through this night. As soon as Linus' chains were broken, both zombie and bonder cocked their heads, hearing a sudden loud, echoing crash that sounded close, just outside the window shutter close. At first, Losnedahl remained pessimistic, praying harder the undead were coming for him, thinking nothing of it; he believed it to be nothing more than just a few more zombies coming to Linus's aid upon hearing Linus's loud, hungry snarls and helping him to finish the job in executing Losnedahl. But then Losnedahl listened to her voice, almost like God's comforting voice telling him that it was okay and that he no longer had to suffer. Only it wasn't God or some realistic representation of something fictional. The voice was authentic and very familiar, and he had wanted to cry. 'That's it, Spot; let's rip this damn thing open. If Henrik's still alive, we're getting him out.' Losnedahl identified the voice of Lisa Ark, muffled but knowing her Australian accent outside cell B-01. He was saved!

Losnedahl's heart began to leap with faith that someone had acknowledged his existence and was coming to his aid! He wanted to cry... someone actually gave a damn about him and couldn't leave him to such a horrendous end. Ark had come to his aid like a good friend would do if you were trapped in a life-and-death situation. She and her outstanding zombie had come to rescue the mute man and then the timid Marilyn Kolen, that's if Ace hadn't devoured her. But for now, the focus was getting Losnedahl to safety as, from the sounds of it, Linus's hunger drug dosage had worn off, and it wouldn't take long for him to view Losnedahl as his next side dish.

'Henrik! If you're still alive, kick the wall or something, so I know I can hear a hungry walking corpse in there!' Ark had commanded Losnedahl. She could hear Linus raging, and she knew that she had to get the mute man out before the boy zombie made a meal out of Losnedahl. If he wanted to get out and see sunlight again like most people, he was going to have to do what the younger woman said. He may have wanted death to retrieve him when he died, but even he could agree that he didn't like to become part of the undead. Losnedahl could hear Linus's menacing growls and snarls, which had given conviction to something disastrous. He looked at his rouge zombie, overseeing Linus almost out of the last chain around his leg. Losnedahl's azure eyes unfolded. Sweat was trickling down his face as well as his back. A childish image of Ark with a billowing yellow cape behind her came to his mind, filling him with a sense that today must have been his lucky day, and Losnedahl wasn't exactly known for them. *Lisa, you beautiful sønn av en pistol!* Losnedahl had now decided that he wanted to live and see daylight and smell the spirited fragrance of pollen from the flowers outside. He readied his foot to kick at the wall, but he took another frightful glance at Linus and gasped without sound. He was out! Linus had finally snapped off the chain and was staring right into Losnedahl's frightened eyes hungrily, drool dripping from those gritted rotten teeth. Losnedahl opened his mouth in another muted gasp, kicking the wall rapidly, stating that he was in a state of panic and that he wanted out and wanted out now! 'Shit!' Ark panicked. 'Henrik, just try to hold off Linus! Spot will try to rip this shutter open if he can. As for me, I'll go find some acid if Spot can't pry open this shutter! Just hold off against Linus for as long as you can, Henrik, I'll be back! Just stay alive!' Ark said, muttering something to Spot before she ran off in the other direction towards one of the facilities labs.

Ark had given a quick, stable order for Spot to stay behind and keep going at the shutter and that she'd be back and hopefully with some acid. Spot hearkened Ark as he always did with his newfound intelligence. He'd put the jar containing his brain near the cell's door.

Losnedahl grabbed a chair and held it in front of him like a shield, as there really wasn't much he could use to defend himself with; a chair would have to do. Linus began twitching in and out from his primitive rabid side to his bonded side, slapping the sides of his face, trying to stop his zombie self (poor little Linus had two sides from being 50/50). But achieving such a feature was torture, and Linus couldn't repress his unquenchable longing for flesh and brains as much as he'd wanted to because that's what he'd been told by his bonder, but he just couldn't. He hurled himself, open-mouthed like a fierce tiger shark, at Losnedahl, crashing into the chair Losnedahl had been using to hold his ground against the rabid Linus, keeping him at a distance, blocking his attacks.

As Losnedahl did his best to hold Linus back with his chair shield, Ark had gone off searching for some acid in the chemistry lab on L4 while Spot was still fighting his way into breaking the shutter to rescue the mute man.

Linus tried getting a hold of himself, snarling, and smacking himself. Linus held out his arms, reaching to grab one of Losnedahl's hands. But instead, he grabbed one of his own and withdrew it back into a penitent hand gesture that he recognised and one that almost made him cry. 'Help me, please, Mr Losnedahl.' This alone had given Losnedahl the message that some of the bonding had paid off during the sessions. Losnedahl was about to lower the chair and check if Linus was trying to control himself, feeling sorry for his zombie. But as soon as Linus had finished making the apologetic hand sign, both Linus's arms were back to where they were initially poised, stretching out to grab his bonder in an attempt to eat him.

While she was inside the chemistry lab next door to the central laboratory. Ark was ransacking through the shelves and drawers, pulling them out of the slots and tossing them away, spilling the tools and equipment all over the floor. No such luck in finding at least a single test tube containing at least an inch of acid. 'Where the fuck is it?' Ark screamed in a whisper, going through everything to find some. She searched through them, her heart pounding, her mind in a sorry state of substantial unrest. I'm not going to fucking make my own acid again; that'll take fricking forever! She thought bitterly to herself. She spun around and saw the desk labelled GROSSMAN. Ark approached the desk and tore the drawers out. 'Eureka!' cackled Ark upon finding a tube that was full of hydrochloric acid! It was the precise stuff she needed to eat away at the steel metal shutter. 'Henrik, you better not be fucking dead, or I swear I'll… I'll,' Ark muttered. She plucked the flask of acid from Grossman's desk and made her way back to cell B-01, but as she attempted to leave the entrance, a silhouette lingered on the wall opposite the lab. Someone was coming. Holding the tube of acid in hand, Ark slid under one of the desks, holding her mouth to stop her heavy, panicked breathing. Her first instinct would be to throw the tube at the intruder and high tail out, but because she needed the acid and wasn't armed with a weapon, the only thing Ark could do was burrow amongst the shadows and pray she wasn't found.

Sam, in no hurry, slithered into view. She took a few steps into the lab and prowled around the area, smelling someone alive. She wandered to one of the desks labelled JAMES, placed her hands down on it and leaned over, sniffing at the air. Ark, thankfully, wasn't underneath that one. She was underneath the desk labelled XIAOQING. Ark knew she stood no chance without a weapon, so she waited soundlessly underneath Xiu Xiaoqiug's desk, tentatively holding the vial of hydrochloric acid. After three heart-stopping minutes, Ark watched as Sam spun around and left. Ark breathed a sigh of relief. She clutched at her heart, regaining her breath before exposing herself from her hiding spot. Ark glanced down at the tube of acid and held it tightly. Knowing what to do, she got to her feet and ran out to help her zombie rescue her mute colleague.

Spot had caused a small hole to appear in the shutter, but because this lockdown shutter wasn't broken like the B-09 shutter, it had to take twice the strength to tear a single hole through it. Ark returned soon after the time struck 9:36. It had taken her approximately an hour and ten minutes to run off in pursuit of finding acid and come back with her hand clutching a vial of the stuff. But something seemed different about her. *Why was this happening? Who is butchering people like this?*

'Spot, let me' she commanded quietly, holding the vial of acid with her left hand; her body began to tremble. Spot looked in the direction of her voice, stepping away from the damaged shutter and picking up his brain jar, hugging it close. Ark studied the flask with her hands shaking. 'Get a hold of yourself, woman,' she cursed, putting her hand on the cork and removing it with a pop. The air bubbles inside the flask bubbled and fizzled up. 'Henrik! Stand back!' she raised her voice in command.

Hearing her outside and still prevailing in his endeavours, Losnedahl launched the chair away along with Linus to the ground. He jumped out of the way from the window. Ark sighted the flask at the window, pushing Spot out of the way so the acid wouldn't bounce onto him, causing more offence to his body (Spot would likely go unchecked from the pain burning his already dead body). Ark delivered the acid flask, and it made contact with the shutter. The glass flask had shattered on impact. The acid made a burning, sizzling noise, which was accompanied by a god-awful stench of burning metal as Ark watched the bubbling acid slither around the expanding hole like a snake, eating away at the shutter and the glass behind it. When the acid had done its work, the crawling came to a hissing cease, smoke vapoured for about thirty seconds, and the disgusting smell of burning metal faded, leaving a gaping hole, big enough for Losnedahl to make his getaway from the famished, violent Linus. Losnedahl gawked, and some hope left him when he saw Linus pushing the chair off him and getting up to continue his advance. Losnedahl hastened to pick it up again and hurl it at him again, temporarily knocking him back down to the ground and, again, giving him a window of opportunity to escape. 'Henrik, come on! Move your fucking arse!' Ark shouted. She put her arms into the hole and reached them out for Losnedahl to take, and when he did, she would pull him out. And when Henrik Losnedahl was out, they'd go and help Kolen out of B-12 and, hopefully, anyone else that was still alive and trapped in the bonding cells. And after that? Well, Ark wasn't actually sure; she supposed a temporary safe place inside the GFOSAR would come to her when she was sure she'd saved all that she could.

After Ark and Spot got Losnedahl out of the cell, they picked up the pace and ran off. Ark was holding onto Spot's arm so he wouldn't be left behind due to the undeniable fact that he was blind and wouldn't be able to find or catch up to them even if he wanted to. They ran far away from the cell, so Linus couldn't catch up to them or find or pick up their scent. The three of them ran into a small storage room, seeking refuge for a few moments and taking a breather before deciding to retrieve Kolen if she was still alive.

Losnedahl noticed the grief inside Ark's expression after she'd returned with the acid and helped him to safety. He tapped on Ark's shoulder and asked in sign language what was troubling her - aside from the self-evident fact that the GFOSAR (a place once viewed as a refuge) had all the so-called safety ripped from its walls, becoming a dangerous place much like the other buildings outside. Ark looked up with tears beginning to drop from her forest-green eyes; stray strings of her golden blonde hair lay in front of her face, showing some of the grief and fear inside her. She was haggard and appeared to have aged about five years. 'Alexander Fredrickson is dead...'

Chapter 25

Marilyn Kolen and the talking crawler, were still trapped inside cell B-12, waiting for some kind of miracle to come and answer the prayer that Kolen had been muttering to herself. But with no help coming their way, the only sounds outside the cell that she could hear were the deafening and haunting echoes of her colleagues as they drew their final breaths, screaming their final sound before they were ultimately silenced for good.

The Dutch woman wasn't sure how long she and Ace had been waiting there for, but Kolen had a gut feeling that it was for a few hours, a few long, agonising hours. She was at the point where she wanted to give up if she'd to wait for another hour, but she heard nothing alive coming past the cell to help her. Ark sat silently, brooding on how things could've gone so wrong in minutes. She checked her breast pocket, pulled out two pills, and closed her eyes. She wished that she'd bought more than five pills for today's session. But like everyone else, no one could've expected the outbreak that would occur; no one could've dreamt the horror of one of their bonded subjects stopping the record of progress. 'I'm running out of hunger drugs, Ace. Maybe I should just let you eat me… because I don't think anyone is coming.' Kolen frowned, putting the pills back into her pocket. She cupped her hands in a praying gesture. She leaned her head on them, sniffling softly, still trying not to lose faith that someone would come to her aid and save her and Ace.

However, as luck would have it, her lucky stars had been granted. Kolen's distressed prayers were about to be answered; Kolen didn't have to wait long because Ark, Losnedahl and Spot were coming from B-01 to recover her from B-12. Hopefully, she'd accompany them and be apt to survive the night alive and unscathed, along with whoever else had joined them. Even if they were bitchy by complaining about everything they saw or if things didn't go their way and were nothing but liabilities, everyone deserved a chance to live; even if they didn't do much for those around them, everyone deserved a chance to see tomorrow. With humanity on the brink of extinction, throwing lives away was petty and callous. No one wanted to die and have their bodies reanimated and representations liquidated (temporarily, thanks to the bonding process), so thankfully, the number of suicides had seen a decrease and were considered rare by today's standards. The only people who'd killed themselves were those unfortunates to have lost everything, family, friends, pets, companions, everything. While Kolen had lost her husband, she knew she now had Ace and wanted to live and see Ace's mind grow into something more human-like.

Kolen had sat quietly, wanting to cry. She took off her glasses and rubbed them with her coat. They'd started to fog from how much Kolen was breathing and the absence of ventilation systems in the bonding cells.

Ark and Company weren't too far away from her cell. It was as if Ark had known that Kolen wouldn't have it in her to orchestrate her own breakout; she was too much of a snivelling little rabbit, displaying any kind of violence wasn't in her and seeing things such as gore had always given Kolen the ticket to the "Golden John".

Kolen and Ace both flinched at the loud crashing sound against the glass window, followed by the clearly audible racket of glass fragments raining down on the floor below. Kolen was frightened. Her first initial thought was that it was her doom beckoning her. Then…

'Marilyn! You in there?' came Ark's voice.

Kolen's eyes widened at the sound of the Australian woman's voice, which, during this current situation, had sounded like she was hearing the voice of a mighty knight from a prophecy who had come to rescue the princess after slaying the dragon guarding her and the cavern of gold. 'Lisa? How did you-?'

'No time for explanations; just get yourself and Ace out!' Kolen glanced behind her shoulder and felt a massive load lift at seeing Ark was on the outside. She reached her arms inside the break-in window, signalling Kolen to climb through the small hole and to be mindful of the glass in. 'Oh, my goodness, Lisa, you are my hero! Thank you, thank you! I will never forget this!' Kolen perceived this chance of escape with Ark and Losnedahl as a once-in-a-lifetime opportunity to see tomorrow (a common goal for the survivors) and knew that it was better to take the ticket instead of idling around, waiting for her pills to be depleted and for Ace to get hungry. But thankfully, she wouldn't have to think of that anymore because she was saved; her fellow colleagues had come to her rescue. A smile of delight swelled on her face at the thought that she was being rescued. Kolen got up from her chair and approached the wheelbarrow Ace was nestled into.

Ace held out her hand, requesting another hunger drug to numb her sense of hunger for brains and flesh. Kolen handed her the last one (Kolen brought five dosages with her during today's bonding session) to Ace and waited for the medication to take effect. Thankfully, it wasn't long before Kolen could carry the paralysed Ace out of the wheelbarrow and present her to Ark. She did that before making her own escape from B-12. 'Marilyn, I don't want to rush you, but we want to make it through tonight without any of us dying an excruciating death.' The Australian woman urged, her voice becoming more impatient. Kolen held onto Ace like a baby. She took the anesthetised crawler over to Ark, who still held her hands. 'Don't worry, Lisa, Ace is on our side. I've just sedated her with the hunger remedy, so she thankfully won't be hungry for a while. Although I think she might know who's behind all this blood-shedding,' Kolen instructed timidly. She held Ace to Ark's arms, transmitting Ace to her. Ark took Ace from Kolen's hands and gently pulled her through the breakage in the glass window. Looking over at Losnedahl Ark said, 'Henrik, we need a wheelchair for Marilyn's crawler Ace. Spot, you stay here and cover me while I help Marilyn out.' Ark's orders were clear.

Losnedahl nodded instantly at the order he was given as if he was in boot camp and was ordered to do twenty laps around the field. He ran off to where the wheelchairs were kept while keeping a close watch on any zombies that were lingering around. While hunting for a wheelchair in the medical ward on L2, Losnedahl's eyes widened; his heart froze when he stopped and saw glimpses of zombies around … six of them about two metres from him, feasting on what remained of bulky security guard Robert Boson's, arms, legs, chest and even face! Losnedahl stepped back and gagged, feeling the intoxicating urge to throw his own guts out upon seeing the zombies ripping away into Boson's ribcage, playing with his bloody internal organs like pre-schoolers with playdough. The brain had already been eaten by an anonymous zombie. Losnedahl expelled his eyes from the disgusting sight, holding onto his mouth to contain his sickness. Slowly and making sure there was nothing on the ground that would give his position away, knocking items over would usually create quite a disturbance of noise to lurking nearby unbonded zombies. Not wanting to risk it, he got on his hands and knees and slowly began to crawl on all fours away from the undead feasting upon the hulking corpse of Boson. He snuck downstairs and into the hospital ward in the GFOSAR, where the wheelchairs were bound to be located.

The hospital ward luckily didn't have many zombies encompassing the area. So that gave Losnedahl the window of advantage to stand up and silently tiptoe over to where the stacked, folded-up wheelchairs on hooks on the walls were located. Losnedahl glued his eyes onto the wheelchairs while still laying a cautious eye to check if (Fredrickson's killer) anyone dangerous was sneaking up behind him, checking and making sure that he was still in the safe zone and remained undetected by the small number of zombies in the hospital ward. Targeting the first one he saw, Losnedahl closed in on the wheelchair rack, taking hold of the one he had marked. Being visual and mindful of his surroundings, he gently began to pull the folded wheelchair up off the hook, watching the ground and anything around him, desperate to not hit it on anything. The slight ping could be fatal. Losnedahl's breathing pace quickened, gripping it tightly. He put the chair underneath his armpit like a surfer with his trusty surfboard, eager to catch the big Hawaiian waves. But this was no beach of beautiful summer breeze; this wasn't a surfer's playground, this wasn't the place where you would hear sounds of the waves crashing onto the rocks around the rock pools and washing up on the shore, with people laughing instead of screaming.

It was good to fantasize about the possibilities and what could happen when the zombie pandemic came to an end, and the extinction of the mortuus carnem became a reality, becoming a fragment of the planet's dark past. But alas, that was thinking far into the future. The year was only 2056, and it was at the peak of the mortuus carnem apocalypse. So, another thirty or so years before the Earth had finally built up the capacity to drive out the parasite and refurbish itself, it became somewhat of a utopia, possibly in the year 2086. A rather funny and futuristic-sounding year. A year that should be full of flying cars and human-looking robots.

Losnedahl shook his head and frowned, returning to the real world, and being shoved out of such a peaceful thought. With a wheelchair under his arm, Losnedahl flipped around, knowing what he had to do. He was about to take his leave right before he was halted in his tracks. His body froze stiff, his eyes wide with dread upon seeing the black-haired zombie with the black shirt and tan shorts who had looked rather pretty and a looker, the apparent sign of the surgery and a bang-up job for whoever had done the surgery. Losnedahl recognised her and wasn't taking his chances of confronting her. His heart skipped a beat upon seeing the zombie emerge from the place that he'd marked as his exit, simply standing in the doorway. He had to hide! He had to get out of her sight. *Oh shit! Oh shit! Oh shit!* Losnedahl's mind shrieked, holding onto the folded wheelchair under his arm tightly, staring at Sam, who fortunately hadn't seen him yet. Thank goodness…

His heart was running laps; he could hear it beating, and he opted to take one hand from the wheelchair to grasp at his heart, hoping that it would at least quiet the sound it made. Losnedahl still kept his grasp on the wheelchair, using the skills he had developed when he was a young boy when his mad, drunken father invited him over to his aunt Annette's house (while she was at work) to finish what he started. Forcing the young, tongueless boy to hide and escape from what could've been a cruel beating. Anytime he was drinking, Joakim would propel himself into Annette's house, knocking Annette down like she was a glass vase that shattered upon hitting a hard surface, he turned his attention to hunting his only son down beat him to unconsciousness every time he saw the small, skinny boy. Lucky for Losnedahl, at times, his aunt saved him from his repulsive father by calling the police and having Joakim arrested and in jail. There, he'd stay for a few months until Annette was confident, he was sober and sane enough to be released, with the only catch being that he was to never come over when he started opening the bottles.

But this wasn't his dad, and the nickers weren't helpful in this current condition. If you wanted to survive still with your teeth, you had to rely on wits and hiding skills. Losnedahl kept his stance, lowering his back so he'd seem insignificant to Sam. It was like trying to hide from Daddy the Bogeyman again, only this time, Daddy was a highly efficient female zombie. It was fruitless to fight back. Fighting against a modified zombie would seem like a death wish, and you'd have to have no sense of self-preservation to do so. Losnedahl knew that he wouldn't have a chance if he tried to fight back and defend himself, waiting and hoping that Sam left the room quietly, giving Losnedahl a chance to flee. Because sometimes, in these scenarios, flight was better than fight.

Losnedahl held the wheelchair, his head drowning with prayers to a formless God about helping him get away from Sam and survive this one thing. He kept his back hunched, moving slowly and soundlessly towards the exit and away from Sam, who'd walked over to a desk, completely ignoring him, or viewing him as a pointless adversary. She pulled out drawers as if looking for something. What? Losnedahl didn't know and didn't care. He seized this moment to escape. Watching her closely, he snuck behind her carefully, and when he was out of the hospital ward, he ran in the opposite direction of her without so much as a glance behind him.

Chapter 26

Ark frequently looked about her, checking if anything dangerous was coming her way as she assisted Kolen from the hole of B-12, clean and straight after Ace. Kolen slid the drugged-up crawler through the hole as Kolen decided that having a talker with them would provide some use. While she hadn't openly expressed this to Ark, she didn't need to as the Australian seemed more than keen enough to get the crawler out first as Kolen soon found out that Ark had her half-headless zombie standing beside her. Ark took Ace and placed her down on the ground gently; she then put her hands through the hole, taking Kolen's hands in her own and pulled as Kolen stepped onto the wall underneath the window with her feet and hopped; Kolen made sure to veer away from the sharp edges of glass to avoid any unnecessary damage. When most of Kolen was poking through the hole, Ark let her hands go, allowing Kolen to carefully climb her way out where upon doing a small somersault to the ground below, had made a swift and easy escape from the cell that could've been her tomb if it wasn't for Kolen drugging Ace and the Australian and her half headless zombie and Losnedahl coming to her rescue.

Kolen landed on her buttocks with very little glass scraping at the skin and only making minor tears into her lab coat, which was a good thing. The roaming undead (not including Spot and Ace) would have a pretty hard time smelling Kolen's blood if it wasn't exposed with an open cut, although the same couldn't be said about her brains. Now, the four played the waiting game, waiting for the arrival of Losnedahl and the wheelchair for Ace. *We're not going to plot our escape until he comes back; Henrik is one of us. He's had a lot of misfortune and deserves at least one good thing. He deserves to make it through this as well as anyone else.* Ark thought to herself as she asked Kolen if she was hurt, wanting to double-check if she was clean of any bites or hadn't been cut by the shards of glass during her escape from the cell. Ark examined Kolen's front and back, feeling satisfaction when she saw that the young Dutch woman was, in fact, clean.

'Lisa,' peeped Kolen. Jerking Ark on her shoulder, Ark looked at her, regarding her petite face that was soaked in dry tears. 'I'm scared; what if something happened to Henrik?'

Although Ark was indeed worried about the mute Norwegian man, she remained hopeful of his return and knew that they had to keep up that hope if she and any others were going to survive this day. 'I doubt that Henrik has been through the mill; remember when he told you in BSL that his tongue was cut out shortly after he was born and that when his putrid dad invited himself into his aunt's place, he'd have to run, hide and wait for him to be arrested?'

Kolen replied with a scant nod.

'I'm sure he'll be okay. The man is a born survivor. Just have faith,' Ark said. Ark peered over and to the opposite of B-12, seeing a small room often used as a breakroom for the zombie bonders during the bonding process's non-working months, allowing more space for recreation. 'Marilyn, the breakroom, we can wait until he gets back with the wheelchair.' Ark pointed and Kolen didn't need anything else to convince her otherwise; anything was better than standing here in the middle of the carnage. So, Ark, Kolen (carrying Ace) and Spot, decided to wait in there for the time being. She hoped it wouldn't be too far and that Losnedahl could find them easily in there so it wouldn't be like abandoning him to a cruel fate. More like hiding somewhere nearby for him to come back. Ark just hoped that it was only Losnedahl that found them hiding there and not the bitch behind the breach because if that was the case, prayers weren't an option.

Knowing the inherent threat her zombie would bring against them when submerged in excessive hunger, Ark ambled over to Spot, digging into her breast pocket, pulling out one of the mild red drugs for Spot, and said 'Spot, tongue up.' She commanded her half-headless zombie, who was standing at a staggering height behind her and holding his brain jar closely, not thinking for a mere second of abandoning it. Ark turned to him, and Spot knelt down to Ark. He was so tall that it was common for people such as Ark to presume he'd been a basketball player in life, notwithstanding nearly the same amount of bulk as Boson had, one would still not want to be on the receiving end of a very tall person, let alone someone who could've been over six-foot-six. So, it was lucky that he was good on Ark, Kolen and Losnedahl's side and not Sam's. Spot lifted his tongue up as high as it would go, allowing Ark to place the pill on his bottom jaw. He would then dissolve the drug from underneath his tongue, rolling it around with his tongue until it evaporated. Then, he'd move his head backwards, causing the dissolved liquid remains to slide into his hypopharynx, where he could swallow the remains and let the drug take effect.

Kolen watched this process with reverence. She'd never seen Spot take a hunger drug and always wondered how on earth he was able to swallow them. 'How can he be alive? He's missing half a head,' Kolen stated, looking up at the towering Spot, who appeared as if he was struggling with getting the drug in the exact place he wanted it, holding his hands up, clenching and unclenching them. He was triumphant and managed to obtain the fluid remains down his throat and swallow it, causing him to fall to the floor, unconscious for the time being, like Ace on the floor.

'It's a long story.' Ark looked at Kolen. Her eyes stung. 'Marilyn... I have to tell you something about Alexander,' she announced, her voice heavy, getting Kolen's utmost attention; anything about Fredrickson was most important to Kolen. Her expression glowed, her eyes were wide and glassy, and her mouth hung open. She patted her hands down on Ark's buttoned lab coat, informing Ark that she was frantic to know anything concerning her dear friend and teacher. Ark breathed in and out, opening her mouth to speak.

Losendahl on his way back to B-12, held the wheelchair closely under his arm and did his best not to trip or step on anyone's severed arms or legs or heads that might cause him to trip. Losnedahl ran up the stairs, seeing L3 printed on the wall at the end of the flight of steps. Losnedahl was about to turn and run to the left when his body froze again upon hearing the sound of a revolver clicking from behind him. Losnedahl turned around slowly, still keeping a solid hold on the wheelchair. He turned and faced the owner of the gun, praying that it wasn't Sam who had tailed him from the hospital ward after finding a gun in one of the drawers.

'Jesus fucking Christ, Henrik! You scared the shit out of me!' Came the jarring voice of the village idiot.

Chapter 27

Winsome lowered the revolver he was holding, putting it back into the back pocket of his pants, feeling a wave of relief in seeing someone else alive. He had something clamped between his teeth that Losnedahl saw what looked like a wallet (he still used one of those old things?) He laid back against the wall and wiped his forehead with the hand holding the revolver. Winsome took the wallet from his mouth and looked into it briefly, muttering something under his breath before folding it back up and shoving it into his back pocket. 'Oi, what's with the wheelchair? Ya surely can't be fussed about some ol' broken legs when people 'ere are dropping like fucking steak and kidney pie?' Winsome cried, pointing to the wheelchair tucked under the mute man's arm.

Losnedahl closed his eyes, also letting out a relieved sigh, feeling his terror lift at the sight of one of his own, even if it was Winsome; at least was better than the undead. And anyone was better than that scary black-haired woman. Most people hated Winsome, and the sick wanted him to die so they'd be free from his inconsistent, ranting, sickish remarks, and verbal harassment. But he'd done the gracious thing after the alarm was set off, bringing a once-safe place full of fresh meat to bully into a danger zone. He let go of his idiocy instead of pushing the older man out of his way, thinking that he'd be a liability slowing him down; he became earnest; determined like everyone else to get through the day alive even if he didn't much like the person, Winsome knew that he'd have to work alongside them as a team. Because Winsome supposed that was the joy of teamwork and survival. Sometimes, you had to work with those you weren't fond of, such as Lisa Ark; the two had a rocky relationship. 'So, whereabouts are you headin? Mind if I tag along?' Losnedahl pointed over, behind Winsome, to show where he came from, trying his best to explain in sign language to Winsome in a way that he'd understand, trying to let him know that there were others still alive and were in hiding. 'Oh, thank fuck. More survivors. Yes! I just came from Allen Bates's office and killed this meat-headed black zombie named Queen, according to Olio, by shooting her in the head and blasting her brains from here to kingdom come,' Winsome verified triumphantly. Losnedahl rolled his eyes at Winsome's bragging. He stepped to his left, looking out to see if the coast was clear and beckoned his fingers to Winsome, telling the younger man to follow him back. Back to where he'd left the two women and two zombies so they could plan their escape, even though it was a considerable risk, but what other choice did they have? They were going to have to leave the GFOSAR. Outside was crawling with that mortuus carnem resurrected carcasses. People thought it was appalling inside, waiting until they tasted the horror that was the outside. While shadowed in a growing cloud of risk and danger, it would be better than staying in here, a claustrophobic environment and waiting to become dinner.

Ryan Winsome tailed closely behind Losnedahl, the revolver tucked away in his pocket, his hand holding the grip, in case both men ran into a zombie that wasn't one of the bonded and executed an attempt to attack them. 'Shit really did hit the fan as soon as the alarm was set off. I just hope there are still women alive for me to fuck when this blows over.' Winsome tried to lighten the mood by bringing the subject of love into the picture when humans repopulated the Earth, but this wasn't the time, and Losnedahl knew it. Losnedahl raised an eyebrow and cocked his head to him. 'That seriously can't be your excuse to survive.' Losnedahl wanted to say. 'Wot? Surely, after this is over, we'll be heroes and will get all the chicks in bed.' Winsome disclosed, making loud, obnoxious kissing noises. Losnedahl rolled his eyes. *You're a sick bastard, Ryan.'* When Losnedahl returned to B-12, with Winsome behind him, he nervously glanced around, dreading the thought of the two women leaving him behind because he was mute. He began to visibly worry about where Ark and company were, hoping and praying that they hadn't abandoned him. He started to shake, and his lips quivered as he darted around, trying to pinpoint the two women.

'Where are they? We can't be the only ones alive? Can we Henrik?'

'Shut up, idiot and let me think!' Losnedahl mouthed to himself as he gripped his chest, feeling his heart pounding frettingly. Where the hell were they? He panicked.

'Henrik!' Ark cried upon seeing him standing in the doorway with the wheelchair slugged under one arm. 'In here!' she called, alerting the two men to her location, along with Kolen and the inert Ace and Spot on the floor. She stepped out of the room where they sought safety and beckoned with her hand for them to enter. Losnedahl entered the room, followed by Winsome, clenching the wheelchair under his arm. He opened and placed the wheelchair on the ground next to Kolen. She nodded with a slight smile, picking Ace up and seating her in the wheelchair, thanking him for putting himself in the line of danger to get a wheelchair here for Ace. Ark and Winsome eyed one another like long-time school rivals meeting each other again face-to-face after years of not seeing each other. 'I see you're still alive, arsehole.' Ark sneered at Winsome, not expecting him to be alive. Winsome stared at her, flabbergasted as well as insulted. 'I don't get a kiss or a hug? I'm disappointed. It's good to see you too, bitch,' he greeted in an unfriendly tone back to Ark, not noticing the knocked-out zombies yet. 'You should watch your tongue around Spot, Ryan; he's sensitive about violation against me,' Ark warned, opening her hand, and counting how many red pills she had left for Spot; much like the late Fredrickson, Ark wasn't keen on Winsome because of his wisecracks, which most people had found suitably irritating at most. As with the case of Ark and Winsome; they viewed each other like rivals all the way from high school. While they didn't hate each other, they weren't fond of each other. 'Fuck off, Lisa! You can't tell me what to do around here. After all, you're just a blonde bimbo! And they always die in horror movies!' Winsome viciously snapped at Ark.' Whatever, Ryan, I'm not dealing with your shit' Ark rolled her eyes, going back to pill counting, counting thirteen. Plenty! Winsome saw Kolen, unbelieving that someone as frail as she had survived. 'And you, Marilyn Kolen, howd'you get here, ay? Did Alex or some barmpot save your arse,?' ridiculed Winsome, taking it a bit too far with the remark of Fredrickson's name. Speaking ill of the deceased was disrespectful and should not be unjustified. Winsome needed to be taught a lesson about manners and knowing his place amongst them as survivors.

Feeling the pressure and tension blowing up inside her, Ark rammed the fistful of pills back into her breast pocket. She propelled out of her seat and landed a hard punch against Winsome's face before seizing the scruff of his coat collar and pinning him up to the wall to express and let out her anger onto him. 'You know what your problem is? You're too much of a charismatic jackass! You think you're so fucking good because people quail every time you open that shit-filled mouth of yours to deliver an insult. Do you even think about others or the situation we're in? When was the last time that dodgy brain of yours worked properly, and you were actually capable of saying something helpful about the good people you work with?' Ark harangued; she stormed over to him and bowled him and his smug face to the ground, kicking him in the stomach, listening to his cries from being assaulted in the stomach. 'H-Hey c'mon lady. I was joking! It was a joke!'

'You're as weak as piss, Ryan, just like Max,' Ark scolded, withdrawing from him while Kolen and Losnedahl gawked at her dumbfounded. She held out her arm to help the man up and find some common ground, but he spat at her and smacked it away. Winsome clutched his aching stomach as she stood up, his legs feeling like jelly and wabbling as he shambled over to the wall, stretched out his arm and steadied himself. 'Let that be a lesson to you, Ryan; if you pull shit like that again, I won't hesitate in breaking your arm. But because we're in a crisis of dying by the zombies out there,' Ark paused, allowing herself to relax a bit before speaking up again; like most, she didn't like Winsome, but she knew that she couldn't just leave him to the mercy of the undead, because that would be against her morals. 'We may not see eye-to-eye, but we have to bypass those rivalries and work together as a team to stay alive in this death-stricken world as best as possible. And we need to work up to beating the infection. If we're lucky, we could drive the mortuus carnem species to extinction. Even if we don't like each other, this is something that we're going to have to do. We need to work together if we will have any chance of making it out alive. Both the living and the bonded undead must work together to stay alive, protect each other, and stop whoever started all this.' Ark declared what they would have to do if they wanted to survive this outbreak. Winsome's eyes widened, feeling a flicker of hope. Half of the pain in his gut seemed to wash away at hers. 'Wait, wait, wait, bonded zombies? You're saying we have zombies on our side? Fuck Yeah!' Winsome inquired, completely forgetting that he had just been assaulted by Ark. He looked up at Ark, holding onto his stomach, striving to regain his ground after he just got his arse handed to him by a woman. Let alone a blonde one. Ark rolled her eyes at Winsome's stupidity; she was still surprised at how dumb the man could be when he wasn't paying attention. 'Yes, Ryan, we have zombies on our side.' Ark told Winsome. 'Now I know what you're all thinking.

And no. I'm not trying to appoint myself as the leader of a group of survivors or some shit like that. All I want is for us and the human race to survive this war and beat the mortuus carnem.' She said to the three humans and two zombies.

Winsome stood up and looked Ark deep in the eyes. 'Well, tough shit, Lisa. I don't see anyone else offering for the job. The votes go to you. It's either we live by your leadership or die by mine, your choice.'

'Sam.' Ace uttered, stirring a bit, waking up to sit in the wheelchair that Losnedahl had provided and Kolen had placed onto. 'It, Sam', she said, thoroughly subduing the effect of the drugs, and waking up in the breakroom with her allies. Spot was still sprawled out on the floor, still doped on the medicines. Kolen looked at her with uncertainty as to what she was on about. 'What are you talking about, Ace? Who is...?

'Oh fuck...' Ark's forest-green eyes widened upon realisation. 'I know what Ace is on about. That would explain Alexander's dead body that I stumbled over while I was on the way back after retrieving some acid to get Henrik out.' Ark gulped, realising the one who started the whole storm on the GFOSAR. Sam was Fredrickson's intelligent female zombie. By the way, Ace theorised it all on her meant that...

'It's Sam. She's responsible for this!'

Chapter 28

Ark's fists clenched as she clearly remembered encountering the body of one such Alexander Fredrickson and the image of Sam turning against him, tearing out his throat and leaving him for dead. *I told him to control his temper and to pull his manners in. I told him, I bloody told him!* She thought, exasperated at the idea of Fredrickson not making it and understanding that he'd perhaps caused his own downfall by not maintaining his temper. Little did Ark know the real story behind Fredrickson's demise at his subject's hands.

It was soon after Ark had made it out of the laboratory, after her brief encounter with Sam, with a flask of acid in hand, hoping to use it to get Losnedahl out of cell B-01. She'd been sprinting while cupping the flask to her chest, hoping Linus hadn't turned Losnedahl into a buffet. Then, she tripped and stumbled over a corpse, making her tumble to the floor. A body she was sure wasn't there before. She luckily held the flask away from the ground, saving it from the impact and shattering over the floor, ruining her chances of saving the mute Norwegian. Ark scampered up to her feet and was about to bypass the corpse as if it were just some hurdle left out for an olympic runner. But that was when she turned around to look at the body and a red trail around it, a trail that came from inside a bonding cell, telling Ark that the body had been purposely moved there. By who? Who is sick enough to move a still-bleeding body and intentionally position it in the middle of the hall in an attempt to trip someone? Ark looked at the number on the cell, and she felt the air being sucked from her lungs when she saw the broad B-35. Then she slowly looked down at the face as if her movements had somehow been slowed down. Her hand instinctively went to her mouth, and her eyes bulged; her heart stopped when she recognised the look of horror on the familiar face she'd seen everywhere in the facility. It was the corpse of Alexander Fredrickson. Ark felt as if she would drop the flask so she could cup her mouth with both hands and stifle a scream, seeing Fredrickson's body with a half-eaten neck that had caked the floor around him with blood. His eyes were huge and full of terror, his mouth agape and blood spilling out of it. He was a fresh kill and was one of the first deaths before the alarm was set off, causing the slaughtering of innocent people to begin.

It made perfect sense!

Ark clutched her head, trying to put the tiny puzzle pieces together. Although Fredrickson was a well-known bonder in the GFOSAR among his pupils and those he tutored into becoming bonders, such as Kolen, he did have flaws and was far from perfect. Ark could see that he was flawed despite his reputation. Yes, he was very strict and had a bad temper that she warned him about, but he was still a good man, just trying to do his job and save the rest of the human race like every other bonder. At least this was what he told people what his plan was, that he wanted to bond with a zombie and make them civil and intelligent enough to be identified as humans. So, why on Earth would Sam mark him as her first victim and start this entire stunt? That part didn't make sense. Why would she kill someone that was trying to help her? Why would Sam go out of her way to start a massacre when she knew that if the military saw her, they'd gun her down in minutes? If she positively had the intelligence of a human being and knew the difference between good and evil, why kill Fredrickson out of all people? Indeed, he was a great and, in some ways, a flawed bonder, but he honestly didn't teach her anything immoral. It made sense that she'd start a massacre upon escaping because it would be an act of natural undead instinct, but it didn't produce any sense of the reasons why

Sam would attack the best bonder in the GFOSAR, let alone kill him. While Fredrickson may have had his flaws as a bonder, Ark speculated that he probably would've made an adept survivor as the man had guts, was a quick thinker and strong sense of leadership.

Ark took her hands away from her head and peered over at the crawler in the wheelchair. It would seem as if Ace had known some things the other humans didn't and couldn't think of the precise way to deliver the information to them. But there was no trouble in asking the crawler about what she knew.

'Tell us more about Sam. Did she do anything to Alexander when he took her out? Anything bad?' She had asked the crawler. The blonde-haired woman approached Ace and knelt beside her, making sure to consume every drop of information Ace could conceive about Sam and the other things she knew. Ace looked up at Ark drunkenly, drooling and one eye twitching. But thankfully, her words didn't come out slurred. They sounded clear and articulate. 'One time, he took out one time. I no know why time, but now I do. She goes by me while I in the cell. First, she looks like me, then she came back looking like you,' Ace replied, pointing to Ark, telling her in her own way that Sam had had the surgery and that had been the only time she'd ever left her cell B-35. 'Keep going, Ace,' encouraged Kolen, staring at her zombie pleadingly, beckoning her to continue. 'I do remember during one of our sessions, you were looking a little strangely at the window behind me. It kinda creeped me out,' said Kolen.

Winsome yawned, seeing these women rely on a crawler who couldn't even speak properly to give them the information they needed on Sam's intentions. It honestly made him want to drop to the deck and sleep until the apocalypse was over. He'd seen better strategies put together in all those zombie movies he watched as a teenager. But the women ignore him. 'Sam look at me when bonder took her back to the cell.' Ace answered Kolen and Ark, sparking their interest further and prompting them to shuffle forward. Winsome let out another loud, annoying yawn, 'WoopiefuckenDoo! Just because she looked at you doesn't tell us jackshit!' Winsome grunted, crossing his arms, huffing, asking if "this dump", the GFOSAR had a packet of cigarettes or a bottle of booze for him to consume.

Losnedahl perceived the impediment in both women's optics, mostly Ark's, because she clenched her fists, ready to deliver another punch to his smug face. Losnedahl stared at Winsome next to him and had decided, 'Oh, to hell with it.' he was sick of Winsome's sarcastic protests and whining, deciding to save Ark the trouble of teaching him a lesson he wouldn't learn. He seized Winsome's right shoulder with a firm man's grip, kicked his foot up with the intention to trip him, and threw him down to the ground next to the paralysed Spot, who towered over him. 'Henrik, what the …' Winsome cried out. Still, his words were quickly turned into incoherent muffles underneath Losnedahl's hand over his mouth, doing everyone a favour in shutting him up and presenting Ace with the opportunity to finish.

Ark regarded Losnedahl and thanked him with a nod, finding satisfaction in seeing Winsome squirm like a fish out of water.

'Ignore him,' Ark said.

'Go on, Ace', Kolen requested, patting Ace on the shoulder, feeling the flaking skin underneath her gloves, making her feel mildly sick. 'Something with that smile she gave, it not friendly and I no like. It look like Sam was thinking something that ended in the bonder lying on the ground; I think Sam plan the bonder death and put everyone in danger.' Ace had concluded, despite the difficulty in understanding the crawler because of the missing words in the sentence, based on what she had told them, Sam's intentions were now manifested as straightforward, and she had to be stopped.

'Shit!' Ark hissed through her teeth. Sam had been planning on killing Fredrickson for a while. She'd been planning on starting a massacre at the GFOSAR for some time. Sam was merely buying her time because of Fredrickson's teachings, waiting for the surgery, and allowing Fredrickson to bond with her. She was waiting for the appropriate moment to start her bloody killing spree, remaking everyone into zombies so that the human race would crumble under her feet. She was genocidal and had to be stopped! The evidence was apparent. 'We have to stop Sam! Kill her. She's the reason so much blood had been spilt. Who knows how much she's killed already and how many more she plans to kill.' Ark told the group what they had to do, her voice high in authority.

Spot stirred for a bit, his fingers and tongue flickering as a sign that he was beginning to wake up and that the pill Ark had given him started to dwindle. Yet, despite being under the influence of the hunger drug, his wired brain had unintentionally caused him to eavesdrop on their conversation. He'd listened to every bit of information about his enemy and was more than ready to stop Sam and help Ark and her friends along the way. He put his hands on the ground and pushed his body up, slowly standing up, and Winsome's eyes enlarged, getting a clear glimpse of Ark's zombie's sheer size, sweet mother of bollocks… that's one tall zombie, he thought to himself.

'B-But Lisa, think about this for a second, she's probably outside the GFOSAR where all the wild zombies are. She could already be terrorising the whole of London as we speak and could have an army of undead against us. Wh-What chance do we have against her?' Kolen whimpered, the fear rising through her body again, her face beginning to drip with sweat. Ark looked at the frightened Dutch woman, seeing the fear behind her glasses and forced a smile, a smile that she hoped would give her some hope. 'Not all hope is lost, Marilyn. There will undoubtedly be survivors out there, people who have adapted to the outside world of walking corpses lingering in the streets. And remember this, Marilyn, we have (a giant) Spot and (a talker) Ace to aid us.' Their goal was clear, and their mission seemed uncomplicated and straightforward; kill Sam and save Britain and perhaps the rest of the countries if they needed help.

'Grab everything you need. Supplies, food, weapons, anything crucial to our mission. We're leaving the GFOSAR.' Ark ordered. She spoke with the voice of a leader.

Chapter 29

She was outside. She breathed in a puff of the air as if it were the first time she'd ever stepped outside after living in quarantine her entire life. She hadn't taken air for over a hundred years, making her smile as she stared out into the foreign, alien landscape that used to be packed-to-the-brim with life. While the streets were paved with the undead and the bloody memories of those who'd tried and failed to survive, there was one thing that was deftly clear to Sam. It sure as hell had felt good to be outside the enclosed walls of the GFOSAR! She was away from the condensed, claustrophobic spaces and the feeling of bumping into people along the way and giving her disgusted looks. The outside was open, with the constant stench of rotting flesh sweeping through the air like a retched perfume that only the undead could tolerate as if it were the latest Shine makeup product. To Sam, she had felt right at home.

Sam wasted no time, with minimal hesitation, about spreading the infection of the mortuus carnem through crimes of the multiple murders she'd perpetrated back inside the sanctuary of the GFOSAR. She had little sympathy, if any, for the human race. Mercy was a foreign word to her. Despite having read all about it in the novels Fredrickson had presented her. Books and novellas about injustice and justice, with characters begging the villain for mercy and heroes saving the day. The difference between good and evil. It made no difference to her. Because Fredrickson was dead, so what did it matter if she was doing wrong? No one was going to stop her. Killing people felt so good; the ever-sweetening lust for blood, the agonising distressed screams of those Sam would butcher and mutilate in various creative ways just to satisfy her zest for carnage.

Mercy was for the weak. Sam had become the opposite of what the bonding process was created for, becoming a symbol of science gone rogue, the embodiment of evil. She'd embraced Fredrickson's dying words with a smile as if to spite him. Sam was indeed a very bad girl, and showed zero signs of stopping her gruesome path of destruction, wiping out the rest of the human race, killing anyone in her way in the most unimaginable ways the human mind could predict. She was a force to be reckoned with and, like Ark had proposed, needed to be stopped. But how could she be stopped when she was still far ahead of Ark and Company?

Sam may just be a simple female zombie with a human appearance, thanks to the surgery (it would be hard to spot her amongst a crowd of people; the eyes might be the only credible evidence that she was dead), but Sam was no ordinary zombie; that fact was apparent thanks to Fredrickson. Sam was a heavily bonded zombie capable of thinking about her surroundings and the scenarios before her. She was scary smart. Sam knew all too well that she'd be hunted down by the ones who'd been lucky enough to have escaped her reign of carnage and terror, with them being fortified in the safety of the bonding cells, along with their bonded zombies. But did she care? No. She knew that the survivors wanted her dead again, and she knew that she'd have to come up with ways of slowing them down; if Sam couldn't kill them, the best she could do was slow them down. She didn't intend to be stopped, so simply, the survivors of the GFOSAR would have to use every ounce of willpower if they wanted to repeal and eviscerate Sam, the zombie.

Sam wondered through the desolate English streets, taking in the sheer amount of decay that had befallen the once-living city. Her pale grey eyes darted from left to right, staring at the many buildings whose windows were broken and replaced with wooden boards. Sam found herself treading over to one of those buildings without much reason, letting her feet carry her in whatever direction they faced. Sam approached one of the windows and examined one of the wooden boards covering it. There were a few splodges of blood dripping from it. Still, nobody around to tell Sam who it could have belonged to, so Sam reached out and took a brief swipe of the red splatter with her finger, bringing it to her mouth and licking it where she could determine that the blood was fresh, meaning it had belonged to a human who must've died recently. The body had been dragged away and possibly eaten there. Sam was about to turn and let herself into the building when a young man with red hair, perhaps around seventeen, leapt out of the doorway, a Remington shotgun clutched in his hands as he stared at Sam as if she was a lost survivor seeking shelter away from the undead, completely ignoring the apparent factor that she was caked in blood.

'H-Hey, lady! What are you doing out here alone? Get inside!' He spoke with a robust and posh accent as he called out to her. Sam didn't have much time to react as the young man already made up his decision, ushering the Remington under his left arm. He strode over swiftly, eyes darting cautiously around his sides, took hold of Sam's hand and attempted to bring her inside where a middle-aged woman with red hair and a younger-looking boy, around five with blonde hair and glasses sat, cuddled one another in the corner like frightened rabbits. Sam stared at them, then at the boy and restrained the urge to grin at him, knowing that he had just unknowingly dug his and the woman's and more petite boy's graves.

'It's dangerous out there, miss. But don't worry, you'll be safe here; the woman over there is my mother, Sabrina, and my little brother Zack. We will take good care of you. You can call me Hamish, Hamish Daniels at your service.

The red-haired older lady looked up at Sam, holding a carton of milk in her hand and the hand of a small boy, about five in the other. 'Pl-Please stay for as long as you like, Mrs, I didn't catch your name.' Sabrina spoke timidly to Sam.

'Mummy!' squeaked the little boy.

'Yes, my little Zackery, what is it, hon? Are you hungry? Thirsty?'

'What's wrong with lady's eyes, and what's the red stuff over her?'

Ugh, kids, such a nuisance... the cover had been blown by a mere five-year-old boy who actually was shown to have more self-preservation than his Mum and big brother as he was the one that saw through Sam's identity as a zombie; he noticed her dead pale, bloodshot eyes and the blood that blanketed her.

The chips were on the ground now as both Sabrina and Hamish stared at Sam; their eyes broad, and their mouths hung low in an almost comical realisation that Sam wasn't a lost survivor at all but a zombie!

'Hamish! Kill her! She's one of them!' shrieked Sabrina, holding her youngest son closer to her chest as he cried. Out of fear, Hamish brought the Remington up and tried to aim and shoot at Sam, but Sam grabbed the muzzle and yanked it out of the teenager's hands. 'What the?' he cried, bawling his hand up into a fist and ramming it towards Sam, hoping to clock her; Sam caught Hamish's fist, grinning now, she pushed it forward with enough force to break his wrist, resulting in an ear-splitting CRACK that made Sabrina, little Zackery, and Hamish all erupt into screams, only Hamish's screams were more deafening as it was his wrist that she'd snapped. Hamish fell to his knees, in tears, holding his broken wrist, which had blood pouring out as his hand flicked around like a detached doll's limb. Sam glanced at the young man, and her smile widened. Sabrina took notice of this and condemned Sam in the same manner as poor Robert Boson had done before Sam ended his life. 'Witch! You leave my son alone!' shrieked Sabrina Daniels. But Sam pretended she hadn't heard the mother's feeble cries as Sam strutted over to the anguished Hamish, who seemed more focused on his broken wrist than on giving Sam any real attention, but she didn't care. She placed a hand on her chest and another on his head and pushed again, with the same amount of force she'd used when breaking the young man's wrist, only this time, she broke Hamish's neck, which had his spine protruding out for his dear mamma and 'lil brother to see in all its bloody glory.

'NO!' Sabrina shrieked, as she clutched her youngest son more closely as he did the same with her, using his tiny arms to wrap around his mother's neck as he tried but failed to evict his glance from the horrific sight in front of them.

'HAMISH!!' cried little Zack as Hamish's now dead body fell to the side. Sam turned her attention towards the helpless mother and young son, licking her lips wickedly.

Chapter 30

A terrifying aura lingered in the GFOSAR. The five humans and two bonded zombies had made sure they had gotten everything they needed for their journey into leaving the walls of the GFOSAR (the only natural source of safety was broken, all thanks to that zombie bitch), guns, first aid kits, food to snack on and drink to nourish them, along with all the hunger drugs they could find and anything else that they knew that they'd need during their perilous journey across the stark landscape of the outside. Standing inside the small breakroom outside B-12, where Losnedahl and Winsome had brought the wheelchair, they consoled each other to double-check if they were genuinely ready to face the horrors of the outside. The undead and unbonded were everywhere, waiting like a tiger in the jungle foliage stalking its prey. It was a scary thought to be leaving the facility where they'd slept for years, and it was even more frightening to be going into the outside world where the atmosphere was completely different and far more dangerous, where anything could kill you if you weren't careful. One would need to have their wits about them if they wanted to survive the dangers of the outside. They couldn't stay here in this dead facility; Ark knew they would need to go outside, as dangerous as it was. It was better to be outside with strangers rather than inside and wait for former friends to wake up into a life full of insatiable hunger for the flesh of the living.

Winsome fisted the air triumphantly, vocally expressing that he was more than ready to go outside and blast any rotting muttons he could see, as he had so boldly stated, but Ark wasn't yet convinced. She rolled her eyes because she knew that Winsome was letting his confidence and cockiness get the better of him. She almost wanted to give him a reality check and inform him that on the outside, he couldn't flap his jaw and would need to stay close and not draw any unwanted attention to himself. Though she also knew that Winsome was never going to change out of his cockiness, and trying to give him some advice that would probably save his arse would be pointless. So, she was sure he wouldn't listen to her. He'd have to evolve to be suited to the outside conditions. It was like the rest of them; they'd need to develop and adapt to the perilous surroundings. Ark's eyes switched between the five standing around her, and she asked if they were ready for the journey into the outside to hunt down the black-haired witch that brought the kingdom down on them. Almost straight after she'd spoken, Spot leaned over, bowing his half-head in the direction of Ark, holding his brain jar with one hand; he put a hand on his chest, then he pointed at her, showing her that he was more than ready to follow her lead. Losnedahl cocked his head to Ark and gave her a dull thumbs up and a less-than-confident grin, stating that he was also prepared, despite having some kind of inkling as to the terrors that would be facing them on the outside. The crawler then peered up in Ark's direction from the wheelchair and said, 'Ace, go outside,' confirming that she was also ready. The last person to say anything was Kolen, who was grasping upon a realistic image of what they'd find outside of the GFOSAR: empty streets with large numbers of hungry zombies looming around, mutilated corpses scattering the street, waiting to be resurrected by the mortuus carnem, pages from newspapers and torn books fluttering in the wind as if they had minds of their own and blood. Lots and lots of blood.

Marilyn?' Ark asked the Dutch woman in a small, soft voice. Kolen looked at Ark with red eyes. She knew that Kolen could always confide her feelings to her or the late Fredrickson. Usually, Kolen's facial emotions were easy to distinguish, but this time, her face was a variety of mixed emotions that Ark couldn't precisely read. Kolen wiped her eyes swiftly before saying, 'Mr Fredrickson's teachings are the precise reason why I'm here and got Ace talking in the first place; if it wasn't for him, Ace might have killed me without so much as lifting a finger. I owe him my life. I'm more than ready to do anything to avenge him,' she said, providing Ark with all the conviction she needed to know that everyone was ready to say goodbye to the GFOSAR and hunt down the zombie named Sam.

Lisa Ark had taken the stand against Sam as the leader of the group. Much to her dismay, she'd been the most voted role for the leader and the one to ensure everyone made it out alive. She knew that no one else would be otherwise suited to the role aside from her. Like everyone else in the group, Ark wanted to avenge the fallen, such as Alexander Fredrickson and others like Cansu Aksoy, Olio Garcia, Robert Boson, Maximillian Engel, Daisuke Kushiro, Quinn Steinmann, Carl Boyle, and so many more who'd been unlucky enough to have an encounter with a zombie doctor, according to Winsome.

Spot had appointed himself as bodyguard to Ark and would be responsible for her well-being and safety. If she ordered him to do something for her and the group, he'd do it without question. Spot's life was in his bonder's hands. She could kill him at any time if he succumbed to violence like the other rabid undead, but that was highly unlikely. Despite his appearance and prominent Death Mark, Spot was far too developed because of how Ark had bonded with him; he'd acquired more than dedication and feelings for her.

Despite his missing tongue, Losnedahl didn't need one in his role of organiser. Losnedahl would be the one to fill the group's supply cash for both human and zombie resources. He'd keep everything in check, making sure nothing went missing or, worse, stolen. Losnedahl would also be willing to run out and fetch more stuff for them if needed and, if lucky, bring more survivors and become like a small army to withstand Sam's.

Kolen was appointed the most accessible and safest role because she wasn't the type to get blood on her hands or go out into a dangerous world. She took the role of keeping check of the supplies and maintaining that they had enough resources and food for their travels. If they didn't have enough of something, Kolen would be sure to inform someone in the group that they were running low and would need to get more of that particular something. She would also be Ace's caretaker.

Ace, upon first impressions, had seemed pretty useless in the group, a liability that opened a window to death; she knew as well as everyone else in the group that she was nowhere near as brilliant as Sam, or even the rest of the group, and the fact that Ace didn't have legs made picking her role complicated. But because Ace was a zombie, like Sam and Spot. She could be competent to convince the other wild zombies to swap sides, turning them against Sam by communicating in English and zombie moans, because there is no doubt that Sam would have an army at her disposal or would be turning the roaming undead into her own personal soldiers.

And as much as everyone hated him for his constant barrage of insults and unnecessary jokes, Winsome had the role of the fighter because it would provide him with the chance to redeem himself and prove he was a brave man, instead of a man with a big mouth and not so much bravery when it came to fighting off attackers. He wanted to own up for all the times he allowed himself to be beaten; he tried to do damage to someone instead of someone inflicting damage on him. And besides, he couldn't pass up the idea of having bragging rights to how many zombies he killed along the way; he knew he couldn't just let his rights to bragging slide. That would be like telling him to stop breathing. Winsome announced that he'd be the one to fend off the dead, killing them and expectedly making sure they don't rise up from their slumber once again with any patrolling mortuus carnem parasites around the recently dispatched zombie. 'The double tap was sure to do the job,' he'd said with a cocky grin.

Holding the needed equipment and supplies, the group left the sanctuary of the breakroom and proceeded to make their way downstairs to L1, praying that they didn't run into any of the undead along their way to the GFOSAR's front door. Upon reaching the entrance of the GFOSAR, which had taken three minutes because they all each had to manoeuvre their way around obstacles, stepping over gaping mangled corpses, some of which had missing limbs and blood, giving the floor a fresh shade of colour, the group had to make themselves scarce, temporarily distancing from one other to watch their steps around the bodies and being mindful not to slip into the blood, making them look like they played a part in a psychopath's sick game.

Because no one else would do it, Kolen was in charge of pushing and steering the wheelchair into which Ace was nestled comfortably. When it came to stepping over the bodies, she had to lean the wheelchair up and over them as well as the limbs, considering she wanted to throw up each time she saw the mangled bodies with the bones exposed and the blood oozing from any openings. 'Guys... I don't think I can do this,' Kolen cringed, holding her mouth; an ugly retching sound came from her throat and eyes broadened behind her spectacles upon seeing the body of a man whose chest had been eaten away, revealing his exposed ribcage with organs still secure inside.

It was Ark who approached her and placed a hand on her shoulder. 'Yes, you can, Marilyn, just try not to think about it,' She encouraged her with that same soft tone that she had used before. Spot peered in Kolen's direction, figuring he should help Kolen without being ordered by Ark to perform a random act of kindness. He held his brain jar with one arm, using his other to grab one of the handles. He elevated the wheelchair over the man with the exposed ribcage and large clump of human body parts before putting it down on the ground and ushering Kolen to follow by gurgling a word that had sounded like "come" before returning to the use of both hands to hold the brain jar. 'Th-Thank you, Spot,' Kolen stammered, not noticing just how tall Spot was and how his towering, looming presence and that tongue that moved about like it seemingly had a mind of its own and drooling at random times had sent chills down her spine. Kolen had always found tall men to be unnerving; thankfully, her late husband Jacob was only a few inches taller and didn't tower over her like Spot had. Kolen closed her eyes and bit her lip as she stepped up the small mountain of bodies and leapt off it, her feet landing in front of the wheelchair and letting out a sigh of relief, knowing the worst was over. And she'd continue to wheel Ace behind the trail of the others in the group who were more than ready to leave the GFOSAR, closing the one deadly door only to open another deadlier door.

'Is everyone ready? Once we leave this building, we won't be able to return and will be knocking on the doorstep of death itself?' Ark declared, wanting to double-check if everyone was really up to the task set out before them.

The group nodded, inhaling one final breath inside the GFOSAR and exhaling. However, Ark had gone outside before to retrieve Spot's prized possession; she knew that going outside this time would hit a more sensitive part of her because once she stepped outside, her fate would be sealed. She understood she wouldn't be able to return to the damaged facility, not with a highly dangerous adversary on the loose.

Losnedahl and Winsome came up from behind Ark, moving in front of her, placing their hands on the glass-pained doors of the GFOSAR's entrance, the place that had previously been known as a sanctuary and the only place in London that was remotely considered safe. After a moment, the men looked at Ark, who thought about what could happen to them and nodded. Both men then stared at each other for a brief moment, pushing the doors outwards, sending a heavy plume of the rotting undead into their snouts. 'Ugh, smells worse than sick, no worse than animal shit', Winsome moaned, holding his nose, endeavouring to block out the stench. Ark was holding onto a rifle that she'd taken, finding it to be suited to her as if it had spoken to her in whispers (*You know we're compatible, Lisa*), had claimed from Winsome's personal stash of guns that he had been carrying in an oversized gym bag when Losnedahl had led him back into the small break room (*your nightmares are just beginning. Better hope that you're equipped to face the horrors before you*). She was the first to step outside the GFOSAR, seeing the United Kingdom's dying nation again for the first time in years. It deeply perturbed her. But going back inside wasn't an option. Not when lives were at stake.

Chapter 31

Outside the GFOSAR's doors, it didn't take long for the group to run into a pack of regular unbonded zombies roaming around, sniffing the air. The first sight they were greeted with was normal staggering, reanimated rotting corpses skulking about looking for food. Luckily for the survivors, they didn't stick around and allow themselves to be set upon or to see where the pack was heading to. It'd be dumb to stay around and to just watch them as if they were wild animals in a nature documentary.

One by one, they followed behind Ark as she moved down the path on her side, seeing it as a much safer option than going straight ahead and into the unbonded territory. Once Ark was sure they were out of sight from their unwanted welcoming party, Ark beckoned that they make a run for it, as far away from the GFOSAR as possible. No one objected to this command as they all ran in the footsteps of the blonde woman for the nearest place (an abandoned shack that looked as if a homeless person had lived in it, by a simple rusted container that would've been used as a heater), that appeared empty and safe enough and away from the prying undead eyes. Standard zombies provided various challenges for the group of four humans and two zombies; it was really all dependent on how old the zombie was. But when it came down to it, the undead's difficulty and threats relied on the person's actions and how heedless and narcissistic they were to the circumstances at hand, such as Winsome flapping his jaw or trying to show off by letting off a few rounds and drawing the enemy to him. But ordinarily, the undead didn't need a whole lot of bullets to put them down; just a few shots to the head and blasting the brain apart with heavy firearms would do the trick, at least, that's what the army had told those fortified inside the GFOSAR. 'One shot wouldn't be enough; the rotten sacks would need at least five to put them down,' Ark had heard someone from the army say as he patrolled the subject collection room. One of the main things that would catch anyone's eye was the ever-disgusting sight of the innumerable managed bodies littered across the streets, unavoidable to the eye, turning a once lively town into a ghost town abundant with the daunting memories of the past not buried.

Remembering that one piece of advice that she'd heard, Ark turned around and reconciled it to the group, though her stern words were mainly directed towards Winsome. Mentioning that one bullet wouldn't be enough and that they'd need a few to put them down, she said. 'This is survival, lads; one isn't enough. Give 'em five, and that should put them down, but don't waste your ammunition; only shoot if you absolutely need to. We need to look after Marilyn, her crawler, and our own skin.' She didn't need to tell Losnedahl again about what it means to survive. He'd been surviving all his life.

Taking these words into account, Winsome actually behaves for once and does exactly what Ark told him to do. Both he and Losnedahl gathered around the Dutch woman and the crawler, huddling around like royal templars guarding the queen against any offence that was aimed at her.

Meanwhile, Ark had been specific about not firing off any guns unless they absolutely needed to. Each of the four members had their own way of killing the undead whenever it came down to it, such as a zombie getting too close to them or if a pack of them had smelt them and came for them, which sometimes Winsome would confidently fire off his Remington without much thought. Some were swift and simple; others were slow and brutal. Ark held a sniper rifle, which she'd later claim as her own, as soon as Winsome revealed that he possessed a secret stash of weapons that he stole from the armoury on L1 and had greedily intended to keep for himself only. But now that he was with the group, his bag of firearms only seemed to grow. He had only opened up about the weapons he claimed he'd nicked from the armoury when Ark questioned him about the contents inside his gym bag. She also asked if anyone else knew the location of the arsenal storage and if they still had any weapons that they could use at their disposal in fighting against the undead. And if luck was on their side, Ark hoped she could snipe that Sam bitch without her knowing, causing an end to her killing spree, and saving countless lives.

Spot rightly wasn't trusted with using a weapon such as a gun or a knife. It was commonly debatable that he wouldn't even be able to use one anyway, as he didn't have any eyes to see where he was aiming, or where he was slashing. As much as Ark was concerned, he could hurt one of them, and he wouldn't know, so she decided that Spot's hands should remain free. The giant zombie would come to use when it came to the role of bodyguard, striving to protect the assembly of humans around him, mainly Ark, from the wild, hungry zombies without the use of weapons because, like Ark, they'd be of no use to him anyway. He'd be able to use his intimidating stature to his advantage, and if it ever came down to it (which it probably would), he could pound zombies to death with his bare hands, tearing their heads or jaws off, often attending to his fists becoming covered in blood. But because he was a zombie, bloody fists didn't mean shit to him; he sometimes licked them off his fingers to give his hunger some satisfaction (even if undead blood wasn't as divine as living blood, it was better than nothing); too which he'd place his hand over his tongue to help him swallow.

Losnedahl was in charge of wielding the revolver that Winsome had almost shot him with when they'd reunited back at the GFOSAR. He didn't want something big and heavy like a shotgun or rifle; Losnedahl felt more comfortable with something small and light like a revolver or a bowie knife. So Winsome did the reasonable thing and handed the firearm over to him, feeling that he'd use it more than him and because he viewed that Losnedahl would be far more suited to small guns than big ones with loud booms.

Winsome was the opposite and found himself suited to big guns when it came to the apocalypse. He favoured the idea of killing swarms of the mosquito-like parasites that flew past him. The mortuus carnem parasites were just as much of a threat as the zombies; they were resurrecting them, so it only made sense for the parasites to be treated as creatures that people wanted to make extinct, a nightmare preserved in historical memory. Losendahl had laid claim to the shotgun. The heavy weapon that was best used for close-range if you really wanted to seriously hurt something or even kill it, but range didn't matter when it came to fighting in a dying world where the dead walked the Earth. Because the undead had a hunger that was never sated and were always on high alert for anything that could be a potential meal for them, and if a zombie had its sights on you, you'd better pray you had enough ammo in your bags to bring it down. Because these zombies didn't mess around, they weren't slow and lumbering like those depicted in most zombie movies; these ones ran when they were in dire need of some brains. And when they ran, they sprinted.

The outside was just as they had expected it to be; a sad, dreary place littered with dozens of dead bodies that were either left unattended, waiting for the mortuus carnem to sniff them out or were in the process of being eaten by the already lingering numbers of the undead. There wasn't a single sign of life amongst the once lively streets. Buildings were in a drastic state of disrepair; windows were broken or bared, and valuables had been stolen from shops when the first zombies had started walking. There was graffiti, written in both black and white coloured paint, even blood, that had been sprayed all across the walls, marking the apocalypse, and that the end was nigh. The sky was a lifeless, depressing grey. The sun had been robbed of its blinding beauty, like the mortuus carnem had infected and killed its glory, because it now hung bitterly in the sky behind a never-ending blanket of grey clouds and even when it did show, its rays had lacked the merit that it once had before, a mere shady ball of light. Big Ben appeared like a titan who had sliced it in two with a giant sword and had taken a large bite out of what remained. Dust billowed in the air, creating small sand tornados that were sure to fill anyone's lungs. Everything was just so stagnant and lifeless. A bleak reminder of what a simple mortuus carnem could do to the country.

'What do we do now, our brave and courageous leader, Lisa?' Winsome whined, seeing the outside state for the first time in six years and wanting to know what they were going to do next, not wanting to wait for death to catch up to them, now that they were outside where danger had lurked. They weren't behind the secured walls of the GFOSAR. They were outside those walls, in the land of the dead. To be more specific, they'd wandered out of zombie sight into an alleyway that, thankfully, was clean enough. Not many bodies were around to lure the starving undead to them, so they were in the clear for now, at least until a rabid zombie skulked past the alleyway, picking up their scent, which would end terribly for the five living members. 'Don't call me "Leader," Ryan. I'm not even close to a leader. I just want us, as survivors, to make it through the next twenty-four hours alive and uninfected by the mortuus carnem,' Ark clenched her fist, staring out into what used to be the city. 'It's all thanks to that motherfucking parasite that the dead are rising from the graves with an ever-present taste for anything that breathes. Or can remotely be deemed as alive. If only it had never been discovered.' Ark sneered with a stern, cold tone. Ark's mind had been transfixed on two things, both stopping that intelligent zombie bitch who murdered Fredrickson and started the massacre. And eradicate the entire mortuus carnem species, once and for all. Giving the deceased the peace they wanted, allowing them to finally enjoy their eternal slumber without worrying about some mosquito-like creature causing them to rise up and feast on the living and friends and family. 'Don't forget that cunt that started the massacre on the place we "once" called a sanctuary. We gotta focus on killing that bitch first! Then we can focus on finding a meteorite for the mortuus carnem.' Winsome enunciated, and for once, Ark had agreed with him, having the same thoughts as he did about Sam and sending the mortuus carnem to the dinosaurs. *Oh yes, Sam, just wait. Just you fucking wait! It doesn't matter how fucking intelligent Alexander made you or how clever you're becoming. One of these days, we'll put an end to your pitiful existence. We'll make sure you don't get revisited by the mortuus carnem; mark my words, you bitch.* Ark's mind had recited, thinking of the many sadistic ways they could dispatch Sam from the face of the Earth. It didn't matter which method they'd use to their advantage; as long as Sam was six feet under, that was all it would take to satisfy Ark and her needs to protect her friends and the rest of the human race as best as possible.

'Lisa, I don't mean to interrupt if you're in the middle of fantasising about our survival in the company of two good bonded zombies. But shouldn't we look for a place to rest and gain our strength for the time being, and if we're lucky, run into some survivors along the way, probably with the same intentions as us?' Kolen hesitated, holding the handles of Ace's wheelchair, which Ace sat impassively in. Ark looked at Kolen with a gleam in her eye. She gave her a nod. 'Good thinking, Marilyn; I got ahead of myself in thinking about ways to put the mortuus carnem to extinction. Glad we have you to worry about our safety,' Ark applauded Kolen, giving her a small smile of hope. 'Um, excuse me, Marilyn, but have you seen *The Walking Dead?* Or any kind of zombie movie? Survivors are bad news and might want to kill us just as much as the undead,' Winsome turned to Ark, flabbergasted, and stunned as if someone had swung a cricket bat into his crotch. 'Also, where the fuck are we gonna go? In case you bitches hadn't cleaned your peepers from the dirt in them, the entire English country is populated with fucking zombies!' Winsome screamed, letting the dread and panic get a hold of him.

'Yeah, we noticed', Losnedahl wanted to say sarcastically, rolling his eyes along with Ark and Kolen, all equally fed up with Winsome bitching like a spoilt brat for not getting what he wanted from the lollie shop. Ark stared at Spot from the corner of her eye. 'Be a dear, would you, Spot? Shut Ryan up,' she'd winked at him, but he couldn't see it, of course, for obvious reasons. 'Wait, what?' Winsome exclaimed. Spot tilted his head in the direction of Winsome's voice; without question, he held his brain jar out for someone to hold onto for him while he shut the whining Ryan Winsome up. 'Gimme,' Ace pleaded, holding her hands out to him. Spot hesitated, unsure if Ace would be the right one to hold something so precious to him. 'Go on, Spot, you can give it to Ace. She's reliable, right Marilyn?' Ark observed Kolen, searching for the truth about Ace's reliability. 'O-Of course she is, sh-she might be a bit of a klutz from having no bottom half, and well, not really crafty when it comes to problem-solving and speech. But Ace is reliable nonetheless from what I taught her and what I have learnt so far up to this point,' Kolen replied, looking down at Ace the entire time, who was looking at

Spot's brain jar eagerly, couldn't tell if with malice or rectitude. Spot obeyed his bonder. He obeyed and lowered his arms to Ace; she had her arms out, ready to meet the jar Spot was lowering down to her. 'Be very careful with that brain, Ace. It means a lot to Spot. I don't think he'd be very happy if you dropped and damaged it, so please be careful, Ace,' Kolen balanced to give the direction upon gazing up at Spot's towering structure and gulping. Must've been a basketball player before death; his size must've been at least seven-zero" when he was alive and had a full head, Kolen thought while glancing up at the tall zombie with half a crown. 'I zombie, I have zombie grip, I cling on for life, count on me,' Ace said back to her bonder (basically saying she had a firm, vice grip and was faithful to her word).

'As long as you know', Kolen assured, wanting to smile. 'Yadiyadayada, can you bitches just shut u-'Winsome was immediately interrupted by Spot taking a firm hold of the back of his light brown coat and yanking him towards him, holding him still and his mouth closed. Turning his bitching into muffled shouts of protest. 'Thank you, Spot. I'll give you a treat when we find some shelter,' Ark responded with a slight smile on her face, glad that someone had finally shut Winsome up and done everyone a favour. Bloody hell, Spot, you're a big boy. Ark's mind wandered off from realising just how dwarfed Winsome looked compared to Spot, and knowing that he would've been taller in life just added another intimidating factor about him (Winsome was only five-seven", Ark was five-eight", Losnedahl was 6'0, Kolen was five-five"). Ark shook her head, resetting her mind, taking it back into the real world at the touch of Losnedahl's hand as he was on alert, telling Ark through sign that he'd heard some faint whispering coming from behind them. The others remained quiet and listened in; they had heard it too. 'I think there's someone behind us,' Kolen rose to a whimper. 'No shit

Sherlock,' was heard from Winsome's muffled mouth from underneath Spot's big hands. 'Sounds like the undead have found us… Get ready,' Ark rustled, holding the sniper rifle up so the scope was up to her eyes. 'Spot, guard Marilyn and Ace', she ordered, stepping in the front of the group with the rifle aimed up high and ready to shoot anything that moved.

Sam, if that's you coming to claim our lives like you did back at the GFOSAR, you bet your arse that we won't lay down so simply; we're a gathered group of four survivors as well as two bonded zombies from the GFOSAR with one mission, to eliminate you from the face of the Earth! So, if it's you, Sam, come out. Make this quick, and let us kill you; you'll pay for what you did in the GFOSAR. Both Losnedahl and Ark's minds had cursed whoever was watching them, making the whispering ruckus in front of them, aiming to distract them, drawing them close enough to the opening so they could be dispatched by the unknown assailant. 'I warn you, I'm armed, and I'm feeling a tad trigger-happy.' The whispering came to a cessation about a minute and a half later, which was unsettling, leaving them in an unwelcoming silence. 'Congratulations, Lisa, you scared the entire pack,' Winsome mumbled from behind Spot's hands. But then, just as Winsome had said that, Ark stopped, thrusting her hand before her, telling them to stop. They did and stared at Ark, wondering why she'd stopped them. Was she seeing or hearing something that they couldn't yet?

'Lisa?' peeped Kolen, 'what is it?'

'I hear something,' whispered Ark, tilting her head back towards those behind her; she put a finger to her lips in a shushing movement. Ark slid her hand up to the leather rifle strap around her, and slowly and quietly, she removed it and held the rifle in both her hands as she told the group to not make a sound just in case her suspicions were confirmed. Then everyone could hear it, the sound Ark was hearing, the sound of faint footsteps behind them, which sounded like someone was running, footsteps echoing in the darkened alleyway, growing closer and closer to the group.

Chapter 32

The footsteps ceased after reaching a certain distance from the group, putting Ark more on edge. As far as she was concerned, this stranger concealed in the shadow could easily be Sam, who was trying to manifest as a survivor from the outside. Ark didn't want to take any chances if the lives behind her were on the line. She placed one finger on the trigger of the rifle and turned around to aim at whoever was behind them, about to shoot the figure stalking them, thinking they were clever to jump them. They hadn't been on the outside for so much as an hour. But despite that, Ark hated being outside, and she knew that anyone who claimed to be safe could prove dangerous. It wasn't like inside the GFOSAR, where she learned the people there were safe and relatively harmless; on the outside, anyone could be safe or dangerous depending on who you met. 'Who the fuck are you? What the fuck do you want?' She snapped, demanding the figure answer her before she immediately pulled back on the rifle's trigger. 'I highly recommend that you back the hell off or tell me who you are and what you want. This thing is loaded, and I have fired one of these before.' The figure fell silent for a few seconds, as if considering Ark's words of retreat, before submitting that he or she was no threat, hoisting up the arms in a surrendering posture, revealing the armaments the figure had been carrying on their person. A simple kitchen knife and a butcher's cleaver, which could've meant that this person must've used close combat, getting up close and personal with the undead so they could kill them; the figure threw the sharp cutlery to the ground with an echoing clanging noise upon impacting the pavement without being told to. But Ark still wasn't entirely convinced that this stranger was friendly; she continued to hold her aim. 'No funny business, mate. I mean it.' warned Ark as she watched the figure take one step backwards, its arms becoming feverish, appearing as if the figure was struggling to keep them up. Either that or the figure had another weapon concealed somewhere and was itching to use it.

'You're alive?' the stranger muttered before he went with pleading and trying to bargain with Ark. 'D-Don't shoot, please, I-I want to help you. I know a place where you guys can hide and use for a safe haven, getting your strength back. Please, I know how bad it is out here; you can trust me,' the figure spoke in a gruff masculine croak, identifying himself as male. 'You can trust me, yeah? I'm unarmed, my weapons are on the ground there.' The acting was on point. If Ark didn't know any better, she'd trust this fellow as he was proposing things that they did need; a place to stay where they'd be safe and regain lost energy, away from the undead sniffing them out, smelling their living skin, and most likely, smelling their brains and being drawn to them like flies are attracted to manure and anything that smells wondrous. Years ago, studies at the GFOSAR revealed that zombies had a far superior sense of smell to humans. They were like humanoid bloodhounds. But for all Ark knew, this man could easily be bribing her into coming with him, and once inside, he would reveal his true intentions, that he was part of some kind of cult dedicated to snuffing out the would-be survivors. It'd be like what Winsome had warned Kolen about from seeing all those zombie movies he'd claimed to have seen in his youth, how some survivors adapted outside had been driven insane from the horror around them. This unknown man presumably would most likely have a party of outcasts with him, waiting to jump and rob them of their supplies and weapons. Then he and his band would leave them to fend for themselves, unarmed and without any medical supplies to patch themselves up for when any of them sustained some kind of trauma. It wouldn't be out of spite or hate for the group; it was natural for urgent people to do reckless things in these rough times. People would do anything to survive. So, thinking about all these possibilities that could happen if she wasn't careful with her decision-making, she kept the rifle poised, keeping a firm aim on this strange man cloaked in a thick layer of darkness, which was only adding to the ominous feeling that he was possibly hiding something wicked. Ark closed one eye and looked down through the scope. 'You sure as hell had better be telling the truth and no porkies, or I'll make you think twice about thinking you could jump Lisa Ark and her companions, so you spill the truth, or you can kiss your arse goodnight!' Ark was upbraided, her arms beginning to shake, her teeth were clenched, and her cheeks starting to drip with stress and perspiration, not knowing what to do with this man. She couldn't tell if he was good or bad, and she couldn't bear fruit to the idea of killing someone, a seemingly innocent man at that. Purposely taking the life of a living person was on a whole different level and was something that Ark wouldn't be able to live with if the choice had come to her and she'd been forced into taking a person's life. Her job was to save lives, not take them.

'I swear on my Aunt Rhonda's grave that my words are genuine. I'm not shitting you in any way. I honestly do know a place where the five of you can rest up and restock on supplies and shit; you can trust me,' the man insisted while he pleaded for life and their trust, still holding up his arms as if waiting to be policed and arrested. 'Woah, Woah, wait!' Ark began to steadily lower the rifle but kept her guard up for any sudden movements the man blanketed in shadow made, watching his hands closely, hoping he didn't have a gun holstered on his knee, one that he'd draw when Ark and the others weren't looking. 'How can we be certain we can trust you, like put our lives on edge for you? And there's six of us, if you count the crawler in the wheelchair operated by Marilyn, yet again you probably can't see her in this dim light, and she's behind both Henrik and Ryan, but that doesn't matter; you better cough up the evidence if you want us to trust you,' Ark finished. She was still on edge, still not ready to trust this man until he gave them some adequate information on why he'd claimed that he wanted to help them and wanted them to follow him to this safe haven of his. For all Ark and the other humans knew, he could be a deviant, trying to lead them into a trap, or waiting for their guard to be down so he could strip them of their weapons. However, that would be tricky as Spot would be able to repel him, just with his height alone, or if he tried anything, Spot would be able to pick him up and hold him until Ark told Spot what to do with him. But who knew, maybe the man actually did want to help them.

The man gulped, slowly putting down his hands. His posture going to the ground and disappearing from Ark's view. There was no way she could be hallucinating things now? It hadn't even been an hour away from the GFOSAR. But then Ark heard the sound of hands rustling on the ground, fingernails clinking on the pavement as if they were looking for something on the ground, maybe the knife and cleaver he'd surrendered. Though he may not be trying to claim his innocence anymore to Ark, she could identify that he was seeking no desire to keep the conversation going forever, as he thought that it was getting absolutely nowhere, which she could agree with. It was getting nowhere, and they were just stalling time. The clinking fingernails continued to search the ground until they seemingly found what they were looking for, the knife and cleaver next there were sharp metal scrapes on the pavement. As the man stood up, he put the cutlery weapons into his cloak of darkness and took a small step backward.

When he spoke up next, he responded with something he knew the group would want to hear. And by the tone of his voice, shuddering and choked, it was something that he didn't want to bring up again because it had been something so shocking and destructive that he could've sworn that he'd borne witness to the devil unbound from the chains of Hell and was wrecking its work on anyone in its way. At least, that was what he thought it was. And what could be more destructive than a demon free from its confinement?

'Look lady, I know how you must feel, I get that, I understand, but listen to me when I tell you this... moments ago, a mysterious black-haired woman clad in a black shirt and tan shorts passed through here not that long ago and brutally murdered most of my friends and the people whom I was hiding out with… this bitch… she… she was smiling… that scary smile as she showed no mercy for them which I'll never forget. She smiled as she slaughtered them in cold blood while I managed to nimbly escape with my life intact. I want to repay that bitch for killing my people by killing her! Those screams of all my companions will be avenged in her death!' the man inhaled through his nose. 'Please if you're going to stop her, I want in. I want to help you get her.' The man didn't need any more explaining in endeavouring to make Ark and her companions understand exactly who he was talking about, just going by his description alone of the attacker that killed his friends: – black hair, black shirt, tan shorts, evil smile. They knew exactly who he was talking about and what he desired. He wanted the same thing as the rest of the group; to find and kill Sam.

Chapter 33

Seeing that this strange man shared a common goal with them was more than enough conviction for Ark. She wrapped the rifle strap over her chest and let the weapon hang on her back like a rucksack. 'It appears we have the same goal. We all want to survive this night. Without any of our party getting bitten, we'll have no choice but to gun her down.' Ark stepped forward, holding out a hand towards the man. Footsteps shuffled closer, and a gruff hand was placed in hers. She bowed her head in confirmation that she and her party's mission was the exact same as his, and they'd both come to a mutual understanding of what they had to do. The man kept repeating his thanks to Ark for letting him into her group, and Ark had to hold up a hand to silence him. Usually, it would be best to keep your guard up and not trust anyone you didn't know, and Ark knew that; she understood that people on the outside weren't like those at the GFOSAR. The outside was dead and an uncontrolled environment where the undead lurked around every corner. At the same time, the GFOSAR did have some level of control and coordination before it was snuffed out by the black-haired witch for whom the group had come outside. Ark wasn't going to trust this strange man unless she was sure he could be trusted. If someone had seen their enemy inflict suffering on others, people close to them, growing a vengeance and a hatred for her, then that was enough evidence that Ark needed to convince her that this man was genuine and that he was just as scared and angry as they were when Sam was in the equation. So, if someone had the same goal as Ark and co. and wanted to stop the black-haired witch, they were welcome in her party.

Winsome had mouthed "bitch," obviously a reference to his loathing for Sam, though some of it was directed towards Ark for wanting to trust some random stranger they'd just met from underneath the tall zombie's grip. He soon grunted as Spot tightened his grip over his mouth, ceasing all sound that was to come from his mouth.

'If you don't mind me asking, lady. But where do you come from? I've never seen your faces before, and I've lived out here in this shithole for years.' The man quizzed.

'We came from the GFOSAR, at least what's left of it. All six of us, zombies included, want nothing more than to kill that bitch, who we know simply as Sam. From what she did to… a good man we knew, and possibly countless others while we were trapped in lockdown. She's half the reason the infection of the mortuus carnem is spreading across London at such an alarming pace. One kill wouldn't be near enough to satisfy her, so it's really no surprise that she's grown a taste for it. Every kill she commits, a new zombie is born, and with two purposes, to eat anyone that's living and to spread the infection further.' Ark explained to the man. She tilted her head to the rest of the group and gestured with her hand for them to lower their guard, that things were safe. 'Stand down; I think we can trust this man, and Spot, you can release Ryan now. You know what to do if he starts again.'

Ark ordered the group to lower their guard against this lonesome civil man but told them not to fully dwindle their guard in case zombies or anyone that wouldn't be as trustworthy as this man was lurking about. What if there were zombies silently closing in on them while they exchanged friendly small talk with this man. Ark told them to be ready in case someone dangerous was behind them, planning their attack as they spoke.

Spot immediately let go of Winsome after he was given the order, and Winsome catapulted himself away from the giant half-headless zombie, seeking support from the nearby wall. Winsome coughed a few times, regaining his composure after being locked under a firm zombie grip with no hope of prying off, forcing him to breathe out of his nose. 'Spread the infection of the mortuus carnem? Are you saying that black-haired bitch is a zombie? Bullshit! Why did she look like she was alive?' The man spat upon rethinking Ark's words in regards to Sam. Winsome then took a step forward, regarded the man's question, looking around with a sheepish face as if he could hear the faint sound of footsteps along with the hungry snarling of the looming undead. 'Look me old china, it's a long story, tell ya later if ya lucky, yeah? Now, are you gonna take us to that place of yours, or are we gonna continue standing around 'ere arguing until we're fucking killed like Tom's tit?!' Winsome hissed, his patience growing thin with all this unnecessary dialogue about Sam and standing around in the opening waiting for something undead to sniff them out. He looked around again, and he froze when he saw a zombie male teenager covered in red strut past; his broken head hung dangerously backwards and dangled around as if it was being held by nothing more than string. Winsome gulped and came to Ark, grabbed her shoulders, and pointed to the broken-necked zombie, knowing that once one had spotted them, it wouldn't be long until others started coming. 'Lisa, don't want to alarm you during your dandy meeting, but we gotta book it, like now!' he shuddered. Ark could feel the trembling fingers on her shoulders, and she, Losnedahl, Kolen and the man peered in the direction and saw it. The broken-necked zombie was now smiling at them. A smile that looked hungry and glad that he'd found them. This gnarly smile was more than enough for Ark and company, to know that now would be a good time to get out of there. 'Yeah, sorry, your friends, right. We don't have much time; come with me; I will show you to the hideout; there'll be time for questions later,' the man urged, beckoning them urgently to follow behind him. Kolen gripped the wheelchair handlebars while Ace clung onto Spot's brain jar, keeping a sloth's death grip on it, holding it close to ensure she wouldn't drop it. Because if one were to drop something of such value to something twice your size, you'd be more than dead if you were to destroy something so precious to the tallest member of the group.

The group started to follow behind the man they didn't know or even his name (he could've said his name). The group stepped over more than a few obstacles in the path, such as puddles of blood that still looked very fresh and ripe that stained their shoes and feet, bundles of slain zombie corpses, which they had to lift their legs over and step over on the other side, which had provided Kolen with a challenge to conquer when it came to mounting the wheelchair over them. Thankfully, with a bit of help from Losnedahl's generous heart, he aided the youngest of them over said obstacle. He'd put the revolver in his pants pocket, grabbing the wheels and lifting it over the heap of flesh. Grateful for Losnedahl's help with elevation, Kolen was able to mount the wheelchair containing Ace over the pile of corpses. Ace sojourned silence the whole trip, not speaking with anyone, even her bonder, having and requesting no part in any of the conversations between Ark and the anonymous man they had encountered. Or rather, he'd stumbled upon them while they'd been searching for a safe place to stay, away from the wild zombies lingering about. From having an absent top half of a head, Spot was never far away from Ark, having been guided by her holding his hand through the obstacles and mountains of rotting flesh and careful not to slip in the many red puddles. Winsome staggered behind, still keeping a vice grip on the shotgun and taking moments to whip around, aiming his weapon and ready to blast anyone stalking them.

As the group followed close behind the man, he led them through the alleyway, avoiding bins and other pieces of trash that had been left unattended, eventually reaching the place he had deemed safe and where the dead ignored, at least that was what the man had claimed. Ark was quite inclined to believe him, as the wood that covered the entrance was coated in a dark red substance, which told her that this man must have killed a 40-year AOR zombie and had used its blood to act as some kind of zombie repellent since individual zombies avoided the smell of other zombies. It was also why Ark's little exertion to the outside to fetch Spot's brain worked, she was covered in clothes that smelt of the undead. This safe-house that the man claimed was no different, and zombies would simply pass by it, smelling themselves rather than someone alive. While the idea initially seemed bright, how long would it take until a certain black-haired zombie figured out that Ark and the other GFOSAR survivors were being kept inside by some stranger? Were they ever really safe inside?

Chapter 34

Linus had successfully navigated his way out of the GFOSAR, searching for people to feed upon, a typical undead's goal. To always feed the hunger that was never satisfied. To consistently search and search for food that was becoming scarcer with each death of a living soul. The young Linus began shambling his way out of the extensive science facility soon after Ark and the others had made their escape. Much like they'd done before, he was aimlessly plodding through the dead remains of the UK, often misplacing his footing and tripping over various discarded limbs of people and zombies and sometimes he'd get his footing caught and fall over, his face landing on the concrete or on something dead.

Linus moaned a sad tune, trudging through the city of corpses and entering the lifeless town of London, not knowing why he was here wandering the dead city and not knowing his purpose and goal. Why was he brought back to life if only to roam the streets brainless and without meaning? Always hungry for those he had viewed as friends and family. Why did Henrik Losnedahl choose him to work with, and why did he give him these feelings. Why was he living in such a cruel, vile world? Why was he even here to begin with? Who was he? What was he?

Linus walked among the dead streets littered with carcasses, glancing at all the distributed body parts and slain victims waiting for resurrection. He dropped to his knees, and gripped his jeans, wanting to cry and moan in sadness; feeling mournful for all those people that had met such a gruesome end, and, of course, the never-ending hunger that plagued all the undead. The prime goal of the undead was to eat everything that breathed. Linus clenched his teeth as the familiar stench filled his nose, beginning to feel a craving for the flesh that smelt like divine nectar to him. Linus tried to resist, wanting to resist getting up and looking for where that smell was leading him. Living as an undead was painful; Linus was a prime example of how bitter it was to wander the streets with a half-human brain and half undead brain. Linus' human side wanted and fought desperately against his undead side; he put his hands on the ground and scraped the grey flesh over his fingers, scabbing them until some dark muscle tissue could be seen. He shook his head violently, trying to shake away the smell from his nose as if it was smoke. But when that didn't work, he shot one hand to his throat and tried to strangle himself, but his other hand had also shot up and ventured to hold his hand back, stopping him from snuffing out his own undead existence. Linus screamed, the hand controlled by humanity punching at his chest, thinking that someone was pulling half his strings and wasn't ready to discard their puppet just yet. Linus couldn't take the conflicting sides in his head; it was like listening to a constant barrage of intrusive thoughts; he didn't know who to listen to; he wanted to make them go away, anything to stop one side from berating him on what he needed to do. Linus looked over at his humanity fist and accomplished in throwing a hard punch at the side of his head, knocking back the human side of his brain for a while, and temporarily getting rid of his undead side.

Linus stood up, shook his head, and continued to wander to an unknown destination as most unbonded zombies do, lingering on the streets without a goal, just set on finding anything they could sink their chops into. However, something made Linus cease in his tracks. Something had caught his scent like a predator being alerted to the sounds of its prey, a robust divine redolence that was greater than those limbs he'd found earlier. It was the same smell that he recognised because he smelt like it, dead and soaked in blood. It seemed to be coming from behind him! Linus whipped around. Seeing a hand drenched in blood, offering a juicy, fresh blood-dripping lump towards him. It was a human brain; there was no mistaking it; it was a smell that his nose had been plagued with. It was the thing that he was searching for. Linus felt his humanity side vanish as if it were a card that had disappeared in some kind of magic trick. No words were exchanged between the two as Linus viciously embedded his teeth into the still-fresh brain, putting massive holes into it and creating a mess of his face and spilling drops of blood and chunks of the brain onto the ground, and the one offering it to him. Upon finishing his feast, completely devouring the brain, only leaving the scraps on the floor, he looked up at who had granted him the brain as a gift, licking his lips. A pale hand came to his cheek, wiping the remaining lumps of brain matter away and putting them into her own mouth; a smirk appeared on the face of the person who'd gifted the brain to him. Linus stared up into the pale, dead eyes of Sam as she resumed to smirk at him as if saying that Linus was now her ally, that he would help her in spreading the mortuus carnem infection further into the country, killing anyone in sight.

Chapter 35

The journey to this safe house that the man proposed had been brief but bumpy if one would count all the obstacles they had to mount over. But when the man had stopped in front of a dilapidated, abandoned-looking building that had defiantly seen better days, they knew they'd reached the strange man's so aptly named safe place, which upon first glance, had looked like a wooden shithole and the place people go to if they need to take a number two in secret. Yes, it wasn't the best and safest looking place out there, but one couldn't be picky during these harrowing times; you took what you could, regardless of how much of a dump it looked like, as long as it was secluded from prying eyes and did well to hide away the scent that the living was inside, that was more than enough for it to be classed as a safe house.

Ark grimaced when she looked at the wooden beams holding the place together and noted how heavily eroded, they looked, making the place appear heavily decrepit and threatening to cave in on those inhabiting inside. And if that wasn't enough to show people that this was not a place for the faint of heart, the outside of the supposed safe house had some sort of sick barrier around it. A fence of discarded body parts gave off a disgusting odour that filled the five human's noses with grime and sickening malice. It, of course, had been Winsome to make a comment about this bizarre and yet cruel border design, accusing the man of being a sicko and that he probably decorated the interior with the remains of his "fellow friends", the ones that he claimed had been murdered by Sam. But the unnamed man had insisted that the horrendous fence of body parts had been collected by him and his former allies over the past few days with the purpose of being installed and used as a way to repel the undead from sniffing them out because the undead would have a hard time exposing the living if they were fortified behind the undead remnants. The man who'd guided them there had implored them, insisting that it was safe enough for them to stay and recuperate despite its looks. He explained that it was indeed sturdy and would be the ideal place to keep the reanimated corpses at bay. At least until they could find someplace else that was better in appearance and was overall safer for them to hide out in. And if they did find something better to camp out in, it would allow them the moments they would need to strategise, think, and plan ways to stop and destroy their enemy.

The unknown man was the first to enter the safe place, going through a crooked door that seemed to be leaning out of position as if it was some kind of art installation of having a wonky but otherwise standard doorframe. The group members watched as he parked himself down on a small log next to a small fire concealed inside a steel bbq canister that was initially made for the sole purpose of roasting marshmallows, bacon and other bits of food used for a campfire and keeping homeless people warm back in the day.

The man patted the hard wooden surface he used as a seat, beckoning the survivors to join him. 'Please, if I wanted to loot you, I would've done it by now. And I'm not the type of man to lower myself into nicking things from armed people. It may be a dangerous place on the outside, but I wouldn't do anything like that, even if I were starving or poor. Plus, I'm lonely; it's a very lonely place outside. I could use some company from actual living people.' His tone was low, and his voice pained. For someone who would've been used to these kinds of conditions, the tone of his voice made him sound like he was still struggling to face the facts that this was the life and world he lived in and that he was trying to understand that if he wasn't careful, he was going to lose more people that he would call his friends.

Ark swallowed, not letting the gruelling design of the fence steer her away from the possibility of safety. She glanced at those who had escaped the ruins of GFOSAR with her, and she unknowingly decided what they should do. She lowered her head and sighed. 'We don't have a lot of options, and we don't know the outside the same way as this man. So, like it or not, we're going to have to take his word for it and trust him. Come on, Spot, let's go first.' Ark approached Spot and held his hand as she guided him towards the wonky doorframe. She whispered for him to duck, considering the condition of the safe house was a total wreck, and people had to be careful when crossing through the doorway. Over time, and due to not having owners attend to it, the building had become rotten and brittle. At least, that was how Ark perceived it based on appearance alone. It had caused the doors and windows to break away from the designed fixtures, becoming small, causing the heavy wooden ceiling beams to blister and collapse onto the floor.

Ark went inside the house first, stepping over and through the crooked door and glancing behind her to watch

Spot, who'd ducked, holding out a hand, blindly feeling about the air until he touched the crooked door frame. He crouched and lowered his height significantly. He stepped through the door and met Ark on the other side. 'Sorry about the mess. It was like this when I found it.' The man said. And he was right; the inside of the place wasn't any better than the outside; it was littered with rubbish bags, and some of the bags were torn, spilling out quantities of trash across the floor. Ark kicked away a mouldy banana skin she was about to step on. The smell was bad but durable; it smelt like cat faeces mixed with a grandma's fart. But at least it didn't have heads on pikes, and trash was better than heads on pikes, Ark decided. She then guided a still crouched Spot over to the bbq canister with the dancing flames inside, proceeding to sit down with him, taking a much-needed wave of relief at feeling some warmth while waiting for the others to enter and accompany her. Once they were both seated on the floor in front of the canister, the man asked the first thing he should've said before he'd led them into this safe house. 'So, what's your name, ma'am?' looking at Ark from the opposite side of her, watching her caress the rifle's scope in her lap. 'Ark. Lisa Ark, the zombie next to me is named Spot,' she responded glumly, looking at him with a look of sorrow and grief from the thought of losing all those people back at the GFOSAR. 'What about you? You haven't told us your name yet,' she asked him in return. 'Slater, ma'am, Darren Slater,' the man had finally introduced himself. Losnedahl had entered shortly after, followed by Kolen and Ace, whom he had helped get inside the entranceway of the safe house. The last one that followed was Winsome, who, despite complaining about the fence outside, had made it inside anyway, a gym bag of weapons around him, still gripping the shotgun tightly, refusing to part with it. Winsome cast his eyes at the state of the interior of the building and put his fingers to his nostrils. 'Peeyuu! Who farted?' Slater ignored him and told him curtly to board the entrance with the pillars on the floor beside the entrance; Winsome did this simple task without much complaint. 'I take it you guys must be zombie bonders, judging by the two docile zombies with you. I didn't see them fully until just now in the fire's light...' Slater began, looking down at his hands that were cupped together; his shaggy bearded face seemed to be swimming with regret; he knew that zombie bonders were scientists and that they worked with zombies, but that was it, he didn't really understand any more of what the bonding process was or if it was really as successful as the rumours spreading around town were. Before Sam had killed his old group, one topic that had been frequently brought up was the bonding process and what really had gone on there.

'I ain't, but these Berkeley hunts are,' Winsome huffed, plopping his arse down on one of the broken, dusty couches while still holding the shotgun close, caressing it like it was his birthright while also using his other hand to rub his crotch. Ark pretended to not acknowledge Winsome's existence. 'We were... now we're just like you, Darren, survivors, people wanting to see the sun again, to feel the soft grass beneath the feet, the soft summer breeze. In other words, we just want to survive.' Ark spoke sadly, staring blankly into the fire inside the BBQ, watching as sparks crackled above. 'That bitch, Sam or whatever the fuck her name is, she made you like this, right? Killing most of your friends and co-workers?' Slater gently requested information, eyeing Ark's haggard face wanly through the flames of the bbq, relating with her and the burden she was carrying. 'Yeah… she did; that fucking zombie will pay for killing all those innocent people just doing their fucking job.' Ark gnarled, clenching her fists slightly at the very perception of Sam. 'Sam is the given name of that zombie that looks human. She had surgery to make her look like that, and zombies usually get the surgery if they're well-behaved and have shown staggering amounts of intelligence, enough for them to be considered human. Believe me, the five of us are still wondering what had caused Sam to develop such a murderous ego. We don't know why she became this monster that kills anyone living. It's one mystery we can't solve,' Kolen had noted, sitting on a plastic outdoor chair next to Losnedahl on the floor, who'd placed the wheelchair on the other side of Kolen. Slater looked at Kolen and eyed the rest of the group as if asking who they were. 'Oh, shoot, sorry, how rude of me. I should've introduced myself as well as the rest of us. It's just we've been so worked up with the idea of killing Sam that we didn't think we would find anyone else alive willing to help us. I'm Marilyn Kolen, and the crawler in the wheelchair is Ace,' Kolen introduced herself, along with Ace, who acted as if they were still talking about Sam. 'Sam is bad,' Ace pronounced, watching Slater as if he didn't know that yet and needed to be confirmed on who their enemy was. Slater gawked at Ace awkwardly. 'Yeah, I figured,' he said, looking back down into his cupped hands, his face telling Ark that he didn't understand how all this could happen to them in just a short period. 'Name's Ryan Winsome,' Winsome stated his name simply. 'The man over there is Henrik Losnedahl; due to a traumatic incident in his childhood, he's being rendered mute.' Kolen said, pointing over to Losnedahl. Losnedahl responded with a light wave, so Slater knew who he was; Losnedahl opened his mouth and pointed into his mouth. Revealing to Slater that he had no tongue and was permanently mute and had been since he was a baby (making him a popular target for bullying at school for being called "tongueless Henrik").

'Jesus…' Slater cringed, sympathising with Losnedahl, tapping the log he was sitting on, gesturing him to come and sit next to him. He did.

'Lisa, if you don't mind me asking, but when you entered, I couldn't help but notice and stare at that tall zombie with a half-decapitated head, and not to sound like a prick, but how the fuck can he hear your every word? I noticed that he takes orders from you,' Slater inquired while studying Spot, who'd been sitting down next to Ark and towering over her, so he could only imagine how tall he'd be when he stood up; he'd probably put a hole in the ceiling. 'Well, if you're morbidly curious, I'll tell you.' Even as Spot sat next to her, she had to peer up at him and lightly tap him on the arm so that he could understand that she was talking to or addressing him. 'Yeah, like how the shit can a half-headless zombie hear your every order. I mean, it's not like he can hear with that fucking brain of his,' Winsome chimed in, also wishing to know the answer, as the thought didn't plague him as much; only until Slater had mentioned it did Winsome start growing curiosity for an answer. 'He does.' she admitted to both males, considering the idea and concept sounded utterly ludicrous, taking a slap on logic and science. Still, this was 2056, and scientific technology had advanced dramatically over the years. One such example was bringing a dead brain back to life and thinking capabilities in a way that was similar to how Victor Frankenstein gave his creature life.

Ark looked away from Slater at Winsome before standing up, walking over to Ace, and gently taking the brain jar from her. Ark held the brain jar in front of her, gently tapping it, gesturing for Spot to stand and collect his brain. Spot did so like a loyal lapdog. Using the ground for support, Spot stood, bumping his sliced head on the ceiling, causing him to react by rubbing his flat, fleshy head. After that, Spot was forced into an awkward hunch. Slater stared at the giant zombie with awe, mouth agape and eyes wide. 'Spot is the zombie I was given during the, how do I put this… ordinary zombie bonding days before everything went to hell. He couldn't think very well during the first few days of bonding because of an absent brain, but overall, he wasn't violent like most zombies, which was the main thing.' She paused momentarily, looking at Spot, who was still hunched, lowering his height, and showing visible discomfort by his legs trembling due to all the years of rot from being unattended for so long and terraforming greenery. The ceiling and walls of the safe house had become unstable, which had caused a significant decrease in the building's former height. Becoming a mere shadow of the glory the once excellent building had been, permitting access and safety for people who were either exact or under six-one; those taller would have to either sit down or hunch their bodies down like Spot had done, as uncomfortable as it had seemed for him.

Ark returned the brain jar to its owner before going on with the rest of the story. 'A thought crossed my mind during the time when most bonders go into their cells to bond with their designated zombies. And that thought was: if Spot had his uninjured brain in close contact with him, he might be able to think more clearly. Now, I know how illogical this had sounded, but it was worth a shot. So instead of going straight to cell B-09, where Spot had waited for me. I dressed in clothes made for the brave, seemingly casual-looking clothes, but they were soaked in undead blood and had pieces of skin and organs stuck to them; they smelt like shit. But it was the best way for bonders to fetch out supplies without harassing the military, despite it being their job. I wasn't the type of woman to rely on others. I knew what I was looking for, and it was something I knew the military couldn't fetch for me. So, I wore those clothes so I could bypass the roaming zombies that were around. I tried my best to mimic the sounds and movements of the dead so that they wouldn't suspect me of being one of the living. Anyway, I headed over to a nearby cemetery. Upon entering, I dropped the whole undead staggering act and started looking around the rows for a particular open grave with the top half of his head inside it.' Ark gestured with her hand to show them what she had meant. 'Of course, I found it, Spot's grave… I tried looking to see the name engraved on the headstone, but most of it had been scratched away due to vandalism or had simply had time to do its work on it. Nevertheless, I got the head out of the grave and returned it to the GFOSAR. There, I conducted a bit of brain surgery since I was a professional neurosurgeon back in my country. I surgically removed the brain from the head.' Ark looked at Spot, who was looking in her direction; his body seemed tense as if he seemed slightly offended at the mention of what his bonder had done to remove his brain. 'Sorry, Spot, I meant no harm to you in any way. That was just something I needed to do in order to extract your brain and get it to function properly. But like I said, I removed the brain and started doing a Frankenstein-like experiment with the brain, with hopes of giving it life. So, it would think and understand words like a normal brain. I attached cords and wires into the living brain's auditory cortex and cerebrum, invisible at first glance, but there nonetheless, hoping that they would function in the same manner as normal ears do and would allow him to think for himself like we humans do. I didn't know that it would work then as I hadn't even done anything like that before, especially to an inept brain. I didn't give two shits if people were gossiping about me as I worked; I was determined to see if my thesis would be a success and continued to go along with it until it was done. I put the wired brain inside a jar with the moss-coloured lung liquid (designed to help once-dead things breathe). I gave it to Spot soon after I arrived in his cell, which is now Spot's most cherished possession, as you already know. That's when I realised what the time was and started to panic, thinking about the consequences of being absent from a zombie during bonding hours. I thought, 'Oh shit! This wasn't going to look good on my record; they were going to give me the sack,' and I wanted to punish myself while verbally abusing myself for what I had done. But Spot stopped me as soon as I could deck myself, and he hugged me. Yeah, you heard right… hugged! A zombie displaying affection seems like a joke, doesn't it? At first, I couldn't process why. He was expressing his gratitude with the emotions he had learned, which is often contemplated as being one of the hardest things for a zombie to learn.

'Wowzers, you must really admire him for coming this far and gaining a significant amount of humanity,' Slater marvelled. His shaggy, bearded mug drowned in amazement at the things that the average brainless zombies strutting about the dead streets (he had grown accustomed to) could learn and individuals they could become with the right bonding and time spent with them.

'So, if I was to go up and tell him that he has Wonder Woman as a bonder, he'd be able to hear it?' he joked, to which Ark responded with a light snicker. 'I think he already knows that Lisa is an amazing woman, d-don't you, Spot.' Kolen said. Spot responded with a nod of the head. 'You damn well bet that I praise him! Spot has my utmost trust!' she confirmed with a stern grin, staring into Darren's brown eyes through the fiery flames of the bbq barrel as he rubbed his small matching brown goatee with immense interest in what the others did and the things the GFOSAR had done and what had caused these workers to leave the safety of its walls. 'Must have lost some good people back in that place where the zombie bonding took place? Otherwise, you wouldn't be out here. I heard the facility was notorious for being a safe place guarded by the army and all that,' Slater said quietly, understanding their pain all too well. Slater stood up, advancing to get some beverages from the fridge in the corner of the mouldy, decrepit kitchen. 'Anyone want a beer?' he called out from the kitchen. 'Yeah, I'll have one,' Winsome replied, calling out, holding his hand out for a glass or bottle; he didn't care as long as he got a drink to soothe his nerves. The rest shook their heads, declining his offer.

'You couldn't begin to comprehend how many corpses are back at the GFOSAR... we lost the great Alexander Fredrickson. I'll never forget his words and teachings,' Kolen sniffed, imagining Fredrickson's corpse lying in a large red puddle of his blood, thinking about what Sam had done to him. Was his body being devoured by their zombified co-workers? Was he a zombie? Those thoughts made Kolen's heart bleed, and she tried to steer her wandering mind away from it but found herself unable. The images were too strong and too wicked to get rid of, so all Kolen could do was cry, hoping that the sound of her tears would drown out those sinful images. Thankfully, Losnedahl answered Kolen's pleas and decided to come to her aid in helping her get away from such horrendous thoughts. Losnedahl got off the log he was sitting on and walked over to Kolen, seated in a fold-up chair beside Ace. He knelt down to her side and placed a hand on her shoulder, presenting her with a piece of cloth he'd kept inside his breast pocket to use as an emergency tissue, beckoning her to wipe the small tears Kolen didn't realise she was crying. 'Oh boohoo, cry me a river, Marilyn! We've lost a lot more! Alex wasn't the only one to die. Have you forgotten about all those corpses back at the GFOSAR?' Winsome snorted, rolling his eyes upon taking his can of London Pride from Slater. 'What about Carl Boyle, huh? He was cornered by a bunch of those fucking zombie bastards and eaten alive. I was with him when a zombified Prezky bit onto his fucking arm, causing his blood to whoosh out like a fucken hose! What about all the others that perished, eh? Do you stop and think about others like that? Are you too much of a fucking pussy that all you can care about is the one who trained you? Christ, Marilyn, you heartless bitch! Always bitching about FUCKING ALEXANDER FREDRICKSON! Christ, he wasn't that great of a guy. If you take a moment to smell the poison, he was actually a real pig of a bloke!' Winsome roared, overpowering Kolen, putting more pressure on her and keeping her mind in that dark place, causing more and more tears to leak from her eyes and onto her glasses. Losnedahl closed his arms around Kolen, embracing her and trying to calm her down without words, while Ace plucked the cloth out of his hand and dabbed Kolen's face with it, wiping away her bonder's tears.

'You know you are starting to get on my nerves, Ryan. So what if he was a pig or not. She greatly admired him. Just let her have this,' Ark snarled, clenching her fists, and glaring at him. She didn't want to fight him, but Winsome wasn't exactly making things easy. He never did make things easy for her.

'Shut up, Lisa! This is between this pathetic little cow and me. It's always Fredrickson this, Fredrickson that, wah-wah-wah. What about the others, Marilyn, eh? What about them, ay? Would you care if Henrik dropped dead in front of you, or you still complain about Fredrickson?' This was the final straw. Ark picked up a nearby rock from the floor and hurled it at Winsome's sleazy face. It hit him on the nose, causing him to yelp and hold his nose, seeing that it was now bleeding and he was now sporting an ugly red cut on his bridge. 'HEY! WHAT THE FUCK, LISA?' he cried, holding his nose. Ark seized the scuff of his coat and held him up, her eyes staring accusingly at him.

'Shut up, Ryan! Just fucking shut up! Do you have a death wish? Because if you do, scream as much as you want and alert the undead to us! Marilyn is fucking harmless! Alexander meant a lot to her!! He's the reason Marilyn became a fucking zombie bonder and the reason why Ace can talk! You complain about her not caring for others when it's you that doesn't care! She's done nothing to you! She's fucking innocent! Innocent!! Can you at least plant that inside that skull of yours before opening your worthless fucking lowlife trap to insult those who aren't as strong as you, or the rest of us?! You're fucking pathetic Ryan!! The very sight of you aggravates me!' Ark took a deep breath. 'Ryan, I'm trying so hard not to lose my patience with you. But you are making it harder every time you flap that jaw, and I'm about one minute away from making your nose hurt more. The only reason you're still alive and tagging along with us in the first place is that I'm generous enough to not leave anyone, no matter how much of a dickhead they are, to such a cruel fate in the hands of Sam or any other zombie as a matter of fact. So, if you want to continue to live, I suggest you shut your trap and lay off Marilyn. She admired Fredrickson; okay, leave her alone, so for the sake of my sanity, Ryan. Please, shut the fuck up,' Ark harangued, screaming at the top of her lungs. 'Fuck me... lady, you're fierce,' Slater mumbled, completely flabbergasted by how mentally powerful Lisa Ark was: for a neurosurgeon and she didn't take smack from anyone. He'd never met a woman with more power in her lungs than Lisa Ark. She definitely was a sight to behold, and most men would do well to keep on her good side.

'Must be silent.' Ace whispered, giving the group an explicit instruction to be quieter and sending an eerie tinge down their backs. *Who let the crawler in charge?* Winsome bickered in his mind, not wanting to say it out loud, risking Ark, or worse, Spot punching his teeth at Ark's order. 'The crawler's right; we should keep our voices down. The dead are patrolling outside,' Slater said, agreeing with Ace and giving everyone small glances. 'We never asked if there are any more survivors like you that want to kill Sam.' Ark wheezed, reacquiring her breath and voice from her loud outburst, and speaking her mind, something she had always wanted to say to Winsome concerning how much Fredrickson had meant to Kolen. 'Guarantee that, Lisa. I have a twin sister named Olivia, or Oli as I like to call her. Who, based on what she'd told me through text, had managed to capture a live specimen of the mortuus carnem. That had been the last I'd heard from her a few days ago. She'd texted me before my damn phone's battery ran out. While not a scientist, she's interested in the field, and based on what she told me, she's been studying the characteristics of the parasite that are similar to those of the common mosquito. I haven't been able to check up on her since my phone died, and there isn't anywhere I can charge it, sadly, since there aren't any places around with power. But I remember her telling me that she was hiding out somewhere close to London city, but that's all I know. I'm worried about her; I hope she's okay,' Slater declared sadly, feeling disappointed that he couldn't help the group much.

After some long seconds, Kolen got up from the fold-up chair she'd been sitting in; her face stained red from all the tears she'd cried. She walked over to Slater. He looked up at her, confused, as she sat down on the log next to him, taking her glasses off, tapping them in her palms, and having a confession to make. 'When we get out of here, we will go look for your sister in London city. All seven of

317

us, and when we do, the eight of us will hunt down that bitch and put her in the ground so deep that she hopefully won't rise up from.' She said, looking down at the glasses in her hands before looking back up at Slater. Officially welcoming him into their group. The rest of the group looked surprised at hearing the word "bitch" come out of timid Marilyn Kolen's mouth and that she wished actual death upon Sam. Everyone had wanted Sam dead because of all the heinous things she'd done back at the GFOSAR; she couldn't go unpunished. But hearing such things come from Kolen was more than a shock because Kolen was the last person to wish death upon anyone; her heart was in the right place, and she believed that everyone deserved a chance at life. Even if they were miserable lowlifes like Winsome.

'Sam here!' Ace elevated her voice a little, warning them that Sam was nearby and that she would likely find them if they continued to sit there without having their guards raised.

'Shit! Hide!' Slater gave a whispering hiss, jumping off the log, rushing into the kitchen and returning with a small bucket of water that he'd gotten from the kitchen faucet, which had surprisingly still worked. He threw the pail of water over the barrel, extinguishing the flames that made a hissing sound, before darting over to the boarded-up window, peeking through the cracks, and checking on the outside, scanning his eyes around the area, looking for her. 'Oh fuck...!' Slater shuddered, prying his eyes away and hugging the wall, staring at the others wide-eyed and trembling. 'That's her,' he said fearfully, 'that's the bitch that murdered my mates,' pointing to the crack in the window, alerting the group to come over and hide with him. Some took a moment to eavesdrop, peeking through the gap in the window. Seeing Sam eerily walking after a wounded man who was understandably in a full-blown panic and who was desperate to survive and escape Sam with his life.

Chapter 36

Their eyes were staring ahead as a man with a limp was spotted, running, and screaming for his life after he had an unfortunate encounter with the intelligent zombie named Sam. It was her alright because the crawler by Kolen's side made a noise that sounded like a gag. Ark's complexion was pale when she saw the man throw his only weapon, a rusted tomahawk, at his pursuer, hitting one of the zombie woman's breasts, tearing through the black shirt and digging fairly deep into the flesh. Ark subconsciously gripped her own breast as if she could feel the sharp impact of the blade puncturing her. Ark watched with her mouth quivering as Sam glanced at the object thrown at her with mild concern, staring at it as if it was something minor, like a paper cut. Sam reached up to grab the handle, and she tugged it away, pulling it out of her breast, which oiled black dust instead of blood. Without glancing at the weapon, she glanced at the axe that had been embedded into her before she tossed it away like a ball of paper. The man gasped at this. 'Fuck off! Get the fuck away from me you bitch!' The man shrieked, his haunting voice solidifying the horrors of the outside and what Ark and Company would have to get used to. And yet, despite knowing that this man wasn't going to live very long now that he had Sam's attention, it was hard to look away from the terror because Ark just knew in her gut that Sam was going to have some fun with him, that she was going to enjoy the suffering which she would put this poor man through. Tears were flying out of the man's eyes as he clutched his wounded leg, trying his hardest to limp away from the human-looking zombie pursuing him, walking at an eerily fast pace after him. The complexion on Sam's face was hard to read, with the curtain of black hair blocking her face. Ark felt something shift to her side, and at the corner of her eye, she saw Kolen gripping one of the wooden boards nailed to the windowpane. Ark stared at her momentarily, seeing the look in her teary eyes. It was a look that gave Ark the impression that Kolen wanted to shout encouraging things at the man, such as, 'Don't give up! Keep going! Use that cinderblock to slow her down!' But of course, Kolen yelling at the man would only create more problems for the group. If Kolen were to yell at the man to keep going, she would be alerting Sam and other zombies to their presence inside Slater's Safe Haven, and that was something Ark knew Kolen didn't want to do. Someone told Kolen to be quiet; it was Slater. Like Ark and the rest, all Kolen could do was stay put and watch. All the seven survivors were unable to pry their eyes away; even if the sight and endeavours they were witnessing were the scariest and most horrific thing they'd seen in their entire lives, it would be like watching a highly intense thriller movie which you just couldn't look away from. They still watched, unable to look away from the unearthly sight, watching with atrocity at just how far and brutal Sam was willing to go into killing each human that came into contact with her, leaving their discarded dead bodies to the mortuus carnem or simply infecting them herself with just a single bite (once bitten, it was all over, as the rumours in the GFOSAR went). Once the infection was transferred into the body, it would spread into the bloodstream like how the venom of a snake travels throughout the circular system, shutting down the red and white blood cells like a cancer, turning them black and slowly and painfully killing the person from the inside out, turning them into zombies sometime later, ready to wander the streets without aim, killing anyone that still breathed and had a heartbeat.

Even if they knew what would happen, the group continued to watch, horrified at seeing the man trip and collapse after trying to jump over a small pile of dumped bodies, which seemed like they'd been purposely placed there causing Winsome's voice to mutter, 'Ya gaddamn sicko.' Ark cringed as she saw the man's wounded, bleeding leg step on a fresh, bloodied intestine that had been torn out from a corpse that had its chest eaten away, leaving a blemished mess of fleshy exposed organs and bones. The long-bloodied cord made a disgusting squelching sound like meat dropped on a tile floor it squirted quite a heavy dosage of blood as the man trod and slipped on it, kicking it up into the air and therefore invoking him to fall into the abhorrent sight before him. Ark's face went taut as she saw the man land face-first into a gruesome collection of bodies, new and old, smothering his face with a foul stench, painting his face with blood and bits of gore. The man looked up and spat gore from his mouth. He was crying heavily. Ark heard an audible gagging sound from Losnedahl, making him turn away and saving him from the rest of the ugliness.

'Yuck… that's fucked up…' Winsome cringed, holding his mouth and audibly moaning. 'Tell me about it… fuck,' Ark rasped, scrunching her eyes with disgust, but she was unable to look away. Her eyes were glued to what was going to be the poor man's final moments. It seemed that the man knew that this was his final stop as well, and with his injured leg, he wasn't going to get very far and knowing that he wasn't going to get far only increased the intensity of his crying. But even so, that didn't stop him from trying to fight back against his aggressor.

'Ms Kolen, I think you may want to look away from this part, I think things are going to get nasty.' Slater gagged still with full eyes on the gnarly sight, politely ushering Kolen to look away. Kolen didn't hesitate to turn away and cover her ears tightly, not wanting access to the unwelcoming screams that were bound to ensue. She fiercely clenched her eyes and teeth shut, even if it was hurting; she didn't want to hear or see anything that Sam was doing to the poor man. She tried to drown out the harrowing sounds by whispering a small Dutch prayer to herself. Ark wished that she could do what Kolen had done and look away, but her eyes stayed put; it was even a struggle trying to blink as she stared at Sam, seeing the black-haired witch gaze down at the terrified man, grounding her arm, reaching, and seizing hold of his damaged leg, yanking him towards her away and away from the mound of bodies that had cushioned his fall. The man screamed loudly, his shrieks echoing through the dead streets as he strived to fight back against his attacker, thrashing his other, healthy foot wildly in the air, hoping to at least land some kind of offence against his attacker. The group watched as Sam's head was knocked backwards as it was realised that he succeeded in kicking her in the face, causing her black hair to dance about in the air before coming back down in front of her face like a diabolical fringe. The hand clutching the man's wounded leg opened, and the man's leg fell to the ground with a loud thud. He grunted, but he ignored it as he felt triumph in managing to kick his attacker. 'Yes!' the group hissed through a forced whisper. 'Yeah! How'dya like that, you bitch?,' spat the man as he crawled backwards and attempted to get to his feet so he could try to get away once more.

'Come on, get up!' Slater hissed.

'Don't just sit there! Throw something at the cunt; slow her the fuck down! Escape!' cried Winsome, watching the man, and refusing to allow himself a moment to blink. However unlucky for the man, Sam recovered quickly, and once she had a bone to pick with someone, she made damn sure that she'd pick it.

'No!' Ark murmured, her eyes started to sting. She put her hands on her mouth as she watched Sam brutally grasp the man's wounded leg again (which, upon closer inspection, had appeared to show a large piece of wrought iron lodged deep into his leg protruding out from both sides, removing it would mean removing the portion entirely) and strenuously dragged him over to her. The man tried to scamper away like a mouse whose tail had been caught by a cat's paw. Sam knelt down to him and was holding him down, preventing him from escaping. It was like watching a predator sadistically playing with its prey.

Sam looked and observed the piece of iron wedged inside the man's leg. She grabbed it almost instantly from the moment she saw it and mercilessly twisted it to the sides while it was still lodged in the man's leg, effortlessly snapping the man's tibia bone in two from inside the skin. The group members - save from Spot and Kolen - watched, wanting to look away but they couldn't; their eyes swelled with terror, and mouths dropped at hearing the hapless man wail in anguish; hearing his own leg crack and break, causing him to be in even more unbearable suffering.

The man screamed an ear-splitting sound, feeling about the ground around him for something he could use to repel Sam, maybe a rock to throw in her eye or mouth or anything, just something that would get her away from him. His face was smothered with tears of despondency as he extended in crying at the top of his lungs, clutching his now broken, ruined leg, screaming out curses at his attacker. But Sam didn't stop there. … Oh no, she took the man's healthy foot, hoistered it up high, almost in a gymnastic splitting position. 'No fucking way...' Ark gasped, her eyes widened, cupping her mouth, grasping an inkling into what was going to happen next, on what Sam was planning to do to him. This added another thing to her sadistic character, which only increased Ark's hatred for Fredrickson's killer. Sam slammed her clutching hand onto the man's crotch, getting a grip on his crotch that, thankfully, was shielded by his black jeans.

The group tried to look away; they really did, but they were unable. Winsome tried covering his eyes with his hands, but he could still see through the gaps between his fingers. It was as if invisible hands were holding their eyelids apart and facing their heads in the direction of the screaming man. Though Losnedahl did get close enough to slam his eyes shut for a moment before they opened again. Forcing them to watch, eyes burning from lack of blinking, Sam, in one traumatising, excruciating feat, ignoring the man's screaming pleads for her to stop, yanked at his crotch area, pulling at his shlong like how a person tugs on something heavy. 'No! Anything but th-' the man's pleas were quickly silenced by the sound of him screaming and crying as Sam continued to yank and pull at his crotch.

That was until a heavy ripping sound ensued, echoing through the streets and the ears of those unfortunate enough to hear. Sam pulled her hand away from the man, clutching a piece of black fabric that was dripping with blood. Blanketed behind the blood-stained jeans fragment was the man's torn off junk. Blood sprayed out from the man's now missing reproductive organ like some cheap 1970s splatter film. Sam dropped the man's fixed foot, where it thrashed wildly on the floor. The man screamed so loud that it made the windows around him vibrate, eventually leading to him provisionally losing his voice. The man tried to clutch down at his missing genitals, but each endeavour he made to sit up just caused more blood to ooze out, drenching the ground and Sam's feet with a fresh coating of living blood. The man had been crying so hard that his face became a nasty-looking red colour, his veins were popped, and his nose was bleeding heavily. He tried yelling out for help, but his larynx was broken, and the most he could produce was a husky rasp that was just above a whisper. But still, Sam wasn't done with him. From what Ark could tell, Sam lived to cause as much suffering to her victims as possible, and that fact was on full display here. She knelt down to his heavily bleeding private area like he was on more than a simple man, period. Sam's face was still curtained by her black hair, but her face wasn't the target of scrutiny. She put a hand on the man's chest as he was unable to do anything but rasp out in agony, feeling nothing but pain and suffering, wishing for someone to come save him and shoot this black-haired witch right in the face and disfigure that kisser of hers. *Fucking Hell, Sam, it's not enough ripping the dude's pecker off! You're going to torture him further? I Swear You Deserve More Than Death! YOU DESERVE TO GO TO FUCKING HELL AND ROT THERE!* Ark's spirit had detonated just from seeing all this occur in such a short time. It was like that time she and her friend Katie's older brother told them that he had borne witness to a man drenched in blood from a street brawl and had been forced into kissing the floor by the police officers on top of him, endeavouring to cuff him and get him to jail. She had been eight, so it had understandably scared her and was something she couldn't look away from. It was like now; she couldn't evict her eyes from such a scary sight. The five watched and gasped Winsome and Losnedahl fought against the invisible hands holding them and drawn back, retreating to the safety of the walls beside them alongside Kolen, who was still muttering Dutch prayers to herself. Ark envied them; she wanted so much to look away, but her eyes weren't letting her. Only she, Ace and Slater were the ones watching as Sam then shoved her hand up the cavity she vigorously made into the man's private parts, which was something that perturbed even the crawler, imploring Kolen to turn her wheelchair around so that she could join the not watching club. So, the only ones watching were Slater and Ark. They weren't so lucky as the rest; their eyes remained savagely adhered to Sam and the man, striving hard to turn away and fight the invisible force holding them in place. 'Oh god... you diabolical...' Slater gagged just as Sam had submerged her hand farther into the man's gentile, generating a disturbing, uncomfortable feeling in Slater's own groin, making him caress it carefully and feeling immense pity for the man. Watching alongside Ark, Sam appeared as if she had grasped onto something from inside the poor man's genitals. Which she proceeded to tug at. Ark and Slater's teeth were clenched, and their eyes were hurting from being unable to look away; their hearts were banging inside their chests, and sweat was dripping ever so swiftly down their cheeks. Ark started to feel queasy and sick in the stomach; she clenched her belly and moaned as if she was about to throw up. Sam pulled the thing harder out through the man's cock, eventually making it surface and making Slater gag before finally upchucking a discoloured awful liquidly mass on the ground.

It was his fucking intestine!

After ten more agonising seconds, Sam pulled the man's intestine out of his crotch, holding it in both hands like it was some kind of offensive Halloween decoration. She stood up again, and a sharp gust of wind blew, causing Sam's black locks to flutter out of her face, and there, the smirk that Ace had shown clear detest for all that her eyes were cursed into seeing. She glanced at the intestine she had ripped out from the man's cock and smirked down at the dying man who started going pale from loss of blood, the tears never-ending. Sam simply discarded the bloody intestine away for the other zombies to eat, once again walking up to the man's fearful, suffering face. Sam grinned at the terminal man, who'd mustered up the strength to spit in her face, which she'd simply wiped off as if it was a bug. She licked the intestinal blood from her fingers. After that, Sam did the man the only decent thing; she stepped up towards him and smirked down at him. She then raised a bare foot above his head and, without hesitation, slammed it down on his face, finally putting an end to the poor man and what probably felt like an eternity of suffering.

Ark and Slater turned away from the scene together, not wanting to see if Sam ate any of the man's squashed brain; Slater and Ark gaped at each other, their hearts pounding heavily and loudly with sheer terror and disgust after Sam had killed the man. They were concerned that she was probably still outside, eating his brains. But they didn't want to see it. Their mouths were quivering and agape, their breathing was very hectic, their pupils were small with horror, and their hearts were beating like no tomorrow. Slater had a small trail of vomit on his scraggy beard and down his brown trench coat, and he looked like he was about to be sick again. Ark had gone pale and dead-looking, her mouth trembling and her forest green eyes bulging.

'We're not dealing with an ordinary zombie...' Slater fearfully stammered.

Chapter 37

It wasn't long after the gruesome demise of that unfortunate man who'd caught the sights of that abhorrent zombie that lunches were dispensed from the mouth. Winsome and Losnedahl ran into separate rooms, and their audible retching was clearly heard throughout the house. Seeing a man die in such a horrible way warranted more than just one batch of puke. The sound of their harsh, violent retching was clearly heard, producing a lacklustre sound that the others didn't want to hear. Especially soon after, they'd become haunted by the man's dying shrieks, playing over and over in their heads, and unintentionally becoming witnesses of something their minds wouldn't forget. 'Oh... fu,' Winsome could be heard groaning from the kitchen, where he'd sought shelter and a place to dispatch his lunch in a liquefied puddle. Losnedahl had returned, looking pale, groggy and a little worse for wear. Shortly after Winsome had unloaded his second batch of vomit, he sat down on the log in front of the barrel, hands on his head. Kolen still kept her ears blocked with her hands, still had her eyes shut and teeth tightly clenched. She was muttering Dutch prayers, thinking she could faintly still hear all those awful outcries from the now dead man. Ark had fought and succeeded in swallowing her lunch. Kept it back down her throat despite the dangers of stomach acid burning the throat if not excreted through the mouth. She did it anyway, not wanting to regurgitate the muck in her throat and desecrate the house even further, prompting Kolen and Slater to become sick and expel their half-digested meals. Drops of puss-coloured vomit leaked out of Slater's mouth. He let out a scanty cough, and it all came whooshing out of his mouth. 'Sorry,' he apologised weakly. 'I couldn't hold it in any longer,' he wheezed, wiping the last remaining drops of vomit from his mouth with the back of his brown leather jacket. You'd think that a man accustomed to living on the outside of the GFOSAR would be used to the horrific conditions of corpses and seeing people die left and right like flies. But after seeing some guy have his penis quite literally ripped off and his intestines pulled out from the cock hole. That was more than enough to churn his stomach. Hell might even stir the toughest of men's stomachs!

Winsome came back into the living room, wiping his mouth with what used to be a clean white dishcloth; now, it was caked in fragments of Winsome's sick. 'What the actual hell was that?' he blurted, wiping his mouth, and tossing the dirty cloth back into the kitchen, where it landed on the counter. 'The hell is Alex doing, creating a monster? He should've been working into making her a hot as babe that would gladly welcome you to the nearest club.'

'That seriously isn't where your mind travels to,' Ark remarked, gasping her mouth, and looking groggily at the ground.

'Look, whaddya expect? I'm a male, and males need to get laid with the girl of their dreams.' Winsome replied, covering his mouth with his sleeve, coughing, and wiping some of his puke against the shin of his pants.

Losnedahl tapped Kolen's shoulder in the way of explaining to her that the horror was over and the man's death screams had been silenced forever. Dead. Kolen flinched, moving her hands away from her ears and resting her teeth, but she still kept her eyes clenched in case something worse was in front of her. It had been Ace to make her fully aware that everything was over. 'It over, Sam, now gone.'

'I don't think I'll be eating for the next twenty-four hours…' Kolen murmured in a small voice, slowly opening her eyes, and seeing the ground, a far more pleasant sight compared to what had lurked out the window. 'Don't think any of us will be eating for the next twenty-four hours, not until this crisis ends. Hell! I don't think I'll be eating for a week!' Slater derided, leaning his back against the wall near the entrance of the safe house, panting wildly and catching his stolen breath, as well as trying to push the ever-present image of that man's brutal fate out of his mind. Ark floundered over to Spot like she was a zombie herself; the sickening feeling was burdensome in her stomach. She dropped into his chest; her body and insides felt weak from that traumatic experience. Spot had recognized her husky breathing approaching him and caught her with his arms as she collapsed onto his chest. He held her. 'Spot, good boy.' Ark mumbled; her face buried in his chest. 'THE FUCK ARE WE SUPPOSED TO DO NOW?' Winsome suddenly cried out, getting everyone's attention with a flinch. Ark undug her face from Spot's thin chest and looked at Winsome tiredly as Spot tenderly placed her back on the ground. Winsome had the expression of bloody murder on his face, like a little boy who just saw his parents get killed in front of his feeble eyes. He had tears streaming down his cheeks. 'Lisa! Everyone listens to you. What the fuck are we gonna do now? That fucking bitch is smart enough to know where a man's weak spot is! Let alone SMILE at the kill! Who knows, Sam is probably way more advanced than all of us combined! What if she knows we're after her? What if she knew we were here, and that's why she killed that guy right in front of us, knowing that we were watching? What if she's planning on doing something even worse to us? Whatever it is, I don't want to wait and find out. No, thank you! I don't plan on dying yet! Surely not at the hands of that fucking bitch!' he panicked, falling to the floor, burying his head in his knees, bawling his eyes out from the intense fear and situation they had found themselves in.

The scary thought then occurred to him. 'Oh fuck! What if she's secretly listening to our conversation right now!' he panicked, looking up into Ark's tired eyes, sobbing. 'Please… what are we supposed to do? Tell me… what do we do?' Ark stared down at the poor man on the ground, his eyes drowning in tears. Although she'd hated him as much as everyone else because of how he whined and carried on, thinking he was above everyone else, she had felt pity for him because she could understand where his fear was coming from. But before Ark could make her move to comfort him (something she'd never do on any other occasion), she was stumped. Kolen had already got up and approached Winsome despite the number of times he'd harassed and bullied her, insulting and accusing her of being an insufferable hodgepodge of tears. 'Ryan,' she began, gently lifting his chin up so he was facing her. 'I know how scared you are; I am too. We all are, but please don't let your thoughts come down like a ton of bricks and think of the inevitable. Don't jump to conclusions about how clever Sam is. We all know she's scary and has incredible intelligence for a zombie, but brainpower doesn't make her invincible. Sam may be, if not the scariest zombie ever to walk the streets, but remember that she's just a highly advanced zombie that's had the surgery. Do you remember when you and Carl gave her to Alexander when she was your average zombie, rotting and all? She was a standard zombie then and still is a standard zombie with typical zombie weaknesses. Think of her like that; Sam will still go down like any other zombie reanimated by the mortuus carnem. Although it might just be a bit harder to understand how mentally superior she is. But I promise you, you'll see the sun again, and we'll put an end to all the killings committed by that evil zombie. We will kill Sam again so she doesn't rise up from another mortuus carnem. Don't give up yet, Ryan, help us stop and kill Sam once and for all.'

This little motivational speech had surprised everyone; those who worked at the GFOSAR knew Kolen to be the timid little rabbit against any form of brutality and harsh language. Everyone was baffled by Kolen's sudden courage, being able to confront the one man who'd always picked on her. Even Ark was stumped by her words and couldn't help but admire her generosity and courage.

Kolen held her hand out for him to take as a sign of forgiveness from the number of times he'd belittled and berated her for just being herself. Telling him that he needed to take a stand up with her and earn the nickname of "hero" instead of "dickhead", lend a hand to the rest of the group and help them to stop Sam and her endeavours of killing and infecting anyone she saw. 'Are we square?' Kolen asked him. Winsome responded by biting his lip and nodding to her, giving her an encouraging punch on the shoulder.

Ark and Losnedahl regarded Kolen with wide eyes. 'Shocking to hear those words from your mouth, Marilyn,' muttered Winsome, drying up his last remaining tear drops from his eyes and winking at her. He took Kolen's hand in his, and the both of them stood up, seeing one another for the people they were and showing respect for one another. Winsome unzipped his gym bag of weapons and pulled out a crowbar for Kolen to use, which she kindly declined, appointing herself Ace's caretaker and not one to do any fighting. 'I insist. You can't keep yourself from not fighting. Please take it in case things get hairy, and we need someone to fight off close encounters.' He spoke gently to her, holding the crowbar in front of her, which she kept denying, holding her hands up and pushing it away. 'Violence isn't in my blood. Besides, I'd just break down when confronted and forced to fight. Trust me, I'm a liability, so I'll just stick with my current job of tending to Ace and food.' She explained to him. Winsome signed, put the crowbar back in his gym bag, and zipped it up. Slater offered to carry the gym bag for him, and Winsome agreed, taking it off and handing it over to the bearded man. Kolen shifted her attention to Ark, who'd freed herself from Spot's clutches, even if he wasn't ready to let her go (he had more than feelings for her) so quickly.

'What is the plan, Lisa? What happens next?' she inquired with a respectful aspect on her face. Ark was utterly speechless by what Kolen said to Winsome and Winsome's act to show her kindness for once and offer her a weapon to defend herself with. She wanted to say something encouraging but couldn't find the right words. Losnedahl approached Kolen and Winsome, standing between the two and giving them both pats on the back.

Finding her voice again, Ark opened her mouth to speak. 'Well…' She started, glancing at Kolen nervously, her mouth agape. 'We'll start off by searching the place. See if we can find anything that could be of use to us before we leave this dump. And after that, we'll go into London city and look for this Olivia Slater, hoping she'll have answers to some unanswered questions about the mortuus carnem parasite and why it goes for the dead.' Slater glanced at Ark as soon as she'd mentioned the idea of finding his twin sister. 'Then, when Olivia is on board with us, we'll then hunt down Sam.' Ark declared, glancing into the eyes of those standing by her. Explaining what they were going to do next and wanting to see it in their faces that they understood her and that they were okay with it. Which they were. Bowing their heads and confirming without words that they were ready to face their fears and fight back against the mortuus carnem apocalypse, just the seven of them, striving to do something no one else had done.

'Right, before we leave this shitheap, police the area. Look around for stuff that might help us along the way, food, drinks, medical supplies, anything that we'll need,' Ark ordered.

'For the first time ever, I like the sound of what you're saying.' Winsome accepted, portraying that he learned his lesson about resilience and willpower to keep fighting from Kolen's speech. Winsome was the first to do as Ark had ordered. He wandered back into the kitchen, this time with purpose. He opened the small fridge and looked at the contents inside before picking out the plastic containers of what looked to be still fresh edible food and cans of fizzy drink and bottles of water, the bottles of water seemed to be healthy and safe enough for consumption, and if it wasn't… well they probably would have to resort to drinking their own urine. He opened one of the drawers under the washbasin and took out a roll of black garbage bags. He tore off one of the bags and shook it to open it. Winsome shoved the food and drink into the garbage bag and tied it up with a knot before scanning through the other cupboards and drawers for more supplies.

Kolen tended to Ace, holding the wheelchair containing her. Slater had disappeared behind a wall leading into a hallway, perhaps searching for supplies in a basement or attic. Winsome returned with the bag of food and drink, and Kolen held her hand out for them. He transferred them over to her, and she took them from him, setting them down next to the wheelchair while she worked to prepping the wheelchair so it would be able to transfer their supplies. She examined the wheelchair, picked up the food bag, untied Winsome's knot, and tied it to the handles of the wheelchair so it would be suitable for transportation and that she'd be able to see and take anything out if the others requested it. Ark gathered Spot's brain jar, which he'd placed on the ground shortly before the man's demise, sensing Ark staggering over and falling into his chest. She returned it back to his hands, giving it a light tap on the glass for good measure. She looked at him, tenderly taking his arm and speaking up at him. 'When we leave here, Spot, I'm gonna need you to be as protective as possible of our group, not just to me but the rest of us. I know you have no way of seeing because of your missing top head half, but you have a working brain with cables inside it to help you think and hear like the rest of us. If you hear Sam or any other bad zombies around, signal us, even if it's a tap or a gurgle … any sign will do. You understand me, boy?' Ark clarified, giving his arm a gentle, encouraging slap. Spot understood, holding onto his brain jar protectively, one of his hands reaching out in front of him, touching and moving up to her face and stroking it gently as if saying: 'I would be honoured to do anything for you, Lisa. The lives of this group will be in my hands. I'll make sure to keep Sam away from us the best I can.'

'Good boy,' she praised, forcing a small smile onto her face for him, although sadly, he couldn't see it. But he didn't need to; he knew when he was doing his bonder proud.

Slater returned soon after, his hands empty of anything of use aside from a small container containing only three antidepressant pills, which he claimed he had plucked out from somewhere in the basement. Slater tilted the container over his head and shook them gently, spilling one of the pills out and tossing it into his mouth. Losnedahl approached him and traded arms with Slater while holding his own hand out, beckoning for an antidepressant, Slater gave him the second last one without protest, and Losnedahl tossed it into his mouth. The mute man then gave the revolver to Slater, and Slater returned him with a bowie knife, granting each other a weapon they both felt more comfortable with.

Losnedahl ventured into another room to look around for more stuff that could be useful to them, hopefully finding some first-aid kits. Slater dug into one of his jacket's pockets and reloaded the revolver with some bullets, which he'd discovered while he'd been out scavenging for wood for the bbq.

'Alright, is everyone ready to go?' Ark announced after reloading the rifle with some spare ammo she'd taken from Slater when he'd offered them to her (Darren Slater was now the ammunition man). 'You bet your fucking cunt we are!' Winsome stated, putting the last remaining shells, kindly taken from Slater, into his shotgun and pulling the fore-end back with a satisfying click. A look of determination unquestionably levelled on his face, wanting nothing more than to find Sam and put a shell in her skull, relishing in the very thought alone.

Kolen concluded by stocking the wheelchair pouches with supplies and was about to confirm that she, too, was ready and had an army load of supplies when the panicked footsteps and heavy breathing of Losnedahl emerged, out of breath and holding up a peculiar rectangular object. Something that hadn't seen the light since 2009, a relic of the past. He held a very old vintage VHS tape with the faded words "Happy birthday" written with pencil on it. Next to the name of the tape was a written year date, but that was far too eroded for Losnedahl to see independently. Losnedahl gave it to Kolen as she was the one with the glasses and would be able to read the eroded message, even if it was very faintly seen by her spectacled eyes. 'An old birthday tape?' Slater studied the name of the tape, confused, wondering how the videotape had managed to survive after all these years, let alone in a decrepit shithole of a house. He looked at Kolen, who squinted her eyes behind the glasses and managed to read the VHS's date: **12th Oct 1980.** '1980? Holy crap! That's seventy-six years ago!' Kolen stared down at the videotape strangely as if it were an alien instrument before handing it over for Ark to study, flipping it over and observing such an ancient specimen from the past and feeling a slight unease at the confirmation of the tape's date. Ark investigated it for a few fleeting seconds before glancing at Slater. 'Is there a VHS player here?' She asked, giving the videotape to him, thinking that the player should also be here if the tape was here, hoping it was still intact and could still play videos. I was not expecting it to be as crystal clear as it used to be back in the day, but I was still able to play them grainy, nonetheless. Slater was about to open his mouth and tell her that there wasn't one, but then he stopped and looked up at the ceiling, hand brushing his beard, thinking. 'I think there's one in the basement; follow me.' He said, leading them all through one of the hallways, telling Spot, led by Ark, to duck, as Slater lifted up an old mattered woollen carpet to reveal a secret door, which he pulled open to reveal a sketchy-looking room that was shadowed in nothing but darkness. Kolen decided it best to leave the wheelchair upstairs, picking up Ace and holding her like a doll.

'Why are we suddenly wasting time with some stupid random videotape from the ancient times?' Winsome questioned, letting the shotgun drop so it flung around in one hand. Ark cocked her head to him. '1980 is seventy-six years ago. Alexander had confirmed when he was still alive that Sam was over seventy-six years old. There's an odd similarity to the date on the tape that's unsettling me.' She explained to him as she, holding Spot's hand, carefully followed Slater down the stairs and into the basement's lucid shadows. 'But what's that gotta do with the price of fish? How is watching some old tape gonna help us stop Sam?' he said, puzzled, but was silenced by Slater flicking and lighting a match, bringing an eerie glow to the basement. He wandered through the dark basement, finding a lantern hanging from a hook near the foot of the basement and lit it before shaking it out. When there was enough light, Slater then made his way over to a light switch on the opposite side of the lantern, still at the foot of the steps and pressed the button, generating a flickering light that illuminated the basement to some degree. The six of them watched Slater fumble around the pieces of junk around the cellar, pulling off blankets of cloth to reveal more piles upon piles of trash from the previous owner of the house when it was still a habitable house. That's when he threw away one specific blanket and unveiled an old box TV with a video player installed underneath. They all watched keenly as Slater rummaged around the back of the old television, flicking on a switch from behind before returning to the front and pressing the big "on" button. The screen on the small box TV flickered for a few seconds, showing nothing but static. Slater fumbled around with the antenna on top of the TV until he was blessed with a signal. A very grainy signal. He knelt down to the old VHS player and pressed the on button, marvelling at finding out that it was still working after all these years of sitting in the basement and collecting dust. 'I'm amazed this piece of shit still works,' Slater mumbled as he inserted the tape into the player, fiddling around with the buttons on the TV, finding a suitable station and backing away from the TV to see what would happen. Except for Spot, the other group members watched the static on the TV for a few minutes out of pure amazement (none of them had ever seen a working VHS player before) before the TV flashed for a second, showing a blue screen for a few more seconds. The word REC flickered on the top left corner of the screen right before the screen flashed again, and a picture started to form, along with faint sounds of people talking.

Outside the house, Sam had finished her meal, licking the blood and gore from her fingers, and taking in the savouring taste of the brain she had just consumed. She blinked and stared at the rundown, abandoned building with the boarded-up windows and the zombie gore that had been positioned in the front, acting as some kind of protective barrier against zombies such as herself. Sam tilted her head as she stared at the side of the building with those boarded windows and zombie heads displayed out the front, and that was when it hit her, and she remembered. She remembered that she'd seen the house before. She may have once lived in it, and the secrets to her past could be locked inside.

Chapter 38

'Jessica, Chantelle, Nathan! Come and say happy birthday to your sister, Naomi!' A feminine voice with a passive British accent was heard from the heavily-grained screen that threatened to flash and stop, leaving them with the same blinding blue screen from before. But through the grained, static footage, there was still a manifested picture to be seen on the TV and supposed that was the main thing the group had wanted, to see a picture of life back in the 1980s as it was written on the tape. Grasping a glimpse into the past, decades before the mortuus carnem was even discovered. Back when life made sense and had a meaning. When life was good. Not only was the footage heavily grained, but it was also shaky like someone was holding the camera. And when one considers the visible distance of the female voice, it becomes a prominent factor that a mysterious woman was holding the camera and was panning it around the outside. The group watched with keen, watchful eyes, seeing this old footage play out like a home movie, which it was Slater who had stated that what they were watching was, in fact, a wholesome home movie from back in the day and by the topic that was happening during the grainy footage, it was a birthday video for someone possibly long-dead, named Naomi?

'Damn, home movies are that ancient?' Winsome marvelled.

'Shush,' Ark hushed him, her eyes staring wide and unblinking into the TV's screen, observing the woman holding the camera as she filmed at what appeared to be an outdoor seating; it was hard to tell from the terrible quality of the footage. But what the group could make out was a lovely-looking banana cake surrounded by colourful balloons, party food and all sorts of party decorations that you'd find at an 80s-style party. The footage on the tape was terrible in that it would briefly lose its signal, causing minor cuts into static and had few dips in colour, sometimes reverting to black and white. But that could be forgiven. The footage was filmed in 1980, and the year was 2056, so it was overlooked for having such lousy quality; it was even a wonder that the film had even managed to survive and still function accurately inside the player. Hell, it was a wonder that the player and TV still worked after all these long, agonised years, Box TVs, video players, and VHS tapes were discontinued years ago, way, before any member of the group was even born, so for them to see this grained footage, was like going back in time and seeing what life was like during the late 20th century. And as far as they were concerned, it looked and sounded far better than the life they were forced into living. It had been Losnedahl who had shuffled closer to the screen and put a finger on the screen as if hoping it would suck him inside and transport him into the world of the 1980s. The world inside of this video.

'Jeremey, can you hold this for me?' The woman holding the camera had requested an unseen man named Jeremey. *Who were these people? Why is this tape even here in the first place? And more importantly, how was it still working after all these years of gathering dust in this basement?* Ark thought as she watched the video. The woman holding the camera wandered off away from the decorations outside, coming into what looked to be the kitchen. Handing the camera out, an orange-haired man with a bushy matching moustache and a long horse-like face came into view of the camera briefly, smiling and taking the camera from what was assumed to be his wife, whom the group still hadn't seen yet.

With the man named Jeremey in possession of the camera, he panned it around a nice-looking dining room as a little girl with black hair, which had been done in plaits in a purple princess outfit came into view of the camera's lens and looked up at who seemed to be her father holding the camera. Her hands were clasped behind her back as she peered from her father to the outside seating, biting her bottom lip shyly as if she wasn't sure whether she should go outside and join the party. 'Go on, Naomi, your brother and sisters will be here soon,' the man coaxed, watching as the little girl named Naomi smiled shyly. The camera then panned up to the outdoor seating. Naomi came back into view as the camera followed her, watching her sit in front of that delicious-looking banana cake that was soon becoming crowded with presents that had been placed on the table around it. This was quickly followed by the sound of children laughing in the background. An older-looking boy with black hair came into view and chose his spot next to Naomi (her brother, Nathan), placing his arm around her shoulder and whispering something to her, which merited a giggle from her. A few seconds later, the woman's voice from before could be heard again; who'd initially been holding the camera had come into view of the camera with two other people, one younger, the other older (Chantelle and Jessica?).

'Alright, kids, come over and take a seat!' Jeremey's voice had shouted. This was followed by the sound of children laughing and the sounds of multiple running legs as about five more children came into view and picked their seats around the table. 'Alright!' The woman's voice from before exulted. 'Let's get this party started by singing Happy Birthday! Presents will come soon,' the woman's voice gleamed with delight, and from what her voice told them, she seemed like a proud matriarch and mother to Naomi, whose birthday video they were watching.

'S'cuse me, honey,' the woman said, shuffling in front of the camera to get behind Naomi in her purple princess costume. Jeremey, the camera holder, walked to the other side of the table, behind five of the younger-looking children and panned the camera up to reveal the woman standing over her daughter Naomi; she smacked a kiss on the little girl's head and beamed at the camera.

The woman had been a mystery ever since the beginning of the footage, and now she was in front of them. It was Slater who had made an audible gasp as if he'd recognised her from somewhere. She had black hair that matched her daughter's, which had been tied back in a ponytail; she wore a golden tiara on her head and a Wonder Woman costume as she stood over the birthday girl, presiding over her and gesturing for her to look at the camera, to look at daddy.

Even so, they continued to watch. The camera at first was panned down at Naomi sitting in front of the cake as everyone around the table jovially sang Happy Birthday to the little girl in the princess costume. The camera zoomed in on her face as her siblings and the other children sang the birthday song. The camera then panned up to the woman singing behind Naomi as the man holding the camera spoke to the audience, calling the woman "the wife" but without giving the woman an identity or saying what her name was. And when it showed a close-up of her face, the group members flinched back with a start, prompting Winsome to fall backwards as if pushed; Losnedahl gaped, Slater and Ark had their words stolen from them, and Kolen stared with wide eyes.

The singing woman on the tape was the spitting image of Sam, the same shade of black hair and the same sharp features on her face! The murderer of countless GFOSAR officials. But this woman was nowhere near Sam in the slightest way possible! This had to be some kind of doppelganger, or maybe Sam had some sort of identical twin back in the day? Who the hell was this woman? Why was this tape here? What kind of coincidence was this? Yes, she had black hair and a face they'd come to loathe, but this no way in hell was Sam when she was alive! This was probably just some innocent video from the 1980s, and the woman in a shot just happened to look like their enemy. There had to be some kind of reason why the woman in the video coincidently looks like Sam. Maybe this video had been purposely put here for them to find? Did Sam secretly lead them to this supposed safe haven, hoping they'd stumble upon this video? Did Sam want Ark and company to see this?

No way! This wasn't Sam when she was alive; this just happened to be some random English mother who just happened to look like her. The woman in the film seemed too sweet and displayed a genuine loving nature to her daughter Naomi, who was now blowing out the candles. The woman was smiling broadly. She hugged Naomi, smothering her cheeks with kisses as the little girl finished blowing out the tenth and final candle on the cake, which everyone had cheered in celebration, congratulating Naomi on her tenth birthday.

This was when the tape had ended, causing the blue screen to appear again, leaving all of the humans in the group agitated about what they had seen on that old harmless VHS tape. It was an innocuous home video and was nowhere near as scary as the gruesome fate of that man, but still… it had raised more and more questions about who exactly they were fighting. Again, they found themselves asking: Who is Sam? What kind of person was she before death? Was that her alive on the tape? How did she die? Was she a mother? Was she actually a good person? These were some of the questions they now had trapped in their heads. More pieces were added to the puzzle, and they had doubted that Sam would be so willing as to hand over those remaining pieces and answer those questions for them about who she was right before they killed her.

'Holy shit… what if that was Sam, and the bonding turned her into a murderous monster?' moaned Winsome, pointing to the blue screen, and staring at Ark fearfully.

'No! Alexander would never teach her anything bad; of course, that wasn't Sam. It couldn't be; that would be too much of a coincidence. It was just some random woman who just happened to look like her, nothing more.' Ark stressed, shaking her head in denial. 'The job of a bonder is to help the zombie and try to make them remember who they are, and if they can't remember, they're given a new name and another chance of a different life.' She shivered. Her mind was jumbled, swamped with questions about Sam's true identity. *Who the fuck was she?* Ark was stressed; she tried to tell herself that the woman on the video was just some harmless lady who just happened to share the same face as Sam. But there was something inside her gut that was telling her otherwise, ratting her and trying to tell her that Sam had possibly left breadcrumbs for them, hoping for them to come into this house and see the video. No, no, no! That was too much of a coincidence… then what? How was it that this place, the place that Slater had taken them to, just happened to have this video? Did Slater know something in which she and co. didn't? Was he some kind of mole, and he had no idea? When Sam killed his friends, was there a reason why she didn't chase him when he escaped? Did she purposely chase him to this place, knowing all too well what was inside? Again, that was too much of a coincidence. But yet again… how much did Sam really know? How much of her past had she remembered? There were so many questions that Ark was scared she might drown in, and there would be no answers to help her out.

'Lisa, we can jump to conclusions later when the world is back in balance again. But right now, our main priority now is to kill Sam, not to uncover the mystery of who the fuck she is. Don't forget that she's killed a shit tonne of people tonight; she ain't gonna kill any more in the next twenty-four hours; we'll make sure of that, Lisa. We can figure out her past after Sam is dead for good.' Slater grabbed Ark's hand and nodded to her. He walked over to the box TV and turned it and the player off before blowing the lantern's candle out and asking everyone to join him back upstairs.

They did.

While upstairs, Losnedahl and Kolen were just as stunned as Ark, but they tried to approach her and gently touched her shoulder, asking if she was okay. She told them she was and that she was just a little frightened by the footage and seeing the eerily similar woman. But it was like Slater had said; none of it mattered now, and there was time to jump to conclusions later on. Shaking her head, Ark recovered quickly and patted the leather strap of her rifle, remembering what Slater had said. Yes, they had a job to do, and that was to kill Sam. One way or another, they were going to destroy the one who had massacred the GFOSAR. She was confident she'd interrogate the man at some stage and find out where he found this place, if Sam had chased him here and if he knew about the video. But for now, they had a zombie they needed to find and kill. 'Let's finish this. Together, for the people at the GFOSAR, for Alexander Fredrickson, for Ace and Spot, for everyone in Britain! Let's go kill that bitch!

PART 2: 24 Hours

Chapter 1

During the first few days before the mass outbreak of the mortuus carnem was officially declared, back around in the year 2032, somewhere in Bulgaria, panic had already ensued around Europe. Evidently, it is finding its way to the rest of the world when social media, podcasts and news broadcasts blew up, depicting frightful stories of the dead, rising from their graves with sweet teeth for brains, attacking the living on sight, breaking into their homes, wandering into local bars and restaurants, and skulking around local cemeteries that were meant to house their final resting place. Videos were posted online, documenting these harrowing attacks. One of the unlucky victims who had his demise posted had been an urban explorer named Clive Keegan, nicknamed The Irish Vampyr, who personally specialised in exploring abandoned cemeteries, mausoleums, crypts, and mansions for the entertainment of his community. He'd been streaming his adventure with his good friend Dolores Walsh, exploring one of Bulgaria's many alleged haunted cemeteries during the outbreak. Hoping to document any undead behaviour as irrefutable proof that the end was indeed nigh and the undead were, in fact, rising from their graves to attack anyone on sight. It would be known as The Irish Vampyr's last video, as Clive Keegan got more than he bargained for when he was talking to Dolores, holding the camera and the audience. A pair of rotting hands had burst from the soil, grabbing him from behind, and started to drag him underneath the dirt where he stood. Clive Keegan wailed in pain and terror as Dolores instinctively dropped the camera, unknowing that the lens was facing the urban explorer (whose death was being recorded). While she tried pulling him away from the pulling hands.

She pulled at him for dear life. That was when a zombified face emerged from the soil, causing both explorers to shriek from terror, their screams echoing throughout the cemetery like ghoulish howls carried upon the wind. The zombified face then sunk its teeth into Clive's foot, causing him to let out a haunting scream that echoed throughout the cemetery like a ghoulish wail and which hesitantly caused Dolores to let go of her friend's hand and run out of the cemetery. She picked up the camera from where she'd dropped it, muttering "feck" over and over and wondering why on Earth she'd taken the camera with her instead of just leaving it and booking it out. The world would need to know about the dangers of the undead. But her escape wasn't without risk, and she encountered many more of the risen undead roaming in her direction as Clive's screams echoed in the background and in her ears.

Dolores managed to escape by entering the car they'd arrived in, drove away and ended the video. That had been one of the wake-up calls, documenting the dangers the world was heading into.

Of course, when the mortuus carnem started reaching other countries, it wasn't long before the military got involved, providing weapons to slow down the numbers of the dead rising by simply killing them, patrolling graveyards, and shooting anything that moved underneath the graves. And when they thought that the corpses would stay stagnant, so they would essentially be reburied inside their graves for another night of eternal slumber. This was before they found out about the mortuus carnem going for even the recently deceased and not just buried bodies. And when it was mentioned that the mortuus carnem didn't discriminate and went for anything classed as dead, that was when numbers of the army were dispatched into the cemeteries either to burn bodies of recent victims or to exhume old ones and burn them on a funeral pyre.

But as long as the mortuus carnem was around (still breathing) and as long as there were dead bodies for it to sniff out, Earth was no longer safe... and the dead would continue to rise.

In just twenty years, most of the living world had died out because all it took to become infected was one bite from one of the undead, and once bitten, it was all over. Humans were scarily decreasing in numbers within every twenty-four hours; Earth was becoming increasingly more inhabitable and a very terrifying place to live in.

If the mortuus carnem parasite wasn't put to extinction by the year 2100. Memories of a once peaceful(ish) Earth would just be a mere figment of a planet that used to be full of life, a dream that could never happen.

By the way things were going, Earth by 2100 would be a dead planet, endlessly drifting in the unfathomable void of stars and emptiness, never to see the light of day again. To never again have any ounce of life, grass wouldn't grow, and the sun would shine on the residue of the past. A barren wasteland where only the dead roamed.

If changes weren't made to change Sam's desired future on Earth, the human race would be nothing but a fossil, an extinct species like the dinosaurs and animals before that. If no one stood up to fight for their home. If the human race were to give up, deciding that hope was indeed lost and that the dead had, in fact, conquered the once beautiful planet that used to be shining with life. The undead would have no struggles, transforming it into something completely different. Terraforming it into an unhabitable ghost planet full of nothing but death and devastation that might have a similar appearance often seen in big-budget Hollywood movies or a horror novel about the end of the world. This was just becoming more of a reality because Sam was increasing her IQ levels by reading through various books on the culture and survival of the human race over the years and reading other pieces from both fiction and non-fiction and the longer she spent outside the doors of GFOSAR and seeing things again with a different mindset, she was remembering things, things she'd once forgotten. She'd make frequent visits inside the remaining lifeless libraries around, often reading things in novels on the downfall of the human race and thinking of ways to incorporate them into her plans. Thinking of the best ways she could eviscerate the rest of the human race. The more creative and the more the victim suffered, the better.

If Sam wasn't stopped and killed along with the other zombies taking her side, and if the mortuus carnem wasn't put to extinction, the human race wouldn't have such a colourful future. Sam's destiny would become a dreaded reality; more zombies would be born every day, and the world will be dead and without humans. Lord help us...

Chapter 2

Back in the abandoned house, Darren Slater checked his watch. An old analogue thing that he'd found on the floor and was surprisingly still working despite a small line running across the glass face. He told the others that the time was just after two in the afternoon. The group had just finished getting organised for the ordeal at hand. They finished loading their weapons with enough ammunition and keeping the spares inside their pockets in case they needed to reload. Or if they ran out of spare ammo, just ask the ammunition man, Darren Slater; he was likely to have satchels upon satchels stored with ammunition for any type of firearm, and if they were lucky, they could find more along their journey.

Supplies were smuggled into the many pockets and pouches strapped onto the back of Ace's wheelchair, enhancing the density by a few pounds. Kolen often required Losnedahl's aid so she could move it along or get over an obstacle without much issue and not slowing them down, for when they'd leave the so-called safe house and be en route to finding Slater's younger twin sister. Slater had confirmed that the last he'd heard from his sister Olivia she'd told him she was somewhere in London. So, her whereabouts could be anywhere as London was a prominent place; Ark hoped that their stars were lucky and they wouldn't have to look far.

As they were getting ready, Kolen looked over and noticed that Ark's movements seemed more delayed than before. Kolen knew that there was something on her mind, and she felt as if she should ask Ark what it was that she was brooding about. Though judging by the wide eyes and the way she stared straight ahead and absently as if she'd seen something she was trying to deny, Kolen sensed that Ark was still thinking of that VHS and the woman dressed as Wonder Woman. Kolen approached her friend and was tender in placing a hand on her shoulder, causing Ark to flinch slightly and shudder. She then looked up at Ark with those frightened bulb-like eyes. Kolen opened her mouth and asked her softly if she was okay. Even if she could clearly tell that she wasn't. 'I'm okay, Marilyn, I'm okay. Just a little uneasy about the coincidence of that video.' She replied with a stammer that sounded like she'd gone into a butcher's freezer and had come out feeling more than just a little chilled. Kolen could clearly understand where her friend was coming from. She, too, had been left completely baffled by the sheer coincidence of the haunting birthday tape, which she and her companions had all witnessed. Still, as she was sure that Ark had been doing, Kolen tried to tell herself that the woman in the video wasn't Sam and it was just some other random woman who'd been unfortunate enough to share the exact features of their enemy. She was just some innocent woman who had recorded her daughter's birthday, and they'd just stumbled across it; that was it! It was just some old random relic from the past that had been abandoned and left in the basement. Thankfully, Slater had been the one to tear them away from their brooding over the video and the haunting image of that woman. It'd been Slater who'd reminded Ark and Kolen of the dangers Sam had opposed, and discovering her identity and why she looked like that woman on the tape would be something they must do later when Britain was safe from her clutches.

Though that face smiling down at that little girl wasn't a face to forget (as much as she might want to), it was like the image had been tattooed into her brain where it would remain forever.

Once again, her confidence had appointed her the leadership role, taking a firm grip on the sniper rifle, glancing at everyone in her party, who, in turn, stared back at her, a distilled flame in their eyes that Ark couldn't help but find serenity in. 'I hope you're ready to face against the dead? The horrors back at the GFOSAR will be far different and outside will be twice as dangerous,' Ark said, wanting to clarify that everyone knew what they were getting into and just how ugly the outside could be. Ark watched her allies' glance at each other, muttering among themselves before returning their gazes back to Ark and nodding, informing her that they were indeed ready to face the horrors of the outside.

'Once we leave here, you all know the drill,' maintained Ark, holding the rifle up with a firm grasp and letting out a long breath. She wanted to affirm with her allies that they were indeed ready to get their hands dirty and venture out into the dangerous world that they had hidden away from. 'Ready as a pouncing cheetah, Mrs Ark,' Slater responded.

'You fucking bet I'm ready to take on that black-haired bitch!' asserted Winsome with a cocky grin, possessing the shotgun, and pulling the fore-end back, making a satisfying clink, sweat dripping from his forehead. He had gained some of the colour that he'd formally lost after watching that poor man die, along with that haunting home video from the 1980s.

'Right as rain, Lisa, I'll keep Ace supported and an eye on the supplies. Just as long as I don't have to fight,' Kolen responded, straightening her white-rimmed glasses because her zombie, Ace, had pointed to them, alerting her that they were fogging up and crooked.

Losnedahl kept the sharp bowie knife in one of the belt's ring around his grey jeans, ready to unsheath it when needed to stab it into a zombie's face. He glanced at Ark and created an *'I'm ready! Let's do this!'* gesture with sign language. 'Zombies?' Ark questioned, looking over at the two zombies and waiting for a one-word answer from them. Spot was holding onto his brain jar closely to his chest like a teddy bear; one of his hands managed a thumbs up, which had surprised Ark, but she thought no more of it, as he indicated that he was ready. 'Let go!' Ace blasted, less than a second after Spot's thumbs-up, representing to the group that she was more than equipped to get going and find Olivia Slater. 'Right! Let's go and kill that fucking zombie!' Ark avowed, making her orders clear. They all nodded. Winsome even cheered in response to Ark's order to hunt and kill Sam right after they were done with Olivia, leading to some of the questions finally getting answered.

Ark looked at Slater and cocked her head towards some wooden pillars in the way of their exit. Slater forgot he'd told Winsome to put them up shortly after his arrival, and having experienced firsthand what Winsome was like when riled up, he thought twice about asking him to remove them. The order was simple: he had to remove those pillars away from the entrance, which, in this case, was their exit. Aiming to compose an easy escape from where they'd come from. 'Anyone got the time?' Winsome wondered, peering down at his wrist, seeing that it was broken; pieces of the glass were missing from the face and replaced with small pebbles of dirt, obscuring the clock's arrows and numbers, rendering it useless upon his arm. 'No good, Ryan, my watch is broken,' Kolen grimaced, taking off her broken wristwatch and dropping it on the floor, finding no use for it anymore, while placing her hands back on the wheelchair handles, ready to move with everyone else. 'It just turned 2:34pm,' Slater answered, looking at his watch.

'Shit,' Ark sighed, 'we'll have at least twenty-four hours to kill Sam before she presumably infects the whole country. Time is short.' Ark frowned, making it apparent they didn't have time to mess around at Olivia's place if they wanted to find and kill Sam. They had to grab the information they needed to stop the mortuus carnem and dwindling its numbers, leading to its demise. Hoping to equip Olivia, praying that she'll join their team of both humans and zombies and aid them in their plans to stop Sam from destroying the country in such a short window of time.

There was a nervous chortle, and once they looked around, they saw it had come from Winsome. 'Twenty-four hours? I'm sorry, call me an idiot, but twenty-four fucking hours? Are you serious? That's all we have? Twenty-four damn hours?' Winsome cried; his eyes were dilated and darting from left to right, his shoulders were hitching, and his breathing was fevered. 'Ryan, please. Remember what I told you. Don't let your thoughts get ahead of you. I know you're scared; I am, too; we all are. But remember, you're gonna make it. We'll make sure you see the sun tomorrow; just have faith. We'll stop Sam and put an end to her wretched life. Mr Fredrickson wouldn't want his bonded zombie to do this; this is the opposite of what he would want. We'll kill Sam for him and the United Kingdom and the rest of the world. Just keep telling yourself that, Ryan, we will be okay,' Kolen had calmly reassured him, deciding that it would be a waste going over to him like she did before and reciting her exact words over to him. 'But think of it from a logical perspective!' Winsome said, raising his voice slightly, seeing no desire to calm down and take Kolen's wisdom to heart. He strode over to Ark, chortling that nervous sound as he whispered in her ear, venting his views on what she'd said. 'Listen to me on this, Lisa, there's no fucking way we can just beat the fucking clock and kill Sam just like that! It's crazy, and even you know it.' He hissed. 'You're basically asking us to dig our own graves, Lisa. And I, for one, am not ready to say goodbye to my beautiful arse. And I guarantee that everyone here has beautiful arses worth saving, right?' he locked eyes with the rest of the group, tears in his eyes now, and he dropped the shotgun to his feet.

'Right?!'

'Fuck this,' Slater grumbled, seating the revolver in the pocket of his jacket, dropping the wooden pillar, which hit the floor with a clang, storming over to Winsome with a clenched-up fist at the ready. Yes, he understood that Winsome was scared to death, but that didn't mean he could waste the very little time they had thinking of the worst and letting his over-paranoia get the better of him; like Kolen had said, he needed to gain a grip on himself, control his fear and have a little faith that they were going to make it through this with their teeth still in their mouths.

Slater seized the collar of Winsome's shirt, bringing him over so close to his bearded face that Winsome could almost feel the bristles of facial hair tickle his chin as he stared helplessly at Slater, eyes wide and speechless. 'Ryan! I have four words for you: Shut. The. Fuck. Up. We're already wasting precious time just standing here listening to you complain. How fucking old are you? Six? Four? Be a fucking man, Ryan, and think before opening your gob. We will end up dead if you continue to bitch on about things way ahead of time!' Slater chided, picking up the shotgun from the ground and shoving it back into Winsome's arms, knocking Winsome back a few steps. Winsome blinked and gaped stupidly at the bearded man. 'Your heart is in the right place, and I get that you're scared, but we're going to make it alright! So, get a freaking grip over yourself, man!' Slater commanded.

Darren Slater didn't like things delayed. He had to grow accustomed to doing things on time; he'd been fortunate to work in the army as a cadet at nineteen for about fourteen years, being trained to fight against the many hordes of the living dead. However, his service for the Royal Military Army (RMA) wasn't due to last forever (good things never do). Because of the increasing outbreak of corpses rising from their graves to kill and becoming increasingly more hostile and violent, sometimes riddling them with bullets wasn't enough to slow them down. They were highly durable, and it wasn't long until Slater and his fellow soldiers would be overrun, forcing them to make a harrowing retreat, because when one found themselves in a hordes' line of sight, running was often regarded as the most sensible thing to do. This not only ended his career as a soldier fighting for the greater good of Britain because of a horde's sheer number of approximately three hundred and fifty runners. But Slater had fortunately managed to flee the massacre of his fellow RMA soldiers after one of his best mates in the army, Xavier Van Ray, had made the heroic sacrifice for his country and charged headfirst into a horde of zombies with a grenade belt attached to him. Van Ray had pulled the keys off the grenade belt as he ran into the crowd, yelling his best war cry while Slater had screamed out for him to stop what he was doing, take off the belt and fall back, but Van Ray was amenable to die for his country in which he heroically did (For Britain). The grenades strapped to the belt, all in unison, had exploded at the same time. Which had not only killed Van Ray but the whole mountain of zombies that were piling on top of him, which had killed them for good, propelling massive chunks of both rotten and alive flesh all over the battleground. This was back in Winchester in 2041. Xavier Van Ray's name was remembered, and he was commemorated as a hero who made that heroic sacrifice for his country. Seeing him charging into that horde and hearing his battle cries still haunted Slater even fifteen years later. *I pray that your remains are resting peacefully inside your grave, Xavier. A good man like yourself needs his rest. I hope your parts are still contained inside your tomb and are undisturbed by that parasite.* Slater's mind had taken a moment of silence to remember his dear friend, who'd chosen to sacrifice himself, something that Slater would never have the guts to do.

'Darren, are you ready to go?' Ark queried, glancing at him as he let go of Winsome and getting some closure of Van Ray's passing.

'Yeah. Let's get to London city and find my sister,' he replied, nodding at Winsome and pulling the revolver back out, holding it at the ready.

Chapter 3

The man with the bushy brown beard shook his head after he'd just experienced a brief flashback of one of his friends choosing to heroically sacrifice himself. He rubbed his eyes with his wrist and decided to remove the last wooden pillar that blocked the exit. Suppose in this kind of world, nowhere was really safe. He went over to the pillar without paying much attention in front of him, instead staring at the floor as he made his way over to the door. Slater was mumbling things to himself, his mind still a little uneasy with all the things he'd seen throughout the day and with the nagging memory of his old friend, he felt something in front of him, a body. He stepped back and looked up, seeing that he'd bumped into the back of Spot, who was awkwardly hunched over; he'd blindly navigated his way over to the door and had already placed his hands on it, although he hadn't attempted to move it yet seeing as the man with the beard had interrupted him. He peered blindly behind him in Slater's direction, curiously wondering who'd bumped him. Slater took another step back, seeing as Spot appeared far taller than he was. 'Woah, easy there, big guy, it's just me, Darren. Lisa requested that I move that out of the way so we can all escape.' He warily explained to the tall zombie. He knew that Spot was docile and loyal to Ark, but Slater still got nervous when confronted by the half-headless giant whose towering presence was enough to intimidate him. So much that when Spot peered down at him, he instinctively swallowed some saliva.

He knew that Spot couldn't see him, but it was still nerve-racking to be gazing upon that sliced head on that imposing tall body. Spot humbled Slater, nodding to him, his tongue dripping with spit. 'We cool?' Slater spoke gingerly to the towering zombie. Spot tilted his head to him before bowing his head again, stepping out of his way and letting the bearded man help him.

After coming to a truce with Spot and seeing Slater as responsible, both he and Slater successfully and safely removed the wooden pillar from the entranceway. They were the first to leave upon Slater, kindly reminding Spot to duck, lower his size considerably, and leave the safe house while holding Slater's hand for that one time. The others soon followed behind them. When Ark was out, she made her way back to the front, taking Spot's hand and leading them away from the governed safe house and back into the outside, where they'd proceeded to make their way into London city. Winsome was trailing closely behind, not even bothering to open his mouth to speak anything out of line. Ark glanced back at Winsome, amazed to see he was silent; she wanted to deliver her own witty remark but didn't bother wasting her breath by asking which cork he shoved up his arse. Not only did she not have anything whimsical to say to him, but she also had no patience for a man who'd slow everyone down with his cowardly pleas just because he was scared. She didn't have time for those who were only in it for themselves; he wasn't the only one who was scared out of his wits: the entire group was scared senseless, including the zombies in the group, even though they were capable of knowing the taste of horror. Mainly Spot, because he feared for the safety and life of his dear friend and bonder. He stressed the possibility that Sam could jump on her and kill her without a moment's apprehension; he couldn't see or smell. Which just made him increasingly all the more paranoid and worried for Ark; he couldn't bear the thought of Sam killing Ark while he remained powerless to do anything to prevent it. Spot owed his life to Ark for retrieving his brain and allowing him to think again. 'I is needing of drug. I feel hungry,' the crawler suddenly said, gazing at her bonder. Kolen watched Ace, then the group walking ahead of her and sighed, coming to a stop and fiddling around with her lab coat's breast pocket. The group were forced to arrive at a dead halt just a few feet away from the safe house, watching Kolen fiddle around in her breast pocket. 'Don't wait for me, I can catch up. I have pills in here, somewhere. I just gotta-' Kolen told them as she dug through her pocket, rummaging around, looking for at least one of the red antibiotics containing the hunger drug.

'Darn it, why can't I find it?' she muttered, her voice becoming increasingly panicked when she couldn't find any. Losnedahl, being impulsive, knew he had some and fumbled through his pockets until he found one. He extracted it from his pocket and was about to tip it over to Kolen to give to the talking crawler, who was licking her rotten teeth, appearing to look hungrier and hungrier the more she went without food or a pill. But Ark already had Kolen covered and had given her a pill from her breast pocket, seeing as if it was wasting time to wait for Kolen to feed Ace the drug. Ark was and remained the most trustworthy of the group to always have a stash of hunger drugs for zombies if their hunger needed to be sedated. 'O-Oh, th-thank you,' Kolen thanked her timidly. Ark repeated a nod back at her and progressed to lead them further away from the safe house and into the dying wasteland of a city, searching for Slater's twin sister, with the former clutching the skin around his heart, praying that his sister was still alive and hadn't succumbed to the mortuus carnem infection, or worse: killed by Sam. Despite not being a religious man, he crossed his heart and pleaded that his sister was okay and still clinging to life, just to be safe.

The group went ahead, and Kolen plopped the hunger drug inside Ace's open mouth. She watched the crawler swallow it in seconds, which had knocked her out for the time being as she lay motionless in the wheelchair, head laid back, eyes wide and staring into the musky colourless sky. Feeling some unease with Ace's blank stare into the sky, she bit her bottom lip and gently closed Ace's eyes, giving the illusion that she was merely sleeping. Glancing up and seeing the group a few steps ahead of her gut churned, thinking of the otherworldly idea that they would abandon her, even though she'd told them to go ahead. Trying to make as little of a racket as possible with the squeaking wheels, Kolen hurried with the wheelchair, not wanting to keep the group waiting for her. She caught up with the two men soon enough, and her stomach felt a weight being lifted when she reached their safety and without much issue. The seven of them continued to wander the lifeless streets of London, looking out for themselves and each other, prowling close together, being sensible and not drifting away from each other. If they were to separate, they would most likely be picked off, like a group of stranded gazelles that were unknowingly being prayed on by a pride of lions stalking them in the tall grass.

'Darren?' Ark cocked her head behind her and asked.

Slater jolted as if someone had grabbed his shoulders from behind in an attempt to prank him by jump-scaring him. 'Uh! Yeah?'

'What can you tell us about your sister? I hope she's as trustworthy as you say she is,' Ark interrogated without looking directly at him as she led the group through the marsh of messy body parts that were scattered around them, keeping her peepers in front of her at all times.

'Oh, she's definitely trustworthy! You can count on that. Though I understand why you'd think otherwise, take my word for it; she's trustworthy and a little eccentric. In a way, Mrs Ark, you remind me of her.' he said.

'Is that so? In what way?'

'You're both outstandingly brave and ain't afraid to get your hands dirty. I respect that in women.' Slater verified.

Ark manufactured a dainty chuckle, seeming to find it amusing that this man had viewed her as fearless and with a lot of balls despite being a female. 'Although I should tell you, Oli can also be a little on the bonkers side of things, and she might rave on about the discoveries she's made and might crack a few jokes here and there about what she's found. She also likes to make people laugh with quips and dry humour.' He paused for a moment, mustering a frail grin. 'I guess you could say that she's a real geek when it comes to the science department of things, though part of me thinks that she would've been more suited being a comedian with how much she used to make me laugh when we were kids.' He looked elsewhere for a bit, rubbing his beard, and letting out his little chuckle. 'He's got you all figured out, blondie. Because that sounds a lot like you, only without the comedian side.' Winsome mumbled under his breath, finally opening his mouth to speak but closing it shortly after and not reopening it until the time was right. 'I doubt it, Ryan; Lisa isn't crazy like you think she is; she's just what do you call it… gutsy and has a lot of… well… balls for a woman. We'll just have to wait and see what lady Slater is really like,' Kolen articulated, peering down at Ace, who just sat there motionless in the wheelchair.

I was being sarcastic, Winsome thought savagely to himself.

'Yeah, whatever, let's just hope Sam didn't fuck her up before we get to her,' Ark murmured to herself, vaguely sure no one heard her.

'I swear,' Slater started, his voice coming out as a violent snarl, 'If that black-haired witch so much as lays a finger on Oli, I'll make sure she meets a brutal, satisfying end!' Slater gnarled morosely to himself, implying that he managed to hear what Ark had muttered about the outcome of his sister if and after encountering the black-haired devil herself.

Chapter 4

Olivia was heading back to her sturdy, reasonably habitable place of refuge after she made the daring act of survival by traversing into the dead city of London to look for food and supplies. She also borrowed a phone charger for her phone from a ransacked phone supplies store so she'd be able to text her twin brother and let him know that she was still alive and that she was still in one piece, unbitten. Olivia hadn't been able to contact him and reassure him of her safety since her phone had died. She had charged it until it was about six percent, just enough for her to text him; *Yo bro, I'm still breathing and still as beautiful and clean as ever despite not having a proper shower in days, lol. I hope to see you soon. I miss you; you won't believe what I got.* She'd charge it fully later, waiting for him to reply. However, she was unaware that his phone was flat and he had no charger.

Similar to her brother. Olivia was very much adapted to the mortal world where life was scarce, resources were limited, and the only colour left in the sky was a dusty, smoky grey. Like others living on the outside, she was used to the air becoming stuck with the sickening, foul stench of the decay carried on the wind. Customary to see the streets coated with blood stains and festering bodies with missing limbs, sometimes with the guts fleshed out over the ground and the sickening echo of bones being chewed into. While they were gut-wrenching to behold, one did get used to it if they are brought up with it, and because it was a common sight to see, people learnt how to deal with it. The Slater twins were a prime example; they'd learnt to live in a world surrounded by the dead, so seeing gnarly states of corpses was equal to seeing someone walking across the street. It had become the new norm.

Is it just me, or are more people getting picked off easily now? There are more cadavers here than there was yesterday; shit... this ain't good, she began to wonder, glancing down with a grimace from seeing all the stacks of mounted bodies that were distributed around the streets. She couldn't help but take in the fact that humans were etching further towards extinction. Despite being used to seeing mutilated bodies, Olivia had always felt sick at the thought. She hoped the human race still had a chance to come up strong. There were rare occasions when she'd come across the corpse of a child, which instinctively made her sick to the stomach. But this was a sight she needed to get used to, especially since she had camped out in an area that was frequently active with the undead. Olivia had come to associate her part of town with the Grey Land, seeing as her surroundings looked like they were from an old black and white photograph; the only colour in the area was, of course, the blood and the splatters of gore.

Olivia took precautions to be careful of the places she treaded, making sure not to accidentally step on something inappropriate that would disgrace the dead or endanger her life. Olivia covered her mouth, keeping herself from being sick, avoiding the mountains of bodies as well as the festering, maggoty piles of scattered limbs that surrounded her. 'Alright, Olivia Judy Slater, just take it slow; you're the snail; slow and steady wins the race,' she whispered to herself, vaulting over the obscuring limbs, striving to make as little noise as possible. 'Okay, almost home and time for tea and cake,' she muttered to herself. But what she didn't take note of was a specific blind zombie stalking her, ghosting behind her, listening closely to her footsteps, keeping her own shuffling footsteps silent so the brown-haired middle-aged woman couldn't pinpoint her from behind. The blind zombie stalked Olivia for quite some time, listening carefully to where Olivia's feet were. So, when the feet came to a halt, the sound of keys tingling had been heard in replacement for the footsteps; that's when the blind zombie knew it was the right time to strike. The blind zombie let out a hungry shriek, leaping at Olivia, causing her to turn around just in the nick of time and jump out of the way, dropping the keys in the process as they clattered to the ground as the blind zombie slammed her face into the door. Olivia quickly scooped the keys back up.

'Ha! Sucke-' Olivia looked down, seeing the blind zombie's hand clutching on her foot, Son of a bitch! Her thoughts hissed. 'Oi, ya old crone, get off!' she tried kicking and stomping at the blind zombie to attempt to get it off. But the blind zombie showed no signs of coming off; it kept its grip on her like a dead sloth clinging to a tree branch. Olivia snarled and tried kicking harder, hissing through her teeth as she did so. 'Get. The. Fuck. Off!' The blind zombie reciprocated the snarl, pulling her leg towards it, provoking Olivia to lose her footing and tumble to the ground, landing on her buttocks with a pained OOF, Olivia tried to violently shake her leg free as she feebly tried to crawl away, but her efforts appeared to have no prevail. 'Goddammit! Get Off!' She cried, kicking the blind zombie in the face, invoking the zombie to grunt, and let go. Olivia felt a wash of relief as she tried to scamper back to her feet, but her advance was halted when she once more felt something seize her, grabbing her leg and sending her back down to the dirt. This time, the zombie didn't mess around as it opened its mouth and bit into her leg. Olivia hissed in distress and tried to kick the zombie off again. Still, the zombie had a death grip, the uncomfortable feeling of teeth buried deep into her, and soon, the sound of flesh tearing was heard as the zombie tore a sizable chunk of flesh from Olivia's foot, making her scream out in anguish.

Chapter 5

The scream was so loud and piercing that it echoed throughout the streets of London like the cries of a white bellbird. It eventually found its way to the group, ringing like a haunting church bell inside their ears. Kolen shuddered at the velocity of the scream and blocked her ears. 'What the fuck was that?' Slater flinched, sensing familiarity, digging his hand into his pocket, and taking hold of the revolver but not pulling it out yet. He darted his head around warily as if suspecting something to jump out and scream at him.

'Sounds like someone's had a fang,' Winsome mumbled in an amused tone, not really being considerate of those around him, thinking they hadn't heard him. Kolen stopped the wheelchair suddenly, the wheels scraping to a stop, and stared at him, flabbergasted and bemused. 'How can you be so damn cruel, Ryan? Seriously, how inconsiderate are you? Someone probably died. Don't you care about that?' Kolen cried, not realising that she'd shouted, her voice bouncing off the walls like a basketball. Silence came through the group as if all their voices had been stolen. It was Losnedahl who put his hand on Ark's shoulder and signed to her if she could hear something. Ark looked ahead, putting her nose up and listened closely. That was when she heard it: the sound of running and… snarling!

'Oh, shit!' Slater cried behind Ark. That was when Ark saw it, too, a horde of the undead coming straight for them. 'Wow, nice one, Marilyn. You just had to open your trap to tell me off,' Winsome jeered, clapping his hands sarcastically at Kolen, who glared at him frustratedly as she began backing up the wheelchair. 'Well, you made a joke about death! It wasn't funny!' she cried, her voice hoarse and sounding on the verge of panic, her eyes showing signs of leaking.

'Shut Up, the pair of you! Get ready. Here they come!' Ark commanded, pulling a small switchblade out from her sock as she stared ahead, seeing a horde of what at first appeared to be around eighty-five zombies coming straight for them, but only ended up being around the fifties. 'Get ready to have your clothes soaked even more with the blood, people!' Slater ordered, joining forces, taking the revolver out, aiming it in front of him, and protecting Ark's rear. Soon, they were quickly overrun with zombies. 'Come on, ya shit smelling bastards! Come, fucking get me!' Winsome imitated his best war cry, punching his chest. Aiming his shotgun up and fired the trigger, repelling some of the zombies back, blowing holes right through them, exposing their broken ribcages along with other fleshy organs. Some of the organs were sucked dry from the flesh-eating maggots inside them, making their appearance all the more grotesque. 'Spot!' Ark commanded to her tall zombie. 'Protect Marilyn and Ace!' she ordered fiercely while fending off a wave of zombies with both knife and rifle, using them as melee weapons to smack and slash at the undead. That was when one zombie leapt out in front of the others, its mouth wide open. Ark saw this at the very last second and shielded herself with the rifle. The sudden pressure of the zombie leaping at her and its teeth hitting the rifle caused Ark to skid backward a bit. Ark cursed, eyes fuming as the zombie's teeth bit down onto the rifle's scope, scraping its putrid teeth against the metal of the scope. She held the gun with both hands so she couldn't plunge the switchblade into the zombie's eye or head to repel it back. At first, Spot hesitated to leave Ark alone to fend off such a strong zombie. But not wanting to disgrace her, he did what he was told and went over to them and protected them from the oncoming horde, standing in front of them with his arms out, guarding them.

At that moment, a small, frail-looking zombie with a chunk of flesh torn from its neck that looked like a child had run up and skirted the tall zombie with a half head, sliding underneath his legs and scampering like a small jungle critter over towards the wheelchair and climbing over the unconscious crawler to get to the spectacled woman as she ushered backwards out of reach, her face, a river of tears as she uttered in a pathetic voice, telling the zombie child to go away and leave her alone, not that it did anything to help her, so when that didn't do anything, Kolen just cried, wishing that someone would come help her. Just as Kolen had said that, Ace's eyes shot open just in time to hear the sound of zombies snarling and the sound of her bonder in a state of sheer terror. Ace stared ahead and saw the zombie child trying to reach over her to get to Kolen. 'Naai!' The crawler attempted to swat the child zombie away as she didn't have legs to kick at the undead child. But because Ace was a crawler, she was of no interest and didn't matter to the zombie child. The child simply ignored Ace as if she were a piece of furniture, climbing up her like she was nothing and heading straight for the Dutch woman, who panicked, moving out of the way of the child's grasp. 'Help!' she cried, her words incoherent underneath her tears.

Thankfully, this was when Spot took notice of the zombie child after hearing Kolen's cry. Just when the undead child was about to climb up onto Ace's head, putting a foot in her mouth delivering a surprise bite onto Kolen's face, leaping at her like a rabid monkey, a deep guttural gurgling came from Spot's throat.

Spot had handed his brain jar over to Ace earlier, just prior to the scream. Ace had relinquished it over to Kolen, which Kolen had placed in one of the wheelchairs' pouches for temporary safekeeping (good thing, too, if the little brat was going to use Ace as a climbing gym); she'd take it back out when the fighting was over and if he requested it. Hence, he was all right fighting in hand-to-hand combat, knowing with relief that his brain was safe. Granted that he had no sight, he wouldn't need it when hearing the distress and panic coming from Kolen behind him. He knew precisely where the zombie child was just by the sound intensity of the snarls and growls. Kolen's panicked cries were enough to tell him the child was right behind him and had gotten past Ace. Disrespecting Ace in such a manner would not go unpunished. Even though his facial animations couldn't be observed, it was evident by the deep gurgles that the tall zombie was fuming. He propelled one oversized hand at the child, seizing hold of one of the child's legs and hulling the child off Ace and towards him as the brat growled and spat and tried uselessly scratching at him.

Ark succeeded in fending off the violent zombie that was biting her rifle while clutching at her shirt. Slater aided her struggles, who, after fending off his share, had aimed his revolver with a quick reflex and shot a hostile bullet straight into the side of the zombie's head. Sending it staggering off Ark, Ark aimed down the rifle's scope and blasted the sorry, good-for-nothing zombie in the eye right before returning to fighting off more of the undead that surrounded them. Winsome garnered a lot of casualties under his belt, killing anything that was charging towards him, and if the others yelled for him to help them, he did so without complaint, aiming, firing, and covering himself in blood. He whooped like he was on a mechanical bull as he blasted limbs and popped heads off, painting his former white lab coat a new dark shade of red. The only thing Winsome needed was limbs strapped to his body; Then, he'd be able to blend in with the rest of the undead, of course. 'Oh, Man! If only I had me a fucking chainsaw!' he shouted while laughing manically at the piles of zombie fatalities he was committing and proud to be stacking up such a large number. 'That's twenty-four less for the military!' He whooped as he started to break up a sweat, but he shook the perspiration off and continued firing shell after shell at the horde.

Spot uprooted the scrambling zombie child towards him and held the child high above the ground by the right foot. The child squirmed and snarled while being dangled upside down by the foot. Spot had taken a sip from the volcanic tea and was on a rampage; he'd be damned if he let anything happen to his bonder or anyone affiliated with her. With his free hand, Spot grabbed the child's left foot and thought about instructing his own little gymnastics lesson to the zombie child, and he knew just what. He decided to teach and provide a comprehensive lesson about doing the splits.

Spot hoisted the legs up of the dead child and proceeded to extend them, pulling them in separate ways. The child shrieked and snarled, hopelessly thrashing around in Spot's clutches. Spot kept pulling the legs away from each other, not caring for how much the little shit screamed. He continued to pull at them, drawing them away until a gruesome ripping sound was heard from the screeching zombie child. But did that make Spot stop? No, it most certainly didn't. Spot stretched the zombie child's legs further away. Spot let out another angry gurgle as the zombie child's stomach started to tear, prompting the intestines and other vital organs to come spilling out, accompanied by a disgusting squelching plop.

Kolen watched with wide eyes and mouth agape. 'Ugh, Dat is grof....' Kolen rasped, gagging her mouth to prevent herself from upchucking while fighting a private battle of her own, to evict her eyes from the uncomfortable sight of watching Spot forcing the undead child to do one last demonstration of the splits.

Bellowing another final gurgle, Spot gave another hard, vicious tug that resulted in ripping the zombie child in two, flinging massive splotches of blood and guts onto him and the group members around him. He blindly stared at the split remains of the zombie child before tossing them away with a sickening splat as the remains of the child twitched slightly like a fish on land before finally ceasing.

Spot growled a guttural sound. If he could talk, he'd say something along the lines of: *Don't screw with me or my friends!* His tongue wiped around wildly as if demonstrating that he wasn't afraid to do the same thing to anyone else who tried to hurt his friends or himself.

A handful of zombies that had seen the brutality of one of their own kind ruthlessly killing another of their kind started to quiver, feeling a strange sensation, a glimmer of humanity ... fear. A few began to shake and stumble over their own feet as they began to topple over one another to make a hurried retreat; a peculiar act showed that they feared Spot like he was some kind of powerful monarch that they couldn't cross, not unless they wanted to be torn apart like that little brat who was now lying in two pieces. So, they fled, knowing they couldn't face off against a tall zombie who was on a streak and seemed more than glad to kill them if they stayed and fought. It was as if some of them had some ounces of their former humanity or if they were simply failed bonded zombies that had survived the elimination in the Elevator to Hell ... it couldn't be! Failed zombies were disposed of with a blow to the head, and when the Elevator to Hell was full, incineration was put in order.

'Ha!' Winsome cheered. 'Fuck yeah, Spotty boy! Yeah! That's right, you bastards! *Go home and cry to Sammy-Whammy!* Ya want to mess with me, old undead China? Ha! Didn't think so!' Winsome cried triumphantly as he danced after finishing off his fair share of zombies around him and exceedingly decreasing the numbers. He poked his tongue out and gave the retreating undead the middle finger. His cockiness didn't last long as there were still more zombies that crowded them. This egged Spot's bloodlust further. He began to beat the remaining zombies to death with his bare hands, and when they tried to mount him and bite at him, he wrangled them off like they were merely flies.

Slater and Ark did their best to fight off the last remaining walking sacks of the undead. Ark defended herself by holding the rifle in front of her as if it were a long rusty pipe or log, forcing the offending zombies to bite it instead of her; all the while, Slater finished them off by pumping more than a few rounds into their heads, about six for good measure. Ace fixed herself after the child crawled on her. Ace spat out some dirt that had been stuck to the child's feet when the child dug its foot into her mouth. Her eyes darted ahead to see a male zombie wearing a torn grey business suit, an eyeball flapping around on its tendons, and a Glasgow grin that looked to have been cut into his cheeks, so when he opened his mouth, his jaw hung far lower than expected. This one targeted Kolen again, seeing her as an easy target and an even easier chance of getting a meal. It was at this moment when Ace decided that she wasn't just going to sit back and be a liability; she was going to do something for her bonder; she couldn't wait to show Kolen just what she could do, to show her that she wasn't as useless as she first initially thought. Ace could, in fact, fight, and she was going to show Kolen just what she could do and just how useful she could be. She waited and watched the zombie charging in her direction. She hoped Kolen was watching because she was going to see something gruesome but magnificent.

'Ace?' Kolen whimpered.

When Glasgow Grin zombie got within a meter from them, Ace flung herself out of the wheelchair like a jumping spider and onto the oncoming zombie's chest, halting its advance on Kolen. Kolen stood baffled. She cupped her mouth, not believing what her eyes were seeing. Ace, with her undead grip, held closely onto the zombie's shoulders and fiercely sunk her chops into the zombie's face, plucking the dangling eyeball and spitting it out; undead flesh tasted disgusting to her, a mixture of dried sponges and dirt, but she dealt with it for her bonder's sake. She tightened her clamp down on Glasgow Grin, tearing pieces of undead flesh and spitting it out, burying her teeth further down the zombie's face, finally reaching the skull. What followed next was the hideous sound of bones snapping as Ace chewed through the marrow until the zombie tumbled backward, taking Ace with it. 'Holy shit...' both Kolen and Winsome marvelled at the disturbing sight of Ace killing that zombie and eating her way through the skull. Ace's mouth and teeth were stained with blood from eating her way through the zombie's face. When she was done, Ace turned around and faced the stunned look on Kolen's face. She wiped her mouth and smiled crookedly. Kolen was speechless. Ace grasped the seat of the wheelchair and hoisted herself up onto it, taking her original place in the wheelchair, holding her hands up, gesturing for the brain jar. Not bothering to question anything about Ace's sudden bloodlust, she took the brain jar from the backwards pouch and handed it back down to the crawler. She then turned away from the group, and a mass of yellowish-green shit exploded from her mouth in vomit form. Kolen groaned, wiping her mouth.

The last remaining zombies of the horde were eliminated by Spot, who tore arms and legs off, ripped hearts and ribs out and stabbed other zombies with them where he could, stomped on their heads, leaving quite a horrid wall of bodies around them; Slater, and Ark. Though it'd been Spot who'd finished off the very last remaining zombie. He grabbed hold of its head and began to squeeze it, putting pressure on it as the rabid zombie snarled and growled in protest, thrashing its arms around in a feeble effort to make Spot stop. But Spot refused to let go as he put more pressure on the zombie's head. The sound of bones crunching was heard coming from the inside, and blood began to weep down the zombie's every orifice. The blood spilled down Spot's fingers, and before the group could tell Spot that it was enough and that he could stop, an explosion of blood and brain mass erupted, completely coverinng their faces with bits of bloody fleshy brain. Slater and Ark stood there in shock as the brain matter slipped off their shocked faces. Slater cringed from the feeling of the brain bits still on his face as they dripped off him like water drops. 'Oh…Fu-' Slater soon cut himself off by plummeting to the floor and retching up his lunch mixed in with some blood; he looked like he was going to sick out his fucking organs! 'Don't…you…fucking die…on me Darren…I…we need…' Ark groaned, unable to get out a complete sentence without panting halfway through.

Ark, her hands shaking, moved them up to her face and wiped the blood and brain matter from her face. She had a look of pure dread, eyes wide, mouth hung low and lips trembling. Ark and Slater and the other group members, aside from Ace, had matching wide-eyes (Kolen was crying, and both Losnedahl and Slater were speechless), agape mouths of dread on their faces, frightened at seeing just how capable Spot was when it came to fighting. If someone crossed the line with them and pissed him off, he wouldn't let them get away unscathed. Spot's bloodlust had thankfully ceased shortly after Slater had finished throwing up and was making minor coughs here and there. The zombie, with half a head, turned his attention to his bonder, alarmed to hear her panicked breathing as she could not move or think straight; her mind was dead set on the unearthly sight she witnessed and seeing what Spot could do when he was angry. He reassured Ark that he was still loyal to her and the others by wrapping his large arms around her and hugging her, squeezing her for a brief moment as if saying, *'I'm so happy that you didn't die; I had to do that in order to save Ms Kolen and the rest,'* before letting go of her and taking his place once again behind her and retrieving his brain jar back from Ace.

Ark stood silent for a few seconds longer, collecting herself. There would be far more blood, gore, and chaos further down the path. And they would just have to become used to it, whether they liked it or not. Winsome leaned over, hands on his knees, and panted before looking over at Ark. 'And here I thought your zombie was a harmless pussy.' Winsome implied with a cocky grin. 'I mean, he's all lovey-dovey towards you,' he established, coughing into his fist, wanting to sound solid. Wishing to act like that sickening sight of blood and brain mass exploding over them didn't bother him, yet though his insides were tightening and churning, making disgusting garbles loud enough that the other members, including the zombies, could hear. 'Ryan, you Vom. No, old in.' Ace suggested. Winsome stared at Ace; seeing her bloody teeth smiling at him, he was almost sure that he could see bits of flesh stuck in between those rotting chops, which unnerved him immensely, accurately causing the vomit to come whooshing out his trap and over the mountain of bodies before him. Kolen saw Winsome throw up, and she instinctively pinched the bridge of her nose, slammed her eyes shut and looked away, hoping it would prevent her from picking up anything. Kolen was never too keen on watching people vomit; it always made her sick, and she was feeling twice as sick upon seeing not only Winsome vomit but also the sea of bodies around them. Blood and guts were streaming out like some deformed inbred snake.

It would have made a good fort for war if all the insides and body parts were replaced with sandbags. Still, she was at least grateful that she was able to manage to hold her sick inside of her and not join in the puke orgy.

Losnedahl cringed heavily at the ghastly surrounding wall of mangled bodies. He pursed his lips together and looked up, putting his attention on the sky and how, since the mortuus carnem outbreak, the clouds always seemed grey and lifeless.

'Olivier, we fine?' Ace interrupted, ignoring that everyone was having trouble with suspending the puke from leaving their mouths. She broke them from the "Who could hold their insides in the longest" competition by telling them it was time to tread further on their mission to get to Olivia Slater's place, or at least where Slater thought she was, based on her directions.

Slater was the first to regain his composure, going on his knees and hands; he'd turned pale, punching his chest, forcing the last remaining drops of puke out before he wiped his mouth with his sleeve grunting for a bit. He stood after and retook his stance again, setting his hand on Ark's shoulder and coughed once as Ark flinched back from the abrupt feeling of being touched. Completely ignoring Ace's mispronunciation, calling his sister Olivier instead of Olivia, he coughed with a closed mouth a few more times before replying to the crawler. 'Yeah… we should head off and take shelter with Oli. But firstly, we gotta get out of this fucking corpse circle; one would think we were part of some satanic cult mounting the bodies for the devil.' He moaned, looking over at Losnedahl and reminding him to get out of the circle first and help Kolen get Ace and the wheelchair over it without tripping and sending the crawler tumbling out. Sure, no problem, Losnedahl thought, seeing Slater point from the corner of his eye. He examined the wall of the body's height and hypothesised the best cause of action to get the wheelchair over without kicking the body out of the way. The very idea alone of kicking those corpses added a sour taste to his mouth, making him cringe. He took a deep breath, prying his eyes down onto the carnage again; the sickening feeling was running rampant in his chest again. Losnedahl clicked his fingers twice behind Kolen to get her attention, then he pointed to the wheelchair and outside the well of corpses. Kolen understood him clearly with a weak nod.

Losnedahl placed the bowie knife back inside a pocket of his lab coat and grasped the wheelchair handlebars away from Kolen. He looked behind her for a brief second and saw a zombie with one of its eyes hanging precariously from the darkened tendons, barely holding it; this sight made him cough up a little some ghastly, sickly, coloured vomit. He looked away from it and tried looking at something else; there weren't much to behold at this time but the sky, and he couldn't rely on the misty sky to ease the burden in his bowels. Everything in his eyesight view was painted red and had pieces of guts. Even the streets outside the circle weren't looking any better and were littered with discarded newspapers, trash, and severed limbs. Still, he endured the appalling sight and dragged the wheelchair over to him, all the while avoiding as much of the disgusting well as he could as he backwards vaulted over the well, taking the wheelchair with him as Ace held onto the seat to stop herself from spilling out.

After Losnedahl got the wheelchair containing Ace over the wall made of guts and multiple slain zombie bodies, he looked away and offered his hand out for Kolen. She took it and held her mouth and nose. Kolen joined him on the other side of the well. Both stood still, not even daring to look back at the repulsive circle of corpses. The pair of them waited outside it, waiting for Ark and the others to exit out of the unholy ring of death. Winsome came out, followed by Spot, who stepped and tripped but kept his footing, holding his brain jar closely to his chest. Finally, Slater and Ark made their exit from the circle of corpses. Proceeding to move as far away from it as possible, wanting to put as much distance from the remainder of their battle with one of the hordes, the nauseous feeling it gave them, and the godawful smell that perfumed it.

'Please tell me we're going to find this sister of yours now?' Kolen moaned, lecturing Slater while still feeling sick from all that blood and carnage from the recent zombie attack.

'Yeah, we'll go find her now. Rest assured, Marilyn, we'll find her.' He explained to the red-faced, spectacled woman. *I hope we'll find her*, he thought naively to himself. 'Let's get going and waste no more time,' Slater said.

'Time, Daz?' demanded Winsome, keeping track of how much time they had left.

'4:56pm,' Slater replied.

Around two hours had passed since he last checked. Which meant they had around twenty-two hours to kill Sam before she became unstoppable, biting and killing everyone on sight.

Chapter 6

Sam was about a kilometre ahead of the group, somewhere in the middle of what was left of London City. She had it planned out to make things twice as hard for the group by creating more obstacles for them to overcome. One such way to achieve this part of her goal was taking her time to communicate in her own way and "bond" with the undead herself so that she could pass on specific tasks to these particular zombies and have them do anything that she required of them. She felt the bulge in the pocket of her shorts and considered using the hunger drugs she'd stolen from Fredrickson and the other bonders she'd slain. She would sedate other zombies' hunger and her own, as it was better to concentrate and think of things when she wasn't hungry.

Hunger was often a course of distraction, and Sam couldn't afford to have distractions if she was going to put her plans to fruition. Sam endeavoured to create her own personal army that would help her succeed in her vision of converting every single British citizen into one of the ranks of the walking dead. But instead of going straight for the prize, for now, she was buying her time, waiting for the decisive moment to strike because, like most carefully thought-out plans, the moment would come sooner or later when she'd unleash the fear and suffering into the hearts of any remaining humans, giving in to her hunger.

She'd play with her food for a little while. Taunting them like rats in a cage. She'd infect them with her bite, torture them by beating and slashing them with anything she could find, cutting pieces of their flesh off to feed to the hungry undead, and slaughter anything that still had a beating heart and still breathes, men, women, and children, even animals (but they weren't as tasty as humans), anything that breathed, as well as the group that crossed her by showing them all the zombies which had converted over into her own personal genocidal army. Sam wouldn't give two shits if she tore families apart, even if they tried to fight her or beg for her to stop. How could she stop if mercy and remorse were foreign words? She knew that she was hated, but she didn't care. She learned the group wanted her head on a pike, but Sam wouldn't be so willing to hand over her head like some kind of trophy; it was like a competition, and they'd have to fight for it, earning their prize and she'd make sure she'd give them one to remember.

Sam would be the one to bequeath their ends. In short, she wanted to eliminate them all; everyone would be turned into a zombie, whether they liked it or not (living as an undead is fun; killing people is twice as fun). Sam smiled wickedly, taking great pride in the thought of dictating propaganda and having all of Britain at her feet, obeying her every order, and treating her like the next Queen. *Britain will be mine. I will spread the infection. I will turn every fucking person into a zombie, and when Britain is dead, and once Britain is mine, I will move to the rest of the world. Just you try and stop me, friends of Fredrickson, just you fucking try, you'll just become part of my army and forever hungry for those who you called friends.* Sam thought evilly to herself; the smirk that Ace hated had once again reappeared on her face. Sam chuckled; the sickening thought came to her of beating Ark and ripping her head off. Showing it to the adoring crowd like a trophy, seeing their faces as she took the first bite of Lisa Lorraine Ark's brains before she tossed the head into the crowd and walked away while "her" zombies fought over Ark's decapitated head.

Chapter 7

Ark buckled over and took a few deep breaths, her hands on her knees and staring at the ground. She put a hand on her chest and could feel her insides soften; her breathing became more relaxed, and her heartbeat steady. Once under control, she turned around and looked at Slater, who was picking off bits of flesh from his beard and grimacing every time he flicked them off his fingers. Ark looked over at the watch on his wrist and nodded. 'Still, plenty of time to do what we have to do with Olivia and equip her as part of the team.' She said, letting out a relieved breath. She then walked over and reached to put a hand on Spot's shoulder. Spot flinched and cocked his head down to his shoulder, he put his hand over Ark's, feeling that it was hers, based on the texture of her fingers, and he relaxed. 'You… did a brutal job, Spot.' She spoke to him, congratulating him on the effort he'd made in going out for the team and saving both Kolen and Ace from that little brat. Ark asked Winsome and Kolen if they were okay; Winsome grunted, but he was otherwise quiet and said nothing else. Kolen was slowly controlling her trembling hands as she gripped the wheelchair's handles, breathing, shaking breaths as she looked up at Ark with the eyes of a child. 'I-I'm okay,' she said, 'just a little shaken up.'

'What about you, Henrik? You, okay?' Slater asked the mute man sitting on his knees, patting the ground, and moving pieces of debris and body parts away, blindly searching for something. Slater asked him what it was he was looking for. When Losnedahl looked up, he spoke with his hands that he had the idea of finding some rope or a leather belt and tying it either around Spot's neck like some kind of human leash so Ark wouldn't have to keep holding his hand or around his hand like a leather bracelet or perhaps he could tie the other end of the rope or belt to Ace's wheelchair or someone else's hand, cuffing him so he wouldn't be able to stray from the group and would always be by Ark's side. She wouldn't have to worry about constantly holding his hand throughout their journey or for her to keep watch of him and to make sure that he doesn't wander off someplace he shouldn't and Ark putting their mission on hold just so they could find him and return him to the group.

Slater scratched the back of his head. 'My sign language is off, but I'm sure it's something good; you should let Lisa or Marilyn know.'

Losnedahl nodded, confirming he would indeed inform Ark about it when they reached the place where Olivia Slater was hiding out. He wasn't having any luck finding anything on the floor, so he stood back up.

Ark exhaled again; she was feeling satisfied knowing that everyone was still with her and that they were recovering from their most recent battle with some of the undead. She looked over and saw her zombie was standing still with his head lowered and strings of drool trickling off his tongue. It seemed strange for him to be acting this way, and Ark thought it was because he needed a hunger drug. She walked over to him and looked at him, 'Hey. Hey Spot.' She called out to him. But she got no response from him. This confused and, in some way, unsettled her that her good, loyal zombie was being unresponsive. So, she called out his name again, her voice quavering; this time, she clicked her fingers in front of his face like she was endeavouring to wake him out of a trance that had left him in this state. Still nothing. 'What the fuck?' Now Ark was starting to get worried and a little scared. She seized her zombie by his arms and tried to shake him, calling out his name and each time sounding more panicked and fevered. And still, when Spot wasn't responding, Ark went to Kolen and demanded a pill from her. But when Kolen said she couldn't find any in her pockets, she went to Losnedahl, who thankfully had one prepared for her when he saw her go over to Kolen looking for one. Then, finally, Spot moved. Ark watched her zombie raise his hands before him so his palms were facing his half-head, watching as they trembled, clenching and unclenching. Judging just by this movement, Ark understood what was going on with him; he was experiencing another emotional sensation – guilt – guilt for killing that child zombie and doing it in such a violent and ruthless way in front of her and the others. From what she saw of how he was blindly staring at his shaking hands; he didn't like the sensation. 'Spot, it's okay. You did a good job.' Ark tried to reassure him in a softer voice. 'If you didn't do what you did, that little brat would've gotten Marilyn.'

'Y-Yeah, you saved me and Ace, Spot, thank you.' Kolen mumbled. She reached out to touch him, but as soon as one of her fingers touched him, he flinched away and made a noise Ark had never heard. A strangled sound that resembled a whimper that a dog who'd been attacked by another bigger dog would make. It was Kolen who had pointed out the strange behaviour as Spot being scared and worried that his actions had made her and the others scared of him and that he was feeling guilt for making them distrust him slightly if that was indeed the case. And as if to confirm Kolen's theory, Spot nodded remorsefully, clenching his shaking fists and increasing the volume of that strangled dog-like whimper.

When Ark touched him again, this time, he didn't flinch; he instead looked in the direction of where her hand was. 'But I will also say this, my god, it was a fucking phenomenal effort, my boy!' She glowed, gazing up at his tall frame, reassuring him, making sure to keep him calm and collected towards the group and not expressing guilt and weakness that might lead to their downfall or him going rogue. Ark blinked.

She took her hand away from him and thought about how scary it was that he was becoming more and more human and how much emotions he was capable of administering. *How was it possible?* She thought. *He was missing half of his head, so how on god's green Earth could he be expressing so much damn emotion? His brain wasn't even connected to him. It was nestled inside a jar full of the murky LUNG liquid. Could it be that he's starting to remember his life when he was alive? Oh, you truly are an extraordinary specimen, Spot. If he's starting to remember his past before death, I'd love to know his real name and who he was!* Ark's cognisance was thinking ahead, imagining the possibilities of what could be causing her zombie to behave so "humanly" that she'd completely forgotten about the brutal deaths that he'd committed. Acting as if the horde attacking them had never occurred in the first place. Spot was Ark's prodigy, and each time he displayed a new form of intelligence, Ark couldn't help but be surprised. And with the thought of Spot becoming smarter planting the seed in her mind, she wondered if it'd sprout and grow into jSpot being able to reach some point of Sam's level of IQ; he might be able to start a new order for the new world, hell he might become the first-ever zombie prime minister! Leading a rebellion against Sam and the nasty zombies, he might be able to bring peace into the world where humans and zombies co-exist. But because of the current political greed that had destroyed the country in the first place before the mortuus carnem discovery and him being without a full head, it would be inconceivable for him to win a seat in the parliament house. But he might be able to get something big like that if he could get a full-blown head surgery, which, of course, would have his working brain inside. He could be the brightest bonded zombie of all time! The thought of Spot's success was giving Ark goosebumps, excited ones that she almost forgot where she was and that she and the others had a highly dangerous zombie that they were on the hunt for.

'Lisa?' Slater intervened, placing his hand on her shoulder, and snapping her out of her future trance about her zombie becoming a recognisable name in the record books under "The first zombie to be awarded Deputy Mayor of London".

Ark responded with a jolt. 'What? Oh, shit, sorry, I may have gotten ahead of myself in terms of praising my zombie,' she chuckled a little, a slight blush beginning to shine on her face; she bit her lip. 'Oooh, someone's got a crush on dear old Darren,' winked Winsome, leaning over to Ark's ear in hopes of embarrassing her, but his efforts were flawed when he was pulled back by Losnedahl and was shoved a piece of cloth to go inside his mouth to shut him up again. 'Thank you, Henrik,' she nodded to him, and he returned a nod and a thumbs-up back to her.

'Now, let's not fuck around any longer; each second is vital. We have a lot to do in the next twenty or so hours,' Ark explained to the group, inquiring about their mission being clear enough by repeating what they had to do. 'We find Darren's sister in London city, and we get her help as well as other people's help, and if we're lucky, we might find some good zombies that are against Sam and want to help us defeat her.' She said, making it clear to them that no matter what the cost was, she was confident that Sam was going to die tonight before 3:00am.

Chapter 8

Wendy, the blind elderly zombie, shambled around the dank streets without goal or purpose, waving blindly at the air in front of her, had finally navigated her way out of the GFOSAR at around 1:10pm, shortly before Ark and the others had left and heard the wolves of the sky, howling in her ears, giving her the evidence that she was indeed outside. She strutted out soon after she had finished devouring her bonder's remains. So, when Wendy finished pickings with him, Maximillian Engel had lost weight and was a mess of bloody bones. She got up and stumbled out of cell B-20, piloting her way out of the GFOSAR with her still-preserved sense of hearing. Wendy wandered around the empty British streets outside the GOSAR, absent of any real aim, not knowing where she was and what she was doing, unable to see and comprehend the course of her destination. She did all she could do, and that was to rely on her sniffer and her eardrums to find her way over to her next feast. Wendy roamed the colourless streets, constantly searching for food, bumping, and tripping over things in her way, flinching at the slightest sound she heard, thinking that it was a potential meal.

She had also just happened to be the one that attacked Olivia Slater after her purposeless ambling led her to London, following her nose. Because she was blind and seemed to have died during her late sixties, Wendy wasn't a runner like most; the best she could do was jog, and sometimes she would stumble over things and trip to the floor as she wasn't able to see things blocking her path, and that was an understandable factor, regarding she was elderly looking zombie around the age of sixty-nine. It was a familiar feat for most of the elderly to not have the strength they had once when they were still living a life of youth. The other easy factor was that she had no visible eyes due to them being stabbed out, leading to a most painful death. Like all dead people, Wendy was eventually resurrected by the mortuus carnem as a blind zombie to be bonded by Max Engel, who had christened her with "Wendy". However, as is a typical case for most bonders, Engel didn't fully bond with her and teach her the basics of being a human again. He lacked the qualifications of most bonders and didn't exactly have the right amount of patience to be a bonder and deal with the undead because of his pushy, need-to-be-perfect attitude. So, if things didn't go his way, Engel would make sure everyone knew about it and blame them for not giving him the right amount of training, when in reality, it was his lack of patience to do the task. That was the good thing about Fredrickson; he may have had little tolerance for people, but he was highly efficient when it came to his line of work and knew how the bonding process worked; therefore, he had the patience for the job. Since the lockdown was initiated, Engel became trapped inside B-20, becoming a male damsel and waiting for his princess in shining armour to come to save him. Sam had been the one to answer his beckoned calls, only she wasn't his princess in shining armour. Sam was the witch that accelerated his torment, entering his cell with a stolen key card, tearing his legs off and preventing him from escaping while she unchained Wendy and allowed her to consume him. And because of Engel's little patience for anything and since Wendy was blind and always hungry (this was the undead curse, to be constantly hungry and craving for the flesh and brains of the living), she didn't have much intelligence, Engel hadn't precisely bonded with her like he was supposed to. He paid for his lacklustre bonding with his life.

However, Wendy's time as a walking corpse was soon to be cut short, as would be with most zombies; someone had their sights on her head. As soon as Wendy was in the process of tearing down the wooden door leading into a panicked and wounded Olivia's safe house a long rifle bullet came whooshing at an alarming speed. It flew straight for the blind zombie and contacted with the back of her head and out her front, stopping when it hit the door. Wendy stood still for a second or two; her brain was bleeding from the inside, and the small hole where the bullet had exited was dripping with blood. Curiously, she tapped the front of her head, which felt moist, smelling the blood on her fingers. She opened her mouth and touched some of the blood with her tongue, but that was all she could manage as she soon fell onto her knees, blood dripping from her mouth and the holes in her head. She sat on her knees for a few more seconds until her zombified body slowly fell to the ground with a thud, blood oozing out and revealing who'd fired the shot and killed her.

Chapter 9

'Woah! Nice shot, Marilyn,' Ark praised Kolen, patting her on the back after she'd handed the rifle over to Kolen on her request, claiming that she had wanted to do something for the group instead of laying back and keeping her crawler under control. Besides, if everyone found some sort of satisfaction in putting a bullet through a zombie's head, she wanted to know the pleasure they felt; she wanted to experience the kick of what it was like to kill a zombie, her first zombie for herself. 'Th-Thanks, Lisa.' Replied Kolen timidly. Losnedahl was beaming at her. *I always knew, inside that frail shell that you show us, you secretly knew how to wield a gun, let alone a sniper rifle; proud of you, Marilyn, and you should be too.'*

He soundlessly reverenced Kolen as he, too, gave Kolen a pat on the back, congratulating her on her very first kill. Although Kolen wasn't precisely feeling victorious about her first kill, she couldn't help but feel a wave of sorrow wash over her as she stared at the lifeless body of the blind elderly zombie, knowing that she was once a normal human and was probably someone's grandmother. 'I know I should feel good about it, but I just can't help but feel bad for killing that zombie… I mean, when you stop to think of it. They were originally alive like us, had feelings like us, felt pain like us, and then they died and... and they were resurrected by that repulsive parasite… though I will admit it did feel good to kill one. Still, it's just the fact that they were just like us, and being dead for so long caused their past lives to be erased. Surely you all can understand my point?' She grimaced, head hung low, handing the rifle back to Ark, who took it and held it over her shoulder like a baseball bat.

Ark placed one of her hands on Kolen's chin, moving it up so she was looking at her glassed eyes behind those white-rimmed spectacles. 'Marilyn, we understand your point perfectly, and I know that Alexander would be proud of you for your bravery and for taking a stand and, of course, how far you've come as a person, but think of killing zombies like this; we are ending their suffering. Each zombie we kill, we are giving the human trapped inside them what they want; we're doing them a favour by putting an end to their undead lives,' Ark articulated, exchanging her chin for her cheek, which she stroked generously, smiling down at her. 'Your glasses have drops of blood on them,' she pointed out. Hang on,' Ark fumbled about her pockets to look for a hanky or a piece of loose fabric she could tear off and give to her. Losnedahl lunged into his trouser pocket and drew out an old scrunched-up hankerchief he had on him, using it for the countless times when he would wake up sweating after reliving the traumatizing abuse at the hands of Joakim; he still kept that hanky after all these years, using it as a reminder of the life he'd escaped and reminding him that he was a survivor. The icing on the cake was finding a home and camaraderie in the GFOSAR, where he became somewhat of a friendly father figure to Kolen whenever she needed some mutual encouragement whenever Fredrickson wasn't around.

'Oh, thank you, Henrik.' Kolen removed her glasses and seized the lace from Losnedahl, where she spat to make it wet and went forth into scrubbing the stained blood droplets away. When she was done wiping her glasses from the red droplets, she breathed into them, wiping them with the fabric of her coat and then putting them back on her face. She looked at the cloth Losnedahl had given to her and handed the damp cloth back to him awkwardly, thanking him for letting her use it, though he didn't take it back from her. He shook his head with a kind grin and pushed her hand, pushing the hanky back to her, telling her that he was giving it to her and that she wouldn't need to worry about returning it. He no longer wanted it.

Kolen smiled timidly, looking at the tissue that had been gifted to her before she put it in her pocket. 'Thanks, guys. I really appreciate you all, and I'm pleased to call you "friends".' She gushed (Winsome blushed, looking away embarrassed). Kolen glanced back down at Ace in the wheelchair, feeling her cheeks starting to heat up. 'Yo,' Winsome muffled, pointing to the zombie casualty Kolen had under her belt. 'I may be wrong, but isn't Marilyn's first kill Maxi's precious zombie, Wendy? Ya know, the old bag that he kept bragging about?' He conjectured, taking the piece of cloth out of his mouth, stating that he recognized the zombie as Wendy and identified that her bonder had been the late Max Engel's. Even Winsome grew agitated by Engel's constant barrage about Wendy, like he was fucking in love with the old hag. 'So, what if it was? Max was an annoying piece of shit who was only in it for himself,' Ark huffed, not caring much for the late Engel or the identity of the blind old dear Kolen had killed. In Ark's books, there is always one person who is worse than Winsome, and that is Max Engel. While Winsome is annoying because he wants a laugh, Engel is annoying because he thinks he is better than everyone and wants to abuse his power over everyone. This was something that even Winsome could agree with, as Winsome didn't have anything nice to say about the late Engel. Prick, Winsome may be, but even he had his limits when it came to how much a man prattled on about something he couldn't care less about.

'Whoever it was, it doesn't matter now; the zombie is dead. The important thing is that zombie was banging on that door, which means someone is hiding inside,' Slater articulated, pointing to the door, which now had Wendy's corpse in front of it. 'Wait!' Winsome exclaimed, his eyes wide with surprise. 'We're in London city, already?' Winsome blurted out his question. Ark whipped her face to him, baffled. 'Ryan, you're fucking British! You should recognize your hometown.' She snapped at him. 'Oi! gimme a break Liis; I would probably recognize it if it didn't look like fucking shit like the Americans dropped another Hiroshima-sized A-bomb on it!' He retorted, ready to start an argument that would most likely end up in him garnering a black eye. 'Shut Up! The pair o'ya! Now is not the fucking time to be squabbling like a bunch of kindergarteners!' swore Slater, stepping in front of the two and putting his body between them. 'Lisa, you made it clear to us that we'd get to London city and find my sister (I hope she's alive), that we'd get her advice and equip her as part of the team! Now, Oli could be behind that door. So, stop this mindless bitching, and let's not keep my sis waiting!' He scolded them both, not only putting Winsome in his place but Ark as well. 'Yes, your right; sorry, Darren, it's just when someone gets me worked up, I need to discharge the anger and have to teach and show them their fucking place in this world; surely you get me on that regard.' Ark spoke bluntly while looking down at the floor, seeing the dust moving along with the wind under her feet; she was clenching her fists bitterly. 'I agree with Darren. We should waste no more time and get inside that house and pray that it's Olivia Slater behind the door and hope that she's more than willing to help us,' Kolen softly shared her agreement with the shaggy older man. 'Oh, believe me, Marilyn, she'll definitely want to help us kill that black haired zombie bitch,' he calmly replied back to Kolen.

'Spot, stand down. It's okay,' Ark had commanded sharply to Spot without looking at him. She could tell he was planning on attacking either Winsome or Slater for raising their voices and yelling so violently at her.

'So, shall we proceed on?'

'Yeah, let's go.' Ark breathed, looking up at the imposing fixture that, based on its outside alone, looked like it could've been a tiny hostel for the neighbouring homeless – before everything went sour when the mortuus carnem turned up – as the building seemed pretty big with boarded up windows and what looked like another floor upstairs. How many beds did the place hold before everything went to crap, Ark thought to herself.

'You can meet and talk with Oli if she's indeed behind that door, while I can reunite and have some belated family time with her,' he contributed, wondering, and hoping that the person behind the door was his long-lost twin sister.

'Yeah, she sounds fun. Let's go and finally meet your sister if it's her.' Ark acquiesced, looking up at him as they made their way over to the doorway of the house, shoving Wendy's inert body out of the way with her feet. Ark and Slater exchanged roles. Slater took the lead for this brief moment; he crossed his fingers before balling it into a fist and proceeded to knock thrice on the wooden door, which had fingernail marks in it, splintered wood and, of course, the bullet that Kolen had fired. His heart was pounding. He wasn't a religious man, but natural instincts made him cross his heart, praying that Olivia was there and would answer the door if she was still alive and hadn't been turned into one of the undead.

If Olivia was dead, Slater would be overwhelmed with the stinging feeling of what it feels like to be well and truly alone.

Chapter 10

Please be here, Oli, please be alive. Slater closed his eyes and prayed, crossing his heart. He couldn't comprehend what he'd do, the emotions swimming around in his head, the actions he'd do if the last remaining member of his family had died, leaving him all alone in this cursed land, the terrible life that the mortuus carnem had put him through. He couldn't cope with being the only Slater left in England. The sheer loneliness that'd pile up on top of him would be overwhelming.

Like most brothers, he loved his sister very much; just as much as she loved him, they were as thick as thieves as children, despite being siblings; they did everything together. Darren and Olivia were the same age, forty-seven; Darren had emerged first while Olivia came an hour later. They were like two peas in a pod. One would often assume they were best friends or boyfriend and girlfriend from all the times they were seen together. It was always very awkward for people to wolf whistle them out for being a couple. Thankfully, Olivia was always the one who silenced them by casually stating that they were siblings, causing people to shut their traps or awkwardly go the other way, humiliated. Darren did everything with his twin sister, until they were adults with big dreams. But things started to change when Darren got employment in the RMA; their close bond was separated, and Olivia was forced to look for work herself without her brother's aid. She did. After discovering she had a love for science, she tried getting into employment based on science, a geneticist, as she became fascinated with family genes.

She studied hard, sometimes day and night, and endeavoured to join the GFOSAR team when news broke out of the mortuus carnem pandemic beginning to rise. She had heard about the work they did with zombie bonding and wanted to be part of the work they did. She thought that she could use her knowledge to an advantage. Olivia had waltzed up to the front door of the GFOSAR, resume in hand and carrying enthusiasm with her. 'You fellas are looking for someone to join your team and save Britain from mortuus carnem. Welp, the person you're looking for is right in front of you,' she had sung confidently as she handed her resume down to be examined. But luck just wasn't on Olivia Slater's side, which had made things sour for the younger Slater sibling.

She couldn't get the position she craved because apparently, Olivia wasn't qualified enough to be a zombie bonder despite her daily studying (dream job) and having no real experience face-to-face with the undead and her overly cocky attitude instead of a professional one. She was dismissed, along with other unlucky people seeking employment and refuge, leaving her not only disappointed but unemployed, forced to fend for the scraps herself. So, her other and only option was to do random independent work to save up the money to afford food and a home for her to stay in. However, as soon as the mortuus carnem apocalypse started in England, the number of the dead rose in staggering numbers when things reached critical. Olivia had unknowingly found herself in a gold mine when she came to the realisation that she didn't need the money anymore (the world was going to shit, and it wouldn't be long until you could walk into the shop and take whatever you desired free of charge). All Olivia needed was basic knowledge of zombie bonding and, of course, a zombie to bond with, thinking that she could spite the bigwigs at the GFOSAR by doing some bonding outside the facility and, furthermore, proving that she was capable. She'd also need some hunger drugs to help her outside for her independent zombie bonding sessions. She'd managed to snag some drugs off one of the nearby black markets, which sadly don't exist anymore, thanks to the increasing number of zombies claiming Earth as their own, so therefore, business was shut down. So, the only place to get the hunger pills was to steal them from the heavily fortified GFOSAR, which was sometimes easier said than done.

'Hello, anybody home?' Slater asked, rapping on the door again, a little louder this time, hoping his knocks would warrant some kind of answer. However, the more his knocks were left unanswered, the more anxious and frightened he became. He was about to rap on the door again when a voice rang from behind.

'Alright, Alright! Keep your testicles between your legs; I'm coming!' A distinct female voice was faintly heard from behind the door as some faint shuffling footsteps approached, growing louder as the female made her way to the door and from the sounds of metal clinging together. Slater could recognise the voice, and his heart leapt, and his eyes twinkled in anticipation. It sounded like the woman behind the door was fumbling around with some locking mechanisms, hence the sound of small metallic chains scraping across metal. Sounds of keys on a belt were also heard clinking and one by one, each key was inserted into a different depression, unlocking the chains barring the door before they were discarded on the floor; the woman could be heard faintly mumbling about how many locks she'd installed. Then the door flung open, and a woman with medium-length brown hair that matched Slater's stepped out; her face seemed frustrated mixed with anguish, almost as if she was in the middle of something and that the group had obviously disturbed her by showing up at her doorstep.

The woman also appeared to be leaning onto a large wooden plank, putting most of her weight on it for support. If you were to glance down below the rod, you would see that she had a missing foot with bloodied bandages wrapped tightly around the stub where a foot would've been. The woman's agitation eased upon seeing Slater, and her eyes widened, and her jaw hung low. The arm that rested on the plank appeared to be trembling as she regarded Slater before her, regarding him like he was her…

'Fuck me… Darren?!' The woman had greeted her brother after not seeing him face-to-face in the past fourteen years since the very early stages of the mortuus carnem panic and the fact that he had to work full time in the RMA, but at least they had been able to contact each other through SMS messages, and that was better than not seeing and contacting at all. Slater watched his sister hobble towards him, her face animated with longing at the sight of him drop the wooden plank as if she had magically grown another leg and flung herself into her brother's arms, her arms wrapped tightly around him, her nose nuzzling his neck. After so many years apart, Slater tried not to tear up upon seeing his sister alive and well. 'Man, bro, aren't you a sight for sore eyes!' she cried, taking her time to embrace him, something that she hadn't been able to do over the past fourteen years they had been separated.

When she was done, she held his shoulders and looked at him; her face had gone red, and her eyes appeared as if they had been made of glass; she was about to cry. Slater reached out and touched her face as if wanting to feel that it was her face and that he could still recognise the exact texture of her face before he'd left to join the army. He felt that he wanted to cry upon realising that it was her face and that the person standing before him was indeed his sister. 'Sis? My God, it's really you; it's been so long, fourteen years since we last saw each other face to face? I was starting to worry that something might've happened t-' Slater couldn't finish his sentence when he looked down and saw it and the discarded plank beside her. 'Oli! Jesus Christ, what happened to your damn foot?!' he exclaimed, pointing at her missing leg, his eyes wide and his mouth agape, understandably showing his concern for his twin sister.

'Uh… about that,' she looked sheepishly at her bandaged stump; the sight made her sick as she made a disgusted face. And by the way, she cringed and shut her eyes, he could tell it was recent and still hurting, still giving her an intense stinging sensation that she had strived to bite her lip and treat it like it was nothing but a wasp sting, a deadly wasp sting that ended in her leg having to be amputated. Oli gingerly peered out of the doorway as if checking to see if any undead hadn't followed her brother and his companion's scent during their trek, realising that the remaining members of the group were still outside, standing behind Slater quietly like vampires, waiting outside to be welcomed. The considerate thing she could do was offer them inside and grant them a temporary safe place to stay. Without being asked to, Slater picked up the wooden plank she had tossed away and handed it to her; she took it and thanked him with a nod. She then shuffled out of the way and held the door open with her back, where she then cocked over into the interior of the house, which at first glance hadn't looked much better than Slater's safehouse from before.

'I'll tell you later, come, come in. Dry yourselves off, I'll put the kettle on; a storm is coming.' She bided them inside, out of the dangers of the outside. She poked her head out the doorway, scanning in both directions again, double-checking if there weren't any zombies nearby. When she was confident that nothing had followed Slater and the rest, she shut the door and reassembled the locks again. Not planning on having any more unexpected visitors.

After Oli was done with securing the door, she took the wooden board by her side and hobbled over to where the group was, humbly asking them to make themselves at home and that the food and supplies were in the kitchen and in a chest under the bed in one of the bedrooms. The interior was in ruins; the ceiling was splintered along with other parts of the wood that held the walls up; there was a white woollen rug that sat in the middle of the living room, though it was caked in dirt and blood and had some pebbles and small wood chips from the ceiling in it. Moss grew on the floor and walls near the wooden splinters. The bedrooms and kitchen weren't that different either, with one of the duvet covers looking like someone had been murdered on it by the sizable red stains. The kitchen appeared to show traces of domestic abuse; perhaps the previous owners used to beat each other there, or the owner had been attacked by a malicious stranger as counters had splodges of blood, some of the cabinets were broken off their hinges and pieces of cutlery stained with blood were strewn on the floor; there was even a severed ear in the sink next to a large lock of hair as if someone had ripped it from the other's scalp. This scene played a haunting reminder of what humans could do to each other, but like the living room, both bedrooms and kitchen were overgrown with green moss and other weeds.

'Names Olivia, by the way, but I guess you already figured that out judging from my reunion with my brother.' she looked at him from across the room, sitting on the floor, his eyes glued to her bandaged stump. 'Speaking of Darren, I guarantee my older bro has been off his head about me, ya know, yakking off about how much he misses dear old me,' she joshed, intending it to get a few chuckles, which ended up being in poor taste and only got silence out of them. She looked over at Darren, who was looking away, feeling a tinge of humiliation, finding her attempted joke more offensive than amusing; they reunited after all these years, and this was how she said she had missed him by pulling one of her wisecracks? Like him, no one was laughing.

'Ain't, you guys a cheery bunch,' she said sarcastically. Slater whipped around and stared at his sister, flabbergasted. 'Well, sue me for ruining your joke Oli, the hug was nice and all, but we haven't seen each other for the past fourteen fucking years. Of course, I'd miss my twin sister; sometimes, I think that you were born ten years after me.' he declared before looking away, feeling his cheeks heating up. He covered his face, trying to hide his reddening face from her; she's still as immature as ever; she'd always been the immature one who often told jokes and wasn't ashamed of humiliating herself in front of him. Oli laughed; she could tell he was blushing, even if she couldn't see it. Slater turned back to her after a few seconds, getting himself in control and stared at his sister with furrowed brows. 'Family time can come soon. Right now, Oli, I want to know what the fuck happened to your leg! I want you to tell me right now.' He demanded, pointing to her stump. Oli glanced at it briefly before she looked at her brother and winked, only causing even more concern. 'Ah, you see, Darren and other people whom I'll know, laron (Olivia Slater's word for Later on), this is a thing I've just discovered. You know that old goat outside my door? Thanks for killing; by the way, whoever took the shot. Well, that old hag bit me on this here leg, and-' she stated plainly. Slater abruptly stood up, and he stormed over to her and seized her shoulders, shaking them, 'She BIT you!' he exclaimed. 'Are you fucking kidding me? First, we reunite, then you make an immature joke, and next, you tell me you got bit! What's next? You're going to turn in an hour, and you just wanted to see my face again before you go ugly?'

Gimme a sec, bro, I'll get to that.'

'Wa-wa-wait, hang on a mo. If you got a bit, how are you? Are you not a rotting meat sack yet? I heard that once you got bit, it was all over.' Winsome interrupted. He may not know much about how the mortuus carnem works and what the bonding process had done back in the GFOSAR, but he did know that once a person was bitten, it was all over, and the person would join the undead ranks.

Oli held her hands up to settle the two men. 'That's the something I've only just discovered before my brother's little fit.' Oli paused, beckoning Slater to let her go and to sit back down and stop worrying. He did hesitantly, sitting next to Losnedahl and watching as his sister slowly and carefully lowered her body to the floor as well, sitting down between Kolen and Ark. She put her board beside her and put her hands on her ruined stump. 'Now I know this is going to sound completely crazy, such as when England beat America at the games in 2032. But I know how to stop the infection from spreading once bitten. Although it's quick and painful, and from what I've read, it usually takes about an hour for the infection to spread throughout the entire body, shutting the body down from the inside like cancer or a snake's venom. But there is a way to stop the infection and take it from me and my missing foot; it hurts like a bitch, and you need to act fast,' Losnedahl and Ark had a brief conception of what Oli was getting at; the concept made them both gulp. Oli held her bloodied stump up, showing the group members what she had done to prevent the infection. 'Do you have to sacrifice the infected limb and kiss it a warm goodbye? To put it mildly, you have to cut it off to stop the spread of infection. I was bitten on the ankle, and you can obviously tell by my bandaged stud that I had to saw off my own leg without numbing it to get rid of the infection in my leg and not turn into a zombie in the same way most people would. You wouldn't be able to comprehend just how painful it was to do, but I did it, and here I am telling this story. So ya! That's my story.

Oh and to answer your question about how I managed to survive out here by myself, it's a thing that people have to get used to since we're on the outside, so we have to adapt to our surroundings, there really is no other way to put it. And as for this place which used to be a two-story unit, I've been staying here for the past three years, and because the place is a right shitbox, no one even considers it having valuables, and that's fine by me. Although, once, some wimpy guy tried to steal the carpet for God knows why, and I told him to beat it and go find another. He'd quickly left.' she closed with a clap.

'So then, who are you guys? If you bonders by the lab coats, I gotta show you what I've got out back! You won't believe what I managed to get.' She began to prattle them with her science business and knowledge, which she'd found out not yet observed the two bonded zombies. Mistaking them for a very tall man whose head was obscured in darkness and a disabled woman in a wheelchair. 'Ryan is the name; Winsome is the patronymic.' Winsome introduced himself, 'You'll come to know me as the handsome one that saves everyone's arses,' yeah, right, keep dreaming, Ark thought bitterly, rolling her eyes. 'My name is Marilyn Arabella Kolen, at your service, Ms Slater, and the man next to me is Henrik Losnedahl. He's mute from an accident that happened when he was a baby,' Kolen had introduced herself and Losnedahl as well, as it was common courtesy to introduce the man who couldn't talk.

'I'm Lisa Ark, and yes, Marilyn and Henrik are bonders, and so am I, well, we used to be bonders. My zombie is named Spot; (she cocked her thumb behind her, Oli looked in the direction, saw him and mouthed her surprise) he's the tall zombie behind me, missing the top half of his head, so we like to call him a half headless zombie. Both Henrik and Marilyn are ex-bonders. Marilyn's zombie's name is Ace. Ace is the crawler in the wheelchair; we don't know about Henrik's zombie, Linus. He's probably dead,' Ark explained to Oli about who they were and what they used to be. Oli stared from Ace to Spot, marvelling at seeing two official bonded zombies in the flesh. Ace waved, and Spot bowed, showing her his half-missing head. But something about the blonde woman's name had struck a chord in Oli, a wave of excitement she had only heard stories about.

'Did I hear that right? Lisa Ark? You're Lisa fucking Ark? I've heard only rumours about you, depicting you as one of the best bonders in the UK. Although judging by your voice, you don't sound like us Brits,' she said, registering Ark's accent different to the rest of them; she could only mildly hear Kolen's Dutch accent, but with Ark, her accent was still heavy of her birth country. She looked down at her fingers, noticing them twitching. 'I was born in Adelaide, Australia. Henrik is from Florø in Norway, and Marilyn is from Middelburg in the Netherlands; we all have our reasons for being here in the UK, but we're on a pretty tight schedule. We have less than twenty-four hours to kill this one zombie called "Sam" and put the mortuus carnem parasite to extinction, or at least we hope to.' Ark explained to Olivia Slater. The latter seemed all the more interested in hearing her side of the story as she spoke with the legendary Lisa Ark herself.

'So, we were wondering if you'd help us? We didn't really know if there was anyone else alive around that would be able to help us, so if it's not trouble, do you think you could join and help us?' Kolen told the rest, courtesy of Ark. Oli stared at Kolen with furrowed brows, 'Do you really think I'd want to lose this other leg?' Ark looked down, feeling a wash of disappointment, but then. 'Fuck yeah! I'll help! You've returned my brother to me after fourteen years of being apart, and I can't thank you enough for that because I love him so much, and I've missed him just as much as he has me. Besides, losing both legs means that Darren can show me his RMA strength by carrying me.' Oli winked at her brother, who sat cross-legged, arms crossed and gave her the bird. 'But before you do anything, you're going to need more help in stopping this zombie Sam or whatever, and ya gonna need more than two zombies. Lucky for you to run into me, cause-' Oli suddenly paused, taking hold of her wooden pole to help her stand up straight. 'I have a surprise to show you. You'll love it, trust me. Wait here.' Oli then hobbled out of the room for about three minutes, which had seemed like an hour. The others stared bemused at each other as Oli could be heard talking to herself or someone hiding in the background? She came out shortly after.

But she wasn't alone.

Standing behind Oli were two male zombies with pale blonde hair, one taller than the other and looking fairly decent without anything missing from their bodies aside from the loose skin that was an obvious sign of decay. But other than the minor signs of decay, they were decent and still had a head, two arms and two legs. The shorter one appeared young, giving Ark, Kolen and Losnedahl the impression that he was a teenager when he died. The teenage one wore a navy-blue long-sleeved shirt and matching blue jeans, while the other was an adult who wore a moss-green hoodie and navy-blue jeans. The pair of them seemed docile enough, like Oli had drugged them before bringing them out for presentation. Oli beamed and fawned at them like they were priceless family heirlooms and wouldn't part with them for even One Billion pounds or for a chance to become the Prime Minister for a week.

'This handsome fellow is Aladar!' She glowed, playfully putting her arm on the adult one's shoulder. The older one gave no reaction. Oli then slithered over to the teenage-looking one and gave it a playful punch on the arm; its pale grey eyes followed her movements drunkenly. 'And this admirable chap is Zinni.' she chirped, like a little girl introducing her dolls to her friend's parents when they come over to pick their kid up. 'Now I know what you're thinking, weird names, I know. But I remember watching this dinosaur movie when Darren and I were kids, and I kinda got the names from that movie. But… anyway! I've been doing independent bonding with these two fine lads; they get a day each like Aladar gets day 1, Zinni gets day 2, Aladar 3, Zinni 4 and so on. Of course, their intelligence isn't as good as your zombies. What were their names again? Oh! Spot and Ace. But whatever, at least my zombies know right from wrong if I tell them,' She explained to them. The three ex-bonders, Ark, Kolen and Losnedahl, were the only ones avidly absorbing her words like a sponge soaking up water.

'They look to be around the 40 AOR. And if that is the case, then holy crap, they're in good nick' Kolen endorsed them, determining their ages by their appearance and state of decay. 'You must really look after them?' Kolen asked.

'More or less,' chuckled Oli, 'really all depends on the crap you can find on the streets.' She explained to Kolen, who adjusted her glasses, staring at the two male zombies as if they were the purest and sweetest eye candy.

'Oh! I almost forgot! Mrs Ark,' She glanced at Ark, who was studying the two blonde male zombies with her eyes. 'Since I've only heard great things about you being one of the greatest non-local bonders, I know I said it before. But can you tell me what makes you so awesome? ('Gimmie a break,' Winsome made a gagging noise in the background, one that thankfully one could hear) I really want more tips from the best of the best on how to better bond with Aladar and Zinni.' Oli chuckled, hands clapped together, but Ark didn't smile back; Ark felt as if she didn't deserve this amount of pleasure and praise. 'Trust me, Olivia, I'm not the best; Alexander Fredrickson is… he was the best.' She answered, looking down at her twiddling fingers.

'Oh, that's right, I forgot all about him and his stable reputation as Britain's best bonder; say I don't see him with you,' she wondered. Ark's eyes didn't meet Oli's as the house fell into an eerie silence. 'He's dead. He was one of the first to die back at the GFOSAR.' Ark concluded, looking up at Oli with a mournful frown.

Chapter 11

A gruelling silence filled the room as eyes followed Ark's direction. 'Oh shit. Jesus... I-I'm so sorry, really. You have my deepest respect.' Oli spoke; she looked down at the floor. Ark and the other ex-bonders nodded sadly. 'I bet he was an amazing man; sorry for bombarding you with questions.' Oli withdrew; her once confident smile immediately dissolved into a frown upon hearing about the death of one of the greatest bonders in the whole country, the one that had taught the three ex-bonders the basics and outcomes of bonding with the undead. The one whose lessons had kept them alive. 'It's fine, Ms Slater. You were just curious as this is the first time you've met actual bonders, so it's perfectly palpable that you'd want to know everything about the bonding process.' Ark explained.

'What made you start doing independent bonding, sis? I mean, you already have two bonded zombies with you, and no doubt you'd have the drugs made for them; how come you're out here bonding and not in that big facility where other bonders bond with zombies?' Inquired Slater, speaking up after a prolonged silence. Oli stared at her brother; her brow raised as if she had been asked a rhetorical question. 'Tch, you wouldn't believe me if I told you I couldn't get a job at the GFOSAR. However, I was lucky enough to have an audience with Charles Mansfield before he moved to Washington, and he said I wasn't "qualified enough" for the job. He said that I had a glint in my eye that he didn't like, and Charlie said he didn't like the vibe he got around me; in his words, I was cocky, arrogant and I wouldn't take things seriously, so he dismissed me, what a snob; those arseholes just didn't like the idea of me "confident and knowledgeable" being anywhere near the zombies, for shit only knows why. I told him I would be back and was right about that. I did come back, bypassed the guards, and stole a bonding manual from Charles' office just after he left; I would've taken some drugs, but I knew that I had to book it, so I did. I had a manual, and I was certain that I would be able to get the drugs in some shape or form, and funnily enough, I did; I managed to snag a medicine container full of them from one of the black markets originally down the street. I use "originally" because it's not functional anymore. Idiots.' She scoffed, looking down at the floor. Slater stood up, prompting the four zombies in the room to glance up in his direction. 'Bullshit! From the little equipment you've worked with and what you've managed with these two zombies! I'd say you're more than qualified to be a zombie bonder. Those fucks had no idea what they were doing when they turned you down.' he shot.

'That's if Sam didn't go bad and kill everyone,' Ark mumbled, pivoting her head slightly to look at her.

'You flatter me, bro. But this was what I was forced into. I wasn't planning on meeting the grim reaper just yet by giving up on my dream of making an attempt to do something grand for the country; that's why I took up independent bonding and actually made some kind of difference in this crappy world. It was the only option left for me. And I think I turned out alright.' Oli stated flatly, averting her gaze from him to look at the survivors of the GFOSAR massacre. 'I'm sorry if I'm asking too many questions, especially ones that strike up the wrong cord… but what's so bad about this, Sam? I heard Lisa mention someone with that name.' Oli inquired, intrigued into who the monster was that they were up against.

'The fucking bitch is EVIL! Pure unshakable evil!' Winsome raised his voice, creating an unnecessary echo throughout the building, stating it in the best possible way, venting his strong distaste for Sam and the very thought of her still skulking around the streets, killing anything that still has a beating heart and can still breathe. He looked around and realised what he had done, so he lowered his head.

'Sam is a true monster; she is what nightmares are made of.' Kolen said softly; her body shivered just thinking about Sam and all the dreadful things she did at the GFOSAR. Losnedahl spoke in sign language, saying, *'She was the one who murdered Alexander and started a massacre on the GFOSAR. We all want to make sure she bites the dust painfully.'* Kolen had done the kindness and had translated his signs for the Slater twins. Both Kolen and Ark knew sign language and could read Losnedahl's signs clearly, as if he was speaking to them with a voice that only they could hear, almost like telepathy. 'I is not smart, but I no Sam, bad.' Ace lowered, admitting her thoughts about Sam and how Sam had frightened her by giving her that grin just after she had the surgery while also taking Oli back a bit.

Surprising her that a zombie was capable of speech and was speaking actual words instead of rambling incoherent moans. Oli, being cognizant of zombie bonding, knew zombies could get bright enough to state their opinions instead of having one thing on their minds (brains). She understood that they were more than capable of remembering their past lives when it came to future bonding sessions. But never in her lifetime of studying bonding had Oli even considered the thought that they could master speech! That their voice boxes could work right and produce actual tangible words.

'We don't exactly know what pushed her into becoming what she is. But all we know is that she has to die; she's already taken so many innocent lives back at the facility, and we can't just sit idly by and let her continue her warmongering. We need to kill her before she kills more people, turning them into zombies and giving the mortuus carnem a host to infect. Speaking of the mortuus carnem, Darren mentioned you captured one and was doing research on it. If you still have it, I'd like to see it; that way, we can both learn things about how and why it goes for the deceased.' Ark spoke to Oli, now showing her undivided interest and attention, wanting to know if Slater was indeed telling the truth and, if so if Olivia really did have an actual mortuus carnem specimen. Like most people, she wanted to see one up close and know what makes them tick. But out of simple curiosity, she liked to learn how Oli had managed to get one in the first place. Obviously, it wasn't something simple and cliché like luck? She suspected some serious thought went into how to capture one.

'Yeah, I still have the little shit.' Oli picked up the pole and stood up; balancing on one leg was more problematic than initially thought. 'Follow me; it's in the basement.' Oli instructed, leaning on the pole to support her missing, amputated leg as she hopped awkwardly over to where the basement was located. Ark stood up as well and followed her. 'Henrik, since you're the oldest, you're in charge until I return. Marilyn, call if you need me back up, and Spot.' The very mention of her calling his name got his strict attention. 'Put Olivia's zombies in their place if they misbehave; Ace will provide you with directions on where they are.' She commanded (knowing Spot, he had a loyalty that couldn't be matched; he'd do anything for her if she decided she'd had enough of him and wanted him disposed of, he'd gladly off himself; it would break his dead heart, but he'd do it all for his bonder). Even without eyes, he would make sure the two zombies weren't misbehaving by listening to the sounds they made, determining their emotions (if they were stressed or agitated or hungry), and Ace would be able to tell him where they were in the room. He gave Ark a nod to show that he understood her command. 'Good boy.' She said before turning her attention to Oli as the two of them left to go down into the basement where Oli had claimed to have allegedly captured a live Mortuus Carnem specimen. If Oli was indeed telling the truth and she did have a live specimen, Ark hoped it would be able to provide her with enough facts that would help to debunk and answer all the questions about the Mortuus Carnem parasite and why it goes for the dead.

'So, Olivia, how did you capture one? If you don't mind my asking.' Ark asked as Oli escorted her into a dilapidated hallway and opened one of the wooden doors. There stood some steps that led into the dimly lit basement. 'I'll tell you in a bit first I'll need to introduce you.' She replied as Ark took Oli's arm and threw it over her shoulder. She aided Oli down the steps until they were at the foot. 'Oh, bug these candles,' Oli muttered, limping over to one of the melted candles and replacing it with another unlit one. Ark watched Oli fumble around the desk of draws, pulling out a box of matches; she couldn't see the brand in this dim light. Oli pulled a matchstick out and struck it on the side. A small flame illuminated the room; she hovered it over the new candle, generating some more light to the dim basement. Welcoming Ark to the insight of Olivia Slater's independent research. Shelves of books and drawings of the titular mortuus carnem parasite, desks and benches of flasks, and even more books on basic and advanced science. Ark felt an ocean's wave of wonderment as she glanced around Oli's private study.

'Over there under that black cloth,' Oli pointed to one of the benches as she continued to light more candles, giving the basement some more light. 'It's in that jar. You know, I'm actually surprised it managed to stay alive for so long inside a small container without holes,' she said. Ark walked over to the bench and removed the black cloth that was covering the jar. And there, buzzing recklessly inside the pot, was a live mortuus carnem parasite in the flesh!

Chapter 12

Ark leered over the creature inside and cringed. Seeing the thing responsible for the nightmare they lived in. 'So, this is the little shit that started it all? They did say that the fucking thing looks just like a common mosquito, and those things are disgusting already. Now we got these. Hideous little shit, isn't it?' Ark snarled, picking up the jar containing the parasitic insect for a better inspection. She'd never seen a live mortuus carnem in the flesh, but she'd seen the diagrams Fredrickson had shown her during her training days. She remembered that one of them had been captured and experimented on to see how it was able to resurrect the dead, but as soon as it was dissected, it died. Its carcass was incinerated. 'Though upon closer inspection, it measured about 2.0 inches.' Ark shook the jar, watching the creature bobble around irritably inside. 'You know what gender it is?' She asked Oli, who, after sorting through her messy piles of papers, had hobbled over to Ark to examine the mortuus carnem specimen with her.

'Bugger if I know at this current stage. But based on what I've figured out from it, it's a hermaphrodite, it is both sexes and can fertilise eggs, carry them, and host them. But right now, I'm guessing it's a female since when it comes to the common mosquito, the bitches are the ones that sting. But hey, suppose Mother Nature decided to create an abomination of a freak of nature. Now it's the males that do the stinging?' She shrugged, hitching her shoulders, and leaning over Ark's shoulder as the blonde-haired woman turned the jar around, making sure to get a view of every angle of the mosquito-like parasite. 'While that does sound possible that it could be a male, but if you look closely, you'll see that it doesn't have a stinger on the back. And it has eight legs instead of six. Its back is black and yellow like a bee or wasp instead of red or brown. The mortuus carnem does have a ubiquitous trait with the common mosquitos (*and I'm not talking about appearance-wise*); they're both little shits.' Ark grunted, feeling an eruption of disgust mixed with anger.

'Damn right there, Lisa.' Oli said. Ark narrowed her eyes at the disgusting creature, watching it ram its drill-like beak into the glass of the jar, trying to free itself. Just staring into those large insectoid eyes was making her sick, and she had the ill thought that it would drill its way out of the glass pot like how they're known to dig into wooden coffins and inject whatever into the undead to make them rise up from their graves.

'Just looking at this little fucker makes me want to puke,' she hissed. Ark put the jar back on the table, concealing it with the black cloth. Fighting the urge to open the jar and pluck it out, like how someone would pick a spider from its web and squish it between her hands (one less mortuus carnem to deal with) and hear a vaguely satisfying squishing sound. So instead, she asked, 'How did you capture it?' with a voice that was yearning and high with anticipation to hearing the story of how Oli managed to capture a live specimen of the creature that turned itself into world enemy no.1.

Oli coughed a laugh. She hobbled over to the pillar with the burning candle and leaned beside it. 'I was patrolling a nearby gravesite because I wanted to get to understand how the mortuus carnem infects the dead since Mr Mansfield rejected me. I wanted to have something to prove, so I went searching for one, no luck at first, past a few graves, either nothing or the bodies had already been resurrected as the graves had holes in them. So, I considered hanging up the towel when, BAM, I managed to spot one zipping around like a fly on caffeine. I had to be quick because the little fuckers are fast, which is what makes them difficult to catch. Lucky for me, I had some

Pet Relax that I stole from a dilapidated veterinary clinic, and I sprayed it on the little bastard. Funnily enough, I only had to wait about two minutes for the thing to drop from the sky, and the prick was all mine.' She looked at the jar and spat on the floor.

Ark bobbed her head in confirmation. 'Huh... interesting. Now I know what the damn thing looks like, and it disgusts me. But my main question is what everyone else has been asking, and that's; Why does it target the dead? Can you answer that, Olivia? Based on this one, do you know the answer to that question?' Ark interrogated, clenching her fist and leaning it on the table, digging her nails into her skin as she could hear the mortuus carnem pinging at the glass. Again, trying to restrain herself from killing it as Oli mentioned that the things were quick and capturing one would prove another challenge on its own. Oli had just been in the right place at the right time to capture hers.

Oli hobbled over to her side and looked at her intently. 'Well, from what I can tell you from the visual research I've conducted on the little shit. The mortuus carnem is bee-like; once it does its work, it dies, exchanging life for another life. I know this because a dear friend told me before he died - his name was Waylon Tarnell. - He apparently got lucky and managed to see one infecting a corpse, seeing a dead person become undead. He told me that it infects the corpses by sucking the fluid out of itself and giving it to the deceased. You get me?'

Ark nodded, drinking at her words. Oli nodded and continued. 'I don't know how or why it does it, or what's inside the fluid that can jumpstart dead bodies. But I do know the fluid from the now-dead mortuus carnem spreads throughout the entire body and reanimates them, hence the absence of the stinger. I also did a few hands-on tests, and the parasite has a very distinctive odour about it. Although unconfirmed why, it smells like... well, dead flesh. My hypothesis is that mortuus carnem goes for the dead because it feels it needs to transfer its smell over to something already dead, much like flies are attracted to shit. The mortuus carnem is attracted to the dead; probably, it's attracted to the smell and could try to mate with them, as disgusting as that sounds. Or it could be that it feels like it needs to sacrifice itself so that another life form can live. But that's just my theory, and from what I personally have learnt about it.' Oli concluded her hypothesis, stating the things that she'd learnt about it since capturing it about a month and a half ago. Finding that it was still alive was a surprise, since she'd expected it to be dead, considering the absence of air holes. But suppose that was another thing to add to the list of unanswered questions about the mortuus carnem: it can survive months without oxygen.

'Also, another thing I should tell you is, like any other insect, they can die by poisoning such as a powerful dosage like Nicorette and Enclove, though they are durable like cockroaches and can survive CO. And I guess if we want to wipe out the species, we'd have to go for the big guns such as releasing some Botulinum, but even I know that would be a stupid idea seeing as Botulinum is one of the most dangerous poisons in the modern world.' she blurted out, 'though getting a large supply of it is the hard part. And, of course, we'd have to be mindful of all the other life out there, such as humans and animals.' She finished.

'Noted, but before we can even consider trying to destroy the mortuus carnem species, we'll need to kill Sam, because she's the one accelerating the mortuus carnem's work. So will you join us in our life-or-death mission?' she asked, holding her hand out. Proposing partnership. 'Fuck yeah, I'll join you. Besides, you helped reunite me with my brother; we were as thick as thieves back when we were kids, and if he wasn't with you, I probably would've kept the door closed. If Darren trusts you, then I do, too. So, Mrs Ark, what do you want me and my zombies to do?' she asked. 'Just tell us what to do, and we'll do it.' The group is now up to ten. 'First, you can call me Lisa.' Ark stated, and Oli nodded respectfully. At this rate, it would be no surprise that they were bound to find more survivors along the way who would be more than willing to join them on this quest for redemption and retribution. After all, Sam was turning the scarce number of survivors out there into zombies within each passing minute, and that wasn't going to go unpunished. She was stripping their living existence, robbing them of life and eternal peace, gaining her own little personalised army of the undead. She couldn't be permitted to live and continue such a heinous rebellion (that's why Ark was dead-set on destroying her in twenty-four hours; she couldn't allow the country to fall to Sam and the mortuus carnem Apocalypse). Sam would utilise her zombified army as obstacles for the group to encounter as they operate their way through the dying city, which would result in the grisly aftermath of blood and gore, turning London into more than a ghost town. All in effort to find the one zombie named Sam and kill her. However, Sam wasn't gonna lay down like a dog and go down without a fight.

A group of six humans and four zombies wouldn't be nearly enough to stop a highly intelligent, sadistic zombie bitch that could know everything they have planned out and counter their attacks simply like a self-defence master. The four survivors of the GFOSAR knew it would be a challenging feat, but one way or another, it was going to happen, and Sam was going to be rotting in a coffin-less grave by the time the day was done. Sam had no such source of pity and mercy. She wouldn't care if a lost puppy or child was trying to escape from other zombified animals or children. Sam would just delay her travels to watch the confronting scene with a smirk on her face as the animal or child cried out in pain. She really was a demon, an embodiment of pure sadism and depravity.

Sam's fire of bitterness was going to be extinguished. She was gonna die, and it would be soon - that was Ark's promise. The group of ten members would make sure of it and uplift Ark's pledge. Ark regarded Oli; her face inspired a bright wash of determination that reminded Ark of herself when her parents had driven her to her school so she could receive her medical diploma back when she still lived in Adelaide. She favoured that determined grin on Oli's face as they made their way back upstairs to join the others who were waiting quietly. 'Keep your zombies in check, make sure they behave and follow your every order. Make sure they don't go rogue and attack anyone. I don't want anyone else dying tonight if I can help it; I've seen enough bloodshed that would churn even the strongest of stomachs.' Ark scripted Oli into the group with her part to play, who confidently nodded her understanding before she hobbled over between Aladar and Zinni, who simply stared drunkenly at her. Ark turned her attention to the rest of the group. 'Right, everyone, listen up! Olivia Slater and her zombies are joining us, and she's in charge of them. Got it?' Everyone nodded. 'Yeah, sure, whatever you say, boss,' mumbled Winsome.

'If we run into any survivors that aren't infected, "Welcome them" into the group, regardless of their background; because of our situation, I doubt survivors would fight each other. We'll have a better chance at killing that bitch if our numbers are increased.' declared Ark, watching their faces light up with a flame of redemption that she greatly admired. 'Hell Yeah! Alright! Let's go murder some fucking zombies!' Oli cackled, showing that she was more than happy with her role in the group and what Ark had instructed her to do, and that was to tend to her own zombie's needs; they were hers, and they were her responsibility, and as long as Oli knew that, Ark was fine. 'Because I have one leg thanks to that blind bitch one of ya killed just before meeting me. I'll let my zombies get their faces bloody.' Oli informed with a sly grin, making sure Ark was alright with that. 'Before you do anything, Olivia, there is another thing I should mention,' Ark said.

Oli turned her head to her; her face was gleaming with hope and admiration for her. 'Anything.' She spoke.

'If we perhaps find any stragglers, undead ones, which I highly doubt because they often hunt in hordes, perhaps...' Ark then shook her head, dismissing the idea that she had.

Oli studied her expression curiously. 'What was it? Tell me, I'm genuinely curious.'

'It's dumb.' said Ark.

'Try me. Can't be as dumb as the shit I used to do as a girl.

'I was going to say that we could capture them and try to bond with them, but we don't have any of our bonding equipment, and we're already scarce on hunger drugs; they're only meant for Spot and Ace, I suppose you already have a supply for your zombies?'

Oli opened her mouth to speak, then closed it, and finally opened it again and said, 'I may not be a professional bonder like you, Marilyn or Henrik, but I did bond with two zombies at the same time, and the only piece of equipment I had were drugs and a shovel, which I would smack them over the head with, knocking them out for a

423

short time, and then I would slip the drug into their mouths, and it would be the first thing they swallow when they wake up. You're probably going to say this as well, but bonding with zombies is sometimes a tedious operation, and it depends on the dormant zombie if they want to bond with you or not. So, I can say that your idea isn't that bonkers; it perhaps isn't best to pluck them out of the street and bond with them right there, not when you said we have an important job to do by dispatching this one named Sam.'

Ark nodded, 'Good point, I can already tell you'd be a valuable asset to the team; even if you can't walk, you've got knowledge and spunk, more spunk than Ryan could ever hope to get.'

'Go fuck yourself, Ark,' Winsome grunted, flipping his middle finger, but Ark ignored him. Oli's cheeks flushed pink, and she swatted the air bashfully before saying, 'You Flatter me, Lisa.' Ark nodded, and Oli thrust her fist in front of her as she stared at her zombies with a face that could best be described as, "You boys ready to kick some arse?"

'Yeah, that's perfectly fine, Olivia; they can help Spot in protecting both Marilyn and Ace. Because Ace is a crawler and, in that wheelchair operated by Marilyn and also because Marilyn doesn't want to fight because she doesn't like the idea of blood on her hands and taking away a life, even if it's undead, which is fine with me. So, she just pushes Ace's wheelchair around. Also,' she points to Winsome in the corner. 'If Ryan started bitching, I start yelling, Marilyn, the one that calms me down.' Winsome winded his fist to show his middle finger directed at Ark.

'Oh, Okay, thanks for letting me know. I look forward to killing this, Sam; all villains need to be vanquished. *Feel the righteous fury of Olivia Slater and her zombie-slaying buddies!"* Oli finished, sounding like she was reciting words from a book or quoting a famous movie line.

Both women consented to each other, confirming that they were at a truce on what they had to do. 'Alright, does everyone know what they're doing, what part they play?' Ark asked her allies, staring into each of their independent faces. They all stare at her and bow their head. Ark was glad.

'Ya got any beer or pot in this dump?' Winsome asked out of nowhere. Oli narrowed his eyes at him, and both Slater and Ark stared at him with brows raised and mouths agape as if he had gone mad. 'What? It's a simple question?' Oli kept her eyes on Winsome, not believing that he just said that. 'Of course, there's no beer or pot here!' she snapped. 'You think I would let everyone else drink my beer? Uh No. I love my beer; as for the pot, I smoked that too (this was a lie; Oli couldn't bear the smell and thought of smoking pot or any drugs). It 'elped me put a smile during these devastating times.'

'Sheesh, lady, (pity if I wanted to smoke some) it was just a question.' mumbled Winsome, looking down at his hands and imagining himself holding a bong or a bottle of Spitfire.

'Well, is there anything to eat? I'm actually quite hungry.' Slater asks his sister, who stares at him perplexed but nevertheless points her thumb into the kitchen, where most foods should be.

'Smartarse.' said Slater as he got up and ventured into the kitchen to look for something decent to sink his chops into. 'Love you too,' winked Oli.

Slater returned a minute later, clutching a ham and vegetable sandwich that he had gotten out of a fridge that looked like it hadn't had power in it in ten years; it was inside a plastic zip-lock bag and appeared to have been freshly made, perhaps Oli had made it earlier with ingredients which she probably "borrowed" from a nearby supermarket that was lucky to still have bread, ham and vegetables, and she perhaps had stored it in the fridge for "laron" consumption, to ensure that it would be protected against mould. He unzipped it and took the sandwich out, discarding the plastic covering on the floor next to him as he ate the sandwich in just under a minute, his stomach sighing in satisfaction.

The six humans sat amongst each other, exchanging idle chit-chat about where they should check for Sam first when they decided to leave the safety of Olivia Slater's chosen residence. The time was 6:16 when their conversations were quickly interrupted by the sound of someone screaming nearby, followed by someone harrowing at the door, demanding to be let in, making them all flinch and dart their eyes over to the door, pondering the possibilities on who or what was behind it.

'Please! Whoever is in there, Let Me In! I don't want to die! The monsters are out here!' A hoarse female voice called, and judging by the quality of the voice, she sounded elderly, possibly around the sixties? Or plan, and simply, the woman was just in too much panic that her voice ended up sounding like a croak. Picking up his shotgun, he got up and threw himself to the wall next to the door. 'We ain't gonna let you in if you're gonna be like in those movies and kill us as soon as we open this door. Cause I sure as hell ain't ready to kick the gutbucket now!' Winsome swore, holding his gun close and refusing to let the woman inside, obviously not trusting her and going by the logic of movies and video games. 'Ryan-'

'SHUDDUP Lisa! I can handle this!' retorted Winsome. 'As for whoever is out there, ya better not be bullshitting me and on shooting us dead. I gotta shotgun, and I ain't chickenshit to use it! So, ya either back da fuck up, or I will use this here.'

'Please. I'm not planning on harming whoever is in there; I'm not armed, and that is the honest truth! There's no one with me; I'm all alone, but I believe I have attracted some of those walking corpses with my scent. Oh god!' The woman sounded more distraught.

'Please let me in! They're coming!' the woman outside wailed banging on the door, sounding more frantic now. Zombie's snarling could also be faintly heard, becoming louder and louder as they seemed to approach the fretting woman outside. 'Are you infected? Answer yes, and I'm afraid that we can't risk your attack-'

'No! I haven't been bitten. I'm not infected!' The woman screamed before Ark could finish. That was enough proof Oli needed to hear as she nodded to Slater to unlock the door and let the terrified woman inside. 'But Oli, what if she's lying?' he tried to protest against allowing some stranger inside. 'Darren, you may be an hour older than me and worked in the RMA, but I was always the smart one, and I can tell if someone is genuine.' Oli snapped back, silencing him, admitting the truth to him; he didn't complain or protest further because he knew it was true. Oli was always the brightest child; one might say she was a prodigy; she would ace her tests and exams in school, while Darren was just like your typical boy and would work out at the school's gym.

Slater took the keys from Oli and walked over to the door, pushing Winsome out of the way. Winsome stumbled backward and landed on his arse. Slater placed his hands on the locks and started to unlock them one at a time, reassuring the woman outside that he'd let her in; the woman outside thanked him. Losnedahl was on edge and had his hand in his lab coat pocket, gripping the knife handle but not pulling it out. While sitting on his sore buttocks, Winsome was in front of Ace and Kolen, shotgun at the ready. Guarding them, which surprised Kolen. She didn't try to open her mouth to question him; she just let him play the protector part. Aladar and Zinni both stood at Oli's sides, watching Slater with his hands on the lock and key. Spot held onto his brain jar closely while Ark stared at the door, her rifle aimed the ready if needed.

Slater unlocked one lock, then the other and then the last two. He then placed his hand on the door handle and looked at everyone, not opening it, as if reconsidering the thought of letting her in. He gulped while the woman outside continued to scream, growing more feverish. 'WHAT ARE YOU DOING IN THERE? STOP MOCKING ME. I'M DEAD SERIOUS; I'M NOT INFECTED! PLEASE LET ME IN! I'M BEGGING YOU!' the woman screeched as the sounds of hungry zombies began to rise, drifting even closer, meaning the woman was really being chased by the dead! and from the sounds of it, there were a lot of them. 'DON'T JUST STAND THERE DARREN! OPEN THE FUCKING DOOR!!' Oli shouted, which seemed to make Slater flinch at hearing Oli yell at him, like his drill instructor had once done. He shook his head and thrust the door open. The woman flung herself inside.

'Close it! Close it! Don't let them in!' the woman squealed, quickly shambling to her feet, assisting Slater to seal the door back up and moving some furniture in front of the door, barricading it so the zombies outside wouldn't be able to break their way in. When the door had been fully secured, the woman and Slater glanced at each other, huffing. The woman then turned around to peruse the group. She had blood covering her face, betokening that she was a survivor of an attack with some zombies, and the blood of the undead had splattered over her face. She was in a mass panic. The trembling of her breathing and how her body fluctuated like she had been exposed to the deathly freezing Arctic cold. The trembling woman then closed her eyes and crossed her heart; she made a small prayer to God to inform him that she was safe and thanked him for delivering rescuers; this was her way of calming down.

'Alright, lady, who the fuck are you!' Winsome used his way of "greeting", holding his shotgun up to the strange religious woman's head, symbolising that he still didn't trust her. 'Ryan, for Christ's sake, put the gun down! Give this woman a chance!' Kolen took it upon herself to stand up to Winsome, grabbing the nuzzle and pushing his shotgun away from the scared woman. 'Please... I... I don't mean to barge in uninvited and disrupt your chances of survival, but I need some shelter as well as some food... please, I'm scared and all alone, and it's quite alright if you mercy kill me later; I'm not cut out for this kind of environment. I just don't want to end up like one of those thi-!' the woman forcefully cut herself off at the sight of Spot. She stared as if she had recognised him from somewhere. 'Ma'am?' Slater tried calling to the woman, but it was like she hadn't heard him.

'No, no, no, no... no! It can't be him... it can't be...' the woman cried softly, taking a few cautious steps towards the giant zombie with half a head.

'Lucas?'

Chapter 13

'Lucas? But his name is Spot, though? At least that's the name you gave him, right Lisa? Or is that his real name?' Kolen glanced at the woman. 'Is that his real name?' she asked the stranger before looking over to Ark, puzzled as if she thought Ark might've surreptitiously know his real name as Lucas the entire time; she had bonded with him and may have kept his name a secret for them. No, of course, that wasn't the case; Kolen was just thinking too far out of the box; besides, when she stared at Ark's face, she could see how it resembled an equal amount of bafflement as everyone else who had come to know the tall half headless zombie as Spot, a name more suited for a dog rather than a human.

Ark pretended she hadn't heard Kolen as she, too, gawked from the stranger and then to her zombie as if trying to pinpoint a connection between the two, trying to work out how this stranger knew her zombie and why she had called him Lucas but could find none. The other thing that was on her mind was how this woman survived the horrors of the outside for this long, considering she looked like she hadn't developed a single ounce of muscle on her petite body. Those thin, spindly stilts for legs on her made it look like she couldn't run fast, even if she wanted to. The woman was small, appeared around Losnedahl's age and meek, around five-five, while Spot was a towering six-seven, and when he was alive, he probably would've been at least seven feet tall, making him a literal gentle giant.

Ark felt an impulse to ask this strange woman how she had gotten here in the first place and how she had managed to survive for this long. There were so many questions regarding this woman that she wanted to ask, and yet, none of them wanted to leave her lips, and all she could do was stare helplessly at her, hoping someone would be able to say something for her. She glanced back at Spot, who seemed afraid – something she hadn't seen from him. His hands shook, his fingers jerked, and his feet stepped backward until his back hit the wall. While he couldn't see or smell her, it was like he could recognise the woman's voice and could only vaguely remember the name "Lucas", but everything along the lines of that was a blur. He didn't want to remember who he was, because he was happy, considering Spot was blind and undead. He had Lisa Ark as his bonder, and he adored everything about her and her dedication to getting nothing but the best out of him. The idea of this strange woman taking him away from Ark and the others and the prospect of stopping Sam after she had identified him had frightened him greatly; he didn't want to leave Ark after everything she had done for him. Holding his brain jar with one hand, Spot brought a hand to his clean-cut bottom head half, distraught gurgles emitted from him as if he was crying. His legs gave way, his back slid down the wall to the ground, clutching said brain jar, and he lowered his half head into it and made more of her those distraught gurgles. He was scared, didn't know what was going on, he didn't know who the strange female voice was, but he felt as if he had recognised it from somewhere, and he didn't know who Lucas was and why the peculiar woman kept calling him that. It was becoming too overbearing for Spot that he started to shake his half head about, wanting the strange woman to leave; the distraught, saddened gurgles became louder the more Spot thought about the name Lucas, and knowing that the strange woman was in the room just caused more stress about him as more images started to encircle him, locking him up in a box of memories and feelings that he didn't understand.

Is he... crying?' Oli questioned; eyes broadened with amazement. 'Seems like it.' Slater replied to his sister. Everyone in the room, aside from Ace, Aladar and Zinni, stared at Spot, eyes wide with wonderment at a zombie emitting sounds similar to crying, again showing another emotion that wasn't thought capable until probably a year and a half work of bonding. The mere sight of her zombie brought her into such a feeble state that it almost brought Ark to tears. She had the urge to ask this stranger to get out and bother someone else with her religious evangelism. But now that she had addressed Spot as Lucas, she couldn't just withhold her curiosity and throw away the chance of knowing Spot's real name and past, one of the main goals for any zombie bonder.

Finally, Ark felt she had control over her body, after it'd been frozen in place from shock. She approached the woman who, like the other humans, had become distracted by Spot sitting on the floor, "crying" at the idea of being forcefully taken from Ark without his say-so. 'Excuse me, Ms? But how do you know this zombie? Was Lucas his real name?' Ark had asked, tapping the woman's shoulder to get her attention. She probably should have interrogated her some more by asking her how she'd found this place and how she'd survived with the undead after her, as she couldn't deny that the woman sounded more than a little panicked when she had banged on the door, demanding to be let inside.

The woman did not look at Ark as she stared ahead of her at the zombie with half a head, cowering to the wall, scared, and confused. 'I'm certain it's him. Oh, my. Oh my. The times I prayed that this would never happen to him… but it did, oh father, why did you forsake my wishes? Why did you let him become one of them?' the woman trailed off, gingerly stepping towards the crying zombie, ignoring Ark and everyone else in the room, as if it was just her and Spot in the room. Ark had to ask again. The woman flinched, placing a hand on her chest, and releasing a startled breath. 'Oh, forgive me, I didn't see you… and yes, yes, this zombie's name is Lucas Fitzroy. I can now tell by

the dirty white buttoned shirt and black overalls, and by
the… by the...' the woman sniffled, unable to finish as she
cupped her face with her hands and bawled into them. Spot
stopped with the sad gurgles and looked in the direction of
the crying woman, seemingly as confused as everyone else.
Whoever this woman was, she seemed harmless enough;
she knew the information Ark couldn't get a hold of, and to
turn her away would seem cruel and heartless, so she
placed her hands on the woman's shoulders and rubbed
them in a comforting way. 'Missing head,' she uttered with
a spin around the head with her finger. Acknowledging
what Spot didn't have only seemed to make the woman cry
harder.

'Not safe, we leave. Sammy.' Said the crawler. But
everyone pretended as if the crawler was invisible, and her
very existence could only be felt rather than seen or heard.
Ark felt as if she could see a connection between her
zombie and this woman, so she delved further into the
investigation, gently asking. 'Who are you, Ms?' while
trying not to upset the already heavily distressed woman
further.

The woman forced herself to stop crying to answer
Ark; she wiped her eyes with her palms, tearfully perusing
Spot, who was now standing behind Kolen and Losnedahl.
His staggering height had dwarfed them both and even
unnerved Losnedahl as he had to look up at him. The
woman then looked back at Ark and said, through her
weeping voice, though she did her best to speak with more
control in her tone. 'Forgive my manners; I should've
introduced myself when I came inside. My name is Heather
Fitzroy… and Lucas is my son.'

Chapter 14

Winsome shot a hand up to talk. 'Excuse me French, but wot da fuck? You're telling me this random old bag, which could easily be trying to trick us, is the protective Spot's ma?' He burst, his voice bouncing off the walls, making Heather Fitzroy shutter and shrink from the harsh profanity; she slinked out of sight, wanting no part of any conversation that would result in a few F-bombs and other nasty animadversions of profanity. 'Seems like a pretty big coincidence for her to just show up, and suddenly, she's Spot's ma.'

'How the fuck should we fucking know!' Slater exclaimed at Winsome. He was then joined by Ark, Oli and even Kolen, who were all debating whether the woman named Heather was really who she said she was and was Spot's biological mother because one thing was clear, Winsome did make a good point about this woman's true intentions. For all they knew, this woman could be trying to lure them into a trap because how did she know that they were even in this place to begin with? Theories ricocheted from one another. Trying to find any discernible evidence that would relate the two together, but so far, their minds were left with nothing but blanks. They'd only just met Heather, and for all they knew, she could be claiming that she knew him or had seen his undead state somewhere, or she'd probably kept him in a personal "rubbish bin" (disposing of any human meat she didn't need) and would address him as her son Lucas. This woman was not right in the head if that was the case. Until Heather spills out her story, the humans were left to gamble on the true identity and intentions behind this strange woman who'd coincidently survived a horde after her.

'I think we should just calm down and try to talk to her in a civil manner.' Kolen suggested, putting her hands up and slowly lowering them, gesturing they lower their tones.

The woman who called herself Heather was trembling at the conflict of conversation that revolved around her. 'Please.' she trembled, hands together, clasping the necklace around her neck.

'Shut up!' Slater hissed. 'We are trying to think whether we should trust you or not.'

Heather was quickly quiet at that. Her mouth closed, and her thoughts jumbled. The only thing she could do was look at the half-headless zombie who was trembling just as much as she was.

Spot stood still in silence; his only movement was his hands, which were twitching and shaking in an uncontrolled manner as if he was feeling cold or had just held a palm-sized block of ice cupped in both hands. He was just as agitated as everyone else, if not even more disturbed and frightened; the emotions and feelings were zipping back and forth inside his brain like a pinball. He started to "see" things that he'd never seen before. Images flashed through the darkness like sunlight's afterimage. It was piling up on him that he felt confronted by them. *Who were these people? What is going on? Why am I seeing this?* These were some of the questions that were going through his mind, questions that he feared wouldn't be answered unless someone told him the purpose for them and why they were happening to him. He began to lose his grip on reality; his brain jar glided and slipped away from his arms. It felt as if his hands were jelly, and keeping the pot in them became a struggle. The harmony of the group members arguing seemed to be nothing more than a few distant mumbles that he could barely understand. They sounded far away even though he was in the same room as them all. 'You think we fucking know everything, don't you, Ryan? Well, we fucking don't! We're just as clueless as you are!' he faintly heard Slater's booming voice; he wanted to reach out to that voice, to let Slater's voice save him, but he could feel as if he was being vacuumed into a place where even if he ran, he could never escape from, could never get away from. He held his brain so tightly that it was a wonder that the glass wasn't splintering; he was scared. So many colours flashed through his head, so many voices interloping one another that he felt as if his head would explode. 'Come on, Lucas! This way!' He heard an unfamiliar voice coming from close by, and for the first time since his death, Spot saw colour! He could see that he was inside a room, a bedroom based on the bed, personalised furniture and posters strewn about the walls. His head almost reached the ceiling. A mirror was in front of him, and he had to go down on his knees just to see the face staring back at him. Spot gazed into what was supposed to be his reflection in the mirror, seeing himself as a rather handsome-looking young man with shoulder-length black hair, matching eyes, and a generous face. No way this was him; this couldn't be. The only explanation he had for these things he was seeing was that he was staring through someone else's eyes, seeing the memories of this Lucas man. Then he could hear Heather's voice calling out to him from behind him. 'Lucas, this way, into the living room. there are some people here who want to meet you.' Why was he being called Lucas? His name was Spot. What was going on? Who was he? Where was he? He looked down at his hands and then saw his face again in the mirror, and then his face became animated with all these emotions, feelings, and images that he had never noticed before. The memories were returning back to him, pooling back in his mind all so quickly that he couldn't keep up with how many of them re-entered his brain. But one thing was now determined. And now he was beginning to understand why he was sent here and why he was seeing these things. He was remembering who he was, how he died, and what his name was. Lucas Fitzroy was, in fact, his actual name. And this woman was indeed telling the truth, and she was undoubtedly his mother! He understood now; he was watching his final moments in real-time play out before him. He was watching his life before it would be taken away from him.

He remembered his name was Lucas Harlot Fitzroy and that he was a twenty-one-year-old man who'd been born with a minor case of gigantism, he was the tallest in his family. He remembered that after his tenth birthday, he'd been gawked at, with one of his uncle's pointing out that he was already five-eight, around seven inches taller than an ordinary ten-year-old boy, and his growth only increased as he got older until eventually, he became the tallest in his family, standing at a towering height of seven-one. One of Britain's tallest men in a while. And yet, despite standing above seven-foot and dwarfing most people his age and getting used to strange looks by his family, he was a mild, soft-spoken man who always treated everyone around equally, even if they were people who would mock and judge him because of his height, he would always see them as equals to him. While he'd been alive, he had also endured a stuttering problem, and his friends would often have to say the words out for him. Because of his giant height, his family and friends always saw him as a basketball player and would frequently motivate him to become one and play for Britain, but he didn't see himself as the sporty type. He always saw himself as something else, away from sports. Instead of training to be a basketball player like everyone had pitched him to be. He had an admiring fondness for music, mainly the piano. Which is what Lucas had become. He may not have seen himself as a basketball player representing the country in games. The gentle giant saw himself as a pianist. He took lessons at a local piano school. Saved up and bought his own moveable piano, where he would practice on and play in front of crowds of people who'd become drawn in by his grace and performance (that is until he stood up and revealed himself as seven-one, which had garnered mixed reactions from those who had watched him).

This was only five years ago, in 2051; the mortuus carnem had been in the country then, but it was better than it was now. Although there were alerts about the mortuus carnem and the occasional zombie lurking around, it wasn't as panic endured as it currently is in 2056.

Lucas had lived a good, average life despite what was slowly consuming the world around him and everyone else. His life had been good until one day, while he had been playing the grand piano at a big concert with the whole stage full of observing eyes. Everyone at the show who had their eyes trained on him as he played the piano that day had gotten more than what they had paid for, and they got to witness his final moments as a human being.

Lucas Harlot Fitzroy was born in 2029 and died in 2051.

The alarm clock chimed, and his hand came down on it like a hammer, and he quickly flung the covers off him. He was stoked about tomorrow, which was just three hours from now. It was nine o'clock, and he couldn't sleep, he did try to, but his efforts in getting some much-needed forty winks were fleeting. He couldn't contain his bubbling excitement mixed in with a spoonful of anxiety that he kept tossing and turning around in bed, knowing that today was going to be the big day for him. On this day, all his hard work and practice would be paying off, and he would show the country his talents and introduce Britain to its latest famed son. His eyes occasionally shot themselves awake, only for him to be disappointed that it was still Friday and not Saturday, the 21st of August. Lucas had been chosen to participate in a big upcoming concert. He had been selected to be the finale, the one to seal the end of the show, and quite possibly, the most important part (well, according to Heather, it was), so he had to make his performance have the most impact, he would have to play songs that would resonate well with the audience he would be playing to. Songs that he already had picked. He was going to play three songs for a vast crowd of attendees. The entire concert hall was going to be staked full of people, all their eyes on those performing before and, eventually, him—all watching him with their utmost attention. The idea of having so many non-family and friend eyes watching him had made him nervous. He had shown off his talent and paid off skills for the piano in front of his friends and family through ZOOM meetings, but never had Lucas actually shown his pianist skills in front of a vast crowd of so many faces whom he hadn't known, so, Lucas would pray that he wouldn't screw this event up. He had made sure to repeatedly practice the songs that he would play at the concert so they would become engraved in his head. Lucas was determined to give everyone in the crowd the best-dammed performance they would ever have the chance to see. So, when the day finally arrived, spilling rays of sunlight into Lucas's room. He sprung to life. He threw the duvet off him and jumped out of bed, bursting with energy. He paraded down the stairs, being mindful to not bump into anything along the way as he went into the kitchen to consume his breakfast, two slices of honey toast prepped especially by his mother. Lucas gushed about his feelings towards his mother, and Heather presented him with a cheery smile. She knew how much this concert had meant to her son, and to see him in such uplifting spirits was painting a rather divine image on her day. He finished his toast, standing up and putting the plate under the faucet. He turned around and knelt down on one foot to kiss his mother, Heather, on the cheek, informing her that he would be picked up by his best friend, Josh Krimmer. 'Will yu-you b-b-be at the co-con-cert?' He stammered, standing up and towering over his mother, who only reached up to his chest. He hated how he always stammered whenever he was excited about something such as this day.

His mother nuzzled his cheek with her fingers. 'Of course, I'll be there. I wouldn't miss my big boys' big debut; I know this concert means a lot to you. I hope everyone else there enjoys the songs you've picked out to play,' she smiles tenderly—the way a dotting, loving mother would. 'Th-thanks, m-ma-mum', he smiled back, going down on one foot again and hugging Heather tightly until he heard a car horn beep from outside, alerting him that Josh had arrived. 'C-See you s-soon!' Lucas got up and waved at his mother, picking up his rucksack with his music sheets, leaving the house, and letting himself into Josh's car, which he had struggled to fit inside and had to awkwardly hunch just to sit down in the backseat. 'I'll definitely be the audience when it's your turn to shine, mate,' Josh spoke, cocking his head to see Lucas in the backseat, uncomfortably hunching his body to make himself appear smaller. 'Th-tanks Jo-Josh.' Lucas bit his lip nervously, glancing around while in Josh's car and wishing he wasn't so tall. Josh had a simple Jackson Suzuki, nothing flash or special.

When Josh parked in the car park at The La Ballerina Theatre, Lucas exited first, thanked Josh, and was hastily ushered out back to where the other performers were, his rucksack dancing in the air as he ran towards the backstage.

Heather came in her car soon after Lucas had disappeared backstage. Josh hollered out for her, calling her Mrs Fitz, and she came over to meet him, beaming. Both are excited to see Lucas play in front of such an astounding number of people.

'You ready, Mrs Fitz?' Josh asked.

'You better believe I am ready! He's going to be spectacular! This is going to be something I won't be forgetting anytime soon.'

*'I'll drink to that, Mrs Fitz!' they both exchanged friendly remarks with each other until they were finally able to enter the theatre. The concert halls were packed; pretty much all the seats had been taken, so Josh and Heather had to pay and book early to reserve their seats before they were sold out. Three acts would be happening during the concert before Lucas would finish up for the day, making it a total of four. The first act was a Native American band from California called the 'Blind Eagles.' They had played a total of four songs so loudly that some people had to hold their ears, and some people, such as Josh, had noticed that some of the lights above them started to become loose due to vibrations. Once they were done, they bowed and thanked the audience for their help and support in becoming who they are, and they were glad to have fans like them from all the way to the United Kingdom; then they left the stage. The second act was a nine-year transfer soprano named Yuri Nazarenko, who didn't speak much English from Kyiv, singing a version of **Suo Gân**. He had a spectacular voice that melted the hearts of some of the women, making them shed a few tears at this young Ukrainian boy's angelic voice. 'You have an amazing voice! I hope you continue to sing more!' A man had shouted from the crowd down to the little Ukrainian soprano. Making the little boy weep tears of joy from being so appreciated and loved, he had to be taken off stage by his translator because he found himself bawling his little eyes out too much from being so overly felicitous. The third was a blind woman from Liverpool named Rani Allen, who sang her take on **Celine Dion's My Heart Will Go On**. She was blessed with a standing ovation from half of the*

audience, and she got whoops from both men and women who were gushing things like. "You're the next Enya!" and "You do CDs yet?" Much like Nazarenko, she had to be taken off stage because she was blind and couldn't see herself off the stage alone. But before the final performer came on stage, a male light technician appeared briefly on the light banister to attempt to fix the loose wiring.

*A few minutes later, Lucas Fitzroy made his appearance. He had stepped onto the scene as Heather and Josh cheered before forcing themselves to be quiet so that Lucas could deliver the much-awaited grand finale; he played three songs on the grand piano. The first song was the infamous **5th Sympathy** by **Beethoven**, the second was a piece called **Last Dance** by an online pianist, and the last was **Unbreakable** by **Two Steps From Hell**. So far, everything was fine, and everyone's eyes remained poised on Lucas and how fast his fingers were. A man next to Heather pointed towards the light technician, speaking with another man next to him about how the technician should've fixed the lights and wiring by now, either that or why they hadn't delayed the show until it was fixed. 'That's my son playing down there,' Heather had said to the man, completely ignoring the technician who looked like he was trying to tame a rather violent and large python, though he couldn't seem to get a good grip on the wire. 'I don't like this,' Heather heard someone behind her mutter, 'I don't like the way those wires are whipping around that young man's head. Shouldn't someone halt the performance until the lights are fixed?' the person behind her said. Heather did not know what this person was going on about; she couldn't see any stray wires around her boy's head; she only saw people trying to distract her from watching her son give out the performance of a lifetime.*

But just because the dodgy lighting mechanism backstage broke, that didn't mean it wasn't dangerous, seeing as it was seen by some of the theatregoers, some even holding the arms of their seats and pressing their backs against the fabric of the chairs, their throats tightened. And because Lucas was really getting into the song he was currently playing, which was Unbreakable, the sound of cables snapping and the lighting technicians screaming in terror was muted by the chime of the piano keys. So, no one could have predicted what would happen next. They definitely would get one hell of a grand finale. It was all so quick and would work in a Final Destination movie. While Lucas had the audience at the edges of their seats, along with his mother and his best friend. The broken cable was unintentionally caused by that loud Native American band, which had begun to swing and swerve uncontrollably around backstage like a wild snake. It then slithered onto the front stage for a few moments, seemingly with purpose, as if jovially dancing along to Lucas's piano playing. Lucas was going wild with the piano music to notice the dancing, whipping cable behind him. Some of the onlookers noticed the snake-like cable, contemplating if they should warn the giant pianist or why the extras behind the scene weren't doing anything about it. Even so, the crowd remained silent, not wanting to disrupt Lucas, just as he was about to beat down on the final keys of the song. He lifted his fingers, and just as soon as they touched the keys, no music came, and he had suddenly stopped playing at the mid-ending of the song, which stumped everyone as to why he stopped before finishing.

Lucas sat frozen on the piano stool, his eyes staring ahead, his body not moving as much as an inch. His fingers were still slummed on the piano keys he had touched but not yet played. Everything was going fine before, until now, when he had suddenly stopped like he just had some kind of brain freeze. Onlookers in the crowd were left baffled, pondering why Lucas had randomly ceased playing; why had he stopped playing, not finishing the song? Everyone in the audience was left questioning what had just happened and why the sudden halt...

Then it happened.

Blood slowly trickled out from the corners of his mouth and around the sides in a straight line. At first, people started chattering amongst each other about this being part of the finale, but their thoughts were soon silenced by the horror that was about to ensue. Unable to keep their eyes away, they watched the top half of his head slowly disconnect itself from the rest of his head, slip off his body and hit the ground with a dead splat of blood. It was quickly followed by Lucas's giant body collapsing to the floor. That was the reason why he had suddenly stopped playing... he was dead! The wild snake-like cable had whipped itself right through Lucas's head, slicing half his clean head off.

The audience that saw this screamed, hastening out of their seats and out of the building. Seeing someone just up and die in front of you, of course, would scare the hell out of you! Especially Heather Fitzroy, a divorced mother, seeing her own child die in front of her, especially to see him get decapitated in what should have been a good moment and cherished memory. 'Oh...my...god...Lucas ...no... Oh my god!' she screeched, fighting her way through the panicked crowd of people with Josh following suit behind her, an equal amount of fear and shock surging through him. As the two of them ran down the stairs to where Lucas's dead body rested, Heather fell to her knees as blood pooled around them. 'Dear Christ...' Josh whimpered, crossing his heart, staring at his best friend's corpse that was now missing half his head. The light operators backstage had come on stage, repeatedly apologising for what happened. Josh dealt with them, berating them about why they hadn't done anything to stop the faulty wire from slicing an innocent man's head off. Heather pretended not to hear Josh as he bickered to the men as she tightly held onto the corpse of her giant son, clearly too distressed and shocked about everything that had just flashed before her. Her eyes were a mess of tears, along with Josh, who was finding it hard to even look at him and was busy harrowing the operators backstage about how he was going to sue them for letting a gentle giant like Lucas Fitzroy die before demanding they be the ones to ring the funeral home for them. Both Heather Fitzroy and Josh Krimmer wailed and mourned for thirty minutes straight until the two of them were forcefully escorted out of the theatre while the recently deceased body and head of Lucas Fitzroy was to be carried away and ferried off to the nearest funeral home. Heather continued to shriek from seeing her son die in front of her and knowing that she would have to pay and attend his funeral and watch his oversized coffin getting buried, joining the rest of the family and friends who had passed away.

It wasn't until about a year later, after his funeral, that the mortuus carnem really infected the United Kingdom country enough to cause panic and disturb the daily peace. And it just so happens that one of the little shits had chipped its way through Lucas Fitzroy's coffin and infected him, transmitting its own life for Lucas's.

Now infected by the mortuus carnem and beginning his new life as an undead, Lucas's half-headless body rose from his grave. Bashing and forcing his way out of his own coffin. He climbed out of his grave and started walking the Earth again. But this time, as a mindless zombie with half a head. One that could've regularly been shot and dismissed as a zombie incapable of being bonded with. But undead, Lucas's luck was beginning to charm. It wasn't until about two years later when he was found and captured by the military, forcefully fed the hunger drug via a tube inserted uncomfortably down his throat.

He was then handed over to an attractive, youthful Australian bonder, who'd unknowingly renamed him after his most common nickname, seeing the circle-shaped mark on his wrist. It was her kindness and dexterity and retrieving his brain back for him, where he became eternally loyal to her and became Spot, Ark's faithful bonded zombie.

Chapter 15

Spot stood in silence; his only sound was a momentary whimper. He'd remembered everything that happened leading up to this point; he'd seen faces that he thought he'd forgotten, voices that he thought he'd forgotten and names that he thought he would never hear again. He remained motionless, his feet planted as if they were encased in cement, as if mourning himself and his life as the giant pianist, Lucas Fitzroy. He was a kind and gentle man who had had his life taken away in a cruel act of fate, leading him into this rotting corpse that carried his own brain around in a jar as if it were a fish in a bag of water. It'd taken him a few minutes to go through this trip down memory lane and witness his death through the eyes of someone reciting his life as if it were a story. Despite not knowing his real name and backstory before, the woman named Heather showed up claiming to be his mother, he'd always wished that he was a generous and kind person in life, hoping that he was like the person Ark had fleshed him out to be with the bonding. He could now confirm that it was true and that he was a kind and overly friendly person in life, although it was too bad that he wasn't successful in becoming famous and known by his would-be future stage name "The Giant Pianist". It really was a shame that his life was so quickly snuffed out, how his big moment had ended up being his death. His sudden death became the thing that he would be known for. How everyone watching had witnessed the abrupt cessation of what could've been Britain's next greatest pianist.

Then, once he started regaining composure of who he was and where he was, the wires connected to his brain worked and were making him hear things again, things around him, such as the faint chimes of a heated argument which had started to become louder, sounding like thunder billowing in a coming storm. Spot could hear that they were still harrowing at each other about the woman's identity, whom Spot could now confirm was his real mother. He couldn't take all the voices yelling all at once, and he wished he could block his ears to silence them. But he knew he didn't have any to cover, and he couldn't exactly pull out the wires in his brain to remove some his sense of hearing. He just got more agitated the further the arguing ensued.

'We need stop, Sam! We go now!' Ace's croaky voice yelled out to them, trying to break up the group's argument and stop their stupid quarrel over something that wasn't important and out of their hands. 'Ace is right. What the hell are you arguing about this crap for? We're just wasting time wondering if this woman is really Spot's mother. It isn't important. What matters is killing Sam and saving Britain! And so many lives along with it!' Kolen fired, which would've come as a shock to the people if they were paying attention to her and Ace – seemingly the only logical ones at this point.

'That's it. I've had a gut full of this old bag.' Winsome spat, aiming his shotgun at Heather, who held up her hands and begged Winsome not to pull the trigger, but knowing Winsome, he didn't listen and continually acted on instinct rather than thinking things through. 'Ryan, for fuck's sake! Put the gun down!' both Slater and Ark ordered; they both tried to wrestle with the cockney man with light brown hair, but he kept pushing and knocking them back with the butt of the shotgun and even threatening to shoot them as well if they don't get out of his way. Spot heard this and started to shake with fury so much that he started to imagine Winsome standing in front of him and only him standing out in the darkness that forever consumed his vision. *You had better not, Ryan. I swear if you hurt Lisa or my mother, I will turn your head into red paste.*

'Say g'night!' Winsome sassed, putting his finger on the trigger. Heather covered her face, a look of sheer terror behind her hands, waiting for the deafening sound and the shells to silence her. But they didn't come. Heather slowly and hesitantly moved her hands from her teary face to see a sight before her that shocked her and seemingly everyone else in the room. 'Let Go! You... You rotten-urk!' Winsome snapped, endeavouring to insult the tall zombie, but Spot wouldn't allow some puny little human man to bully him or his mother anymore. He shot a hand, clutched Winsome by his neck, and hoisted him two feet from the ground, his tongue lapping wildly in the air. Winsome gagged, dropping the shotgun as the others stepped back. Winsome began to feebly punch Spot's hand, trying to make him let go, but Spot was tired of this man's childish behaviour and pointless insults and wanted to give him his own private punishment without being told to. He growled angry gurgles while holding Winsome up by one hand and making movements with his other hand that Losnedahl recognised as him demanding an apology.

'He wants you to say sorry.' Kolen had translated. Winsome glared at her fleetingly and then back at Spot. 'Go to hell, Spot.' He rasped.

Big mistake.

Spot made another angry gurgle as he tightened his fingers around Winsome's throat, so much that Winsome had trouble breathing. It started to show with Winsome beginning to turn purple, making hideous choking sounds while he had to claw at Spot's firm fingers to make him let him go, though it didn't work as Spot just kept his hand firmly around his neck. 'Fuck!' Slater cried out, seeing that Spot was aiming to choke him to death. He ran over and tried intervening by prying Spot's fingers away from Winsome's throat. 'Spot! Stop it; you're killing him!' Slater shrieked with effort, trying to pull away those sturdy but spindly-looking fingers. Oli had been silent throughout this entire ordeal. She didn't have anything to say to intervene, and her efforts to intervene would seem useless as she would have to hop around on her unstable one leg.

'Lisa, do something! He's going to kill him!' Kolen cried.

'Spot! Let him go! Spot!' Ark bellowed.

'Apology... Now!' Spot roared.

'Okay! Okay, sorry, I'm sorry!' gagged Winsome, fearfully staring at Spot's agitated tongue, swishing back and forth. Instead of dropping him, Spot respectfully lowered him to the floor and let go of his throat. Winsome held his throat and coughed. Slater went over to help him, but Winsome rudely smacked him away, denying his assistance. Winsome fished his shotgun from the floor and drew it at Spot, who now showed zero attention to him. 'I called it, I fucking called it! You should've disposed of him sooner, Ark. The sonofabitch nearly killed me.' Winsome declared loudly. Pointing an accusing finger at the tall zombie.

'But as soon as you apologised, he gently put you down; you should be lucky he didn't drop you.' Ark informed him, and Winsome mocked her with a pouting face before glancing at Kolen from the corner of his eye and looking away each time she looked at him.

'Look!' Kolen pointed. The group did, diverting their attention to where she was aiming. They watched Spot slowly advancing towards the old woman. They had expected, after Spot's lesson to Winsome, the old woman, to retire and back away from the zombie she had claimed was her dead son, back from the grave. But surprisingly, Heather remained where she was standing as the half-headless zombies approached her, staring down at her blindly but still knowing where she was. Heather stared up at the zombie, breathing heavily but not running away from him because deep down, she knew in her conscious mind that it was him, that her son had returned from beyond the grave.

'Lucas?' she simply asked, staring at the giant zombie. Spot reached out and grabbed Heather by her arms; Heather flinched. Losnedahl unsheathed his bowie knife, but Ark silently gestured to him to put it back and watch. Spot then quite literally fell to his knees; his shoulders were trembling. The memories and emotions were so overwhelming that he felt like he wanted to die again just to stop the painful onslaught of emotions he was feeling. Heather gingerly called his name again. Next, Spot flung his arms around the woman and embraced her, confirming to everyone that Heather was indeed his mother and that, like any son spending the last five years separated from his mother, he had missed her dearly and was elated to know that she was still alive.

'Spot, is this your mother? Is Lucas your real name?' Ark asked; she had been the only one to gain the courage to speak after she had nearly seen her protective and normally docile zombie almost erase Winsome from their living group. She marvelled at the sudden change of pace and saw her zombie embrace this woman whom they all had just met. Kolen and Oli appeared moved by this sudden change of affairs, mostly because she was surprised to see a zombie express such deep emotion for someone he had not seen in a few years. It was genuinely ground-breaking to watch this play out, almost like striving to come up with a suitable name for a newly discovered species of dinosaur or prehistoric creature. Oli had felt like she was bearing fruit to one of humanity's most significant scientific jumps ever. Even Heather herself was astonished by this sudden embrace. Admiring how quickly he had gone from almost snuffing out Winsome's life plainly out of blind rage and loathing for him, exhibiting the factor that he could just outright kill an innocent woman who disapproves of and because he feels like it. To kneeling to her height and embracing her with his dead cold hands, which had, for some odd reason, felt pleasant and warm (*I'm home, mum, sorry I'm late, hope you still have leftovers for me*) like she was receiving an inviting welcome from someone alive. She felt like she'd wanted to burst into a chorus of tears from being reunited with her son, even if he was a half-headless, bonded zombie.

Spot responded with a slight tilt of the head. If he had eyes right now, he'd be crying from either melancholy or delight. Spot made constricted gagging sonances mixed with a slight whimpering, giving the impression that he was weeping, happy to meet his mother again and unhappy that he had to reunite with her in his undead form. 'Oh Lucas,' moaned Heather, putting her arms around Spot, 'Why did you have to be infected by that demon of a parasite?' she lamented from seeing her son again, but as a zombie, so the most comfortable of family reunions.

Heather turned to stare at Ark; her eyes were dripping with tears. 'Are you the one that bonded with him? I've heard of you zombie bonders.' Heather cried, almost as if accusing her of changing her son and bonding with him without her say-so. Ark regarded Heather, and judging by the flagrant expression on her face, she tried to utilise a smooth serenity with her words, 'Yes, Mrs Fitzroy, I am the one that bonded with him; I had named him Spot, and because of that mark on his arm. I tried my best to train him in the best way possible,' Ark paused, seeing the exoticism in Heather's eyes, washing out the accusing flare she once had. 'And I can say he's a living miracle, the real deal; you would expect it from a zombie with half a head that he wouldn't have any chance of learning anything. I can tell Spot still wants to keep a grip on his humanity, and he doesn't want to live like Sam and the other walking corpses out there. He really is a special zombie… and well... I'm very proud of him.' Ark narrated to her, peering at the ground, thinking that information would upset the grieving mother.

Heather withdrew her arms from Spot and he moved his arms away from her. She stared at Ark, and went to her, cupping her face, glimmering with an expression that could best be described in one word... gratitude. She launched herself into Ark's arms and hugged her. 'Thank you! Really! For bringing my son's feelings back to him! You have no idea how happy that makes me. Seeing him again makes me happy. Even though seeing his undead state, not going to lie, was a bit of a shocker, the fact that he has emotion and still remembers me as his mother. That is honestly the greatest thing a mother can ask for, especially in a world where death awaits around every corner.' she smiled through her tear-stained cast. Ark, not knowing how to respond to being swiftly hugged by a stranger, awkwardly glanced around at the faces the others were casting upon her, 'Uh... your welcome?' Ark drawled. Heather let go, apologising and gushing about how she was grateful that Ark didn't leave Spot to rot with the other unbonded zombies. 'Uh… I hate to ruin this family reunion, but Lisa, we kinda have to kill Sam and wipe out the mortuus carnem parasite.' Slater stated rigidly behind her.

'Fuck, excuse my profanity, but we're on a tight schedule at the moment. We have to find this highly intelligent zombie named Sam and kill her sometime before 3am. Because we fear she might.t infect what's left of the English population.' Ark remembered and described to her.

'I understand; end one life to save dozens. I like you, Mrs.'

'Lisa Ark'

'Mrs Lisa Ark. You are a headstrong woman, and I admire that. It's hard to find women like you who will take a stand for the worst. I won't join you as much as you may want me, and as much as Lucas wants me to stay with him, I won't. I'll just be a burden to you all, and I'll get you all killed. Please don't debate me and let me off this one. Lucas seems very fond of you, Mrs Ark, and friends. You have my deepest gratitude. Feel free to call him Spot as much as you want; that was his nickname when he was alive; his best friend Josh used to call him that.' Heather stared at the barded door where she'd come from and signed, knowing that she would be heading back out that door and back into the dangers outside. 'I should be heading off now; you have a job to do, and I don't want to be a burden by slowing you down. Besides, there's someone else that I need to look for.' She faced Spot. 'Lucas, this, let's hope, won't be the last time we see each other. Promise me that you'll stay loyal to your bonder and kill that demon they call Sam.' Heather gently ordered, wiping her tears away and giving her still, very tall, zombie son one last hug. 'I love you so much, Lucas,' she said her final goodbyes to Spot, heading over to the barricaded door. Slater came over with the keys and unlocked the locks again before opening the door for Heather. The zombies that had chased her had wandered off, allowing Heather to escape safely, but not before glancing back at Ark and her companions. 'I hope to see you again in the future, Mrs Lisa Ark.' Smiled Heather before she left the house, running off into the decayed city until she was out of their view, unknown when she would be seen again.

'You okay, Spot? I understand this might be hard for you at the moment, having to meet your mother again as an undead, but we need your and everyone else's help to survive this nightmare and see a brighter future for the human race.' Ark observed Spot with a concerned look on her face, genuinely worried for her zombie.

Spot stood still for a moment as if heartbroken. He was staring ahead, thinking about Heather and that he might never get to see her again. He responded to Ark shortly after, shuffling his way over to her and giving her another friendly hug, symbolising that he still trusts her and has high emotions and feelings for her. After all, he found out who he was and his real name, even discovering that he had a mother who was very much alive and well. 'Any more reunions?' Winsome taunted, leaning against the plaster mantel of the main room, yawning, heavy apathy in his voice, desiring some fast-paced action and more brain splattering, again glancing at Kolen absently.

'There might be later if we reencounter Heather. But for now. Let's kill that bitch called Sam. Safety in numbers, right?' Oli smirked, giving her zombies Aladar and Zinni a small order to follow behind as the group's now ten members.

'Now I like me the sound of that! Let's do this!' Winsome applauded, resting his shotgun in his arms and pulling the fore-end back with a satisfying click, declaring that he was ready for anything. The group prepped themselves with more supplies, such as sandwiches in the zip-lock bags from the fridge and drinks from one of the chests that Oli had hidden under a bed that was overgrown with moss and weeds and first aid kits from the lavatory's mirror and sink cabinets and anything else they could carry like sticks and poles off the ground for close combat purposes, they didn't bother with getting any blankets or towels out of the cupboards, as they wouldn't have time to sleep. Instead, they worked into stuffing the food and drinks into Ace's wheelchair bottom pouch and putting the first aid kits into an orange and white backpack with the Fanta logo stitched on its front, which Losnedahl had found under the bed with the massacre stained on its duvet. They got themselves ready once more to leave the house and hunt down the zombie that massacred all those people back at the GFOSAR and infected all those people. Aiming to kill that one zombie who sought to spread the mortuus carnem infection faster.

Chapter 16

Slater went over to Oli, who was still using the old cane to keep her balance and muttering about how she had taken walking with two legs for granted. 'Oli, I'll help you. You have one leg and can't walk properly.' He said, worried for his sister's safety. 'And I doubt you'd want to carry that stick everywhere you go like some broken cripple who couldn't afford a decent cane or wheelchair.' Oli took a step away from him, looking at him as if he was on drugs. 'Bro, this really is unnecessary to carry me around like some fairy-tale princess; how are you supposed to fight?' She inquired, leaning her weight against the dirty wooden pole. 'I won't be. The others will have to fight for me since I must attend to my handicapped twin sister. Or, with any luck, my handicapped sister could do some fighting for me, at least until we find you something better.' He said, walking over by her side; he gently took her arm and hulled it over his shoulders for extra support. Slater hoped he could find a better, more firm cane for his sister to use along the way.

Oli smiled slyly, something that just made Slater roll his eyes. 'Naw, thanks, bro.' she giggled. 'Now, this might sound bat-shit crazy, possibly the most bonkers thing I'll ever ask anyone, but can you hand that gun over to Zinni or Aladar? I want at least one of them to be useful in this battle of survival.' Oli announced, discarding the wooden pole to the floor.

Slater played around with his sister's request on the outside by giving her a light, playful chuckle, but on the inside, he wasn't sure about the two zombies; right up to this point, they hadn't done much aside from sway around on the spot with their tongues out as if they were dehydrated and stranded in the Sahara Desert. So, while he didn't thoroughly trust them with any kind of weapon, he did trust Oli because she was his sister, his only remaining family member and Oli, as mental as she could be at times, wasn't the type of person who'd lie to him, and if she wanted one of her zombies to be armed with a weapon, suppose he'd have to take her word for it and put his trust in her to be able to control them and teach them to use the said weapon on the enemy and not on any of them. So, if Oli was able to control her zombies as well as Kolen and Ark controlled theirs, he wouldn't have a problem with them. He wished that Oli was genuine to her words and that Aladar and Zinni were just as loyal to her as Spot was to Ark.

'Still as crazy as ever, sis,' he pulled a small pocket knife out of his coat's breast pocket as he didn't have any other firearms on him besides the revolver which he had commandeered from Winsome who for some reason, found himself staring at Kolen again. But he didn't tell Oli that. 'I said gun, not flimsy butter spreader.' Said Oli in a tone that Slater recognised was trying to be funny, but he wasn't laughing, and neither was anyone else. He looked at her firmly, his eyes hard set upon hers as if he were a professor giving out a lecture to students in detention. 'I trust that you'll be responsible for them and will maintain their loyalty to you because I don't want to be responsible for having to take one of them out for your safety. So, until I can see some proper control and loyalty in the pair of them, such as the crawler and the half-headless one, I'm not trusting any of them with a gun; they can use this for now.' He flipped through the bladed trinkets installed inside it, flipping up the sharpest blade in it, which he stared at for a moment; glancing at his reflection in the blade, he glanced at Oli for a fleeting second and sighed, hoping that she knew what she was doing as it was one of his best Gerber's and that she wouldn't dare betray him. He glanced at her momentarily, waiting for his sister to say something witty in return. However, all she said was for him to trust her and that she knew what she was doing. If she didn't, she wouldn't be alive, fighting for survival and trying to bond with two zombies simultaneously. Slater sighed at this and gave the pocket knife to Oli, who in return handed it over to Zinni, the young zombie.

'Now, Zinni, don't be a moron with that knife, a'ight? Don't go stabbing things you're not supposed to and dent the blade. I know how much Darren loves his pocket knives; he'll be royally pissed off if you broke it,' winked Oli. Slater rolled his eyes. Sometimes, he wished that his sister didn't have so much of a funny bone as she did and would take things a little more seriously.

'Not to break up this family moment, but Henrik says we have places to be and not to waste any more time,' Kolen said. 'I agree. We ought to get outta here and pop more heads off.' Added Winsome. Slater noted this. He plopped his revolver down Oli's bra, feeling the fleshy lumps of her breasts against his hand. Usually, he would've liked this feeling, but because it was his sister's breasts, he quickly retracted his hand after he was sure that the revolver was tucked away safely. 'Op!' yelped Oli as Slater leaned over, one arm around Oli's neck, the other touched her thighs. 'Please don't tell me you're planning on fucking me when this is over. You do know that's incest.' Oli raised a brow, awkwardly pulling the revolver out of her bra and inspecting it for scratches. 'Oh, be quiet, sis,' Slater sneered at her, who returned another cocky wink to him. 'Oli… use your leg to jump into my arms. It'd be quicker to move around this way, that's if you haven't been stuffing your face with doughnuts.' Slater instructed her. Oli looked at him with cheeky eyes, her tongue licking her lips in a playful, seductive way. Been watching too many kinky movies, I, see?' Oli stated, chuckling a bit before giving her brother a light punch on the bicep as if remembering what he had said about her and doughnuts and wondered where on earth he'd gotten such a ludicrous idea from since all doughnut shops were closed and had been for about twelve years, so how the hell was she supposed to have stuffed her face with them if they didn't exist? 'I don't even like doughnuts!' She'd said as she nudged Slater with her elbow. The group were gathered around them. Winsome and Ark both made a frustrated huff, and Winsome glanced down at his wrist to check the time on an invisible watch, waiting impatiently to leave. 'Yo, can we go now? My feet are starting to go numb.'

Oli could see it in their faces; a firm eagerness had masked them as they waited for her to get into her brother's arms. She complied with Slater's wishes and hopped using her one foot into his arms as Slater's eyes bulged and his cheek pursed at the sudden shift of weight on his arm, but as soon as he lifted her and stood up, he shrugged her weight off as she weighed around 87lbs, a reasonably average weight for a woman. 'Just like a princess with her prince charming, oh my, what a sturdy-built man my prince is.' Oli grinned; her brown eyes twinkled cheekily after being carried in a bride-style by her brother. Slater rolled his eyes again, forgetting that Oli had liked to crack jokes and embarrass him in front of people with her sly and witty remarks. Slater grunted in reply. 'We're ready.' Slater gave the word to Ark, indicating they were ready to step into the wrecked city again.

'Finally.' Ark mouthed. 'Within each passing minute, we waste, someone dies, and a new zombie is born. We gotta go and do this now. Time anyone?' Ark told them. She wanted to double-check that everyone understood what they had to do and who they were against. Her words were replied with a nod.

'Seven, zero, three, pee em,' Ace replied, peeking over at Slater's arm, and seeing the numbers on his digital watch (*Nice try, Ace*). *Thank you, Ace.* '7:03pm.

Approximately sixteen hours until Sam and her zombies infect the entire country. When that happens, we won't be able to stop her; also, thanks, Ace.' Ark once again informed the group of the consequences if they didn't finish what Sam started and put a stop to her plans. Ark signalled Losnedahl. He came to her, and the pair stood on opposite sides the doorway from which they came from, the one that Heather had also come and gone from, listening. Making sure there were no suspicious sounds outside. Nothing, just the eerie howl of the wind, which had struck Ark as odd, but she didn't want to comment on it in case Sam was on the other side, buying her time by being silent, wanting to lure them into a trap by making them think that the coast was clear and that they could go outside, only then would she jump them. But Ark shook away that scary thought as absurd because how in the hell would Sam know where they were and the exact place they were hiding? Yes, she was an undead and had advantages that the group couldn't even comprehend. The idea of Sam knowing where they were at all times was stupid because, for all Ark knew, Sam could be somewhere in York or Cheshire or bloody Scotland right now.

Right now, the only thing Ark could do about the silence outside was to see it as the perfect means of getting out of the house and roaming the streets undetected; the best she could do was continue leading them.

Losnedahl regarded Ark, who bowed at him. Losnedahl gulped and pulled it open, being cautious that no zombies were around to take the jump on them. Losnedahl peaked his head outside before motioning to the group that the coast was clear for them to leave.

Ace glanced up at Kolen; she held her right arm up and tapped onto Kolen's breast pocket, beckoning for a hunger drug to last for the road. Kolen reached into her lab coat's breast pocket and fished out one of the pills; she handed it down to Ace, who took it plainly from her and placed it into her mouth, where she swallowed it. Kolen pulled two more out of her pocket and nudged Oli, who sat comfortably in Slater's arms. 'Here.' She said, 'Some spares for the road, don't worry, I still have three more.' Said Kolen as she transferred the two hunger drugs to her. Oli thanked her, stating that she already had two drugs for them, but otherwise thanked her for giving her some spares in case she needed to provide them with to Aladar and Zinni. She took them from Kolen and dropped them down her bra, where they would stay until she could find some kind of satchel or fanny bag to put them in. She smiled at Kolen.

The group's six humans and four zombies bowed at each other as they left the house Oli had claimed and treaded further through the blood-stained city. Ark led the way, Losnedahl and Winsome behind her, followed by Kolen wheeling Ace, Zinni drunkenly but keeping a firm grip on the pocket knife, and Slater carrying Oli. And finally, Spot, holding Aladar's hand as Aladar led him in the direction the others were going. Not wanting to lose them.

However, strangely enough, Ace wasn't as doped out on the drugs as the previous times she'd taken them. Whenever Kolen gave them to her now, she reacted very mildly to them, almost as if she hadn't been given it at all. Was the pill she'd been given this time around not as strong as the other drugs she'd taken? Or was it because Ace had started growing conventional to having them and could be having a change of appetite? The latter seems plausible enough. The only real thing this dosage did was turn her into a brainless noodle. She was awake and could see, hear, and feel everything. But she was just unreactive to her surroundings. It's as if someone bumped her in any way.

Ace would simply look at them and possibly smile like she was a crazed mental patient in one of those loony bins of history. Looking up at the ceiling, a dazed expression on her face as she sat slumped back in her wheelchair with a straight jacket around her body. At the same time, drool congested inside her mouth, emerging out of her intoxicated gaping mouth and landing on the floor in small splashes. Ace did that to Winsome while in a disorientated state where Ace couldn't think straight. Ace kept staring at Winsome, making him feel an uncomfortable tension in his gut each time he looked back and saw her staring and smiling at him for no particular reason; he glanced from Kolen to Ace, back to Kolen and Ace and finally back to Kolen, his Adam's apple bumping up and down in his throat. And it was staring at Winsome that she could tell that he couldn't shake the wretched thought that Ace was eying his brains and was secretly planning on scoping them like ice cream out of his skull and devouring them in front of his frightened, dead face. To distance himself from that ghastly grin, Winsome dove into his pocket for his wallet and opened it to the photograph he had placed inside it; he did that for a few seconds before closing it and putting it back in his pocket, resuming to look at Kolen. Ace also recognised that Winsome might have something for Kolen, feelings perhaps, as she'd noticed the way he had kept staring at her.

Chapter 17

'For the love of God, can you stop staring at me, Ryan? You've been staring at me ever since Spot almost killed you. Seriously, can you stop? It's giving me the creeps.' Kolen said, exasperated, finally catching him casting glances at her and feeling a potent discomfort from seeing his eyes upon her, studying her as if she was the most fascinating magical creature he had ever witnessed. His staring made her shiver more than the cold October breeze had. Either way, Kolen did not approve of being stared at so much, especially by the one man who'd gone out of his way to mock and tease her about everything.

It only made things more awkward for her when she saw Winsome's shoulders tense at knowing that he'd been caught and immediately reverted his stare back to Ace, where he made a loud gulping sound, biting his bottom lip, failing to pretend that he hadn't been staring at her at all. Kolen saw this and furrowed her eyebrows at him. Something was going on with him, something that she recognised as strange for Winsome. Usually, when he stared at her, it was because he was brewing up some kind of insult. Still, this time, when she'd seen him staring at her, he'd looked away instantly, seeming frightened and sheepish as if there was something new inside him that was opening up, something that she could tell was feeling just as strange to him as it was to her.

'Sheesh, what on earth is the matter with you, Ryan.' Kolen asked, expecting him to look at her again and to throw out some comical and foolish rebuke at her and humiliate himself yet again, but there was nothing; he said nothing; he didn't so much as cast a cheek to her. He just continued to stare at the crawler, pretending that she wasn't there at all and that it was just him and the crawler in the room, conducting an intense stare-off.

'I'm fine.' He simply said in a flat voice. 'I just don't like the look Ace is giving me.' He mumbled so that she couldn't hear him, though she did still hear him, but didn't say anything in response as she looked at Ace, who appeared relaxed in the wheelchair, staring at Winsome with dead pale eyes that didn't blink. In a way, this is what it was like for zombies when they were doped out on the hunger drug. Doped or intoxicated zombies were known simply by the term 'dead'. They had similar factors to when a human is knocked into unconsciousness during a pub brawl or simply being too drunk and needing to sleep the alcohol off. Mostly, they had their eyes closed as if asleep, though it was rare when their eyes were open when they were drugged up. According to something that she'd heard from the late Olio Garcia, *eyes open and little reaction to the pill often means that they are either remembering something from their past or that they are starting to become tolerant of them and that it should be time for you to work of changing their appetite into something more human.*

Another thing that can sometimes happen when the doped zombie is in the unconscious state; much like humans do when they sleep off the drink in their system, they'd be transported to a dream-like world where anything would happen, where nothing is as it seems. Like humans, zombies can also dream crazy and wild things when they are doped on the hunger drugs, and it seemed that Ace had reached this stage, Kolen assumed. It seemed that Ace was daydreaming about something, or maybe, just maybe, she was actually remembering her past, or at least some kind piece from it. A piece that would help Kolen solve the puzzle, unlocking her zombie's true identity. Kolen fiddled with the ring on her finger, remembering the reason why she'd called her crawler Ace in the first place. Remembering how her late husband had loved card games and always got excited whenever he got an ace card. She'd named Ace in honour of her late husband and the one who'd made her safe and happy. How she'd sometimes wish he was still here with her. He would be able to help her with so many things.

'The crawler looks retarted.' Winsome stated out of nowhere whilst staring at Ace, who remained slumped in the wheelchair, eyes drifting away from Winsome as if they were controlled by some remote control. She was now staring at the dismal, gloomy sky (it was getting dark and very soon, the freaks would unveil themselves) with fixated interest like she'd never seen the sky before, like an animal who'd been bred in captivity and hadn't known what the sky looked like. Ace likewise had drool plopping from her mouth, seeping through the holes in her teeth, making her look more than the part of a mental patient. Ace even chuckled at nothing, which, based on the way Winsome had raised his eyebrows, was confusing and creeping him out.

'Yo Marilyn, is this normal?' he questioned her softly, studying Ace, a little freaked out by Ace's drugged-up behaviour; it was like her dopey expression had reminded him of someone important, a friend of his who had the same look as Ace whenever they were sick with the flu. Kolen rolled her eyes and gave out a huff of annoyance from Winsome's foolish question. *Did you seriously just ask me that? Of course, it's normal for zombies to look droopy when they're under the influence of the drugs. Maybe if you paid more attention to our work and read our daily reports, you would understand this better instead of insulting our intelligence with stupid questions.* Kolen had felt like saying in response to Winsome's stupid inquest (everyone that operated in the GFOSAR knew what the zombies were like on the hunger drugs), but it wasn't like her to abuse and call people out for asking dumb questions. She wasn't the type to resort to yelling and cussing. Kolen was too sweet and innocent for that. Kolen was a good girl. 'Yeah, it's perfectly normal for zombies like Ace to look like that; I must have given her a mild dosage of the drug; either that or she could be remembering something from her past, such as a funny memory with the way she is lightly laughing to herself.' she replied back to him with a better answer and a lot less heated. She looked back at Ace, who had ceased in the light laughter and was simply staring at the sky and the clouds that blanketed the sky.

'Ah, right, I should've known.' he gingerly rubbed the back of his neck. He felt stupid and a need to better himself, especially to Kolen, because he knew that he didn't hate her; he just... just wanted a feeling of dominance, and Kolen had seemed like the perfect candidate for him to walk over. 'I probably sound like a huge nitwit for asking that. I mean, I did work at the GFOSAR, so I should've known better. Fuck, I'm a moron. Sorry for asking you such a retarted question, Marilyn, and I'm sorry I've been a huge bollocks.' He said before glancing away and smacking himself with his fist as if thinking about himself and reflecting on how much of a prick he had been. This surprised Kolen, Ark, and Losnedahl *(someone hit pause on the earth's remote! Ryan Winsome has officially apologised to Marilyn Kolen! This is something everyone needs to know)*. But they pretended they didn't hear Winsome and resumed walking as if nothing had happened. Kolen, meanwhile, peered up at him; her mouth was open with reverence; the fact that Ryan Winsome- the village idiot and the one everyone hates, had just apologised, and admitted his mistakes to meek, little Marilyn Kolen. He had often targeted the individual since the two weren't the best of allies and were more rivals than anything. So, it was a shock that Winsome had warmed up to her enough to apologise and speak in a civil, respectful manner. Was Winsome hoping to turn a new leaf and change who he naturally is for the people he's stuck here with? The people shielding him and keeping him alive? Kolen hoped that was the case and Winsome was finally willing to grow up and become a better man.

'It's fine, Ryan; we all ask silly questions we didn't believe we asked, here and there. It's part of what makes us human.' Kolen smiled, sounding like she had the sun inside her voice and that any wisdom that came out of her mouth would be enough to put a smile on anyone's heart.

'You may not believe it, but I've said some pretty dumb things to Lisa and Alexander; I once had been so humiliated about something I said to Alexander during my lectures with him that I couldn't sleep that night, and the next day I worked up the courage to confront and apologise for making a fool of myself and him. But they always understood and forgave me and gave me a thorough explanation of things that I didn't quite understand, so I understand. But right now, it isn't really the time to contemplate simple things that happened in the past; we have to focus our minds on saving the country and the future of mankind once Sam and the entire mortuus carnem species have been eradicated.' Kolen articulated her perspicacity to Winsome, again making him understand what they were dealing with and making him feel better about himself.

Kolen was always the one to create and keep the best peace. Winsome stopped, allowing Kolen and Ace to pass him. He started walking alongside them, eyes looking at the ground, hands holding the shotgun wanly. He resembled a man who regretted all his life choices and wished he could go back in time and tell his younger self to not be a bully and find ways to be a good person and one people look up to and come to for help. 'Look, I know we don't have time and all, but I just want to get this off my chest and wash my hands. But y'know, I'm really sorry about all the things I said about Alexander. I know he was a really great guy who was just trying to do his job, and I disgraced his name every time I opened my fat gob. I… I don't know why I did it or what was even wrong with me. I don't know why I was such a prick to everyone.' Winsome said wistfully, expressing that he wished Fredrickson survived instead and for him to have died in Fredrickson's place; because Fredrickson had accomplished so much and was far superior, he had his life planned out and knew what the hell he was doing. He'd no idea where he wanted his life to go and hadn't the best achievements on his record; he's just a piece of gum on Fredrickson's boot.

'At least you've had the decency to realise your mistakes, Ryan (Engel certainly wouldn't, that's for sure), and we can admire that and for you to make that apology. I, Lisa Lorraine Ark, hereby make my own apology to you for all the times I've roasted and threatened you,' Ark responded, glancing back at him from the front. Indicating that she, too, was at a truce with him. Winsome gave her a wan smile, mumbling thanks under his breath. He went over to the two women, and he threw his arms around them one by one and hugged them. Kolen first, then Ark, thanking them both for understanding him, for putting up with him, and for letting him continue to be a part of their group.

The group travelled further through the dead streets of London's capital; soon, they would be at the Heart of London, The unshakable air smelt foul and putrid like the smell of rotten, cooked meat, while at the same time, the winds started to pick up, bringing a crisp and chilling breeze, billowing small dust devils here and there, picking up pieces of trash such as plastic bags, clothing rags, and discarded newspapers dating back to early 2052 and the late 2040s when the apocalypse had really started. The entire planet was put on lockdown, declaring the end was officially nigh and the dead were walking amongst us as businesses began to fall, people were put out of work and then came the purge.

People started going mad with fear that they're going to die, so they broke into shops for things they needed and fought others who tried to stop them. While people didn't kill each other, some were forced into doing such a thing when a deceased loved one came back as a rotting corpse, and people had stood in their way, trying to defend their loved one, foolishly believing that their humanity was still inside; (which they were, but they had to be reached out to first, and defending them on the street riddled in panic wasn't it), and that they were just scared. Yeah, right, more like starving. Buildings were breached by crowds of people who sought to hide in them. But most of the time, large quantities of people had invited death through the front door because as soon a zombie smelt and broke its way into the supposed safe place, it wouldn't take long until the bodies started piling up and more zombies to be born. It wasn't until 2053 that the United Kingdom became the devastated landscape that it is now, with only a scarce number of people seeking shelter away from the always-hungry undead.

The group trudged even further through this lifeless world, keeping their eyes ahead of them and paying no attention to the frequent dust devils that swelled up around them, blowing pieces of junk around them and blowing their hair and clothes as they followed the trail behind Ark, who had her mind set on going straight, hoping for a sign left behind by the monster which they were following.

It wasn't 'til a long red object, obviously made of fabric, came fluttering their way gracefully, appearing and mounting one last sign of hope and peace in zombie-ridden world vibes. The group initially didn't think much of this scant red piece of fabric, assuming it was just another piece of clothing caught in the expanding wind as they kept walking. But to Ace, it resonated with something familiar inside her. She stretched her arm and caught the red portion of fabric out of the air as if it were a tennis ball. As soon as she regained her senses from the small dosage of the hunger drug, she woke up and saw the piece of cloth fluttering her way like some kind of peaceful butterfly.

Chapter 18

Ace sat in her chair, her body was bobbing up and down over the rickety pathway that Kolen pushed her over. She felt some moist droplets touching her head and arms. It dawned on Kolen that it was starting to rain and they'd need some shelter and wait the rain out, as the sky only seemed to get darker and darker with the closer to the night they were getting. They wouldn't want to be outside in the cold rain when the light disappears from the sky. However, Ace hadn't reacted to the droplets of rain that hit her, nor did her bonder inform the group of the changing weather. Most of Ace's functions had vanished upon coming in contact with the thing in her hand. She sniffed, stared, and examined the piece of red cloth that appeared torn at the sides with holes in the middle, flayed with a few missing strings. It was also smeared with dirt, darkening its shade of red; now it appeared to resemble a dirty bloody tint like it'd been doused in a puddle of the horrendous crimson liquid. Ace held the red fabric close to her eyes and smelt it closely, turning it over in her hands and making sure to sniff and examine every single strand of string from it. She came to a conclusion and identified the blood-red object as a piece of an old bandana, and precisely one from the late '90s to early 2000s; by the patterns printed on it and the quality of how old and tattered it looked, it seemed like it had quite a story to tell during its journey of flying with the wind and making it to the wheelchair-bound crawler. Ace had brought it to her nose so close, touching and smelling it, and her eyes widened as if she'd just remembered something from her past. But to just clarify that it was what she thought it was, she sniffed it again, taking in a hefty waft of its scent and her suspicions were confirmed because the dirty rag smelt accurately like her, or at least matched a close description to what people assumed the crawler in the wheelchair had smelt like (no one likes to sniff the undead). The bandana had almost given the crawler an eerie feeling as if the red bandana had been hers in another life, or perhaps she'd been buried with it. Rotting with her 'til the time came when Ace was infected by the mortuus carnem. It'd then flown off her head when she'd fought her way out of her grave, fluttering freely in the crisp breeze, only to meet her again after years of being needlessly carried in the wind like insincere trash. But Ace knew as soon as she'd seen the object coming towards her that it wasn't trash and that seeing it was almost like it was calling out to her.

The group just assumed Ace was having one of those episodes where she saw something interesting flying in the air and wanted to have a closer examination of it. They continued to navigate their way through the harsh deadlands of London city, not looking at Ace.

However, the group was unaware of just how much Ace had kept her dead attention on a simple ripped-up, dirtied bandana. There was just something about this red bandana that resonated inside the crawler in the wheelchair. Could this bandana be well and truly hers? Ace proceeded to stare at the red, rubbing and caressing it, putting it to her ears as if a faint but haunting sound of torturous screaming of a woman and mocked laughing that sounded masculine had entered her mind. *"Where ya goin, farmgirl? Ya still got one last cow to milk!"* a disgusting male voice echoed through her head. Ace's eyes broadened once again, and she felt as if she would let the rotting ribbon go from shock to realisation. Ace then started to do something out of character for her, something very human-like. She started hyperventilating; she clutched onto the bandana closely, staring up at the backs of Losnedahl and Winsome. Her mouth fell, and her eyes felt tears dripping from them with each blink, feeling the harsh memories beginning to intrude into her brain. She could see ghostly holographic images in the pattering rain, a woman in a bright red bandana swinging an empty pail and whistling a tune to herself. And now, this is where Ace understood and remembered she did have a name; she was someone and not a talking crawler in a wheelchair, like most zombies like her; she used to be human, she used to have her own personality, her own things, and this bandana reminded her of the one which she had worn when she was alive. The memories of when she was very much alive, living as a reclusive woman named Evelyn Davis (*Yes! That was my name! I remember Ms Kolen*), living on her own land and farm, and, of course, the violent memories of when she had died... no, when she'd been violated and murdered.

Evelyn Davis lived on her own private property as a farmer, deciding she wanted to live her own on a farm away from society when she was old enough and had gained enough independence and money from her family, who were very supportive of their eldest daughters wishes and left her their old family farmhouse. At the same time, they continued to live in the city of London because Evelyn hadn't been a people person much to begin with. So, Evelyn could continue to spend her new life as an adult, living on her family's secluded farm and frequently obtaining money by selling fresh milk, which she'd extracted from the cows in their stables. Evelyn Davis was a tomboy with firm features who was commonly seen wearing a greenish-grey tee shirt and simple grey slacks and was always seen wearing a red bandana around her brown, messy, long hair. Although at just the young age of twenty-nine, and a looker to most males. She barely got any visitors on her farm, but that was more than satisfactory as she didn't mind being alone. Evelyn Davis much preferred to be isolated and away from society and people because she always found that she had connected more with animals rather than people. So, living on a farm with animals to tend to was the perfect environment for Evelyn Davis; she had everything she could possibly want. She had the resident animals to keep her company, which, like any farm, contained animals like cows, pigs, sheep, horses, a cat named Prince Yarn and a dog named Blinky. The usual animals you'd find on a conventional farm. And it made Evelyn happy to live on this farm with so many animals to watch over her.

But it wasn't until one day after completing the daily tasks of tending to the animals' food and milking cows that Evelyn Davis milked her last cow and breathed her last breath.

Evelyn Rita Davis was born in 1981 and died in 2010.

Evelyn sat on her couch, remote in hand, flicking through the channels for something decent to watch. When she flicked it to the news channel, she remembered something she had read somewhere in yesterday's paper, also appearing on the news at around seven that night. 'Remember to be careful around the farm, from now on, Evelyn, those papers and that news reporter Dexter Williams had said there were (swindlers) worthless dickheads lurking around the London and Cheshire districts, looking for trouble.' Evelyn recited to herself as she watched the news and got more insight into what was happening around her area. Aside from Liberal and Labour politicians creating pointless arguments about things people didn't care about and a few reported break-ins all around the UK, nothing wasn't anything that worried Evelyn. The news wasn't as exciting as it used to be, but Evelyn had supposed that 2010 wasn't the most exciting year for Britain. She switched her television off after becoming bored of hearing the same stories they had played yesterday and the day before. Evelyn put the remote on the glass end table beside her, heaved herself off the armchair, entered the kitchen, and pulled three stacked medium-sized tin buckets out of the drawer under the faucet, ready to begin her daily chore of milking the cows in their stables. Evelyn whistled merrily to herself as she swung the buckets in her arms, skipping over to the cow stables, buckets in hand. 'Hey Marcy, Daisy, Leela, and so on, are you ready for your milking?' Evelyn gleamed with a blithe smile as she approached one of the stables with the name MARCY carved on it. She unlocked the latch and welcomed herself inside, tenderly stroking Marcy's soft, tender fur as Marcy lowed pleasantly at her human friend.

However, little did Evelyn realise that she'd unnecessarily caught the attention and was being stalked by a trio of local jackarses for the past day and a half, looking to stir up chaos and impede on Evelyn's peaceful and sequestered life. 'There she is. The hawt cowgirl,' one of the lowlifes with a long shaggy beard and shaven head named Bobby Jenkins, sniggered, pointing over to Evelyn from a hole in the cows milking stables; he sat hidden behind some bushes with two other equally sketchy looking men. One was tall and fat and balding, while the other appeared the same height as Bobby Jenkins, only his face was clean of a beard, and he looked to be a well-built man. 'Ayup, she'll be milking more than one cow by the time we're finished with her.' his brother Albert, the clean-faced, well-built one, had grinned an unsettling smirk as he stared at the lone farm girl as she began milking Marcy, whistling calmly to herself. 'Oi Gordon, get over there and pull down those grey tights of hers and bring her to me.' Albert ordered the tall, fat member of this little gang and friend of the two lowlife Jenkins brothers. 'My pleasure.' Gordon Macintosh licked his cracked lips, rubbing his palms together like he was preparing for a big meal at a restaurant.

Evelyn finished squeezing the drops of milk out of Marcy's utters. She left her stable and looked at the second cow, still smiling. The thought of being stalked by a six-

three fat man with balding patches on his head never once crossed her mind. 'Now you, Daisy.' Evelyn beamed at the second cow, holding one of the empty buckets, about to open the stables latch. 'No... me.' Gordon smirked down at her, breathing his disgusting cigarette stench odour down her neck as he harshly took hold of some of the tuffs of her brown hair and gagged her so she couldn't cry out for help. Not that she could anyway... Evelyn Davis did live alone. But even if she tried calling Blinky, he was locked up inside the house and possibly in a deep sleep on her bed. Evelyn kicked and thrashed around in Gordon's firm grip, but he was psychically overpowering, and Evelyn didn't have much she could do if she wanted to get away from him. Gordon had managed to get Evelyn away from the cows, who were lying down casually as if nothing was happening. Gordon took her, kicking and muffling, screaming outside the barn, dragging her against her will to where the Jenkins brothers were.

'Ey baby, why doncha be a good little dairy cow, and I'll be the bull... why don't we make a calf together?' Albert hummed, pulling Evelyn's hair from her face, admiring the beauty in those hazel pearls. Albert then trailed his eyes down to her tights and smirked. 'Animals don't wear pants, so drop them.' Albert purred in a demanding yet seductive voice. Evelyn knew what they were planning on doing to her. She could tell by Albert Jenkins's voice and the words he delivered to her. Like any reasonable woman being forcefully nabbed and demanded she drop her pants, she wanted nothing of it. 'Whaddya say farmgirl?' Albert asked the rhetorical question, beckoning Gordon to remove his hand and let her speak. Gordon did, and Albert knelt down to Evelyn, looking her right in the eye. Instead of giving the twisted man what he wanted, she swished her tongue around inside her mouth. Albert took it as a sign that she was thirsting for him, and his smirk broadened, then Evelyn let it out and spat a shell of spit at

him. 'Fuck you!' she censured him aggressively. 'Feisty little bitch ain't ya when you're not around your cows,' Albert simply said, wiping the bullets of saliva off his face. 'Drop those pants for me, Bobby, and Gordon, dig a hole.' Albert ordered his younger brother and his fat henchmen. The two men nodded, dirty grins creaking onto their faces. Gordon went and picked up a nearby shovel from the cow stables and began to dig up a human-sized grave in front of the barn. Meanwhile, Bobby and his long, messy beard pushed Evelyn just after Gordon had dropped her to the ground. Bobby then sat on top of her legs as he began to unbutton her tights, licking his lips and attempting to slide them off her legs. 'NO! YOU FUCKING RAPIST! GET FUCKED!!' Evelyn screamed. She tried holding her tights on, but that's when Bobby threw a smack at the side of her face, causing Evelyn to yelp out to touch the side of her face, which now threatened to swell. This gave Bobby the bittersweet moment to emphatically yank her pants from her legs and shoes, so all that remained now was her undies. 'Oh, I am sweet-tits. I'm gonna get fucked right now because you're gonna fuck me right now and I'm gonna like it very much,' he chuckled. Bobby got off Evelyn. She took this moment to try and scamper her way to her feet and hopefully into the house, where she would barricade the door and immediately ring the nearest Police Station. But she couldn't get very far as she felt someone land a kick into her back, knocking her back down. Evelyn was then vigorously turned over so she was facing Albert and his sickening mug.

He held her still with the weight of his knees. He then proceeded to tear Evelyn's undies; Evelyn heard them ripping as Albert tore them off and allowed himself unwelcome access to her. He then unzipped his fly as his junk protruded (the fucking cunt wasn't wearing any fucking undies!) out of his trousers and uncomfortably touched the hairs on Evelyn's vagina. Evelyn screamed.

'NO, GET OFF ME, YOU DISGUSTING PIECE OF SHIT!!!' she roared while trying to fight against the endeavours of Albert Jenkins, who was on top of her, holding her arms down with his hands and her legs down with his knees. Albert then shuffled himself back an inch, but he soon brought himself back into Evelyn's vagina in a sick up-and-down gesture. He repeated this over twenty times in her front while closing his eyes and moaning at the sky erotically, picking up his penis and jostling it into Evelyn's vagina... The feeling of a man's wet slimy pecker being forcibly inserted into a women's birth hole was unbearably disgusting, and Evelyn couldn't do anything to stop it. There wasn't anyone she could call out for help. She was all alone, all while Albert was making sexual moaning sounds. 'Ooh man, I'm so fuckin horny right now,' Albert slurred, continuing to violate Evelyn's virginity. Evelyn had tears engulfing her red cheeks, one of them throbbing from when Bobby had slapped her. Albert slurped up her tears with his tongue, his bottom half still working it on her. 'Yeah, I like that cowgirl.' Albert moaned, temporarily getting off her to turn her around so she was facing the dirt, and her back was meeting him; he made the same movements on her buttocks. He jammed his penis into her buttocks, snorting loudly as a way to block out the sound of Evelyn's cries and pleads for him to stop. He moaned, savouring the feeling of his penis inside her buttocks as he fucked her hard. 'Oh! Oh! Ah! Oh, YES!' Albert groaned, jacking off into Evelyn, throbbing his cock into the poor farmer's arse. The only thing she could do was scream, 'Fuck you fuck you fuck you fuck you fuck you.' Evelyn cried as she was being forced to endure the displeasure and rape at the hands of some lowlife scum and his equal lowlife brother and friend.*

Because he enjoyed the feeling a bit too much for sensible words to describe. Albert began to lose his concentration on the natural world and his sense of thinking (if he even had any, to start with), sinking into a dream-like trance where all he felt was pleasure and the awful echoing sound of his own erotic moaning. This gave Evelyn the perfect opportunity to fight back against her attacker! She used what strength she had to free a foot from his hold when he faced her, her back to the front and slurring erotic phrases at her. She hurled a fierce kick right into Albert's penis and kicked him off her. She covered the hairs of her lower half as she forcibly got to her feet to scamper straight for the house. Albert's eyes widened, and he snapped back into the real world, groaning, clutching his now sore junk. Bobby came to his brother's aid, and Albert told him to fuck off. 'Fucking bitch!' he rasped, presenting a furious and distressed order to Bobby and Gordon to bring her back so he could finish what he started on her. 'Where ya going, cowgirl.' Bobby taunted her while Gordon, belly dancing around like jelly, chased after her.

It didn't take long for Bobby to catch and bring her back, which he had done by launching himself at her, causing her to fall to the ground with a hard thud and spitting dust up around them. Gordon had gone disappeared to enter one of the barns around the house and quickly returned with some chains connected to the feet of two horses. Albert saw them and smiled briefly before clutching his aching junk as he put it back inside his pants and zipped them up, but even inside his pants, they throbbed like hell. The farmgirl was going to pay for hurting Lil Wiggles with her life, and that was something Albert promised. Fuck the farmgirl. Fuck her! 'Yes...' Albert hissed like a desert rattlesnake. 'Kill that bitch, fucking kill her!' Albert screamed, holding his crotch as he endeavoured to stand up on one foot. Evelyn was kicking and screaming, cursing at her captors while in a desperate struggle to get away from these three fuckers, call the cops and land their arses in jail, but the two men were just too strong for her. They picked up the chains tied around the horse's back legs around her arms and legs. The only thing she could do was scream and thrash around against them as they tried chaining her up. 'FUCK PIG RAPIST BASTARDS!!' she bellowed at them, sounding an echo throughout the farm, which startled the animals as they broke into a chorus of howls, caws, and other furious if not scared, noises. 'That's it, lads, chain the bitch up. Rip her apart...' Albert growled.

'They'll hang you all for this!' Evelyn condemned the three. 'Op! sorry cowgirl, but hanging has been banned since the 60s; the last person to be given the rope within 1964.' Gordon winked. Evelyn's eyes widened; tears dribbled out. 'Whoopsies, sorry, did I crush your dreams? My bad.' Gordon and Bobby laughed as they both gave the two horses one hard slap on the back, sending the horses through a frenzied state of panic. Both horses started in opposite directions. Gordon, Bobby, and Albert watched, their faces sharing the same sick expression of wonderment. At the same time, Evelyn was held defenceless, tied to horses like that some old 1700s torture method and brutal display of execution. Evelyn Davis screamed at the top of her lungs until her voice box started crackling, the ungodly feeling of her limps stretching and her insides tearing themselves apart! Her spine disconnected itself from her pelvis, serrating howls of pain throughout her body; she kept screaming as the horses tried to run in opposite directions. Evelyn's anguished, teary face contrived to look down, her screaming becoming more horrendous and agonising. She could see that her skin was ripping itself away like the times she would tear plastic coverings off bought meat, spatting drops of blood up to her top part and creating an awful red puddle beneath her. Evelyn couldn't scream anymore; her voice box was broken, and what replaced the screams were ugly husky rasps. After a turbulent splitting noise, Evelyn was pulled into two pieces. She could only watch as her legs

*were being dragged off by one of the horses across the
ground, spilling her bloodied intestines across the field
until the horse came to a stop a few feet away from where
the horse carrying her top half had galloped off to.*

*Albert, Bobby, and Gordon laughed at this... the
sickos.*

*Evelyn didn't know why and how she was still
(barely) alive... With the last flakes of strength, she
managed to unbuckle herself from the chains around her
hands. Her bottom half was gone, halfway across the farm
now... and she was left with only her arms as her only
mobility. She turned herself over, it hurt like hell... and
tried crawling across the dirt, even if she knew her efforts
were pointless; she was standing on death's door, and she
was marked to die very soon.*

*'Fucking bitch is still alive!' squawked Bobby,
seeing Evelyn slowly drag what was left of her away; as
blood trailed out from her body, covering the grass red
with her blood. She was due for death very shortly. She'd
bleed out. Bobby and the two meatheads decided to do her
a decent amount of kindness by ending her suffering and
killing her swiftly. Both Bobby Jenkins and Gordon
Macintosh sauntered over to Evelyn; meathead Gordon
then picked up one of her arms and dragged her like a
discarded, broken Barbie doll back with him. Without
needing Albert to tell him what to do next, he tossed Evelyn
into the hole he'd dug earlier like a piece of waste, and
Bobby, who had picked up the shovel next to the cavity, he
began to bury her alive! All while Albert in the background
chuckled at the grieving sight, still holding his throbbing
crotch area. Evelyn's life was snuffed out shortly after
Bobby had tossed the first spade of earth upon her. Her life
had been ripped from her. She was robbed of her*

exemplary life as an isolated farmer. Furthermore, she was deprived of her virginity in the process.

It was sometime around 2047 that the mortuus carnem found its way to her grave and infected her, urging a crawler, a destroyed version of Evelyn Davis, to rupture out from her coffin-less tomb. Shortly after rising from her grave, the military got her. They'd been alerted to an abandoned farm where the legends of an unfortunate woman who'd allegedly been raped and torn apart took place. They knew that when the woman rose, she would make a good subject for bonding because she had a story to tell, a rather gruesome but nonetheless interesting story to know for when she remembers and is ready to say to them. So, they waited by her gravesite for her to be infected. They camped by her grave, dressed in the rotting garments that Ark had worn during her previous mission to Spot's grave. They had forced themselves to get used to the smell of the disgusting garment as they waited for when the day came, as they were armed with drugs and a dog catcher's leash. When the day did come, and Evelyn emerged from the soil, a decayed crawler; they had her, quickly grabbed her, and took her back to the GFOSAR. While inside, they kept her in the Z-Storage for another nine years until she was ready to be handed over to the rookie bonder Marilyn Kolen, where she would be christened with her new zombie name, "Ace." Evelyn Davis had become the timid Marilyn Kolen's first zombie and, even better, a talking crawler named Ace.

It was in that moment of remembering her past life when Ace had remembered that grudge which she had for the three men, and she clenched her rotting, flayed fists, wanting this one chance to enact her revenge for Albert and his cronies. Not only was Evelyn Davis a simple woman living a simple life on her quiet farm, but now she was Ace,

a crawler who wanted vengeance against the men who took
everything from her.

Chapter 19

'Davis.' Ace spoke finally after being silent since she had been drugged; her voice was fairly muted but still distinguishable. Kolen glanced to look at her, wearing a face of puzzlement by what her crawler zombie had just said out of nowhere. Ace's eyes weren't meeting hers as the crawler stared absently into space. Her mind was still transfixed on the nightmarish memories of being forcibly raped and torn in half, and for what? A good laugh? 'Davis? Who's Davis? Is that someone you used to know?' Kolen coaxed Ace to continue talking. She then peered down and saw the piece of red fabric in the crawlers' hands, clenching it like a valuable inheritance. Ace was still clinging to the red bandana. She didn't endeavour to reply to her bonder as if she didn't hear her. Ace just stared ahead; her eyes wide and had tiny drops of tears leaking from them. The bandana was only a few inches shorter than it originally was when Ace, formally known as Evelyn, used to wear it, but even so, it was still wearable around forty or so years later. Ace cocked her head down and placed the bandana around her head (remembering how to put them on), tying it around the back of her head into a tight knot and keeping it underneath the hair, the way she used to when she was alive.

Kolen was amazed and confused by Ace's unnatural actions, so she asked the crawler again who Davis was. This time, she got her reply. 'That be my name, Evelyn Davis. I remember that name because of a bandana I always used to wear; this bandana was similar to the one I used to wear a lot. I know by its smell because it has same scent as me.' Ace spoke a complete sentence, sending the group members to a striking halt, enough for them to fixate their gazes upon Ace in the wheelchair (well, how about that? Zombies can remember their pasts without help). Kolen's expression was tied in shock and excitement while

Oli observed between her zombies, wondering if they might be able to remember their original selves before death. 'Well, I'll be damned, zombies can speak full sentences, and something as simple as a red piece of rag can grant them a free pass down memory lane.' Slater sounded both amazed and sarcastic as he kept kicking up his pace with the group and behind Ark. Ark was internally glad that Ace had remembered who she was and was feeling the same amount of pleasure as Kolen felt. Still, she didn't show it in vivid colour because she was further focused on exterminating Sam, avenging Fredrickson, and the rest of the people she's killed back in the GFOSAR. And to top it all off, the mortuus carnem species are put to extinction. 'When Sam is killed. Ace, you will have every treat that I can find for remembering your name and who you were. My whole intention as a bonder was to get you to remember your past life! And you did it!' Kolen jovially saluted Ace's success, remembering who she was before death. On the other hand, Ace wasn't feeling the same kind of merit as her bonder. Her death was excruciating to comprehend; moreover, hard to think about, without getting upset or astonishing the bonders further by bestowing them the once inconceivable fact that zombies could indeed produce tears. Knowing what they were and why they were crying instead of thinking, "Why is water coming from my eyes?" Ace didn't care much about being rewarded for remembering something that would fit most in a graphic horror novel. The sooner they stopped gushing about her past life, the better; Ace didn't want to relive the disgusting faces of those men, Gordon Macintosh, Albert, and Bobby Jenkins, who'd assaulted her, violated her, and murdered her. 'Not focus on me. Focus on killing Sam.' Ace grimaced, not wanting the people to see her and thank her just because she remembered the torturous pain of her insides tearing and ripping themselves apart, separating her top half from her bottom half. Only then was she finished off by being buried alive in a coffin-less tomb, her body open to flesh-eating maggots began to feast upon her decomposing dead flesh. The more she thought about her death and saw those laughing faces, just fuelled the fire in Ace, making her wish she became a ghost and could haunt her killers until the day they died and finally knew of the suffering they had inflicted upon her. But Ace didn't have enough luck as she became a useless crawler who could only speak broken English and couldn't do much in a way to help her bonder and her friends. The more Ace thought of Evelyn Davis, the more she hated herself and wanted to expire early; Evelyn had it all; she had legs, could speak English well and could actually do things for herself; Ace couldn't do any of those things. Ace was legless, spoke broken sentences and was next to useless in the group. The more she thought about it, the more hurt she became. Ace wanted to live like she had and contribute more to Kolen and the group's aid. 'But Ace or I should say, Evelyn, I'm really proud of you!' Kolen couldn't contain her tears of joy, so much so that she wanted to take them out on Ace and hug her. Ace wasn't feeling the same joy that Kolen was feeling; however, remembering her past just made the crawler depressed, so much that she wished she could just disappear and that Kolen would just forget about her.

'As much as I'd hate to admit this, Marilyn, and tear you away from this tender moment, but I agree with the crawler. Don't get ahead of yourself in glorifying her for remembering something she probably doesn't want to think about. I know exactly what it's like to be emotionally sickened. Your crawler probably died a brutal, fucked up, inhuman death; as for me… when I lost my best friend, I was visibly shattered.' Winsome sighed sadly, raising his voice and answering the question no one had asked. 'Yeah, I HAD a best friend, even arseholes like me can have friends too. So, rest assured, I wasn't always a dickhead.' Ark huffed irritably, and this time, it was she who started an unwarranted assault on Winsome. 'Yeah, yeah, we all know that you were gay for Max Engel and loved Carl Boyle, hence why you were always around him; really, no surprise there, Ryan.' Ark rolled her eyes, stepping over a charred corpse in her way and warning everyone to watch where they danced and be careful not to trip. Winsome stared, confounded at what Ark had just said to him. 'Shut up, Lisa! What do you fucking know about anything? Why don't you just be quiet and not butt in other conversations.' Winsome said, exasperated. He took a deep breath after he had said this, and both Kolen and Losnedahl could see and understand that he was trying to make an effort to keep himself at head level and not allow himself to become masked in the pointless game of fury. Slater looked at Ark and was biting his lip.

'That wasn't cool, Yo, I think you should apologise to him,' said Oli morosely. 'Keep calm, Ryan, just keep calm, she didn't mean it, she was just dicking around, she didn't mean it.' Winsome's breathing was shaking, his lips were trembling, and his grip on the shotgun was wavering. He really was trying to control and convince himself that it was just some cruel joke and that Ark didn't mean what she said about him being gay for the late Max Engel. But try as he did, and the more he thought about Ark disrespecting the most important one in his life in such a spiteful way, the harder it was for him, and he knew that he just couldn't let this one go unpunished. Ark had hurt him in ways that he had never thought possible. When Ark turned and looked at him, that was when she noticed that what she'd said was wrong, very wrong and that she'd been the one who'd spoken out of line. 'Yeah, I agree with Olivia; that was very uncalled for, Lisa. You know Ryan is passionate about things, and to make assumptions that someone is gay isn't right, and look at him, you can tell that he really is trying to redeem himself.' Kolen translated for Losnedahl. She looked nervously at Winsome, who looked like he was trying his best to fight back against the intrusive thoughts and images that were plaguing his head. But before she could come clean and apologise about what she said about his "best friend" and that she didn't mean it the way she did, Winsome's candle had already been lit, deciding he'd had enough of Ark ordering him around like some dog by the way he was hitching his shoulders and gritting his teeth. Sick of the way Ark thought she knew every bit of him and used them against him to make herself feel more powerful and untouchable. Winsome was about to show her that she wasn't indestructible and still human, just like he and the rest of the six humans. He hated being the one who was always wrong, and she was always right.

Winsome abandoned his shotgun; it landed with a loud thud that echoed through the pouring streets, and he flung himself at Ark when she wasn't looking at him; he balled his hand up into a fist, stormed at her and held a readying fist before her, but he was able to stop himself, breathing heavily with droplets of spit flying out of his gritted teeth, so, instead of hitting her, he seized her grey tees collar and pulled her towards him, where he ensued to vent at her. 'I'm trying so hard, Lisa, trying so hard to be better and calmer. Christ, I've been trying to be a better person ever since your zombie almost killed me. But you aren't making things easy for me! I have news for you, Ark! I hate it when you think of yourself as hot shit just because you have more experience with things because you're the leader; you think you know everything about me and the people who I consider friends? I mean, honestly, how goddamn inconsiderate, and selfish can you be? Yeah, I'll admit Carl Boyle was a dear friend of mine, almost like a brother, but it doesn't mean shit that I was ever in love with him, and I was not gay for Max, and to let you in on a secret, I actually didn't like him all that much, and I actually found him to be an even bigger prick than me. I was only really around him because it was part of my job. So, don't you dare make assumptions that I was ever gay for him or anyone without the proper evidence?' Winsome roared. 'I would hit you if I could, but I'm not going to, I'm going to let you sit on what you've done.'

'Ryan, calm down! You didn't even give her a chance to apologise!' Slater shouted as he and Losnedahl struggled to keep Spot at bay. Aladar violently tugged onto Spot's arm, and Spot flew back in Aladar's direction. 'I'm sorry, okay! God, you don't even give people a chance to fucking apologise if they speak out of line! And I know I spoke out of line and offended you and those you were affiliated with, and I'm sorry. But don't you go off at me for not being given a chance to say "sorry" you didn't tell us about this best friend of yours, so that's why I said that. I had just assumed, and it was wrong of me. So don't you dare accuse me of something I was about to admit was wrong?' Ark had shouted her apology to Winsome, admitting that she was sorry for what she had said and that he shouldn't go around antagonising people who are rethinking the words they had said and how those words had affected others.

He began to calm down after about three minutes of heavy but controlled breathing. 'Okay, I'm good now, Lisa... sorry.' Winsome spoke softly, lowering his head. He went back to his place beside Losnedahl, picking up his shotgun from the ground and holding it incompetently, thinking about everything irrational thing he had done up to this point and muttering curses to himself.

Ark let out a deep-sounding sigh. 'Now then... without any more interruptions as we have already wasted enough time standing here and bickering like a bunch of kindergarteners. Let's find Sam and kill her, even if that means killing other zombies on the way,' she said softly, giving her final order; for now, more orders would come later, depending on how things turn out.

Chapter 20

Somewhere inside the Heart of London city. The place where the dead mostly roamed around. One might even go as far as to say that it was an undead hotspot; one of the most populated places in the United Kingdom had ended up becoming one of its most dangerous, and unless people had a death wish or were suicidal, they were more than welcome to tread into the streets. The insufficient number of the living population would know to veer clear away from the city of London as words could not describe the horrors one would find while wandering the dead streets alone, armed with only a pistol or a knife, mere toys against a horde of the undead that would mostly take shots and stab wounds as if they were splatters of paintballs.

It was also the perfect place for Sam to get to work where she could focus on putting her plans to fruition.

She had plans of creating her own personal undead army and aiming to wipe out most of Britain's living civilisation, saving a few humans where she'd be treating them like cattle, meat that needed to grow and mature and then be harvested for those who were hungry. Once she was able to get herself a cult-like following, she was confident that not even the scarce military numbers would stand much of a chance against her because she would often always lead the undead, and set them up in a particular area to search for anything that Sam would see as food, or enlist them in her goal of rebuilding a world that was safe and respectful for the undead – a world where the undead were the reigning species and where the humans were the ones that were the slaves – that humans were the bonded experiments to be played with. Sometimes, Sam liked to play with her victims, such as about an hour and a half after she had found the wandering Linus. She and him skulked the colourless, bleak streets where Sam decided on doing some conning to get some food or to simply just kill people just to satisfy her intense desire to see blood running through her fingers. She'd told Linus to stay back and watch her, which he did. Firstly, she'd cleaned herself and her clothes with cleaning supplies stolen from a nearby pharmacy to get rid of the stench that clung to her and tearing off a piece of clothing from a nearby corpse that hadn't woken up, she clawed a deep gaping hole into the body and doused the piece of rag in the blood, then she wrapped the blood-soaked rag around her neck tightly as if it were a gauze to help cover up a broken bone or a large gaping wound such as her throat being ripped out, which would be able to explain why she'd be unable to talk. Sam practised in front of Linus, acting like a scared and helpless woman who'd just survived a vicious attack that ended in her losing her voice box in a desperate effort to get away. It was almost foolproof, and if she would be able to play the act right, she could bend the stupid and gullible humans to her will, and when the time was right – dinner time. Humans can be so naive. Sometimes, Sam picked off stragglers of these small groups. She'd make sure that Linus was watching. Once she had gotten close enough to someone that if she could breathe, it'd be felt on the neck, she'd take the bite of fate and then disappear, before anyone knew what had happened and passing the infection onto them, so when they die from the inside, they will awaken as one of the unbonded and turn against their formers, that'd be when Sam knew that her work was done. She'd leave them to look for other lives to steal. It was all part of the game that Sam created and took great delight in, and she'd continue to play this game until she either grew tired of it or if her goal was being realised. However, one thing she was still a little uncertain about was why the group continued to push forward and try to stop her when she knew their efforts would just seem foolish, seeing as there were less than fifteen of them against what Sam was hoping to create an army of over fifty or more.

Overpowering the group in not only numbers but in sheer strength, as the average zombie was about seven times stronger than the average human, and the average zombie was around 12%, or sometimes 43% more durable than the average human and could reasonably shrug off large quantities of punishment and frequently shrug off losing limbs and broken bones. So, unless you knew how to wield a gun and aim it properly, you'd stand little to no chance against the zombies that had been resurrected by the mortuus carnem and especially the ones that shrugged bullets off as if they're nothing short of paintballs.

Like always, since she left the ruins of the GFOSAR, Sam was one step ahead of the group of ten. But instead of going back and killing her enemies, she thought she'd play with them some more and make things a little harder for them by creating new members for her undead army. Sam aimed to completely terraform the once beautiful country of the United Kingdom into nothing but an empty ghost-town full of blood and misery, stopping the peace and killing anything that shows even the slightest glint of life. The only signs of life were the occasional scared human tied to a post or on a chopping block as a zombified chef, slices and cuts into their flesh and prepares it for his undead punters. A place where the grass never grows green, where the blooming flowers never blossom into vibrant colours. Where the sun is permanently shadowed behind grey melancholy clouds. The once pleasant sound of happy dogs barking and playing is nothing more than a figment of a person's imagination, and the only sounds dogs would make are the hungry growls of undead dogs as they fought over a slab of meat. Birds never chirped or tweeted sweetly in the trees unless they were crows or ravens. The only sound present was that of the ghostly howls of the wind and an eerie silence that would often drive people insane. There was an unchanging rotting stench that threatened to never lift from the air, creating an ungodly smell for the living that took residence in the still habitable houses, along with the streets constantly being drenched with blood and sometimes littered with discarded zombie limbs. Sometimes, you'd be unlucky enough to find guts that'd been turned inside out, painting the entire city of London red (Welcome to the London City, the city where you die). Sam aimed to abolish the UK country before the clock struck 3:00am, which is why the group of ten had to hurry if they wanted to stop and kill Sam and save the country. Snuff out one life to save millions.

Not long now, Mr Fredrickson, and your precious position. I hope you are watching from the spot in Hell where you reside. You are the reason your homeland is going to shit because you made me the way I am, and no one else can say that because I was the one you were "bonding" with; people may look upon you and think of you as an amazing, brilliant man; but in reality, after reading through those papers that you so just happen to drop into my cell, and when you saw me holding them up to you. The face you made when you saw that I had read them, you called them your "sins" Oh, the things I'd read in those papers. I knew that you were secretly a bad man, a sinful man, the ways you belittled me and threatened to dispose of me even if I was your first success story. The cruel way you fell in love with that stray, your "wife", Deborah. You mentioned that the only reason you married her was that you were too much of a narcissistic sociopath who couldn't give an arse rat about her feelings because you wanted to be the dominant one and wouldn't allow her to have what she wanted because you knew that your heart wasn't big enough for the other strays Deborah had in her family. You wrote that you only married her because she was "a sexy hot babe," a selfish reason to marry anyone if I do say so myself. But oh no, the sins don't end there, because you clearly stated the fact that you had a thorough hatred for the homeless and would treat them like they weren't even human and just a "stain on your coat". You claimed that you'd bash and threaten them in your notes, then it came to Deborah, oh dear sweet naïve Deborah Mikalsson. "But Deborah was different; she was an angel trapped in tramp clothing," you'd said in those notes; you'd declared that you wouldn't have any pity for her if she wasn't pretty and that she'd just be another parasite living on the street like the rest of the Mikalsson's. Oh, Mr Fredrickson, if only you could see what I'm doing with your beloved country; you'd be, of course, like any other pathetic human being; you'd beg me to stop what I'm doing because you're my bonder and that I have to abide by your orders and blah blah blah. Well, guess what, Mr Fredrickson, times have changed. I'm tired of being the saint Mary that you wanted me to be. I make my own choices; I make my own rules. In a way, Mr Fredrickson, I should be thanking you for giving me all this amount of intelligence and such a vast insight into how exhilarating killing is, and no one, not even those "friends" of yours, is going to stop me. They will just become part of my army and my vision for a better future for the undead. A future where we are at the top of the hierarchy. The top of the food chain.

The number of deaths I'm committing is almost cathartic; it's like when humans hunt for ducks, geese, and deer. It purifies the mind and soul, and damn, it feels good to see the sheer terror on the face of a human as I take their breaths from them. If you'd been better to me and were the genuine person everyone sees you as, I could've been the zombie everyone wanted me to be, a goody-two-shoes, a saviour of humanity. But where's the fun in that? What's so fun about being a goody-to-shoes. I like being bad. It makes me learn more about the world, makes me more creative, and know about my surroundings and who I'm up against. But remember, Mr Fredrickson, I know about you more than anyone else. I read through your "Sins", and I'm doing you a favour; by 2063, every single homeless person in the UK will be dead and rotting walking corpses. And at least by tomorrow, Lisa Ark and her group will have no chance of stopping me. Britain will belong to the undead. Sam articulated to herself in her twisted mind after thinking about her idea of the country's future. Sam may be a simple zombie over the 76-year AOR, but she looks human again with the surgery, and she's highly modified in intelligence. She was devoted to her mission and wouldn't quit or pause for any reason. Sam cherished her goal and the idea of a positive future for her and the rest of the undead, and she didn't care how many lives she would take; no one got in the way of Sam achieving her goal by any means necessary.

Chapter 21

The two of them took solace in an old rundown church that still had the stained-glass figure of St Lucy with her dish of eyes. Linus stared up at the holy figure, and he wished that someone would come and take out his eyes, his ears, and his tongue so that he wouldn't be able to see or hear the things Sam would do in front of him when she finds some human survivors – or taste blood and flesh on his lips as Sam would force him into eating something he didn't want. He wouldn't wish this life upon anyone, zombie or not. Being Sam's pawn was like he was being shackled around the neck and left to rot inside this dark and tiny room surrounded by your own faeces, with your own friend being a small rusted garden trowel which you'd use to carve away and eat your own flesh to keep yourself fed. Working for Sam was like being trapped inside that prison-like room without the trowel and forced into breaking. At least, that was how it felt for Linus. The worst part was that he couldn't run and escape her because he knew that she'd hunt him down and bring him back kicking and screaming and then she'd hurt him some more, his punishment for trying to betray her. Sam was keeping him in this room to break him down, to strip him away from his humanity and the progress that Henrik Losnedahl had made, and to turn him into a ravaging hungry monster whose only goal was to kill and eat anything that breathed, anything that still had a beating heart. He was petrified of her, of the sheer authority and command she had over him. He wanted to get away and escape her. Still, he knew that once he'd accepted that *gift* from her, he'd unknowingly and unwillingly bound himself to her service, to the torture in which she'd put his humanity through to mentally break him beyond repair.

He'd been sitting on his knees, flicking the tiny pebbles around him with his finger, watching them flatly as they skit across the concrete when the huge overarching doors leading into the church creaked open. She strutted inside, her bare feet stepping and pushing away broken pieces of glass and stone as they pattered up the aisle towards him. Linus cringed at the sight of her, at the sight of that grin plastered on her face and the way she had drawn the curtain of black hair from her face as she approached him. But as soon as she reached about two metres from him, he ducked his head down, avoiding that scornful gaze. Then he remembered how he'd ended up with her in the first place, how Sam had taken him away from the aimless moaning, softly wandering and craving for something he couldn't reasonably perceive what, she'd found him of all people and been the one that had enlisted him, and starting up what would be her army. Until this point, he was a lost soul, doomed to wander the streets forever, searching for something he couldn't quite understand. But then, the thing he'd been unknowingly striving for had come in the form of Sam, who'd offered him that tender, sweet, juicy brain from one of the humans she'd recently snuffed out. Linus' humanity wished he could've resisted the offer of that brain, and he knew that his bonder would've wanted him to resist it, too. Still, Linus couldn't deny the fact that he was ravenous and that he hadn't eaten anything decent since he'd been captured by the guards to be used as a bonding test subject. And so, knowing that some food was being handed out to him as if it practically had his name engraved on it, the primitive and hungry side of Linus took over, and he snatched the brain out of Sam's hand and ate it messily in front of her, sealing his fate in her hands.

-The Good Side - the human inside him, pushing through to try to take the wheel of control and do the right thing. The side that the imaginary voice Losnedahl strived to reach. The side that Sam wanted to get rid of.

-The Bad Side - the zombie in him, controlling his hunger and fogging up his sense of thinking and reason, the side that's in most zombies and the side Sam wanted more. The side that was more useful to her.

She wanted to make Linus just as intelligent and violent as her; that way, he'd have no issues killing innocent people just like her, giving more into his zombified nature and embracing Sam's immoral mind. However, with him being half-bonded, his two conflicting sides were troublesome for Sam, and he knew that by whenever he'd stare into those hating eyes, he'd see her trying to mould up an idea that would be stronger this time, one that would break the spirit of the Losnedahl voice.

The good side of Linus had a strong sense of justice and right from wrong, it also shared a heavy dislike for Sam's genocidal intentions to dispatch an entire country of its living population. He unintentionally had the same motives as Henrik Losnedahl and the rest of the group. Yet, Linus's bad side drank up Sam's plans like drinking blood from a goblet, following her every order (even if it was in zombie language), even if it meant killing certain people in their way and not giving them a chance to defend themselves, if the prospect of getting food was in the deal, then his zombie side would obey without question, because as far as Sam and he knew, there were no other bonded zombies roaming around London, Linus was the one that she'd found and the one that she thought would be the most useful in her gains. His zombified side overpowered his humanity, and he had more control over his actions. In contrast, his humanity just had to watch through the boy's dead eyes, powerless to do anything against Sam's wishes, and that is one of the reasons why the boy suffered a lot while working with Sam. He'd captured people for Sam; if she wanted specific individuals, he'd get them, cutting them with anything sharp he could find and extracting blood into small cups which Sam had thrown down at him from their screaming bodies that'd been beaten almost to death by Sam herself as she was brutal when she'd beat them. To avoid ending up like the beaten, Linus had no choice but to cut fingers and toes off and small cubes the size of tea bags of meat and suckle onto them like a lollipop. He'd do this not for himself but for other zombies that came into the building with Sam, farming humans for food. When Sam gave him the swipe over the neck, he'd use said sharp object to carve into the human scalp and skull while they were still alive and remove their brains, which he would pass to Sam, as she's one who always got the best parts. The rest of the suffering human would be for the rest of the starving undead.

He hated it, but he couldn't do anything to help it, and that was his curse, the curse of being undead and having Sam as his boss.

The good side of Linus had come out around the time of 7:50pm. He sat underneath the figure of St Lucy, hesitantly lowering his head towards his master like a servant towards his cruel, barbaric king. Then Linus heard another female voice, and he looked up, scared to see that his master was currently dragging a defenceless human woman and a younger-looking woman, which could've been her teenage daughter, behind by their legs. He jolted back, startled when Sam tossed the two women in front of him like they were bags of trash, and watched as the two frightened females scattered to their knees, coming close and holding each other closely while darting their petrified eyes towards him and their captor. Linus looked up at his master, and judging by the way she'd grinned that horrible smile at him and lowered her eyes in a sneer at him, he could tell what she was hinting for him to do, and god almighty, he'd loathed this next part. He'd done it once already, which was enough for him to grow an unyielding hatred for this next process. It was his job to flay off pieces of their skin, to cut and drain blood from open orifices, and sometimes amputate limbs, with both Sam and Linus feeding on those parts themselves or feeding them to any hungry zombie that lurked around like some twisted charity for the undead.

He looked down at his pale hands, which were still soaked with the blood of the brain Sam had offered him previously. He observed the fresh red tint mixed with his darkened blood and the dirt smeared on his palms, and he wanted to rub his hands clean from those abhorrent colours. Linus's good side resented the sight of blood on his palms, and therefore, he couldn't bear the knowledge that he's killing people just for this witch's sadistic pleasure; he might as well be a tyrant's pet and say goodbye to his own free will. But because of being dead and his zombified hunger caused him to lash out at someone simply out of starvation reason. Try as he might, try as he may, he couldn't resist the urge to lick the blood off his hands because for any zombie to have such ripe living blood on their hands was like getting one's hands into the targeted cookie jar when the folks weren't observing. Accomplishing the master plan of successfully stealing some cookies from the pot. Linus licked at the blood on his hands, turning his hand around and licking it all around like it was some hand-shaped icy pole. Yet, that wasn't even close to enough to sedate his ever-expanding hunger (he needed more than just crimson liquid), and Linus started taking nibbles at pieces of loose dead skin hanging from his fingers. He even went as far as to bite and tug away at the skin on his hand, assaulting himself until a piece of dead skin was torn off his hand where it hung loosely from his teeth. Linus then swallowed it, eating away at himself. It wasn't common for the undead to start eating and flaying away at themselves, but at the same time, it wasn't unheard of. It would often be found in bonders' reports, depicting why zombies eat themselves and that they tend to do it only because they can't sniff out anything living, and they have no other options but to eat the putrefied flesh from their own bodies. Disgusting thought, but the undead would go to extreme lengths for a decent meal, and Linus tearing at his own body was no exception. Sam watched him for the first part and simply shook her head. She didn't mind him eating away at himself and the uncomfortable chewing and flesh-ripping noises accompanying him. She didn't care what he did to himself as long as he wasn't in her way and doing anything to provoke a violent reaction from her. Linus, from the other side of the room, stopped devouring himself shortly after he'd torn off quite a large portion of skin off his forearm and had almost choked when trying to swallow it, so he ended up spitting it out where it landed on the floor like a deflated balloon. Eating himself did nothing to soothe the growling desire in his stomach. He needed living blood, needed skin, and needed brains. He looked at the petrified woman with blonde hair and her equally frightened daughter with dyed purple strings in her brown hair as they held onto one another, tears streaming down both their cheeks as they stared at Linus, fearing the hungry glint in his eyes.

'I don't want to die, mum.' The purple-haired girl murmured to her mother, who held her closely, not saying anything soothing in return. Linus was in pain; he wanted to rip himself apart and tear his own ribcage out before he could lay a hungry finger on the two women. He desperately fought with himself, clutching his head, groaning as his feet carried him, stumbling over to the two humans Sam had captured. The two scuttled away from him as best as they could, trying to hide their presence by making themselves appear smaller as they huddled even closer. Linus fell to his knees, fingernails digging into the concrete platform. He gritted his teeth and smacked himself in the face in different directions, even smashing his head down on the concrete floor below until he'd opened up a new orifice on his forehead, prompting some dark red blood to dribble out. Linus glanced up at the smooth-faced mother as if begging her to do something she didn't know how to do. Then Linus held up his hands, which had felt heavy like he was trying with all his might to rebel against a puppeteer holding his arms back with wires. Still, despite the uncomfortable tugging in his wrists. He pushed forward, reaching his arms out. He began to lift his hands and fingers up to communicate with them in BSL as that was what he'd been taught by his former bonder Henrik Losnedahl, trying to hint to them on basic gestures, wanting to prove that he hadn't wanted to do all these barbaric things that Sam was making him do. If Linus had his way and could think as clearly as Sam could and didn't have to worry about his bad and hungry side, his good side would make him rebel against Sam and give this woman and her daughter a chance to escape with their lives. Something they wouldn't get another chance at. Linus wanted to tell the women to get up and run as far away from here as possible (find a man without a tongue. He can help you; find him; I don't know how much longer I can hold back). But the woman and her daughter hadn't understood any of the forms of basic Sign Language that Linus tried communicating in. Both mother and daughter just kept themselves huddled together like they were trying to assimilate with each other, mother and daughter sharing the same body (that's a sci-fi horror in a half). They both scuttled away in terror, wanting nothing more than to be as far away from him as possible. Fearing the black-haired tyrant's 5-year AOR corpse in front of them. Let alone the one that captured them and brought them here to be farmed and fed to a bunch of hungry zombies patrolling the outside.

Linus whimpered. He knew they were afraid of him. He knew it, because it hurt him, more than Sam could ever do to him. He knew the words he wanted to say to them, never mind the matriarch, I'll deal with her. You just get yourselves to safety and away from here. Linus wanted to speak; he tried to convey his message so severely and tell the women to get away while Sam was distracted and that he'd personally take the punishment of degression from Sam. But he didn't know how to, mainly because his ex-bonder was a permanent mute. So, Linus had to make do with what he'd learnt from the short time he was with Losnedahl. Young, broken-minded Linus shifted his index finger up to his mouth. He bit at the tip of the finger hard enough to cause himself more pain and make himself bleed a mahogany shade of red, wanting to show them that he could still bleed and could still be hurt just like any other person. The woman backed up even more, letting out a disgusted yelp as she held onto her dyed purple-haired daughter closely at what Linus did. But the fear inside them was beginning to relax and both females cocked their tear-stained faces over to scrutinise what Linus was doing now. He was using the blood from his bitten finger to write a clear English message in blood to them, hinting that he was one of the bonded zombies from that old building simply known as the GFOSAR. Further informing them that his good side still had some shards of humanity and that he meant no harm to them. However, his evil side was clearly hostile, and he wouldn't think twice about lashing out at them and turning them into some kind of meal.

To keep the message clear, Linus would have to gnaw at his finger just to make it bleed more, allowing him to continue using it as a pen, much to the disgust of the women huddled close, watching his every moment with sheer terror stitched to their faces.

I know you are scared of me because I am dead, and you have been brought here so I can torture and feed to that scary zombie named Sam. I am sorry; I do not want this; I wish I could do

He was about to finish his little blood message by
telling them that when they find Losnedahl, his zombie
Linus says, "I'm sorry." When Sam, who'd secretly been
eavesdropping from the obscured shadows of the night after
she'd quickly decided to utilise the mortuus carnem to
awaken some formally dead animals and sick them out onto
their former owners. She'd taken an interest in what had
caused Linus to become too quiet. So, she peered over to
see him with those humans she'd captured and to make sure
he's unsuspicious of her. Sam thought about sinking herself
inside the shadows to watch him, curious about what he
was doing with those two humans. So, one can quickly
assume that she wasn't very impressed by Linus's actions;
watching him trying to communicate with his food was like
imagining a spider helping a fly out of its web. It was
foolish, and Sam didn't like it. So, like any disciplinarian or
parent, Sam thought the best way to make Linus realise
who he was and who she was and that she doesn't take
treason lightly was to punish him psychically.

Sam narrowed her eyes. She stepped out from the
shadows, looming behind Linus as the women let out
another fearful yelp, pointing, alerting him of Sam's
presence behind him. Linus swung his head around to face
Sam, narrowing her eyes down at him for disobeying her
strict order about not speaking with his food. Linus's eyes
broadened; he was about to usher the woman and her
daughter outside to where they could be safe and where
they could run away. But Sam had other intentions for
them, evil intentions.

She stormed over to Linus, who tried to back up along with the mother and daughter. Sam seized him by his navy-blue tee shirt and hoisted him off the ground as the boy zombie's dangling feet kicked and his fists punched at Sam's wrists. Sam showed little reaction to Linus's weak attempts to thwart her; her eyes just narrowed as she retracted her hand back and forth, hurling the boy zombie at the two huddled females who finally decided to make a last-minute breakaway as they both jumped to their feet at the same time, refusing to let each other go. But the woman's leg ended up being caught underneath Linus as he was being launched right into them, causing her leg to twist back so far and so violently that the bones had become dislodged, giving the woman a searing feeling in her leg. The woman hissed from the pain as her daughter tried to crawl over to aid her now-injured mother, temporarily ignoring Sam as she advanced onto Linus once more like an imposing horror monster. Sam picked up Linus again, this time by his neck and shot him like a fired bullet at the wall behind the two humans. Linus, still lodged in his good side, hit the wall and instantly fell to the ground; pebbles of plaster and dust rained down on him as Sam's powerful throw caused quite the damage to the wall, creating a small crater. Linus didn't have anywhere near as much energy, not even as much as the power Sam did, so there wasn't much he could do when it came to fighting back against a highly modified zombie. However, despite her skinny physical appearance, Sam was more innovative and more powerful than him, and she'd easily win any fight with him or anyone else if it came down to it.

At this point, Linus had given up trying to fight her, as he knew he couldn't win, so he just allowed any sort of pain to befall him. Sam picked him up by his tee-shirt once more, and with a short swing, she tossed him like a ball of paper to the floor where he lay there sputtering out blood and spit, unable to do anything, just admit defeat and allow Sam to do whatever she pleases.

Sam, of course, knew that the humanity sleeping inside Linus was going to be troublesome to her and her plans. Still, she'd never expected him to commit such a shameful act of trying to help humans around her presence. Sam had presumed that killing an innocent teenage girl along with her protective mother would damage Linus's good side to an extreme that it might even cause his bad side to be unleashed from seeing all the blood spilt, all the blood that was his for the taking. Sam glanced over at the beaten Linus before turning said attention to the blonde mother and dyed purple-haired daughter, the daughter of whom, in tears, was hastily in the process of making a splint out of some of the wooden sticks that were lying about for her mother's dislocated leg. Sam brought her gaze back to Linus, who was staring at her timidly, knowing that she was going to kill them in front of him by the way she wore that smirk, that damn smirk. Then, still glancing his way, Sam approached the humans and forcefully tore the daughter away from her mother; the handmade splint flung out of the teenager's hands as Sam chucked her out of the way while the mother screamed out for her daughter, screaming out the name, 'Lauren!'

The mother's screaming was swiftly silenced by Sam, who held the mother by her jawline and rammed her fist down the woman's throat, causing the woman to make unpleasant choking noises as Sam's fist moved sharply down the throat. All while Lauren shrieked from the horror of seeing her own mother being snuffed out. The woman was slowly and painfully dying from air loss as her face started to go a slight blue, purplish tint. Sam glanced at Linus's disturbed, twitching face while her fist was still inside the woman's mouth; she removed her fist from her jaws as the woman's colour slowly started to return to its original colour. But that wasn't enough suffering to satisfy Sam. Before the woman and her daughter Lauren could think about what she was going to do next, Sam threw her fingers into the woman's throat again and ripped out the woman's tongue, as well as knocking a few of the teeth out from their gums.

Sam stared wickedly at Linus, holding the tongue out to him as if teasing him with it, while the woman wailed in choked agony (*Oh look! Losnedahl has a female counterpart*! Sam thought dastardly to herself). Linus was whimpering and even making constricted cries, trying desperately to keep a fair hold of his good side and not give into his undead instincts, but the hunger inside him was too great. He got off the ground upon finding the energy and, like some primitive, uneducated person, snatched the slithering warm human tongue from her and energetically shoved it into his mouth, consuming it like a treat. Sam smiled evilly at that. That evil, disgusting smile that everyone instantly knew that Sam would commit vile murder in a most brutal, inhuman way! Sam clutched the woman by her chin, forcing the woman to face her and to stare into the lifeless eyes of the devil herself. She dug her fingers back inside the woman's trap; the woman wailed, gagged screams in excruciating pain as her own blood poured out of her mouth and filled her throat with nothing but the disgusting red liquid coating Sam's fingers. Sam clutched the bottom jaw and the top half of the woman's head and smiled a scary, rotten grin. Sam merely smiled at this and pulled away at the woman's jawbones. Lauren blocked her eyes with her hands, but even that wasn't enough to snuff out the gruesome ripping sounds that were heard coming from the woman's jaws; Lauren could only imagine what Sam was doing to her mother and wished it could just stop, wishing she had a gun to shoot herself with. Sam pulled more, spit-spattered her face, and finally, she ripped the woman's jaw off her skull. Brutally killing her, inducing in the blood to come gushing out like a volcano of blood, spraying anything crimson in the way. Lauren, although thankfully hiding her eyes from the sight, had screamed at the top of her lungs from hearing her mother's anguished screams, the horrible tearing noise and the sound of liquid hitting the floor, hinting that her mother had had her jaw torn off and her blood was spilling around her. Sam next went over to the screaming Lauren, shovelled up one of Lauren's feet and snapped the bone inside, sending Lauren on a glass-shattering wave of screams. But Sam, now tired of hearing the same anguished song, instantly silenced the screams by firmly dragging Lauren's foot away so that Lauren lay screaming in front of her. Next, Sam raised her bare foot above Lauren's head and bore it down on her head, splatting Lauren's head apart like a watermelon being caved in by a hammer.

Just as Sam had predicted, Linus's good side was shut away instantly from seeing just how far Sam was willing to go when it came to killing people. His nasty, killer side was quickly unleashed. Despite Linus's travails in trying to keep a firm grip on his humanity, Sam had evidently won over his bad side again and continued ordering him around like a dog.

Chapter 22

The group had arrived in the middle of London now. Yet, for some reason, it was eerily quiet compared to what it had been; the rain had been temporary and had ceased about half an hour ago, and along with that, the sounds of the undead eating and shuffling along the streets, dragging their broken legs behind them couldn't be heard as if they had either moved on to another area of London or perhaps, more eerily, Sam had planned something for them and that she'd probably conveyed a message to the neighbouring undead's to be silent as if she'd known the group would end up around here at some stage. There'd be some kind of explanation for the hauntingly quiet atmosphere that they'd wandered into. Winsome and Oli both had come up with the same similar idea that the undead were indeed skulking around London, but they were hiding in the alleyways or abandoned buildings, feeding soundlessly behind closed doors, distracted by what they currently had in their clutches and paying no attention to the humans walking around outside. Winsome had also conveyed a quiet message that he didn't like the quiet, he didn't trust the serene, and that was something that Ark had agreed with. She didn't like the quiet that the Heart of London produced. Whatever the reason behind the stillness of the Heart of London, it furthermore created a nasty taste in their abdomens, and they knew that they'd better find someplace safer.

Better get ndoors soon before a zombie dog or cat sniffs them out, alerting the resident zombies to their location. Another reason why the group needed to flee the Heart of London was that they wouldn't want to wait around and see what would happen if the zombie animals found them. Maybe that was the reason why it was quiet; perhaps the Heart was where the zombified animals came out; maybe it was the place where they sniffed around for anyone unlucky enough to be caught in their scent. Undead animals could be a lot quieter and more discreet than regular human zombies, as was discovered about a year ago when the late Kushiro tried to bond with an undead cat, so that would make some sense and would provide some explanation behind the city's haunting silence.

But that was only a remnant of what Sam had in store for them. What she'd planned to slow the group, and she had an idea of who she had on her list of victims to toy with. During those days when Sam was still undergoing the bondation period with Fredrickson, Sam succeeded in peaking her ears and eavesdropping on a particular conversation between some male bonders she didn't know who were discussing random topics. Things like work, their own zombies, dinner plans, and even going as far as mentioning an ongoing rumour about Losnedahl wanting to meet his dead mother for the first time (how her corpse was smuggled and bought to be sold on the black market and that she was buried somewhere in the cemetery across from the GFOSAR). How he wanted a chance to bond with her so he'd finally understand the concept of what she was really like for himself since his ma had blown her brains out with a shotgun shortly after he was born. "Why? Because Henrik doesn't want to quote-on-quote, talk about it. He's very delicate when people discuss his father and the death of his ma. And who could really blame him? Like the man got his tongue literally fucking cut out soon after he was born after his mum had offed herself. So, whatever you do, Jayden, don't mention anything about what I've said to Henrik or Ryan because you know how that cockney prick gets when it comes to rumours." Sam had remembered that conversation between those two, and the very idea of resurrecting Losnedahl's dear mother had become an aspiring if not a cruel, dream. The opportunity to reunite son with his mum was just too great to pass up, and she wouldn't need to fret about giving the deceased Eir

Losnedahl any orders about hunting down her son and the others he accompanied. Sam would just use the mortuus carnem on her and let her go with the flow. If she found and killed Losnedahl, it was a bonus, and if Losnedahl killed her, either way, Sam didn't really care. When Sam had evidently escaped from the confinement of her cell, she didn't even bother going to the nearby cemetery those bonders had spoken of. The one labelled ANGEL'S REST CEMETERY. Sam concluded that catching just one of the mortuus carnem parasites would be a chore on its own, even if she did strive and succeed in capturing one, only to sacrifice it for Eir Losnedahl's life. She might've already been awoken by the mortuus carnem way before Sam had even gotten to her (mummy wants to see her little boy now). So, instead, Sam's mission was to find the wondering Eir Losnedahl and to purposefully take her into the Heart, where she would position her right in the middle of the Heart where Eir Losnedahl would stay and soundlessly wait for her son's eventual appearance as like the discussions she had heard outside her cell, Losnedahl, despite never getting the chance to meet his mother in person, had a deep connection with her and the memories that had been told to him about her.

So, Sam thought that she'd grant him his wish and reunite the mother and son for a one-time family reunion. The significance of what would happen when the two eventually meet doesn't have any meaning for Sam. She hadn't much relished keeping Eir Losnedahl as one of her own personal lapdogs; to Sam, Eir Losnedahl was just as expendable as every other brainless zombie that hadn't had a trip to the GFOSAR. Sam didn't care if she got killed by the group or another survivor; hell, it wouldn't imply any importance if Losnedahl had managed to bond with her! Though it would take some time, due to both Losnedahl's missing some kind of body part, bonding would be next to impossible, and Losnedahl wouldn't have much joy in bonding with her, even if he tried and tried. So, when it came down to the facts, Eir Losnedahl was just another expendable zombie to wander the streets of London, just another obstacle for the group to vanquish. However, much like Sam had planned, she expected Eir Losnedahl to lure her son to her, and then she'd deliver the blow and reunite with him in their undead life.

Chapter 23

Losnedahl travelled loosely behind Kolen, escorting Ace through the red crimson marshes of blood and guts. He was primarily used to the grisly sight of fresh entrails, but there would always be something about them that'd make him feel sick in his stomach. But he cringed in silence because that was all he could do. He then threw an arm around his chest and rubbed under his armpit in a feeble and desperate attempt to keep himself warm, but it didn't seem to work for him; Losnedahl felt eerily cold, right now, like the hands of the unresting ghosts had grown a fascination with him and were caressing him and it wouldn't matter how much he'd tried to maintain a decent sense of warmth throughout his body. He suddenly stopped and looked around; the sickening feeling was back in his stomach, and the ominous feeling that he was being watched – that all of them were being watched by someone hiding in the shadows of the long-abandoned department stores.

Losnedahl quietly walked up to Kolen and tapped her on the shoulder to get her attention. She looked back at him and asked what was wrong, and he explained that he just didn't feel right and that he could feel eyes on him, watching him. Watching all of them. Taking his dreadful words to thought, Kolen looked about her, and he witnessed her shuddering and breathing into her hands to try to warm them up. 'Ooh, it's fresh, isn't it. You think we should go into one of the stores and borrow some coats?' she asked, and Losnedahl quickly replied by shaking his head. Losnedahl pushed Ace closer to Kolen, and with a free arm, he draped it over Kolen's shoulder and pulled her close to him to keep her warm; she held him back and thanked him for looking out for her. Losnedahl nodded, but he didn't look at her; his eyes continued to scan cautiously around as if he were a robot taking in the environment where it'd been positioned; he kept his eyes in front and around him, not thinking for a second about his gaze falter as he pushed Ace's wheelchair forward, while also keeping Kolen safe and warm under his bulk, which wasn't much, he wasn't a heavy or broad man. He took a deep breath, which only led to his breathing becoming irregular, waiting for something to jump out at them. 'Hey, you two okay, back there?' Oli had wondered in a soft, concerning voice, making him flinch, breaking the prolonged eerie silence as she held the revolver in one hand and used the free hand to envelop her older brother's neck so she wouldn't fall from his arms as he carried her.

Losnedahl signed a reply to her, expressing his deep dislike of how it was too quiet, that something felt unnaturally off about how silent it was and that it'd almost seemed like a pure coincidence that the temperature had suddenly dropped as if they'd wandered into the playground for the neighbouring ghosts and other phantoms that wanted him to come over and join them in their little game. 'What'd he say, Mrs Kolen? My BSL isn't up to date, sorry.' Oli quizzed.

'He said he doesn't like how silent and still it is and how it seems oddly too cold here; he gets the feeling that something doesn't feel right.' Kolen translated. Oli looked around also and hugged her arms. 'Yeah, I can agree; something feels off. Usually, London would be crawling with the undead and the sounds of eating. Nope, I don't like this… Whatever the hell this Sam witch has planned for us, I don't like it… the thought alone of what she might be cooking up gives me the creeps. As for this silence and odd temperature drop… It's an obvious sign of something amiss. I don't know much about the weather, but I still don't trust this. Best everyone be on guard.'

'Lisa. I don't want to be that guy who suggests we dismiss from the task at hand, but it's gotten a bit too cold. Do you think maybe we should go look for some coats and extra layers? And you, wait it out until something comes along our way?' Winsome asked Ark in a small voice. Ark considered the idea of putting a halt to their mission to go look for some extra clothing. But feeling the same way that Losnedahl was feeling, she wasn't taking any chances and didn't trust the abandoned stores; something dangerous could lurk behind the doors and welcome signs. Very much like Losnedahl, she didn't like the fact that the Heart of London was so... well... empty. Based on the knowledge that she knew, London City, usually known for blossoming with packs of people with bags of shopping, now as she and company passed through, she saw that the city was lifeless, nothing compared to the stories she'd heard about the once famous city. The darkened black sky gave off a haunting yet dangerous feeling; soon, it would be completely dark, and no one wanted to be out in the open for when that would eventually happen. The light from the lampposts conjured little but durable light. Everything had felt safe and tranquil, yet at the same time, deadly and scary. It gave one the constant gut feeling that they weren't alone and someone was behind them, watching them from among the darkness, wearing some night-vision visors on their heads as they stalked their preferred target.

'Jeez, it's so cold.' Kolen shivered. '-and for Autumn, is this normal?'

'Not really,' said Oli. 'We've had cold Autumns before, but this feels different.'

'Almost like winter?' shivered Ark.

Oli nodded, rubbing her arms with her hands. 'Yeah, like winter. Maybe, and here's hoping we find someplace that we can rest up and get out of the night and the terrors it'll bring, we can find some extra layers there that we can have.'

'That sounds like a fantastic idea. But before it gets dark, we should walk under the lampposts.' Winsome finished.

Ark agreed with Winsome and escorted them over to the line of lampposts where she and co. pressed on through the Heart, trying to keep their heads underneath the light of the lampposts as the night's light would only become more invigorated as the day closer to a close. Then, the group suddenly came to a ceasing stop when Oli was alerted to the familiar groans of her zombie Zinni calling out for her attention. 'Eh? What is it, Zinni?' she said, seeing Zinni make his way through the crowd of people before him and stopping in front of Slater carrying Oli. Zinni handed something to her. Oli dismissed the jokes tentatively, putting the revolver down her shirt, taking the cylinder-shaped item from Zinni's offering hands and examining it in her own before flicking a switch on its side. A powerful and bright gush of light burst from the cylinder object, right into Oli's eyes, causing her to shield her eyes and yelp 'OH!' a bit before coming to the apparent conclusion that it was a torch and something they'd very much needed at this time. 'You okay, Olivia?' Ark questioned after hearing her yelp before Oli fingered the flashlight off button. 'My eyes are in my brain!' she whined, holding the flashlight out for someone else to grab and operate. Zinni took it back from her and, on Oli's command, had given it to Winsome, who then gave it to Ark, who put the rifle around her as she took the flashlight from Winsome, clicked it and lit up the grisly, blood-soaked path before them. 'It's got some intensity to it, just what we need.' Ark said as she turned on the torch, stopping in her tracks when the light of the torch illuminated; a peculiar headless zombie in a blinding white dress that seemed made of silk staggered out of the shadows behind one of the many ruined shops into the flashlight's line of view. There was something otherworldly about a particular headless corpse shrouded in white, something that didn't sit well with the group members and gave them a haunted vibe, almost like they were seeing the ghosts of the residents, and that was going to have to get used to the idea that seeing these ghostly residents was going to be a common sight for them.

London truly was a haunted place.

'Oh shi- we're dinner!' cried Winsome. 'You want me to take it out?' he asked her, but Ark just held up her fist to stop him. 'No, this one is headless; if we're quiet, we can move around without trouble.' Ark insisted in a soft, hushed voice.

Losnedahl's blue eyes locked on this zombie that stood dreamily in the flashlight's beam, having no reaction to its blinding flare as it was without a head (similar to Spot, but he still had his bottom jaw and tongue). Therefore, making it permanently blind like that old crone. Kolen had dispatched before the group's eventual meeting with the eccentric Olivia Slater. His heart skipped two beats, and he felt as if his life had just prematurely flashed before his eyes.

"Even if you did meet your mother again, Henrik, which is probably a never. You'd be greeted by a horrifically botched corpse of a woman with her head looking like a squashed tomato, and that's something I don't ever wish upon you, dear Henrik, considering the abuse and trauma Joakim has put you through. The last thing I'd want my nephew to see is the rotting headless body of your mother." The calm yet ominous advice of his late aunt

Annette replayed in his head, reminding him of what he'd see if he met his reanimated mother wandering across the dank streets of dead London. He stared, body frozen with shock and eyes dripping with tears at the headless zombie woman, whose head looked very much resembled that of a squashed tomato, and that white shroud that dragged behind her in the freezing breeze; he remembered something his aunt had told him, that his mother had been buried in a long, white silk cocktail dress with dried splotches of blood, seeing as that was the outfit which she'd taken her life in. There was no mistaking that the walking body in front of him fits the description his Aunt Anette had warned him about. Her words had never been more accurate than at this point in time, as she had said; the aging Henrik Losnedahl got the horrific surprise he was warned about and could immediately put identification on it. Losnedahl saw his mother for the first time, even as a headless zombie; he could tell it was her, and he felt like he was gonna bawl from seeing this (*You bitch... you positioned her here for me to find. How dare you. When I find you, I'll gut you like a slaughtered pig*). Without his control, he pulled the bowie knife from his pocket, gripping the handle tightly as he started to slowly advance forward. He knew what he had to do. 'Mr Henrik?' Ace had been the first to question him, seeing the troubled Losnedahl pass her and approach Slater and Oli; without looking at them, his eyes remained fixed on the headless zombie before him; he beckoned his knife out to her.

Losnedahl had tears stinging his eyes; he tried to hold the tears back, but eventually, they came out, and it was like he'd turned into a young boy at this very moment. The man whom Ark, Winsome and Kolen had come to know had seemed to vanish. It was as if Losnedahl had been reverted back into a mere thirteen-year-old boy who'd only started having dreams of a time when the apparition of Eir Losnedahl would be calling to him in her ghostly form, beckoning him to end the pain and join her. Losnedahl couldn't help but let the tears fall as he stared at what remained of his mother. The woman who'd conceived him right before cashing herself out early and leaving him at the mercy of the brutish Joakim. *'The amount of times I would imagine this moment playing out in my head, the sheer number of times I would envision what you would be like if you finally got the chance to meet your son, as I, too, am finally meeting my mother at this very millisecond... I only pray that you will allow me to help you to regain your humanity again; others may tell me that it's preposterous, but fuck'em, I'll do my best. I have longed so long for this moment.'* Losnedahl's thoughts had trailed off as he drove ever closer to the headless zombie. The sound of his footsteps merited the zombie's attention (even without visible ears, she could hear, yet again, feel his presence). *'It's me, Henrik Eir Losnedahl. You don't know me because you sadly took yourself out before you got a chance to adequately meet me in person. Your older sister Anette was the one who named me after she took me away from Dad. She had told me all about you, and her words have forever been stuck in my head. Filling my head with dreams and thoughts of what would happen if this moment became a reality. Although sadly, I can't talk to you like how an average person would because my bastard of a father had blamed me for your death, and he cut out my tongue as a punishment, leaving me permanently unable to speak.'* Losnedahl had moved his mouth into the words he was saying. He imagined responses from her in his mind. Almost as if he was engaging in the very much-desired conversation with his dead mother, whom he'd waited forty-plus years to meet.

'Oy!' Winsome called out to him. 'Henrik, are you fu-'

'Shut up, Ryan! That's his mother (*at least I hope it is for Henrik's sake*); let the man have this one thing. He's been waiting for this moment his whole life.' Ark hushed Winsome by throwing her palm over his mouth. She knew what zombies were like when they got startled; they went into a violent frenzy. So, the quicker she shut Winsome up and let Losnedahl have this moment to himself, the better, though she did keep the light on the zombified Eir Losnedahl, plainly for Henrik Losnedahl's safety. But Losnedahl had forgotten all about his friends as he now stood in front of Eir's walking corpse. Eir turned to face his direction upon hearing his footsteps come to a halt, which sounded close, determining that Losnedahl was right in front of her and that he was hurting as much as he was elated to finally meet her in person and not in his dreams. Losnedahl slowly stretched out his arm to touch the white silked fabric his dead mother wore on the shoulder, which had extended below her feet; hence, she was wearing her white death shrouds; his hand was open, his fingers spread out. Slowly and gently, he made his first physical contact with his mother; he'd placed his free hand on her shoulder and began stroking it placidly as his face became more contorted with the more tears that fell from his eyes. *'I love you so much, Mum, even if you are this horribly disfigured zombie, I'm... I'm just so happy I got to finally meet you in person...'* he lip-synced with his thoughts, even going as far as to try and recreate it in words, but it came out as an obscure mesh of sounds. 'A-Ah ru-ruve o-o-ou mu-mu-a-am.' which had taken a heap of energy out of him if he even tried to speak normally for the first time in about fifty-five years.

The tears were really flowing now. He gently pulled Eir over to him in a hug, careful not to startle her to the point where she viewed him as a threat, and her first natural instinct would be to spring into the action of attacking him. Losnedahl sobbed like a little baby; his head was planted into Eir's dead, rotting shoulder as he cried. A grown man tearfully embraces the headless body of his deceased Mum. He tried to control his tears by wiping them with his fingers, or to at least stop them from pooling out of his eyes at such a feverish speed, soaking his already blood-soaked cheeks and creating the illusion that he was crying blood. But who'd blame him for wanting to get the waterworks flowing? This moment had meant everything to him! He'd dreamt of meeting his mother in person for over forty years. Even if she did visit him as a ghost, that was more than acceptable for him. As long as Losnedahl wasn't in a dream-like state. His mind being crystal clear. His body was awake and aware of the freezing temperature that Eir Losnedahl had brought with her when she finally came to visit her little boy, who'd grown into a respectable yet fairly handsome-looking, fifty-seven-year-old man. *'I'm so happy! Yet, I'm also really sorry, but I have to do this.'* Losnedahl sobbed; he held the revolver in both hands, examining it like it was an egg that the mother bird had abandoned, still with a vice grip, but his hands were shaking; he didn't know what sensation he was feeling. But he knew that he couldn't let his mother continue to wander the streets like this forever, doomed to never see her son's adult face for the first time, doomed to never experience the loving embrace of peace. Losnedahl knew what he had to do... he had to put his mother out of her misery for good. Losnedahl, as much as it hurt him, stepped away from the cold yet welcoming embrace of his undead mother; with the revolver clutched in his shaking fingers, he brought it up and aimed it at where the heart was. His heart was bleeding, his mind was in a violent state of unease, and he wished to God that there was another way that Eir Losnedahl could be saved, he had wished that there was a way that he could bond with her and make her better, but there wasn't, he hated that, and this was the greatest mercy he could offer her.

But then Losnedahl dropped aim of the revolver, where it slipped out of his fingers and hit the floor. He couldn't bring himself to shoot her in the heart. At this point, Henrik Losnedahl wanted to give himself to God, pick up the revolver from the floor and shoot himself plainly in front of the group's horrified faces. But that was when the flashlight's beam started to become brighter, and the circle of light began to jog and bounce as footsteps approached him. Ark had carefully and calmly addressed him, still holding the case of the flashlight. Ark fished the revolver from the ground without saying anything and put it in her dusted lab coat's breast pocket as she regarded miserably the broken expression of her Norwegian friend. Ark put her fist tenderly on his shoulder. Losnedahl didn't look at her. Ark then handed the bowie knife that she'd taken back from Oli and held it in front of him. Losnedahl stared at her saddened face; his own was a harsh red shade, and he was an ocean of tears. Ark nudged the knife in front of him. He took it soundlessly from her, bowing her thanks, bent one in return in a reminder of what he had to do. Losnedahl sighed, wiping his eyes as he looked at the lingering Eir Losnedahl standing still. Ark placed an arm on his shoulder, giving it a light pat before she moved backwards, keeping the light's beam trained on Eir Losnedahl's still frame and that haunting white dress that lit her up.

Losnedahl stepped towards the white dress and the dried blood patches that accompanied it. Knife in hand, he embraced for the final time before mouthing in his native tongue, *'Jeg er lei for det, mamma. Jeg elsker deg.'* He then raised the knife, trembling a bit, and plunged it into Eir's back, sending Eir through a hostile frenzy as she let out a pained gurgling noise that sounded disturbingly like a female version of Spot if Ark were to stab him in the back. Eir made an unpleasant, angry growl as she sheathed her arms around her only son's neck in an attempt to choke him with her firm zombie grip. Losnedahl made unhealthy rasping noises as he started to lose breath; his disturbed cries were made worse by the gurgled sobs that mingled his tears. 'Hold on, Henrik, we'll help!' Kolen and Ark had both shouted, abandoning their posts to rush over to help their friend. But the pair didn't get very far as they were both held back by Aladar and Zinni by their coat collars on Oli's mono order. 'He'd more than likely want to do this himself, you said it yourself, Mrs Ark, that's his mother, so let him do this without disruption, let him put her out of her misery by himself… I can understand his pain all too well.' Oli spoke sadly, now completely devoid of jokes and witty remarks. The female Slater stared at them, feeling sorrow and compassion for Losnedahl having to go through the anguishing task of killing his own mother, whom he'd finally got to meet despite her being a walking corpse that's far beyond the help of zombie bonding. Losnedahl wrenched the knife out of Eir's back, opening up a new gaping wound in her back for dark blood to dribble out of. He swapped hands; the blade now sat in his left hand, and he used his right hand to hold his zombie mother back, feebly trying to stop her endeavours to scrap her nails across his skin.

The Eir zombie maintained to make those awful growling, gurgling noises as Losnedahl proceeded to fight back as much as he could. Finally, he let out a raspy but definite scream of guilt and fear as he gripped his mum by the neck and slammed her to the ground, where he then fell on top of her, knees pinning her down as she punched and flayed her arms at him to knock him off. Losnedahl now seized the bowie knife in both hands. He gritted his teeth and hissed before he let out another rasped scream as he bore the blade down into Eir's chest, screaming and crying a tsunami as he plunged the knife over and over into Eir's chest and neck. And to make sure she was really dead, he picked her up by the shoulders and cast what was left of her head down upon a large piece of broken debris, which splatted her head and neck entirely, coating the trash as well as the ground and himself with dark red blood.

It was done.

He'd done the right thing, and the one thing that if his mother could see him here from the heavens, she'd be pleased with him for ending her suffering and that she could finally rest in peace with her sister Anette and the rest of the pure family members who'd fallen. Losnedahl accumulated the knife again and continued to jab it into Eir's undead corpse, thinking she was still alive and was still going to attack him if he let his guard down, even for a mere second. *Fuck*! His mind cried through each stab of the motionless body under his knees. *Fuck*! he wept again. *Fuck*, he repeated again. *Fuck…* he deplored the last one. But just before he could land another jab into his mother's splattered neck, Kolen came up from behind and enveloped him in a tight hug, her tears fused with his tears as she held the hand holding the knife still. 'It's okay now, Henrik. You can stop now. She's at peace. If she could see you now from the heavens, she'd smile, proud of you for putting her out of her misery.' Kolen spoke to him softly; even through her sobs, she masked them for Losnedahl's sake and sanity.

Even though Losnedahl was, in fact, a fifty-seven-year-old man, his bewailing was that of a child. He squandered his strength on the bowie knife, and he dropped it on the ground next to him, where it landed with a clink from the blade hitting the hard debris below. Losnedahl crossed his heart; his sclera commenced changing its colour from the usual white into a pinkish tint from the sheer number of heavy tears in his eyes. The tears of a man who's done the unthinkable yet gracious thing of putting a beloved family member to eternal rest.

'It's done now, Henrik… it's done, it's over. Please, Henrik, we need you.' cried Kolen, holding onto him tighter as she did her best to soothe him and dry his tears that showed minor signs of ceasing. Ultimately, it took him around thirty or so minutes to fully calm down and face the terms that he'd granted his mother Eir the peace that she had craved ever since the terror of the mortuus carnem was brought into the light of the media. He thanked Kolen with a sign, and she helped him stand up and walk him back to the group, who all expressed their deep condolences and grief for him. Informing him that what he did was excruciating to watch and that he admittedly had shown a strong sense of bravery with commencing to kill his mother's undead form and permit her passage to heaven… Winsome had actually exchanged some kind of wisdom with him, saying that no child, no matter the age, should ever have to go through killing their parent, regardless of whether they're undead or not. If the parent was loving and nurturing, no child should ever have the duty of killing them like Henrik Losnedahl. Because something as wicked as that can take a heavy turn on the person's subconscious mind. One thing was on Losnedahl's mind then, as clear as ever; he'd never be able to forgive Sam for this. Ever.

Chapter 24

It was upon observing the emotional moments of Losnedahl meeting and killing his undead mother, whom he'd dreamt of meeting in person and doing her the kindness of putting her in the ground once more, this time officially, he hoped. It'd been Winsome who'd started feeling a little sick and horrendous himself, almost as if all the times he'd been a complete douche were coming at him like punches all over his body, as if they were mocking and beating him up for the irrational way he'd been behaving Each one of his insults hurting more than the last. Upon hearing his words and insults punching and piercing through him like needles, he began to realise that he didn't feel good about what he'd done; he felt so insignificant and petty instead of feeling grand and high like they'd initially made him feel. His mood suddenly went sour, and he'd lost the traits that'd made him unique, such as his sly wit, tendency to say something inappropriate, and sense of humour. He'd lost it all; he felt empty, devoid of happiness and bitter at this time. The only thing he felt was the dread and dissatisfaction with his recent actions up to this point. He almost felt a chain pulling at his neck, pulling him towards the cliff – prompting him to let himself go – to give up on his chances of survival. He stared at the particles of dust billowing and dead leaves floating in circles in the small cold tornados around his feet. His arms and legs sagged; he wanted to drop the shotgun and fall to his knees, wishing that things weren't the way they were. Then that was when they returned to him like a slap in the face that woke up from a nap. Then came the flashbacks that had begun to plague his head, bad flashbacks, emotional flashbacks, distressing flashbacks, flashbacks of his deceased best friend, the one he had hinted to Kolen previously but knew it would be too emotional to actually talk about him fully in words; his loyal German Shepherd's, final moments. The tearful moments that'd remained stitched to his brain and ones that weren't kind to him when he thought about them, he wished he could pull them off, but pulling them off his brain would mean it would hurt the outer layer in which it was stitched to. So, for better or worse, he'd have to deal with and wear it. But even during those tough times during his best friend's final breaths, like any dog owner, there'd been some grand ones; in fact, most had been good, and he just needed to think of them. Oh, how much he had missed him, how much he had helped him during the bad times in his life. How much he had missed it whenever he would come through the front door, and Bear would be at the door to greet him with licks to his face, happy to see him home. Winsome closed his eyes and recalled the times when things made sense in his life. A time when Ryan Winsome was happy and wasn't a jerk to everyone.

He was only around five weeks old, when Winsome, at just twenty-three years old, had been looking for a four-legged companion to help him wake up in the mornings, someone to coax him into getting out the door for his daily exercise, someone whom he could tell things to without the idea of being judged, had gotten Bear from one of the kind breeders who treated his dogs with love and care, keeping them inside a well-ventilated house, feeding them good quality food and overall making sure they were okay and were treated like royalty, instead of holding them in pitiful cages and left outside, sometimes in the garage when it rained and only keeping them around just to breed them. No, this man, Russell Esposito, whom Winsome had read about in a newspaper ad about German Shepherd pups for sale, was a humble old man who always sought the wellbeing of the dogs he had raised and bred once every three years. Winsome and Esposito shook hands and exchanged pleasantries, and Winsome was soon escorted to a room in the man's laundry where the pups were; there were about five in total, happily bounding and yapping from their little confinement at the new person who had come to see them. Winsome loved dogs, and when he saw those little tails wagging. Those jovial little yaps, he wanted to take them all, but he didn't have the space for all five pups, and he felt a stabbing sensation at the thought that he only had to pick one, one special puppy would be calling for Winsome, one special pup was going to go to a new home. And it wasn't long until he caught sight of those darling little puppy eyes. Winsome knew that fuzzy little puppy was for him! He could tell that they were going to be more than just good friends as soon as he saw the desire to play in the pups' eyes as his little tail wagged, tongue panting, and his little paws held onto the bars of the crate in which his brothers and sisters were enclosed inside of. Bear was the runt of the litter of seven other puppies. He was the most adventurous and playful out of the litter, a perfect match for a much younger Ryan Winsome, and because of Bear being the smallest of the seven puppies, Russell offered a five per cent discount for him, making him a grand total of £475. Winsome was instantly sold and was glad to leave without £475 because money wasn't necessary when he now had a loyal puppy dog with him, whom he loved to pieces and was always seen with, walking on a blue lead down the street, a four-legged friend who was always around to help Winsome during his blue days. Sometimes, Winsome would frequently be spotted in dog parks, happily engaging in a conversation with anyone who complimented Bear or who had simply loved dogs just as much as he did. So basically, Winsome was a modest man enjoying a simple life with his dog.

'Oi Ryan, Ya with us?' Slater strained, leaning over to him whilst still holding Oli in his arms, showing signs that his arms were getting tired and that he needed to put Oli down or find her some kind of steel cane for her to hobble on without his aid.

'Yeah, you right? You look like you just witnessed your own ma's funeral,' said Oli. Slater snapped at her, hearing the fault in his sister's words. 'Oli, it ain't the time to be cracking jokes. Not when Henrik just had to put his mother out of commission.' He scowled at her.

'I wasn't crack-'

'Can you two shut up... please, I just... I just need to talk to Lisa. I... Something came up...' Winsome murmured; 'Yeah, you're right, bad time. Sorry, Ryan.' Said Oli, but Winsome didn't hear her as he walked up to Ark and gently placed a hand on her shoulder, something that wasn't likely expected of someone like him. If he wanted something from you, he wouldn't be tender with garnering your attention. Ark looked at him, surprised at knowing how tender he was around her. 'Lisa… I need to talk to you,' he frowned; his voice sounded authentic and not full of crackhead jokes that were intended to annoy and poke at the controlled fire inside of people. His head was low, his shoulders hitched, and his hands grasped his coat's fabric. He appeared mortal and lost like he didn't know how his life had gotten so low, and he wanted to wash his hands and atone for all the pointless shit he's done throughout his years of acting like the village idiot. 'It can wait. What's the time anyway?' Ark asked without much emotion that irritated Winsome to some extent, but he didn't fight the fire unprotected. Instead of bursting into a song of fury and going down the path of shameless venting, Winsome offered a more minimalistic approach to discussing what he'd wanted to say to her. He tightened his grip on her shoulder and planted his feet on the spot, causing Ark to stop. His voice was trembling, and the way he kept blinking rapidly at her told Ark that he was trying to save his eyes from crying, something which Ark had basically never seen Winsome do, like ever. 'Lisa, please. We have plenty of time. Don't be a bitch and shut me out like you always do.

I'm not cracking any jokes or complaining. I'm just asking that you please just listen to me for one fucking minute! I… I need to say this, I need to wash my hands and tell you something that I've tried to keep locked up.' This abrupt change of Winsome's usually annoying, childish nature for a more serious and mature tone shocked Ark. If one were to assess each depressing and gruesome moment that has happened around them without much thought. Winsome, unfortunately, was always the one caught in the middle.

But this time, when Ark turned around to face him, she was moved, stunned actually to see him without the Idiot's mask and to see him for his true self. A somewhat likable and modest fellow who owned a face that she and others could relate to was Fear and a strong desire to help those around him. But he just didn't know how to enable them based on how others perceived him and how he often lashed out an insult at someone without thought. But with those factors aside, he looked genuinely scared beyond hope and heartbroken, like someone had just dug a knife deep into his chest and pierced it through his heart, making it bleed. 'Seeing Henrik react like that to his dead mother triggered something in me, something I'd never thought I'd see again. If you will, call it a flashback about someone very important to me, Bear, whose name was. He meant the world to me, and I feel like I need to confront my deepest thoughts and finally talk about him and move on, you know what I mean?' he declared to her, still wearing that frown and those watery eyes, which gave out the impression that he wanted to give in to his weakness and cry in front of her, something that wasn't expected from someone like Ryan Winsome, furthermore, stating that he has often tried and failed to move on from losing his best friend. Ark's face resembled one of confusion dwindled in grief as she regarded those hurting brown Winsome eyes. 'Who's Bear?' she asked, her voice not matching her face as it sounded lifeless and dull while her face was constricted, trying to work out what Winsome was trying to tell her.

'My dead dog… my sweet, beautiful dog.' he sniffled, the first few tears starting to trickle from his brown eyes and down his reddening cheeks.

Ark looked away a little, sighing to herself, knowing that she had better give the man what he wanted, before looking back at Winsome, indicating she was listening to whatever he' had to say about his departed dog, Bear. 'Okay, Ryan, I'm listening. What about your dog?'

Chapter 25

Since the mortuus carnem parasite infects the dead, and remember sometime last year when that Japanese guy (*Dai-something*) tried to bond with an undead cat that had ended up in the feline being disposed of? And I know that we haven't seen any undead animals yet. But... I just had the horrible feeling that it got to my sweet pooch just like how something got to Henrik's mother, who I remembered getting buried instead of getting him cremated like a decent dog owner.' Winsome's head was low. 'You know Lisa, if the time came, if it ever did. I can guarantee you that I would NEVER be able to gun down the zombified version of my dear German Shepherd, or any dog for that matter; I would be more suited to cowering and crying than to doing anything bad to a dog... I love dogs, and I hate seeing them harmed in any way. The way they look at you and whimper... it just breaks my heart.' He paused, looking down at the ground before his eyes once again met with Ark. Ark looked down and saw that he was holding her hands, and when he spoke next, he sounded wounded, like the very idea of finding any undead animals was hurting him. 'I admire and look up to Henrik. I admire his stomach and being able to do something as brave as killing his own mother just after he had just met her for the first time in fifty-seven years... I can't even imagine how hard that was for him to do that. But, hey, I guess I'm just owning up to what you said about me; I really am a pathetic, weak sack of shit... I see that now; I know that I'm a sniffling coward. I may have sounded like a man, by the way; I would always ask for carnage, and I wanted to spill some blood of the undead. The way I behaved; how stupidly childish I was. But in reality, I was just putting on a brave face, and deep down inside, I felt the same way as Marilyn, and wanted to be sick every time I saw gore. I was basically asking to kill the undead in hopes of not sounding weak and to come off as something that I wasn't... But seeing Henrik do that to his zombie mother just made me realise just how much of a sniffling piss-bucket I really am; what I'm saying is that you were right all along, Lisa. I could never bring myself to do such a thing, even if someone had strapped my hands to a post and made me hold a gun up to my dog with the intention of killing it. I would never be able to. In short, I just wanted to say that you were right the entire time about me and when the time comes. I'm too chickenshit... I want you to please do the duty for me.' He pleaded, staring right into her forest-green eyes. 'Please, I'm begging you, Lisa Ark, please do this one thing for a man's final redeeming wish.' He looked down and let go of Ark's hands. 'Because this would be one thing that I just know that I'll never be able to do. And hey, I don't think I'm going to survive the night. I'm still surprised at how I've made it this far.'

Ark stood planted; the torch with its intense beam threatened to slip from her fingers. Throughout all the years, she'd worked at the GFOSAR and had known Winsome as the man no one liked. But she never in her life thought she would hear him confess himself, appointing himself as the helpless victim instead of the brave hero who wins and gets the girl, as well as fame and fortune. So, she was unmistakeably taken back by what Winsome told her, admitting himself as the one in the wrong and that he admittedly was a sorry excuse for a human being. She wanted to tell him that he's being silly and that, of course, he would survive the night, but her mouth was dry, and Winsome wasn't finished saying what he'd wanted to say. 'And you know what, I understand if you're sick of me and want me out; I know I've been hard to deal with; I see that now, and I regret it. So, if you want me out of the group, just say, and I'll be on my way.' He added sadly, feeling that he should put his gloves away and retire.

'Ryan, don't you dare go on spouting that kind of BS when we're only just starting to get used to having ya around. Sure, you were a real twat at times, but everyone deserves a chance at life.' noted Oli. 'Am I right, fellas?' Losnedahl, Kolen, Slater and the zombies nodded, though Aladar and Zinni seemed like they didn't really know what was going on and were simply nodding just because their bonder was nodding. Ace even went on to chip at the ice, hoping to make an ice rendition of Michelangelo by saying. 'You, a good man.' However, it was Ark who was instantly overcome with sympathy, and she felt bad after hearing this come from the ordinarily complicated Ryan Winsome. Winsome spoke to the crawler next, thanking her for her attempt at complimenting them but unintentionally rubbing salt at his own wounds by furthermore saying that he wasn't a good man and didn't deserve to be alive. This then ensued in Kolen speaking up about everyone needing to have at least one chance at life; it doesn't matter if they're useless or not; everyone deserves a chance to live, similar to what Oli had said. Losnedahl was silent. He's still shocked by what he'd done, which was understandable. Spot, who probably had more of an excuse to dislike him after he'd stupidly and irrationally threatened to kill his mother, even he'd come clean with him and had given Winsome a thumbs up, expressing that they're now on good terms.

Finally, it'd been Ark who was at a loss for quips or wisdom. She, as well as everyone else, knew that it was against Winsome's code to exploit his weakness to a bunch of girls, let alone Lisa Ark. She was the one woman in the group with whom he didn't share much zest, although he admired the fact that she had more balls than he did. Often at times, he was jealous of her for that exact reason. Ultimately, when she had the right amount of moistness in her mouth to speak to him and when she did open her mouth, the words just came out without much consideration or thought. 'Ryan, when the time comes, you will have t-

'Please, Lisa! Look, I've already admitted that I have no balls and am not man enough for this task, unlike you; please do this one thing for me when the time does come (*which I hope it doesn't*).' He interrupted her, protesting that she had to be the one to kill a zombified version of his dog for when and if it happens. 'That is one thing that I just can't do; no matter how much preparation I do, I could never do it.'

'Okay, Ryan, okay, I'll do it...' She ultimately gave in to him, nodding dismally to him before tapping him on the shoulder to tell him to go back to his post. 'Thank you, Lisa,' he sobbed a little; he wrapped his arms around Ark and gave her a small hug before letting go and going back to his post at the end, beside the Slater twins and Losnedahl. 'The time is 8:42pm.' Slater called out. Ark nodded wanly, the thought of killing Winsome's undead dog nagging in her head. 'Hey, look on the floor! Footprints.' Kolen said, pointing to the floor where the torch beam was. Ark and the others looked down at the red human-shaped prints facing them on the ground, and it was Slater who concluded that the prints were made with blood. Winsome made an audible grimacing sound as Ark shone the beam up to follow the bloody footprints and saw they had led to another secluded house. 'They look like they have come from that house over there, so whatever was in that house is gone now. Or if we are lucky, we can find better supplies to help us.'

'Lisa...' moaned Winsome. Ark looked at him, seeing he was trembling and pointing at the prints. Ark shone the light on them again, and she saw more prints that were going in the opposite direction of the human ones; only they looked a little faded compared to the human-shaped ones that looked a little fresher. Ark knelt down to study these new prints and realised they weren't human. These new prints appeared animal-like, with a centre pad and four smaller ones above it. These prints fit the footprints of a dog, and they are pretty big ones. Ark looked back at Winsome, shining the light on him. Winsome closed his eyes and let out a whimper-like moan, knowing that he and the others would go into the house and follow the dog-like footprints.

Chapter 26

Nighttime came in an orderly fashion, backing out the colour, which was foreboding, harrowing and deathly cold. It carried a grim breeze with it, and along with the draft came a ghastly howl as it billowed through the abandoned English streets, casting up particles of dust and carrying them up and around in small dust twisters. Yet because of the ghostly howls carried along with the wind, it would function as a haunting, consistent reminder that another living life has been forcefully snuffed out, and their final cries of torment were traversed along with the chilling air.

Sam thrived in this harsh weather; she closed her eyes and sniffed at the air with a smile on her pale face; listening to those dramatic cries as someone died was like walking to the nearest cafe and hearing her favourite song playing on the radio. The sound of terror was simply music to her. It's as if Sam's very existence had placed a curse upon the sky and the environment around her like a servant of death, she carried it wherever she went, tainting things good in her wake; she was a monster who acted in a very similar way to Jack the Ripper, simply dispatching her victims just because she wanted to and she didn't care what people would think of her, because she'd ensure that they never speak and start another rumour again.

Taking the traumatised Linus with her, dragging him across the dirt by the arm like a sack of potatoes, Sam had abandoned the chapel and had gone outside shortly after killing the mother and daughter and leaving their remains to Linus, whom she might have forced him into eating by peeling away a slab of meat and trying to force it into his mouth until the boy buckled under her force and ate what was forced upon him. Dragging Linus behind her, Sam ventured back into the dank outside where the night surrounded her. The only light around her was the light from the lampposts and the faint glow of a quarter moon. Sam inhaled a breath despite not needing to. She felt like it, so she did it anyway. While on her walk and carrying the zombie boy behind her, she was not bothered if the broken concrete slabs were digging into the boy's pale grey skin and cutting him here and there; for Sam, the pain was one way she could teach the boy to become more desensitised to it, so the next time he's cut, he'd simply be able to shrug it off as a simple cat scratch.

During her trek through the dark chill of the night, Sam would take some simple-minded zombies roaming around the district under her order because she'd need to start somewhere if she's going to build her army and create some version of her vision, a place where humans were hunted like animals and the undead were the ones that carried the hunting rifles. Sam communed with her recruits, leading them to a place under the dirt of all places. She'd found a large, long, abandoned subway station that'd been given new access thanks to three-magnitude earthquake two years back, which had caused the wall of the station to collapse; it was the perfect place to set up shop and to work on creating her soldiers, advisers, and followers. The station, which held the former title of Limberg Station, was now under Sam's ownership; it was the place that she'd used for her own benefit where Sam sat down with some of them and fed them one of the hunger drugs that she'd previously stolen from the GFOSAR before she had left it in ruins. There was a reason why she'd taken them in the first place, and this was that reason. Sam assumed to conduct her own independent bonding experiments with them privately. Bonding with them, zombie to zombie, rewriting their minds, giving them personalities, goals, and simple objectives to follow, such as finding a human and infecting them with their bite. Often, the price of their loyalty and work would be Sam rewarding them with a brain or the entire corpse of someone they killed. Sam worked steadily to turn them over to her (which didn't take all that long, about forty minutes at least; she would release them as soon as they knew what they had to do.

So, while a bonder's job was to make zombies feel human again, Sam's job was to turn them into murderers and feel a divine sensation when they took a life) that would aid her in snuffing out the rest of the country's living inhabitants, save for a few lucky ones that would help to feed the hungry. She would not only give them personalities that would differ from the ones they previously had in life, but she would feed their minds with lies, turning them away from the former person they once had been in life. Sam created new memories completely of her own fabrication, giving a formerly mindless husk something to think about other than running into the line of fire and ending up in bloody pieces. She taught them to smile whenever a human screamed, showing them by bringing in one of the captured wailing humans with her and smiling her evil grin as she plucked their eyes out or broke their fingers while they screamed and licked one of them; Sam would only smile in satisfaction when she handed the human over to the zombie under her direct bonding order, watching with a parted grin as the zombie either snapped fingers off hands with a violent cracking bone sound or gripped onto the humans headed and started squeezing it, causing the human to holler out in anguish until Sam told the zombie to stop and finish the human off by biting it and leaving them to die from the inside and wake up about an hour later as one of them and with no memory of what had happened to them. She gifted those flesh husks the ability to plan their attacks and surprise their living targets whom they had marked as their next dinner. Sam was undoubtedly far superior to them that even the plain old rotting unbonded corpses they knew who was in charge of them, and some were even afraid of her. It was as if Sam's proximity had awakened the once thought-dead emotion of terror inside them, causing them to veer away from her whenever Sam was in the vicinity, carrying a chariot of misery behind her. Most common zombies were slow and lumbering when it came to movement and following orders, so Sam would have to give them the order twice before they would give a moan suggesting that they understood, but that was okay; she knew that those brainless husks would bloom for her in time. Sam returned to the rubble that led into her lair and captured another breath as she glanced up into those unforgiving grey clouds before exhaling the breath while steam billowed from her cold lips. Sam peered down from the shadows in the sky to stare behind her, and she grinned. Her ghastly dead pupils observed the zombies under her wing. She watched this display of zombies around her. The sight of zombies dragging in screaming panicked humans by their feet or arms, regardless of their age or race and were savaging into them on her very plain and simple order, such as digging their decomposing fingers into their stomachs and their skulls and pulling out their vital organs and brains to fest on. She'd greeted with her titular evil smirk. Sam would have the brains delivered to her because she's the most powerful and the most feared of them, and the most dominant one gets the best stuff. At the same time, the other zombies would be left with the scraps and things like the organs, the blood, and the skin which they sometimes flayed off a person who's still alive, causing them to holler in anguish as they're slowly torn apart and eaten.

Sam looked to her side as she could hear the heavy shuffling of feet behind her. Normally, it would be unwise to sneak up behind Sam. But Sam could recognise who these heavy footsteps belonged to, a sturdy black female zombie dubbed Queen, who's under Sam's mental confinement after Sam had encountered her about an hour ago while she's still camping in the chapel with Linus.

Queen had originally come from the ruins of the GFOSAR. But unlike Linus, she didn't have two sides; she wasn't as bonded as him despite her former late bonder (Olio Garcia) being able to talk, making Queen quite a curious case who'd developed a cult-like devotion to Sam and ultimately refused to disobey her, viewing her as some kind of biblical entity. Queen was a hard-born survivor (sitting up shortly after Winsome foolishly thought he'd killed her by shooting her in the throat) who'd murdered her kind and young bonder, beating the defenceless Spaniard to a pulp with her bare hands and caving her face in upon itself. Sam turned around and looked at her cult-like follower as she bowed down to her. Sam smirked at her. She looked at the dried-up flakes of blood around the huge black zombie's fists, and thought of the wordless story Queen had told her when she had found her. When the lockdown was initiated, Queen conveyed that she'd easily broken free from the chains bounding her because of her robust build, tied in with her undead strength. Queen then sought to take her rage out on her bonder and hurled herself at the skinny Spanish woman. She pinned her to the wall, seizing her throat with her giant hand, then proceeding to harrow punches into Garcia's pretty face until her face was left completely battered and her skull crushed and unrecognisable. But before she had done that, Garcia had tried to obtain leadership over Queen, trying to make her stop by holding her arms up in protest and shouting things at her like, "Stop It, Queen! I'm trying to help you! If you'll just let me help you" while she covered her face like a shield. But her efforts in trying to ward off her aggressor had their faults because, without any real effort, Queen had taken grasp of the petite Spaniard's arms that were masking her face and had swiftly torn them off of her body, causing Garcia to drop to the floor harrowing in agony. At the same time, her hostile zombie tossed her useless arms away. Garcia screeched, eyes extended, observing the blood gushing out of her arm studs, seeing her bones protruding out of her stumps. That was when Queen released her undead strength on her bonder, showing her just how strong she really was by using one arm to pick up Olio and pin her to the wall by her neck, as Garcia could not do anything to stop her. So, she just tearfully accepted her fate in the hands of Queen and proceeded to shut her eyes and clench her teeth. Waiting for Queen to finish her by punching her in the face a few times before finally bestowing the final blow. Delivering a boulder-sized fist at the speed of a bullet right at her face, it exited from the back of her head, creating a crater in Garcia's head. This resulted in a nasty painting of spattered brain tissue, prompting blood to pulse out of her smashed head, drowning the ground beneath her, painting it a violent crimson. Sam had grinned at this story of strength and gore, taking Queen with her as Sam understood she would need some muscle and someone to help intimidate her enemies.

While out to get more hostages, Queen delayed herself from her duty in knocking some "logical" sense into some of the hostages whom she'd captured trying to loot a nearby bar for some drinks, as well as money, not that money, was of any actual worth these days. Queen liked to loot anything that was shiny. She found two men trying to break into the register; one was black, the other white. They both were lugging oversized duffel bags over their shoulders that would possibly be full of supplies and bottles of stolen wine and booze. Queen didn't go for the silent approach. Her footsteps hammered on the broken tiled flooring as she ventured towards the two men with her arms reaching; the white male was the one who whipped his head around and saw her. He alerted his mate to stop trying to open the register before pulling out his 38. Glock from his knee holster and fired three bullets into Queen to slow the giantess down, but Queen pursued, simply brushing off the pain of the bullets as if they were pebbles. Queen picked up the register the black male was trying to break into and hurled it at the white male, knocking him into unconsciousness, while throwing a vicious backhand at the black one, knocking him into unconsciousness. Queen picked up both men and transported them on her shoulders, bringing them back to Sam as the holes where she'd been shot three times had started to leak out crimson, colouring her lime green shirt. Queen could crush a man's skull with just one hand if she wanted to. While searching through the white male's pockets, she found and took the 38. out of the man's pocket where Queen seemed strangely memorised by the newfangled weapon. Turning it around and inspecting it like it was the latest addition in an adult series of realistic American toy guns (Kids love'em! Kids wan'em! Kids can't have'em! Sorry Timmy, but you'll have to stick with the plastic ones!). 'Hey! Give that back! Fucking nigger zombie!' The white man screamed as his black friend still remained unconscious on the ground next to him, unable to do anything to save his friend from Queen. The white man leapt at Queen, trying to reclaim his Glock, but was kicked back to the floor by Queen. She held the front of the barrel to her face; her finger unknowingly resided on the trigger. 'Pull it! Blow ya gitting dirt for brains out!' The man fumed, provoking Queen, prodding the fire inside her with a stick. Queen slowly turned her head to stare at the white man. She sealed the 38. inside the back pocket of her grey cargo shorts. 'Oh fuck,' the man gulped, watching Queen advance to him, leaning down, and outstretching her hand around the man, locking her fingers around his neck, her thumb resting just above the Adam's Apple. Queen looked at the man, growling, showing brown rotting teeth at what he'd said to her. Queen stiffened her grip around the man's neck, causing the man's face colour to heat up and his breathing to become husky as he tried to thrash his arms and legs around, punching at Queen's stalwart arm foolishly hoping that it'd prompt her into putting him down. 'Fu-k-ck yo-oo,' he spat into Queen's dark scabbed mug. Queen growled again at the man, so much so that she started to excrete spit from her mouth and onto the man's face; while she was still clutching onto the man's neck, her thumb traversed to sit under his chin. She gave the man's chin a flick with her thumb (like how a person flicks a coin for a head or tail), snapping the man's spine with a loud, unpleasant crack. Death was instantaneous. The man's broken neck caused his head to drop backwards like a ragdoll. Queen released her grasp from the dead man's broken neck, letting the lifeless body fall to the floor like a child discarding a broken toy. There Queen wandered off away from the corpse. That dead man and his black friend would be eaten by the other zombies around, zombies that would sniff them out and call to the black man's beckoning cries.

Queen fished the 38. out from her shorts pocket and continued to fiddle with it like a child, curious about how the device worked. *Maybe the pale one knows*, Queen thought. She marched over to Sam, who was sitting on a small throne of mangled corpses made from recent victims, torsos, arms, legs, and heads that each bore a different face. Still, all wore the same anguished mask of mouth wide and agape, eyes widened and fearful, some torn out, even full bodies that stood atop the growing pool of blood, all placed in an area that at first resembled a small mountain. Still, when Sam started using it as a seat, it became her throne of victims. Queen knelt down to her like some kind of dark prophet or Messiah and presented her with the Glock she was so perplexed about, trying to ask her through finger gestures if she knew what it was and would be able to show her how the instrument worked. Sam studied the trinket contributed to her. Sam grabbed the Glock from Queen and observed it closely. Sam took the magazine case out and peered at it. Seeing the gun was fully loaded with bullets, before shoving the magazine back up into the grip and looked at Queen with downcast eyes and a frown to match the appearance of "Sorry, Queenie, but I'm just as bummed as you are as to what this thing is. Looks like you brought me a dud." Queen addressed Sam with a disheartened moan, discouraged by the thought that the mighty intelligent Sam didn't know what a gun was and that she couldn't teach her how to use it because Queen thought she'd use it to fight the rest of the living population. Disappointed in herself, Queen turned to walk away. Sam pulled back the slide of the 38. She heard it make a clicking noise as she loaded it and was ready to shoot something with it to check if it wasn't jammed, but what? What was Sam going to shoot? Sam stared back at Queen while still holding the 38. her index finger was resting on the trigger; she aimed it at Queen. Queen had heard the click of the slide and had turned around to face Sam, who was now smiling, her usual evil smile that said, "Sorry, Queenie, nothing personal, just wanting to test the toy out," the grin Ace often associated with evil. Before Queen could process what, her boss was planning, a loud BANG had come from the 38. followed by a blinding flash as Sam's malicious smile.

At first, Queen displayed an absence of a reaction, but that was until she peered down at her stomach, seeing some vaguely fresh red blood dripping from the newly made orifice. She groped at her brick-like stomach for a few fleeting seconds before bringing her fingers up in front of her, examining the crimson liquid on her dark-skinned fingers. Queen looked down at the floor, seeing a red puddle starting to form around her legs. Now Queen had commenced in becoming distressed. The shots fired by the two men she'd captured prior had meant nothing, simple pebbles against a boulder, but to be shot by the one she looked up to had been a real gut punch; it's as if she'd driven a large machete right into her chest. She whimpered at the sickening feeling of the blood dripping out of her body; she stared up at Sam again, dropping to her big knees with an expression of utter bafflement. *Why Mistress? I never made any attempt to disobey you. I thought I was your most loyal.* But saw that the 38. Glock was aimed right at her forehead where her brains were. Queen's pale eyes trailed up to where the muzzle was aimed and wanted to make a plea for Sam not to dispose of her so quickly. However, Sam was unable to listen to some half-bonded zombie blubber about how she didn't want to die in Zomblish (zombie language, a mixture of incoherent moans that the undead could read). She didn't allow Queen much time to fight back as her finger remained fastened on the trigger, not tilting from it, or moving the muzzle away from Queen; whoever Queen was in life and whatever she did in life didn't matter because Sam was going to send Queen to hell as soon as she fired. Sam seized Queen's throat and hoisted her up, causing her forehead to touch the Glock's muzzle. Goodbye Queen, you were a big help to me, but as I'm sure you've already concluded. Besides, I wonder if killing a fellow zombie will provide the same satisfaction as killing a human, so adios! Maybe in another life, you won't horde any more useless junk. Tell your bonder to send me a postcard. Sam snickered; she taunted the massive female zombie, her finger slightly pulled back on the trigger of the Glock, teasing her. Queen's teeth and eyes were clenched shut. Like a terrified human, she was breathing heavily from those gritted rotting chops, preparing for a bullet to pass through her skull and out of her brain, ending in death. Even for a powerful zombie built like a brick wall, the Queen always had one human weakness: fear. The one shred of humanity she had in her was that she had Thanatophobia, a Fear of dying.

But nothing happened. Sam didn't go ahead with pulling the trigger. What followed was nothing... just the sound of Queen's panicked breathing and Sam chuckling cruelly.

Sheepishly, Queen opened her eyes like a fearful rabbit and looked at Sam. Sam had moved the gun away from Queen's head and was chortling playfully as if to say that she got her, planning on scaring the daylights out of her, experimenting with her, and wanting to see if someone as sturdy as Queen could feel dread and terror. Sam held her hand out to Queen and winked at her, gesturing to Queen that she wasn't planning on killing her trusted zombie tank! Queen resembled a young, innocent child in the face, scared whenever she heard her parents fighting in the kitchen, Queen blinked hesitantly, slowly moving her hands from her face and staring at Sam with a mask of anxiety, prompting Sam to burst into an uproar of laughter at this cruel joke she'd pulled on Queen. Queen glanced around sheepishly; her face still resembled a naive child who still didn't understand the meaning of the prank that her older friend had pulled on her (*You're so easy, Winnie*). Finally, she peered back at Sam and then commenced to give her own zombified chuckles at the joke as well, not wanting to sound like the butt that always ruins the fun for everyone. If one were to think of things from a bonded zombie's perspective, Sam would've had no issues in gunning down a fellow zombie. After all, Sam did just shoot Queen in the stomach without so much as a sweat of remorse or a flicker of hesitation. Furthermore, threatened to shoot her head and kill her before revealing that she'd played Queen like a violin, and that was already a scary thought on its own factor. Queen then saw Sam's hand and took it gingerly, to which Sam had helped her up to her feet, standing two inches taller than her. Sam was addressing Queen with a friendly smile this time, furnishing her with a light and warm tap on the shoulder. Sam eyed Queen's pale grey eyes and beckoned with her fingers for Queen to leave and go back into her daily routine of capturing any living being she could find and returning them back to Sam, where she'd either infect them or kill them straight up. Yet, because Queen didn't have as much intelligence as Sam, Spot, Ace and even Linus, acting stubbornly to her bonder before the time was right and killing her, therefore Queen hadn't learnt about grudges as well as other emotions and feelings. Because Queen had ended Garcia's life before she could be taught more about human emotions and what it meant to "hold a grudge". So, henceforth, Queen had spontaneously forgotten what Sam had done to her, treating her bleeding wound as nothing more than an injury sustained during patrol. It was as if Sam's character change had wiped Queen's memory of what could have been her untimely demise. She turned her back to Sam and began to walk away from her; her mind was set on doing exactly what Sam had ordered, playing the pawn role to its fullest.

That's when Queen met her official end.

Watching Queen as she turned around and started to leave her, Sam's once familiar smile twisted back into its original wicked smirk. She pointed the loaded 38. up to her head. This time, she did pull the trigger, propelling a loud flying bullet pelting through the back of Queen's head, punching through the skull, tearing into the brain, and killing her before she hit the ground, falling to her knees and finally, planting on her face. The feeding zombies around Sam saw this scene play out of Sam killing one of her own and had withdrawn from her, knowing it was ill-advised to take her on, or she might do the same thing to them, or worse, see them as human and attack them like one before eating them.

See, even some regular zombies feared for their lives; it wasn't just bonded zombies that were part of the zombie bondation process; ordinary unbonded zombies sometimes feared death. But in reality, and if a person were to grasp it in a scientific view, it all depended on the AOR of the zombie; it was mostly the young zombies over the 5-

year AOR that had a fear of death, ones that had only a few loose threads of humanity. It'd be an unbelievable story or rumour if word got out of a zombie over the 40- or 70-year AOR feared for their lives and actually retreated from the person welding the firearm to their head. You didn't have to be a GFOSAR bonder to comprehend the knowledge that zombies over 40 and 70 AOR had lost all remnants of their humanity many years before; the older the zombies were, the less human they mentally were.

Sam steered the 38. up to her mouth, gently blowing at the billowing steam emitting from the Glock's muzzle. She peered over at Linus standing by the half-devoured skeletal corpse of the Haylock girl, who resembled an appearance of pure, unending terror, clutching the base of his pants and staring wide-eyed into the corpse lying in front of him at Sam; he looked like he's going to start shitting bricks. Still wearing the jester's mask of evil, Sam shot a few more times into Queen's now undead carcass, each bullet hitting the body, making Sam's grin widen. Killing zombies was just as satisfying as killing humans.

Linus gulped as he stared at the fallen titan, then fearfully at Sam, who pointed directly to the nearest wall, fundamentally telling him to move the cadaver out of her way. His body was stuck in his bad side, and his face was glued with the mask of pain and fear that humans feel. Linus didn't hesitate to disobey her, although he's wary of her nonetheless, now coming to the understanding that if she wanted to, she could shoot and be done with him, dispatching, and disposing of him like she'd done with Queen. Linus went over to the titan's motionless body, lifting up one of her legs and taking a portion of flesh from Queen's left leg as he hulled the giant ox of a zombie out of Sam's passage. She thanked him with a simple nod.

Sam stayed in her own abandoned station where she planned her next move. Maybe now that she had a firearm with her, perhaps now it'd be time for her to pay a visit to the group. She looked at Linus and hoped that the next time she saw him again, he'd be far too mentally broken upon seeing Sam kill Queen simply because she wanted to test out her new toy. She hoped that he'd be the zombie she wanted him to be when she saw Linus again.

Chapter 27

An hour had passed since Ark had last asked for the time. He asked again and Kolen had delivered, but not before she'd yawned, peering down at Slater's wristwatch, observing the electronic numbers on the watch which told the exact time. It said the time was 9:42pm; they still had plenty of time before midnight and far more time before daylight and 3am. If they were lucky, they might be able to find and kill Sam before the clock strikes midnight, but that seemed unlikely because none of them had any idea where Sam was or any idea where she was last seen. They were trekking behind the paw-like prints that Winsome had spotted and reasonably seemed hesitant to follow them in the first place. London City may be a ghost town with barely any signs of life. However, it was still a prominent place flowering with places to hide and the undead roaming around the alleyways and abandoned shops, waiting for someone unlucky enough to stumble upon them. But suppose anything was possible if you put your mind to it, and maybe trapping Sam could be possible if the group had put their minds into how they were going to do it. Because trying to hunt down someone you had no possible idea where they were, you'd be at the game for hours, and in those hours, you would still be left with nothing. So, waiting for her to come to them seemed like a better and less risky operation, though the other obstacle posed was the probability of waiting hours or maybe days before Sam eventually came their way. To wait around for something that they weren't one hundred per cent confident of happening.

It'd seem lax to sit and wait around for it if they knew that the chances of Sam just randomly wandering into their sights were stupid because Sam wouldn't be that dumb enough to show herself so easily if she'd some kind of insight that she's being hunted down by people who had firearms on hand.

'Lee-Lisa, I-I can't' came the heavy puffing voice of Slater when Ark had turned around, shining the flashlight upon the twins; she saw the brother was on his knees, his arms spilled before him, and Oli had rolled out of his arms and was lying on the floor, her leg curled up and her arms on her chest, she yawned too as her brother huffed and panted, he's now exhausted from carrying his twin around for what seemed like hours. Slater cussed to himself as he huffed heavily over the form of his sister. Winsome walked up to Ark and asked her if they could stop for a bit to rest their legs and relax, even if their place of encampment was that house in which the prints were leading. 'I mean, look at us; Darren is utterly exhausted from carrying his sister, who looks like she wants to pass out, Marilyn can't even walk in a straight line, and she looks like she wants to fall over. Henrik is still visibly traumatised by what he had to do earlier, and I imagine for his age, he's not used to walking this long. As for me, I might've done a lot of walking when I was younger and when I had Bear, but I am not that man anymore. I can feel blisters on my feet. I bet they're red as well; I need to sit down. I think we all do. As for the zombies? I can't read them as well as the others.' He may have been living under the local idiot blanket. Still, once that blanket was lifted, Ryan Winsome was a sincere man who looked out for the wellbeing of those around him and knew that not just his but everyone in the group needed to replenish their strength and their energy for when they'd hopefully confront Sam if she wanders to where they were. Though the idea of her wandering to their mist seemed very unlikely.

Slater grunted loudly, wiping his head as his body tilted and swayed drunkenly. 'Yeah, yeah, I agree… we… can't keep walking through London… if… we've no idea where she is… let's rest up. I don't think I can carry you for a while, sis.' He'd told her. 'Exactly, I mean, she could be somewhere behind us in Oxford, Cambridge or hell, somewhere in Edinburgh, and if that's the case, we should get our strength back and wait for her to come to us.' Winsome explained, making the few occasional glances behind him, and seeing the tiring faces of Losnedahl, Slater and Kolen, knew, just by their faces, that they agreed with him when they had their strength back, they could fight her, kill her, and put the country to a must deserved rest in knowing that the local she-reaper wasn't around to put the country in the dirt and make it the place that exists in a child's, no an adult's nightmares. Slater then ultimately fell backward and was breathing heavily and laboriously, his chest heaving with each breath. Winsome felt sorry for the man when he looked at him; his mind was a mixture of things regarding the country's current state. Instead of having Welcome to the United Kingdom on the occasional billboard around the local airports and ship docking bays, he imagined it being spray painted with The Land of the Dead. After the massacre of the GFOSAR (formally one of the safest places in Britain), it wouldn't be a surprise to see something painted on the doors resembling something from the American TV show *The Walking Dead*, **Don't Go to Britain; it's a zombie wonderland. If you want to go**

there and join the ranks of the undead, be my guest. graffitied on walls in different parts of the world. The idea hurt him; Britain had been a fairly nice place when he was a young lad. Oh, how quickly did the mortuus carnem come and ruin everything.

Ark looked as if she was considering his proposition because she looked down at her own feet and felt them throbbing in her shoes. She could do with a sit-down as well, but then the image of that boy came to her mind, and the look of the boy's parents stunned, horrified faces when she told them about their son who wouldn't be walking out of the hospital with them. She shook her head. 'We don't want to let Sam infect the country and, by extension, let her win. We really should press on if we hope to find and kill her for Fredrickson and for all the others whose lives she has taken.' Ark replied patiently to him; most of her anger had deserted her after the speech he had reported to her, furthermore admitting his flaws and that he's well and truly a coward that only brought them down (That boy's face again the dread of seeing the light leave those small defenceless eyes). Yet because of him discharging his feelings about himself to her, Ark had found that she had come to a mutual understanding with him and was now viewing him in a more positive light, seeing him as a human being and not some twat who's all bark and no bite. She respected him now, and because he decided to make amends with her, she was willing to tolerate him and keep him in the group. As irritating as his vexes were, he was part of their group, part of them to the very end. And because of that factor, his life warranted saving as much as the other lives of the group. He's part of the group from start to finish.

Winsome looked wounded when he stared at her now, and Ark felt a pang of guilt that was telling her she was overworking her friends and that she needed to let them have their moment of rest like Winsome was trying to explain to her. 'I know, Lisa, but with all due respect, hear me out.' He pointed his thumb to the back, gesturing to the party behind him. Oli was curled up in a cat-like ball, yet despite sounding full and alert before, her eyes fluttered like she was fighting the urge to pass out. Slater was lying on his back, clearly exhausted; Kolen was tilting and struggling to keep her balance while Losnedahl stared ahead, eyes vast and unblinking, still visibly shaken from the ordeal with Eir. The zombies stood quietly; the crawler looked at Ark contently; Spot had one of his arms around Kolen's shoulder, while Aladar and Zinni just looked at Oli, confused. Ark said nothing to this, as if she was considering his proposal and if she should actually go through with his recommendation, as Winsome did sound desperate and honest with her.

And eventually, Winsome had won her over. Her face seemed lax, but it still maintained some alert wakefulness. 'You know, I actually agree with you, Ryan; you can sometimes be a huge feckle that would really cheese me out. But you washed your hands and… (she sighed) I agree that we really should rest up for a bit. Going by your evidence and experience with her in the GFOSAR, it'll take some fervour to bring Sam down. And going from the little that I saw of her when we first met and when she killed that guy and slaughtered all of my previous acquaintances...' she said and cringed, thinking back to the sickening feeling he had in his stomach as he watched that poor man has his junk torn from his bowels. 'She seems very formidable and the type to read movements, so we should lay back and formulate a plan that she won't expect. We'd make easy pickings for her if we don't strategie things and don't have much energy to even put up a fight… besides. Carrying Olivia for twenty-four hours is a real struggle and really takes the steam outta me.' Slater panted as he strived to keep a grip on his sister while backing up Winsome's claims by agreeing with him, saying it would be wise to regain their strength by hiding out in one of the disowned buildings that were all around them.

'Ay! I'm not that fat…' Oli mumbled in what seemed like dipping in semi-consciousness. Slater panted some more, though he'd gotten most of his breathing under control as he laid on his back, looking up at the night sky and the small white dots. 'Remember when we were kids. You would always stuff your face with the cheeseburgers and Big Macs at McDonald's.' Oli's eyes now opened with a snap, and she peered over at her half-exhausted, conscious brother. 'Yeah! Well, the Macca's burgers were awesome! You were the one that would always hog the McFlurry's!' She barked back at him. 'That's because they soothed my throat; remember, I had that gastro-oesophageal reflux disease between twelve and nineteen.' **(GERD- burning sensations in the throat)**. Oli was about to deliver another comedic remark in reply. But she resigned and proceeded to shut her gob because the topic of Darren having GERD would periodically shut her up. Because it was a sensitive topic for her to think about, she often tried to think of other things to sponge out the thought of her brother's throat becoming inflamed. Oli could remember one scary-arse day of 2020 clearly. Her dad, Lance, her mum, Christine, Darren, and herself were having lunch at one of the local Italian restaurants (during the devastating and restricted events of that pandemic that swept through the rest of the world) in the area. When Darren's throat became so congested that he had difficulty breathing, causing him to fall into a writhing fit on the floor, clutching his throat while gasping for air. 999 was quickly phoned, and he was soon taken to the hospital in a stretcher in the back of an ambulance, which had greatly frightened a twelve-year-old Olivia Slater and something that an adult Olivia Slater would never soon forget. That was when twelve-year-old Darren Slater was officially diagnosed with GERD. The terminal fear and dread spread throughout Olivia's rigid body from observing her brother going through some kind of epileptic fit, grasping his neck, and striving for breath, only for him to be lifted onto a stretcher and taken away to the nearest hospital. Such a sight would be unbearable for any sibling to watch. While at home, Oli believed that Darren would surely die if he didn't get the needed treatment or if he didn't look after himself by being mindful of the temperature of his throat. Although the Slater's not been the religious type, Olivia had prayed for Darren's life and for him to overcome the disease that had plagued his throat. God finally answered during his ninetieth year on Earth when he found out how to keep the condition at bay and not let it impede his day-to-day activities.

Oli was silent after Slater had mentioned the previous episodes he had when his GERD was uncontrolled. Slater continued to lay on his back for a prolonged amount of time. 'My legs are fucked; if you want me to move, your gonna have to drag me, or someone will have to team up in carrying me,' he said to the other members of the group admitting he was deprived of his energy. He stared up at Oli, blinking tiredly, who remained quiet '-like a roasted swine over a handmade barbecue.' He stated, trying to make his own Oli-styled quip.

'Well… if we want to rest up, we should follow the prints and get to that house over there.' Ark stated. 'It's safe.' Said the crawler.

'How can you tell?' Winsome's voice questioned.

'Smell,' Ace simply responded with.

'Right, we'll rest there for now and regain our strength.' Ark dictated, putting the rifle down and around her back with the leather strap attached to it. She navigated her way to the back and took Spot's arm away from the sleepy Kolen's shoulder, where she led him into the shambled wreck of a house first since he was blind and couldn't see with his brain. This was then followed by the rest. The next four inside were the Slater twins and Oli's zombies, whom she had directed with the understandable and straightforward commandment. 'Aladar, pick up Darren and help him inside, Zinni you do me.' Unprotesting and without any other conflicting thoughts, Aladar shifted his body through the crowd of humans in front of him, approaching behind Slater, who was stationary on the fractured cement. 'Hoi Ali...' Slater mumbled in a hammered voice, hearing Aladar's shambling footsteps linger behind him. Slater continued to sit as if glued to the ground, staring absently at the pebbles of broken cement in between his stretched-out legs. Aladar was bearing down Slater's back; he reached and seized Slater by the back collar of his oversized leather trench coat. Aladar tugged on the trench coat, and Slater followed. Aladar took one of his hands while still clasping his collar. Slater fell on his back, releasing a repressed groan as his back hit the floor. This lifeless action prompted Aladar to his knees; the hand clutching the collar went up to Slater's brown tee shirt; he embraced it tightly and lifted it, and the other hand went to grab Slater's crotch. 'Ooh! Easy on the pisser there, bud,' groaned Slater as Aladar lifted both the fabric over his chest and crotch. Heaving him off the ground and flipping the knackered middle-aged man onto his shoulders, where he lay under the buckle of Aladar's arm wrapping around him, holding him in place much. The sight of Aladar carrying Slater over his shoulder somewhat resembled an image of World War I when Allied troops were fighting in Gallipoli, and soldiers would have to transport the wounded over the shoulders and carry them to safety inside the trenches, away from all the gunfire. 'Thanks, Ali,' Slater mumbled sluggishly in the zombie's ear, even though Aladar displayed frail reactions to his gratitude and grunted. Aladar kept Slater over his shoulders safely, keeping him secure and holding him close so he wouldn't fall off. As for Slater, he couldn't shake away the intoxicated feeling in his head as his belly lay perched on Aladar's sturdy shoulder. Zinni did the same for Oli.

'You can put him down here next to me if you want, Aladar.' Ark spoke, tenderly scooting over to Spot more and allowing Aladar to bring Slater over. Spot put his arm around Ark's shoulder after she'd scooted over to him. Aladar flipped Slater off his shoulder as if he were a simple inanimate object and gently posed him like a model car down on the right side of the lounge next to Ark; Slater grunted and hissed from his sharp and sudden landing, rubbing his buttocks as he regarded Ark with bidding eyes. Aladar joined them, making himself at home by setting himself down on a tattered floor rug that had been smeared in the dirt (sadly, it used to be a beautiful zentangle pattern of an Indian elephant and would've looked stunning before the apocalypse began) next to Spot as he waited for the appearance of Zinni and their bonder Olivia Slater. Outside, Zinni was strutting over to Oli, his hand still gripping the pocket knife when he reached out for Oli's hands, but she recoiled out of the natural paranoia that Zinni would accidentally stab her through the hand. 'Zinni, please hand the knife to me. I don't want you accidentally stabbing me while you carry me.' Oli told him reasonably, holding her palm out to him like an offerings pedestal. Zinni did as he was directed; he moved his wielded hand and hovered it over hers for about five seconds before dropping it into Oli's opened palm. 'Thank you,' she mumbled softly to him. Like a prince usually depicted in those old Disney movies, Zinni transferred his arms underneath Oli, grasping her buttocks and her back in the same manner as Slater did with her before. Oli put one bladed side of the pocket knife in her mouth as she wrapped her arms around Zinni's neck while she still held onto the pocket knife with her teeth. Oli yelped as she felt herself being lifted off the ground by such extraordinary strength; her buttocks slipped from Zinni's dead grey hand and fell backwards so that her thighs were now in Zinni's grasp, her leg and stump hung loosely. Zinni transported Oli to the secluded house where Ark, Spot, Slater and Aladar waited. Oli was then carefully placed on the ground next to the lounge on which her exhausted brother sat, the latter which looked between zombie and bonder, envious that she had gotten the safer landing while he got the hard one. Zinni went over to join Aladar on the floor, and he, too, commenced playing the waiting game, waiting for the last four to make themselves known.

Losnedahl remained standing and staring outside for a little longer until he returned to the world with Ace, asking if he was okay. He shook his head with a start, looked at the crawler, bit his lip and nodded. He went to grab the handlebars of the wheelchair, but Ace held up a hand to stop him. 'Is okay, I'll take myself there; you just focus on getting Marilyn inside.' Said Ace, surprising him with how her English seemed to have improved a little. He watched Ace fling herself out of the chair and carry herself, walking on her hands towards the house to join the rest. Now it was just him, Kolen and Winsome left outside. Losnedahl looked at Winsome, who said nothing; he just nodded, gesturing for him to lead the tired and sleepy Kolen inside to join her crawler. Losnedahl returned a nod to him and threw one of Kolen's limp arms over his shoulder. Kolen didn't wake up or move; she simply groaned lethargically, and Losnedahl knew that she was asleep. He took an inhale through his teeth as he put his other hand over Kolen's side and started walking her to the house to join the others who were waiting for them. Finally, Winsome was the last to enter the house; he'd taken a moment to fold and pick up the wheelchair, lug it under his arm and bring it into the house, open it and set it down and shut the front door, which hung loosely off its hinges behind him before sitting down in the middle of the zentangle elephant rug. Ace crawled towards the wheelchair and climbed into it. He felt petty and sour about bringing up the topic of Bear; as much as he'd cherished his dog with all his heart, he kept his memories of Bear repressed in a box for the sake of his sanity. Because whenever he would think of, or worse, mention Bear, he'd be discharged into an overflowing stream of darkness; the subject of Bear's passing was still so raw despite it being years ago, Winsome just couldn't bring himself to bandage his scars and get over it. But after Losnedahl had killed the zombified remains of Eir Losnedahl, he felt like the time was right. The time to fill in the gaps and let Ark and the others in on the information about the best damn dog in Britain (according to him). He's sitting on the elephant carpet, thinking of all the idiotic and childish complaining he used to do and how he had earned the nickname of *The Dickhead*, wishing he could take everything back and wished he could've been a more decent guy to be around with. He sighed at the idea that he'd wasted his life.

Chapter 28

As expected, the interior of the house was what they'd come to expect and grew accustomed to, a dimly lit place that looked to have seen far better days. The furniture was torn and smothered with dust. A small pine end table existed near one of the walls that had a plaster outing that, over time, appeared to be chipping, with the wooden pillars holding them together appearing all rotten and overrun with moss; this seemed like one of the earliest houses that'd been abandoned, even before the reign of the mortuus carnem. Some of the lights weren't working due to broken bulbs. The windows were obscured with wooden boards, and the floor was filled with trash and discarded objects the previous owners had left behind before evacuating to a much safer place to hide out with other survivors just looking to see the tomorrow morning's sun. So, in other words, it was just like any other home one would find in these dark days.

Ark stood up after sitting in the torn, foul-smelling couch comfort for a total of four minutes. Her eyes scanned about at her area, and she sighed deeply. 'Does anyone want a drink? I'm parched.' She articulated with intention, progressing over to Ace's wheelchair, opening the attached pouch's flap, and taking out a bottle of fresh purified water before going back to the comfort of the vile-smelling couch as Kolen lay curled up on the floor, sleeping peacefully, her head on a cushion that Losnedahl had given her from one of the dusty couches. Ark screwed the lip off and took large gulps of the cool distilled water, signing in deep relief and satisfaction at the feeling of the cold liquid streaming down her throat, one of the first times she had had a nice cold drink since she and co. had left the GFOSAR. 'If there's Meantime, Raspberry Wheat, I'll have that; I could do with a trip to DazLand right now.' Slater replied groggily while doing mild foot exercises, twitching them, and bending them up and down to check if they were still functional, that the batteries hadn't fully depleted on him. 'Same, I could really dig some beer at the moment,' answered Winsome, corresponding with Slater, though he didn't sound as enthused as the bearded man; he just sat there twiddling his fingers or stroking the cool metal of the shotgun. 'Sorry, but we didn't pack any beer, wine, vodka, or any kind of alcohol; I couldn't find any in Darren's old place. There's only bottled distilled water and a few empty cans of fizzy.' Ark articulated, remembering the assorted bottles she'd seen in the wheelchair pouch.

'Fuck my luck,' Slater moaned, laying on his back and delivering a big deflated sigh.

'You men and your alcohol; pass some water over here, anyone.' Oli requested, holding out her bare hand. Losnedahl stepped over the sleeping Kolen, looked through the pouch, took another bottle of distilled water and tossed it to Oli, who caught it with both hands before hollering her thanks to the mute Norwegian man. Ark stood up from the planted position between Spot and Slater on the lounge, walking about the home to look for the house's kitchen. Ark quickly found it by the cracked tiled floor that was distributed with broken window glass. 'Careful when entering the kitchen, ladies and gents, the floor is swimming with broken glass.' She warned the others about the glass shards in case anyone came into the kitchen to look for some refreshments and something to chow down on. Raking at the glass with her feet, she made it to the fridge and opened it. There, Ark's forest-green eyes scanned around at the contents inside it. Eventually, her eyes caught sight of five dark purple-coloured bottles with the label MEANTIME on the bottom. She smirked as she pulled out two full bottles of the Meantime Raspberry Wheat beer, knowing it'd appear to the men's pleasure. 'You're in luck. The fridge had gallons of the stuff.' Ark called out to them. She placed the two bottles of English beer on the ground, away from the glass shards in front of the fridge, dug herself back into the refrigerator, and pulled out a bottle to taste. Winsome leapt off the couch and met Ark in the kitchen, brushing the fragments of glass away with his foot. He aided Ark by taking two of the bottles from the floor, saving her the trouble of escorting three bottles into the trashed living room. Ark thanked him. 'Though maybe she should just have one if this stuff is strong; we don't want to be hammered for when Sam or anyone bad comes our way. So, I say we just have one. We still need to be awake and alert.' Ark stated. Winsome responded with a nod, taking the two bottles of Meantime Raspberry Wheat and handing one to Slater, who took it respectively from him. 'Cheers, mate,' mused Slater as he popped off the cork and began glugging it down like some dehydrated man who lived on seawater's bitter, salty taste. 'You hear what Lisa said, bro; you're only allowed one, so no trip to DazLand.' Said Oli.

Slater said after already drinking half the bottle before burping. 'Pity, I would've loved to go to DazLand and experience bliss for the first time since the world went to fuck. But oh my, this is the shit!' Slater thought out loud, kissing the dark purple bottle while drops of Meantime dripped from his mouth. Ark returned shortly after, and this time, she sat down on the small end table made of pine in front of one of the chipping plaster walls that began to overgrow with mossy vegetation. Ark crossed one leg over her knee, glancing down at the British beer; a meagre grin found its way to her face. 'I've never had any beer from Pommy-land before, might as well give it a go and see what it's like,' she muttered softly to herself, popping off the cork and taking her first mouthfuls of the supposed raspberry-flavoured beer.

Ark swallowed the substance, and her eyes ultimately broadened with the intense sensation her mouth and taste buds were feeling. *No wonder it's as "raspberry", and no wonder it's craved and loved by the Brits; this stuff is better than James Boag, Coopers, and VB all together.* She thought with wide eyes, staring dreamily at the bottle as she compared the British beer to the beers back in her home country, confirming that the beer was far superior and knew how to add favourable taste to their beer. Losnedahl, who'd been watching Ark's face as she drank from the bottle and witnessing her face light up in what could only be described as pure bliss, had become curious as to what this raspberry beer had tasted like if Ark liked it, gives no reason why he shouldn't. He got off the tarnished floor, ventured into the kitchen, being mindful of the glassed floor, opened the fridge and pulled out a bottle of Meantime; setting it down beside him, he closed the refrigerator and went rummaging through the drawers and compartments until he found what he was looking for. A shot glass in one of the counter compartments near the faucet. Losnedahl returned to the living room and sat down near Kolen, bottle and shot glass in hands. Like Slater, Winsome and Ark had done prior, he pulled off the cork and carefully poured the contents from the bottle into the small shot glass, putting the bottle down beside him. He then raised the glass of Meantime to his lips and drank it in one gulp, not taking another. One shot of Meantime Raspberry Wheat was enough for Henrik Losnedahl (he'd never been the alcoholic type, growing a hatred for the stuff because of what it did to Joakim, escalating his already volcanic temper. But Losnedahl had thought that at this time, having some alcoholic liquid in his system wouldn't hurt so much and decided to try some for the first time in forty-one years. They're bound to be picked off one by one, might as well get pissed and die happy!), and he fell backwards in a dazed state of mind.

'Weak Henrik! So weak!' Slater slurred, still sounding sober. He looked at his empty bottle, grunted with irritation, threw it away, making it shatter, and woke Kolen up with a start. 'What's going on? Where are we?' she wondered, rubbing her eyes tiredly. Losnedahl rolled his eyes and took another small sip. On the opposite side of the floor, Winsome was drinking responsibly and wasn't boasting about how good his first bottle was; like Slater, no, Winsome was taking miniature sips from his bottle of Meantime. When he got about halfway, Winsome looked at the bottle sullenly before putting it on the ground, where he saw more of those ghastly prints, giving him a particularly horrible image in his head. He then sniffled, wiped the snot from his nose, and started to actually cry, putting his face in his hands, and wailing to them as if crying into them would provide some sort of comfort, even if it was fleeting. The others looked at him with wonder. 'What's the matter this time, Ryan,' Oli asked. Winsome looked up at her, his face red, contorted and soaked with tears. 'This.' He blubbered, 'This is wrong, everything, it's all wrong.'

Slater belched loudly, patting his chest. 'What are you carrying on about? You haven't finished your bottle.'

As if he'd been stabbed by those words, Winsome growled, seized his half-drunken bottle furiously and hurled it at the wall where it shattered loudly, raining glass and spattering raspberry-flavoured alcohol over it. Slater cried out from the suddenness of Winsome's aggressive behaviour towards the bottle, asking him what his problem was and why he had taken it on the bottle that would take his problems away. Everyone looked at him, even the zombies, who were alert and curious about what'd caused Winsome's sudden outburst this time; Spot was a little more on edge from the others as if he could sense more violence bubbling in the uneasy man. Winsome was breathing heavily, staring at the splatter on the wall he'd created. Then without looking at anyone in particular, he said, 'I don't need some fucking bottle of beer to help ease away my problems. For the love of god! How can you just sit here and drink and expect your problems to blow over? I, for one, am not a fan of this, I know I said that I would be better and wouldn't cause trouble for anyone. But Christ! Look at the world we're living in? Look at what that fucking thing has put us through; think about what Sam would do if we just sat here and drank like it's happy hour. Wake up people! We shouldn't be sitting here drinking our sorrows away; we should be talking, planning, mapping things out and how we plan on putting a stop to this fucking nightmare that we've been put through. Look, I'm sorry for causing another scene like I've done before. But I'm just frustrated, sick of going from house to house and talking about nonsense. Look, I know I suggested that we come here in the first place, but I didn't expect any of us to find and get hammered before the day was done. We may still have plenty of time with us, but I, for one, am not going to rest until that fucking bitch is six feet under. I will gladly stay away throughout the whole night and watch out for her if I can.' He paused himself for a bit, taking a breather for a minute before continuing. 'All I'm saying is that we shouldn't be wasting time drinking beer and talking about useless information; we should be gathering around each other and mapping things out, planning on how we are actually going to stop Sam and save the country.' Losnedahl sat up and signed that he agreed with him and that they shouldn't be sitting here drinking their sorrows and nightmares away; they should be stepping towards them and learning how to confront and face them.

'Exactly my point, Henrik.' Winsome said, nodding towards the mute man.

Losnedahl nodded.

What followed after this was a little quieter, but it wasn't prolonged when Oli had put her hand up, wishing to say something. 'If that is how you two think, maybe before we plan our final battle out, is there anyone who wishes to confide and tell their story? I mean, we might not get another chance to do so if Sam finds us or we find her. We might not make it out of tonight, so if anyone has anything to say, now would be the best time.' She declared sternly, though it was still evident that she and the rest of them were scared and didn't know if she or the others might make it through this night alive. It was better to clean things up now or never get the chance to again.

The Norwegian man put a hand up and offered to convey his story first and in the best way he could, reciting his tale for what he would assume would be the last time and in front of what had become his dearest and closest friends. "I can't remember how old I was when I moved from Norway to the UK. But I know, based on what I had heard stories from my late aunt, Anette Næss. My mother, who was that headless zombie I took out, was the kindest, most loving woman in Florø, my hometown in Norway; I knew that I wanted to meet her in person. Even though the idea was impossible back then because my mum had died soon after I was born by shooting herself, this was way before the mortuus carnem was discovered, back during the late 2000s and early 2010s when I was still a young boy. Another reason was that I wanted to be as far away from Joakim... dad... as possible, because I'll come to the reason why soon. If I remember correctly, I think I threw a party when I found out about his death... because I hated his guts, he was the one that cut out my effing tongue and the reason I've been mute for my entire life. The reason for him to do such a thing to a newborn baby boy is beyond me, and quite frankly, I don't give a shit as long as he's where he belongs and can't hurt anyone. But anyway, back to when the mortuus carnem problem had started to get high around Norway, and that word got out of people trying to reverse the infection and get the zombies back into humanity in the United Kingdom. I realized that this would be an excellent opportunity to meet my zombified mother in person, who I had heard so many good things about; that was partly a reason why I chose to become a zombie bonder. So, pretty much the main reason I had moved to the UK was because of a childish wish to see my mother for the first time in the real world and not in my dreams… and you're probably wondering how I found out my mother's body was here in the first place? Rumours were spreading around about a headless Norwegian female getting illegally smuggled over to the UK. If that wasn't enough, it wasn't long until more rumours spread about her corpse being bought and sold to the local necrophiliac's here on black markets. Sick effers buying corpses to eff with; that shit is the lowest of the low... So yeah... that's basically why I'm here, but since I… you know... I don't really know what else to do after we finish what Sam started… might consider going back home to Florø, so yeah, that's my story." Losnedahl signed the final part of his story and laid his hands down on his lap, feeling understandably miserable. Kolen was aghast by what he's saying in sign language and couldn't help but feel more sympathy for him, so much so that she started to tear up. She knew that he'd lived a troubled life in Norway, but she had never heard the part about the rumours about his mother's corpse being sold off to sickos looking to have their way with a headless foreigner. Kolen enveloped her hands around Losnedahl's shot-free hand and held them affectionately, exhibiting contrite concern with what'd happened to him during his childhood and that killing his zombified mother had been the icing on the cake. To Kolen, it seemed that melancholy followed Losnedahl wherever he went and that try as he might, he just couldn't escape the tragedy that stalked him throughout a good reminder of his childhood to adulthood.

'Fuck, man, that's rough. For a father to cut out his newborn son's tongue... I can't even begin to comprehend the trauma you must've felt. It's honestly amazing that you survived and didn't choke on your own blood.' Oli recoiled, looking down at her amputated foot.

'No blame self, Mr Henrik,' said Ace. Losnedahl glanced at Ace and nodded his thanks to her for her kind words. His face wore the expression that told everyone that his mother had intended to set them both free from Joakim's wrath, but Losnedahl was unfortunate to survive and reignite the flame of his father's brutality. Oli looked away sadly.

'There are just some sick bastards out there. Some of the things purchased on black markets are utterly criminal… The only thing I bought on the black market was just some hunger drugs for Aladar and Zinni since people like me can't exactly get them from the GFOSAR without breaking in and stealing some.' Oli assured herself; she looked up at Losnedahl. 'I'm really sorry about what happened to your mother; learning that her corpse was violated like that brings out the F in fucked up,' she made a tender apology to him, considering that she had nothing to do with Eir Losnedahl or Losnedahl's life for that matter.

Kolen put her hand up next. 'I'll go next. The main reason I moved from Middelburg in the Netherlands to the United Kingdom was because I was too much of a coward to gun down a zombified version of my husband, Jacob. He died from a stroke a few days before I was ready to break the news that I was ready to try for a baby and become a mother, as it had always been a dream to become a mother and have children... you can bet that I cried like a child upon hearing the news of his death. I can't precisely remember, but I think I even went as far as musing suicide just so I could be with my dear Jacob. I think I even wrote up a suicide note and had a crafted noose made from a rope we had in the shed, ready to hang myself. But it was as if Jacob could sense the distress and heartbreak I was going through because, from what I can remember, he'd returned home just as I was about to loop my head in the noose. He shambled into the bedroom, looking like he'd just crawled his way out of his own grave. He was smeared head-to-toe in dirt and still wore one of his best business suits. If we had the zombie bonding process back home in the Netherlands and if someone had returned his memories and personality back to him, informing him that his wife is in bad shape due to hearing about his death. It'd almost be like this if Jacob could talk. He'd be saying, "Marilyn darling. What the bloody hell are you doing trying to kill yourself? I'm here now, babe; everything is going to be alright now, honey. I was told that you were ready to become a mother by these high-ranking officials, so why don't we make those dreams a reality and consummate our love once more in bed?" but of course.' Kolen lowered her head, wiping her eyes underneath her spectacles. 'He wasn't saying that because he wasn't a talker, and he most certainly wasn't a bonded zombie… the stress and terror that I felt was just too great. It was too much for me to handle... I suppose you could say that I was one of those stereotypical girls who always panicked at seeing anything dangerous back then. I always needed a man to come and save me from a tower guarded by a fire-breathing dragon, like in those European fairy tales. I couldn't bring myself to even pick up a knife or fire-poker to defend myself against the undead Jacob. So, I simply just ran away like a coward from the house, taking all the money we currently had and forcibly buying my escape out of Middelburg and the Netherlands. I didn't care where I went as long as it was away from my zombified husband and the Netherlands. I soon ended up on Canvey Island in the United Kingdom, where I was quickly informed about the GFOSAR. A safe place where people were conducting experiments to bring the dead back to life with a process called zombie bonding. I qualified for the job and was trained by the amazing late Alexander Fredrickson. My first zombie just happens to be Ace here. My reason for naming her Ace was because of Jacob… he loved card games when he was alive, all kinds, poker, blackjack, go fish, you name it, and his favourite card was the "Ace", so that's why I named my first crawler zombie Ace, in honour of my late husband, Jacob. I think he would be proud of me.' Kolen looked down at the floor, fiddling with some of the strings in the elephant carpet. Ace stared at Kolen in stunned silence after hearing the reason why her bonder had christened her as Ace. It's because of her late husband. Ace wished she had legs so she could walk over and give Kolen a hug, an action that was something Spot was all too familiar with.

'Well, at least you can say that you're more open to violence now and will openly defend yourself even if you don't want to; you can't control your instincts. They make you fight back against your attackers. That's an achievement, Marilyn, and don't you doubt that for a second. When you return to the Netherlands, you should give Jacob the peace he deserves, or if someone already has, find, and visit his grave and confide in the achievements you made during your time in the UK. I bet he'd be really proud of how far you've come Marilyn. I mean it, you've come a long way from when we first met.'

Ark gave her a friendly nod, complying with her seedings for the future after Sam's death and when the mortuus carnem had been wiped out.

'Yeah, I should... thanks, Lisa' Kolen said sadly. Small tears dripped from her brown eyes and onto her white-framed glasses, but she didn't bother wiping them away. She just let them flow, knowing it would be wise to let them cease independently. Kolen looked glumly down at her hands, which she'd cupped on her lap in some kind of praying gesture. Losnedahl repaid Kolen for the hug she'd given him when he was going through the struggles of retelling his tale of woe, of how he lost his tongue not long after he was born and thought it was a good time for him to give her one in return. To be able to retell something that you tried so hard to forget was bound to be a heavy task, but Kolen showed courage and endurance, keeping herself well-collected as she told her story.

'Damn, I feel ya, girl.' Acknowledged Oli, though her mind was thinking a different thing entirely. *You never mentioned anything about you being married and that the reason you left was that your husband became one of the undead! Well, I hope your husband finds peace soon.'* Winsome added softly, coming to her front, kneeling down, and putting a gentle hand on her cheek and rubbing it with his thumb in an amicable manner as if to say everything will be alright Marilyn; I promise you that, Luv.*

'What about you, Lisa?' Oli asked, curious as to know if she had an interesting story that she needed to tell. 'Do you have reasons for coming to this country? Did you come to escape something? Did you have a choice?' She asked gently, looking up at Ark as she took the last mouthful of her first bottle of Meantime Raspberry Wheat beer.

'My story isn't all that special and isn't a heart throbber like Henrik and Marilyn's. I only really moved here for a job, and that's basically it. But if you want my story in full, I'll deliver,' she said, placing the now empty bottle of Meantime on the wooden end table she sat on. 'Spill, even if it's the most uninteresting origin story ever. I'm curious, nonetheless. I want to hear about this job that got you here.' Oli requested, sounding like she was genuinely interested in hearing a brief summary about Lisa Ark and her past. It almost reminded Ark of when she was a little girl in preschool when she and her classmates would sit cross-legged on the floor in front of the teacher as she reads from the picture book about the Dingo looking to find and stew a Wombat, but is outsmarted and poisoned by the Wombat's mates.

'I was born in Adelaide, Australia. I worked as a senior neurosurgeon at the Royal Hospital of Adelaide, and not to brag. But I was known as the most renowned surgeon there. I was infamous for fixing numerous patients whom many of my colleagues had deemed incurable. Lucky for them, I was always around to tend to them, taking note of their issues and working to the fullest to cure them and bring them back to their families. But anyway, my boss, Edward Arlen, confronted me during my break. He invited me into his office, where he explained that he had received a call from the GFOSAR, all the way in the United Kingdom, and about this one patient that only one woman could fix, that woman being me. At first, I was a bit reluctant to take the offer because I wondered what would happen to the other patients at home. But Edward had assured me that the Royal was in good hands and that the employers at the GFOSAR desperately required a brilliant and dexterous neurosurgeon capable of curing almost anything! Cancer wasn't included. I personally didn't think I was that good and didn't deserve half the recognition that I got because… because…' Ark stopped, the boy's face again, the straight line, those lifeless eyes, it was too much, too confronting to go back there. Still, she had already started to tell it, so she might as well finish it, even if it would cause her serious grief. Ark bit her lips, took a deep breath and forced herself to go on. 'There was a boy, about ten, who came into my ward with a paediatric tumour in his brain. My team and I did everything we could to remove it, to help the poor boy, even to the stage where I was drinking cup upon cup of coffee to stay awake; I remember sweating profusely, and I kept staring at the heart-rate monitor, panicking each time the line dipped. My surgery partner was trying to tell me that the boy was gone and that the surgery was pointless, but I didn't listen, and I kept trying to save this young boy, even if it meant days and hours without sleep. I was determined; I used everything I'd learned in this young boy's brain, doing everything I could to remove that tumour. Eventually, I was left to work on him myself because I demanded to be left alone with him. But each second, I remained with him, the more stress I was putting on myself and then, what I assumed was over fifteen straight hours, I was mentally and psychically exhausted and about to pass out. I looked at the monitor, and my heart sank when I saw the straight line and the dreadful monotone beep. When I looked back at the boy, I opened his eyelids and shone a light on them, and that's when I knew that I'd failed... the boy had died, and I'd failed my job as a neurosurgeon; I had failed the boy's parents, the boy and myself. Never again, I thought to myself, never again would I allow anyone to die on my watch, never would I let myself fail... So, when Arlen came to me with the job, I accepted because the GFOSAR had offered to pay direct flight fares and declared that my cooperation would deal with an immense quantity of assistance. That was when Arlen had reminded me of something I'd often spoken about during break time and that I'd planned on moving to the United Kingdom to live, a change from the usual sights of Adelaide. But yeah, despite worrying about the outcome of the Royal and the patients in my absence, the other reason why I was a bit hesitant was because I didn't have the right sum to pay for the airfares. So, that's why they offered to pay for me because I couldn't exactly afford it and because they knew that I was the right person for the job and that it was only fair if they had paid for my flight ticket over. But like I said, I accepted and became a head doctor at the GFOSAR and a zombie bonder after hearing about the experiments they did on the undead and when the mortuus carnem had started to become quite a problem for Britain... So yeah, that's mine. I know it's nothing special... aside from that... that hiccup.' Ark said in a strangled voice. Talking about the death of that young boy (Nolan Edgerton Jr.) was always hard for her, and it always haunted her even all these years later. It's still the one recurring nightmare she had at night. Ark shook her head and got up from the end table. She took the empty beer bottle of Meantime and inserted it in an electronic recycling bin, resting against one of the flaking plaster walls near the hallway shrouded in darkness, leading to what Ark assumed was the bedrooms, bathroom, and laundry. Seems like whoever had lived in this house before age had caught up with it and, before it was evicted, must have savoured having things clean and was lazy enough to have one of these silly things in their house.

'Damn... I didn't know...' murmured Winsome at the thought that Ark had failed to save that young boy.

'Even if your story isn't as tragic as Henrik and Kolen's, it's still interesting. But hey, I'm sorry about the boy. But everyone fails from time to time; it's part of life. I mean, I failed to get into the GFOSAR.' Oli responded, trying to shed light on the shadows that followed Ark. 'Flattering Olivia, but like I said, not that special.' Ark replied wanly.

'We should get going now.' Winsome spoke softly. 'I've had my rest, and my strength is back, for now at least.' He seemed more than eager to finish the job and get through the day alive and see tomorrow, and who could blame him? After everything he had seen in the GFOSAR and seeing just how low Fredrickson's zombie had gone, he's more than ready to see an end to this endless nightmare. Winsome accumulated his shotgun from the ground next to him and stood up. Slater nodded at Winsome, reached into his trench coat pocket and fished out some ammo cases for the group members armed with guns.

Ark didn't need to reload her rifle yet; she'd barely used it in the first place, but she knew that she had one loaded bullet to use before she'd need to reload it. But she had doubted that she'd use it until the time was right and

Sam's head was in the scope's view. One could say that Lisa Ark was saving her one bullet for Sam and Sam only.

Oli put a hand down her bra and fished out the revolver, and returned it back to Slater. He took it and loaded the bullets into the holder. Oli spoke up, making her commandments clear to both her pale blonde-haired zombies. Aladar moved over to Oli, knelt down, shovelled his hands underneath her back and legs and hoisted her up without much trouble while she clung onto his neck with one arm; the other arm held the pocket knife.

But before Ark could ask if everyone was ready to end this, Winsome left the living room for good this time. He went over to the front door with its crooked hinges and sighed heavily, knowing that things would get nasty, and that innocent blood was bound to be spilt. But he was a different man, a decent man who would fight for the safety of his friends to the bitter end; he wasn't going to run away from this; no, Ryan Winsome was going to own his share of the plate and face these demons that wandered the streets. Even if things got ugly, he wouldn't back down.

Breathing in again and breathing out, Winsome placed his free hand on the door and turned it.

Chapter 29

The door flung open so forcibly with the power of a strong gust of wind brought on by a terrible storm, which was brought along with the fury of the night almost knocking him over, Winsome batted the rouge door away with his hands. A grotesque howling ensued from outside, making Winsome cover his ears. Then it came for him like a truck, and Winsome's energy was knocked out of him by a potent force pinning him down to the ground. A set of solid teeth was biting into his shotgun, which Winsome held up to block the fast, strong creature pinning him down with... with paws instead of hands!

'Jesus! Get offa me!' he screeched, 'I could really use some help' he called out desperately to his friends as he darted his head around to avoid being spat on or, worse, bitten. The creature that was pinning Winsome down and clamping down on his shotgun, of course, was a zombie by its exasperated fierce nature and how it kept trying to bite its way through Winsome's shotgun. But this time, it wasn't originally a human; based on the paws it employed to claw at the gun and Winsome's chest, it was an animal. A medium-sized dog, to be exact, and by its matted, furry coat, it looked like it was a German Shepherd. However, Winsome couldn't determine if it did have an owner or was a stray when it died and was infected; the creature was snarling, barking, and growling viciously as it tried to get to Winsome, not giving him the time to check if the creature had a collar. All he knew was that it was a German Shepard dog, and it snarled fiercely at Winsome, raining droplets of slobber flickered about, and some were falling onto Winsome as he tried his best to hold the undead mutt off while the paws dug into Winsome's chest. 'Help me out here!' Winsome called out again. And answering his call, Ark and Losnedahl appeared behind him, seeing the animal pinning the man down.

'Jesus Christ!' Ark cried out the lord's name when she saw the creature on top of Winsome, digging its mangled paws into Winsome's chest, tearing his clothes as Winsome grunted and squeaked in pain, still trying his best to hold the creature away from ripping his throat out. Ark and Losnedahl glanced at each other, both scared and lost. They both wanted to help their friend, but they didn't know how they could be of much service in getting this highly aggressive dog thing off Winsome. The zombie dog appeared to have a devastating case of mange; heavy patches of the tan and black fur were missing. One might've suspected that the dead dog had killed quite a large number of people as well as other animals, feasting on their entrails while at the same time infecting them. The very sight of the zombie hound further bodes for a horrible idea that the zombie dog had sought pleasure in rolling around the blood of its victims. Leaving the remaining scraps of the dog's once handsome coat covered in grime mixed in with the blood of all those that'd fallen victim to those crimson-soaked fangs and paws, furnishing the zombie hound with an unbearable stench along with the persistent stench of death of its breath. The dog's chest was flayed like it'd been shredded from the outside, dug into by clawing hands and eaten, creating a nasty complexion of an exposed ribcage; the organs were there; they stood unquestionably visible, encased inside that cell of bone. Two of the dog's back toes were gone, with the bone stump protruding like a piece of bark on a spoiled tree. The dog had missing skin, much like the stomach; the bones were clearly visible to anyone viewing. One of its ears had been torn off, its muzzle had lacerations, and its once brown admirable eyes had fresh, warm blood dripping from them like bloody tears; the poor thing was in horrendous shape. The zombie dog persisted in the attack, even using its reddened claws to dig into Winsome's chest as he cried out in pain. He tried to shove the shotgun up into the dog's mouth in a feeble effort to break some of its teeth. But the dog's teeth seemed to be made of titanium; they just wouldn't break or even splinter! Advancing in more terror to ensue within Winsome's body. Losnedahl looked around him and yanked a dusty, cobweb-covered picture from the wall and being either brave or stupid, he stepped forward, picture raised above him and slammed it down upon the mutts' head; glass, dust and spiderwebs flickered out. Winsome spat some of the dust out of his mouth. The dog then looked at Losnedahl and snarled a furious and hideous monstrous noise; it left Winsome and leapt at the mute man. Losnedahl's eyes widened, and he hugged the wall; Ark jumped away from the wall, ending up back in the living room with the rest of them as the dog flew past them, disappearing in the dark. There was another crash as the dog hit something in the hall's darkness, giving Losnedahl just enough time to help Winsome to his feet. Winsome thanked Losnedahl; he held his ruined chest where he had been clawed at and stumbled into the room with the others. Losnedahl heard the sound of Kolen squeaking as Winsome went back into the room while he dealt with the dog that'd eventually come charging out of the darkness. The dog made a haunting guttural growl, and then there were some light tapping sounds of the dog's claws getting to its feel. Losnedahl looked to his sides, thinking of slamming another picture down upon the mutt's head, but that seemed ridiculous as he thought that the dog would probably be expecting him. He panicked, feeling about him, patting his pockets, which was when he remembered that he had the blade on his person. He unsheathed his weapon and held it with both hands, which were shaking tremendously. More pattering and tapping of the paws, the dog leapt at Losnedahl with another of those guttural and hideous growls. Losnedahl knew he needed to be quick and to time this just right if he was going to succeed in winning. He saw the dog fly towards him, bearing its ugly teeth, and Losnedahl raised his weapon. He could feel the paws touch him first in what felt like slow motion. Losnedahl yelled a muted cry as he swung the knife, gritting his teeth and jamming the bowie right into the side of the dog's neck, opening his mouth to yell a soundless cry as the dog made a sound that was a mixture of a pained yelp and furious growl as it fell to the ground with a hardened thump. Losnedahl jumped out of the way as he watched the thing get back to its feet again; the dog shook its mattered and broken body, seemingly a little dazed from the landing, causing blood to flicker out as the blood trickled down the handle. The knife remained wedged deep into the dog's neck even as it shook, but this zombie dog wasn't going to lay down and die so swiftly. Slater came into the hallway next and saw the creature; he had the revolver in his hand, pointed it at the dog and pulled the trigger without a moment's hesitation; the dog retreated with a startled and horrible yelp as the bullet went through one of its dead white eyes, just as it'd turned its sights back on the mute man and was about to leap at him again for the third time. Blood streamed down the empty socket as the dog made a disheartening, anguished howl followed by whimpers of pain as it grievously tried to paw at its eye as if trying to claw the bullet lodged deeply inside its socket out, but to no avail; the shot refused to budge. Slater went to fire another shot at the mutt, but the gun clicked – it was jammed! 'Sonofabitch! The guns jammed!' Slater roared as he tried to shoot the mutt but kept getting that same dismal clicking sound. Losnedahl pushed Slater and himself back into the living room, away from the dog's sight. They wouldn't stand a chance at going against Sam if this dog wasn't dealt with.

'What's going on out there?' Kolen whimpered when she saw the two men fall into the living room and scamper to their feet and away from the hallway. 'Henrik. Help me here; cover the doorway with this couch! Quick before the thing recovers!' Slater boomed, going over to one of the couches and trying to push it towards the opening. But it wasn't Losnedahl that came to Slater's aide.

It's the three undead males who had taken measures into their own hands to protect their bonders without needing to give them the order. Aladar helped Slater push the couch in front of the doorway, even though it seemed pointless as the dog could just jump over it. Spot had handed out his brain jar to the nearest person; it was Ark who took it and handed it down to Ace. Spot moved over to the couch and climbed over it; he recovered and fell around blindly. Spot's biggest allies were his hearing at his touch as he felt about the room for the dog's mattered fur and paying attention to how close it was to Ace and his brain jar. Zinni had followed him and found the thing first, grabbing its tail and yanking it backwards away from Spot and the couch. 'Ali, help me board it up with anything we can use! We only want Zin and Spot coming out of it.' Slater ordered from behind the barricade. The dog growled again, turning around quickly, and came at the young zombie boy, latching on and biting a large portion of flesh away from his hand. 'Zinni!' cried Oli as she had seen it behind the building barricade. Zinni let go of the tail to examine with groggy eyes at the offence the zombie dog had caused him. His hand had a flayed layer of skin that dangled and jellied around when he moved. He had bite marks going deep into his gaunt hand, and some of the muscle in his fingers had been torn away, leaving some bone and tendons to show in a ghastly display. He looked at it curiously as if trying to access the damage himself and work out what the bones that connected his fingers together were. But when he looked ahead to see Spot, who was now wrangling with the mutt, holding its muzzle shut, he knew that he needed to abandon his examination of his hand to help him. Zinni ran at the beast as Spot let the muzzle go. The beast barked to frighten the boy zombie, but it did not work, and Zinni came at it with his arms spread out. He crashed into the beast, digging his fingers into the beast's mattered hide while kicking freely at it. Then Spot came onto it again, utilising teamwork. While Zinni had wrapped his body around the undead dog, weighing it down, Spot had grabbed its tail and pulled at it, pulling, and dragging the beast back into the darkness and far away from the group and the barricade. But even with David and Goliath working together to restrain this dog, its strength was superior to them both! The dog threw itself at the walls to loosen Zinni's grip. Then it threw itself down on its side and on Zinni's back and rolled over, jamming Zinni's fingers and arms under its weight and causing him to let go while also peeling away that piece of flayed skin off his hand and bleeding quite profusely. As for Spot, who still kept holding its tail with one hand, the dog thrashed its tail around until Spot let go and fell on his buttocks. As the dog roared in pain, he felt something in his hand, and although he couldn't see what it was, he knew by the way it felt and the roar that it was some of the dog's tail; he had pulled half of it off. The beast zipped to Spot and leapt on him and began violently tearing and ripping away at his chest as if revenge for tearing off its tail. Spot kept fighting back, his tongue flashing about like it was its own wild animal; he held the dog away by its jaws, trying to keep it up, away from his chest, which now had bite marks. Zinni recovered and came over to help Spot. He came at the beast and pelted it with his foot as if it was a soccer ball. The beast ignored Spot then and went for Zinni, running and jumping, but Zinni hit the floor, and the door went straight into the barricade, knocking over the wooden chairs and small tables that had been used to hold it up. To the horror of the humans, the dog seemed more than a little dazed after it crashed into the living room. It staggered to its feet and shook its ruined body, and when Ark shone her torch on the beast, there was a glint of silver hanging down its neck and what looked like a blue-collar around its neck, which now had blood stains on it.

Winsome was standing still next to Kolen and Ace. Not only was he viciously attacked, but he could've easily been killed if it wasn't for Losnedahl and Slater's quick thinking. But he was inundated by a hurricane of fear and oppression. He couldn't help but stare, teary-eyed, at this horrible scene playing out, watching this zombie dog that almost made dinner out of him wobble and shake as it got to its feet. Aladar came to the dog and pinned it down, knocking it back to the ground where Winsome could get a good decent look at the beast and the glint of silver that hung from its blue collar. Then, as if he'd been shot. He recognised this zombie dog... not just because of its breed, but because the dog was still wearing its florescent blue collar and nameplate, which, when Winsome cautiously stepped to closer inspect it, had the name "Bear" engraved onto it... He knew it now; he'd been fighting what remained of his...

'Ba-Ba-Ba-Be-Bear...' Winsome managed to utter a fearful tremble, saying the name his dog had always wagged at. The other group members couldn't hear Winsome's timid cries as their ears were directed at the unfriendly snarls and growls emanating from the dog named Bear's mouth as he tried to wrangle Aladar off him. Winsome whimpered the name again, a little louder and this time Bear heard it, hearing his name and the familiar voice. It's the voice of his master, the man who had treated him like the king of dogs. Bear responded to his name and fellow master by turning his attention away from Zinni to him like he'd recognised him, and he seemed confused by tilting his head at him. The malice was gone in his face as he stared into Winsome's scared eyes. This very occurrence of seeing what'd become of his dog had sent Winsome through another troubled state. His feet were cemented, and he's experiencing another episode where his throat felt dry, and his eyelids had been sewn open. Winsome could've sworn he was hearing the hurt, scared whimpering of his old dog Bear, who was trapped inside a rabid, zombified version of himself, not wanting to hurt his master or anyone for that matter. Winsome then looked into the dog's remaining eye and could see that despite his actions, he was in pain and confused and didn't know what he was doing. Winsome's heart was aching as he could almost hear Bear speaking to him in a human-like voice.

(Master, help me! I'm really scared! I don't know what's wrong with me; why do I feel so hungry? What is going on? Why am I hurting people? Master, why do you look so scared? I don't like seeing you scared. Can we go back home and play? Master? Please, master, I'll be a good boy. Can you please take me home?)

Oh, Christ... why did it have to infect Bear? Why Bear? Winsome thought while tears rapidly started to flood down his reddened cheeks. Winsome knew what his dog would want, that Bear wanted to be put out of his misery so he wouldn't be able to hurt his master's friends or anyone, but... he just couldn't do it… it was just like he'd requested to Ark before they had come into this house; there's absolutely no way that Winsome could cope with the idea that he had to kill his infected dog. He's too much of a coward to even hold a gun to a zombified Bear, so having the duty of killing him was on another level of anguish. He may have died years ago and reanimated as a violent zombie in the same way as other shambling corpses around. But it was still his dog; it was still his Bear. It was still his dog under those dead pale eyes and malicious behaviour. It was still his dog trapped under the influence of the mortuus carnem. The diseased and disgusting mortuus carnem.

'RYAN!' screamed a voice behind him. 'What are you doing standing there? Shoot the damn thing!' shrieked Ark. She tossed the rifle aside to help Aladar and was clutching what remained of Bear's tail, making him yelp, trying the pull him away from Winsome as Bear's attention was now fixed on Winsome. He ignored the zombies that were trying to fight him earlier. Bear wanted Winsome, so he attempted to get to him, but Ark and Aladar kept him back by holding his tail.

(Master, she's pulling my tail too hard, it hurts!)

Winsome shuddered, prying his eyes away from the grieving expression in that dead white singular eye; he was a blubbering mess; he couldn't bring himself to even look at what had happened to his dead dog.

'LISA! BE CAREFUL!' shrieked Kolen and Oli.

'RYAN!' Ark screamed at the top of her lungs.

He knew it was him... as much as he wanted to deny it and leave the task up to Ark, Ryan Winsome knew that it had to him, that he had to put Bear six feet under. But how was he supposed to do it when he couldn't even bring himself to hold a gun up to Bear's head and swiftly pull the trigger, plunging Bear into darkness? Winsome didn't know but knew that if he didn't kill the zombified Bear, they'd be dead before Sam could even rear her head in and crack her wicked smile at them.

Winsome continued to stand there feeling hopeless, submerged in fear and melancholy, blubbering like a child in his mother's arms after finding out his dad died in a crash due to drinking. That was when they started to flash in his conscious mind the sweet memories of him and Bear playing and spending time together before the devastating day when Bear died at twelve. This painful memory of Bear's final moments had triggered Winsome's eyes to discharge even more tears than was originally humanely thought possible.

(Am I still your Little grizzly Bear?)

(*Always...*) It was clear from the apparent fact that the zombified Bear had the intention to kill Winsome and the rest of the group because it was just natural for the undead to hunt the living, so animals were no different. But Winsome just couldn't shake the haunting thought away that his lovable dog was still inside, trying to communicate with him, trying hard but failing to control his rabid hunger and lust for flesh. Trying to reach out to the man who'd soaked his fur with kisses and warmed his body with hugs. Winsome couldn't stop himself and shut himself down, thinking of all the moments he'd had with his dog, his best friend, his little grizzly bear.

Chapter 30

'RYAN!!' Ark continued to scream at him, trying to force him out of his dazed dream-like trance. 'GET YA HEAD IN GEAR! SNAP OUT OF IT!!' She exclaimed, but Winsome showed no signs of returning to the real world. He's trapped in the past, where everything was more manageable, and he didn't need to worry about looking out for his hide; he wasn't even blinking, which by itself was a course for concern. Winsome knew what he had to do, but he couldn't bring himself to do it; he just couldn't do it yet. He couldn't even look at the beast that wore his dog's collar.

'Lisa needs you! Come back to us, Ryan! Please!' This was Kolen, who screamed, trying to bring him back. But to Winsome, both she and Ark had zero sound; it was like someone had muted their voices. Hell, even the Bear thing's vicious growling and distorted barking were muted; the only thing Winsome was hearing was the slowed, laborious breathing Bear had been making during his final minutes in front of that cosy fireplace as Winsome lay beside him, stroking his fur and humming a tune to him – a tune which Bear would bark and sing along to while Winsome would usually dance around the living room, holding Bear's front paws as they tapped their feet across the varnished wood. *Come home to me, Bear. Come home…*

'Come home to me, Bear.' He lamented. This was when Kolen relieved herself as Ace's carer to seize Winsome by his shoulders and shake him violently out of his trance into the dark side of memory lane while sometimes clicking her fingers at his unblinking eyes. But Winsome's body didn't move so much as a flinch; his eyes were wide, his body was stiff, and he was drooling; in his current state, he was nothing but a vegetable with a forever frightened expression inked on it.

It was as if he had...

Spot climbed over the broken barricade, closely followed by Zinni, and joined his bonder (Ace was holding his brain jar) in the struggle to repeal the undead Bear, helping to keep the vicious zombie mutt away from his former master. Not wanting to face seeing the dog tear Winsome's face off. Yes, Winsome may not have been the most likable member of their party. There have been many negative thoughts about keeping him in the group. But that was before Winsome had pardoned himself, apologising and owning up to his every mistake by aiming to become a different man, a better man, a man that he and everyone else had wanted to be. Furthermore, because of his desire to change, Ark made it apparent to the rest of the group that Winsome was one of them to the very end and that his life was just as valuable as everyone else's.

Joining the fight again. Only this time, it was with his bonder, the woman he loved dearly. The giant half-headless zombie tightly wrapped his arms around Ark's waist, lifting her off a few inches from the ground and pulling her backwards. Keeping her way above ground, away from the teeth if Bear had decided to dart around, lashing those blood-soaked fangs into her hands like he had previously done to Aladar. At the same time, she maintained her purchase onto Bear's still bushy German Shepard's tail, sweating and holding the snarling zombie dog away from the petrified Winsome, who finally blinked.

He blinked some more, and Winsome's body regained life; his colour returned to him, and he started to move again like someone had flicked his ON switch. He was trembling like a shy, frightened rabbit, his cherry face was a mess of tears, and he had snot dripping out of his nose. Winsome sniffled, trying to keep the snot inside his nostrils while he cried. This time, Winsome had managed to bring out the strength within him to hold the shotgun up, pointing it directly at Bear's snout. Then he slowly moved it up between the eyes as a fusion of deep, angry growls and terrified yelps came from Bear's gob, which was dripping with a vibrant blend of slobber and blood.

'Bear… dear God… I'm so fucking sorry…' he moaned weakly; his lips were quivering, and his eyes were starting to sting from how much he was crying, staring down at zombie Bear still trying to get to him.

'Ryan!' Ark screamed, making him jolt as she and Spot gave out one more strained tug to the point where Ark started screaming out from the extensive strength she was using. That was until all the power in her arms had left her. She knew that she couldn't keep up this tug-o-war battle forever. Spot made a strained gurgle noise, and he pulled Ark back so hard that the flesh and bone that connected Bear's tail to his buttocks came off with an unearthly splitting sound accompanying it. Ark and Spot both went toppling backwards on the floor. Spot hit the ground; Ark was safely enveloped in his long, thin arms. Ark looked up, observing what was tightly clasped in her fingers was now a mattered, disconnected dog tail with blood squirting out of it, painting Ark's grey tee with another fresh coat of red; she knew what this meant, and it wasn't good for them. 'Shit!' Ark had nothing but full-blown terror in her voice. She understood that ripping that tail off meant something terrible. They had just infuriated the zombie mutt as Bear gave out another ungodly howl right before whipping his head around to face her, bloody teeth bared his mattered flesh contorted with fury. 'Oh fuck,' Ark mouthed as she blocked her ears from the harrowing sound, eyes broadening, and her mouth hung aghast at the sheer scale of hatred that was illustrated on this dog's tattered face.

She dropped the detached tail with heavy disgust and reacquired her stance again, helping Spot up in the process, clutching his arm tightly while backing up; her face was submerged with fear, and she commenced shouting at Winsome to do the final blow and be that hero he wanted to be! *Goddamn mutt just won't play dead and stay playing dead*, the impure thought occurred into Slater's mind after realising just how much damage they had put into this one zombie dog. If this dog provided a chore for them, he could only imagine what other zombie animals would do to them if they were given the right moment and time. 'Ryan, if you want to write yourself as the hero of this story, you know what to do!' Slater yelled. And yes, Winsome did know what he had to do, but he didn't know if he could do it. This was his dog, for crying out loud.

'Be-Bear!' Winsome cried; his features were so anguished that he almost looked like a different person.

Bear shot his attention back to Winsome; his mug was a never-ending canvas of wrath. To see such fierce emotions from what used to be his best friend hurt Winsome to the core, and he didn't think he would ever be able to recover from this. After dispelling the shot, he might hang up the belt and call it quits on life.

'I'm so, so, SO sorry! You will always and forever be my little grizzly Bear'. Winsome blubbered, tears and snot streaming down his face. He bit his lip so hard that he could taste his own blood. He lifted his trembling hands up, holding the shotgun up and put his finger on the trigger, blubbering on about how sorry he was over and over with each second the gun was pointed at Bear. The dog let out a demonic-sounding roar at Winsome and furiously assailed at him, ignoring everyone else in the room; his one dead white eye was full of a powerful, inescapable bloodlust, intending with each fibre of his undead being to tear Ryan Winsome apart. His former owner.

Winsome closed one eye and aimed. 'God have mercy on my soul.' He snivelled.

Bear jumped.

Winsome pulled the trigger.

BLAM!

Then silence.

Bear collapsed onto Winsome with a terrible firework display of blood, sending both man and dog falling backward onto the ground, and everything became still... the only sound being the shocked, panicked breathing of the man who lay underneath the bloodied corpse of the dead dog.

'Ryan!' Ark and Slater said as they panted and ran over to Winsome's side to help him. Slater gave Bear a light prod with his foot for good measure to double-check if he was well and truly dead. He was still, which meant that he was. Bear was dead, for good. He nodded towards the blonde woman.

Ark gave Slater a slight dip as the both of them knelt down and pushed the inert zombie dog off Winsome's trembling, blood-soaked frame, who was staring up at the ceiling with huge, frightened eyes. As if seeing his dog die the first time wasn't bad enough… Everyone glanced down at Winsome, who was lying still, shaking, and breathing heavily.

'Ry-' Kolen began softly but was quickly interrupted by Winsome screaming back to life before he flung himself up off the ground and shuffled backward, pushing with his feet until he hit the plastered wall and jumped when he felt the wall. He threw his arms over his bent knees and bawled while rocking back and forth, crying heavy tears onto his knees. Winsome was in shock from what he had done, something that he'd never thought he would have the guts and mental capacity to do. He had blood and bits of flesh staining his body, painting his entire formally white lab coat a violent crimson. His face wasn't only covered in liquid because of his own tears, but he also had a red, slimy substance mixed around his cheeks. Before Bear sustained the war that was brought upon his rotting corpse, the kind-hearted dog inside him had made the very last effort to thank his master by licking him on the cheeks as if he were to try and lick away his master's tears.

'Hey, hey, it's okay... you did it, you did it.' Ark cooed gently as she helped Winsome up to his feet with the help of Slater, who had taken one of his arms and placed it tenderly over his shoulder. Winsome jumped when they touched him, panicked, and moved away with haste, 'Don't touch me!' he whimpered in a child's voice. 'Get away!' The poor man was frightened beyond repair. Once they consoled him, he allowed himself to be helped. They took him by the arms, carefully lifted him up without any sudden movements and placed him gently on the couch without complaining or hassling him to get over it; they stayed by his side and waited patiently for him to mentally recover after being forced into killing the zombified version of his sweet dog. As expected, it had taken quite some time for him to recover from what he had just done to his undead dog's remains, as Winsome was in too much shock to do or say anything at this moment. He could only cry and listen to the warm things his fellow friends had to say about the feat he had just done and that he had been brave for doing it and not getting his way out of it. Or taking the coward's way out by turning the gun on himself and shooting so he could avoid having to kill Bear, even if Bear was a zombie. Talking about Bear was already hard enough for him. When one considered the evidence that he had just shot two hard shells straight into Bear's already exposed chest and blew apart his back and spine, shattering his ribcage and organs inside. If Winsome had fired one more shot, he would've blown the zombified Bear into two pieces. So, one could only begin to imagine just how Winsome was feeling.

Ark glanced at the now stagnant dog named Bear on the ground with blood pooling around it, seeing the work that one shotgun blast had done and knowing that that dog had once been Winsome's beloved pet

Ark was known by those around her as a strong-minded woman and a woman who had an even stronger gut when it came to things ghastly. She actually had tears welling in her eyes, but she wiped them away before anyone could see them. Kolen was blubbering, blowing her nose with her sleeve at the sight of Bear's mangled, lifeless body in the ever-expanding puddle of blood. The thought of, what if that were my dog or cat? Came to them. Oli and Slater contained their sorrow on the outside. But on the inside, they were feeling the same way that Winsome had like someone dear had been taken away from them; Oli was shedding a few tears here and there, while Slater didn't share any; his eyes remained dry. But that didn't mean that he didn't feel remorseful for the former arsehole of the group. Slater held Winsome's hand in his, softly tapping it and telling him that everything was going to be alright, that he did the right thing and that he was fearless for getting it done, even if it hurt.

The zombies just stood in the back and stared, though Spot was the one that was feeling the most sympathy for the man he didn't like at first. Ark came over and sat down next to Winsome, who continued to sniffle and stare at his shaking hands. 'Lisa, can you hold me?' Winsome said again in that small child's voice. Ark stared at him for a bit but didn't say anything. She just put her arm over his shoulder and pulled him close to her without a word. He dug his face into Ark's chest and cried out Bear's name. Still, Ark didn't say anything, nor did anyone else, as Ark rubbed his back to calm him down; whilst doing so, she wiped away his tears the best she could with her thumbs. The way an indulgent mother does to her child after they hurt themselves.

Chapter 31

After he was done crying, Winsome turned away from the blonde woman, wiped his face, and sat in silence, staring absently into space for what seemed like hours, even though it'd only been around twenty minutes, according to Slater's wristwatch. Most of his tears had become dry with the help of Ark, who helped to clean them with her thumbs. At the same time, she tenderly consoled him about his dog, explaining how he'd done the right thing by not allowing him to suffer any more as a rotting pile of mattered fur. Winsome said nothing. Ark's way of comforting Winsome was almost, if not dubiously, similar to how Kolen had often sympathised with Losnedahl when word of his mother was mentioned, even for a split second. Ark continued to comfort Winsome by rubbing his back and informing him that it was done and that he wouldn't have to worry about doing something like it again. Winsome nodded wanly. He knew and understood that what he did was the right thing, but it still didn't make him feel any better about it. He thanked Ark with a nod. 'Can someone remove him. I don't want to see what I did to him,' he mused, refusing to look at the carcass on the floor. Slater and Losnedahl did this without another word. The men both grimaced as they moved the body around in the bloodstained carpet, and then they rolled the rug up with the dog's carcass inside it, and Slater took it away from Losnedahl, rubbing his beard and carrying the dog and the carpet out of the room and out of sight. He returned shortly after, nodding at Winsome that it was gone, who returned one thankful glance back to him.

'God, this is so fucked up…' Oli said dryly. 'What the fuck has happened to this world? What did we do to deserve this?' No one replied to her; they just sat and listened to the wind brushing against the house, causing eerie creaks throughout the house, which none of them reacted to, accustomed to it already.

It was like this for a few minutes until a voice spoke up. 'Not to interrupt or like I'm rushing things. But are we still gonna finish this? I can sense something coming; we better get a move on.' Ace said softly, only this time it was a complete sentence with good punctuation and no gaps; she sounded... human... at any other given time, this would have astounded the group, who'd stare at the crawler with broadened peepers, particularly Kolen because those words had come from Ace's mouth. Ace was her zombie, let alone her first zombie! She was now speaking proper, fluent, English without sounding broken that Kolen sometimes thought to herself that she might not need the use of the drugs anymore. But it wasn't the first time she'd spoken a complete sentence. Losnedahl remembered hearing her say something eloquent to him after he'd killed his undead mother. So, it didn't come as much of a surprise to any of them when she was capable of doing it before, and the only response the crawler got was Ark staring at her for a second before returning her attention to the broken man lying helplessly on the floor. 'Ace is right, Ryan; we can't afford to waste any more time mourning over losses. We have a job to do.' Ark registered softly, placing a hand of comfort on his shoulder, but Winsome just stared, not moving; his face read, *What's the point? We are going to be picked off one way or another; what's the point of fighting anymore?* Ark was deeply saddened by this, seeing that Winsome had pretty much given up. She rubbed his shoulder. 'Please, Ryan, we need you in this. We can't do this without you.' Ark divulged with a tender tone, which did have some force to it. Ark knew better than anyone else if she had force as a means of encouragement. He would very likely snap back into his ball of complaints. Calling her out for being heartless and lashing out at her out of unstilled anger, verbally abusing her in any way he could.

If it came down to it, he might even pick a fight with her physically punching and kicking her until Ark was a bloody pulp, or she begged in a blubbering voice for him to stop. Showing weakness to him by allowing herself to be beaten up by him and the others, unable to do anything to contain or at least extinguish his fury. In a way, Winsome had the cognisance of a child. He would often open his mouth to say something out of line without thinking about others and the things he had said. But Ark couldn't deny that he had a good heart, and seeing him as a broken man was honestly hard for her to grasp because she had never seen or known Winsome to be like this. Still, here he was, sitting silently, with a wan expression on his usually sly canvas.

Ark sighed with a gloomy expression that matched Winsome's. 'We need your help in finishing this, Ryan. Please, don't give up now. I know we've had some disagreements during the past few hours, but you're one of us; we need you.' she urged him gently, placing another reassuring hand on his back and putting her head on his shoulder, urging, and begging him to not give up just because he had to take out the zombified remains of his dog.

'I hate to be the one that sounds insensitive, but Lisa's right, Ryan.' Oli urged him sadly, followed by Kolen, who had shuffled towards him on her knees and put her hands on his knees. 'We can't let Sam win by infecting all of Britain; we need to finish this with y-'

'I'll kill her...' Winsome suddenly gnarled, disrupting Kolen and making her flinch slightly from his sudden deliverance of the threat that was evidently aimed at Sam since she was the prominent reason why everything was worse instead of better. She was meant to be a game-changer and help restore the country… None of them were present during Fredrickson's bonding sessions with Sam, so none of them knew the true extent of what he'd done to her, what he'd unintentionally created, the monster he'd given life to. Ark, Winsome, Kolen and Losnedahl could only guess what the deceased bonder had actually done to Sam while he was bonding with her. Was he genuine? Or was he abusive? If he was the second, that could explain some of the reasons behind why she had such a hatred towards people.

Ark commented on his threat towards Sam and took it as a means of encouragement, to motivate him, to move him out of this dismal wreck slumped on the couch. 'That's the kind of spirit we ne-'

Winsome shot to his feet. Kolen fell over. His face was contorted into another grisly image, only this time he was furious then sad. 'That motherfucking bitch! I'll Fucking end her!' He roared. Winsome took a step forward and just collapsed, falling on his knees and hands, Slater and Losnedahl went over and attempted to help him to his feet, and Slater told him to not get excited yet when he was still recovering. But Winsome shovelled some of the dirt from the floor and tossed it at them furiously, prompting both men to step back, sputtering the dirt that had been thrown at them and letting Winsome have this one rant. And this one would be well deserved; after what he'd done to the zombified Bear and all the other horrors he'd seen throughout the night, it was only natural for him to express his vexation and disdain for the black-haired zombie that had massacred and brought torment and suffering to so many good people. Carl Boyle had been one such individual, as well as so many others, who didn't deserve to die in such gnarly and horrible ways at the hands of the black-haired witch.

Winsome sat on his knees, threw open his mouth and screamed. He was beginning to understand the purpose behind Eir Losnedahl and his dog Bear; he understood the prints that had led them to this house. Sam had planned this all along! 'She's fucking toying with us! Toying with our emotions and using the things we love and hold dear against us! That clever cunt! I won't be satisfied until Sam is **DEAD**! YA, HEAR ME! D.E.A.D! WITH BULLETS RIDDLED IN EVERY CORNER OF HER DISGUSTING FUCKING BODY!! I WON'T BE SATISFIED UNTIL SHE SUFFERS AND IS TORN TO RIBBONS IN HELL!' Winsome erupted, balling his hands into fists and clenching them so hard that the knuckles showed flakes of white. He pounded the ground so violently that a small shockwave sent some minuscule dirt pebbles into the air. Kolen backed up against Losnedahl, frightened of the volcano that had erupted. 'SHE DID THIS TO BEAR! SHE'S READ OUR FUCKING RECORDS! I'm sure of it BECAUSE SHE FUCKING KNOWS ABOUT OUR WEAKNESSES AND IS USING THEM FUCKING AGAINST US!! SHE TURNED MY BEAR INTO A ZOMBIE, AS WELL AS HENRIK'S MUM!! HOW MANY OTHERS HAS SHE TURNED! How many friends and family members she had turned against... Sonofabitch! I'LL END HER!! I'LL FUCKING KILL HER!! WE WILL KILL HER! WE'LL SEND HER TO A GRAVE WHERE SHE WON'T BE DIGGING OUT OF!! CEMENT THE FUCKING THING! AND THEN WHEN SAM IS DEAD AND ROTTING IN A FUCKING FIERY PIT. WE'LL EXTERMINATE THE ENTIRE FUCKING SPECIES OF THOSE LITTLE SHITS!! THEN! ONLY THEN! WILL I BE SATISFIED!!! Only then will all those good people and animals be avenged!' Winsome exploded, figuring that it was none other than Sam that had sent Bear and Eir onto them, hoping that either one of them would kill them. Because what other zombie was smart and had a bone to pick with them? He had delivered a whopper of a rant that Ark and the others agreed on. Hell, they even contemplated joining him and his raving, but because they were in the

Heart of London and, more importantly, the wonderland for the undead, yelling was a definite death wish. And yet, despite the ferocity and aggression of the rant, Ark couldn't help but feel inspired and delighted with it because she was feeling the same way, and she was glad that he vented the same amount of hatred for her as she had. However, it was the crawler who spoke in a softer voice, reminding him of the dangers they were in if he kept raising his voice to rave about something that he and everyone else in the group hated with such a ripe passion. 'I can smell her... she's here! Mr Winsome, you have to lower your voice, we will finish this, but you have to qui-' the crawler tried to speak, but Winsome just ignored the crawler, as he wasn't finished with what he wanted to say.

'NO! I WON'T FUCKING SHUT UP!' he shouted again, running over Ace's soft words. 'I WON'T UNTIL SAM IS DEAD! ROTTING IN A FUCKING GRAVE! YA FUCKING HEAR ME!?!?! I WILL KILL THAT MOTHERFUCKING ZOMBIE CUNT! I'LL KILL HER TILL SHE DEAD, DEAD, DEAD, DEA-' Winsome's words were abruptly cut off, followed by the heart-stopping sound of something punching and ripping and Winsome gagging and the sight of red liquid sputtering out of his mouth. The human group members stepped away from him because not only was blood seeping out of his mouth like he was having some kind of blood seizure. But the blood dripping from his mouth wasn't even a shade of what they'd seen when they looked down at his chest. There was a growing red puddle soaking through Winsome's lab coat and tan-coloured shirt, and... when Oli and Kolen saw it, they almost fell to the floor; Kolen screamed and covered her eyes, and Oli crossed her heart and muttered something under her breath. When Ark, Slater and Losnedahl saw it, their hearts skipped two beats; Losnedahl coughed a few times as if forgetting how to breathe; Ark flew off the couch and gripped the area where her heart was beating, and Slater had his voice taken away from him. A hand washed in Winsome's blood had punched right through his chest! Someone with a vendetta had broken in while Winsome was having his vent, and the others were fixated on such a vent and had assaulted him; the identity was a mystery as the owner of the hand was blanketed in shadow.

She slowly and gingerly removed her hands from her eyes, and behind those white-framed glasses, Kolen's eyes widened, and her own breathing commenced to become unsteady. 'Oh… my…' she squeaked. She wanted to look away again, desperately trying to look away, but she couldn't. Such a task at this point seemed impossible. Her head wouldn't move, and her eyes wouldn't shut; she could only watch like the others, feeling a dire urge to faint when she saw that the hand bathed in Winsome's blood was holding onto Winsome's... still... beating... heart!

Thump, thump... thump, thump came from the bloody heart.

Winsome glanced down at himself, marking his own heart for the first time that was right in front of him. Winsome's eyes widened, and he felt like screaming in horror and pain from this gruesome sight, but his voice was gone, much like Losnedahl; he couldn't cry or make any sound. The only noises coming out of Winsome's blood-dripping lips were unhealthy gags and coughs. He tried to talk, but he only ended up oozing more of the pulsing blood out of his mouth, down his chin and clothes. Blood was merging around him as the hand holding his fresh, warm, still-beating heart refused to move or even flinch. It just stayed there, letting the blood drip from it. Winsome's face contorted into one of sheer horror the more he stared at the sight of his own heart out of his chest. He was crying, but his weeping was replaced by his constricted gags as more blood pooled out of his mouth.

His teary face glanced up pleadingly at Ark and the others before he slowly glanced back down at his gradually beating heart... he didn't want to go out like this. He didn't want to leave the group members so soon; he'd only begun to see them as friends and was willing to fight for them.

He didn't want to die like this.

He didn't...

The group members could only watch, utterly paralysed by their own shock and quivering fear, unable to move or dismiss their eyes away from the grim sight.

Winsome continued to choke as blood pooled in his mouth, obscuring his throat, and making breathing hard. He could feel himself starting to become weak. But that wasn't all; he could feel someone exhaling a deathly cold onto his neck, as well as feel the touch of freezing dead skin caressing his cheek, making him shiver. The hand of death then went and took his shoulder, gently reeling him back so that the freezing cold breathing was directly in his ear, billowing more uncomfortable cold air into his ear.

'Sam is dead, died seventy-six years ago.'

Chapter 32

Ark listened and stared. She tried to feel around for the torch she dropped when the monster dog made its ugly appearance, but she couldn't find it. All she could do was listen in the dark, unable to see the figure behind Winsome as a voice that had uttered those chilling words sounded feminine with a standard RP British accent that sent shivers down the human's spines and even Ace's, because before Winsome had been attacked, she had stated that she could smell her, that she could smell danger, but no one listened to her. It sounded cold, seductive, and instilling nothing but a pure, unkempt bloodlust and a sick joy in installing pain to those around her as you could hear it by the way she'd spoken those words, they had sounded cruel and, in ways, had sounded playful and malicious as if the owner was savouring the delight in the helplessness of her victims. Ark wanted to tell her friend to stay calm, but that'd sound stupid as Winsome's bloody heart had been straight up torn from his chest, and it wouldn't be long until he'd enter shock and eventually, the blood would stop pumping into his brain. Ark knew this because she'd been in the theatre once to assist a heart surgery a lifetime ago, counting the seconds and minutes Mrs Donna Lake's heart was removed from her heart, counting four minutes until Mrs Lake took her final breath. Building to minutes, those seconds were ticking away in her mind as she listened to the slowing thumps and Winsome's laborious breathing. It wouldn't be long until she realised that she had failed him as she fruitlessly tried to find the torch to reveal Winsome's killer to them. Neither she nor anyone could do anything to help him. Winsome's very life existed in this freaky woman's hand (quite literally), and it wouldn't be long now until his heart officially stopped beating (fifty seconds). Ark knew that if he wanted to speak with his friends one last time, he had to make it swift, and it had to be now because he wouldn't have long until the blood pumping to his brain would stop for good, and he would go into cardiac arrest. But talking provided a considerable challenge, and breathing under the faint din of the overhead lamp that had only faintly illuminated the ten of them. Ark panicked upon seeing his face change colour as he stared at her with his big frightened eyes as more blood spilled out of his mouth and the gaping hold in his chest; he was dying, and he knew it. They all did (Nolan's face), but even so, he kept trying to cling to the remaining strings of life (one minute and thirty seconds). Winsome coughed up his own blood, grunting and whimpering in pain, which made the other group members back up further, paralysed by their own terror, watching with unshaken eyes, watching Winsome's fearful eyes turned in the direction of the woman's head where her voice had come from. Oli gagged. She opened her mouth to say something in response to what her eyes were seeing but couldn't muster even a hiss or whisper, so she closed it and continued to watch, unable to look away or say anything as Winsome clung to life. And it wasn't just Oli who wanted to open her mouth to say something; they all did, but like Losnedahl, their voices were nothing but a chorus of rasps and shaky breaths that had come out of quivering lips. *It's her! Oh, Christ, she's found us already!* Losnedahl thought fretfully, having the grim intuition that the queen of death was here with them and she had taken another victim, had taken one of them. Because it was in the middle of the night, and the house they'd been staying in only had a few dim lights turned on, as well as some of the neighbouring lights from the outside street lamps. Ark wanted so badly to tell Winsome to remain calm, but she knew that she couldn't; it was pointless (another thirty seconds). Winsome's breathing became increasingly unsteady as his eyes shifted to his right in sheer panic. Ark's mouth trembled when she saw him look up; she couldn't make out much, but he managed to see the woman's messy black hair that hung loosely over her shoulders. One of the last things he saw. Even Ark could see those black hair strings hanging over his shoulder (two minutes, ten seconds). His painful eyes had managed to turn back and face Ark's equally terrified expression, where he managed to utter, 'Li-Lii-Li-see-a. Sh-She-es he-ear…' out as his last words, right before he heard the woman chuckling a sinister and evil snicker. One that'd haunt the ears of everyone in the group. Still holding Winsome's heart in her hand, the woman forced him to stand up as more blood trickled down her fingers and coughed out of his mouth. During this feat, Winsome was losing the healthy pace of his breathing. He was breathing haggard while keeping his petrified eyes trained on the black-haired woman, slipping in and out of consciousness. Oli, Losnedahl, Slater and even Ace had their mouths open with grimaces; Kolen and Oli cupped their mouths as tears dribbled down Kolen's cheeks; Aladar and Zinni just stared, unaccustomed to the dangers that Winsome's killer would pose them, Ark's eyes were twitching and her fists clenching and unclenching with a whole mixture of emotions flying about in her head. The group all watched the woman, still heavily coated in a shroud of darkness, place something on Winsome's back and give him a slight kick forward, pulling her arm as well as the heart out of his chest cavity, which was beating very, very slowly now, a ghastly wave of drawn-out Thump...Thump...Thump… came from the heart as Winsome fell to the floor with a horrible-sounding splat where he lay, motionless and dead, blood pouring out of him with a constant expression of fear on his face. The woman then tightened her fingers around the slowly beating heart and crushed it into insignificant pieces inside her hand, dripping blood and gore out of her fingers. Cutting the last remaining strings of the man's life, what followed was instantaneous.

Ryan Winsome was dead.

'RYAN!' shrieked Kolen as blood spilled out around Winsome's pale, bleeding body, like a growing bruise, trickling all over the floor. The nine of them regarded their now-dead friend with dismay and terror before they all looked up and could vaguely see the woman's gory hand peeking out from the darkness and the remains of Winsome's now-destroyed heart. Ark's fingers found the torch, and she picked it up, but it felt heavy in her hands. 'Oh my god…' Oli whimpered with her hands over her mouth. 'That's brutal.' Slater croaked. Losnedahl was clutching his chest as his heart was beating at an uncontrolled pace. The detail of the rest of the woman's body remained obscured by the night of the wooden boards capping the window. Then came the snickering, prompting Ark, Kolen, Losnedahl, Slater and Oli to look up and try to squint and focus their eyes in front of them and could make out a sharp feminine silhouette that could've belonged to the woman who'd murdered Winsome in cold blood. The woman then cold-heartily dropped the now destroyed remnants of Winsome's heart on the ground, where it landed next to Winsome's corpse, hitting the ground with a horrible SPLAT. A small puddle of blood formed around it, merging in with an already growing pool of blood around Winsome. The woman's silhouette tilted her head, and she seemed to acknowledge the missing elephant carpet, which had the remains of the dog wrapped inside it and discarded somewhere out of the room. 'Such a pity, he was such a loyal dog,' the woman articulated mockingly, giving off the impression that she was the one wh'd orchestrated everything when it came to Bear's impromptu appearance and attack on the group. She sounded like she'd been the one that told Bear to "sick'em", making him go after them after she'd led the zombie dog to them and had watched the dog attack them through one of the boarded windows. She'd been outside, watching the attack the whole time!

That very conceivable thought alone made Kolen and Ace shudder, and when Kolen held Ace for comfort, she could feel the crawler shaking in her arms, feeling the crawler's dread. Even the mere voice of this woman sent chills down the group's spines as they felt a cold whisper of air pass through them every time she spoke. It was like they were hearing the seductive and crude voice of Lilith, the queen of Hell. A voice that gave the impression that she immensely enjoyed inflicting suffering on those around her.

'Oh well, at least Mr Ryan Winsome can join the ranks of his beast again in the afterlife; oh, and while he's there, he should give Mr Fredrickson my regards.' The woman snickered scornfully. The group watched, frozen on the spot, as the female with the chilling voice took one step into the light, followed by another, and then the rest of her body came. Finally, Ark was able to lift up the torch and shine it towards the woman, revealing her in her blood-soaked glory to the terrified group's wide-eyed gaze. It was her! It was the nightmare personified!

'Tell him that Sam said Hi.' Sam spoke down to the mangled, horror-struck corpse of Ryan Winsome.

Chapter 33

Kolen let out a yelp, gaping her mouth and her eyes wide. 'Oh god, *you monster! You evil, evil monster! Why did you have to take him? Why Ryan?! He was a good man.* yu-you can ta-talk?!' Kolen exclaimed. Her trembling hands had unintentionally released her grasp of the wheelchair handles, and she ended up falling backwards at the very sight of those wavy black locks, those sharp and attractive features and that simple black tee and tan shorts. Still, the main attraction that was most alarming to her was the apparent fact that she could talk! The entire time, the group had thought Sam was mute because she'd never once made an effort to speak, so it was assumed that she was just like 91% of the other zombies and that Ace was one of the few rare 9% success stories where a zombie could speak with English words instead of mindless moaning and groaning. Had she been able to talk this entire time and just fooled them into pretending that she couldn't? It seemed likely that until Winsome took his final breath, he'd been the one who had figured it out that she was toying with them and taking a sinister delight in doing so. Ark held the torch up to the ghastly face, though keeping the light steady was hard; her hands did nothing but shake; even when she held the torch with both hands, she couldn't maintain a decent, steady grip.

'Well, obviously, Ms Kolen.' The black-haired woman said with a snigger, lifting up the bloody hand and licking some of Winsome's blood off it. Kolen felt sick.

Slater moved in front of her, his hand out in front of her in a protective gesture. Despite watching the man whom he'd come to know as a friend had just had his heart torn from his chest, he tried to maintain his courage in the face of this vicious black-haired monster. 'How the hell did you get in without us knowing?' He blurted, and Sam shot up a finger in his direction without so much as glancing his way, gesturing him to be patient and that she'd answer his question soon. 'Fuck you! You'll pay for what you did to Ryan!' he cursed at the monster. Sam smirked at Slater's attempt to threaten her as her cold, lifeless eyes glanced at Kolen; Kolen's skittish breathing accelerated, and she gulped, almost feeling the need to soil herself. She sniggered, and Kolen whimpered, taking a step back and clasping her mouth with her hands as more tears ran down her cheeks. Just the sight of the monster behind the nightmare was enough to make Kolen want to tear her eyes out of her sockets so that she wouldn't be able to see that horrible grin on that twisted and pale face. Sam took a step, and Slater held his ground, his fists raised, ready to fight hand to hand if needed. 'Don't you come any fucking closer, you bitch!' Sam just chuckled as she took another step towards her. Slater growled through his teeth and made to throw a punch at his enemy, but Sam had countered it, much to everyone's surprise, when they saw Slater's fist caught in the palms of Sam's. The grin broadened, and still holding onto his fist, Sam swifty flung her arm behind her and Slater went stumbling past her, his footsteps fighting for decent purchase, but he was unable, and Slater came crashing against the wall near the broken barricade where the fight with Bear had once ensued between the good zombies. Slater let out a cry as he hit his head on the plaster.

'Darren!' Oli cried out; she went to go over and help her brother but was grabbed by Losnedahl, who shook his head, not wanting her to go near the monster.

Sam walked towards Kolen, who whimpered high, mouse-like noises, shuffling against the ground, as Sam knelt down to her, still wearing that abhorrent grin. Kolen wished she was blind at this point. 'You think I'm stupid, Ms Kolen? If Ace can talk, I sure as hell can. I just never did it because I was waiting for the precise moment when I could.' Sam said balefully; she reached out a long, pale finger and poked Kolen's ankle with her nail. Kolen whined and hugged her legs, bringing them away from Sam. She watched with moist, fearful eyes as Sam giggled a nasty, sickly sound, and she stood up and peered down at Ace in the wheelchair and smirked that infamous smile that she had done to her back in the GFOSAR after she'd gotten the surgery to make her look like this. 'Or should I say Evelyn,' she mocked the crawler by knowing her real name. Kolen's eyes became the widest that she could get them, and she was confident that after this night, she'd be sporting some strands of white in her hair. She watched Ace, who started trembling, and a sickly, husky breathing sound came from her, and Kolen understood that something was changing in her crawler's decomposing mess of a body. It was a seething surge of anger; she was starting to experience what Spot had experienced: emotions. 'Ace?' Kolen squeaked in a faraway voice that she herself barely heard. Until this point, Ace had been like Aladar and Zinni and hadn't felt much emotion, but when it came to Sam, she felt nothing but pure, enduring fury for her enemy. If her blood was alive and pumping through her body, it would be boiling over the pot with an unsanitary hatred for Sam.

Sam leered down to the crawler, hands on her knees as if she was talking to a child about how they need to learn their manners. 'Oh yes, indeed, I know your name, Miss Davis. I have my spies, who have been tracking you and your party for the past few hours. They report back to me on their findings, such as when you'd found that little piece of rag that made you remember your name; once that was discovered, the info was conveyed back to me, and therefore, I know you're name, same with the big teddy bear named Lucas.' She smirked. Spot's hands were clenched. Kolen couldn't make out Ace's face, but she expected it to be contorted with sheer rage. Kolen tried calling out to her crawler again, but her voice was even more muted than the previous time. However, Kolen suspected that Ace wanted out of the wheelchair and wanted Sam's undead brains; she wouldn't care if they tasted stale; she would make cannibalising an exception for this one moment, wanting Sam's brains for herself! As disgusting as that thought was for Kolen.

Kolen was shaking all over; she had goosebumps all over her body as she stared at the black-haired witch who opened her mouth. 'And to answer your question, Mr Darren Slater, while you were all listening closely to the village idiots' little rant, I snuck in because you all seemed to forget that it's in the middle of the night and breaking into places is almost child's play, and one of my tricks. I happened to sneak in just as Ryan finished declaring my suffering in hell. Bless his pathetic little heart. I decided to buy my time and wait until Ace told him to be quiet because the legless bitch had smelt me. So, I waited patiently as if for paint to dry. I wanted for the right moment where I could strike and cut him down to size; now look at him,' Sam tilted her head towards the body on the ground. 'Big Ryan Winsome ain't so big now; he quite literally lost his heart to live. That is what he gets for flapping his jaw instead of doing what the crawler wanted and shutting up.' Sam snickered as if to taunt them about the death of one of their own. Kolen hated all that she was hearing; she wished she could just make a wish, count to five, and when she woke up next, she'd be back in the arms and safety of her beloved as they welcomed a daughter or son into the world – becoming the family that she'd always dreamt of. But, of course, that didn't happen. Jacob died before she got the chance to tell him that she wanted to have a child.

There was an echoing clank as if something metallic had been dropped to the floor. Kolen shuddered, scampered on fours, and picked up the torch and shone it. She saw Ark's eyes radiate an intense blue flame that became orange, then a violent shade of red at Sam, providing another valid reason for her loathing towards Fredrickson's subject.

'You, You *Bitch*! I'll! I'll kill You!' Ark exploded. She directed her rifle up towards Sam's head; her eyes red with an intense fire. She didn't care if the range was close. The opportunity to end this evil witch's life was among them! Kolen clasped her ears, knowing the coming shot would be piercingly loud. She looked at Sam, who just watched her; she displayed no fear in her face, still wearing that grin. She drew the trigger back; her eyes were drowning in hatred. All logical sense of thinking vanished; she had a distinguished intention to exterminate Sam right here in front of her. Kolen closed her eyes, blocked her ears, and gritted her teeth.

'This is for Ryan! You cu-' *click*. 'Wha?' *click* again. 'What the Fuck?!' Ark caterwauled as the remaining bullet that she thought she had loaded hadn't come out of the rifle; it didn't matter how many times she tried to fire it. It just made the same clicking sound as if it was jammed. *'FUCK*!!' she screeched, realising her fatal mistake, that while she had a bullet with Sam's name on it ready, she had forgotten to load it into the rifle; it was sitting restfully in her lab coat's breast pocket, along with Spot's hunger pills. Pills that she hadn't given to him in a while. '*SONOFABITCH*!!' she screamed. Kolen crawled over to her and looked at the empty weapon with trepidation. Kolen offered to load it, but Ark ignored her, her teeth clamping down on the gums.

'Oh dear, it'd seem that you've forgotten to reload your weapon. How tragic, Mrs Ark, your every chance to end my life was right in front of you, but the attempt was shammed by you forgetting to reload.' The intelligent zombie taunted the infuriated woman, pointing out a fatal mistake to reload to everyone else in the group. Ark took the fleeting moment to dig through her coat's breast pocket for that one bullet. Kolen's eyes went back to Sam; she moved the torch's light to her, watching as she looked across the living room regarding the remaining traumatised human members of the group, who all took a step back as soon as she looked at them. The smile cracked on her face again, and Kolen knew by the smile that she was planning something, only she didn't understand what, and she probably didn't want to learn. 'Ah, the Slater twins, I've heard things about grubs like yourselves, how you, Darren, abandoned your whittle baby sister to fend for herself.' Sam pretended to cry, hovering a fist above her eye and pouting.

Kolen looked at Slater, who appeared more than a little insulted by this comment, using his days in RMA as an excuse for him to leave Oli behind. 'And how you, Olivia, couldn't make it into the GFOSAR because you weren't qualified enough. I will agree and say that those wealthy slums of the GFOSAR didn't know what the bloody hell they were thinking when they gave you the flick. Because I don't doubt that you have a talent for zombie bonding. You got two loyal zombies by your side. I can guarantee that if you were a zombie, you would've made a valuable addition to my army.'

'How dare you talk to her! Don't you fucking dare talk to my sister like that, you cunt!' Slater rebuked. Oli was silent, her eyes staring, and Kolen thought that she didn't know if she felt flattered or scared by Sam giving her a compliment, showing her that she did have the talent for bonding. 'But... (there is always a but) did you make an attempt to ask them about their past lives, like most bonders were meant to? As I'm sure you are aware of the purpose of zombie bonding. The bondation progress wasn't to turn us, zombies, into your servants. It was to make us remember our past lives, to turn us back into humans. But why be a pissy weakling like a human? Always following the goody-two-shoes role and being good? Why do what the humans expect of you when you can be your own free, independent being, free to eat and do anything as you please without the living telling you what to do. That was Mr Fredrickson's mistake; he thought he could control me, he thought he could use me like I was his puppet, but you knew what happened to him.' Kolen wanted to run away, but she couldn't listen to anything else that came from the monster's mouth. *Click*! Neither did Ark as she finally loaded the rifle and returned to training it at Sam.

'SHUT UP! **YOU SHUT THE FUCK UP!** RIGHT NOW! You killed Ryan, you killed Alexander, you killed so many countless lives and started a massacre on the GFOSAR! The only place in Britain that was considered safe! The fuck would you know about bondation? You fucked it up! Secondly, how the fuck do you know so much about us without even meeting any of us in person?!' bellowed Ark, interrogating Sam on her knowledge; how did she know who they were, their pasts and weaknesses like how Winsome had ranted, screaming it out right before his life was cut short and was murdered by Sam.

'Well, seems like you're all most eager to kill me, dispose me into a hard coffin and foil my plans, so I'll be kind enough to give you a brief summary of how I know so much, maybe after I kill you and make you mine, I'll give you a good spot in my army.' Sam spoke, the sly, wicked grin never leaving her mug. The group stared and waited eagerly; Ark's expression was painted with pure, unadulterated hatred. Sam smacked her lips with her tongue before she spoke. Ark was still wary of her and held the weapon to her head. But Sam seemed unperturbed. 'Mr

Fredrickson is the reason I know about you, Lisa, Marilyn, Henrik and… of course, the dead Ryan Winsome here. He mentioned you during some sessions when he was having one of his rare good moods.' Ark clenched her fists and teeth at how Sam had chosen to mock Winsome's corpse. She was growing even more unbridled hostility toward Sam. 'As for the Slater's, I remember seeing them wandering the streets shortly after I departed from the GFOSAR; I thought about killing them, especially you, Darren. You remember that? Of course you do; I can see it on your face.' Sam eyed him with such a scornful lust that Slater couldn't help but gulp at these words. Slater's eyes shared the same scorn and hatred, but his lips were fearfully quivering. He did his best to hide his swelling fear for this black-haired witch. But he was also sure that she could see it. 'I'm sure you remember our little dance that ended in your old party dropping to the floor; you got away from me, so here I am to finish the job.' She said, again, her haughty smile never failed to leave. Oli stared at her brother in fright; her blood ran cold at hearing that her older brother had been one of the lucky individuals to have had an encounter with Sam and managed to escape. But at the cost of losing his friends and other survivors, he had been with, facing the ever-present uncomfortable tearing feeling in his gut that he had abandoned them. That he was left to face the music by growing accustomed to their screams as Sam had torn them apart and eaten them. That was one thing of his days in the RMA that had clung to him like a flesh-eating tick; the screams of his comrades had followed him wherever he went, refusing to leave him, reminding him of those he couldn't save.

Sam's pale eyes scanned the scorned and unrested eyes of the group; her smile extended, and she relished in the knowledge of her being feared. 'I know you all saw me when I ripped off that man's junk and tore his intestines out from the hole, and I saw you enter this house. I had been outside, watching as you fought the mutt; you might say that I've been stalking or had others stalking you this entire time while tending to my own duties in the shadows. But believe what you will, the living are blinded by their own personal benefits. I will say this; when I was still Fredrickson's bitch. He had some paperwork that he had dropped on the floor during the end of one particular bonding session; it had details about your places in the GFOSAR, as well as documenting personal information about how the position as a bonder had personally made him feel. Speaking of that paperwork, you may think Fredrickson was a good man who cared deeply about his colleagues and "those" under his care. Well, allow me to blow your minds; from what I had read on that written paperwork that he had dropped and from what I had seen when interacting with people, he was far from a good man. He wasn't the saint that you often depicted him to be, and you know why, because he had called the paperwork his "SINS", and it had pretty much everything that you would imagine from paperwork called Sins. Fredrickson mentioned that he had an unchecked hatred for the homeless and the beggars you'd find on the street asking for coins. Fredrickson went on to say that the real reason he had married homeless Deborah Mikalsson was that she was, and I quote, "A lewd canvas with the one perfect arse that would do wonders for his sexually deprived shlong." He liked to bitch about being a nourishing husband by spoiling her with gifts fit for the late Queen, but in truth, if you were to take his comments on her booty into consideration. He was a poor excuse for a man, a crude blockhead looking for a virgin lady to have sex with; in other words, he was a sexual predator. So, when you ponder about his views on people and his loathing of those with nothing but scraps. I'm turning the homeless and other people into zombies so there will be no more living homeless people around. So, I'm just doing him and you a favour,' She glanced at Kolen, and her grin broadened, 'because when it boils down to it, Marilyn, men are scum, can't trust them with anything because when they see you at your most vulnerable, they'll come to stab you in the arse and make off with another whore. Fredrickson was no different. After all, he was the one who bonded with me. Therefore, he is the reason I am who I am. I became self-aware of how he would treat me and those around him.' Sam stated casually, the smile still never leaving her dirty face. It was infuriating to hear such disdainful words about such a prolific man out of an equally contemptuous mouth. It was indeed a miracle that everyone had managed to keep their bodies still and not lash out at Sam. Kolen looked at the floor for a moment, then she looked up, eyes scared but forcing bravery that just made Sam laugh. 'Shut Up! Alexander was a brilliant man!' she cried, though she immediately felt violated as soon as she had opened her mouth. Sam simply glanced at her and said savagely. 'If he's so brilliant, why hasn't he cured cancer? Why did I end up like this?' which had sent Kolen into a frenzy of denial and fear.

'I!' She stammered over her words, trying to come out with a sincere answer.

'Enough Talk!' bellowed Slater; his face was a complex canvas of fury, shock, and tremor, but one thing was sure, he was more than ready to see this bitch on her knees, writhing in pain. He threw his hand into his trench coat pocket, extracting his revolver to shoot Sam. But as soon as he had fished it out and had it drawn to Sam's head. She had pulled out her own firearm and, without a moment's hesitation, had instantly pulled the trigger, shooting him in the leg as well as hand, causing the human group members to yelp in shock and Slater to let out a cry of pain. Prompting him to drop the gun in a matter of seconds where it landed a few inches away from Winsome's corpse. Slater clutched his bleeding leg, which oozed and stung from the pain, not bothered about the hole in his hand that had blood flowing out of it. 'Darren!' cried Oli, reaching her arms out to him, but she was out of reach. The group of nine hurried over to Slater's side to help him. Kolen assessed the bullet's damage while working to tear some of the fabric off her lab coat to wrap around Slater's bleeding hand and leg.

'I swear to god, you will die by the end of this fucking day!' Oli snarled at Sam; she had tears oozing from her eyes, seeing her brother being shot twice in front of her and that it was his blood that was staining her fingers. 'You will be sorry for hurting my brother!'

'Is that so?' Sam smirked another smile of mockery at the younger Slater twin, throwing the simple pistol out of the way. She knelt down, took the shotgun, and held it up as if examining it; she chuckled at her newly declared toy, keeping it in both hands. Snickering, she aimed it down at Ark's head; one shot to the face would definitely kill her. Sam's dead grey pupils and lightly bloodshot eyes were wide and full of focus into shooting Ark as well as everyone else in this room, as killing them all and letting the mortuus carnem resurrect them would feel better on her part, she wasn't dumb enough to try biting one of them if she knew she was crowded by them, so shooting them and leaving them for the Mortuus Carnem seemed better for her, and maybe the last one standing would provide a feast for her where she wouldn't eat just the brains, but everything else until they were a bloody skeleton. She'd have a buffet on her hands. She'd dine like a Queen before twelve o'clock in the morning. Britain's last hope would be eradicated, and there'd be no one and nothing left alive to stop her if the group should end up falling victim to Sam and her violent malice.

'Stop me if you're fit too,' she smirked, ready for anything the group would do to stop their foe. She would be prepared for sore knuckles and the taste of blood in her mouth. 'Which one of you is brave enough to take the first shot?' cackled Sam, tracing the barrel of the shotgun to the frightened but fuming faces of each group member, teasing them, wanting to know who was brave and willing to make the first move on her and get a mug full of lead.

It was Spot.

The half-headless zombie stood up without Ark's orders to do so and moved around the crowd of people and zombies, lightly moving Slater out of his way, causing Slater to glance upward like Winsome had done plenty of times before. Slater was marvelling at the half-headless zombie's height and how, if he was with a whole head, his head might actually be touching the ceiling or, for the most part, be a few inches away from it. He couldn't shake away the feeling of dwarfism whenever Spot stood next to him. Despite Slater being the average standard height for an English man of his age, he felt like he was fourteen again when comparing his standard size of six-foot-two to Spot's tall, imposing six-foot-six frame.

'Spot! No! The bitch's too dangerous!' Ark barked at him; panic had clearly made a home in her voice. But even the sound of the dread in her voice didn't make her zombie flinch in reconsideration. This action of Spot disobeying her was most alarming to Ark, so much so that she wanted to throw herself in the line of danger, seize Spot's arm and pull him out of the way. Because despite Spot being a zombie with half a head, he was part of their group, and his life was just as vital as the rest of them. She'd be dammed if she'd let his modest demeanour be snuffed out so swiftly because the way Ark had considered it, Spot was the most human out of the zombies; he had feelings and emotions, and that factor alone was worth fighting for. Zombies to display such heavy emotion was extremely rare and for Spot to exhibit such feats without a complete head was absolutely remarkable. And with those facts in the bucket, Ark couldn't allow such an incredible specimen to die so quickly. Not if she could do anything about it. 'Spot, this is an order! Fall back! You can't beat her by yourself!' ordered Ark, furiously demanding that he back down and get away from Sam until she and the rest of the group had pummelled Sam down to her knees and flagged her with everything that they had at their disposal. But much to Ark's surprise and horror, this was one order that her loyal, well-behaved zombie, Spot, refused to obey much to Ark's horror…

'Spot!' Ark cried. '*Goddammit!*' But Spot didn't move or make a sign to reassure her that he was fine and that he'd sort this evil zombie out. Spot kept his tall frame in front of them and screened the barrel pointed to his chest. Spot didn't need eyes to know that Sam's pale mug was wearing that sinister grin and that she had the shotgun aimed right at his chest where the heart had resided behind the cell of bone; he knew one thing that Sam didn't predict, something that she overlooked, something that rested in her...

Spot stepped up to Sam, halting when he felt the hard metallic muzzle of the shotgun touch his chest as he towered over Sam, where his eyeless expression peered down at her. Spot knew she was there even if he couldn't see or smell her. Sam stood her ground, unphased by this giant zombie gazing down at her. In fact, she was more interested in his size rather than intimidated by it. Sam was the same height as Fredrickson, who had currently stood at six feet at the time of his death and being around six feet was considered tall for a female since the average height for a woman was around five-six to five-nine. Still, even so, much like everyone else who came in contact with Spot, she was dwarfed by him. He wore the crown of the tallest group member with pride, a giant of a zombie with an outstanding feat of strength and would be able to crush a person's skull with his bare hands if he wanted to. Yet, while Spot did hold some psychic power under his belt, that would take some firm power to beat. He certainly wasn't as strong as Aladar, the adult male zombie with the pale blonde hair that was rarely seen without the teenage, Zinni, had proven himself to be the muscle of the group, lifting a grown man with ease and able to shrug off most damage to his skin membranes. If one were to give Aladar the opportunity and chance, he could punch his way through a person's body, resulting in a somewhat beautiful yet grim discharge of blood.

Sam complimented on Spot's decision to ignore his bonder's worried cries as she continued to call out his name, her voice becoming more hysterical each time she called out "Spot". Sam continued to stare up at Spot, mesmerised by his bravery or foolishness; the smile remained plastered, unfaltering.

'Disobeying your bonders orders, I see, my, my isn't that a change of heart for someone who doesn't rebel. Still, you've got guts, and you understand orders well for a zombie with only half a head.' Sam's smile broadened evilly. 'Oh well, say hi to your bible-bashing mum when you meet her in the afterlife.' Sam had her steady fingers firmly gripped on the shotgun's trigger, and she pulled them.

Nothing... just a simple click.

'Oh, bollocks...' Sam's smile melted away into an irritated frown. *Forgot to load the bloody thing, didn't you, Ryan?* Sam thought wickedly to herself. Spot made a hideous growling noise that caused the human group members to take a step back. *'Don't you dare mention my mother, Heather! I swear to god if you've hurt her I will be very angry!'* Spot felt his brain speak as if he could telepathically yell to Sam, expressing just how much he hated her, condemning her to the bottomless pits of torture in Hell. 'I've underestimated you, congratulations,' she stated with high sarcasm, imagining herself giving the tall zombie a slow and uninteresting standing ovation. She was gazing up at Spot, who was now reeling amidst rage, composing a song of angry gurgles with his only bottom jaw and trembling tongue. To witness a mild-mannered zombie experience such an alarming rate of anger caused Ark and the others to take another step back from him. Spot threw his hands out in an attempt to clasp Sam's thin neck, where he'd then choke her and slam her head into the walls. But Sam blocked his attacks, holding the shotgun in front of his hands, preventing the giant zombie from reaching her neck. So, Spot opted for a different approach, working to disarm her. So, he pulled at the shotgun, pulling it towards him, away from Sam, endeavouring to wrench it free from her hands so he could proceed with whatever was on his mind, for when he does manage to successfully remove it from her pencil-thin fingers. He'd then use it like a baseball bat, reeling it above his head, then sending it crashing down on the side of her face until she either fell to the floor or pieces of her fractured skull had started to show themselves to the group. Then, once Sam is on the floor, Spot unleashes all his bottled-up anger and stomps a foot down on her head, killing Sam once and for all and saving Ark and the others from such an exhausting and raw task. But such an obligation was easier said than done because Sam wouldn't be a good girl and lie down if you told her to do so; Sam would be sure to give the group a fight to remember and one that wouldn't be clean. Additionally, Sam had yielded knowledge to them that she had spies prowling about the Heart of London and that she, herself, had been secretly stalking them from within the shadows. So that was to say that she knew how to incapacitate them and use their loved ones and current knowledge against them.

Sam winked. 'Nice try, Mr Fitzroy, but no fill for you,' Sam's nasty grin returned, which, much to the group watching with dismay, had made Spot freeze in place at the mention of his name, the name he'd been known as before his life was severed during that fateful musical concert. Sam had found out Spot and Ace's identities from her top spy. The bad side of Linus when he'd been out hunting for humans to farm on, and he happened to encounter and listen into Heather Fitzroy's frightened ramblings about how her only son was cursed to wander the Earth as a zombie missing half his head. How she prayed that a woman named Ark would protect him and not let his devilish hunger befall him, to not let him fall into the darkness where he might never be able to return.

This gave Sam the upper hand, playing out just as she had planned if the shotgun wasn't loaded; she took the chance, while Spot was dazed, perplexed by the feature of Sam knowing about his mother or his real name for that matter.

'She's lying!' Oli tried to scream and get Spot's attention. Still, Oli's efforts didn't mean squat as Sam clasped the fore-end and handle and heaved them upwards. Flipping both the shotgun and Spot, still grasping onto it, over her shoulders. Propelling both the gun and the tall half-headless zombie into the wall behind her, where Spot and the shotgun landed with a hard crash, raining plaster chips down upon Spot's body. This gave Losnedahl a chance to make a move! To do something rather than stand around and be useless.

Because of his absent tongue, he couldn't muster any deafening noises that were sure to garner Sam's attention when she had been temporarily distracted by the tall zombie who showed signs that he wanted to get up, putting his hands on the ground in front of him. But his weakened body wouldn't allow such an exercise, and his arms just gave out on him, sending him back on his chest again. So, the best Spot could do was sit this one out and wait until his energy was restored. Only then would he be able to fight for his bonder and his still-breathing friends.

As for Losnedahl, while Sam's gaze was fixated on Ark and Kolen, Losnedahl bent down slowly, hoping to not invoke any sudden movements that'd cause Sam to notice him. Watching Sam's face and actions closely, he carefully extracted the knife from Bear's lifeless corpse, where he slowly got back into a standing position, knife clutched at the ready.

'Eight against one, my, what is a girl to do?' Sam mocked. Losnedahl charged forward. Like some warrior featured in one of those movies set in the Middle Ages where armoured knights charge ahead of them, a sharp sword above their heads, screaming a battle's cry as they plunge themselves into a horde of resurrected foes. Losnedahl ran forward, flaying the knife around Sam, hoping to at least get a hit and make her bleed. But at this point, Sam had become used to people charging head-on in an attempt to kill her; that was the mistake Slater's crew had made before she had slaughtered them all. They had all come at her with knives and other melee weapons, so one by one, she countered them and killed them. So, who was not to say that she half expected one group member to come at her with a knife, coming at her without any strategic thought, acting sorely out of blind rage. Which, from her own personal experience and battles with other humans, had never worked when it came to defeating her.

If one were to defeat and kill her, one would have to be innovative and think outside the box rather than proceeding with the idea that Sam was just another simple zombie that would fall after one blow to the head. So, she bought her time, waiting for someone brave enough to try taking the jump on her, and that's exactly what she got from the oldest group member. In the form of Losnedahl, coming at her, knife cutting through the air with an angry aspect that was masked in sweat glands, making his aging wrinkles pop. Sam's grin extended as she ducked out of the way of the blade. She took Losnedahl's hand and squeezed it. Sam then hauled it up behind him and bent the palm back into the wrist; Losnedahl hissed as he tried prying his hand free from her grasp, but his efforts were futile, and there was a loud crack that came from his wrist, followed the sound of hushed screaming. Sam broke Losnedahl's hand. She then took the knife away from him and plunged it deep into his own stomach. Losnedahl rasped a pained cry at the blade getting wedged into his stomach; he tried to reach down to pull it out, but Sam had other plans for him and removing it wasn't one of them. She had one hand gripped tight on the handle, digging it deeper into Losnedahl's stomach as blood seeped out, while her other hand tightly wrapped around his neck in an attempt to strangle him.

At this point, Losnedahl craved the urge to pull the knife out of his own stomach and jam it right into Sam's eye; he didn't care which one, anything, to make Sam feel pain. But sadly, he couldn't accomplish such a task while he was at her mercy. Sam was choking him, and to make matters worse, he couldn't reach down to grab the knife because Sam had her fingers clenched around the handle, and if he tried to attempt to take her hand, she'd just dig the blade more into him, causing massive discomfort. The only thing he could do was feebly try to pry Sam's vice-undead fingers away from his neck, even though he knew it was pointless since he was old and his strength wasn't what it

used to be. Losnedahl was nearly sixty and was considered
to be reasonably elderly, being at fifty-seven years old.

(*Mother*).

Seeing Losnedahl under such discomfort was
causing mental harm across the group; they wanted to help
their old friend, but they knew that they couldn't, not when
he was under Sam's mercy. 'Don't move, don't fucking
move. If you move so much as a fuckin inch as much as
blink, I will pull out the knife and stab the old codger in the
heart! And I know you wouldn't want that to happen to
someone like Mr Losnedahl here, would you, Marilyn,'
Kolen was flabbergasted, you bitch... you cunting bitch.
'You admire this old mute quack because I murdered your
former love interest.' The four humans and Ace were still;
their bodies were trembling as they were shitting
themselves from being face-to-face with Sam, the demon
behind the GFOSAR massacre. But despite their
overpowering levels of fear, one couldn't help but point out
their extreme off-the-charts level of fury and hatred that
they all equally shared for this one zombie. Ace peered
over and saw Spot, now lying motionless on the ground
with flakes of white plaster coating his large body. She
knew that Spot wasn't dead, dead. No, that wouldn't kill
him. She knew that he'd just passed out from being
viciously launched at the wall. The one irrefutable fact that
the group had come to understand was that zombies in the
highly bonded category, rediscovering what it meant to
have emotions and independent feelings again, were prone
to feel more physical pain like anyone else that was alive.

'Let him go; if you want to kill someone, it should
be me!' Kolen thought it was time for a sacrifice, making a
brave stand against Sam, throwing herself in front of Sam,
relieving her duties as Ace's carer, and offering her own life
in exchange for Losnedahl, who was starting to go pale.

Losnedahl temporarily removed a hand away from his neck to wave it diffidently at Kolen, beckoning for her not to try bargaining with someone who desired to kill them all in the first place. Ace's eyes widened in horror that her bonder would want to throw away her life like this. The Slater twins both shared the same unblinking expression of hysteria that they didn't know what they wanted to do. Did they want to help the young broad, or let Sam decide her fate. Spot was out. Zinni and Aladar didn't know Kolen and the other group members well enough to develop a personal bond with them. Ark was having a mental breakdown. Her heart was throbbing; she clenched her chest and clamped her teeth together. Ark had begun to view Kolen as her best friend, and for Kolen to offer her own young life in exchange for a man who had seen quite a lot during his time, she just couldn't take it. No matter who Sam decided to kill. Everyone in the alliance against the Mortuus Carnem had proved a place for her. She was willing to view them as part of her family; her parents, Michael, and Lorraine Ark, had died during the early years of 2030.

Sam grinned sadistically, taking great pride in tormenting the young, naive Dutch woman. 'I don't exchange lives,' moving her mouth up to the back of Losnedahl's head. 'Say hi to Dad and Mum, and be sure to send me a family photo.' Sam snickered, opening her mouth as drool came slobbering out. Everyone knew what this meant! Most of the group just stood modified, unable to do anything! Of course, they wanted to help their friend out of Sam's diabolical clutches, but they found themselves unable to make a move on Sam as they knew that she wasn't bullshitting, and she would kill Losnedahl if anyone laid so much as a finger on her. She was baiting them, seeing how long they would last until someone made their move, prompting Sam to cut the old Norwegian's violin soundless strings. Losnedahl could feel the bitter wetness of Sam's dribbling saliva touching his neck; such an uncomfortable feeling was making him recoil; he wanted to throw up.

Behind those white spectacles, Kolen's brown eyes were the size of giant marbles. *'OH,GOEDHEID! SOMEONE DO SOMETHING!! HENRIK'S GONNA GET EATEN!!!'* she shrieked, putting her hands to her mouth; she still didn't have the will to pick up a weapon, arm herself and attack Sam herself; she didn't know what else she could do to help her mute friend, if bargaining with the Devil didn't help, what else could she do? Kolen resumed her original position, slinking back behind the shadows of the others, staying where she belonged, in the background, yelling out words of support and pointing out areas where Sam was vulnerable, preferring to keep her hands clean. Picking up the rifle and shooting that blind Wendy was one thing; Sam was another completely different thing. Kolen thought that if she dared to try to shoot Sam, Sam would move Losnedahl's head to the trajectory of the bullet, making Kolen shoot and kill him instead. So Kolen thought it was best if she never picked up a firearm while Sam was holding one of her friends hostage. *Why don't you show Fredrickson what you're worth by getting up and fighting me, Marilyn? Instead of crying like a whiny little bitch, get up and help your friends fight me! At least they won't have to deal with your screaming and having to listen to "Oh, help me, Lisa! Save me, Darren, I'm too much of a chickenshit to fight myself" if you're joining the ranks and earning your official place.* Sam felt like saying this to Kolen, but she didn't, as it would interrupt her feast on Losnedahl. Her teeth were already touching his greying black tufts of hair, and more of her spit was dripping down his head, making Losnedahl utter a rasped shriek of panic. Still, he was unable to do anything to fend her off as she still kept the knife deep inside his gut and her hand tightly clenched around his throat. He clenched his eyes and teeth shut as his face lost more colour, causing Kolen and the others to panic. Suddenly, Slater quickly picked up the revolver again and furiously aimed it at Sam. His own teeth were sealed tight, with drops of saliva escaping out the gaps in his teeth, coating his impressive beard with his drool. Slater's eyes were spacious; his eyebrows were furrowed into an intense expression of utter rage. 'SAAAAAAAM!!!!' he roared, drawing the trigger about three times, which sent three bullets hoarding towards Sam, and without him properly thinking where he was aiming before shooting, they headed towards Losnedahl at the time. Sam made a sarcastic huff, rolling her eyes and removing her teeth away from Losnedahl's head, then proceeded to move his body in the direction of the shots. Turning Losnedahl into a meat shield. Therefore, making it so that it was Losnedahl who got shot three times instead of her. During the whole feat, the smile stayed smelted on her face. As for Losnedahl, he was in tears and showered in his blood. He was looking at Slater with a pleading look as he could feel his blood leak out of the holes where he had been shot.

Left leg.

Right shoulder.

Right arm.

Slater hissed; he was given yet another reason to detest Sam. It was as if Losnedahl didn't suffer enough physical pain throughout his life, so much so that being hurt would become a daily occurrence for him, but now he had been used as a meat shield and was wearing the unwanted scars of friendly fire. 'FUCKING SHIT, SORRY, HENRIK!!' Slater screamed, lowering the revolver, not wanting to risk firing any more shots into the mute man. This was when both zombies, Ace & Zinni, took things into their own hands, Ace out of her own free will and Zinni because Oli had pretty much screamed at him, 'Lads! Kill her! FUCKING KILL HER!' First up was Zinni (Aladar was missing); he was snarling at his enemy, charging forward at Sam, who had shown no fear like she had displayed many times. Ace leapt out of the wheelchair and crawled her way over to Sam's feet. Her intestines were dancing across the ground as she moved with such an alarming speed. If Ace wasn't on the group's side, this would've terrified them as well as made them wildly kick at the ground, trying to kick her away like some kind of decayed flesh soccer ball. Hell, it would scare anyone to see a hungry and angry crawler coming at them at such a scarily fast pace.

This was good! Sam couldn't maintain her focus on three things at once; no one could. There was a thing called multitasking, but to focus on holding a mute man hostage while watching out for a crawler and zombie teenager coming both at her, such a task was remarkable and a little overboard. Sam desired strategic planning. Sam was going to get some damn fine strategic planning and force. Everyone was going to have a chance at punishing Sam. Everyone would have a turn (Roll up! Roll up! Take a shot and hurt this zombie in any method of your choice!). Where the hell is Aladar! Oli thought. We need him!

Ace came up to Sam, seized her foot and sunk her teeth deep into Sam's leg, granting attention to her. The injury on Sam's foot had caused the once constantly seen evil smirk to merge into an angered scowl. Sam growled as Ace mounted down more on her foot and refused to let go. 'Yes! Atta girl Ace!' cheered both Oli and Kolen. Sam peered over at Zinni, ejecting his body at her, and she took the opportunity to be rid of the mute man by thrusting the bleeding Losnedahl at Zinni in a way to stop him in his tracks. But before Sam had done that, she took the knife out of Losnedahl's stomach, unplugging the hole, causing more blood to spill out of Losnedahl's body. She threw Losnedahl at the teenager, and as a result of having a grown man thrown at him, Zinni was knocked to the ground by Losnedahl, who was now bleeding out of four separate wounds.

This paved Sam with enough time to pry Ace away from her foot. Sam seized the crawler by the spine and tufts of hair and pulled so hard that some of the clumps of hair started to free themselves from her crest and that some of the surgically (you've truly outdone yourself, Vinnie) grafted flesh had begun to tear off Sam's foot. Even so, she successfully managed to rip Ace off her foot; remnants of surgery were clumped in her mouth. Ace flayed around frantically in Sam's clutches. Sam gawked, reared back, eyed Oli, who was currently tending to her brother's injuries when Sam had shot him twice in the leg, using the first aid kit that Kolen had installed into the wheelchair, and threw the frantic Ace at her. Oli went down with Ace, falling backwards, with Oli having to utilise some reflexes if she planned on catching Ace in both hands. But she was too slow, and Ace fell on her face, knocking her backwards. Seeing Sam throw a crawler at his bonder and sent Zinni through a deleterious frenzy, one that was kindled with nothing but hate and a lust for carnage.

He shifted the limp but still living Losnedahl off him; Losnedahl let out a rasped groan as both Kolen and Ark advanced to each of his sides and helped pull him up and move him out of the danger's beckoning call. Kolen went and extracted more bandages, along with a knife and scalpel. As much as it was making her heart sick.

She knew that she'd have to conduct surgery on him, that she'd have the duty of removing the bullets herself instead of waiting for the hospitals to become functional again... which might be a never, with the way the world was at the moment.

But thankfully, Kolen wasn't alone. Ark was a former neurosurgeon; she knew her way around medical procedures around the brain and some local knowledge about treating deep wounds, but she was needed in the fight. So, she provided Kolen with the crucial guidance and tips needed to complete the surgery without killing Losnedahl! Because one wrong move could be fatal, and Losnedahl could end up dying from either blood loss or stress, causing cardiac arrest. Ark took Losnedahl's lap coat and unbuttoned it. Then, she carefully removed the wounded shoulder from the shirt's collar, giving Kolen access to it.

'Just try not to rush it, Marilyn; I'll be right here if you need me to take over. But I also do need to help Zinni and Spot.' Ark explained to her. Kolen nodded hastily as she glanced at Losnedahl wearily. Clutching the scalpel in her fingers, she bit her lip. 'This might hurt Henrik,' she swallowed her own nervous spit as she brought the scalpel down on his shoulder.

This movement happened while Zinni had once more bolted over to Sam. A ripe but malevolent energy was coursing throughout his whole body. Zinni's young, bloodshot eyes and Sam's entire body were glowing a rich shade of red. He propelled himself at Sam, arms out and fingers grabbing. But even with all this blinding potent fury, this had granted Sam the chance to grab Zinni by the arm and spin him around, lugging his arm downwards and making his body droop; then she wrapped her arm around his throat, putting him in an undesired chokehold. Sam then, without any hesitation and without saying a word, opened her mouth and rammed her teeth down into Zinni's neck like a fictional vampire sucking the blood out of its victim. Sam's sunk her chops deeply into the zombie teenager's neck, and she made sure to suck out as much blood out of his neck as she could. Her teeth had spent less than ten seconds in his neck before she tore them out of his neck along with a large chunk of his decaying neck, granting sight to his spine connecting to the base of the boy's skull.

Sam claimed another unintentional victim.

She dragged Zinni over to her and held the tufts of his pale blonde hair, digging her fingers into his dead skin; the other hand was holding his right shoulder. And with one terrible undead yank, Sam cleft Zinni's head right off his body and tossed the head away like it was nothing but a broken deflated football.

She dropped Zinni's headless body simply and kicked it out of her way.

Chapter 34

'ZINNI!!' Oli cried loudly; her heart was pounding; her reddened face was moist with the tears of seeing the sudden and gruesome death of one of her loyal bonded zombies. Oli felt the urge and wanted to approach and pick up the remains of Zinni's head so she could mourn him; he'd been good to her, he and Aladar both (where the hell was he?) were good to her, and they'd always listened to her instructions whenever she'd ask for them to grab some food or first-aid kits or the small times she'd go on a plunder for supplies with them. But if she had moved so much as a toe in the direction of his head, Sam would know, and she'd take her movements as an invitation that she wanted to die next, that she wanted to end up like her precious teenage Zinni. Slater moved away from the wall he'd been thrown into and came up to his sister's side and held her close; he knew how much that boy zombie had meant to her, so he simply let her bawl on his shoulder without needing to exchange any wisdom to her. However, despite Oli exhibiting an overflowing sorrow at her zombie's demise, her strong emotions couldn't even cut when it came to the heavy emotions that her other zombie was feeling. Aladar wasn't exactly known for dispensing emotions like Ace and Spot, nor was Zinni. Still, one thing was apparent: if anything, ever happened to Zinni, Aladar would be targeting them like a dad who finds out his daughter has been hit by a man; he'd be really mad if anything happened to Zinni. And that was what Aladar was (wherever he was).

There was a reason why Aladar and Zinni had such a strong bond with each other, and the main reason they were rarely seen separated was because of a family bond that had been firmly lodged inside them, inside those hearts that didn't beat. Even as zombies categorised in the 5-year AOR, they carried that bond with them even in death, the desire to protect and be with each other forever until one or both of them were to die. In other words, Zinni was Aladar's biological son... and like any father who viewed his son as his best friend. Seeing his own son by blood die in front of him would be guaranteed to tip him overboard when it came to becoming an eruption of hostility and wrath. Aladar wasn't as well bonded as Zinni was. If one had to ascertain an exact percentage of how human they were, Aladar would be about a seven while Zinni would be around twelve, but that meant little when it came to being out with the group and surviving with them. At least he could still follow orders and knew who was an enemy and an ally, and Sam was the ultimate enemy. As long as Aladar knew that, it was fine. It made things more transparent to him, knowing that Sam had taken the life of his son.

He made a resounding, intensified undead roar that sounded awfully like "Miles" at hearing the intense grief in his bonder's voice and that Zinni's snarls had become silent, which had only meant that he... Aladar came assailing out of the hallway. Showing himself to the group again, he skidded on the floor for a second before recovering swiftly. He headed straight for Sam, eyes blazing, teeth tensed, similar to one furious rhino with an already lousy temper problem. Aladar came pelting himself at the queen of hell in undead form, totally disregarding his own broken undead life. The only thing covering his clouded mind was seeking vengeance on the bitch that murdered his son. Aladar extended his arms out to Sam, blinded by revenge that shadowed all rational sense, bent on taking her head for himself and having her brains all to himself. After all, it wasn't like zombies' dead brains had tasted any different from a normal, alive brain. Sure, they'd be a little bit shrivelled up from being old and, well... inept. However, the brain would still be protected by a hard skull and would still be considered pristine enough for the undead's liking, sinking their teeth in, and feasting upon the brain's juicy residue. Unless the brain was exposed, sitting outside of the skull, that would cause the brain to rot over time, making it almost inedible, but if zombies were starving, they wouldn't linger at the thought of digging into some tender brains, rotten or fresh.

Around ten years ago, a Canadian man named Kurt Galahad uncovered this piece of information on the difference between inept and living brains while working in his own private, secluded lab somewhere in Yellowknife. He had posted it on his local forum after he had conducted the experiment. Kurt had been working on the rawness of human and zombie brains, doing his scientific investigations on an undead test subject he had named Pig, where he would note Pig's mental changes and how Pig would react to the brains, he had prepared for him. Kurt Galahad had been the one who had concluded and spoken up about the skull performing as a fridge to the brain, protecting it as well as keeping it fresh. If the skull was penetrated in any way, bacteria and other microscopic germs would find their way into the brain, sometimes with differing effects. Still, one thing always remained the same, during the ticking of time, the brain would gradually become stale, and diseased brains didn't have as much juicy nourishment as fresh brains. So, thanks to Mr Galahad's research, it was concluded that the reason the undead was that their brains were rich in flavour, just like how sugar gives things more taste.

Aladar bounded at Sam; pale eyes were ripe with a volcanic red. However, this activity and display of aggression from Aladar had caused Sam to just sigh. She had begun to grow tired of zombies charging upon her without thought; trying to be the hero, bounding dead hard at the villain, had never worked. Aladar had foolishly done the same thing, and instead of avenging Zinni, he was going to join him.

Sam stepped and moved out of the way of the angry zombie. Aladar zoomed past her, heading toward Ark and Kolen as they worked to patch the heavily wounded Losnedahl. But before Aladar could crash into them and probably kill Losnedahl, Sam fired her hand up to the back of Aladar's neck and tossed him backwards. He skidded; shoe heels contacted Spot's arm just as the tall zombie started getting up. Aladar's teeth tensed; he glared at Sam with pure, seething hatred. He came at Sam again. 'Aladar! Don't!' shouted Ace, but her words were in vain as Aladar rushed at Sam. Sam threw up her foot and kicked him hard in the chest, enough to knock him into the wall, making plaster crumble down on him. Spot, although he was blind, knew by instinct that he had to get out of the way, and he did with a leap just as the adult zombie came crashing into the wall. Aladar shook his head, got back to his feet, and once more headed for Sam, but she had strutted over to him before he would bolt towards her again; she grabbed him by the shoulders and forced him to turn around. Aladar protested, but Sam kept a firm grip on him. She seized the pale blonde hairs on his head and pushed him back towards the wall. Aladar's hands were outstretched on the chipping plastered wall as Sam pushed Aladar hard against the wall. However, Aladar still had some fight remaining in him, so Sam did it again, ramming his face into the wall, creating a red stain on the chipping plaster. This time, when she retracted it, Aladar's face had a broken, bleeding nose, and some of his teeth were missing; now, most of Aladar's strength was gone; he just couldn't keep up with Sam's. Letting out a shrill howl. Sam hurdled Aladar's face into the wall one more time, so hard that his entire head exploded in a disgusting bloody mess, raining massive chunks of dead flesh and brain matter, splattering blood all over the wall and around her face and upper body.

Sam retracted the destroyed headless undead corpse of Aladar away from the wall and glared at it before thrusting it down.

Remnants of brain matter slid down the wall as the remaining seven group members all shared the exact amount of terror and shock at Sam's sheer brutality. Oli was wailing, 'Oh god… Aladar…' She was clutching pieces of debris from the floor, dropping them and picking them up again as tears dropped on her knuckles. Both her zombies had just been slaughtered before her eyes, and she hadn't been able to do anything to prevent it; she had just sat there and watched helplessly.

'How the fuck are we gonna do this? Seriously? How are we gonna beat her? She's already killed both of Olivia's zombies in under five minutes!' Slater yelled in a hushed whisper to Kolen, Ark, Ace, and Spot, even though his body was at the other side of the room near Kolen's side, so in form, he could hear Slater perfectly. Ark glanced at Sam, who thankfully had been distracted by the bloody stain on the wall that was caked in pieces of Landon/Aladar's brain.

'We have to outsmart her; Sam can read our moves like she's studied methods of fighting and blocking,' Ark whispered back in reply to Slater.

'Not to mention that she looks like she's done some committed form of karate, from how agile she is with dodging the attacks made by Henrik and the zombies combined, and she knows where it hurts,' Slater whispered back at her. Slater, Kolen and Ark kept their voices down, watching gingerly as Sam cocked her head down to the still twitching undead corpse of Aladar, distracted by it, then to eavesdrop on the four humans as they pondered on ways on how they were going to kill their foe. Aladar appeared to be still clinging to his undead (barely) life by twitching his arms and legs. This caused Sam to make a most irksome noise as one of Aladar's twitching hands clamped around Sam's ankle. 'Please just die already and join your son in death.' she huffed before she well and truly finished Aladar off by stomping down on his chest, making the wittered ribs inside him break and pierce through his already non-beating dead heart, killing him finally. But at least now he was with his boy. Oli saw all this, tears forming in her eyes as she just sat there on her one leg, staring helplessly at the carnage that had been her two zombies, all that hard work, gone…

Chapter 35

Sam turned to them so quickly that her neck made a ghoulish snapping noise, which grabbed the attention of the remaining members of the group; they stared, except for Losnedahl, who had his eyes closed and was clinging to life, breathing slowly, and Oli, who was staring and weeping down at the bodies of her life's work as an independent bonder, with sweat trickling down their faces. Sam grinned. She tilted her head to the side, and the joints created a loud cracking sound. The women grimaced, and Sam relished seeing their fear. Slater commented on the cracking sound being disgusting while Oli continued to blubber and shovel and drop the pieces of debris around her as she mourned. 'I'll give you credit for turning these zombies against me… it's smart but hopeless to fight fire with fire because fire spreads. But too bad you humans won't be inheriting this already fucked up Earth forever, as it's about time for a change; it's time for a new leader, a world where the undead are the masters and the humans are the pets. When the cards are laid down and the facts are dispensed, You, humans, are the reason why the world is like this. Dead. Everything was beautiful when I was alive. Everything made bloody sense. And now look at it, now look what happened to this world and what you selfish humans have done to it.' Oli continued to stare at the bodies of her zombies. Still, her tears had stopped, and she was becoming enraged with Sam for taking her zombies away so mercilessly. Hearing her talk about how she wanted to make the world an undead paradise made her sick. Oli fiddled about the ground for a tool to use to her advantage; a sharp pike of wood would do nicely, or even a piece of glass or, even better, a small carving knife; eventually, her fingers bumped on an empty bottle of Meantime next to the end table, the bottle that Ark had drunken out of. She grabbed it slowly so as to not raise any suspicions and held it behind her back while she continued to glare, this time at the ground where the elephant zentangle with the dog's corpse had been before her brother had wrapped it up and moved it somewhere out of site. She'd ruthlessly taken her zombies, who were more than zombies to her; they were her friends. She'd shot her brother and almost killed Losnedahl; for all that Sam had done, she knew that she couldn't be forgiven. Oli knew she'd never forgive her, and as sick as it made her, she needed to bide her time. Oli glanced up where Sam stood about a metre and a half away from her and her brother, waiting for the moment to break the bottle and stab it into her foot. 'Humans were already turning the world into shit by their selfishness and pointless greed around money and craving lust for power, wanting everything to be adapted to a paradise, a so-called perfect utopia. Wanting to create this politically correct world. Well, congratufuckinglations, this is the future that you've written for yourselves! You, humans, will become an extinct species one day, the new dinosaurs… imagine that. I'm just speeding up the process.' Sam explained to the group with a sickening glee that it was almost a wonder how everyone had managed to hold back their fury to all go at Sam and have their pickings with her; though Oli seemed more than ready to have a go first, she'd seen more than enough corpses to last her a while. 'Look around you; look at the beauty that is to become better for the undead,' Sam turned around, spreading her arms around her to face the carnage and the slain bodies of Ryan Winsome, Zinni and finally, Aladar. Sam made an inhaling noise, taking in the ripe stench of death that was around her. 'You know… all this death and bloodshed reminds me of a book that Fredrickson gave me when I was with him. What was it called again? Oh, that's right, Macbeth.' She turned around to face the group again; her voice was full of accusations, blaming Fredrickson for giving her a book full of malice, paving the way for her descent into chaos, giving ideas on how and the many ways she could go about with her brutal murders. 'Wouldn't you agree that letting a zombie read *Macbeth* was more than a little *foolish*? He really should've done his job correctly and given me something more light-hearted to read, or maybe he should have chosen for me; he was scared of me, a spineless coward that he couldn't even choose the correct book for his precious little subject to read. Pathetic!' The word pathetic was drawn out teasingly, almost the equivalent of scraping a blade over a metal oven. It was piercing. 'You took them from me; they were my mates, and you took them from me.' Oli mumbled angrily, gripping the bottleneck, waiting for her moment.

'And I'll gladly take more if you oppose me.' Sam replied casually.

But her moment didn't come because Kolen had risen to her feet so quickly; it was like someone had hit fast-forward on her that Oli almost didn't realise that the bottle had been stolen from her until she'd looked up and had seen it in Kolen's hand. She had taken the moment. 'Marilyn?' Ark asked anxiously. She took Kolen's hand gently to pull her back, but Kolen moved her hand violently out of her grasp; her blood was tipping out of the pot, and her mind lost all its sense of reason. Behind those glasses,

Kolen wasn't crying because she was scared; she cried out utter blinding hatred. Kolen wanted to make Sam see that she wasn't weak and that she could be motivated to cause some damage when pushed.

Kolen let out a livid, ear-pricing banshee-like shriek at Sam; Ark blocked her ears as she was the closest to Kolen and about a metre away from the black-haired monster. Sam had once again mocked her teacher, whom she idolised and viewed as a very dear friend. Her heart was beating like a startled rabbit, her breathing was rampant and shaky, and her banshee-like shriek had sent the other members into a phase of shock as if they'd become paralysed by the screech alone; Oli felt like her body was encased in a block of frozen ice by this sudden shift of Kolen's personality. She and her brother hadn't known Kolen for long, but they knew this was out of character for the ordinarily timid and fretful Kolen; they'd known her to be the last person to jump into angry hysterics. But here she was right in front of them, gritted teeth and eyes blazing. She made Oli's fury look like a childish pout, that even just bearing witness to the ticking time bomb that Kolen had become had caused Oli's ferocity to drop.

Oli watched, now overwhelmed with nothing but a monstrous desire to bash someone's face in; Kolen leapt from her crouched position, brutally taking ownership of the nearest object, a piece of rotten wood with a sharp spike on the front, and had the bottle she'd stolen from Oli in her other hand. She unbottled her emotions and set forth to Sam with a firm intent to pike it through Sam and kill her or bash her head with the bottle, even if it meant her own demise. But if skewering it through her gut didn't work,

Kolen thought about bashing the bottle into Sam so many times until either Sam was dead or a portion of the bottle split on her and then she would repeatedly stab her with it. Although she didn't say it directly, you could tell that Kolen was cursing Sam, internally screaming damnations of, "I'll kill you!" all over in her head. From being in front of her with her eyes focused on her, Sam had almost instantly caught sight of this sudden and strange behaviour coming from the usually calm and timid Marilyn Kolen. It'd been granted with both shock and excitement from Sam as her smile just became wider with joy. This was a Kolen that Sam could waste energy in fighting. Oli looked bemused when she crawled towards the flashlight Kolen had swapped for the pike, picked it up and glanced at Kolen, who, during this very moment, Kolen didn't even look like Marilyn Kolen anymore. It was like she'd transformed into a completely different person with a completely different personality, but who'd shared the same body with the Kolen that everyone else knew. In a way, she resembled Ark when she was angry. Her brows were knitted together with scorn, her eyes hateful, and her teeth were borne; she spat through them as she clutched the wooden plank. The very sight made her sick, and her voice made her want to rip her ears off, but she knew that it wasn't the time to cower away in fear. Kolen wanted to show her friends what she was capable of if pushed, and Sam had pushed her too far.

Kolen screamed again; her scream, this time, rang inside the ears of Slater, Oli, and Ark and resting and wounded Losnedahl like a haunting battle cry.

Kolen then charged at Sam with the broken piece of wood tugged under her right arm, the bottle raised above her head in the left. Full of adrenaline, Kolen flung herself forward at the monster Sam with the broken piece of wood and bottle. At first, she thew the bottle at the monster. Sam caught it with one hand and crushed it, indifferent to the pieces of glass poking out of her hand. Kolen then leapt up in the air as if she were to dunk a ball; she unbound the pike from the right side of her body and hooked it at Sam with a vice-killer intent as she came down. Sam simply stepped away, and Kolen hit the ground, her knees piercing some of the bottle's glass; Kolen hissed from the stinging feeling in her knees. Kolen dropped the pike and rolled on her backside, fumbling to pull the pieces of glass from her knees.

'Oh please… is that really the best you can do?' Sam rolled her dead grey eyes with disappointment, releasing yet another bored, unsatisfied huff at Kolen's brave but hopeless attempt to attack her. She had high hopes for Kolen actually being able to strike her, but like the zombies had done before her, she'd made the same mistake of storming at her with blunt force. Sam knelt down and seized Kolen's right arm, and forced her to stand. Kolen's eyes were wide and helpless as they stared into those cold, dead eyes. Sam pulled Kolen close to her and said something in her ear, which chilled Kolen so that her flesh bubbled with goosebumps. 'Consider this a badge of achievement for overcoming your extended fear of violence.' Sam simply stated without much turmoil, holding onto Kolen's arm. 'You disappoint me.' She pushed it to the back of her wrist with a force that what happened was instantaneous, and it took Kolen a moment to look down and realise with vast horror what Sam had done to her; her hand had been turned inside out, and the back of her hand was touching her wrist, making the bone project from the base of her wrist; any more pressure and Sam would've wholly torn off Kolen's entire hand as if it was a simple Christmas cracker. Blood was issuing out of Kolen's destroyed hand while Kolen looked at it, screaming a blood-curdling shriek at the top of her lungs from the immense pain and sight alone, seeing her bones out of her skin. Ark and Oli had screamed with her. Slater had cupped his mouth to stifle his cry, and Losnedahl gasped weakly.

Sam grabbed Kolen by her chin and yanked it up so the speckled woman was looking at her. Kolen was back to crying out of fear. Sam sneered at her. 'Do you really think you could stand up against me, Marilyn? Tch, get real. You're as weak as piss, a liability, and always will be! Just like Mr heartless on the floor there. Why don't I just put an end to all that worthless pain and send you straight to Fredrickson? I'm sure he's lonely down in hell.' Sam dropped her before peering right through Kolen's spectacles into her brown eyes with no pity or remorse whatsoever. Only a bittersweet craving for generating pain for those around her.

The smirk was back, making its return. 'Even better, I'll eat you all; I am feeling a little peckish since I removed Winsome's piece from the board.'

Ark and the others couldn't take it anymore. In just a short window of time, Sam had killed three of them and had broken Kolen's wrist, rendering her unable to contribute more fighting or heavy lifting; they desperately wanted to get on their feet and help Kolen, hell it might just be safer to not risk it anymore and run away, run as far away from Sam as they could. But Ark knew they couldn't run away; they had come this far to give up now, and they weren't about to let Kolen's mistake defeat them. They were still a team right up till the end. If they're going to defeat Sam, they had to do it as a team. One wouldn't be enough.

Sam knelt down to the blubbering Kolen, who had descended down on her knees, cradling her broken wrist gently as blood poured out of the base. Sam held her hands to touch Kolen's face, caressing it like the paw of the grim reaper's head. Kolen cringed, flinching at Sam's icy cold fingers. Kolen cringed, looking away. 'Sam, I swear if you break another bone, we'll destroy you!' Ark threatened (*oh yeah as if I haven't heard that a dozen times already out of, ya pie*). But Sam displayed zero signs that she was listening. Sam just snickered, creeping her hands up to Kolen's forehead and the back of her head before glancing up into Ark's infuriated red face, still making those sickening giggles. Her malevolent intention was to snap Kolen's neck like she previously had done with the Turkish woman. 'It'll be over soon, Marilyn; everything will be over soon.'

'NO!!!' roared Ace, resembling a sound that sounded scarily human, without the deep croaking she originally had in her voice.

Ace had recovered from being thrown at Oli and began slithering back over to Sam, moving at an unnatural speed for a crawler (studies showed that crawler zombies start off slow, but as they get more used to their surrounding area, their rate gradually increases). Ace crawled over to Sam. But Sam saw her and lifted her leg back in an attempt to kick her away like a football, but this action was soon flawed as Ace flung herself from side to side like a pinball, making Sam dart her eyes around. She had become distracted by the crawler, watching her every move, and trying to work out when Ace was planning on leaping at her; Sam had unintentionally provided the open window of opportunity, feeding the group a chance to put her down. This was it! This was their moment! Now or never!

'That's it, Ace, get her!' Lisa Ark cried out triumphantly, pumping her fists in the air while watching the crawler showing zero signs of giving up; she just kept bouncing back like a never-ending pinball that wouldn't stop bouncing off the slingshots. Then Ark heard it, footsteps on debris. She demanded the torch; Oli rolled it to her, and she took it and shone it up. There was Spot, projected in front of her, casting a giant, imposing shadow on the wall behind him. Ark smiled thinly as he came up from behind Sam, looking like the rising silhouette of a giant scary monster usually conjured up in a child's nightmares and in her mind, she was cheering him on, knowing that there was a reason why Spot was her zombie, she had put her love and care into him, and he was repaying that care by protecting her and her friends.

Ark returned the torch to Oli, who looked at her brother and whispered something to him, Slater nodded in agreement and had snuck up from behind the bleeding Kolen, hooking his arms under her shoulders, and he dragged her away from the three remaining zombies. Spot and Ace would be able to hold Sam off for the time being.

Slater beckoned to Ark, and she came over, assessing the damage to Kolen's hand. Ark was appalled by the state of Kolen's palm and how Sam could do something so cruel to someone as kind and lovely as Marilyn Kolen; Ark personally wasn't sure if it would have any chance of healing. Her hand might have to be amputated, but she didn't want to tell her that because that might make her panic more. Slater tried his best to coax Kolen into staying calm and said that she had to be strong if she wanted to survive this night. Losnedahl shuffled over and aided Slater. He held Kolen's shoulders and pleasantly rubbed them as a way to soothe her nerves. Slater thanked him. Kolen eyed Ark pleadingly, 'I'm sorry, Lisa, I'm really sorry that all of you have to do this. Sam is right; I am hopeless. I am a liability, I-I'm gonna get you all killed.' she said while clutching her destroyed wrist.

Slater clicked his fingers before her, and she looked at him weakly. 'Hey, you shut up, Marilyn, you are NOT a liability! Take it from me and my days in the RMA. I know a liability when I see one, and you, ma'am, are far from one. Fuck Sam! You are going to make it; Lisa is gonna patch ya up! Right, Lisa?' Slater told her. Losnedahl nodded in agreement as well; his body was aching from having the bullets removed, but he was grateful that he was alive and that Kolen had done well in listening to Ark's words, being able to successfully treat his wounds.

Ark stared into Kolen's melted canvas with a portrait of dismay. 'I warn you, Marilyn, what I'm gonna do will hurt... a lot, but hopefully, it will help your hand heal.'

Kolen took Ark's words to heart, and it hurt Ark to see her mentally prepare herself for what was to come.

Slater saw what would happen, and he tore a piece of fabric from his trousers and handed it to Kolen. Kolen took it and put it in her mouth. Slater and Losnedahl, who had heaved his aching body over to her, they both worked together to keep her calm while Sam and Ace fought in the background; Oli would be watching them, so if Sam somehow fought off both zombies, Oli would let them know, warning them if Sam was targeting one of them. But right now, they were okay, as Ace was still zipping around Sam like a fly evading the swatter. Ark tore some fabric off her black cotton trousers and wrapped it around her fist as she gently cradled Kolen's arm and a broken hand. Ark exhaled a deep breath and blinked. Ark then bent the broken hand back into place, ensuring the bones connected without causing Kolen's skin to tear. Kolen wailed a muffled cry as she clamped down on the piece of rag handed to her. Ark unravelled the ribbon of black cloth from her own palm and hastily wrapped it tightly around Kolen's before sealing it up by placing the end into a sleeve, turning it into some kind of makeshift sling for the time being. Kolen might have to go to the hospital (if there were any functioning ones) after they kill Sam, and the fate of her hand would be officially decided there because Ark didn't have any equipment with her to be able to professionally perform on her friend.

'There, that's the best I can do for now without the proper equipment for the sake of your arm, Marilyn. Keep it safe; don't damage it until you get proper medical treatment.' Ark strictly explained to Kolen, who was now in the process of wiping her eyes and nodding. 'I'll try. By God, I'll try. Thanks, Lisa.'

'Come on, Spot, give the bitch what for!' whispered Oli, balling her fists and watching the three zombies in front of her. Spot had knelt down and, grabbed one of Sam's legs and hoisted her up off the ground, causing Sam to dangle in the air upside down like a piece of meat on a fishing rod hook and was tightly holding onto it. Refusing to let her foot go so she could crash back down to Earth, where she would ignore Ace and Spot and instead focus her bloodlust on the humans. But that thankfully wasn't going to happen, not while Spot held her foot tightly, not caring how many times Sam kicked him with her other foot; he wasn't going to let go, providing Ace with the open window to attack her again, to launch herself and sink her teeth once into her. But this time, she seized one of Sam's shoulders, sending a mound of sharp pain throughout her shoulder and neck. 'Woo! Hell yeah, Ace!' cheered Oli. Sam hissed in pain and flailed around under Spot's undead grip, kicking him in his half-head while trying to uproot Ace from her.

Fuck! Fuck you, Fredrickson, fuck you for making me tolerable to pain! Sam's thoughts ran wild from the hurting feeling of Ace sinking her teeth deep into her shoulder. She had never much liked her former bonder during her time as his pupil, but now she hated him, dammed him, wished she could kill him again and again.

'Now, Lisa, Mr Darren, and Mr Henrik! Take her out while we have her distracted!' If he could talk like Ace, Spot would be yelling that out to his bonder, encouraging her and the men to seize this chance to go for the kill, to end this nightmare! 'Go! While she's being kept back by the two! Let's put an end to this bitch's life!' Oli screamed out to Ark and the two men. Slater did say that his sister was a

bit eccentric, and it was as if she had heard Spot tell Ark to take the shot as if he had spoken to her by telepathy.

'You heard my sister!' Slater declared, getting up to his feet and helping Losnedahl to his, taking up a rock from the ground, hoping to cave Sam's head in with it.

'I think not!' snapped Sam, shovelling her palms underneath Ace's neck, and digging her fingers into her decayed flesh, causing sheer discomfort for Ace. Ace clamped shut her eyes as Sam's fingers wiggled around inside her neck, touching her spine, and grabbing it from the inside. Ace, the crawler, was forced into letting go of Sam's shoulder, tensing her teeth and eyes with signs of severe distress. Sam threw her away. Still dangling upside down in Spot's vice grip, Sam looked at the ground above her, waving her hands around the dirt, wood, and plaster; she uncovered a small carving knife from under the debris and picked it up; she wiggled around in Spot's grasp, as Spot stepped back and forth, trying to keep his grip on her. But Sam wasn't making things easy for the tall zombie. Furthermore, she had shimmied around so much in his grasp that she was able to spin around and use the knife on Spot, driving it deep into his chest and forcing Spot to utter a surprised gurgle. He shambled backward from the sudden pang in his chest, initiating Spot to release Sams foot. Sam broke her fall by settling her hands above her so that she could land gracefully and, in doing so, booting the knife sticking out of Spot's chest, plunging it deeper while in doing so, sending him crashing back into the wall that was stained with Aladar's blood and brain matter.

Sam now studied the group. Her pale features resembled an erupting volcano of how infuriated she was.

Oh, how she detested each one of them, how she hated them for allowing them to get the upper hand on her and how she had been so foolish enough to let them outsmart her by utilising the zombies to fight her as a means of distraction. While they tended to their own if they were injured by her. Sam had reverted back into her former self before the bonding process a few weeks back in the GFOSAR; she had her zombie rage and uncontrolled bloodlust back. She craved nothing more than to rip their throats out, dine on their entrails, and

(Die)

Treat herself to their brains.

Sam got on fours like some crazed animal with rabies. She had drool dripping out from the holes in her rotten, decaying teeth; the tiny red veins inside her sclera were becoming more bloodshot from the mass adrenaline of anger swelling inside of her. Intelligence and appearance aside, Sam was still a zombie and a ruthless one who dispatched and ate her victims without a whiff of remorse.

'Fuck! She's pissed now. What do we do?' Oli gulped, peering at Sam's flaming anger with despair.

'Don't worry, Olivia,' whispered Ark. 'I have a plan.'

Chapter 36

Yes, indeed, Ark did have a plan, but she wasn't going to say it while Sam could still listen. Her plan needed to happen when Sam had been weakened enough. Ark glared at Sam and scoffed, finding some kind of amusement in Sam's wild appearance. Ace took another bite out of Sam's leg, making the black-haired witch hiss through her rotting teeth. Ark found it joyous to appreciate that she was wearing a different mask, one that was angry instead of that disgusting smile that mocked them every time it was seen on that wicked mug; seeing this one suited her more because it told Ark that she was beginning to understand the importance of their teamwork and that there would be some zombies that she'd never be able to convert over to her side. Ark could now understand why Ace had shown an exceptional distaste for it; every time she smiled that evil grin, Ark's stomach churned like she'd been punched in the gut. God, she had hated that smile. Sam scowled back at Ark in return, teeth gritted, eyes bulging red from an intense prejudice. Ark was the one that grinned this time, relishing in the anguish that the two good zombies were giving her. *How's this for a taste of your own medicine,* Ark thought savagely as she picked something up from the floor and held it behind her. Sam flung herself at Ace on fours, scooped her up in her violent palms and thrust her over at Spot to knock him back down to the floor when he made an effort to get up and pull the knife out of his chest. But the tall zombie couldn't get the knife out in time as Ace came crashing into him, prompting Spot to hold his hands in front of him, catching Ace in his arms as Ace groaned. He gently rolled the hurt and spent crawler on the floor next to him and proceeded to twist and tear the knife from his chest, inducing a small amount of blood to spill out before he dropped the carving knife on the floor next to him and clutched the bleeding gash.

Once they were out of commission for the time being, Sam brought her social awareness to the humans, specifically Ark, as she was the one in charge. She went on all fours again, snarling like an animal and got herself ready to propel herself at the group like a leopard that had plagued the country during 2020, desiring to rip them a new one, wanting to eat them alive when she kicked, thrashed, and screamed for her to stop because it was always more fun and satisfying when the food wriggled and screamed and begged for help. Sam didn't acquaint well with offers of mercy; remorse was a foreign word for her, and she showed little interest in learning what it meant because mercy was no fun if you wanted to turn the country upside down and make the undead the dominant species. She only knew how to kill and kept killing for food because she simply enjoyed it too much. Once, the humans of the group were either dead or chosen to act as a food source. Then she'd turn her attention to the two zombies, Spot and Ace, and destroy them as if they were humans themselves for betraying their kind and siding with the enemy. They sided with them, so it was best to treat them as if they were human, so what if it was cannibalism. They had sided with humans; the smell of humans would be rubbing off on them, and she would eat them as if they were humans. Sam even thought of cruel methods for taking the lives of the two zombies affiliated with the group:

Take the gentle giant's precious brain jar and throw it against the floor, then pick the lump of flesh from the ground and tear away at it, ripping her teeth into the thing while her hands closed around the brain, squishing it in her hands as she ate away at it – Spot.

Mercilessly cleft off the arms and the head, dropped the head on the ground and bounced on it to spatter it into a massive bloodied stain that'd be grander than the stain that'd been Aladar's head, smashing the skull into pieces, then she could take a nibble out of the arms and enjoy a nice snack – Ace.

Sam threw herself at the group, mouth open. But she didn't touch anyone as when she looked down, Ark had shoved something inside her chest; Sam looked at her, and Ark spat at her. Sam stepped back and looked down at the thing that'd been stabbed into her. She grabbed what felt smooth and pulled it out, realising it was the neck of the bottle she had broken. Ark had picked it up while she'd been distracted by the annoying crawler. Sam examined the bottleneck and then shot out a laugh; she threw it away where it clinked on the ground. 'I may have underestimated you lot. Even so, don't get cocky; even if you do kill me, you WON'T put the entire mortuus carnem species to extinction; they still reproduce like any other insect. They'll keep infecting the dead, and I'll still have a legacy. So, I'd still win.' Sam seethed and ran at the group full of uncontrolled, adulterated bloodlust!

Ark then leapt out, rolled across the ground, snatched up the revolver near Winsome's corpse, loaded it and aimed it eagerly at Sam, closing her eyes and firing shot after shot and not caring how many times she fired the weapon, just caring that the bullets hit the target. Ark wanted to see her riddled with bullets; she wanted Sam to be a pin cushion of holes. And it wasn't just Ark who wanted her dead. All of them wanted to see Sam dead. All of them wanted to see this growing nightmare come to an end, even if Fredrickson, Winsome and the rest of Sam's list of victims couldn't be present to watch this moment play out before this band of survivors and two bonded zombies. They knew that on this day, on this night, in a few moments, Sam was going to meet her maker; Sam was gonna die! Tonight! Ark had promised it, and she'd see fit to keep her promise for Fredrickson, for Winsome.

Chapter 37

Sam's body jerked back six times as each of the shots Ark had fired into her, her body flung back limply each time one of those loud six bullets punched through her, inducing her to cough up black dust and for the same black dust to slowly trickle out of the holes where she'd been shot; it was hurting her (*good! keep up the pressure!* Ark thought), but she wasn't making many noises to signal her anguish, just a few grunts here and there. The smell of smoke and lead filled the living room of this trashed, dimly lit house. Ark had gritted her teeth ferociously as she fired the six caps at her enemy until the revolver was empty, making absent clicking noises each time she fingered the trigger, but at least those six caps had slowed her down and repelled her back to some degree. But one thing was still apparent, she was still standing her ground, still remaining firmly planted as she glared into the eyes of each human group member. The stench of lead filled the room, Ark's ears were ringing from the thunderous bangs of the revolver, and she was sure that everyone's ears were ringing too, and the smell of lead was filling their noises. Ark coughed wetly and swatted at the smell of lead as if she were pushing away the smell of a particularly brutal, rotting egg. She was scared, petrified, but she tried to mask it behind a face that she hoped was instilling hope into the eyes of her friends, knowing that whatever would happen, even if she did fail, there would always be someone to take a stand against Sam and her wicked dream.

Sometimes, showing a false and fake sense of hope against all odds was the best that someone could do in this kind of situation. Considering the thought that maybe some of them weren't going to make it through this night, such as Winsome – she was determined to try to get them through – even if it'd mean her own death. She'd help her friends no matter what; she would help them and be the saviour that she had wanted to be. Ark might not have been able to save that young boy whose name is forever engrained in her head, Nolan Edgerton Jr. She might not have been able to save him or Winsome. But that didn't matter now because she still had her other friends, and she was wholly fixated on saving them. She might not be able to save all their lives, but as long as she could save most of them, that's all that she needed to do.

Ark then looked up at the zombie she'd shot and watched her stagger and examine the holes where Ark had shot her. 'I refuse to go down easy.' Sam spat, coughing up more of that black dust over the floor. Ark shouted for more ammo, and Oli hastily went through her injured brother's pack, fished out more ammo, and tossed them towards Ark, signalling their location with the beam of the torch. She managed to catch some, but others had escaped her and fell to the floor; that was okay, she at least needed some that she could use and she closed one eye and fired another three into her; one missed, hitting the wall just over her shoulder, but that didn't matter, because each lead cap was making her stumble and move backwards, coughing and spitting more of that ashy substance onto the floor. 'I can take it; I can take every shot you propel at me. Come on, instead of hiding behind those guns. Fight me like a man.' She coughed, swiping away the smoke and the lingering smell of lead. She glared at Ark, and Ark wished that she could punch it, though she was still too jittery to actually approach her to make the punch herself. It was best to keep her distance.

It didn't matter how many times she was shot and how much of that black dust she spat out. She continued to stand her ground, refusing to bend a knee and submit her defeat. She even shuffled a slow and lumbering foot towards them, though her movements seemed a little more sluggish than before (this was good). The sluggish movement was good because it meant that she was becoming weaker, and soon, she'd have to bend a knee to compose herself. But she still refused to do so; either this was courage or foolishness. One thing Ark couldn't deny, however, was that she did admire Sam's resilience and inability to want to back down and accept weakness and failure; in some strange way, Ark saw a bit of herself in Sam; the intolerance to failing was something that had always plagued Arks mind and something she just couldn't escape from. Sam was like that. She seemed intolerant to failure and refused to let things beat her. Ark couldn't help but admire that trait; it really was such a shame that Sam had chosen this path instead of siding with them and trying to rebuild and repair the world. 'I can take it; I can take anything you throw at me! I will never stop coming for you!' Sam said balefully. Ark was stripped of her thoughts, and she yelled for more ammo. Oli nodded and went through the satchel, 'Oh shit…' she shuddered at what she found instead of revolver caps. Ark yelled at her, demanding to know what it was, and Oli looked at her dismally. 'Nothing, there's no more caps left, you're out.'

Ark's eyes widened with horror. 'How can there be no more! I thought Darren filled it to the brim?'

'He did, but you used it all just then.' Oli murmured, lowering her head.

'Fuck!' Slater growled. 'Shit, shit, shit! Ju-Just hang on, I'll see if I can find anything useful.' Slater panicked, dragging his limp and heavy body away from the battle. He got to the wall and the hallway where he'd dumped the rugged-up body of Bear, staggered, but got up to his feet and wobbled down the darkness. There was a loud thump and a pained grunt that came from the hall as Slater had tripped and fell over something (the rug and the dog), but there was the sound of him getting back to his feet and walking further down the dark. As Slater had stumbled out of the room to find something "useful," Ark sat back, the revolver slipped from her hands and rolled to the floor. She was staring, mouth agape at the horrible sight before her. She was confident that she had fired at least a hundred shots into Sam's body because it sure as hell felt like she was firing a constant barrage of lead into her body, even if the total sum was a quarter of what she imagined. But even with that staggering amount of lead injected into her thin, pale frame, the witch just wouldn't fall over and die! She did stagger and stumble a bit, but she didn't fall; she remained standing firmly on her feet like a building that stubbornly refused to come down despite how many times it was hit with the wrecking ball. Sam's physique was caked in bullet holes, and all had the black dust seeping out of them like how sand flickers out of the hands when a person shovels a handful. Her teeth were relaxed, but her eyes were still dead-centred on the group, still housing a caged, agitated animal inside those lenses.

'A very… KOFF valiant effort…' She spoke softly, 'Well done for getting me this battered,' she said sarcastically as she choked up more black dust, hating herself for complimenting them, especially Ark, who had harrowed her with a seemingly endless supply of bullets.

'But the world is still dead; killing me won't change anything. You can't wipe out an entire species that reproduces just as well as rabbits.'

Ark swallowed; she didn't like how her fear was making her sound weak because she couldn't deny it herself. Sam did have a point about wiping out an entire species, like how the meteorite had wiped out the dinosaurs. Still, Ark didn't forget the critical information taught in science class during her years in high school. How humans were responsible for the extinction of many species of animals, such as the New Zealand Moa bird, the Dodo, the Quagga, the Woolly Mammoth, and so on? The evidence was there. Humans could indeed put a race of animals to extinction if they banded together. So, with that said, Ark tried to tell herself and the group that they had to be positive and could rally up the rest of Earth's living population, and with their help, they might be able to turn the horror of the mortuus carnem into a fairy tale, and reserve fossilized remains in local museums. She still needed to instil hope and faith because such a future without the mortuus carnem could and might happen someday. However, just like with everything else, it all bottled down to patience because putting an entire insect species to extinction wouldn't happen overnight. It required patience and actually finding the little buggers before they did their work on a nearby corpse.

Thinking of that possible future for them had changed Ark, and she suddenly felt braver, like she could do anything she had put her mind to. 'Maybe not... but we'll sure as hell try! Because that's what humans like us do, we fight for our planet and for those we care about.' Ark declared with such power in her voice that it was motivating the rest of the group, exposing that hope was not all lost and that they still had chances of success, showing no such ounce of fear while staring into Sam's empty eyes. Lisa Ark was going to show Sam that it was possible that she could be defeated; even if it took Ark to the age of ninety-six, the mortuus carnem would be extinct! She'd be lying on her deathbed, smiling at what she and this small band of survivors had started and finished; her legacy was made, and she could pass on in peace. That was a future worth dying for.

'I respect your tenacity, but you're not superhuman, Lisa; you're just a simple human being; you all are, except the ones you call Ace and Spot, but even so. Wiping out an entire species of parasite is an impossible task for a mere human.' Sam asserted evenly, still maintaining her ground, still staining through all the holes coating most of her body.

Ark took a brave step towards Sam despite the others warning her not to. Once she was almost touching Sam with her nose, she finally came to ask the question that had been on everyone's mind since this whole nightmare began.

'Why are you doing this? What could have caused you to become so... so bloodthirsty?' Ark questioned the one individual she hated the most, wounded, the one individual standing before her, horribly battered but dangerously attractive. 'Every villain is motivated to do what they do; they see something incorrect with the world and the citizens around them. Mine is similar to that. When I was alive, I thought that the living was a disgusting race. The living are full of the corrupt and the cruel. Back when I was alive, the country was full of life, joy, and children's laughter… but as soon as the years went by, I was rotting away in that grave and when I was finally resurrected by the mortuus carnem sometime during the 2040s. I saw that the Earth had started to lose that joy, and the rightfulness that made it great was gone. It was a husk of what it used to be. The life in it was dying. And when I saw what the living were doing to it, I was convinced. I came to the conclusion that the living was doing this. They were destroying the world with their greed and everlasting need to shape the world into their own image; it makes me sick. So, I'm eradicating the planet of its disgusting living humans, saving some that will be used to feed the hungry undead, I know that the Earth can't be fixed, and once something dies, it's irretrievable. But as if I would tell you, my past. You're not worthy of knowing what happiness was like.' Sam spat.

Ark felt like she'd been stabbed; she was flabbergasted by these words, and she was sure everyone else was, too. But Ark was the one to speak up about it, 'What would you know about happiness? All you're doing is killing innocent lives; yes, while I do agree that some people can be corrupt, not the entire human race is corrupt and cruel!'

'Says the one who was born around 2020.' Sam disputed in retort. Ark's eyes widened, and her mouth was agape, clear signs that she was outraged. 'The fuck does the year in when I was born have to do with anything?'

'You were born in it.' said Sam.

'Your death will be satisfying. Not only to us but to the rest of the people you killed,' Ark growled, tensing her fists.

'Lisa!' Slater's voice called out from somewhere. Ark had almost forgotten that he'd gone off somewhere. She looked to her side, following Oli's and Kolen's gazes, and she saw Slater make an appearance out of the darkness; the torch beam was on him, and Ark saw that he was holding something reasonably significant in his hands as he stumbled out the hall and meeting his sister on the floor. He dropped to his knees; the object hugged to his chest. 'Lisa, I got something. I found a canister of acetone. Full too!'

This was brilliant! Now Ark's plan could come together!

Chapter 38

'Do you really think you can win?' Sam teased, cocking her head to the side, and vaguely watching Ark from the corner of her eyes as Ark went over to Slater and took the canister from him, lightly shaking it and listening to the sloshing of the flammable liquid inside. 'Ha. That'll be a story for the young 'uns. As long as my body is still intact, not resembling something in a dog's bowl, and as long as my brain is whole, the mortuus carnem can infect me as much as it wants. I can continue to rise again once more to hunt you all down. One by one and devour you,' she said with a faint chuckle to intimidate them. Kolen had whimpered, but Ark ignored this and unscrewed the lid off the container of acetone, smelling the waft of the liquid's intensity and manifesting no signs of being afraid like she had been before until Slater had found this here canister. She wasn't scared anymore because now she had a plan, and the flammable liquid was a part of it (*God bless you, Darren*), and she was deafly sure that this plan of hers would work.

Ark wasn't going to let Sam's monologues and ridicules gorge her like the maggots that ate (*keep them socks on, friends, I've got a plan*) her while she rotted away in that grave. Ark just had to ensure the group was collected and that everyone did not listen to Sam's chaff. Otherwise, their lashing out at Sam for telling lies could prove disastrous for Ark's method of undermining Sam's energy enough to the point where she was immobile, allowing Ark to grant the final blow. That was the plan, to make her weak enough so that Sam would just lay there motionless and helpless, unable to do anything to fight back. Sam was already suffering from the amount of lead inside her body. Still, Ark was planning on causing her more pain, hoping to force Sam into experiencing the right amount of agony that all her victims had felt and feeling a sense of satisfaction as she administered the torture.

Ark demanded the torch, and Oli tossed it to her instantly. Ark picked it up and beamed it at the white canister in her hands for about a minute, reading the bold word ACETONE – HIGHLY FLAMMABLE – KEEP AWAY FROM FIRE. Sam faced Ark, who was peering up at her with a monotone expression. At this point, Sam concluded that Ark was planning on lighting her up like a druid wicker man. Sam thought about reaching out to foil Ark but decided not to; she wanted to see if Ark had what was needed to start a fire. Instead, Sam went about digging her fingernails into a hole in her chest for a few seconds, pulling out one of the revolver bullets and cocking her head back to the blonde woman with a sly grin as she held the bullet up for Ark to see, Ark cringed, Kolen expressed her disgust in Dutch, Losnedahl closed his eyes and both the Slater twins stared up at the dust-covered shot. Sam extracted each cap from her body and dropped them on the ground with a blunt metallic Tink. Their faces were washed with a solid, putrid wave of disgust and horror, seeing that Sam was willing to tear into her own skin and extract the caps out of them in a display that was to show them just how far she was willing to go to remove the bullets from her body without the cost of surgery.

'That's fucked up, and I've seen my fair share of fucked up things,' Oli thought out loud.

You and me both, sis,' Slater mumbled in response.

Ark shook her head, shaking off the image of Sam removing the caps from her flesh and standing up, holding the canister with both hands and the torch in her mouth. Sam looked at Ark, watching with hatred as Ark started to splash her with the flammable liquid from the container for a few minutes until Sam was drenched entirely in the stuff, cleaning up some of the crackled blood from her previous victims. Sam just stared at Ark intensely, eyes burning into the eyes of the blonde woman. 'Do you seriously think that burning me will decrease the chances of the mortuus carnem returning back and infecting me again? Have you not listened to a fucking word I've said? You can't stop what I've already achieved!' Sam commenced raising her voice, reaching, and seizing Ark by the scruff of her lab coat collar and bearing her teeth at her. Ark pursed her lips together and cringed from the odour of those red teeth. Her mouth worked to say something.

'We've listened. We will still foil your sadistic plans, you sick fuck!' Surprisingly, it wasn't Ark who had said this. It was Kolen who said it with a harsh bitterness, still carefully caressing her broken wrist; her makeshift gauze was completely soaked red with her blood. Her face was stained with tears, but her expression was that of vengeance, which was almost motivational.

The others joined in what was now going to become a chant of words of triumphant and encouragement to Ark. 'Burn the fucking bitch, Lisa! Burn her 'til she's nothing but ash!' Slater threatened as his wounded face contorted into one of anger.

Oli moved around on the ground uncomfortably, 'I want to hear her fucking scream in agony! Fuck her reasons!' Oli snapped, pounding the air as if she could already smell the victory that was just around the corner.

'Avenge the lives that she's taken; you got this, Lisa!' Losnedahl signed confidently.

'The other zombies can have what remains,' Ace added, rubbing her palms together like she was preparing to dine on a massive restaurant meal. All were persisting that Ark ended it all and burned Sam while she stood covered in holes. 'Lisa?' Kolen's voice. Ark cocked her head to the side and saw that Kolen was now standing next to her, her good hand on her shoulder; her face reminded her of herself; she had the face of a strong and sturdy leader. Kolen then took off her glasses briefly, and Ark was suddenly blown back by how attractive and firm she looked – she resembled someone to look up to. 'Send her to Hell, right where she fucking belongs.' Kolen hissed, her good hand clenched onto Ark's shoulder. A mark to prove that Marilyn Kolen was becoming much stronger, showing everyone that she was coming out of her shell and that she could be valuable and fight alongside them with a gun in her hands. If Winsome and Fredrickson were still alive, they'd be proud of her.

The moment was now; Sam was going to pay for everyone she'd killed, for all the suffering she had caused, the fruits she had rotted. Ark was going to make sure that all her victims were going to know true peace. She'd grant them the solace and savour in the thought of knowing that their killer, Sam, is dead and burning.

'Go ahead, Lisa, do it.' Sam pestered Ark. Ark reached into her pockets for some matches and a matchbox to light them with; she remembered taking one from the hostel where they'd equipped Oli and her zombies as part of the team. She dropped the empty container; her face was shining with pride as she dug her hands through her pockets, looking for said box. She pulled out the box and opened it, set on waking up from this nightmare and putting Sam in the dirt.

But then her face suddenly turned sour and pale, her mouth dropped, quivering like the weather had suddenly dropped to minus ten degrees, the colour had abandoned her, leaving her looking like a frightened, lost puppy and just like that, all the spark and confidence had left her. She was standing there wondering how she could've screwed up again, forgetting something so crucial to her plan. 'Shit...' she squeaked.

'Lisa, what is it?! What's wrong!?' Slater called out, noticing this sudden change in Ark's expression and behaviour, not knowing if he should begin to join her grimace or encourage her. Even so, her trembling expression was most concerning for them. Kolen put her hand back on Ark's shoulder, and Ark flinched with a high-pitched gasp.

Ark was staring absently into space, utterly petrified. Sam's wicked grin appeared yet again, and she snickered evilly. She knew this was the case and waited for Ark to realise it, and she wasn't disappointed with her reaction.

Ark turned to the group with dismay, showing the empty matchbox carton to them. She was as pale as snow. 'I- I have no matches...' she whimpered.

Chapter 39

Ark dropped the empty box with a jolt as if she'd been touched by something unbelievably cold. She had failed. She had done the one thing that she'd worked so hard to avoid. She then peeped out and said "I'm sorry" to her friends, staring at the empty box as if expecting it to magically start filling up with matches. This side that had come out of Lisa Ark had stumped them, especially Kolen, who'd known her for the longest. It was new for them to see Ark wearing a face so profoundly hardened with fear that her typically sharp eyes looked as if they might leak tears. She didn't even look like the Ark they knew, but rather someone else who looked like their Ark but wasn't their Ark. Ark gripped the pockets of her lab coat and was subconsciously pulling at them. She took a frightened step away from her friends and shook her head, not wanting to believe that she'd failed them.. She kept staring at the box, wishing, and praying that matches would magically materialise.

But it was like Oli had told her; the world wasn't always entirely of human triumphs and achievements and prosperity; everyone failed from time to time after she had told her about Nolan and those cold, dead eyes that refused to leave her mind. But despite knowing that, it never made accepting failure and the ability to fail easy for her. The world and its inhabitants can be cruel and unforgiving, made worse by some people preferring not to change their ways so they would be able to benefit from the ever-growing changes around them. Sometimes, the strong-willed could be broken down eventually; their shells weren't entirely invaluable. Once they were cracked open, they'd be left as fragile husks, paranoid and untrusting to those around them, casting themselves out as the person who caused their friends and family to die because of a stupid mistake they'd made. The world was unforgivable to those who failed. Lisa Ark was a prime example of this. She hated failure and the very idea and possibility of her failing ever since the passing of Nolan Edgerton Jr. Why did she have to screw it up now? Why now? She had this moment to put a stop to everything. But she'd forgotten the most crucial thing in setting her plan in motion. Why hadn't she checked the box to see if it was complete rather than just looking at it as a matchbox and taking it with her? How could she be so careless not to open and check? How? How? *How*?! Ark was known well by those around her as tough, stoic, and the last to jump into frightened hysterics; she would remain robust and calm, dispensing no fear for her enemies even in the direst of situations. Whenever faced with a grim situation, she'd just hit her inner red button and get angry, even if it did sometimes blanket her rational thoughts. But seeing her retreat back into this soft pillow was utterly new for the group, and to Ark, it just reminded her of that day and Nolan on her table and the stress building up in knowing that she *needed* to fix him, to make him right, to make him better. But now it was revealed to the group so freakishly raw that it was terrifying them that Ark could allow herself to become this delicate and fragile, that one wrong move could cause her to completely crack like glass. Ark then dropped to her knees and made an uncomfortable and painful sniffling sound as she started to cry, droplets leaving her eyes and hitting the ground. Hating herself for this huge mistake that had most definitely spelt doom for her and her friends.

'Such a pity, such a fucking pity! You forgot the matches; out of all the things you could forget, you forgot a packet full of bloody matches. Did you not check the weight decency before you picked the damn thing up and shoved it into your pocket. Seems like you didn't.' Sam threw her head back and began hollering a haunting cackle that rang in Ark's ears, conveying the message that she'd failed again; she'd failed to protect her friends from this demon. 'This is all my fault,' she sobbed, staring at her hands, the hands that wore the blood of many zombies she had destroyed, 'I instilled so much false hope, oh Christ, I'm so sorry…' her lips were trembling, and she was feeling a freezing chill pass through her skin, causing goosebumps to bubble on her pale skin. She felt like she knew that this was something that could never be forgiven.

The others widened their eyes in disbelief at this sudden shift of pace. However, Slater seemed to be the most furious and in disbelief about this. After all, he'd seen Sam butcher most of his friends in cold blood and watch as he fled like a coward. 'How the shit could you have forgotten a box full of the damn matches?!' Slater yelled, exposing it as unbelievable that the brutal, take-crap-from-no-one former high-classed neurosurgeon Lisa Ark had forgotten the one thing that could have granted Sam an early passport stamp to Hell. Ark cried, feeling the same amount of disdain and hatred for herself. *Damn you, Ark, God fucking damn you, Ark!* Ark blasphemed herself. Ark had never hated herself over failure as much as at this moment. She forgot the matches! Her ticket into putting an end to Sam's reign and this whole fucking burden that they all carried with them! Out of all things she could forget, it just had to be the damn matches! She didn't smoke; she had picked up that box during the meeting with Oli, knowing that she had some kind of plan to use them against Sam and just having a gut feeling that it would be complete, slipping the box into her pocket. Why didn't she properly check the box before claiming it? That was an incredibly stupid thing she had done.

Sam was sniggering at this, not bursting into a full song of laughter, but a simple leering snicker that drilled into Ark's skull like a screwdriver. 'Oh, deary me, Lisa, this must feel like a right gut punch to you right now. Better luck next time. If you do confront me again, be sure to tightly screw ya brain on inside your skull. Oh, wait a mo. there won't be a next time.' Sam chuckled, not caring if there was still more of the black dust coming out of her; she proceeded to drill her fingers into her surgically grafted flesh, uprooting the bullets out of her and dumping them to the ground with a light tinkling noise. The last shot lodged somewhere in her breastplate was extracted by Sam and examined. She grinned at it for about five seconds before flicking it away, where it ricocheted off the wall and then landed on the floor. As if Sam wasn't already drenched in enough blood from the many people she'd killed and eaten, she was covering herself with her own! Bathing herself in her own shrivelled dust that had once been red blood, rooting off pieces of the grafted skin and playing with the dust that trickled out, grabbing a handful of the blackened dust, and smearing it over her face, even looping her tongue out to lick the scraps near her mouth. The sight was repugnant, to say the least. The group had thought that Sam couldn't become any more disgusting when it came to her methods of killing. She surprised them and disgusted them with each encounter, playing and gorging herself on her own dried blood mixed with the acetone from the container, painting an even more disturbing portrait than the painter had initially intended. Not to mention, she had smelt worse than ever! rotting flesh caked in acetone couldn't evoke a pleasant fragrance.

'What have I done? What have I done?' Ark moaned. She looked up, her face soaked with tears, seeing Spot first and seeing that he had taken a step towards her, but Losnedahl's arm was gripping his wrist. Ark felt like she deserved this, that she deserved to be the one to fall next. After all, she had failed them in the worst way possible. Spot took another step towards her, tugging away Losnedahl's hand. 'No, boy, you stay. You stay with the good people who won't fuck things around like I did.' Ark wept, looking down at the ground and crying more tears into the floor.

Sam shuffled behind her on her knees and placed a hand on Ark's shoulder. 'Nice try in trying to foil my plans, but Fredrickson made me this way. He made me this intelligent enough to surpass you; this was his parting gift.' Sam made one final smirk at Ark's friends before she grabbed a handful of Ark's blonde locks and seized it, pulling her by the chin and hair and forcing her to see into her evil eyes. Ark had no choice but to stare at those eyes, crying, wishing that she had checked the matchbox before taking it with her. She just hoped that Sam would take her and leave the rest alone. 'As a result of your abysmal failure, I'll let you all live. You can see this country you know and love so well die in front of you, and you will be powerless to stop it. You'll become cattle for my army, food for the starving undead.' Sam grinned before yanking the hair backward and tossing Ark backwards, prompting Ark to fall to the floor, her head banging on the headless body of the young zombie boy that Oli had named Zinni.

'Guys, what the fuck are we doing? We have to help her?' cried Oli.

'What can we do?' Kolen fretted. 'Look at us, do we look like we stand a chance of helping Lisa, let alone stopping Sam. If Lisa can't do it, we can't either. She's already killed your zombies and Ryan.' Said Kolen thinly. Oli screamed angrily in response.

How could I have been so careless and forgotten the damn matches? Out of all things! Why the matches? I had the box ready. Why the matches? Ark condemned herself once more, knowing that this was the end. She had ruined everything! Ark had killed the group! She had destroyed their last chance of cleaning up the death and destruction caused by Sam. Foiling their last opportunity to kill Sam (*I'm sorry, guys*) to send the demon back to Hell!

(*Please, God, please save them*).

Ark knew this because of her fatal mistake. Because of that mistake, she had jeopardised the entire group and the human race. This kind of screw-up was unforgivable, and she'd be wearing it for the rest of the time she'd be alive. If there were survivors still around the group's vicinity they would find her corpse and the corpses of the other group members. Without the drugs to sustain their hunger, Spot and Ace would be killed off like any other zombie, even if they tried to save people from being attacked, and Ark wouldn't be viewed as the so-called saviour of the human race and Sam's killer. She'd be reflected as the failure, the woman who let all her friends die because of her stupid mistake of forgetting some damn matches. The woman who damned the world to Hell. The woman who failed in ending Sam's post-apocalyptic rein once and for all… The woman who had watched that little boy die in front of her on her operating table. Ark closed her eyes, unable to face the faces of her companions; even seeing Kolen was a challenge that she couldn't complete. *I'm so sorry, guys, I fucked up! I was so focused on the guns and medical equipment that I didn't even bother getting a full matchbox to start a fire. Get out and leave me here. You all deserve to live. I deserve to sit here and get eaten alive.* Ark had felt like blubbering out her final words of sorrow to the group. She wanted to plead for them to forget they had even met her, as she wouldn't want them to carry the burden of being affiliated with the person who had doomed the rest of the UK's living population. She didn't want them to remember the person who had failed them. Ark couldn't bear the thought of anything terrible befalling her friends if they were found by other survivors, other more heavily suited survivors.

But not all hope was lost. Footsteps, nearby. Someone who'd been lurking nearby had come and heard Ark's lament. Someone had come to rescue the group, to give them a second chance at life, like how those real-life heroes did on the news. Some people go to save some stranded survivors who had faced the wrath of nature like a tsunami or hurricane and were left clinging to their lives as they sought refuge in a house, waiting for help to come. Some people were too altruistic to put themselves in danger for others, and it seemed like this person was happy with doing just that – as long as Ark's and the other's lives could be spared. Sam was the first to see the group's saviour, and when her eyes locked on with the eyes of this saviour, she wasn't exactly pleased; as a matter of fact, she was far from pleased. Sam's face had contorted into one of fury and disgust at the identity of this person who'd come to save the group, and when she'd growled and snarled through her teeth, she spat; this time, she resembled a wild animal that was frothing around the mouth after it had contracted a rather dangerous version of rabies.

'Traitor...' She growled at the slender figure looming in front of her; a small stick was held between the figure's index and thumb as the figure stood in the doorway in silence. Her eyes boiled from looking at the figure that the group couldn't fully see yet; most of the features and identification details were enveloped in shadow, but from what they could make out in the dim light of street lamps above, it was a slender silhouette of a male, a boy.

Then Sam spoke the name of the saviour, no... the name of the zombie boy standing before her, spitting the name out like it was the worst insult to ever say.

'You're a fucking *traitor*, Linus.'

Chapter 40

Losnedahl released the half-headless zombie's wrist and shot his head up in surprise from hearing the name of his zombie, whom he was sure had been killed off back in the GFOSAR. How the hell did he manage to get around London without being seen, or in the worst case, shot by the occasional human survivor looming in the shadows? He thought as he looked at the silhouette of the boy with whom he thought he was getting nowhere. But it seemed like he was getting somewhere with the boy zombie, as here he was standing before them.

'So, you've let your humanity take the wheel? I should've expected this from a mere child battling with his personas. (*He was battling sides?* Losnedahl thought) I'm very disappointed that you'd come here and finish something that you weren't even part of!' Sam snarled at Linus. Sam pointed accusingly at Ace and Spot. 'Like these two, you'd rather betray your race rather than work with me to create a brighter future for them.' The others looked up at Linus' silhouette, who stood planted in silence. Whoever was holding the torch now, raised it and then it was that moment when he raised up a hand and Ark realised that he was clasping onto a long finger-sized stick in one hand, while the other hand held onto an equally small box that looked like the one, she had carried, this one with a bigger by an inch. It was another matchbox, and this one actually had matches! Sam growled a guttural sound at this. She took a slow and pained step towards him. 'You wouldn't dare! I fed you! Remember that brain? I got that for you; if it wasn't for me, you'd still be wandering the streets, lost and aimless. You'd be dead if it wasn't for me.'

Linus grunted and shook his head as if he was battling a headache. He didn't care if Sam insulted him. He

683

didn't care how much she belittled him with threats. He didn't care if Sam threatened to kill him. He just didn't care anymore because he'd had enough of Sam and her evil ways. He'd had enough of living as a rotting husk that would slowly decay over time. Sam made and forced him to do things he hated, tortured him, and made him kill and eat brains, and if he didn't do as she ordered, she'd brutally take a human life and pin their deaths on him. He couldn't take it anymore, couldn't take following orders from someone so immoral; he was at his limit where he might go crazy if he continued to follow Sam and her wicked ways. Losnedahl was trying to teach him to be a human again. Linus wanted to do good. He wanted to be human again. He wanted to be with his bonder again – he was kind to him – he wanted to help him, he wanted to feel that connection again. However, one thing that being with Sam and seeing how she did things taught him something, she taught him about ambitions, and he discovered that he, too, had a wish, a goal, an ambition that he wanted to see through. Linus wanted to be human again; he wanted emotions and love, wanted (*who am I?*) to be good, and wanted to find out who he was. *Help me, Henrik, get me away from this creature!*

During his peculiar time with Losnedahl, he hadn't thought much about him as Linus was one of those cases who'd learn one day but wouldn't the next day. During his time with Sam, he'd begun to miss his time with Losnedahl and craved to see him again because Losnedahl was considerate and patient with him. Linus liked that, so much so that he wouldn't ever forget the kindness Henrik Losnedahl had given him. Linus was still Losnedahl's bonded zombie, and Linus just couldn't allow a kind man like Henrik Losnedahl to meet such a terrible end (Father figure); he'd already lived a never-ending life of suffering. So, now Linus was here, holding this match and staring at the monster who'd tortured him. Before he struck the match, he thought about how he'd ended up here and to this point where he was standing here confronting his former master.

He'd entered the scene shortly after witnessing a break in one of the boarded windows. He'd been wandering around the Heart, searching for Sam, wanting to act vengeance for all the people she made him hurt; the cries of that mother and daughter scarred him and seeing her take out the loyal titan made him realise that no matter how loyal Sam's followers were, she'd still off them because she felt like it. And with that in his mind, he knew that he'd need to follow her lead for a certain amount of time until she grew tired of him. So, when she had gone off on her own, Linus was left to himself, but he didn't stay behind like she had told him to; he had discreetly followed her. He was then alerted by the sound of her wicked voice and another female voice with a funny accent (Ark's) coming from nearby. He looked and saw her and Ark in the hole in the boarded window and knew that this would be the perfect chance to take his revenge on her. He remembered how he'd stolen a box of matches a few hours prior while out of one of his patrols around the Heart, taking the jump on an unsuspecting middle-aged man, biting him in the arm and causing him to drop the matchbox that he currently had held in possession. He had picked it up and looked at it curiously before putting it in one of the back pockets of his jeans. Then he went about shambling through the dead London streets until he evidently came to the house where the group had once taken refuge before the zombified dog and Sam had shown up to ruin everything. An undead cat had approached him, sniffed him, and then wandered away. He had shown up at the window, watching Ark drench Sam with the flammable acetone liquid. He shook his head, managing to keep a grip on his good self after Sam had left their so-called human farming base, and after about thirty minutes of fighting with himself, he decided to follow her.

And now Linus was here, holding the match and with his humanity taking much-needed control. He'd had enough of Sam's hellish torture and being forced into killing innocent people. Linus concluded that it was finally time for Sam to repay for all the pain and suffering she had caused by meeting her, feeling her pain, and listening to her suffering instead of others. Sam may have fed him, but that still doesn't justify all the people she had influenced him like a shoulder devil into killing people. He couldn't forgive her for that.

'Linus got out?' Kolen queried Losnedahl, who just stared at her; his face matched the same amount of bafflement that Losnedahl's boy zombie had survived for this long. He looked at the woman with the glasses and nodded once, telling her that he did, in fact, get out and that he'd also been unfortunate enough to act as a temporary pawn for Sam.

'Who's Linus?' Slater asked.

'This little shit, who seems to have forgotten who butters his bread.' Sam snarled, watching Linus lift up both hands in front of him. She took another heavy, weighted step towards him. Sam and Ark now understood that he'd come with the matches that Ark needed in order to finish Sam off. *Come on, Linus, light it, help us send this bitch to where she belongs*, Ark thought hopefully, clenching her fists, and staring intently at the boy zombie. Sam took more weighted steps towards the boy, her legs sluggish with all the wounds they had sustained. Ark was biting her lips. She scrambled up off the floor and went to stand by Spot's side, grabbing his hand and shuddering. Spot held her close and comforted her by rubbing her hair. Ark thanked him with a slight whisper. Her eyes never left the sight of Linus and Sam.

'Stupid boy, go ahead and starve. You won't be able to do it for long. You'll give in and attack the living and will be killed by the living.' Sam scorned as she reached Linus, reached out her arms, and seized his shoulders, digging nails into his grey flesh. Linus grunted, and his teeth showed. Losnedahl took a step forward and aided his zombie, but the Slater twins held him back, the brother holding a wrist, the sister holding an ankle.

'Go on, strike it. See where it'll get you,' Sam condemned; she rubbed her arms and heavy legs around Linus, dousing him with some of the acetone before she took a heavy step backwards. Losnedahl squeaked and tugged at the arms holding him back. He wanted to save Linus, to get Sam away from him before he struck the match and set himself on fire.

Too late!

Linus scraped the bud of the match across the side of the matchbox. Sparking at first, he scratched it again, and this time, he got a tremendous burst of flame. Sam narrowed her eyes with hatred at Linus for issuing in this kind of stunt and betraying her, but there was a sick glint in those eyes as if she knew that he'd panic at the burning match or drop the match and light himself up instead of her. But that didn't happen, and Linus stood motionless like a statue, holding the flickering match. The group watched the mesmerising flicker, then at Linus's blank expression with utmost focus; as for Linus, he kept his dead eyes fixed on Sam, whose eyes were burning with damnations for the boy, how she was predicting his death. How she thought of the time when Linus finally snaps after starving himself too much. No more.

He flicked the burning match.

The movement of this match was fast and spun in circles, the fire consuming the wooden match as it travelled towards Sam, but it was like they say; time had seemed to slow down for Sam, as the match crossed in the air towards her in slow motion. Sam was going to move, but her legs felt too heavy, and it felt like they'd become glued to the ground. Sam made a lion-like growl as she tried to move her wounded legs, eyes fixated, preparing for the hellish feeling that was about to rupture throughout her body; even so, she'd take it; she'd take anything that was thrown at her. When moving did nothing, Sam just stared, lips pursed. She seemed to be hypnotised by the fiery stick hurdling right for her as if wanting it to hit her and light her up like a hellish Christmas tree.

It struck her left foot, and just like Ark had predicted and savoured, Sam's entire body blew up into a furious blaze of fire, turning her into some kind of mobile wicker man.

Being burned alive is said to be the most painful way to kick the bucket. To Sam, it was only a papercut of what else she had coming to her.

Almost immediately, as soon as the flame radiated off her entire body, lighting up a good portion of the house they were in, Sam began to yell, shout, and wave around to try to put herself out. She flailed her arms around in a desperate effort to put out the flames, but due to her body being so thoroughly soaked in acetone, extinguishing herself proved impossible. Sam shrieked, banging into various objects, all trying to put herself out. But her efforts were in vain. There was nothing she could do to put herself out. The roaring flames were attached to her like how fleas are attached to the sweetness of animal blood (how nits were attracted to the safety of the human head, how mosquitos were attracted to the smell of fresh blood, just like how the mortuus carnem was drawn to the dead). The group watched their enemy burn with satisfaction; hearing her excruciating cries was like listening to an ensemble of Britain's best sopranos. Linus didn't feel sympathy or regret for betraying Sam; if anything, he smiled at seeing her suffer. He stepped over to the group and grinned, watching Sam burn like his fellow bonded zombies as well as the humans, feeling a profound sense of delight at seeing her burn and hearing her screams as her surgically crafted skin bubbles and blisters. Sam thrashed around against the flames, throwing herself at walls and rolling around on the floor, trying to put them out. But the fire just kept consuming her like acid burning through metal, which had invented a disgusting odour of burning rotten meat, and it was all around the room, making the human group members cover their noses. But even throughout the awful stench perfuming off Sam's burning body. They were grinning. They grinned as if they were witnessing the single most important thing that mankind could ever lay its eyes upon. It was beautiful. Oli wished she had a camera so she could record this moment, savouring it, and then email it to the rest of the human group members later on. So, in the future, if they needed to be reminded of their tremendous act on this day, 1st Nov 2056, 12:10 a.m., they could watch the video and smile, knowing that they'd been there and helped save Britain from its most notoriously feared killer. And their victory was all thanks to Losnedahl's boy zombie who had returned and let his humanity win over his hunger. Losnedahl wanted to reach the boy and give him a hug for saving them against the monster.

Sam wanted to curse, but what came out was an unhealthy "UCK OO" as the fire made its way inside her mouth, burning it along with her voice box. She shot her gaze at the group, and with eyes that were burning as much as her body, she charged at them, forcing the group to disperse and leap out of her way. The only one who didn't get away in time was Slater, Sam crashed into him, burning him a bit, but he was saved by Losnedahl, who kicked the burning zombie off him and helped him to his feet. Sam wailed. The group watched with satisfaction, keeping their distance from each way she stumbled and shambled, knowing it was happening to Sam and not the rest of them had provided them with a bitter comfort; once again, it left her with a raspy moan. Sam started to lose her sense of mobility, shambling around like the rest of her undead folk. Still, despite fighting the eternal flames and screaming from the pain, Sam had another trick up her sleeve and wasn't going to let the ground stand and watch her burn like a skewered pig over a campfire. If she was going to meet her end here in this building, she would take the group with her! Sam flailed around more erratically, purposely stumbling into things to make them catch fire. She flung herself into walls to blister the chipping paint and plaster and burn the wooden pillars holding them together, causing the entire house to catch fire the more she moved and interacted with the environment around her.

Slater had caught a notion of Sam's erratic behaviour and hastened, despite his own screaming aches, over to Ark and pulled her to her feet, where he seized her arm and worked in bringing her back to the safety of her zombie whom he, Darren Slater had ordered to pick her up and keep her above the fire or anything that felt hot. Spot instantly followed Slater's (protect Ark with your life) order and easily picked Ark up, holding her protectively in his long arms. 'The bitch is trying to burn the house down with us!' he bellowed, watching with wide eyes as the fire grew around them.

'It'd seem your idea didn't turn out well according to your fucking plan! You really are fucking stupid!' Sam hissed through her burning voice box. 'You cunts will all burn to fucking crisps inside this burning shithole! You signed your own death certificates! Lucky fucking you! Burn with me! Burn!' she hissed again, still covered in flames. Linus flung himself at Sam, engulfing himself in some of the flames, but he didn't care. He charged her, threw his arms around her stomach, and pushed her out through the boarded window, slowly but surely engulfing the rest of the rotting wood around him. He pushed and pushed and pushed into Sam until there was a loud crashing and shattering sound as the boards fell apart, and both the fighting zombies rolled into the cool outside and under the faint glint of the moon. Linus rolled off Sam and rolled around on the pavement to put himself out. Sam did the same, though her movements were far more sluggish.

The group couldn't afford to give up now and let themselves fall to what was supposed to be a swift end to Sam's existence; they had to press on and leave this burning house. The group wanted to behold Sam's death more than anything else. So, they attempted to follow her outside and away from the flaming debris that would threaten to fall on them if they weren't careful. Slater, fighting through his own pain like he had been taught during his rookie days in RMA, had picked up his sister Olivia in his arms. Darren Slater led the charge out, running over to the front door and kicking it hard. They didn't want to risk skirting the flames that both Linus and Sam had created near the boarded walls, so they went through the door that seemed like the safest way.

It wouldn't budge. 'Shit!' Slater cussed, readying his foot and kicked it hard again. This time, the door gave way and burst off its hinges, granting them an escape, 'COME ON! LET'S FINISH THIS!' he yelled at the others, giving them some motivation before he left the crumbling building first, carrying Oli in his arms. Losnedahl gently caressed Kolen, holding the frightened Dutch woman close to his chest, mindful of her broken hand. Losnedahl and Kolen went on the same path as Slater, trailing behind him, seeming to ignore Linus standing absently near the windows at first until they joined the Slater twins outside in the darkened twilight. Losnedahl made an effort to disband from Slater and Kolen to go fetch Linus, but he was told to stay by Slater and Oli. Not long after them was Ace, who made her appearance out of the smoke. She was out of her wheelchair, so she heaved her legless body after them as fast as she could, her intestines dragging along with her. As for Ark, she was helping Spot out of the house while he carried her, directing him where to go by voice and tapping his shoulders if she wanted him to go left or right. But before the both of them even considered leaving, Ark looked around for Spot's brain jar amongst all the roaring flames; she knew that Spot wouldn't want to go without it, so she knew she had to find it for his and her sake.

'Goddammit, where is it?' Ark's voice rang, sounding panicked. That's when a hand reached up to touch Spot's arm.

Spot darted around in the direction of where he had been touched, and Ark, acting as his eyes, saw Linus standing before them, looking a little burnt, Spot's brain jar balanced on his palm. He had returned through the flames to fetch the brain jar and to help them. 'Linus, you handsome little shit,' gushed Ark; she took the brain jar away from the boy zombie's palm and rested it on her chest. Then, the two of them followed behind the others out of the house. Linus was the last to depart from the burning house, walking wanly after them with his head low and fingers clapping together. Shortly after leaving, it collapsed, succumbing to its extensive burns, puffing out waves of dust and ash all over them, leaving quite a glorious fiery pit over the remains. This was also when Sam stopped burning; the cool twilight and chilling night breeze had extinguished the flames for her. The humans in the group coughed out the smoke. Kolen looked behind her to see an empty but burning pile on the ground. 'Where did she go?' Kolen asked. But she was soon answered by a haunting, abhorrent screaming sound, and the group turned to see Sam on her feet, charred black and charging and roaring at them with a stone slab in her hand. But then there was a disgusting cracking sound as Sam instantly fell to her face, the stone slab being knocked out of her hand. Most of the flames had gone out, and when Sam weakly pushed herself over, she resembled worse than when she had first arrived in the GFOSAR. She was completely black with ash and smoke, and the smell was one of the worst things, like barbecued rotten flesh.

The group and Linus gathered around the charred-up body lying motionless on the pavement, checking if they had well and truly won by finally killing Sam. But no; Sam was still undead, but it was barely; she couldn't move a single part of her rotting smoking body, leaving her in a catatonic state. The only part she could move was her head, tilting it slightly in the direction of the group members; her eyes were heavily bloodshot but were still ripe with a searing hatred.

(This is for you, Mr Fredrickson).

'You've lost Sam; your reign of horror ends here; the time is 12:23. am, 2nd Nov This is where you will die.' Ark sneered down at the fading bonded zombie Sam, who stared at her as her burnt body was steaming profoundly.

'I… told y-you...' Sam rasped softly, staring at Ark coldly. 'If ma...my body isn't a ma...ma...me...mess…I will... rise again with the mortuus car...nem.' Sam struggled to deliver this; her voice sounded pitiful; it was raspy like she was being suffocated by the invisible hands of an unknown assailant. Linus came up behind Ark and held out a now-loaded shotgun to her, a final memory of Winsome. Ark didn't deny this chance; the gun was loaded, and Sam wasn't going in a rush anyway. It was now or never. She took the shotgun from Linus and aimed it at her head. Her thoughts when she held the weapon were that of Winsome and that she'd dedicate the final blow to him and Bear, two innocent lives who were turned upside down thanks to Sam. *This is for you, Ryan.*

'I will rise again.' Sam spoke softly, trying to get it through to Ark's head that no matter how battered or how much her body was destroyed, the mortuus carnem would always be around to resurrect her from her grave. One thing was on Ark's mind, and that was the death of Sam. The death of the zombie that Fredrickson had intended to be his most remarkable work, the zombie that'd change everything, the zombie that'd save humanity.

Ark didn't flinch; her face was empty of expression as she held the shotgun above Sam. Sam closed her eyes and managed to crack one last grin.

Without hesitation. Ark pulled the trigger.

Chapter 41

It was done… it was finally done. The body of nightmares incarnate; Sam was lying in front of them, a large gaping hole in one side of her head. Ace held the torch, and she handed it to Linus, who beamed it on the steaming black cadaver. She wasn't entirely headless; she still had an eye and half a mouth but seeing half her head next to her in bloody dusted chunks and half of her brain joining those bloody lumps. It was more than a satisfactory sight for them to see, because it gave them the evidence they needed to know that their most despised enemy was finally dead and had both feet in the grave. But Losnedahl didn't seem convinced initially; he strode up to the steaming carcass, booted it in the chest, and snapped a bone. The body didn't move or even twitch. He bent over the body and spat at it; *that was for Ryan, you monster*; then he was satisfied then and went back to his position. The witch that had started the massacre on the GFOSAR had finally met her maker. All the lives she has mercilessly taken were now able to rest in peace, without the worry of Sam killing and infecting more people, aiding in the mortuus carnem apocalypse. Sam's victims' graves will have flowers resting above the soil; they will be remembered as they were in life, and they will finally have a taste of true peace as they have their eternal rest, hoping that the mortuus carnem doesn't sniff them out and stomp on that contentment.

The eight of them were still gaping upon the undead withered cadaver of Sam. 'Anyone else want to spit on it and finally take peace in knowing that the nightmare is finally over?' Ark suggested after watching Losnedahl. She walked up to the body, and so did Kolen and the Slaters. Each one of them gathered around the body. The zombies and Losnedahl stayed behind. Slater put his sister down next to Kolen, and the four of them gathered around the steaming body as if they were conducting some kind of cultist ritual. The body illuminated by the torches beam, still laid there, heavily burnt, with a bone poking out of the leg she had tripped over and a large gaping hole in the side of the head. Eyes then looked upon Lisa Ark, who held her hands out, suggesting that everyone join hands with her. They did. Ark closed her eyes for a moment, inhaling the smoke, and while it did smell utterly horrendous, it was enough to satisfy her desire to see Sam's light extinguished. Ark then reopened her eyes and looked into the faces of those she had come to know as her friends. They nodded at her, and she nodded with them. They each drew their heads back before shooting large quantities of spit onto the carcass. 'That was for Mr Fredrickson and all the other countless lives you have taken, you heartless bitch. I hope Hell is far hotter than the fires that sizzled you here.' Kolen snorted; she kicked some dirt and pebbles into the body, and then she broke away from the gathering to stand beside Ace. Oli then looked up at Ark and then at the body from her sitting position on the ground; she was a little sceptic about her really being dead, as she had seen some zombies get up and walk away from harsh battering and torture as if nothing happened. 'Is it over? Is it finally over? Is she dead?' she wondered, not taking her eyes away from the charred, half-headless remains of Sam. The smell was awful, but knowing she wasn't moving was bliss.

'Not sure,' said Ark as she transmitted a stomp on one of the arms, seeing if the body would move or twitch in reaction to being hurt. Nothing. Good. Ark scoffed at it, also breaking from the gathering. 'Yeah, I don't reckon she'll be getting up anytime soon.' Ark announced, confirming one part of their mission had been completed. 'Even if she did get back up, we'll just find and kill her again.' Ark then shivered, showing that the winter weather was approaching her. Kolen shivered also, blew into her hands, and rubbed them together to warm them up.

Losnedahl pulled her into his chest and held her to keep her warm. Slater then picked up his sister and went over to join them. Now, it was onto part two: eradicating the mortuus carnem. But first…

Slater let out a relieved sigh, which had been the first one in a long time. 'I think this calls for a celebration.' Slater proposed with a relieved smile. Everyone looked at him, slightly puzzled by this suggestion. 'Why not? We beat that black-haired witch and saved Britain from becoming another dead country and avenged so many lives by checkmating their killer! I'd use a trip to DazLand and, generally, have something to be victorious about. How bout we head to the nearest pub and drink some Meantime or anything alcoholic until we're hammered? It would be a toast to humanity and a step further in saving this planet from dying!' Slater encouraged, tossing Oli up in the air before catching her. Oli's eyes widened as she was thrown up and caught simultaneously. She clapped both hands around her brother more tightly, not wanting him to launch her in the air again as an obvious sign that he was a bit too invested in his excitement for finally being free from Sam's mass-murdering rule! Once he was done tossing her in the air, Oli reacted to this by smacking him across the face and demanding that he not do it again because she was a fragile package. Slater boomed a laugh because he felt like he had just won the one-billion-pound lottery, fuelled with such adrenaline that he felt like he could tap dance on top of Sam's roasted body. Ark tilted her head in his direction, pursed her lips and nodded. 'I'll admit, I like me the sound of that idea. I could use a drink or two. It's been so long since I've felt a genuine sense of joy and victory.' Ark said, also feeling a sense of warmth in her from finishing the deed. She hadn't felt a sense of true joy in a while, and she was more than grateful to be feeling it now at this moment, so much that she smiled heartily at Slater. It was a smile that warmed not only his heart but the others (Ace was feeling a thought-forgotten sense of what it was like to be alive) in the group because it was a smile of hope (pity that Spot couldn't see it), pity that Winsome wasn't alive to see it, he would've loved it, genuinely loved it.

'How about you, Marilyn, Henrik? Think we deserve a drink for achieving this victory. Just think of the positive outcomes that will happen because of this moment. Sure, it'll take a long arse time, but we will fix this dying planet and wipe out the entire mortuus carnem species from the face of the Earth. Turning it into a scary story for the kids of the next generation.' Ark grinned at them, giving them a sign of optimism; even if the next task appeared almost impossible, at least Ark had given them a symbol of confidence, a token of resilience. 'I may not be one of alcohol, especially after hearing the many ways and adventures my brother has when he's making love with various objects. But what the hell. I'll drink to our victory.' Oli confessed, confirming that she'll join them in alcohol consumption despite her dissing alcohol of any kind. She'd drink with her brother this one time because, like the others. She felt it was necessary, and why wouldn't it be? They've dispatched Sam and saved the country from her reign; who wouldn't want to accept this opportunity to get pissed on the good stuff.

Kolen glanced up at Losnedahl, who was beaming; he was more than happy to drink a few cups of beer at a pub to lighten up his mood and send him into a drunken bliss, flying off to Valhalla, where all those who've died in battle reside to spend their afterlives. He would communicate with the Vikings of legend until it was his time to return to the real world and wake up sober.

'Well... I guess I could have one shot... maybe two.' Kolen had crawled back into the shell of her usual timid self; the power she had before she vanished, leaving behind the timid Marilyn Kolen they had come to love. She was more than compensated with the death of Sam, but after Ark had delivered the final blow, she'd just fallen back to her old ways, and that was understandable because Kolen wasn't a robust-minded person like the rest of them. It was in her blood to be shy and meek, and there was no problem with that because it was what made Kolen who she was.

'Then it's settled!' boomed Slater. 'We'll go to the Earl of Lonsdale; matter not of thy pub condition! We shall go thee, and we shall become intoxicated on thy spirits!' Slater began speaking like a character in a Shakespearian play, one that revolved around the characters going into an inn, getting utterly smashed on ale and spending the rest of the night giggling like idiots on the floor because, like Ark had stated, she needed to feel a genuine sense of joy, even if it would be through getting tanked.

So, with Slater taking the lead this time, still carrying Oli, they abandoned the sizzling cadaver and set forth toward this pub named Earl of Lonsdale.

Once, the eight of them were inside the abandoned pub, which still looked in reasonably good shape and like it originally was, all things considered. It was just dark from some of the lightbulbs being broken, and the electricity was creating a dim light over in the pub. A few trees were growing from the floor, and Earth was growing into the walls and floor. Each member of their group took a seat on a barstool, and Slater, who was acting as bartender, was going through the bar, fetching, and mixing drinks for himself and his party, zombies included. Whatever was available, Slater mixed it up and gave it to anyone who asked for it, even the zombies.

Kolen and Oli were apprehensive about taking a swig at first, but ultimately, Oli took the first shot. She waved at Slater to pour her a shot of Meantime; he did without question, and Oli drank it in one gulp, getting the strong raspberry flavour in her mouth. Her eyes widened, and her mouth was flowering with such taste that she waved for Slater to give her another shot; again, he did it without question. He only smiled at her. 'Whoooo... Holy frickafrack, where the fuck have you been, Olivia Slater?' Oli belched as she started to feel a little tipsy; she glanced at Kolen, two seats from her left, one eye open and the other closed. She held her shot glass up, coaxing Kolen into joining her while also demanding her brother pour her another drink. Even better, get her a bottle.

Slater came over to Kolen and poured her a shot full. Kolen glanced at Oli nervously before picking up her glass and inspecting the liquid inside. Then, she glanced up at Slater, who simply winked at her. Kolen stared at the small half-pint, gulping before she shrugged her shoulders and drank it; like Oli, her mouth exploded with flavour, but unlike Oli, she didn't demand another. Spot was sitting on a barstool. He was so tall that his feet were touching the ground, but despite that, he could still sit on it like an average person. Because of his apparent absent head's top half could only have one, he couldn't join the others in bliss as much as he wanted to. He held an empty shot glass out with one hand, his brain jar slugged under his arm, and Ark approached him; she took his brain jar gently from under his arm and carefully placed it on the bar table in front of him. 'Here,' she said to her tall zombie, gently grabbing his wrist with the spotted birthmark, and she poured a bottle of Meantime over the pint before she released him, which had told him that it was complete. Spot glanced down in the direction of the pint glass in his hand, swinging it around lightly, causing the liquid in the pint to sway around in a circular motion. Ark watched her zombie drink his first shot of alcohol with childlike anticipation as she drank from her bottle. 'Atta boy, mate, chug it down.' Ark encouraged him, watching his every movement with sharp eagle eyes; her solid Australian accent had distinctly come out as she persuaded her zombie to bring it down and get his first sweetening taste. Spot reached the hand holding the pint up to his tongue, lifted it up, and then slowly spilled the alcoholic liquid down his throat; his tongue fell back down, and he struggled a bit, but eventually, he was able to swallow it. Spot recoiled a little from the cool liquid travelling down his throat, down into his digestive system, and the tall zombie almost dropped the pint glass. Luckily, he kept his grip on it before he put the glass on the table as his body stiffened from the incredible sensation that was happening inside his body.

Ark applauded this with a shriek of joy. She flung herself off her stool, a little intoxicated from five shots of Meantime and half a bottle, and bear-hugged Spot, making him almost fall off the seat from the sudden perception of being grabbed and locked into a hug. 'I love you, Lucas.' she slurred, concealing her face into the tall zombie's dusted white buttoned shirt. Spot didn't know what he was thinking, let alone what he felt; he didn't know if he should be weirded out or feel more love for his bonder. It didn't matter either way; he tried to lower himself down for her, but that was when the barstool toppled over, causing both of them to fall to the floor, Ark on top of him. Ark smiled cheekily as she rubbed the side of her face over the fabric of his shirt as if she were a cat brushing her scent over him; she continued to hug him tightly. He wrapped his long arms around her and hugged her passionately in return. Once Slater and Losnedahl had both started Ace on the Meantime beer, she was hooked. She couldn't get enough of the material, not that she was drunk or anything; zombies couldn't get drunk, right? Well, that was most certainly not the case with Kolen's crawler. Ace tossed herself at people, but not to attack them, but to take their Meantime pints, to scoff them all down for herself, and she wouldn't feel drunk at all; she'd just feel thoroughly delighted! 'Ayuh, that's roight biscuits! This 40-year-old crawler can get drunk! betcha didn't know dat!' Ace belched, tumbling off the table and straight into the sober arms of her bonder, who was now drinking from a simple can of lemonade Sprite; one shot was enough for Kolen.

Kolen swayed her head with a captivating smile on her face. 'Bonded zombies can get drunk. You learn something new every day.' She giggled at her zombie, drunkenly flailing her arms around in the air.

'I dead, I no drunk, I no get drunk. You no why? Because I 'appy!' Ace started with the broken English again.

'Oh, dear.' Kolen shook her head as she chuckled. Finally, finding a purpose to laugh and smile again. One thing she was confident about was that it felt good to smile and laugh again for real and not have to fake one. It was a good time to be alive.

Chapter 42

After getting everyone drunk and partying like total loons at the Earl of Lonsdale pub to celebrate their victory by bringing the hammer down on the evil zombie woman. They had ended up falling to the floor, sleeping off the alcohol in their system, and it wasn't until Linus' stomach grumbling loudly that it signalled that it was time to get up, waking up around four hours later at 4:23am, according to the digital clock that glowed white above the bar. Celebration time was over; it was now time to get back on the road and commence business that was at hand. It was still very dark outside, with most of the light outside coming from the faint din outside from either the moon or the lampposts. But it would become light in about an hour or two, and the sun would be gracing them as if congratulating them on their victory. That was if there were still dank grey clouds blocking out the sun. Moreover, when they did wake, it wasn't without a thumping headache. They were sober, but they had something to help them remember what they had done a few hours ago. Losnedahl was the first to open his eyes and get up, rubbing his eyes and sitting up and looking over at Linus; he was the only one who hadn't been drinking and the only one who was still awake; he was holding something in his palms and when Losnedahl adjusted his eyes, he realised that he was holding some hunger drugs and had a dull and hurt expression on his small grey face and his lips were quivering. Concerned, Losnedahl shuffled to his feet and walked over to him; this was then followed by Kolen, who groaned a bit before she opened her eyes and woke up, then Ace, then Spot, Oli, Slater woke up with a splitting hangover and finally Ark had fallen asleep next to Spot and had her arm around his chest. When she did open her eyes up and groaned, she was rubbing her head softly, trying to hush the screaming inside her head. She had had headaches before, but this one felt different, more brutal and nagging.

She wished that she had some Panadol with her that she could take to ease the pain and the consistent nagging in her head.

'Fuck...' she groaned, drawing the word out, putting her palms on her eyes and rubbing them. Spot was holding her to his chest, still raking his long fingers through her hair. 'I guess we overdid it.' Slater grunted, holding an icepack to his head, which Kolen had taken out of the small mini freezer underneath the bar counter for him. Linus had been awake the entire time, leaning by a four-seated table with his arms crossed. He had taken a pill and was chatting in sign to Losnedahl, mentioning something that caused Losnedahl to utter an audible gasp, which caused Ace and Oli to look over at him. *The time was now*, he signed. He relaxed his arms and wandered over to Olivia Slater, who had been in the custody of the revolver for the time being (while Darren Slater had escorted her in his arms). He held out a hand to her, asking for it. At first, Oli didn't understand, but Losnedahl tried to sign and mouth the words, but she still didn't understand, so translator Kolen did her best, telling her he wanted the gun. 'Huh? Oh sure, no killing any of us though, that'd be really mean,' Linus ignored her and acquired it from her hands, checked if it was loaded (learning this from Sam), where he handed it to Losnedahl, speaking to him of what he must do in sign language, giving him the explicit order that he and the other two zombies must go through much to Losnedahl's obvious hurt. *'You must do this, Mr Losnedahl; working for Sam was nothing but a nightmare. She was just so cruel, so vile... so evil that you cannot even comprehend it; she tortured her victims relentlessly, killed many, forced me to go along with her killings and hurt me bad when I wouldn't do as she wanted. I can't live like this anymore. I can't live knowing that I have taken lives for her pleasure just because she wants a world where the undead are superior. I've helped her destroy things, and I'm not proud of it; I have a violent side. A side that aspires to kill more and desires the suffering of people. So please, Mr Losnedahl, I implore you to pull the trigger and kill me. Please put an end to my undead form; let me have a chance to rest in peace.'* Linus had signed. Linus then looked over to the other two good zombies and sighed a harrowing and painful sound before he looked back to his bonder and signed, 'The same goes for those two. Once the drugs wear off, there is no telling what they'd do when they get hungry. Our hunger is horrible; there is nothing worse than the feeling of always being hungry, and no matter how much you eat, you are never satisfied. They'll have to go as well, for the safety of you and your friends. I am sorry, but you will understand my point. As much as he hated to admit his crimes during his partnership with that evil witch, he knew he couldn't let it go unannounced. And upon being granted the chance to see his bonder alive and well, he knew that the time was inevitable, that he couldn't continue to live a life where he hurt people just for food. His heart wanted to stay with Losnedahl, to help him, to see the end of Sam. But his mind wanted to die, wanted the torture of his undead existence to come to an end. He knew it in his blood what had to be done, and it would start with him.

Losnedahl was the oldest human in the group, making him the wisest, but even so, he was shocked at what Linus had asked of him. He put his head in his hands, making the harrowing decision that he had to take out Linus, his zombie who had returned and saved them from being killed off by Sam.

'What did he say, Henrik?' Oli asked softly, but Losnedahl didn't hear. He looked down at the gun resting in his hands, stroking it with his thumb; this would hurt him just as much as killing his zombified mother did. But this time was different; unlike his mother, he actually had a gun this time. He had to shoot Linus in the head, but he just couldn't. He couldn't even bring himself to raise the gun to Linus' head because Linus was still a young boy. Losnedahl couldn't go through with the idea that he was about to shoot a boy who appeared no older than sixteen. Losnedahl shook his head to tell Linus he couldn't do it, so Linus assumed he would help his bonder with this task. Sighing sadly, he walked over to Losnedahl and grabbed the gun inside his bonder's hands. Linus stared into Losnedahl's despairing face as he directed the muzzle to his head. The other group members gasped, but Linus closed his eyes, turning the corners of his lips into small grim, as if he was bottled up with a sense of composure, waiting for his pain to finally come to an end, that he was going to die valiantly by his bonder's hands and not in disgrace by Sam… Losnedahl hesitated and flinched back. However, Linus still held the revolver muzzle to his head, silently and patiently waiting. Losnedahl didn't want to go through with this, even if Linus could switch to his corrupt side and lash out at them at any given moment in one last effort to seek vengeance on them for killing his master. The glaring fact that he was still just a young boy was unmoveable; killing him would be like killing an innocent child. Losnedahl was lost in his mind, trapped in a never-ending prison of mixed emotions. He stared at the others, asking them through BSL what they thought he should do in regards to keeping Linus alive because he clearly didn't know what to do himself. As wise as he was, this was one thing he couldn't make up his mind on; this was something he needed help with. He clenched his eyes shut like he had done with his mother and wiped away at his eyes.

Ark took a step towards him. Her complexion was calm and soothing, but Losnedahl could tell that she was hiding a certain kind of sadness within it. 'It's alright, Henrik, if he wants it, you to do it, do it, let him suffer no more, grant the boy peace.' Ark consented to him, blinking, and nodding once for him to go along with it and kill Linus, as that is what Linus wanted from him. Losnedahl licked his lips gingerly before returning his gaze back to Linus, the sorrow and guilt building up inside of him and swaying around like a runaway wooden cart of bricks. He didn't want to go through with this, but it was the way Linus was staring at him with a scant smile and those words he was signing. 'It's alright, Henrik, I always saw you as a father, and so I must ask you to do this one thing for me. I will miss you, Henrik; furthermore, I will always be here.' Linus smiled, but a whimper had emerged from behind his quivering lips, wanting to show Losnedahl that his death would be a blessing from all the curses that Sam had hexed upon him. He placed a hand on Losnedahl's chest, where the heart sits underneath. Wanting Losnedahl to understand that he was happy to welcome death, and wherever he goes after that, whether it's heaven or hell or buried in the ground or stone, he didn't care, as long as he got his rest and didn't have to worry about coming back, as long as he wasn't walking the Earth as a rotting corpse, he was more than happy with that.

Losnedahl glanced at Linus as two small tears leaked out from his blue eyes before he nodded, biting his lips, saying he was gonna do it, that he would go along with it, that he would send Linus to the place where he wanted to go so badly. His hands were shaking. He strived to keep a grip on the revolver while his heart was a chorus of weak beats. Henrik Losnedahl closed his eyes and sniffled. Henrik Losnedahl's breathing was unsteady, *come on Henrik, you old drink, you can do this, Linus wants this, you can do this.'* but despite that, he kept his aim on the boy zombie; he bit his lip, closed one eye, and pulled back on the trigger, exposing a shot out in a cloud of steam that flew towards Linus's head. It hit Linus on his temple, and Linus's head bobbled back from the sharp impact of the bullet entering his head; dark red blood slowly trickled out of the hole in Linus's head. But before Linus cashed out, he musted one last smile towards his bonder before he fell backwards to the ground, inept. Like he expected, it was a harrowing thing to do; killing average unbonded zombies was one thing. But killing someone whom you knew was different, let alone a child of sixteen, well, that was on a whole other level of guilt. But it was done now. Henrik Losnedahl had granted the boy zombie the escape he had sought...

Linus was dead.

Now, it would either be Spot or Ace to die next. As much as their bonders couldn't bear so much as the idea of killing them, they knew that it had to come one way or another. Keeping Lucas Fitzroy and Evelyn Davis trapped inside their undead lives was close to torture, damming them into an eternity of pain that always had felt an intense hunger for the living that could never be fulfilled. It wouldn't matter how much they ate; they would be cursed to forever be hungry. So, it would mean that killing them would be the kindest thing Kolen and Ark could possibly do for them, to give them a merciful death that would be remembered and missed. Perhaps both zombies will have new gravestones engraved in the future, having their human name, zombie name, DOB, DOD, DOR (date of reanimation) and a little message underneath detailing a reason why they would be missed. Example: helped the survivors to win a seemingly impossible battle. Losnedahl turned to his friends and signed to them on what Linus had told him, that Spot and Ace had to part along with him because they were zombies.

Furthermore, the rest of them were human, and Ark and Kolen knew deep down that they couldn't keep their lovable bonded zombies around as much as they wanted to, knowing that it would be perilous and a risk to the safety of the Slater twins and to any other human survivor they come across. Especially when they ran out of drugs to feed them if either of them felt the tearing hunger sensation, making them have a craving for anything that still breathed (their bonders), quite possibly the most promenade risk of keeping them alive. Therefore, Spot or Ace turning on their bonders out of starvation would kill them mentally. Mainly Spot, who had seen his bonder Lisa Ark as more of a bonder, but a friend, no, more than a friend, someone he feels a genuine affection and love for. So, for a zombie as gentle as Spot to turn on her, kill her, only to realise what he had done after would devastate him to the core that he possibly might try tearing his own guts out from his chest, acting out of guilt for what he had done. The same goes for Ace; the crawler could not even begin to express her gratitude towards Kolen; Ace would still be a brainless zombie that transported her legless body by crawling if it wasn't for Kolen bonding with her and teaching her how to speak again, to remember what it was like to have a voice to talk actual English words instead moaning in Zomblish, that and the bond that they had together, Ace couldn't even begin to thank the timid Dutch woman for all she had done into getting her this far.

With those facts out, as much as Kolen and Ark wanted to take their zombies along with them during their journey to wipe out the remainder of the Mortuus Carnem species, they knew that Linus had a point and that having them around would not only be risking their lives. But the people they try to save. So, as much as the thought pinched them like a knife in the gullet, they knew it had to be done. Keeping them alive was just as bad as exposing one's body to radiation burns. It was a living Hell for them.

'Linus is correct on what must be done.' Ace pointed towards Ark and Kolen. 'You two may want us to go with you… but I'm afraid this will be the end of the road for us both; you can't keep pumping us with hunger drugs; you will need all the human help possible. You must kill us next. Unless you can find some way to change our diet, we will just keep getting hungrier and hungrier, and we might eventually turn on you. We have to go next. I am sorry.' Ace explained their situation, giving them more accurate details on why they couldn't come along with them.

Ark and Kolen glanced at each other and sighed miserably, knowing that it was time for them to say goodbye to their most loyal undead companions because they couldn't deny that Linus did have a point and that without the administering of the hunger drugs, there was only a matter of time because Spot and Ace would revert back to their primitive zombie starving states.

Ark hissed as the question was passed through hers and Kolen's minds on who would be the first to die: Ace or Spot?

Chapter 43

'Jesus…' Ark said glumly, lowering her head and scratching through her hair. She glanced over at Kolen again, and she could understand that she thought of the exact same word when it came to the factor of who they were going to pick, which zombie to die first. The choice wasn't an easy one as both zombies had provided some kind of help towards the group; Spot showed his loyalty to the group by fighting against his enemies, while Ace was about to sense and smell when danger was about. Both women turned to the others to get some kind of input from either of them about what should happen and who should decide to take the lead first. 'Guys, what do you two think?' Ark questioned the Slaters and Losnedahl, wanting to get their personal opinions as she and Kolen found themselves unable to decide because they both had a deep connection to their zombies. Ark looked at Spot, who slid his brain jar from the bar counter and held it sadly at the thought that he could no longer accompany Ark and her friends; like Ace, he would have to die and would be given a merciful passing.

After about a minute, they decided to go outside, believing that the cool breeze and the early rays of sunlight might be able to help motivate them on this difficult choice of who would be the one to die first. Ark grabbed Spot's arm and led him outside while Ace went around on the floor, dragging herself behind Kolen and Spot as the wheelchair that Losnedahl had specified for her had sadly been lost in the fire. The one that had weakened Sam enough for Ark to kill her, the fire that had become Aladar (Landon Wyatt) and Zinni (Miles Wyatt), Bear and Ryan Winsome's tomb.

Once outside and standing underneath one of the lampposts, they talked amongst themselves for a moment, discussing things until Oli blurted out. 'Fuck killing them! Both are awesome with equally amazing qualities; Ace has speech and intellect, and she can sense danger! Spot has comprehension too and a mass loyalty and is more than willing to fight for those he cares about!' Saying her clear thesis on why the two zombies shouldn't be killed off like any plain zombie shambling the London streets. 'Not to mention Spot would have been a real cutie when he was alive.' She gushed, looking at the tall zombie dreamily, fantasying an image in her head of what he would've looked like in her head, and the picture she thought of when she stared at him was of an attractive young man in his late twenties with brown hair, blue eyes and smooth, kind facial features and of course being really tall. Spot's tall, lumbering frame flinched. He made a slight noise, and he turned away, feeling a flush of embarrassment. If he had a full head, Oli was sure that he would be bringing colour to it by his cheeks going red. He clung to his brain jar shyly, like a child holding onto a teddy bear for support.

Slater twiddled his fingers, looked down at the din that was on his shoes and kicked at the tiny pebbles of pavement. 'I've never been good with making good choices and decisions… so I'm afraid you two women are on your own with this one, sorry. I really wish I could be more help, but this isn't up to me. So, I'm taking a step backward.' Slater yielded a dispirited shrug of his shoulders while Oli rested in his arms. Her eyes were broad, and she was looking at him with a wide, renouncing expression, not wanting to believe what her brother was saying.

'I've grown to honestly like both of them and would love for them to be by our sides as we continue through our Mortuus Carnem eradication mission. But I will admit that I do agree with that boy zombie that Henrik had to execute; keeping them alive and with us is risky, especially when either of you two runs out of that hunger stuff, we can't afford that risk when we have already come so far. Speaking of, when was the last time either of them had one of those drugs?' Slater sighed sadly, confirming he did not want to see any of the two zombies go so quickly, providing the knowledge that over the hours they had been around him, he had grown quite a bond with them as if they were his army mates from the RMA days that were finally able to reunite with him. Losnedahl closed his eyes and looked away with no comment, signing and declaring that it was sadly not his decision on who should die first. Ace was Kolen's zombie, and Spot was Ark's zombie and as unfair as it sounded, they couldn't decide or choose. It was just unfair that the day and their short-lived victory over Sam had come to this.

Ark threw her palms to her head and clenched her eyes shut, seeming to be in pain, like she was having a headache. And that wasn't far off the truth. Her mind became a rollercoaster of disembodied voices and the butterfly effect. She thought about all the things that would happen if Spot, no, Lucas, was to die first. It was just so unfair. But the main obstacle that blocked her was the thought of Heather Fitzroy. That sweet old lady (who may be religious) wouldn't want to be faced with the idea that her only child had to be killed off again for the sake of the country; the very essence of mother having to watch her only child die again wasn't a comforting thought to picture, she wasn't a mother herself, but she could imagine the pain it would cause. But yet, Ark couldn't escape it. It was engraved in her mind just the memory of her father, Michael Ark, telling her that her own mother, Lorraine Ark, had died from a concussion in her brain after falling down some steps while on what should have been a lovely holiday to Singapore with some of her work friends. That had been a hard thing to stomach and to cope with. Then, of course, there were Nolan's parents, whom she had to ring up and tell the devastating news that their son's next trip was to the hospital morgue with a white blanket over him and a nametag around his toe.

Ark clenched her fists and gritted her teeth. 'Goddammit, shit, I don't want to go through with this; I made a promise that I would never let anyone I care about die (I promised myself that I would never fail); what about his Mum, Helen, or was it Heather or Harper? She wouldn't want her son to die again.' She took a feeble step backward, shaking her head. 'I'm sorry... I... I can't do it. It's like watching Nolan's eyes staring up at me again, hearing his words, "Don't let me die, Miss Ark, I don't want to go; I'm not ready to go." I... I can't do it. ' The sensitive, feeble side of them came out, and she started to tear up. She wiped them away with her lab coat sleeve, but they wouldn't stop, so Ark rubbed her eyes thoroughly until her eyes started to throb and sting, and she felt humiliated for letting her friends see her this way. Kolen then approached her and placed a hand on her back, and Ark jolted out of instinct. 'Look at me, I... I can't bring myself to hold even a tool for killing... (*I'm so pathetic*), so please, Lisa, whoever is first to die... Ca-Can you be the one to kill Ace? Because I don't think I'll be able to; killing that blind zombie was hard enough.' Kolen sniffled; tears were unquestionably draining out of her brown eyes behind those white-framed specs. Ark was too lost in her own crisis to care about trying to convince Kolen otherwise about the duty of killing Ace. So, she simply agreed, 'Alright, Marilyn. I will do for you.' Ark said wistfully behind her own streaming tears, wishing the gloomy feelings in her head would just go away and leave her alone. The chilling wind was billowing through her, but she was too locked in her thoughts to care about the goosebumps forming on her skin. She had a hard decision to make, and all eyes were on her to make that decision.

Faint footsteps could be heard emerging out of the darkness of the night, followed by an audible shiver to indicate the cold. Holding the torch, Oli shone the light towards the two figures approaching them. 'Lucas. It should be Lucas that goes first. It's what my son would want. A boy like my boy wouldn't want to continue living in this accursed body that the devil has bestowed upon him. So, would you do him the kindness of freeing him?' The familiar voice of Heather Fitzroy was heard approaching them, along with the mutterings of another voice that had accompanied her. This other one was a slender-looking male with a head of rough brown hair, which was shaven on the left side. Ark shot her head up and darted around. Just the darkened sky had started to become a dark, greying tint, meaning that the sun would soon rise up behind the clouds, rise upon them. There, emerging out of an abandoned Indian restaurant with a flickering neon sign above it, which read *Little India* and coming outside into the greying sky, which slowly got became lighter within every ten minutes, came two figures. Ark could make out the familiar form of Heather Fitzroy (Spot's Ma) and the young man who was the owner of the other voice she had heard before. Oli turned the light off with a click. Ark squinted her eyes to get a closer look at the male figure as the two of them approached, and Ark could see that the man still looked young, appearing around twenty-seven to thirty; either way, he looked around the same age as Kolen, he was holding onto something in both hands and Ark saw that it was a black crowbar.

Ark was taken back, and the old woman had managed to survive this long. 'He-Heather! Ha-How long were you listening? And where did you even come from?' Ark asked the older woman as she came towards the group, with the other man following closely by her side, not saying anything. 'I was in the neighbourhood; Josh and I were hiding out in Little India over there; we were saying goodbye to a friend of Josh's who had taken his own life from stress. Then I saw fire and could smell the smoke, and I asked Josh to investigate; when he came back, he said that there were burned ruins, and the only thing he could make out, which seemed out of place, was a wheelchair and I somehow just knew that it belonged to the crawling one. At first, I thought that you all had perished in that fire until Josh told me that he had faintly seen figures in the Earl and three zombies with them. He reported back to me, and I thanked God that he had spared you. So, when Josh and I decided to come join you, you were already outside, and we could hear you and Mrs Kolen debating on which one of the bonded zombies should die first. And I couldn't help but notice that you were having a tough time deciding, so I took the liberty of deciding for you. And I think it should be my son who dies first. I remember-' Heather stopped herself upon realising the absence of one of their party members, the snarky fellow who had almost killed her with a shotgun. Her eyes widened, and she cupped her mouth. 'Oh my, where is the man whom I remember you calling Ryan? Did he not make it?'

Ark looked at Heather sadly, then down at the floor. She opened her mouth to speak, but it was Kolen who spoke for her. Kolen took off her glasses and wiped her eyes; there, she explained what had happened to Ryan Winsome. How Winsome was viciously killed by the black-haired demon after he had been forced into killing a zombified, hostile version of his beloved German Shepard. 'Oh, my goodness... I-I'm really sorry for the loss of your friend. My prayers be with him up in Heaven,' Heather said softly and then crossed her heart. 'You have my condolences.' She said miserably. 'We can't seem to escape death in this kind of world (maybe God has, in fact, abandoned us). But I still hold faith that God and Jesus will protect us, that he is still watching over us and ensuring that we survive.'

'Yeah, but the important thing is to keep fighting, to keep pushing forward, we are the human race, we don't back down, we never give up.' Slater added.

'I agree with you, Mr..?'

'Slater milady, Darren Slater at your service.' Slater then introduced Oli to her in case Heather had forgotten. Heather bowed her head towards Oli and introduced herself as Heather Fitzroy, to which Oli nodded in response, saying that she remembered her during their first meeting back at Oli's place.

'Heather, what were you going to say about... Lucas? you remember?' Ark's voice chimed in softly; she still felt a sting of depression at calling her zombie by his real name.

Heather glanced at her, a little confused, before she nodded with an "oh", signalling that she remembered what she was going to say. 'I remember telling him stories when he was little, that when he dies, he will go to a place full of everlasting happiness, no corruption from this unclean country, no greed, no war, nothing bad at all, nothing but bliss. So, for my son's sake and happiness, please send him to that happy place I would always tell him about.' Heather stated with a disheartened frown on her face, wishing nothing but the best for her gentle giant son. The young man who had been silently standing next to Heather suddenly walked up to Spot, contemplating up at his tall structure as Spot towered over him like the school bully guarding the toilet stalls. The man then reached out to touch Spot on his neck. Spot flinched. 'Remember my voice, Spot'o'buddy? Heather told me that you were resurrected, and I... honestly believed her, as much as I didn't want to... Do you remember me? Remember the voice of your best friend Joshua Krimmer and how we did everything together in school.' The young man with Heather had said, identifying himself to the group. Josh looked down at the brain jar clutched in Spot's hands, understanding that his brain was the source of his undead life, and without it, he would die. Josh only came up to Spot's elbow, but that didn't stop Josh from pushing Spot's arms and the brain jar up. He then thrust his arms around the giant's lean body and pushed his face into his chest, sniffling. 'I've really missed you, buddy. Life just wasn't the same without your shy charm. Even if you can't see or hear me, I know that deep down inside that big un-beating heart, you remember us, and you don't want to spend the rest of your days as a rotting half-headless corpse...' sobbed Josh, stepping back, stealing the words right out of Heather's mouth. His tears were moving, and his words were every bit as authentic as their friendship had once been those five-plus years ago. Ark couldn't help herself; her eyes were now streaming with tears, wetting her already anguished red face and making the choice all the more painful.

Josh had made things more complicated for Ark now because Spot had been chosen for death next. But now she had his mother and his former best friend to watch it; the two people who had seen him die were going to watch him die again.

(*Goddammit, why do Josh and Heather have to be here?*)

'Are you sure that you want to be here and watch Lucas die again? Once he dies again, you know that he won't be coming back.' Ark warned both of them.

'Yes, Mrs Ark, we know that this time he won't be returning back to us, that is fine. We will give him one last farewell to him before he leaves us for good. Because at least this time, we are prepared for it.' Fitzroy sniffled, same with Josh, who also thoroughly understood the consequences of what would happen after Spot was killed. Even if the idea of losing such a friendly, sweet, kind, and loving person again was a real punch in the gut. The first time was sudden and far more depressing, so at least they were prepared for this one; as heartbreaking as it would be for them to see Lucas Fitzroy die all over again, they were ready for their eyes to flow with tears.

Ark sadly walked over to Losnedahl, took the revolver from him, and pushed out the cylinder, checking how many rounds were housed inside. She sighed when she saw that the cylinder held only two. God has a funny and yet cruel way of putting things out for them.

'There are two bullets left. One for Spot and one for Ace.' Ark stated grimly; she strolled over to Spot and, took away his brain jar and held it underneath her left arm, where she fought a desperate struggle of trying to aim the revolver at the wired brain inside the pot so she could execute him. So, she could send him to the place of bliss that Heather had frequently informed him about. The place that was simply known as Heaven.

Spot was almost immediately overwhelmed with a prolific sadness as soon he felt Ark's hands and the removal of his brain jar, knowing that his bonder was going to put an end to his undead existence. But that he was not only going to leave her but his childhood best friend, Josh Krimmer, and his devoted mother, Heather Fitzroy, behind. He couldn't allow Ark to kill him without saying goodbye to her. He didn't want to go without at least giving her an insight on just how much she had meant to him, just how happy he was when he was around her, how much he had loved her.

Spot thrust his arm out towards Ark. Losnedahl caught sight of what the tall zombie was about to do and quickly worked to fish the brain jar out from under Ark's arm to prevent it from flying out of her grasp and shattering on the ground. Spot's hand seized Ark's shirt collar, and he yanked her swiftly up towards him in a staggering display of strength while her feet dangled precariously in the air, which caused some alarm in the Slater twins, who gasped. But Ark, in some ways, expected this. Spot threw his arms around her tightly, burrowing his bottom jaw into her shoulder, giving her one last loving hug. What issued was a chorus of heart-wrenching saddened gurgles coming from Spot's lower jaw and tongue, meaning that... that he was crying…

'I love you, Lisa Ark. You are an amazing woman! You have done so much for me! Words cannot describe the strong feelings I feel for you! I don't want to go... I don't want to die yet, knowing that you, Josh, and Mum will be gravely saddened by my passing... I don't want you to be sad. I want you to be happy. I like it when you are happy because it makes me happy in return.' Spot gurgled morosely; even though he couldn't speak, Ark got a clear idea that he would be saying this to her if he could. Heather then came up next to Spot as he held Ark up in the air, hugging her, and she wrapped her arms around him to embrace him. Krimmer joined in, coming in for seconds. Who could really blame him for wanting a second round of zombie cuddling?

After about fourteen minutes of embracing and final goodbyes (the sun was now pushing its way through the clouds, giving the field the group was standing in some well-needed light), both Josh and Heather pulled themselves away from Spot. They both stepped wistfully away from him to go to the back of the group, where both of them gave Ark a slight nod, granting her permission to kill Spot. Spot gently put Ark down on the ground, where Losnedahl approached her and handed the brain jar back to her. Ark took it from his hands absently. She felt like her mind had been hit with a shovel, leaving her with a mishmash of broken thoughts.

Ark stood planted on the cracked pavement, hyperventilating; she really didn't want to go through with this, but she knew that she had to. Ark knew it in her heart that it had to be done. Now she understood how Winsome had felt when he was faced with the duty of having to kill his zombie dog. Now she understood how Losnedahl had felt when he had to end his dead mother's suffering. Now she finally understood it all, what it meant for someone dear to die by your own hands.

'Please don't cry for me, Lisa. It will be alright; I will watch over you when I'm in Heaven. I will be your guardian angel; I will always be in your heart.' Spot craned his height down slightly and pointed at her chest, where the heart was located. This action just made Ark ugly cry even more, but she knew she couldn't keep this lingering on forever; if Spot was going to bite the dust, it was here in this moment. Spot had wanted it, and so did Josh and Heather.

'Thank you, Spot –oh, sorry. Lucas.' Ark cried, using the hand holding the revolver to wipe away her tears. She clutched the brain jar with one hand, which kept wobbling, but she strived to keep her arm steady so that she wouldn't drop it. Ark then lifted the revolver up, placing it on the side of the glass jar and pointing it towards the wired brain. Tears were brimming down her cheeks. But despite this, she held on; she didn't let herself falter. Spot/Lucas Fitzroy may be a half-headless zombie, but he sure as hell had more stability and compassion than some living people out there. And because of that fact, Ark had loved him, and he had loved her back with outstanding exhibits of emotion that he would frequently show her and the others during their path of redemption against Sam. Ark and the others knew that she wouldn't forget him anytime soon, neither would the rest of them because Spot had such a significant impact on them, and such a substantial impact wouldn't be left forgotten.

'Goodbye, Spot...' Ark lamented her pained final words to her loving zombie who stood still, emitting those sad gurgles that made Ark's heart wrench. She closed her eyes and bit her lip, her finger pressed down on the trigger, sending one of the two bullets shattering through the glass and passing through Spot's brain, killing him before he hit the ground. Ark descended to her knees soon after, dropping the revolver in the process; her breathing was heavy, her body was shaking, and her eyes were pink from the sheer number of tears that left her peepers. Losnedahl, Kolen, the Slater twins, Josh, and Heather gathered around Ark to console her as she cried and screamed hysterically over the loss of one of her most trusted friends and companion. Her unique zombie who was capable of even the most complex of emotions.

Thank you, Lisa. Thank you for putting me to rest. Ark could have almost sworn she could hear Spot speaking to her through her conscience, trying one last final effort to reassure her that everything was okay and that he was happy where he was.

Ace was patient (it was her turn), waiting for her death that would be coming soon. But before Ark took to retake control of herself. Kolen plucked up the courage to pick up the revolver, forgetting what she had said about making a clear point about her never being able to bring herself to wield any kind of instrument of violence. But she did; she had fought away the struggle and the tears to do the one thing that she had vowed she would never do. Ace crawled towards her, putting her head in the line of the revolver's muzzle.

'It was an honour to meet you, Mrs Marilyn Kolen; thank you for giving me this intelligence and the capacity of speech. But you have a mission to do; you need to save the world from the Mortuus Carnem. You need to put an entire species to extinction. Look after yourself, Marilyn Kolen. So, this is my adieu to you as my bonder.' Ace gave Kolen a nod and a smile with her withered lips. At this, Kolen raised the gun up to her Ace's head, waiting for the second nod to pull the trigger. Kolen sniffled the more she kept the gun aimed at Ace, but like Ark before her, she didn't falter; she wouldn't allow herself to slip backwards.

'Goodbye, Lisa Ark. I hope you continue to lead the group in my absence. Goodbye, Henrik Losnedahl, Darren & Olivia Slater, but mostly. Goodbye, Marilyn Kolen; thank you for everything, thank you for gaining the courage to kill me. Mr Fredrickson would be proud at how far you have come as a person.' That final mention of Fredrickson would have likely sent Kolen into a fit of tears, but not this time. Kolen held onto herself; her eyes showed Ace that she was keeping a grip, and it was making her happy to see how far her bonder was willing to go in hopes of doing the right thing, how much she had changed since their escape from the ruined GFOSAR. Fredrickson would indeed be proud of her. She wasn't going to let herself crawl back into her frail shell. She had the gun in her hand and would do it either way.

Through her own hyperventilating tears, Kolen gave Ace a small smile as if saying "Thank you," and shortly after that, Ace gave her the second nod, giving Kolen permission to shoot her. And she did. Kolen pulled the trigger and killed her crawler, Ace/Evelyn Davis.

Completing the feat.

Both Spot and Ace were now dead. First, it was Sam, then Linus, and now Spot and Ace.

Chapter 44

After the ordeal was over in a few minutes, many tears were emitted, hugs were transmitted and received, and the group looked up at the sky. The sun was now upon them, rising up from behind a far hillside. It had now pushed its light through the dreary clouds and was now giving the group some much-required sunlight. It was a welcoming sight for them, even if the sun was beaming down in a not-so-welcoming environment. It was still lovely to see that the sun hadn't died and that it could still fill their hearts with faith, still granting them a taste of warmth instead of the consistent lingering chill the never-ending winter had given them. Heather closed her eyes and took in the sun, stating that it was God's work, that he was congratulating them for besting their enemy and surviving through the night. She put her arm around Josh's shoulder and breathed in. Ark did also, taking the air and seeing the sun creep out over the horizon. She savoured the moment of seeing the sun rise up, feeling a sense of satisfaction that she had felt before when she had taken the shot that silenced Sam. She had – no – they had done it. They had survived the night, and they had dispatched Sam and her wicked rule. Ark closed her eyes and breathed another breath through her nose as the sun crept onto her face, casting light upon her. The others did the same, taking a moment of silence to relish in the sunlight that was once thought to have been forgotten.

'So, ma'ams and sirs, what are we supposed to do now?' Joshua Krimmer had asked them, but the question was mainly addressed to Ark as Josh wiped away the last stray droplets from his red cheeks. Ark opened her eyes and glanced over at the young man. Her face was still disturbed from having to say goodbye to Spot and Ace, but her eyes held some valour to them that Josh had greatly admired, valour at the thought that she and the others had made it, that they had survived the night and left Sam with a gaping hole in her head behind. It told him that Ark was a strong woman who carried the mind and soul of a leader; as much as she thought otherwise, Josh and many others could see it inside her, how a former neurosurgeon was born to lead a group of survivors in this poisonous world.

'What now, Mr Joshua Krimmer? Well, I'll tell you what we are supposed to do now. We're gonna welcome you as members of our party.' Slater spoke up in front of Ark, but it wasn't long before Ark answered her portion of his question. She narrowed her eyes, and Josh was greeted with the fantastic image of the strong, stoic woman that he imagined her to be. 'We're gonna wipe out the entire mortuus carnem species.' Ark sneered, her face showing a deep and unyielding hatred towards the creature that had caused this whole nightmare to begin, not just for her but for the rest of life on this planet.

Josh's eyes widened. 'Pardon my French, Heather,' he quickly said to Heather before turning back to Ark. 'No offence Lady, but are you fucking crazy?! I-I mean, you can't just wipe out an entire species of those *necroquito* bastards that have infected like ninety-nine per cent of the whole world!' Ark shot those eyes full of vigour towards him like a cat eying its prey. Josh took a step back, intimidated. Ark took a step forward, eyeing him with purpose.

'Yeah, I am! I am fucking crazy! But we'll do it. No matter how long it takes, we will eradicate the parasites and wipe them off the face of the Earth! We WILL save the world! We'll do this for Evelyn Davis (she pointed to the body of Ace), for Lucas Fitzroy (pointed to the body of Spot), for Linus (Losnedahl raised his hand to show that Linus was his zombie), for Aladar & Zinni (Oli raised her hand), for Ryan Winsome and his dog Bear and for

Alexander Fredrickson who taught us so much. But most importantly, we will do this for planet Earth! No matter how long it takes us, we will wipe out those bastards! Humanity will have a future; mark my words! We will wipe them off the face of this Earth!' Ark recited the words of a true leader! Confirming that was their new mission. Phase 1 was completed, Sam was dead, so now it was onto phase 2: Extinction of the Mortuus Carnem parasite!

Ark shifted her feet around so that all the faces of the group stood in front of her. 'So, other countries can get a boost; I suggest the six of you head off to other parts of the world and help the locals. I'll stay here, in Britain in Europe; I'll try to give the bodies of our allies here a proper burial; I'll also work into gathering up any survivors that'll help us wipe out the parasites here. How about the rest of you.' She declared triumphantly.

'We'll head off to Africa and wipe those lil fuckers out there.' Slater spoke adamantly, confirming his and Oli's location for bug killing. 'We'll aid the local Africans and give them a boost of courage because they could sure as hell need it.' Oli added in the same tone and manner that her brother utilised. It made her feel stable like her brother and immensely enjoyed it.

'I guess Josh and I will go over to Asia and gather up a cult following to help us.' Heather stated that although Josh and she had just arrived, they were already treated as group members. Therefore, like the zombies and Winsome had done before them, they would go along with any task at hand. No matter how complicated it sounded, as long as they were engulfed by Ark's wisdom, they would be heavily coated with a resilience that wasn't so quickly dissipated.

'I'll head over to Oceania.' Kolen simply said. 'I guess you can say that I've always found New Zealand and Australia interesting... so it would be nice to go there... even if the cities are dead.'

'North and South America for me.' Losnedahl replied, communicating with the usual sign language as that was his only method of interaction with people.

'Then let us make haste, let's waste no more time and head off to those continents, either it is through plane or boat, I'm sure they'll have working planes and boats that will take you to your destinations. But for now, we'll need to split up. Yeah, yeah, I know that splitting up is a shit idea that often gets people killed, but as long as you keep on your toes and are wary of your surroundings, you should be fine. But with that said, it was a pleasure working with you all. God bless you all. I hope we achieve this thing by wiping out the species and giving humanity a chance to rebuild themselves. That is all I have left. So, for now, I bid you all a safe journey and farewell.' Ark spoke bravely. She put her hand out before her, indicating that she was ready to see the mission through to the very end. One by one, hands joined hers, and then, after a final nod. Ark wished them good luck and turned her back, taking her leave. One by one, the rest of them departed from the group to find their own ways to get to their chosen locations. Their hearts were a lantern, fuelled by Ark's light. Yes, the idea was ludicrous to think about. Still, again, they were guided by the Ark's lamp, and that gave them the right amount of courage and resilience to press forward in their goal; no matter how difficult it may get, as long as they were guided by the Ark's light, they couldn't be defeated. They would urge on because humanity deserved a future. The din from Ark's lantern would protect them to the very end.

During this discussion between, the group of putting an entire species of this parasite to extinction, hoping to prevent any more zombies from rising from their graves and wreaking havoc across the world. One of the parasites found its way to a particular charred corpse that still had steam billowing off it, a corpse that was missing half its head, lying motionless on the ground. The Mortuus Carnem landed on the carcass and did its work on the corpse before it rolled off the steaming body, dead. For a few seconds, the body remained as still as a gravestone, just steam billowing off the body, but then one of its arms twitched.

Acknowledgements

Firstly, to the person with a copy of Mortuus Carnem, I want to thank you for purchasing and taking the time into reading my book, I have autism and this is a huge thing for me and I thank you from the bottom of my heart! I want to thank my Mum, Natasha who has been my biggest fan from the moment I started writing, she has been nothing but a pure beacon of hope and praise and I wouldn't have reached this far without her.

I want to thank my developmental editor Flavia Young for helping to train me into developing the skills in learning the authors language. I want to thank my stepdad Jaimes Wiggins for raising funds to help make my dream come true. I also want to thank my friends and family for staying by my side and helping me throughout each step of the way.

Thank you to Andy Gall, who helped develop my idea of the Mortuus Carnem.

About the Author

Madelyn Elisa Lahey was born in Hobart in March 1999. She is the only child of Gregory and Natasha. Her parents separated when Madelyn was just 3 years old. During her upbringing she didn't have a lot of support around her Autism, due to lack of understanding from others. She found this quite difficult and struggled with many things growing up, which left her with her own imagination most of the time. As she got older people started to understand her more and encouraged her to use her imagination as best as possible – writing. Since 18 she has been constantly writing and is always inventing new book ideas.

Although Madelyn suffers with social anxiety alongside her Autism she strives to overcome the barriers these things bring. She strives for success in her writing and is passionate about using her gift of imagination to create something readable for her readers.